The Complete Dr. Thorndyke

Volume I:
The Red Thumb Mark
The Eye of Osiris
The Mystery of 31 New Inn

The
Complete
Dr. Thorndyke

Volume I:
The Red Thumb Mark
The Eye of Osiris
The Mystery of 31 New Inn

By
R. Austin Freeman

Edited by
David Marcum

ISBN Hardback 978-1-78705-390-8
ISBN Paperback 978-1-78705-391-5
AUK ePub ISBN 978-1-78705-392-2
AUK PDF ISBN 978-1-78705-393-9

These works are in the Public Domain in Great Britain
Portrait of Dr. Thorndyke by H.M. Brock (1908)
Illustrations for *The Mystery of 31 New Inn* by Edwin J. Prittie

Published in the UK by
MX Publishing
335 Princess Park Manor, Royal Drive,
London, N11 3GX
www.mxpublishing.co.uk

David Marcum can be reached at:
thepapersofsherlockholmes@gmail.com

Cover design by Brian Belanger
www.belangerbooks.com and *www.redbubble.com/people/zhahadun*

CONTENTS

Introductions

Adventures

The Red Thumb Mark

The Eye of Osiris

(Continued on the next page . . . .)

The Mystery of 31 New Inn

The Complete Dr. Thorndyke

Volume I:
The Red Thumb Mark
The Eye of Osiris
The Mystery of 31 New Inn

Dr. John Thorndyke

99

5A King's Bench Walk
in the late 1890's when
Thorndyke would have moved in

5A King's Bench Walk
Photographed by the Editor
during his
Sherlock Holmes Pilgrimage No. 3
(September 8th, 2016)

Meet Dr. Thorndyke
by R. Austin Freeman

My subject is Dr. John Thorndyke, the hero or central character of most of my detective stories. So I'll give you a short account of his real origin – of the way in which he did in fact come into existence.

To discover the origin of John Thorndyke I have to reach back into the past for at least fifty years, to the time when I was a medical student preparing for my final examination. For reasons which I need not go into I gave rather special attention to the legal aspects of medicine and the medical aspects of law. And as I read my text-books, and especially the illustrative cases, I was profoundly impressed by their dramatic quality. Medical jurisprudence deals with the human body in its relation to all kinds of legal problems. Thus its subject matter includes all sorts of crime against the person and all sorts of violent death and bodily injury: Hanging, drowning, poisons and their effects, problems of suicide and homicide, of personal identity and survivorship, and a host of other problems of the highest dramatic possibilities, though not always quite presentable for the purposes of fiction. And the reported cases which were given in illustration were often crime stories of the most thrilling interest. Cases of disputed identity such as the Tichbourne Case, famous poisoning cases such as the Rugeley Case and that of Madeline Smith, cases of mysterious disappearance or the detection of long-forgotten crimes such as that of Eugene Aram. All these, described and analysed with strict scientific accuracy, formed the matter of Medical Jurisprudence which thrilled me as I read and made an indelible impression.

But it produced no immediate results. I had to pass my examinations and get my diploma, and then look out for the means of earning my living. So all this curious lore was put away for the time being in the pigeon-holes of my mind – which Dr. Freud would call the *Unconscious* – not forgotten, but ready to come to the surface when the need for it should arise. And there it reposed for some twenty years, until failing health compelled me to abandon medical practice and take to literature as a profession.

It was then that my old studies recurred to my mind. A fellow doctor, Conan Doyle, had made a brilliant and well-deserved success by the creation of the immortal Sherlock Holmes. Considering that achievement, I asked myself whether it might not be possible to devise a detective story of a slightly different kind – one based on the science of Medical Jurisprudence, in which, by the sacrifice of a certain amount of dramatic

1

effect, one could keep entirely within the facts of real life, with nothing fictitious excepting the persons and the events. I came to the conclusion that it was, and began to turn the idea over in my mind.

But I think that the influence which finally determined the character of my detective stories, and incidentally the character of John Thorndyke, operated when I was working at the Westminster Ophthalmic Hospital. There I used to take the patients into the dark room, examine their eyes with the ophthalmoscope, estimate the errors of refraction, and construct an experimental pair of spectacles to correct those errors. When a perfect correction had been arrived at, the formula for it was embodied in a prescription which was sent to the optician who made the permanent spectacles.

Now when I was writing those prescriptions it was borne in on me that in many cases, especially the more complex, the formula for the spectacles, and consequently the spectacles themselves, furnished an infallible record of personal identity. If, for instance, such a pair of spectacles should have been found in a railway carriage, and the maker of those spectacles could be found, there would be practically conclusive evidence that a particular person had travelled by that train. About that time I drafted out a story based on a pair of spectacles, which was published some years later under the title of *The Mystery of 31 New Inn*, and the construction of that story determined, as I have said, not only the general character of my future work but of the hero around whom the plots were to be woven. But that story remained for some years in cold storage. My first published detective novel was *The Red Thumb-mark*, and in that book we may consider that John Thorndyke was born. And in passing on to describe him I may as well explain how and why he came to be the kind of person that he is.

I may begin by saying that he was not modelled after any real person. He was deliberately created to play a certain part, and the idea that was in my mind was that he should be such a person as would be likely and suitable to occupy such a position in real life. As he was to be a medico-legal expert, he had to be a doctor and a fully trained lawyer. On the physical side I endowed him with every kind of natural advantage. He is exceptionally tall, strong, and athletic because those qualities are useful in his vocation. For the same reason he has acute eyesight and hearing and considerable general manual skill, as every doctor ought to have. In appearance he is handsome and of an imposing presence, with a symmetrical face of the classical type and a Grecian nose. And here I may remark that his distinguished appearance is not merely a concession to my personal taste but is also a protest against the monsters of ugliness whom some detective writers have evolved.

2

These are quite opposed to natural truth. In real life a first-class man of any kind usually tends to be a good-looking man.

Mentally, Thorndyke is quite normal. He has no gifts of intuition or other supernormal mental qualities. He is just a highly intellectual man of great and varied knowledge with exceptionally acute reasoning powers and endowed with that invaluable asset, a scientific imagination (by a scientific imagination I mean that special faculty which marks the born investigator, the capacity to perceive the essential nature of a problem before the detailed evidence comes into sight). But he arrives at his conclusions by ordinary reasoning, which the reader can follow when he has been supplied with the facts, though the intricacy of the train of reasoning may at times call for an exposition at the end of the investigation.

Thorndyke has no eccentricities or oddities which might detract from the dignity of an eminent professional man, unless one excepts an unnatural liking for Trichinopoly cheroots. In manner he is quiet, reserved and self-contained, and rather markedly secretive, but of a kindly nature, though not sentimental, and addicted to occasional touches of dry humour. That is how Thorndyke appears to me.

As to his age. When he made his first bow to the reading public, he was between thirty-five and forty. As that was thirty years ago, he should now be over sixty-five. But he isn't. If I have to let him *"grow old along with me"* I need not saddle him with the infirmities of age, and I can (in his case) put the brake on the passing years. Probably he is not more than fifty after all!

Now a few words as to how Thorndyke goes to work. His methods are rather different from those of the detectives of the Sherlock Holmes school. They are more technical and more specialized. He is an investigator of crime but he is not a detective. The technique of Scotland Yard would be neither suitable nor possible to him. He is a medico-legal expert, and his methods are those of medico-legal science. In the investigation of a crime there are two entirely different methods of approach. One consists in the careful and laborious examination of a vast mass of small and commonplace detail: Inquiring into the movements of suspected and other persons, interrogating witnesses and checking their statements particularly as to times and places, tracing missing persons, and so forth – the aim being to accumulate a great body of circumstantial evidence which will ultimately disclose the solution of the problem. It is an admirable method, as the success of our police proves, and it is used with brilliant effect by at least one of our contemporary detective writers. But it is essentially a police method.

3

The other method consists in the search for some fact of high evidential value which can be demonstrated by physical methods and which constitutes conclusive proof of some important point. This method also is used by the police in suitable cases. Finger-prints are examples of this kind of evidence, and another instance is furnished by the Gutteridge murder. Here the microscopical examination of a cartridge-case proved conclusively that the murder had been committed with a particular revolver, a fact which incriminated the owner of that revolver and led to his conviction.

This is Thorndyke's procedure. It consists in the interrogation of things rather than persons, of the ascertainment of physical facts which can be made visible to eyes other than his own. And the facts which he seeks tend to be those which are apparent only to the trained eye of the medical practitioner.

I feel that I ought to say a few words about Thorndyke's two satellites, Jervis and Polton. As to the former, he is just the traditional narrator proper to this type of story. Some of my readers have complained that Dr. Jervis is rather slow in the uptake. But that is precisely his function. He is the expert misunderstander. His job is to observe and record all the facts, and to fail completely to perceive their significance. Thereby he gives the reader all the necessary information, and he affords Thorndyke the opportunity to expound its bearing on the case.

Polton is in a slightly different category. Although he is not drawn from any real person, he is associated in my mind with two actual individuals. One is a Mr. Pollard, who was the laboratory assistant in the hospital museum when I was a student, and who gave me many a valuable tip in matters of technique, and who, I hope, is still to the good. The other was a watch- and clock-maker of the name of Parsons – familiarly known as Uncle Parsons – who had premises in a basement near the Royal Exchange, and who was a man of boundless ingenuity and technical resource. Both of these I regard as collateral relatives, so to speak, of Nathaniel Polton. But his personality is not like either. His crinkly countenance is strictly his own copyright.

To return to Thorndyke, his rather technical methods have, for the purposes of fiction, advantages and disadvantages. The advantage is that his facts are demonstrably true, and often they are intrinsically interesting. The disadvantage is that they are frequently not matters of common knowledge, so that the reader may fail to recognize them or grasp their significance until they are explained. But this is the case with all classes of fiction. There is no type of character or story that can be made sympathetic and acceptable to every kind of reader. The personal equation affects the reading as well as the writing of a story.

4

R. Austin Freeman
(1862-1943)

5A King's Bench Walk
in the early 1900's when
Thorndyke was in practice

Dr. Thorndyke: In the Footsteps of Sherlock Holmes
by David Marcum

When Sherlock Holmes began his practice as a "Consulting Detective", his ideas of scientific criminal investigations caused the London police to look upon him as a mere "theorist". He was perceived as an amateur to be tolerated, often with amusement – until, that is, his assistance was required. Then they were more than willing to come knocking upon his door, asking for whatever help that they could receive. And usually this help took the form of brilliant solutions to bizarre and otherwise insoluble problems.

Holmes espoused methods and ideas that were considered ludicrous in the late 1800's. For instance, his frustration knew no bounds when a crime scene was disturbed. Holmes realized that so much could be determined from the physical evidence – footprints, fibers, and spatters. The police were happy to trod into and disturb the evidence as if they were herds of field beasts, with the equivalent level of intelligence.

However, Holmes's methods, and the science behind catching criminals, eventually won out and became so important that it's hard to now imagine the world without them. Many of the exact same techniques and methods that he advocated are now standard practice. From being an amateur with unusual ideas, Holmes is now recognized around the world as The Great Detective. In 2002, Holmes received a posthumous Honorary Fellowship from the British Royal Society of Chemistry, based on the fact that he was beyond his time in using chemistry and chemical sciences as a means of solving crimes.

And before that, in 1985, Scotland Yard introduced *HOLMES* (*Home Office Large Major Enquiry System*), an elaborate computer system designed to process the masses of information collected and evaluated during a criminal investigation, in order to ensure that no vital clues are overlooked. This system, providing total compatibility and consistency between all the police forces of England, Scotland, Wales, and Northern Ireland, as well as the Royal Military Police, has since been upgraded by the improved *HOLMES 2* – and like the first version, there is absolutely no doubt as to who is being honored and memorialized for his work in dragging criminology out of the dark ages.

Many famous Great Detectives followed in Holmes's footsteps – Nero Wolfe and Ellery Queen, Hercule Poirot and Solar Pons – each with their own methods and techniques, but before they began their careers, and while Holmes was still in practice in Baker Street, another London consultant – Dr. John Thorndyke – opened his doors, using the scientific methods developed and perfected by Holmes and taking them to a whole new level of brilliance.

Meet Dr. Thorndyke

Dr. John Evelyn Thorndyke was born on July 4th, 1870. We don't know about where he was raised, or if he has any family. At no point will we be introduced to a more brilliant brother who sometimes *is* the British Government. He was educated at the medical school of St. Margaret's Hospital in London, and while there, he met fellow student Christopher Jervis. They became friends but, after completing school in 1895, they lost touch with one another. Over the next six years, Thorndyke remained at St. Margaret's, taking on various jobs, hanging "about the chemical and physical laboratories, the museum and *post mortem* room," and learning what he could. He obtained his M.D. and his Doctor of Sciences, and then was called to the bar in 1896.

He'd prepared himself with the hope of obtaining a position as a coroner, but he learned of the unexpected retirement of one of St. Margaret's lecturers in medical jurisprudence. He applied for the position and, rather to his own surprise, it was awarded to him. (He would continue to maintain his association with the hospital, going on to become the Medical Registrar, Pathologist, Curator of the Museum, and then Professor of Medical Jurisprudence, all while maintaining his own private consulting practice.

It was when Thorndyke was named lecturer that he obtained his chambers at 5A King's Bench Walk, in the Inner Temple, that amazing and historic area between Fleet Street and the River. Founded over eight-hundred years ago by the Knights Templar, it is one of the four Inns of Court, (along with the Middle Temple, Lincoln's Inn, and Gray's Inn.) The buildings along King's Bench Walk, and particularly No.'s 4, 5, and 6, have a great deal of historical significance – and not just because Dr. John Thorndyke practiced at 5A for a number of years.

Thorndyke was quite fortunate to obtain a suite of rooms on multiple floors at this location, which leads to speculation about his influence and resources – a question which has no answer. In any case, it was there that he opened his practice and began to wait for clients and cases. He also made the acquaintance of elderly Nathaniel Polton, that man-of-all-work with the crinkly smile who ran the household, as well as Thorndyke's upstairs laboratory.

Like Sherlock Holmes during those early years in the 1870's when he had rooms in Montague Street next to the British Museum and spent his vast amounts of free time learning his craft, Thorndyke also found a way to make the empty hours more useful. He had the unique idea of imagining increasingly complex crimes – often a murder or series of them, for instance – and then, when he had planned every single aspect of the crime, he would turn around and work out the solution from the other side. While doing this, he made extensive notes of each of these theoretical exercises, and retained them for their later usefulness when encountering real-life crimes.

His first legal case was *Regina v Gummer* in 1897. Sadly, no further information about this affair is ever revealed to us, but we may be certain that Thorndyke used his considerable skills to bring it to a satisfactory conclusion, adding to his reputation as he did so.

In the meantime, Jervis had a more unfortunate story. As his time at school ended, his funds ran out rather unexpectedly, and after paying his various fees, he was left with earning his living as a medical assistant, or sometimes serving as a *locum tenens*, moving from one low-paying and temporary job to another, with no prospects of improvement.

Jervis is unemployed on the morning of March 22nd, 1901 when he encounters Thorndyke a few doors up from 5A King's Bench Walk. The two friends are happy to see one another, and before long, Jervis is involved in an investigation that will change his life in several ways, as recounted in *The Red Thumb Mark*.

But it should not be assumed that every Thorndyke adventure is narrated by Jervis in a typical Watsonian manner. In fact, the very next book, *The Eye of Osiris*, is instead told from the perspective of one of Thorndyke's students, Dr. Paul Berkeley. It is one of several that provide a look at Thorndyke – and Jervis – from a different perspective. But Jervis returns as narrator in the third novel, *The Mystery of 31 New Inn*, and we see Thorndyke through his eyes for a good many of both the novels and short stories.

Here a word might be mentioned about the Chronology of the Thorndyke stories. For some this is an irrelevant factor, but for others – like me – understanding the correct chronological placement of the stories is very important. Like the volumes that make up the Sherlock Holmes Canon, the Thorndyke stories aren't published in chronological order – a case set in 1907 (such as "Percival Bland's Proxy") might be collected before one that occurs in 1908, ("The Missing Mortgagee"), or it might not. For instance, *The Red Thumb Mark* (1907) is set in March and April 1901. (This chronological placement, by the way, is determined by

9

noticing that a specific date is given three times in the book – in the British fashion of day before month – *9.3.01* – or *March 9th, 1901.* The dates for the events of the rest of the book can be carefully worked out from this fixed point.)

The next book, *The Eye of Osiris* (1911) is primarily set in the summer of 1904 (with Chapter 1, something of a prologue, taking place in late 1902.) Then, the next book to follow, *The Mystery of 31 New Inn* (1912), jumps back to the spring of 1902, about a year after the events of *The Red Thumb Mark,* and before *The Eye of Osiris.* And one of the short stories, "The Man With the Nailed Shoes" occurs in September and October 1901, between the first two books. Clearly, there is a great deal of material for the chronologicist in the Thorndyke Chronicles.

As Jervis becomes a part of Thorndyke's world, following their reacquaintance in March 1901, he meets others in Thorndyke's circle, including policemen such as Superintendent Miller and Inspector Badger, lawyers like Robert Anstey, Marchmont, and Brodribb, and other physicians like Dr. Paul Berkeley and Dr. Humphrey Jardine. He also has more opportunity to learn from his friend as he begins his own studies in order to become a similar specialist in the medico-legal practice – although he'll never be another Thorndyke.

Through Jervis's eyes – as well as others along the way – we build up our knowledge of Dr. Thorndyke. In appearance, he is tall and athletic, just under six feet in height, slender, and weighing around one-hundred-and-eighty pounds. He is exceptionally handsome – and has been called the handsomest detective in literature. He has no vices, except – perhaps – that he enjoys a Trichinopoly cigar upon occasion when he is feeling especially triumphant – although there is one time when the criminal's knowledge of this fact leads to a clever attempt at Thorndyke's murder . . . .

There are several instances where Thorndyke displays a marked resemblance to Sherlock Holmes – and not just in his scientific approach to crime. The two men sometimes say similar things – such as when Holmes says *"It is quite a pretty little problem,"* (in "A Scandal in Bohemia") or *". . . there are some pretty little problems among them"* (in "The Musgrave Ritual"). Thorndyke mimics this in *Felo de Se? ("There, Jervis," said he, "is quite a pretty little problem for you to excogitate")* or *"Ah, there is a very pretty little problem for you to consider"* (in *The Eye of Osiris*).

And who can forget the many instances when Holmes refers to *data*:

- *"It is a capital mistake to theorize before one has data. Insensibly one begins to twist facts to suit theories, instead of theories to suit facts."* – "A Scandal in Bohemia"
- *"I had,"* said he, *"come to an entirely erroneous conclusion which shows, my dear Watson, how dangerous it always is to reason from insufficient data."* – "The Speckled Band"
- *"No data yet,"* he answered. *"It is a capital mistake to theorize before you have all the evidence. It biases the judgment."* – A Study in Scarlet
- *"The temptation to form premature theories upon insufficient data is the bane of our profession."* – The Valley of Fear
- *"Still, it is an error to argue in front of your data."* – "Wisteria Lodge"

Thorndyke's version? *". . . believe me, it is a capital error to decide beforehand what data are to be sought for."* – from *The Mystery of 31 New Inn*. There are others.

Then there is Holmes's quote from "The Man With the Twisted Lip":

"You have a grand gift of silence, Watson," said he. *"It makes you quite invaluable as a companion."*

Here's the Thorndyke equivalent:

"It has just been borne in upon me, Jervis," said he, *"that you are the most companionable fellow in the world. You have the heaven-sent gift of silence."*

And then there is the time, in "The Anthropologist at Large", that a client – expecting a Holmes-like performance as based on "The Blue Carbuncle" – presents Thorndyke with an object for examination:

"I understand," said he, *"that by examining a hat it is possible to deduce from it, not only the bodily characteristics of the wearer, but also his mental and moral qualities, his state of health, his pecuniary position, his past history, and even his domestic relations and the peculiarities of his place of abode. Am I right in this supposition?"*
The ghost of a smile flitted across Thorndyke's face as he laid the hat upon the remains of the newspaper. "We must not expect too much," he observed. *"Hats, as you know, have a way of changing owners . . . ."*

11

Another area of intersection between Holmes and Thorndyke is the assembly of information. Recall Holmes's *"ponderous commonplace books in which he placed his cuttings"* as mentioned in "The Engineer's Thumb". We find, also in "The Anthropologist at Large", that Thorndyke does the same thing:

> *[H]is method of dealing with [the morning newspaper] was characteristic. The paper was laid on the table after breakfast, together with a blue pencil and a pair of office shears. A preliminary glance through the sheets enabled him to mark with the pencil those paragraphs that were to be read, and these were presently cut out and looked through, after which they were either thrown away or set aside to be pasted in an indexed book.*

No doubt and examination of Thorndyke's lodgings at 5A King's Bench Walk would reveal – in addition to a series of indexed commonplace books filled with clippings – a number of other items and aspects that would remind one of 221b Baker Street.

Like many locations where the detective's residence is almost a character in and of itself – Sherlock Holmes's London address at 221 Baker Street, and the New York homes of Ellery Queen on West 87th Street and Nero Wolfe's Brownstone on West 35th Street – Thorndyke's rooms at 5A King's Bench Walk are a living and vibrant place – from the entry way, where a heavy door known as "The Oak" leads visitors into a most comfortable wood-paneled sitting room, located on the (British) first floor, one flight up from the ground floor. On the next floor up, Polton has his laboratory and workshop, containing everything that is needed (or what might be manufactured) in order to solve the case.

On the next floor, underneath the attic, are bedrooms belonging to Thorndyke, Jervis, and Polton. Even after Jervis has married – and now you know that he does get married! – he continues to reside a good deal of the time in King's Bench Walk. As he explains in *When Rogues Fall Out* (1932, with the U.S. title of *Dr. Thorndyke's Discovery*):

> *Here, perhaps, since my records of Thorndyke's practice have contained so little reference to my own personal affairs, I should say a few words concerning my domestic habits. As the circumstances of our practice often made it desirable for me to stay late at our chambers, I had retained there the bedroom that I had occupied before my marriage; and, as these*

12

circumstances could not always be foreseen, I had arranged with my wife the simple rule that the house closed at eleven o'clock. If I was unable to get home by that time, it was to be understood that I was staying at the Temple. It may sound like a rather undomestic arrangement, but it worked quite smoothly, and it was not without its advantages. For the brief absence gave to my homecomings a certain festive quality, and helped to keep alive the romantic element in my married life. It is possible for the most devoted husbands and wives to see too much of one another.

Thorndyke's Other Appearances

Through the years, Thorndyke's reputation continues to grow, as presented through a number of adventures. Surprisingly, in light of the tens of thousands of Post-Canonical Sherlock Holmes that have come to light over the years, as discovered by latter-day Literary Agents taking over Watson's first Literary Agent, Sir Arthur Conan Doyle, stopped literary-agenting, there have been almost no additional Thorndyke cases brought to the public's attention. The few exceptions to this statement are *Goodbye, Dr. Thorndyke* (1972) by Norman Donaldson, and *Dr. Thorndyke's Dilemma* (1974) by John H. Dirckx. Both narratives deal with Thorndyke and Jervis in their latter years, and each is written by an expert in the field of Thorndyke scholarship.

Donaldson also wrote what might be the final scholarly word on the subject, *In Search of Dr. Thorndyke* (1971). In fact, he had intended his pastiche, *Goodbye, Dr. Thorndyke*, to be published as the conclusion to this book, but it ended up appearing separately.

To my knowledge, "The Great Fathomer", as Thorndyke is sometimes known, has rarely appeared in other locations. He is mentioned in the Solar Pons tale "The Adventure of the Proper Comma" by August Derleth, which finds Dr. Parker returning "from Thorndyke & Polton with an analysis of the capsules Mrs. Buxton had carried with her . . . ."

In my own book of authorized Solar Pons stories, *The Papers of Solar Pons* (2017), Thorndyke makes two appearances. "The Adventure of the Additional Heirs" has Pons and Parker visiting King's Bench Walk:

At 5A, we learned that our friend Thorndyke, the medical juris-practitioner, was out on some investigation or other, but Pons handed the papers, sans *photograph, into the care of Polton, his crinkly-faced laboratory technician, with a detailed explanation of what he wished to learn. The man*

*nodded and smiled, and without any extraneous chit-chat,
shut the door, freeing us to return to Fleet Street. We paused
at the edge of the walk to look at the photograph, still in
Pons's hand.*

Later Thorndyke sends Pons a detailed report that helps toward the solution of the problem. And in "The Affair of the Distasteful Society", set in July 1921, Pons and Parker attend the first meeting of a group gathered to honor Sherlock Holmes, where the following conversation occurs:

*"I see that you invited Thorndyke, and that little Belgian
over on Farraway Street," said Rath.
"And Sexton Blake as well," replied Sir Amory.
"Sexton Blake is a fictional character, Sir Amory," said
Pons with a smile.*

In my story, "The Adventure of the Two Sisters", to be included in an upcoming Solar Pons anthology, Dr. Parker writes:

*Pons was not the only detective who offered his services
to the London populace, although he might have been the most
well-known. We were friends with several others, including
the former Belgian policeman who lived in Farraway Street,
and another rather mysterious fellow in nearby Bottle Street.
And of course, Pons went way back with Thorndyke, whose
chambers were across town. It wasn't unusual for Pons and
the others to regularly confer on investigations, or simply to
sit down and share a few drinks and professional anecdotes.*

Thorndyke doesn't just appear in some of my Solar Pons adventures. He's also been referenced off-stage in a couple of Sherlock Holmes adventures that I've pulled from Watson's Tin Dispatch Box – and it's more than likely that others will follow. In "The "London Wheel"", contained in *The MX Book of New Sherlock Holmes Stories – Part IV: 2016 Annual* (2016), Holmes, looking through some documents, states:

*"I believe," said Holmes, "that I have enough amateur
legal training that I can get a sense of the implications of the
clauses in question in both of these documents." He pulled the
folded pages from his pocket. "I thought about sending a
message to my protégé Thorndyke in King's Bench Walk for*

14

his opinion, as he could have been here very quickly, should
he be at home at all and not out on his own business. However,
I don't believe that will be necessary.

Perhaps it is a point of interest that Thorndyke is referred to Holmes's protégé. Possibly more information will be forthcoming, such as that which is hinted in my forthcoming story, "The Coombs Contrivance". Set in 1889, when Thorndyke was nineteen years old, Holmes and Watson are discussing a precocious Baker Street Irregular:

> *[Holmes] pinched the bridge of his nose. "Do you trust Levi's judgment, Watson?"*
> *I considered. "For an eight-year-old, he's remarkable perceptive – as much as any of the other Irregulars who have assisted you. The Wiggins family, or the Peakes, or Thorndyke, before he went away to university."*

So was Thorndyke, perhaps, a gifted Irregular who learned from The Master, and then went on to create his own successful practice, taking what he learned to a next very successful level? Possibly. As Robert Downey, Jr. succinctly stated when playing Holmes in 2009's *Sherlock Holmes*: "Food for thought!"

Thorndyke is also mentioned in Bob Byrne's Holmes story, "The Adventure of the Parson's Son" (*The MX Book of New Sherlock Holmes Stories – Part III: 1896-1929*), wherein Holmes, examining a piece of evidence, cries:

> *"Ha! I believe we have discredited the coat entirely. Though I wish I could get Thorndyke to examine it. Would that we were back in London."*

And it isn't just Thorndyke who has appeared elsewhere. His lawyer friend Marchmont has assisted Holmes and Watson in a small way a couple of my own forthcoming adventures, *Sherlock Holmes and The Eye of Heka* and "The Coombs Contrivance".

Although I have encouraged these Thorndyke cameos in my own stories or in Holmes and Pons books that I edit, his appearances elsewhere are much more fleeting. In the 2015 BBC radio series *The Rivals*, Inspector Lestrade, Holmes's most frequent associate at Scotland Yard, is placed into the events of the Thorndyke short story "The Moabite Cipher". And Thorndyke has only had a handful of other media appearances. In 1964,

15

the BBC produced seven episodes (now mostly lost) of *Thorndyke*, starring Peter Copley. The episodes were:

- "The Case of Oscar Brodski'
- "The Old Lag"
- "A Case of Premeditation"
- "The Mysterious Visitor"
- "The Case of Phyllis Annesley" – Adapted from "Phyllis Annesley's Peril"
- "Percival Bland's Brother" – Adapted from "Percival Bland's Proxy"
- "The Puzzle Lock"

From 1971 to 1973, Thames TV aired *The Rivals of Sherlock Holmes*, and two stories were adapted: "A Message from the Deep Sea" starring John Neville (who had also played Holmes in 1965's *A Study in Terror*), and "The Moabite Cipher" starring Barrie Ingram. Except for a 1963 BBC Radio adaption of *Mr. Pottermack's Oversight*, and a few on-air readings by a single performer, there have been no other Thorndyke adaptations – which is a terrible shame, as the stories certainly lend themselves to visual and audible interpretations. Perhaps a new generation will discover Thorndyke, Jervis, and the rest, and they will find popularity once again, as they did more than a century ago.

Copley, Neville, and Ingram as Thorndyke

A Few (Hundred) Words About R. Austin Freeman
Thorndyke's Chronicler

Richard Austin Freeman was born on April 11, 1862 in the Soho district of London. He was the son of a skilled tailor and the youngest of five children. As he grew, it was expected that he would become a tailor as well, but instead he had an interest in natural history and medicine, and

16

so he obtained employment in a pharmacist's shop. While there, he qualified as an apothecary and could have gone on to manage the shop, but instead he began to study medicine at Middlesex Hospital.

Austin Freeman qualified as a physician in 1887, and in that same year he married. Faced with the twin facts of his new marital responsibilities and his very limited resources as a young doctor, he made the unusual decision to join the Colonial Service, spending the next seven years in Africa as an Assistant Colonial Surgeon. This continued until the early 1890's, when he contracted Blackwater Fever, an illness that eventually forced him to leave the service and return permanently to England.

For several years, he served as a *locum tenens* for various physicians, a bleak time in his life as he moved from job to job, his income low, and his health never quite recovered. (These experiences were reflected in the narratives of Doctors Jervis and Berkeley.) However, he supplemented his meager income and exercised his creativity during these years by beginning to write. His early publications included *Travels and Live in Ashanti and Jaman* (1898), recounting some of his African sojourns.

In 1900, Freeman obtained work as an assistant to Dr. John James Pitcairn (1860-1936) at Holloway Prison. Although he wasn't there for very long, the association between the two men was enough to turn Freeman's attention toward writing mysteries. Over the next few years, they co-wrote several under the pseudonym *Clifford Ashdown*, including *The Adventures of Romney Pringle* (1902), *The Further Adventures of Romney Pringle* (1903), *From a Surgeon's Diary* (1904-1905), and *The Queen's Treasure* (written around 1905-1906, and published posthumously in 1975.) The specifics of the two men's writing arrangement are unknown to the present day, although much research was carried out by Freeman scholar Percival Mason ("P.M.") Stone, who was actually able to confirm Pitcairn's involvement and influence. Following this association, which apparently helped to train Freeman to be a better writer and to focus on a recurring character, his luck changed, and he was able, within just a few years, to abandon the practice of medicine, which had never been successful, and become a professional author.

In approximately 1904, Freeman began developing a mystery novella based on a short job that he had held at the Western Ophthalmic Hospital. This effort, "31 New Inn", was published in 1905, and it is the true first Dr. Thorndyke story. In it, we meet narrator Dr. Christopher Jervis, working as a *locum tenens*, moving from practice to practice in the same bleak existence that Freeman had experienced. Jervis becomes involved with a patient that may or may not be in danger. Unsure what to do, he recalls his former classmate, the brilliant Dr. John Thorndyke.

17

Curiously, this novella, (included in Volume II of this newly reissued collection *The Complete Dr. Thorndyke*), has numerous references to the events of the first Thorndyke novel, *The Red Thumb Mark*, which would not be published until 1907. Much of Freeman's life is obscure and unknown, including his writing processes and milestones, but clearly, with so much already clearly defined in this novella about Thorndyke and Jervis, he had firmly established not only fixed aspects of their histories, but the plot of *The Red Thumb Mark* as well, several years before the book's publication. One wonders why he chose to first publish "31 New Inn", since it occurs chronologically a whole year *after* the events of *The Red Thumb Mark*.

Interestingly – at least to a chronologicist such as myself – the original novella of "31 New Inn" is specifically set in April 1900, as indicated internally. However, when it was later revised to become the third Thorndyke novel, *The Mystery of 31 New Inn*, (1912, and included in Volume I of *The Complete Dr. Thorndyke*), the narrative's date is changed to 1902 – which fits, since the events definitely occur after *The Red Thumb Mark*, which takes place in March and April 1901.

Like Rex Stout's Nero Wolfe, who seemed to have sprung fully formed from his creator's brow, Thorndyke and his world are well-defined and immediately real. Although certain characters are added to the circle through the years, the basic layout – with Thorndyke, Jervis, and Polton (the man-of-all-work crinkly-smiled assistant) are always at 5A, ready to spring into action when Jervis – or one of the other varied narrators who show up throughout the series – arrive with a curious problem.

Freeman had found his voice with the Thorndyke books and short stories, and he was able to make use of his lifelong interest in medicine and natural science – often conducting extensive experiments to work out exactly how the solutions in his stories could be discovered. And in Thorndyke's early days, Freeman was able to turn the literary form inside out with the creation of the "Inverted Mystery Story", wherein the criminal is known from the beginning – the motive is explained, the planning and execution of the crime are observed, and the miscreant is left to believe that all is well and that he'll never be caught. And then, in the second part of the story, Thorndyke enters to inexorably follow the trail that is completely invisible to everyone else, scraping away, layer by layer and point by point, until the truth is inevitably revealed.

As Freeman explained:

> *Some years ago I devised, as an experiment, an inverted detective story in two parts. The first part was a minute and detailed description of a crime, setting forth the antecedents,*

motives, and all attendant circumstances. The reader had seen the crime committed, knew all about the criminal, and was in possession of all the facts. It would have seemed that there was nothing left to tell. But I calculated that the reader would be so occupied with the crime that he would overlook the evidence. And so it turned out. The second part, which described the investigation of the crime, had to most readers the effect of new matter.

This format went on to be used by a great many authors through the years. For example several of the Lord Peter Wimsey narratives come close to being this type of story, and television's *Columbo* used this type of story-telling as its basis.

While these volumes are an attempt to reintroduce the modern reader to Thorndyke, and are a celebration of him and his world, it must be discussed at some point that Freeman held views that are unacceptable. Unlike Sir Arthur Conan Doyle, who spent his last decades championing spiritualism but never allowed it to creep into the Sherlock Holmes stories, Freeman sometimes did let his own prejudices make their way into the Thorndyke tales. In his book *Social Decay and Regeneration* (1921), he expressed his rather nationalistic view that England had become an "homogenized, restless, unionized working class". Worse, he inexcusably and detestably supported the eugenics movement, arguing that people with "undesirable" traits should not be allowed to reproduce by means such as "segregation, marriage restriction, and sterilization". He referred to immigrants as "Sub-Man", and argued that society needed to be protected from "degenerates of the destructive type."

Some have attempted to excuse his beliefs as being a product of his times. For instance, it has been written that he had a distrust of Jews because of the competition that his father, a tailor, had faced when Freeman was a boy. Later, he served in the Colonial Service in Africa during some of the worst years in terms of treatment of natives by the British, and as an older man, he existed in the Great Britain between the two wars when great upheavals disrupted much of what he had known and expected.

Sadly, there are occasional racial stereotypes and references in the Thorndyke books. As I explain in the *Editor's Caveat*, some of these stereotypes had to be unfortunately maintained within the story in order to accurately reflect the plot and the characters of those times. However, there are some words or phrases that were used in the original stories – vile racial epithets that have no business being repeated or perpetuated

19

anywhere – that I have cheerfully and happily removed. (There weren't many of them, but any are too many.)

These books are intended to bring Dr. Thorndyke and his adventures to a new generation – and not to be an untouchable and sacred literary artifact, with every nasty stain preserved and archived for the historical record. As I warn in the *Caveat*, if readers find that they want to experience the original versions as they were first written, with those hateful words included, then they would be advised to go and seek out the original books, because you won't find that filth here. These versions celebrate Dr. Thorndyke and Dr. Jervis – who do not use the awful stereotyped language, I'm glad to say! – and as such, I felt no need whatsoever to include and perpetuate the objectionable and offensive material

From Thorndyke's creation until 1914, Freeman wrote four novels and two volumes of short stories. Then, with the commencement of the First World War, he entered military service. In February 1915, at the age of fifty-two, he joined the Royal Army Medical Corps. Due to his health, which had never entirely recovered from his time in Africa, he spent the duration of the war involved with various aspects of the ambulance corps, having been promoted very early to the rank of Captain. He wrote nothing about Thorndyke during this period, but he did publish one book concerning the adventures of a scoundrel, *The Exploits of Danby Croker* (1916).

Following the war, he resumed his previous life, writing approximately one Thorndyke novel per year, as well as three more volumes of Thorndyke short stories and a number of other unrelated items, until his death on September 28th, 1943 – likely related to Parkinson's Disease, which had plagued him in later years.

Upon learning the news, *Chicago Tribune* columnist Vincent Starrett wrote:

> *When all the bright young things have performed their appointed task of flatting the complexes of neurotic semi-literates, and have gone their way to oblivion, the best of the Thorndyke stories will live on – minor classics on the shelf that holds the good books the world.*

Raymond Chandler wrote in his famous essay, which initially appeared in a couple of magazines and then was published in the book of the same name, *The Simple Art of Murder* (1950):

This man Austin Freeman is a wonderful performer. He has no equal in his genre, and he is also a much better writer than you might think, if you were superficially inclined, because in spite of the immense leisure of his writing, he accomplishes an even suspense which is quite unexpected . . . There is even a gaslight charm about his Victorian love affairs, and those wonderful walks across London.

In the introduction to *Great Stories of Detection, Mystery, and Horror* (1928), Dorothy L. Sayers, Chronicler of Lord Peter Wimsey, stated:

Thorndyke will cheerfully show you all the facts. You will be none the wiser . . . .

Discovering Dr. Thorndyke

I first encountered Dr. Thorndyke in a rather backwards way – in passing only – and it took several decades to correct that mistake. In approximately 1980, my dad gave me Otto Penzler's *The Private Lives of Private Eyes, Spies, Crime Fighters, and Other Good Guys* (1977). This wonderful oversized book has biographies of twenty-five well-known heroes, along with lists of the original books featuring each one.

My dad bought it for me because it had a chapter about Sherlock Holmes. There were a few others in there that I recognized or had already read about– Ellery Queen and Perry Mason – and soon I would become fanatical about a few more – Nero Wolfe and Hercule Poirot. Over the next few years I would also find the chapters on James Bond and Lew Archer indispensable, and later than that I would come to appreciate the entries about Philip Marlowe, Sam Spade, Miss Marple, Philo Vance, and Lord Peter Wimsey. But there were a few that, to this day, I've never bothered to read – such as Modesty Blaise or Mr. Moto – and a few others that I skimmed but otherwise ignored. And one of these was the biography of Dr. Thorndyke.

That fact was easily understandable, as throughout the entire time that I was growing up in eastern Tennessee – and in the years since as well – I've never come across a Thorndyke book for sale here in the wild, either in a new bookstore or in a used one. If I'd found one, I might have bought and read it, liked it, and then sought out others. Instead, I was bound to discover Thorndyke by way of Sherlock Holmes.

I've been collecting traditional Sherlock Holmes pastiches since the same time that I discovered the Sherlockian Canon, when I was ten years old in 1975. Since that time, I've collected, read, and chronologicized literally thousands of them. It never gets old, and I'm constantly looking for more – and that means checking Amazon to see what new releases are on the horizon.

In 2012, someone – and I've never determined who – began releasing a variety of Holmes stories for Kindle under the author name *Dr. John H. Watson.* This wasn't too unusual – there have been a number of pastiches that officially list Watson as the author, rather than putting the editor of Watson's papers first. Of course, after determining that these latest entries weren't going to be available as real books, I bought the e-versions, and then printed them on real paper. (I cannot stand e-books – ephemeral electronic blips that you lease instead of buy. I'll only buy those titles if they aren't going to be released as legitimate books – and in this case, it's a good thing that I did, as each of these Kindle stories that I found and paid for were soon withdrawn.)

As I read these latest "Holmes" stories, I noticed that each had a definite style that captured the writing from the late 1800's or early 1900's. (No matter how modern pasticheurs try to achieve that, they never quite pull it off.) But in one of the first two or three titles that I read, I caught a couple of mistakes. In one story, Holmes and Watson leave 221 Baker Street and are immediately in the area around The Temple and Fleet Street, rather than in Marylebone, where Baker Street is properly located. On another occasion, the story's policeman – who had been identified up to that point as Inspector Lestrade – was inexplicably named *Superintendent Miller* – but only in one instance. And in another place in one of the stories, Holmes's address was stated to be *5A King's Bench Walk.*

It was then that some vague memory triggered in my head, and I realized why these stories had captured the style of the late Victorian and early Edwardian eras: *It was because they had actually been written then.* I recalled – from reading Otto Penzler's book of biographies so long ago - that 5A King's Bench Walk belonged to Dr. Thorndyke, and not Sherlock Holmes. Someone was taking the original Thorndyke stories, which I had never before read, and simply changing names: Dr. Thorndyke, Dr. Jervis, and Superintendent Miller became Sherlock Holmes, Dr. Watson, and Inspector Lestrade, respectively.

Between 2012 and 2014, the anonymous author continued to load new Kindle editions on Amazon of Thorndyke-converted to-Holmes stories, and I continued to buy them. As soon as I had one, I would read it, and then try to figure out the original Thorndyke story from which it was taken. When I'd done so, I'd post a review, identifying what this editor was doing, from where he or she was taking the story, and urging that person, whoever it was, give credit to R. Austin Freeman instead of listing the author as Dr. John H. Watson.

Soon after each of my reviews would appear, the story would be withdrawn. I don't know if it was because the editor had made enough money from the initial sales, or if my reviews alerted him or her that they're game had been uncovered. In any case, I still have the printed copies of each of these converted stories – possibly the only copies that are still in existence.

For the record, over that two year period, this editor produced sixteen converted tales – four of the original Thorndyke novels, and twelve short stories. One of the original short stories, "The Mandarin's Pearl", was converted twice, with slight variations – initially published as "The Dragon Pearl", withdrawn, and later revised and reloaded as "The Oriental Pearl":

- "The Bloodied Thumbprint" – Originally the first Thorndyke novel, *The Red Thumb Mark*;
- "The Eye of Ra" – Originally the second Thorndyke novel, *The Eye of Osiris*;
- "The Cat's Eye Mystery" – Originally the sixth Thorndyke novel, *The Cat's Eye*;
- "The Julius Dalton Mystery" – Originally the ninth Thorndyke novel, *The D'Arblay Mystery*;
- "The Green Jacket Mystery" – Originally "The Green Check Jacket";
- "Mr. Crofton's Disappearance" – Originally "The Mysterious Visitor";
- "The Coded Lock" – Originally "The Puzzle Lock";
- "The Duplicated Letter" – Originally "The Stalking Horse";
- "The Bullion Robbery" – Originally "The Stolen Ingots";
- "The Talking Corpse" – Originally "The Contents of a Mare's Nest";
- "The Blue Diamond Mystery" – Originally "The Fisher of Men";
- "The Dragon Pearl" – Originally "The Mandarin's Pearl". (This story was also reworked and published again as a Holmes story under the title "The Oriental Pearl");
- "The Ingenious Murder" – Originally "The Aluminium Dagger";

23

- "The Bloodhound Superstition" – Originally "The Singing Bone"; *and*
- "The Magic Box" – Originally "The Magic Casket".

For quite a while, I was happy to have these as Holmes stories, and I even considered converting the rest of the Thorndyke adventures into additions to the extended Holmes Canon as well. (For at that time I cared nothing for Dr. Thorndyke.) It was partly with these converted stories in mind that I was motivated to go ahead and publish *Sherlock Holmes in Montague Street* (2014, 2016), which did the same thing to the Martin Hewitt stories, making them early adventures of Holmes before he met Watson and moved to Baker Street. I had long before decided to my own satisfaction that Martin Hewitt *was* a young Sherlock Holmes, with his identity changed through the preparations of a different literary agent than Sir Arthur Conan Doyle.

The taking of old public-domain stories featuring other detectives as the main protagonists and switching them so that Holmes is the main character has also been done by Alan Lance Andersen for his collection *The Affairs of Sherlock Holmes* (2015, 2016), wherein various non-series Sax Rohmer stories from nearly a hundred years ago were reworked as Holmes tales. Other non-Holmes authors have sometimes done the same thing. Raymond Chandler revised some of his early short stories so that the original characters' names were changed to Philip Marlowe. Ross MacDonald – (Kenneth Millar) also rewrote his old stories as well, making them into Lew Archer cases instead. More recently, the British ITV series *Marple* has taken non-Miss Marple Agatha Christie stories and converted them into episodes featuring that character.

So I had no problems with this type of change – and still don't. In fact, in my foreword to *Sherlock Holmes of Montague Street*, I wrote that I would rather have these converted Thorndyke stories as Holmes adventures, because I would rather read about Holmes than Thorndyke. But gradually my mind began to change, and I became more curious about Thorndyke, as presented in the proper fashion.

In 2013, I was able to go to London, as well as other places in England and Scotland, on the first (of three so far) Holmes Pilgrimages. For the most part, if a location wasn't related to Holmes, I didn't visit it. There were a few exceptions – I did intentionally visit Solar Pons's house at 7B Praed Street, Hercule Poirot's two residences, James Bond's flat in Chelsea – but everything else was pretty much pure Holmes.

One day, during my Holmesian rambles, I was making my way east down Fleet Street, and I visited both of the possible locations of "Pope's

Court" (as featured in "The Red-Headed League"), Poppin's Court and Mitre Court. (The latter is also one of the locations where Denis Nayland Smith and Dr. Petrie had quarters in some of the Fu Manchu books.) I decided that Mitre Court was certainly the original of "Pope's Court", and I passed through it to find myself unexpectedly in The Temple.

That's the amazing thing about a Holmes Pilgrimage to London – one travels to a site and finds two more very close by. I had planned to visit The Temple, but hadn't realized that I was so close. And now here I was – and more interesting was the fact that I was walking along King's Bench Walk, which runs downhill from the Miter Court passage. I recalled that Thorndyke had lived at 5A, so I made my way there – but without too much awe on that day, because I hadn't actually read any Thorndyke adventures yet – just some converted Holmes stories.

After I returned home, the thought of that side-trip to Thorndyke's front door stuck in my mind, and I sought out and read the first novel in the series, *The Red Thumb Mark*. I was so impressed that I kept going, and discovered a wonderful series of books and stories – fascinating characters and mysteries, and very evocative descriptions of both the London and the countryside of those times.

When I returned on my second Holmes Pilgrimage in 2015, I took the second Thorndyke book with me, reading it while there – while also reading Holmes stories too, of course! This one, *The Eye of Osiris*, has a great deal of London atmosphere, and I spent part of one late afternoon tracking down locations in this book – or what's now left of them – in the area around Fetter Lane to the north of Thorndyke's home in The Temple. It was truly unforgettable.

And of course I made an intentional stop at King's Bench Walk on that 2015 trip, and again on Holmes Pilgrimage No. 3 in 2016. By that point I was a Thorndyke fan, and I took the trouble to write to the current occupiers of 5A before I traveled to see if I could step inside and perhaps spend a moment in Thorndyke's old quarters. Sadly, they did not respond – either because it was simply beneath them to do so, or possibly because they get too many people like me who want to make a literary pilgrimage to what is a functioning and thriving business location.

While making photographs at Thorndyke's old doorway, I had several chances to go inside when someone else would enter or leave – My ever-present deerstalker and I could have simply been bold enough to slip in and then talk my way onward. It worked at other places on my Holmes Pilgrimages – the laboratory at Barts where Holmes and Watson met, for instance, and the site of the (former?) Diogenes Club at No. 78 Pall Mall, where they acted just oddly enough to make me think that the club is still there. But for some reason, barging into Thorndyke's old chambers without proper permission didn't feel quite right. But if or when I make Holmes Pilgrimage No. 4, I'll definitely make an even greater effort to see the doctor's former rooms.

The Editor and his deerstalker at 5A King's Bench Walk
September 2016
With many thanks . . . .

These last few years have been an amazing ride, and I've been able to play in the Sherlockian sandbox more than I'd ever imagined. (And subsequently, the Solar Pons sandbox, and now Thorndyke, too! Along the way, I've been able to meet some incredible people, both in person and in the modern electronic way, and also I've been able to read several hundred new Holmes adventures, as well as to be able to share them with others.

Still, what is most important is my amazingly wonderful wife (of over thirty years!) Rebecca, and our truly awesome son and my friend, Dan. I love you both, and you are everything to me! I am the luckiest guy in the world.

I have all the gratitude in the world for everyone that I've encountered along the way – It's an undeniable fact that Sherlock Holmes authors are the *best* people! I'd like to thank those who offer support, encouragement, and friendship, sometimes patiently waiting on me to reply as my time is directed in many other directions. Many many thanks to (in alphabetical order): Brian Belanger, Derrick Belanger, Bob Byrne, Roger Johnson, Mark Mower, Denis Smith, Tom Turley, Dan Victor, and Marcia Wilson.

In particular, I'd also like to especially thank Steve Emecz, who is always supportive of every idea that I pitch. It's been my particular good fortune that he crossed my path – it changed my life in a way that would have never happened otherwise, and I'm grateful for every opportunity!

I hope that these books will provide pleasure to those discovering Dr. Thorndyke for the first time, and to others who have known him for a long time. As always, I approach these matters from a Sherlockian perspective, so of course these stories, to me, are a peripheral extension of Holmes's world, and as such they are just more tiny threads woven into the ongoing Great Holmes Tapestry. However, they are wonderful on their own, and however one reads them, I wish great joy upon the journey.

David Marcum
October 2018

Questions, comments, and story submissions
may be addressed to David Marcum at
thepapersofsherlockholmes@gmail.com

5A King's Bench Walk
in the late 1890's when
Thorndyke was in residence

Editor's *Caveat*

These stories have been prepared using modern text-converting software, and as such, occasional deviations in punctuation have occurred. Those who absolutely must have the original version, down to each jot and dash, should understand that this version was created in order to present Dr. Thorndyke's adventures to a modern audience, and not to preserve an absolute pristine model for the historical archives.

Similarly, these stories were written in a time when racial prejudice and stereotypes were much more common than today. While some of these stereotypes must be unfortunately maintained within the story in order to accurately reflect the plot and the characters of those times, there are some words that were used in the original stories – vile racial epithets that have no business being repeated or perpetuated anywhere – that I have cheerfully removed. (There weren't many of them, but *any* are *too many*.)

If readers find that they want to experience the original versions as they were first written, with those hateful and ignorant words included, then they would be advised to seek out the original books. These versions celebrate Dr. Thorndyke and Dr. Jervis – who do *not* use the awful stereotyped language, I'm glad to say! – and as such, I felt no need whatsoever to include objectionable and offensive material simply for the sake of honoring or archiving the historical record.

David Marcum
Editor

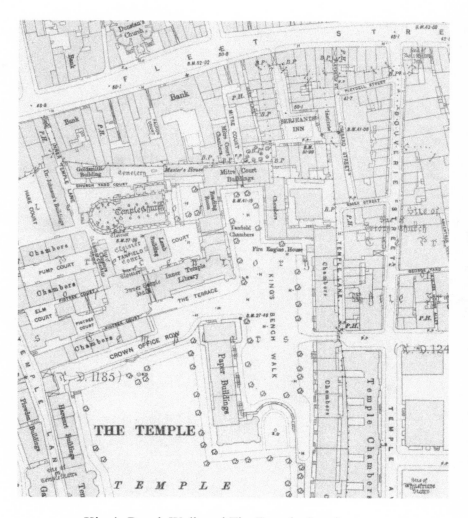

King's Bench Walk and The Temple, London
circa 1900

33

The Red 🗡 🗡
Thumb Mark

By
R. Austin
Freeman

1907 Collingwood Brothers Cover

Preface

*I*n writing the following story, the author has had in view no purpose other than that of affording entertainment to such readers as are interested in problems of crime and their solutions, and the story itself differs in no respect from others of its class, excepting in that an effort has been made to keep within the probabilities of ordinary life, both in the characters and in the incidents.

Nevertheless it may happen that the book may serve a useful purpose in drawing attention to certain popular misapprehensions on the subject of finger-prints and their evidential value, misapprehensions the extent of which may be judged when we learn from the newspapers that several Continental commercial houses have actually substituted finger-prints for signed initials.

The facts and figures contained in Mr. Singleton's evidence, including the very liberal estimate of the population of the globe, are, of course, taken from Mr. Galton's great and important work on finger-prints, to which the reader who is interested in the subject is referred for much curious and valuable information.

In conclusion, the author desires to express his thanks to his friend Mr. Bernard E. Bishop for the assistance rendered to him in certain photographic experiments, and to those officers of the Central Criminal Court who very kindly furnished him with details of the procedure in criminal trials.

R.A.F.

Chapter I
My Learned Brother

"*Conflagratam An° 1677. Fabricatam An° 1698. Richardo Powell Armiger Thesaurar.*" The words, set in four panels, which formed a frieze beneath the pediment of a fine brick portico, summarised the history of one of the tall houses at the upper end of King's Bench Walk and as I, somewhat absently, read over the inscription, my attention was divided between admiration of the exquisitely finished carved brickwork and the quiet dignity of the building, and an effort to reconstitute the dead and gone Richard Powell, and the stirring times in which he played his part.

I was about to turn away when the empty frame of the portico became occupied by a figure, and one so appropriate, in its wig and obsolete habiliments, to the old-world surroundings that it seemed to complete the picture, and I lingered idly to look at it. The barrister had halted in the doorway to turn over a sheaf of papers that he held in his hand, and, as he replaced the red tape which bound them together, he looked up and our eyes met. For a moment we regarded one another with the incurious gaze that casual strangers bestow on one another. Then there was a flash of mutual recognition. The impassive and rather severe face of the lawyer softened into a genial smile, and the figure, detaching itself from its frame, came down the steps with a hand extended in cordial greeting.

"My dear Jervis," he exclaimed, as we clasped hands warmly, "this is a great and delightful surprise. How often have I thought of my old comrade and wondered if I should ever see him again, and lo! Here he is, thrown up on the sounding beach of the Inner Temple, like the proverbial bread cast upon the waters."

"Your surprise, Thorndyke, is nothing to mine," I replied, "for your bread has at least returned as bread, whereas I am in the position of a man who, having cast his bread upon the waters, sees it return in the form of a buttered muffin or a Bath bun. I left a respectable medical practitioner and I find him transformed into a bewigged and begowned limb of the law."

Thorndyke laughed at the comparison.

"Liken not your old friend unto a Bath bun," said he. "Say, rather, that you left him a chrysalis and come back to find him a butterfly. But the change is not so great as you think. Hippocrates is only hiding under the gown of Solon, as you will understand when I explain my metamorphosis, and that I will do this very evening, if you have no engagement."

"I am one of the unemployed at present," I said, "and quite at your service."

"Then come round to my chambers at seven," said Thorndyke, "and we will have a chop and a pint of claret together and exchange autobiographies. I am due in court in a few minutes."

"Do you reside within that noble old portico?" I asked.

"No," replied Thorndyke. "I often wish I did. It would add several inches to one's stature to feel that the mouth of one's burrow was graced with a Latin inscription for admiring strangers to ponder over. No, my chambers are some doors further down – number 5A," and he turned to point out the house as we crossed towards Crown Office Row.

At the top of Middle Temple Lane we parted, Thorndyke taking his way with fluttering gown towards the Law Courts, while I directed my steps westward towards Adam Street, the chosen haunt of the medical agent.

The soft-voiced bell of the Temple clock was telling out the hour of seven in muffled accents (as though it apologised for breaking the studious silence) as I emerged from the archway of Mitre Court and turned into King's Bench Walk.

The paved footway was empty save for a single figure, pacing slowly before the doorway of number 5A*, in which, though the wig had now given place to a felt hat and the gown to a jacket, I had no difficulty in recognising my friend.

"Punctual to the moment, as of old," said he, meeting me halfway. "What a blessed virtue is punctuality, even in small things. I have just been taking the air in Fountain Court, and will now introduce you to my chambers. Here is my humble retreat."

We passed in through the common entrance and ascended the stone stairs to the first floor, where we were confronted by a massive door, above which my friend's name was written in white letters.

"Rather a forbidding exterior," remarked Thorndyke, as he inserted the latchkey, "but it is homely enough inside."

The heavy door swung outwards and disclosed a baize-covered inner door, which Thorndyke pushed open and held for me to pass in.

---

* EDITOR'S NOTE: In the original text, Thorndyke's residence is identified here – and in no other location throughout the entire Thorndyke Canon – as *6A King's Bench Walk*. This has long been considered to be a mistake by Freeman, and is discussed more thoroughly in Chapter X of Norman Donaldson's *In Search of Dr. Thorndyke* (Bowling Green University Popular Press, 1971). For consistency and correctness, the true address is used here.

"You will find my chambers an odd mixture," said Thorndyke, "for they combine the attractions of an office, a museum, a laboratory and a workshop."

"And a restaurant," added a small, elderly man, who was decanting a bottle of claret by means of a glass syphon, "you forgot that, sir."

"Yes, I forgot that, Polton," said Thorndyke, "but I see you have not." He glanced towards a small table that had been placed near the fire and set out with the requisites for our meal.

"Tell me," said Thorndyke, as we made the initial onslaught on the products of Polton's culinary experiments, "what has been happening to you since you left the hospital six years ago?"

"My story is soon told," I answered, somewhat bitterly. "It is not an uncommon one. My funds ran out, as you know, rather unexpectedly. When I had paid my examination and registration fees the coffer was absolutely empty, and though, no doubt, a medical diploma contains – to use Johnson's phrase – the potentiality of wealth beyond the dreams of avarice, there is a vast difference in practice between the potential and the actual. I have, in fact, been earning a subsistence, sometimes as an assistant, sometimes as a *locum tenens*. Just now I've got no work to do, and so have entered my name on Turcival's list of eligibles."

Thorndyke pursed up his lips and frowned.

"It's a wicked shame, Jervis," said he presently, "that a man of your abilities and scientific acquirements should be frittering away his time on odd jobs like some half-qualified wastrel."

"It is," I agreed. "My merits are grossly undervalued by a stiff-necked and obtuse generation. But what would you have, my learned brother? If poverty steps behind you and claps the occulting bushel over your thirty thousand candle-power luminary, your brilliancy is apt to be obscured."

"Yes, I suppose that is so," grunted Thorndyke, and he remained for a time in deep thought.

"And now," said I, "let us have your promised explanation. I am positively frizzling with curiosity to know what chain of circumstances has converted John Evelyn Thorndyke from a medical practitioner into a luminary of the law."

Thorndyke smiled indulgently.

"The fact is," said he, "that no such transformation has occurred. John Evelyn Thorndyke is still a medical practitioner."

"What, in a wig and gown!" I exclaimed.

"Yes, a mere sheep in wolf's clothing," he replied. "I will tell you how it has come about. After you left the hospital, six years ago, I stayed on, taking up any small appointments that were going – assistant demonstrator, or curatorships and such like – hung about the chemical and physical laboratories, the museum and post mortem room, and meanwhile took my M.D. and D.Sc. Then I got called to the bar in the hope of getting a coronership, but soon after this, old Stedman retired unexpectedly – you

41

remember Stedman, the lecturer on medical jurisprudence – and I put in for the vacant post. Rather to my surprise, I was appointed lecturer, whereupon I dismissed the coronership from my mind, took my present chambers and sat down to wait for anything that might come."

"And what has come?" I asked.

"Why, a very curious assortment of miscellaneous practice," he replied. "At first I only got an occasional analysis in a doubtful poisoning case, but, by degrees, my sphere of influence has extended until it now includes all cases in which a special knowledge of medicine or physical science can be brought to bear upon law."

"But you plead in court, I observe," said I.

"Very seldom," he replied. "More usually I appear in the character of that *bête noir* of judges and counsel – the scientific witness. But in most instances I do not appear at all – I merely direct investigations, arrange and analyse the results, and prime the counsel with facts and suggestions for cross-examination."

"A good deal more interesting than acting as understudy for an absent g.p.," said I, a little enviously. "But you deserve to succeed, for you were always a deuce of a worker, to say nothing of your capabilities."

"Yes, I worked hard," replied Thorndyke, "and I work hard still, but I have my hours of labour and my hours of leisure, unlike you poor devils of general practitioners, who are liable to be dragged away from the dinner table or roused out of your first sleep by – confound it all! Who can that be?"

For at this moment, as a sort of commentary on his self-congratulation, there came a smart rapping at the outer door.

"Must see who it is, I suppose," he continued, "though one expects people to accept the hint of a closed oak."

He strode across the room and flung open the door with an air of by no means gracious inquiry.

"It's rather late for a business call," said an apologetic voice outside, "but my client was anxious to see you without delay."

"Come in, Mr. Lawley," said Thorndyke, rather stiffly, and, as he held the door open, the two visitors entered. They were both men – one middle-aged, rather foxy in appearance and of a typically legal aspect, and the other a fine, handsome young fellow of very prepossessing exterior, though at present rather pale and wild-looking, and evidently in a state of profound agitation.

"I am afraid," said the latter, with a glance at me and the dinner table, "that our visit – for which I am alone responsible – is a most unseasonable one. If we are really inconveniencing you, Dr. Thorndyke, pray tell us, and my business must wait."

Thorndyke had cast a keen and curious glance at the young man, and he now replied in a much more genial tone, "I take it that your business is of a kind that will not wait, and as to inconveniencing us, why, my friend and I are both doctors, and, as you are aware, no doctor expects to call any part of the twenty-four hours his own unreservedly."

I had risen on the entrance of the two strangers, and now proposed to take a walk on the Embankment and return later, but the young man interrupted me.

"Pray don't go away on my account," he said. "The facts that I am about to lay before Dr. Thorndyke will be known to all the world by this time to-morrow, so there is no occasion for any show of secrecy."

"In that case," said Thorndyke, "let us draw our chairs up to the fire and fall to business forthwith. We had just finished our dinner and were waiting for the coffee, which I hear my man bringing down at this moment."

We accordingly drew up our chairs, and when Polton had set the coffee on the table and retired, the lawyer plunged into the matter without preamble.

Chapter II
The Suspect

"I had better," said he, "give you a general outline of the case as it presents itself to the legal mind, and then my client, Mr. Reuben Hornby, can fill in the details if necessary, and answer any questions that you may wish to put to him.

"Mr. Reuben occupies a position of trust in the business of his uncle, John Hornby, who is a gold and silver refiner and dealer in precious metals generally. There is a certain amount of outside assay work carried on in the establishment, but the main business consists in the testing and refining of samples of gold sent from certain mines in South Africa.

"About five years ago Mr. Reuben and his cousin Walter – another nephew of John Hornby – left school, and both were articled to their uncle, with the view to their ultimately becoming partners in the house, and they have remained with him ever since, occupying, as I have said, positions of considerable responsibility.

"And now for a few words as to how business is conducted in Mr. Hornby's establishment. The samples of gold are handed over at the docks to some accredited representative of the firm – generally either Mr. Reuben or Mr. Walter – who has been despatched to meet the ship, and conveyed either to the bank or to the works according to circumstances. Of course every effort is made to have as little gold as possible on the premises, and the bars are always removed to the bank at the earliest opportunity, but it happens unavoidably that samples of considerable value have often to remain on the premises all night, and so the works are furnished with a large and powerful safe or strong room for their reception. This safe is situated in the private office under the eye of the principal, and, as an additional precaution, the caretaker, who acts as night-watchman, occupies a room directly over the office, and patrols the building periodically through the night.

"Now a very strange thing has occurred with regard to this safe. It happens that one of Mr. Hornby's customers in South Africa is interested in a diamond mine, and, although transactions in precious stones form no part of the business of the house, he has, from time to time, sent parcels of rough diamonds addressed to Mr. Hornby, to be either deposited in the bank or handed on to the diamond brokers.

"A fortnight ago Mr. Hornby was advised that a parcel of stones had been despatched by the *Elmina Castle*, and it appeared that the parcel was an unusually large one and contained stones of exceptional size and value.

44

Under these circumstances Mr. Reuben was sent down to the docks at an early hour in the hope the ship might arrive in time for the stones to be lodged in the bank at once. Unfortunately, however, this was not the case, and the diamonds had to be taken to the works and locked up in the safe."

"Who placed them in the safe?" asked Thorndyke.

"Mr. Hornby himself, to whom Mr. Reuben delivered up the package on his return from the docks."

"Yes," said Thorndyke, "and what happened next?"

"Well, on the following morning, when the safe was opened, the diamonds had disappeared."

"Had the place been broken into?" asked Thorndyke.

"No. The place was all locked up as usual, and the caretaker, who had made his accustomed rounds, had heard nothing, and the safe was, outwardly, quite undisturbed. It had evidently been opened with keys and locked again after the stones were removed."

"And in whose custody were the keys of the safe?" inquired Thorndyke.

"Mr. Hornby usually kept the keys himself, but, on occasions, when he was absent from the office, he handed them over to one of his nephews – whichever happened to be in charge at the time. But on this occasion the keys did not go out of his custody from the time when he locked up the safe, after depositing the diamonds in it, to the time when it was opened by him on the following morning."

"And was there anything that tended to throw suspicion upon anyone?" asked Thorndyke.

"Why, yes," said Mr. Lawley, with an uncomfortable glance at his client, "unfortunately there was. It seemed that the person who abstracted the diamonds must have cut or scratched his thumb or finger in some way, for there were two drops of blood on the bottom of the safe and one or two bloody smears on a piece of paper, and, in addition, a remarkably clear imprint of a thumb."

"Also in blood?" asked Thorndyke.

"Yes. The thumb had apparently been put down on one of the drops and then, while still wet with blood, had been pressed on the paper in taking hold of it or otherwise."

"Well, and what next?"

"Well," said the lawyer, fidgeting in his chair, "to make a long story short, the thumb-print has been identified as that of Mr. Reuben Hornby."

"Ha!" exclaimed Thorndyke. "The plot thickens with a vengeance. I had better jot down a few notes before you proceed any further."

He took from a drawer a small paper-covered notebook, on the cover of which he wrote "Reuben Hornby," and then, laying the book open on a blotting-pad, which he rested on his knee, he made a few brief notes.

"Now," he said, when he had finished, "with reference to this thumb-print. There is no doubt, I suppose, as to the identification?"

"None whatever," replied Mr. Lawley. "The Scotland Yard people, of course, took possession of the paper, which was handed to the director of the finger-print department for examination and comparison with those in their collection. The report of the experts is that the thumb-print does not agree with any of the thumb-prints of criminals in their possession – that it is a very peculiar one, inasmuch as the ridge-pattern on the bulb of the thumb – which is a remarkably distinct and characteristic one – is crossed by the scar of a deep cut, rendering identification easy and infallible. That it agrees in every respect with the thumb-print of Mr. Reuben Hornby, and is, in fact, his thumb-print beyond any possible doubt."

"Is there any possibility," asked Thorndyke, "that the paper bearing the thumb-print could have been introduced by any person?"

"No," answered the lawyer. "It is quite impossible. The paper on which the mark was found was a leaf from Mr. Hornby's memorandum block. He had pencilled on it some particulars relating to the diamonds, and laid it on the parcel before he closed up the safe."

"Was anyone present when Mr. Hornby opened the safe in the morning?" asked Thorndyke.

"No, he was alone," answered the lawyer. "He saw at a glance that the diamonds were missing, and then he observed the paper with the thumb-mark on it, on which he closed and locked the safe and sent for the police."

"Is it not rather odd that the thief did not notice the thumb-mark, since it was so distinct and conspicuous?"

"No, I think not," answered Mr. Lawley. "The paper was lying face downwards on the bottom of the safe, and it was only when he picked it up and turned it over that Mr. Hornby discovered the thumb-print. Apparently the thief had taken hold of the parcel, with the paper on it, and the paper had afterwards dropped off and fallen with the marked surface downwards – probably when the parcel was transferred to the other hand."

"You mentioned," said Thorndyke, "that the experts at Scotland Yard have identified this thumb-mark as that of Mr. Reuben Hornby. May I ask how they came to have the opportunity of making the comparison?"

"Ah!" said Mr. Lawley. "Thereby hangs a very curious tale of coincidences. The police, of course, when they found that there was so simple a means of identification as a thumb-mark, wished to take thumb-prints of all the employees in the works, but this Mr. Hornby refused to sanction – rather quixotically, as it seems to me – saying that he would not allow his nephews to be subjected to such an indignity. Now it was, naturally, these nephews in whom the police were chiefly interested, seeing that they alone had had the handling of the keys, and considerable pressure was brought to bear upon Mr. Hornby to have the thumb-prints taken.

"However, he was obdurate, scouting the idea of any suspicion attaching to either of the gentlemen in whom he had reposed such complete confidence and whom he had known all their lives, and so the matter would probably have remained a mystery but for a very odd circumstance.

"You may have seen on the bookstalls and in shop windows an appliance called a 'Thumbograph,' or some such name, consisting of a small book of blank paper for collecting the thumb-prints of one's friends, together with an inking pad."

"I have seen those devices of the Evil One," said Thorndyke, "in fact, I have one, which I bought at Charing Cross Station."

"Well, it seems that some months ago Mrs. Hornby, the wife of John Hornby, purchased one of these toys – "

"As a matter of fact," interrupted Reuben, "it was my cousin Walter who bought the thing and gave it to her."

"Well, that is not material," said Mr. Lawley (though I observed that Thorndyke made a note of the fact in his book), "at any rate, Mrs. Hornby became possessed of one of these appliances and proceeded to fill it with the thumb-prints of her friends, including her two nephews. Now it happened that the detective in charge of this case called yesterday at Mr. Hornby's house when the latter was absent from home, and took the opportunity of urging her to induce her husband to consent to have the thumb-prints of her nephews taken for the inspection of the experts at Scotland Yard. He pointed out that the procedure was really necessary, not only in the interests of justice but in the interests of the young men themselves, who were regarded with considerable suspicion by the police, which suspicion would be completely removed if it could be shown by actual comparison that the thumb-print could not have been made by either of them. Moreover, it seemed that both the young men had expressed their willingness to have the test applied, but had been forbidden by their uncle. Then Mrs. Hornby had a brilliant idea. She suddenly remembered the 'Thumbograph,' and thinking to set the question at rest once for all, fetched the little book and showed it to the detective. It contained the prints of both thumbs of Mr. Reuben (among others), and, as the detective had with him a photograph of the incriminating mark, the comparison was made then and there, and you may imagine Mrs. Hornby's horror and amazement when it was made clear that the print of her nephew Reuben's left thumb corresponded in every particular with the thumb-print that was found in the safe.

"At this juncture Mr. Hornby arrived on the scene and was, of course, overwhelmed with consternation at the turn events had taken. He would have liked to let the matter drop and make good the loss of the diamonds out of his own funds, but, as that would have amounted practically to compounding a felony, he had no choice but to prosecute. As a result, a warrant was issued for the arrest of Mr. Reuben, and was executed this morning, and my client was taken forthwith to Bow Street and charged with the robbery."

"Was any evidence taken?" asked Thorndyke.

"No. Only evidence of arrest. The prisoner is remanded for a week, bail having been accepted in two sureties of five hundred pounds each."

Thorndyke was silent for a space after the conclusion of the narrative. Like me, he was evidently not agreeably impressed by the lawyer's manner, which seemed to take his client's guilt for granted, a position indeed not entirely without excuse having regard to the circumstances of the case.

"What have you advised your client to do?" Thorndyke asked presently.

"I have recommended him to plead guilty and throw himself on the clemency of the court as a first offender. You must see for yourself that there is no defence possible."

The young man flushed crimson, but made no remark.

"But let us be clear how we stand," said Thorndyke. "Are we defending an innocent man or are we endeavouring to obtain a light sentence for a man who admits that he is guilty?"

Mr. Lawley shrugged his shoulders.

"That question can be best answered by our client himself," said he.

Thorndyke directed an inquiring glance at Reuben Hornby, remarking, "You are not called upon to incriminate yourself in any way, Mr. Hornby, but I must know what position you intend to adopt."

Here I again proposed to withdraw, but Reuben interrupted me.

"There is no need for you to go away, Dr. Jervis," he said. "My position is that I did not commit this robbery and that I know nothing whatever about it or about the thumb-print that was found in the safe. I do not, of course, expect you to believe me in the face of the overwhelming evidence against me, but I do, nevertheless, declare in the most solemn manner before God, that I am absolutely innocent of this crime and have no knowledge of it whatever."

48

"Then I take it that you did not plead 'guilty'?" said Thorndyke.

"Certainly not, and I never will," replied Reuben hotly.

"You would not be the first innocent man, by very many, who has entered that plea," remarked Mr. Lawley. "It is often the best policy, when the defence is hopelessly weak."

"It is a policy that will not be adopted by me," rejoined Reuben. "I may be, and probably shall be, convicted and sentenced, but I shall continue to maintain my innocence, whatever happens. Do you think," he added, turning to Thorndyke, "that you can undertake my defence on that assumption?"

"It is the only assumption on which I should agree to undertake the case," replied Thorndyke.

"And – if I may ask the question – " pursued Reuben anxiously, "do you find it possible to conceive that I may really be innocent?"

"Certainly I do," Thorndyke replied, on which I observed Mr. Lawley's eyebrows rise perceptibly. "I am a man of facts, not an advocate, and if I found it impossible to entertain the hypothesis of your innocence, I should not be willing to expend time and energy in searching for evidence to prove it. Nevertheless," he continued, seeing the light of hope break out on the face of the unfortunate young man, "I must impress upon you that the case presents enormous difficulties and that we must be prepared to find them insuperable in spite of all our efforts."

"I expect nothing but a conviction," replied Reuben in a calm and resolute voice, "and can face it like a man if only you do not take my guilt for granted, but give me a chance, no matter how small, of making a defence."

"Everything shall be done that I am capable of doing," said Thorndyke, "that I can promise you. The long odds against us are themselves a spur to endeavour, as far as I am concerned. And now, let me ask you, have you any cuts or scratches on your fingers?"

Reuben Hornby held out both his hands for my colleague's inspection, and I noticed that they were powerful and shapely, like the hands of a skilled craftsman, though faultlessly kept. Thorndyke set on the table a large condenser such as is used for microscopic work, and taking his client's hand, brought the bright spot of light to bear on each finger in succession, examining their tips and the parts around the nails with the aid of a pocket lens.

"A fine, capable hand, this," said he, regarding the member approvingly, as he finished his examination, "but I don't perceive any trace of a scar on either the right or left. Will you go over them, Jervis? The robbery took place a fortnight ago, so there has been time for a small cut or scratch to heal and disappear entirely. Still, the matter is worth noting."

He handed me the lens and I scrutinised every part of each hand without being able to detect the faintest trace of any recent wound.

"There is one other matter that must be attended to before you go," said Thorndyke, pressing the electric bell-push by his chair. "I will take one or two prints of the left thumb for my own information."

In response to the summons, Polton made his appearance from some lair unknown to me, but presumably the laboratory, and, having received his instructions, retired, and presently returned carrying a box, which he laid on the table. From this receptacle Thorndyke drew forth a bright copper plate mounted on a slab of hard wood, a small printer's roller, a tube of finger-print ink, and a number of cards with very white and rather glazed surfaces.

"Now, Mr. Hornby," said he, "your hands, I see, are beyond criticism as to cleanliness, but we will, nevertheless, give the thumb a final polish."

Accordingly he proceeded to brush the bulb of the thumb with a well-soaked badger-hair nail-brush, and, having rinsed it in water, dried it with a silk handkerchief, and gave it a final rub on a piece of chamois leather. The thumb having been thus prepared, he squeezed out a drop of the thick ink on to the copper plate and spread it out with the roller, testing the condition of the film from time to time by touching the plate with the tip of his finger and taking an impression on one of the cards.

When the ink had been rolled out to the requisite thinness, he took Reuben's hand and pressed the thumb lightly but firmly on to the inked plate, then, transferring the thumb to one of the cards, which he directed me to hold steady on the table, he repeated the pressure, when there was left on the card a beautifully sharp and clear impression of the bulb of the thumb, the tiny papillary ridges being shown with microscopic distinctness, and even the mouths of the sweat glands, which appeared as rows of little white dots on the black lines of the ridges. This manoeuvre was repeated a dozen times on two of the cards, each of which thus received six impressions. Thorndyke then took one or two rolled prints, *i.e.* prints produced by rolling the thumb first on the inked slab and then on the card, by which means a much larger portion of the surface of the thumb was displayed in a single print.

"And now," said Thorndyke, "that we may be furnished with all the necessary means of comparison, we will take an impression in blood."

The thumb was accordingly cleansed and dried afresh, when Thorndyke, having pricked his own thumb with a needle, squeezed out a good-sized drop of blood on to a card.

"There," said he, with a smile, as he spread the drop out with the needle into a little shallow pool, "it is not every lawyer who is willing to shed his blood in the interests of his client."

50

He proceeded to make a dozen prints as before on two cards, writing a number with his pencil opposite each print as he made it.

"We are now," said he, as he finally cleansed his client's thumb, "furnished with the material for a preliminary investigation, and if you will now give me your address, Mr. Hornby, we may consider our business concluded for the present. I must apologise to you, Mr. Lawley, for having detained you so long with these experiments."

The lawyer had, in fact, been viewing the proceedings with hardly concealed impatience, and he now rose with evident relief that they were at an end.

"I have been highly interested," he said mendaciously, "though I confess I do not quite fathom your intentions. And, by the way, I should like to have a few words with you on another matter, if Mr. Reuben would not mind waiting for me in the square just a few minutes."

"Not at all," said Reuben, who was, I perceived, in no way deceived by the lawyer's pretence. "Don't hurry on my account. My time is my own – at present." He held out his hand to Thorndyke, who grasped it cordially.

"Good-bye, Mr. Hornby," said the latter. "Do not be unreasonably sanguine, but at the same time, do not lose heart. Keep your wits about you and let me know at once if anything occurs to you that may have a bearing on the case."

The young man then took his leave, and, as the door closed after him, Mr. Lawley turned towards Thorndyke.

"I thought I had better have a word with you alone," he said, "just to hear what line you propose to take up, for I confess that your attitude has puzzled me completely."

"What line would you propose?" asked Thorndyke.

"Well," said the lawyer, with a shrug of his shoulders, "the position seems to be this: Our young friend has stolen a parcel of diamonds and has been found out – at least, that is how the matter presents itself to me."

"That is not how it presents itself to me," said Thorndyke drily. "He may have taken the diamonds or he may not. I have no means of judging until I have sifted the evidence and acquired a few more facts. This I hope to do in the course of the next day or two, and I suggest that we postpone the consideration of our plan of campaign until I have seen what line of defence it is possible to adopt."

"As you will," replied the lawyer, taking up his hat, "but I am afraid you are encouraging the young rogue to entertain hopes that will only make his fall the harder – to say nothing of our own position. We don't want to make ourselves ridiculous in court, you know."

"I don't, certainly," agreed Thorndyke. "However, I will look into the matter and communicate with you in the course of a day or two."

He stood holding the door open as the lawyer descended the stairs, and when the footsteps at length died away, he closed it sharply and turned to me with an air of annoyance.

"The 'young rogue,'" he remarked, "does not appear to me to have been very happy in his choice of a solicitor. By the way, Jervis, I understand you are out of employment just now?"

"That is so," I answered.

"Would you care to help me – as a matter of business, of course – to work up this case? I have a lot of other work on hand and your assistance would be of great value to me."

I said, with great truth, that I should be delighted.

"Then," said Thorndyke, "come round to breakfast to-morrow and we will settle the terms, and you can commence your duties at once. And now let us light our pipes and finish our yarns as though agitated clients and thick-headed solicitors had no existence."

Chapter III
A Lady in the Case

When I arrived at Thorndyke's chambers on the following morning, I found my friend already hard at work. Breakfast was laid at one end of the table, while at the other stood a microscope of the pattern used for examining plate-cultures of micro-organisms, on the wide stage of which was one of the cards bearing six thumb-prints in blood. A condenser threw a bright spot of light on the card, which Thorndyke had been examining when I knocked, as I gathered from the position of the chair, which he now pushed back against the wall.

"I see you have commenced work on our problem," I remarked as, in response to a double ring of the electric bell, Polton entered with the materials for our repast.

"Yes," answered Thorndyke. "I have opened the campaign, supported, as usual, by my trusty chief-of-staff, eh! Polton?"

The little man, whose intellectual, refined countenance and dignified bearing seemed oddly out of character with the tea-tray that he carried, smiled proudly, and, with a glance of affectionate admiration at my friend, replied, "Yes, sir. We haven't been letting the grass grow under our feet. There's a beautiful negative washing upstairs and a bromide enlargement too, which will be mounted and dried by the time you have finished your breakfast."

"A wonderful man that, Jervis," my friend observed as his assistant retired. "Looks like a rural dean or a chancery judge, and was obviously intended by Nature to be a professor of physics. As an actual fact he was first a watchmaker, then a maker of optical instruments, and now he is mechanical factotum to a medical jurist. He is my right-hand, is Polton. Takes an idea before you have time to utter it – but you will make his more intimate acquaintance by-and-by."

"Where did you pick him up?" I asked.

"He was an in-patient at the hospital when I first met him, miserably ill and broken, a victim of poverty and undeserved misfortune. I gave him one or two little jobs, and when I found what class of man he was I took him permanently into my service. He is perfectly devoted to me, and his gratitude is as boundless as it is uncalled for."

"What are the photographs he was referring to?" I asked.

"He is making an enlarged *facsimile* of one of the thumb-prints on bromide paper and a negative of the same size in case we want the print repeated."

"You evidently have some expectation of being able to help poor Hornby," said I, "though I cannot imagine how you propose to go to work. To me his case seems as hopeless a one as it is possible to conceive. One doesn't like to condemn him, but yet his innocence seems almost unthinkable."

"It does certainly look like a hopeless case," Thorndyke agreed, "and I see no way out of it at present. But I make it a rule, in all cases, to proceed on the strictly classical lines of inductive inquiry – collect facts, make hypotheses, test them and seek for verification. And I always endeavour to keep a perfectly open mind.

"Now, in the present case, assuming, as we must, that the robbery has actually taken place, there are four conceivable hypotheses: (1) that the robbery was committed by Reuben Hornby; (2) that it was committed by Walter Hornby; (3) that it was committed by John Hornby, or (4) that it was committed by some other person or persons.

"The last hypothesis I propose to disregard for the present and confine myself to the examination of the other three."

"You don't think it possible that Mr. Hornby could have stolen the diamonds out of his own safe?" I exclaimed.

"I incline at present to no one theory of the matter," replied Thorndyke. "I merely state the hypotheses. John Hornby had access to the diamonds, therefore it is possible that he stole them."

"But surely he was responsible to the owners."

"Not in the absence of gross negligence, which the owners would have difficulty in proving. You see, he was what is called a gratuitous bailee, and in such a case no responsibility for loss lies with the bailee unless there has been gross negligence."

"But the thumb-mark, my dear fellow!" I exclaimed. "How can you possibly get over that?"

"I don't know that I can," answered Thorndyke calmly, "but I see you are taking the same view as the police, who persist in regarding a finger-print as a kind of magical touchstone, a final proof, beyond which inquiry need not go. Now, this is an entire mistake. A finger-print is merely a fact – a very important and significant one, I admit – but still a fact, which, like any other fact, requires to be weighed and measured with reference to its evidential value."

"And what do you propose to do first?"

"I shall first satisfy myself that the suspected thumb-print is identical in character with that of Reuben Hornby – of which, however, I have very

54

little doubt, for the finger-print experts may fairly be trusted in their own speciality."

"And then?"

"I shall collect fresh facts, in which I look to you for assistance, and, if we have finished breakfast, I may as well induct you into your new duties."

He rose and rang the bell, and then, fetching from the office four small, paper-covered notebooks, laid them before me on the table.

"One of these books," said he, "we will devote to data concerning Reuben Hornby. You will find out anything you can – anything, mind, no matter how trivial or apparently irrelevant – in any way connected with him and enter it in this book." He wrote on the cover "Reuben Hornby" and passed the book to me. "In this second book you will, in like manner, enter anything that you can learn about Walter Hornby, and, in the third book, data concerning John Hornby. As to the fourth book, you will keep that for stray facts connected with the case but not coming under either of the other headings. And now let us look at the product of Polton's industry."

He took from his assistant's hand a photograph ten inches long by eight broad, done on glazed bromide paper and mounted flatly on stiff card. It showed a greatly magnified *facsimile* of one of the thumb-prints, in which all the minute details, such as the orifices of the sweat glands and trifling irregularities in the ridges, which, in the original, could be seen only with the aid of a lens, were plainly visible to the naked eye. Moreover, the entire print was covered by a network of fine black lines, by which it was divided into a multitude of small squares, each square being distinguished by a number.

"Excellent, Polton," said Thorndyke approvingly, "a most admirable enlargement. You see, Jervis, we have photographed the thumb-print in contact with a numbered micrometer divided into square twelfths-of-an-inch. The magnification is eight diameters, so that the squares are here each two-thirds-of-an-inch in diameter. I have a number of these micrometers of different scales, and I find them invaluable in examining cheques, doubtful signatures and such like. I see you have packed up the camera and the microscope, Polton. Have you put in the micrometer?"

"Yes, sir," replied Polton, "and the six-inch objective and the low-power eye-piece. Everything is in the case, and I have put 'special rapid' plates into the dark-slides in case the light should be bad."

"Then we will go forth and beard the Scotland Yard lions in their den," said Thorndyke, putting on his hat and gloves.

"But surely," said I, "you are not going to drag that great microscope to Scotland Yard, when you only want eight diameters. Haven't you a dissecting microscope or some other portable instrument?"

"We have a most delightful instrument of the dissecting type, of Polton's own make – he shall show it to you. But I may have need of a more powerful instrument – and here let me give you a word of warning: Whatever you may see me do, make no comments before the officials. We are seeking information, not giving it, you understand."

At this moment the little brass knocker on the inner door – the outer oak being open – uttered a timid and apologetic rat-tat.

"Who the deuce can that be?" muttered Thorndyke, replacing the microscope on the table. He strode across to the door and opened it somewhat brusquely, but immediately whisked his hat off, and I then perceived a lady standing on the threshold.

"Dr. Thorndyke?" she inquired, and as my colleague bowed, she continued, "I ought to have written to ask for an appointment but the matter is rather urgent – it concerns Mr. Reuben Hornby and I only learned from him this morning that he had consulted you."

"Pray come in," said Thorndyke. "Dr. Jervis and I were just setting out for Scotland Yard on this very business. Let me present you to my colleague, who is working up the case with me."

Our visitor, a tall handsome girl of twenty or thereabouts, returned my bow and remarked with perfect self-possession, "My name is Gibson – Miss Juliet Gibson. My business is of a very simple character and need not detain you many minutes."

She seated herself in the chair that Thorndyke placed for her, and continued in a brisk and business-like manner, "I must tell you who I am in order to explain my visit to you. For the last six years I have lived with Mr. and Mrs. Hornby, although I am no relation to them. I first came to the house as a sort of companion to Mrs. Hornby, though, as I was only fifteen at the time, I need hardly say that my duties were not very onerous – in fact, I think Mrs. Hornby took me because I was an orphan without the proper means of getting a livelihood, and she had no children of her own.

"Three years ago I came into a little fortune which rendered me independent, but I had been so happy with my kind friends that I asked to be allowed to remain with them, and there I have been ever since in the position of an adopted daughter. Naturally, I have seen a great deal of their nephews, who spend a good part of their time at the house, and I need not tell you that the horrible charge against Reuben has fallen upon us like a thunderbolt. Now, what I have come to say to you is this: I do not believe that Reuben stole those diamonds. It is entirely out of character with all my previous experience of him. I am convinced that he is innocent, and I am prepared to back my opinion."

"In what way?" asked Thorndyke.

"By supplying the sinews of war," replied Miss Gibson. "I understand that legal advice and assistance involves considerable expense."

"I am afraid you are quite correctly informed," said Thorndyke.

"Well, Reuben's pecuniary resources are, I am sure, quite small, so it is necessary for his friends to support him, and I want you to promise me that nothing shall be left undone that might help to prove his innocence if I make myself responsible for any costs that he is unable to meet. I should prefer, of course, not to appear in the matter, if it could be avoided."

"Your friendship is of an eminently practical kind, Miss Gibson," said my colleague, with a smile. "As a matter of fact, the costs are no affair of mine. If the occasion arose for the exercise of your generosity you would have to approach Mr. Reuben's solicitor through the medium of your guardian, Mr. Hornby, and with the consent of the accused. But I do not suppose the occasion will arise, although I am very glad you called, as you may be able to give us valuable assistance in other ways. For example, you might answer one or two apparently impertinent questions."

"I should not consider any question impertinent that you considered necessary to ask," our visitor replied.

"Then," said Thorndyke, "I will venture to inquire if any special relations exist between you and Mr. Reuben."

"You look for the inevitable motive in a woman," said Miss Gibson, laughing and flushing a little. "No, there have been no tender passages between Reuben and me. We are merely old and intimate friends. In fact, there is what I may call a tendency in another direction – Walter Hornby."

"Do you mean that you are engaged to Mr. Walter?"

"Oh, no," she replied, "but he has asked me to marry him – he has asked me, in fact, more than once, and I really believe that he has a sincere attachment to me."

She made this latter statement with an odd air, as though the thing asserted were curious and rather incredible, and the tone was evidently noticed by Thorndyke as well as me for he rejoined, "Of course he has. Why not?"

"Well, you see," replied Miss Gibson, "I have some six hundred a year of my own and should not be considered a bad match for a young man like Walter, who has neither property nor expectations, and one naturally takes that into account. But still, as I have said, I believe he is quite sincere in his professions and not merely attracted by my money."

57

"I do not find your opinion at all incredible," said Thorndyke, with a smile, "even if Mr. Walter were quite a mercenary young man – which, I take it, he is not."

Miss Gibson flushed very prettily as she replied, "Oh, pray do not trouble to pay me compliments. I assure you I am by no means insensible of my merits. But with regard to Walter Hornby, I should be sorry to apply the term 'mercenary' to him, and yet – well, I have never met a young man who showed a stronger appreciation of the value of money. He means to succeed in life and I have no doubt he will."

"And do I understand that you refused him?"

"Yes. My feelings towards him are quite friendly, but not of such a nature as to allow me to contemplate marrying him."

"And now, to return for a moment to Mr. Reuben. You have known him for some years?"

"I have known him intimately for six years," replied Miss Gibson.

"And what sort of character do you give him?"

"Speaking from my own observation of him," she replied, "I can say that I have never known him to tell an untruth or do a dishonourable deed. As to theft, it is merely ridiculous. His habits have always been inexpensive and frugal, he is unambitious to a fault, and in respect to the 'main chance' his indifference is as conspicuous as Walter's keenness. He is a generous man, too, although careful and industrious."

"Thank you, Miss Gibson," said Thorndyke. "We shall apply to you for further information as the case progresses. I am sure that you will help us if you can, and that you can help us if you will, with your clear head and your admirable frankness. If you will leave us your card, Dr. Jervis and I will keep you informed of our prospects and ask for your assistance whenever we need it."

After our fair visitor had departed, Thorndyke stood for a minute or more gazing dreamily into the fire. Then, with a quick glance at his watch, he resumed his hat and, catching up the microscope, handed the camera case to me and made for the door.

"How the time goes!" he exclaimed, as we descended the stairs, "but it hasn't been wasted, Jervis, hey?"

"No, I suppose not," I answered tentatively.

"You suppose not!" he replied. "Why here is as pretty a little problem as you could desire – what would be called in the jargon of the novels, a psychological problem – and it is your business to work it out, too."

"You mean as to Miss Gibson's relations with these two young men?" Thorndyke nodded.

"Is it any concern of ours?" I asked.

"Certainly it is," he replied. "Everything is a concern of ours at this preliminary stage. We are groping about for a clue and must let nothing pass unscrutinised."

"Well, then, to begin with, she is not wildly infatuated with Walter Hornby, I should say."

"No," agreed Thorndyke, laughing softly, "we may take it that the canny Walter has not inspired a grand passion."

"Then," I resumed, "if I were a suitor for Miss Gibson's hand, I think I would sooner stand in Reuben's shoes than in Walter's."

"There again I am with you," said Thorndyke. "Go on."

"Well," I continued, "our fair visitor conveyed to me the impression that her evident admiration of Reuben's character was tempered by something that she had heard from a third party. That expression of hers, 'speaking from my own observation,' seemed to imply that her observations of him were not in entire agreement with somebody else's."

"Good man!" exclaimed Thorndyke, slapping me on the back, to the undissembled surprise of a policeman whom we were passing, "that is what I had hoped for in you – the capacity to perceive the essential underneath the obvious. Yes, somebody has been saying something about our client, and the thing that we have to find out is, what is it that has been said and who has been saying it. We shall have to make a pretext for another interview with Miss Gibson."

"By the way, why didn't you ask her what she meant?" I asked foolishly.

Thorndyke grinned in my face. "Why didn't you?" he retorted.

"No," I rejoined, "I suppose it is not politic to appear too discerning. Let me carry the microscope for a time. It is making your arm ache, I see."

"Thanks," said he, handing the case to me and rubbing his fingers, "it is rather ponderous."

"I can't make out what you want with this great instrument," I said. "A common pocket lens would do all that you require. Besides, a six-inch objective will not magnify more than two or three diameters."

"Two, with the draw-tube closed," replied Thorndyke, "and the low-power eye-piece brings it up to four. Polton made them both for me for examining cheques, bank-notes and other large objects. But you will understand when you see me use the instrument, and remember, you are to make no comments."

We had by this time arrived at the entrance to Scotland Yard, and were passing up the narrow thoroughfare, when we encountered a uniformed official who halted and saluted my colleague.

"Ah, I thought we should see you here before long, Doctor," said he genially. "I heard this morning that you have this thumb-print case in hand."

"Yes," replied Thorndyke, "I am going to see what can be done for the defence."

"Well," said the officer as he ushered us into the building, "you've given us a good many surprises, but you'll give us a bigger one if you can make anything of this. It's a foregone conclusion, I should say."

"My dear fellow," said Thorndyke, "there is no such thing. You mean that there is a *prima facie* case against the accused."

"Put it that way if you like," replied the officer, with a sly smile, "but I think you will find this about the hardest nut you ever tried your teeth on – and they're pretty strong teeth too, I'll say that. You had better come into Mr. Singleton's office," and he conducted us along a corridor and into a large, barely-furnished room, where we found a sedate-looking gentleman seated at a large writing table.

"How-d'ye-do, Doctor?" said the latter, rising and holding out his hand. "I can guess what you've come for. Want to see that thumb-print, eh?"

"Quite right," answered Thorndyke, and then, having introduced me, he continued: "We were partners in the last game, but we are on opposite sides of the board this time."

"Yes," agreed Mr. Singleton, "and we are going to give you check-mate."

He unlocked a drawer and drew forth a small portfolio, from which he extracted a piece of paper which he laid on the table. It appeared to be a sheet torn from a perforated memorandum block, and bore the pencilled inscription: "*Handed in by Reuben at 7.3 p.m., 9.3.01. J. H.*" At one end was a dark, glossy blood-stain, made by the falling of a good-sized drop, and this was smeared slightly, apparently by a finger or thumb having been pressed on it. Near to it were two or three smaller smears and a remarkably distinct and clean print of a thumb.

Thorndyke gazed intently at the paper for a minute or two, scrutinising the thumb-print and the smears in turn, but making no remark, while Mr. Singleton watched his impassive face with expectant curiosity.

"Not much difficulty in identifying that mark," the official at length observed.

"No," agreed Thorndyke, "it is an excellent impression and a very distinctive pattern, even without the scar."

"Yes," rejoined Mr. Singleton, "the scar makes it absolutely conclusive. You have a print with you, I suppose?"

"Yes," replied Thorndyke, and he drew from a wide flap-pocket the enlarged photograph, at the sight of which Mr. Singleton's face broadened into a smile.

"You don't want to put on spectacles to look at that," he remarked, "not that you gain anything by so much enlargement, three diameters is ample for studying the ridge-patterns. I see you have divided it up into numbered squares – not a bad plan, but ours, or rather Galton's, for we borrowed the method from him – is better for this purpose."

He drew from the portfolio a half-plate photograph of the thumb-print which appeared magnified to about four inches in length. The print was marked by a number of figures written minutely with a fine-pointed pen, each figure being placed on an "island," a loop, a bifurcation or some other striking and characteristic portion of the ridge-pattern.

"This system of marking with reference numbers," said Mr. Singleton, "is better than your method of squares, because the numbers are only placed at points which are important for comparison, whereas your squares or the intersections of the lines fall arbitrarily on important or unimportant points according to chance. Besides, we can't let you mark our original, you know, though, of course, we can give you a photograph, which will do as well."

"I was going to ask you to let me take a photograph presently," said Thorndyke.

"Certainly," replied Mr. Singleton, "if you would rather have one of your own taking. I know you don't care to take anything on trust. And now I must get on with my work, if you will excuse me. Inspector Johnson will give you any assistance you may require."

"And see that I don't pocket the original," added Thorndyke, with a smile at the inspector who had shown us in.

"Oh, I'll see to that," said the latter, grinning, and, as Mr. Singleton returned to his table, Thorndyke unlocked the microscope case and drew forth the instrument.

"What, are you going to put it under the microscope?" exclaimed Mr. Singleton, looking round with a broad smile.

"Must do something for my fee, you know," replied Thorndyke, as he set up the microscope and screwed on two extra objectives to the triple nose-piece.

"You observe that there is no deception," he added to the inspector, as he took the paper from Mr. Singleton's table and placed it between two slips of glass.

"I'm watching you, sir," replied the officer, with a chuckle, and he did watch, with close attention and great interest, while Thorndyke laid the glass slips on the microscope stage and proceeded to focus.

61

I also watched, and was a good deal exercised in my mind by my colleague's proceedings. After a preliminary glance with the six-inch glass, he swung round the nose-piece to the half-inch objective and slipped in a more powerful eye-piece, and with this power he examined the blood-stains carefully, and then moved the thumb-print into the field of vision. After looking at this for some time with deep attention, he drew from the case a tiny spirit lamp which was evidently filled with an alcoholic solution of some sodium salt, for when he lit it I recognised the characteristic yellow sodium flame. Then he replaced one of the objectives by a spectroscopic attachment, and having placed the little lamp close to the microscope mirror, adjusted the spectroscope. Evidently my friend was fixing the position of the "D" line (or sodium line) in the spectrum.

Having completed the adjustments, he now examined afresh the blood-smears and the thumb-print, both by transmitted and reflected light, and I observed him hurriedly draw one or two diagrams in his notebook. Then he replaced the spectroscope and lamp in the case and brought forth the micrometer – a slip of rather thin glass about three inches by one-and-a-half – which he laid over the thumb-print in the place of the upper plate of glass.

Having secured it in position by the clips, he moved it about, comparing its appearance with that of the lines on the large photograph, which he held in his hand. After a considerable amount of adjustment and readjustment, he appeared to be satisfied, for he remarked to me, "I think I have got the lines in the same position as they are on our print, so, with Inspector Johnson's assistance, we will take a photograph which we can examine at our leisure."

He extracted the camera – a quarter-plate instrument – from its case and opened it. Then, having swung the microscope on its stand into a horizontal position, he produced from the camera case a slab of mahogany with three brass feet, on which he placed the camera, and which brought the latter to a level with the eye-piece of the microscope.

The front of the camera was fitted with a short sleeve of thin black leather, and into this the eye-piece end of the microscope was now passed, the sleeve being secured round the barrel of the microscope by a stout india rubber band, thus producing a completely light-tight connection.

Everything was now ready for taking the photograph. The light from the window having been concentrated on the thumb-print by means of a condenser, Thorndyke proceeded to focus the image on the ground-glass screen with extreme care and then, slipping a small leather cap over the objective, introduced the dark slide and drew out the shutter.

"I will ask you to sit down and remain quite still while I make the exposure," he said to me and the inspector. "A very little vibration is enough to destroy the sharpness of the image."

We seated ourselves accordingly, and Thorndyke then removed the cap, standing motionless, watch in hand, while he exposed the first plate.

"We may as well take a second, in case this should not turn out quite perfect," he said, as he replaced the cap and closed the shutter.

He reversed the dark slide and made another exposure in the same way, and then, having removed the micrometer and replaced it by a slip of plain glass, he made two more exposures.

"There are two plates left," he remarked, as he drew out the second dark slide. "I think I will take a record of the blood-stain on them."

He accordingly made two more exposures – one of the larger blood-stain and one of the smaller smears.

"There," said he, with an air of satisfaction, as he proceeded to pack up what the inspector described as his "box of tricks." "I think we have all the data that we can squeeze out of Scotland Yard, and I am very much obliged to you, Mr. Singleton, for giving so many facilities to your natural enemy, the counsel for the defence."

"Not our natural enemies, Doctor," protested Mr. Singleton. "We work for a conviction, of course, but we don't throw obstacles in the way of the defence. You know that perfectly well."

"Of course I do, my dear sir," replied Thorndyke, shaking the official by the hand. "Haven't I benefited by your help a score of times? But I am greatly obliged all the same. Good-bye."

"Good-bye, Doctor. I wish you luck, though I fear you will find it 'no go' this time."

"We shall see," replied Thorndyke, and with a friendly wave of the hand to the inspector he caught up the two cases and led the way out of the building.

Chapter IV
Confidences

During our walk home my friend was unusually thoughtful and silent, and his face bore a look of concentration under which I thought I could detect, in spite of his habitually impassive expression, a certain suppressed excitement of a not entirely unpleasurable kind. I forbore, however, from making any remarks or asking questions, not only because I saw that he was preoccupied, but also because, from my knowledge of the man, I judged that he would consider it his duty to keep his own counsel and to make no unnecessary confidences even to me.

On our arrival at his chambers he immediately handed over the camera to Polton with a few curt directions as to the development of the plates, and, lunch being already prepared, we sat down at the table without delay.

We had proceeded with our meal in silence for some time when Thorndyke suddenly laid down his knife and fork and looked into my face with a smile of quiet amusement.

"It has just been borne in upon me, Jervis," said he, "that you are the most companionable fellow in the world. You have the heaven-sent gift of silence."

"If silence is the test of companionability," I answered, with a grin, "I think I can pay you a similar compliment in even more emphatic terms."

He laughed cheerfully and rejoined, "You are pleased to be sarcastic, I observe, but I maintain my position. The capacity to preserve an opportune silence is the rarest and most precious of social accomplishments. Now, most men would have plied me with questions and babbled comments on my proceedings at Scotland Yard, whereas you have allowed me to sort out, without interruption, a mass of evidence while it is still fresh and impressive, to docket each item and stow it away in the pigeonholes of my brain. By the way, I have made a ridiculous oversight."

"What is that?" I asked.

"The 'Thumbograph.' I never ascertained whether the police have it or whether it is still in the possession of Mrs. Hornby."

"Does it matter?" I inquired.

"Not much. Only I must see it. And perhaps it will furnish an excellent pretext for you to call on Miss Gibson. As I am busy at the hospital this afternoon and Polton has his hands full, it would be a good plan for you to drop in at Endsley Gardens – that is the address, I think –

and if you can see Miss Gibson, try to get a confidential chat with her, and extend your knowledge of the manners and customs of the three Messieurs Hornby. Put on your best bedside manner and keep your weather eye lifting. Find out everything you can as to the characters and habits of those three gentlemen, regardless of all scruples of delicacy. Everything is of importance to us, even to the names of their tailors."

"And with regard to the 'Thumbograph'?"

"Find out who has it, and, if it is still in Mrs. Hornby's possession, get her to lend it to us or – what might, perhaps, be better – get her permission to take a photograph of it."

"It shall be done according to your word," said I. "I will furbish up my exterior, and this very afternoon make my first appearance in the character of Paul Pry."

About an hour later I found myself upon the doorstep of Mr. Hornby's house in Endsley Gardens listening to the jangling of the bell that I had just set in motion.

"Miss Gibson, sir?" repeated the parlourmaid in response to my question. "She *was* going out, but I am not sure whether she has gone yet. If you will step in, I will go and see."

I followed her into the drawing-room, and, threading my way amongst the litter of small tables and miscellaneous furniture by which ladies nowadays convert their special domain into the semblance of a broker's shop, let go my anchor in the vicinity of the fireplace to await the parlourmaid's report.

I had not long to wait, for in less than a minute Miss Gibson herself entered the room. She wore her hat and gloves, and I congratulated myself on my timely arrival.

"I didn't expect to see you again so soon, Dr. Jervis," she said, holding out her hand with a frank and friendly manner, "but you are very welcome all the same. You have come to tell me something?"

"On the contrary," I replied, "I have come to ask you something."

"Well, that is better than nothing," she said, with a shade of disappointment. "Won't you sit down?"

I seated myself with caution on a dwarf chair of scrofulous aspect, and opened my business without preamble.

"Do you remember a thing called a 'Thumbograph'?"

"Indeed I do," she replied with energy. "It was the cause of all this trouble."

"Do you know if the police took possession of it?"

"The detective took it to Scotland Yard that the finger-print experts might examine it and compare the two thumb-prints, and they wanted to keep it, but Mrs. Hornby was so distressed at the idea of its being used in

65

evidence that they let her have it back. You see, they really had no further need of it, as they could take a print for themselves when they had Reuben in custody. In fact, he volunteered to have a print taken at once, as soon as he was arrested, and that was done."

"So the 'Thumbograph' is now in Mrs. Hornby's possession?"

"Yes, unless she has destroyed it. She spoke of doing so."

"I hope she has not," said I, in some alarm, "for Dr. Thorndyke is extremely anxious, for some reason, to examine it."

"Well, she will be down in a few minutes, and then we shall know. I told her you were here. Have you any idea what Dr. Thorndyke's reason is for wanting to see it?"

"None whatever," I replied. "Dr. Thorndyke is as close as an oyster. He treats me as he treats everyone else – he listens attentively, observes closely, and says nothing."

"It doesn't sound very agreeable," mused Miss Gibson, "and yet he seemed very nice and sympathetic."

"He *is* very nice and sympathetic," I retorted with some emphasis, "but he doesn't make himself agreeable by divulging his clients' secrets."

"I suppose not, and I regard myself as very effectively snubbed," said she, smiling, but evidently somewhat piqued by my not very tactful observation.

I was hastening to repair my error with apologies and self-accusations, when the door opened and an elderly lady entered the room. She was somewhat stout, amiable and placid of mien, and impressed me (to be entirely truthful) as looking rather foolish.

"Here is Mrs. Hornby," said Miss Gibson, presenting me to her hostess, and she continued, "Dr. Jervis has come to ask about the 'Thumbograph.' You haven't destroyed it, I hope?"

"No, my dear," replied Mrs. Hornby. "I have it in my little bureau. What did Dr. Jervis wish to know about it?"

Seeing that she was terrified lest some new and dreadful surprise should be sprung upon her, I hastened to reassure her.

"My colleague, Dr. Thorndyke, is anxious to examine it. He is directing your nephew's defence, you know."

"Yes, yes," said Mrs. Hornby. "Juliet told me about him. She says he is a dear. Do you agree with her?"

Here I caught Miss Gibson's eye, in which was a mischievous twinkle, and noted a little deeper pink in her cheeks.

"Well," I answered dubiously, "I have never considered my colleague in the capacity of a dear, but I have a very high opinion of him in every respect."

"That, no doubt, is the masculine equivalent," said Miss Gibson, recovering from the momentary embarrassment that Mrs. Hornby's artless repetition of her phrase had produced. "I think the feminine expression is more epigrammatic and comprehensive. But to return to the object of Dr. Jervis's visit. Would you let him have the 'Thumbograph,' aunt, to show to Dr. Thorndyke?"

"Oh, my dear Juliet," replied Mrs. Hornby, "I would do anything – anything – to help our poor boy. I will never believe that he could be guilty of theft – common, vulgar theft. There has been some dreadful mistake – I am convinced there has – I told the detectives so. I assured them that Reuben could not have committed the robbery, and that they were totally mistaken in supposing him to be capable of such an action. But they would not listen to me, although I have known him since he was a little child, and ought to be able to judge, if anyone is. Diamonds, too! Now, I ask you, what could Reuben want with diamonds? And they were not even cut."

Here Mrs. Hornby drew forth a lace-edged handkerchief and mopped her eyes.

"I am sure Dr. Thorndyke will be very much interested to see this little book of yours," said I, with a view to stemming the tide of her reflections.

"Oh, the 'Thumbograph,'" she replied. "Yes, I will let him have it with the greatest pleasure. I am so glad he wishes to see it. It makes one feel hopeful to know that he is taking so much interest in the case. Would you believe it, Dr. Jervis, those detective people actually wanted to keep it to bring up in evidence against the poor boy. My 'Thumbograph,' mind you. But I put my foot down there and they had to return it. I was resolved that they should not receive any assistance from me in their efforts to involve my nephew in this horrible affair."

"Then, perhaps," said Miss Gibson, "you might give Dr. Jervis the 'Thumbograph' and he can hand it to Dr. Thorndyke."

"Of course I will," said Mrs. Hornby, "instantly, and you need not return it, Dr. Jervis. When you have finished with it, fling it into the fire. I wish never to see it again."

But I had been considering the matter, and had come to the conclusion that it would be highly indiscreet to take the book out of Mrs. Hornby's custody, and this I now proceeded to explain.

"I have no idea," I said, "for what purpose Dr. Thorndyke wishes to examine the 'Thumbograph,' but it occurs to me that he may desire to put it in evidence, in which case it would be better that it should not go out of your possession for the present. He merely commissioned me to ask for your permission to take a photograph of it."

"Oh, if he wants a photograph," said Mrs. Hornby, "I could get one done for him without any difficulty. My nephew Walter would take one for us, I am sure, if I asked him. He is so clever, you know – is he not, Juliet, dear?"

"Yes, aunt," replied Miss Gibson quickly, "but I expect Dr. Thorndyke would rather take the photograph himself."

"I am sure he would," I agreed. "In fact, a photograph taken by another person would not be of much use to him."

"Ah," said Mrs. Hornby in a slightly injured tone, "you think Walter is just an ordinary amateur, but if I were to show you some of the photographs he has taken you would really be surprised. He is remarkably clever, I assure you."

"Would you like us to bring the book to Dr. Thorndyke's chambers?" asked Miss Gibson. "That would save time and trouble."

"It is excessively good of you," I began.

"Not at all. When shall we bring it? Would you like to have it this evening?"

"We should very much," I replied. "My colleague could then examine it and decide what is to be done with it. But it is giving you so much trouble."

"It is nothing of the kind," said Miss Gibson. "You would not mind coming with me this evening, would you, aunt?"

"Certainly not, my dear," replied Mrs. Hornby, and she was about to enlarge on the subject when Miss Gibson rose and, looking at her watch, declared that she must start on her errand at once. I also rose to make my adieux, and she then remarked, "If you are walking in the same direction as I am, Dr. Jervis, we might arrange the time of our proposed visit as we go along."

I was not slow to avail myself of this invitation, and a few seconds later we left the house together, leaving Mrs. Hornby smiling fatuously after us from the open door.

"Will eight o'clock suit you, do you think?" Miss Gibson asked, as we walked up the street.

"It will do excellently, I should say," I answered. "If anything should render the meeting impossible I will send you a telegram. I could wish that you were coming alone, as ours is to be a business conference."

Miss Gibson laughed softly – and a very pleasant and musical laugh it was.

"Yes," she agreed. "Dear Mrs. Hornby is a little diffuse and difficult to keep to one subject, but you must be indulgent to her little failings. You would be if you had experienced such kindness and generosity from her as I have."

"I am sure I should," I rejoined, "in fact, I am. After all, a little diffuseness of speech and haziness of ideas are no great faults in a generous and amiable woman of her age."

Miss Gibson rewarded me for these highly correct sentiments with a little smile of approval, and we walked on for some time in silence. Presently she turned to me with some suddenness and a very earnest expression, and said, "I want to ask you a question, Dr. Jervis, and please forgive me if I beg you to put aside your professional reserve just a little in my favour. I want you to tell me if you think Dr. Thorndyke has any kind of hope or expectation of being able to save poor Reuben from the dreadful peril that threatens him."

This was a rather pointed question, and I took some time to consider it before replying.

"I should like," I replied at length, "to tell you as much as my duty to my colleague will allow me to, but that is so little that it is hardly worth telling. However, I may say this without breaking any confidence: Dr. Thorndyke has undertaken the case and is working hard at it, and he would, most assuredly, have done neither the one nor the other if he had considered it a hopeless one."

"That is a very encouraging view of the matter," said she, "which, had, however, already occurred to me. May I ask if anything came of your visit to Scotland Yard? Oh, please don't think me encroaching. I am so terribly anxious and troubled."

"I can tell you very little about the results of our expedition, for I know very little, but I have an idea that Dr. Thorndyke is not dissatisfied with his morning's work. He certainly picked up some facts, though I have no idea of their nature, and as soon as we reached home he developed a sudden desire to examine the 'Thumbograph.'"

"Thank you, Dr. Jervis," she said gratefully. "You have cheered me more than I can tell you, and I won't ask you any more questions. Are you sure I am not bringing you out of the way?"

"Not at all," I answered hastily. "The fact is, I had hoped to have a little chat with you when we had disposed of the 'Thumbograph,' so I can regard myself as combining a little business with a great deal of pleasure if I am allowed to accompany you."

She gave me a little ironical bow as she inquired, "And, in short, I may take it that I am to be pumped?"

"Come, now," I retorted. "You have been plying the pump handle pretty vigorously yourself. But that is not my meaning at all. You see, we are absolute strangers to all the parties concerned in this case, which, of course, makes for an impartial estimate of their characters. But, after all, knowledge is more useful to us than impartiality. There is our client, for instance. He impressed us both very favourably, I think, but he might have been a plausible rascal with the blackest of records. Then you come and tell us that he is a gentleman of stainless character and we are at once on firmer ground."

"I see," said Miss Gibson thoughtfully, "and suppose that I or someone else had told you things that seemed to reflect on his character. Would they have influenced you in your attitude towards him?"

"Only in this," I replied, "that we should have made it our business to inquire into the truth of those reports and ascertain their origin."

"That is what one should always do, I suppose," said she, still with an air of deep thoughtfulness which encouraged me to inquire, "May I ask if anyone to your knowledge has ever said anything to Mr. Reuben's disadvantage?"

She pondered for some time before replying, and kept her eyes bent pensively on the ground. At length she said, not without some hesitation of manner, "It is a small thing and quite without any bearing on this affair. But it has been a great trouble to me since it has to some extent put a barrier between Reuben and me, and we used to be such close friends. And I have blamed myself for letting it influence me – perhaps unjustly – in my opinion of him. I will tell you about it, though I expect you will think me very foolish.

"You must know, then, that Reuben and I used, until about six months ago, to be very much together, though we were only friends, you understand. But we were on the footing of relatives, so there was nothing out of the way in it. Reuben is a keen student of ancient and mediaeval art, in which I also am much interested, so we used to visit the museums and galleries together and get a great deal of pleasure from comparing our views and impressions of what we saw.

"About six months ago, Walter took me aside one day and, with a very serious face, asked me if there was any kind of understanding between Reuben and me. I thought it rather impertinent of him, but nevertheless, I told him the truth, that Reuben and I were just friends and nothing more.

"'If that is the case,' said he, looking mighty grave, 'I would advise you not to be seen about with him quite so much.'

"'And why not?' I asked very naturally.

"'Why, the fact is,' said Walter, 'that Reuben is a confounded fool. He has been chattering to the men at the club and seems to have given them the impression that a young lady of means and position has been setting her cap at him very hard, but that he, being a high-souled philosopher above the temptations that beset ordinary mortals, is superior both to her blandishments and her pecuniary attractions. I give you the hint for your own guidance,' he continued, 'and I expect this to go no farther. You mustn't be annoyed with Reuben. The best of young men will often behave like prigs and donkeys, and I have no doubt the fellows have grossly exaggerated what he said, but I thought it right to put you on your guard.'

"Now this report, as you may suppose, made me excessively angry, and I wanted to have it out with Reuben then and there. But Walter refused to sanction this – 'there was no use in making a scene' he said – and he insisted that the caution was given to me in strict confidence. So what was I to do? I tried to ignore it and treat Reuben as I always had done, but this I found impossible – my womanly pride was much too deeply hurt. And yet I felt it the lowest depth of meanness to harbour such thoughts of him without giving him the opportunity to defend himself. And although it was most unlike Reuben in some respects, it was very like him in others, for he has always expressed the utmost contempt for men who marry for a livelihood. So I have remained on the horns of a dilemma and am there still. What do you think I ought to have done?"

I rubbed my chin in some embarrassment at this question. Needless to say, I was most disagreeably impressed by Walter Hornby's conduct, and not a little disposed to blame my fair companion for giving an ear to his secret disparagement of his cousin, but I was obviously not in a position to pronounce, offhand, upon the merits of the case.

"The position appears to be this," I said, after a pause, "either Reuben has spoken most unworthily and untruthfully of you, or Walter has lied deliberately about him."

"Yes," she agreed, "that is the position, but which of the two alternatives appears to you the more probable?"

"That is very difficult to say," I answered. "There is a certain kind of cad who is much given to boastful rhodomontade concerning his conquests. We all know him and can generally spot him at first sight, but I must say that Reuben Hornby did not strike me as that kind of man at all. Then it is clear that the proper course for Walter to have adopted, if he had really heard such rumours, was to have had the matter out with Reuben, instead of coming secretly to you with whispered reports. That is my feeling, Miss Gibson, but, of course, I may be quite wrong. I gather that our two young friends are not inseparable companions?"

"Oh, they are very good friends, but you see, their interests and views of life are quite different. Reuben, although an excellent worker in business hours, is a student, or perhaps rather what one would call a scholar, whereas Walter is more a practical man of affairs – decidedly long-headed and shrewd. He is undoubtedly very clever, as Mrs. Hornby said."

71

"He takes photographs, for instance," I suggested.

"Yes. But not ordinary amateur photographs – his work is more technical and quite excellent of its kind. For example, he did a most beautiful series of micro-photographs of sections of metalliferous rocks which he reproduced for publication by the collotype process, and even printed off the plates himself."

"I see. He must be a very capable fellow."

"He is, very," she assented, "and very keen on making a position, but I am afraid he is rather too fond of money for its own sake, which is not a pleasant feature in a young man's character, is it?"

I agreed that it was not.

"Excessive keenness in money affairs," proceeded Miss Gibson oracularly, "is apt to lead a young man into bad ways – oh, you need not smile, Dr. Jervis, at my wise saws. It is perfectly true, and you know it. The fact is, I sometimes have an uneasy feeling that Walter's desire to be rich inclines him to try what looks like a quick and easy method of making money. He had a friend – a Mr. Horton – who is a dealer on the Stock Exchange and who 'operates' rather largely – 'operate' I believe is the expression used, although it seems to be nothing more than common gambling – and I have more than once suspected Walter of being concerned in what Mr. Horton calls 'a little flutter.'"

"That doesn't strike me as a very long-headed proceeding," I remarked, with the impartial wisdom of the impecunious, and therefore untempted.

"No," she agreed, "it isn't. But your gambler always thinks he is going to win – though you mustn't let me give you the impression that Walter is a gambler. But here is my destination. Thank you for escorting me so far, and I hope you are beginning to feel less like a stranger to the Hornby family. We shall make our appearance to-night at eight punctually."

She gave me her hand with a frank smile and tripped up the steps leading to the street door, and when I glanced back, after crossing the road, she gave me a little friendly nod as she turned to enter the house.

72

Chapter V
The "Thumbograph"

"**S**o your net has been sweeping the quiet and pleasant waters of feminine conversation," remarked Thorndyke when we met at the dinner table and I gave him an outline of my afternoon's adventures.

"Yes," I answered, "and here is the catch cleaned and ready for the consumer."

I laid on the table two of my notebooks in which I had entered such facts as I had been able to extract from my talk with Miss Gibson.

"You made your entries as soon as possible after your return, I suppose?" said Thorndyke, "while the matter was still fresh?"

"I wrote down my notes as I sat on a seat in Kensington Gardens within five minutes after leaving Miss Gibson."

"Good!" said Thorndyke. "And now let us see what you have collected."

He glanced quickly through the entries in the two books, referring back once or twice, and stood for a few moments silent and abstracted. Then he laid the little books down on the table with a satisfied nod.

"Our information, then," he said, "amounts to this: Reuben is an industrious worker at his business and, in his leisure, a student of ancient and medieval art – possibly a babbling fool and a cad or, on the other hand, a maligned and much-abused man.

"Walter Hornby is obviously a sneak and possibly a liar, a keen man of business, perhaps a flutterer round the financial candle that burns in Throgmorton Street, an expert photographer and a competent worker of the collotype process. You have done a very excellent day's work, Jervis. I wonder if you see the bearing of the facts that you have collected."

"I think I see the bearing of some of them," I answered, "at least, I have formed certain opinions."

"Then keep them to yourself, *mon ami*, so that I need not feel as if I ought to unbosom myself of my own views."

"I should be very much surprised if you did, Thorndyke," I replied, "and should have none the better opinion of you. I realise fully that your opinions and theories are the property of your client and not to be used for the entertainment of your friends."

Thorndyke patted me on the back playfully, but he looked uncommonly pleased, and said, with evident sincerity, "I am really grateful to you for saying that, for I have felt a little awkward in being so

73

reticent with you who know so much of this case. But you are quite right, and I am delighted to find you so discerning and sympathetic. The least I can do under the circumstances is to uncork a bottle of Pommard, and drink the health of so loyal and helpful a colleague. Ah! Praise the gods! here is Polton, like a sacrificial priest accompanied by a sweet savour of roasted flesh. Rump steak I ween," he added, sniffing, "food meet for the mighty Shamash (that pun was fortuitous, I need not say) or a ravenous medical jurist. Can you explain to me, Polton, how it is that your rump steak is better than any other steak? Is it that you have command of a special brand of ox?"

The little man's dry countenance wrinkled with pleasure until it was as full of lines as a ground-plan of Clapham Junction.

"Perhaps it is the special treatment it gets, sir," he replied. "I usually bruise it in the mortar before cooking, without breaking up the fibre too much, and then I heat up the little cupel furnace to about 600° C, and put the steak in on a tripod."

Thorndyke laughed outright. "The cupel furnace, too," he exclaimed. "Well, well, 'to what base uses' – but I don't know that it is a base use after all. Anyhow, Polton, open a bottle of Pommard and put a couple of ten by eight 'process' plates in your dark slides. I am expecting two ladies here this evening with a document."

"Shall you bring them upstairs, sir?" inquired Polton, with an alarmed expression.

"I expect I shall have to," answered Thorndyke.

"Then I shall just smarten the laboratory up a bit," said Polton, who evidently appreciated the difference between the masculine and feminine view as to the proper appearance of working premises.

"And so Miss Gibson wanted to know our private views on the case?" said Thorndyke, when his voracity had become somewhat appeased.

"Yes," I answered, and then I repeated our conversation as nearly as I could remember it.

"Your answer was very discreet and diplomatic," Thorndyke remarked, "and it was very necessary that it should be, for it is essential that we show the backs of our cards to Scotland Yard, and if to Scotland Yard, then to the whole world. We know what their trump card is and can arrange our play accordingly, so long as we do not show our hand."

"You speak of the police as your antagonists. I noticed that at the 'Yard' this morning, and was surprised to find that they accepted the position. But surely their business is to discover the actual offender, not to fix the crime on some particular person."

"That would seem to be so," replied Thorndyke, "but in practice it is otherwise. When the police have made an arrest they work for a

74

conviction. If the man is innocent, that is his business, not theirs. It is for him to prove it. The system is a pernicious one – especially since the efficiency of a police officer is, in consequence, apt to be estimated by the number of convictions he has secured, and an inducement is thus held out to him to obtain a conviction, if possible, but it is of a piece with legislative procedure in general. Lawyers are not engaged in academic discussions or in the pursuit of truth, but each is trying, by hook or by crook, to make out a particular case without regard to its actual truth or even to the lawyer's own belief on the subject. That is what produces so much friction between lawyers and scientific witnesses. Neither can understand the point of view of the other. But we must not sit over the table chattering like this. It has gone half-past seven, and Polton will be wanting to make this room presentable."

"I notice you don't use your office much," I remarked.

"Hardly at all, excepting as a repository for documents and stationery. It is very cheerless to talk in an office, and nearly all my business is transacted with solicitors and counsel who are known to me, so there is no need for such formalities. All right, Polton. We shall be ready for you in five minutes."

The Temple bell was striking eight as, at Thorndyke's request, I threw open the iron-bound "oak", and even as I did so the sound of footsteps came up from the stairs below. I waited on the landing for our two visitors, and led them into the room.

"I am so glad to make your acquaintance," said Mrs. Hornby, when I had done the honours of introduction, "I have heard so much about you from Juliet – "

"Really, my dear aunt," protested Miss Gibson, as she caught my eye with a look of comical alarm, "you will give Dr. Thorndyke a most erroneous impression. I merely mentioned that I had intruded on him without notice and had been received with undeserved indulgence and consideration."

"You didn't put it quite in that way, my dear," said Mrs. Hornby, "but I suppose it doesn't matter."

"We are highly gratified by Miss Gibson's favourable report of us, whatever may have been the actual form of expression," said Thorndyke, with a momentary glance at the younger lady which covered her with smiling confusion, "and we are deeply indebted to you for taking so much trouble to help us."

"It is no trouble at all, but a great pleasure," replied Mrs. Hornby, and she proceeded to enlarge on the matter until her remarks threatened, like the rippling circles produced by a falling stone, to spread out into infinity. In the midst of this discourse Thorndyke placed chairs for the two ladies, and, leaning against the mantelpiece, fixed a stony gaze upon the small handbag that hung from Mrs. Hornby's wrist.

"Is the 'Thumbograph' in your bag?" interrupted Miss Gibson, in response to this mute appeal.

"Of course it is, my dear Juliet," replied the elder lady. "You saw me put it in yourself. What an odd girl you are. Did you think I should have taken it out and put it somewhere else? Not that these handbags are really very secure, you know, although I daresay they are safer than pockets, especially now that it is the fashion to have the pocket at the back. Still, I have often thought how easy it would be for a thief or a pickpocket or some other dreadful creature of that kind, don't you know, to make a snatch and – in fact, the thing has actually happened. Why, I knew a lady – Mrs. Moggridge, you know, Juliet – no, it wasn't Mrs. Moggridge, that was another affair, it was Mrs. – Mrs. – dear me, how silly of me! – Now, what was her name? Can't you help me, Juliet? You must surely remember the woman. She used to visit a good deal at the Hawley-Johnsons' – I think it was the Hawley-Johnsons', or else it was those people, you know – "

"Hadn't you better give Dr. Thorndyke the 'Thumbograph'?" interrupted Miss Gibson.

"Why, of course, Juliet, dear. What else did we come here for?" With a slightly injured expression, Mrs. Hornby opened the little bag and commenced, with the utmost deliberation, to turn out its contents on to the table. These included a laced handkerchief, a purse, a card-case, a visiting list, a packet of *papier poudré*, and when she had laid the last-mentioned article on the table, she paused abruptly and gazed into Miss Gibson's face with the air of one who has made a startling discovery.

"I remember the woman's name," she said in an impressive voice. "It was Gudge – Mrs. Gudge, the sister-in-law of – "

Here Miss Gibson made an unceremonious dive into the open bag and fished out a tiny parcel wrapped in notepaper and secured with a silk thread.

"Thank you," said Thorndyke, taking it from her hand just as Mrs. Hornby was reaching out to intercept it. He cut the thread and drew from its wrappings a little book bound in red cloth, with the word "*Thumbograph*" stamped upon the cover, and was beginning to inspect it when Mrs. Hornby rose and stood beside him.

"That," said she, as she opened the book at the first page, "is the thumb-mark of a Miss Colley. She is no connection of ours. You see it is a little smeared – she said Reuben jogged her elbow, but I don't think he did. At any rate he assured me he did not, and, you know – "

"Ah! Here is one we are looking for," interrupted Thorndyke, who had been turning the leaves of the book regardless of Mrs. Hornby's rambling comments, "a very good impression, too, considering the rather rough method of producing it."

He reached out for the reading lens that hung from its nail above the mantelpiece, and I could tell by the eagerness with which he peered through it at the thumb-print that he was looking for something. A moment later I felt sure that he had found that something which he had sought, for, though he replaced the lens upon its nail with a quiet and composed air and made no remark, there was a sparkle of the eye and a scarcely perceptible flush of suppressed excitement and triumph which I had begun to recognise beneath the impassive mask that he presented to the world.

"I shall ask you to leave this little book with me, Mrs. Hornby," he said, breaking in upon that lady's inconsequent babblings, "and, as I may possibly put it in evidence, it would be a wise precaution for you and Miss Gibson to sign your names – as small as possible – on the page which bears Mr. Reuben's thumb-mark. That will anticipate any suggestion that the book has been tampered with after leaving your hands."

"It would be a great impertinence for anyone to make any such suggestion," Mrs. Hornby began, but on Thorndyke's placing his fountain pen in her hand, she wrote her signature in the place indicated and handed the pen to Miss Gibson, who signed underneath.

"And now," said Thorndyke, "we will take an enlarged photograph of this page with the thumb-mark – not that it is necessary that it should be done now, as you are leaving the book in my possession, but the photograph will be wanted, and as my man is expecting us and has the apparatus ready, we may as well despatch the business at once."

To this both the ladies readily agreed (being, in fact, devoured by curiosity with regard to my colleague's premises), and we accordingly proceeded to invade the set of rooms on the floor above, over which the ingenious Polton was accustomed to reign in solitary grandeur.

It was my first visit to these mysterious regions, and I looked about me with as much curiosity as did the two ladies. The first room that we entered was apparently the workshop, for it contained a small woodworker's bench, a lathe, a bench for metal work and a number of mechanical appliances which I was not then able to examine, but I noticed that the entire place presented to the eye a most unworkmanlike neatness, a circumstance that did not escape Thorndyke's observation, for his face relaxed into a grim smile as his eye travelled over the bare benches and the clean-swept floor.

From this room we entered the laboratory, a large apartment, one side of which was given up to chemical research, as was shown by the shelves of reagents that covered the wall, and the flasks, retorts and other apparatus that were arranged on the bench, like ornaments on a drawing-room mantelpiece. On the opposite side of the room was a large, massively-constructed copying camera, the front of which, carrying the lens, was fixed, and an easel or copyholder travelled on parallel guides towards, or away, from it, on a long stand.

This apparatus Thorndyke proceeded to explain to our visitors while Polton was fixing the "Thumbograph" in a holder attached to the easel.

"You see," he said, in answer to a question from Miss Gibson, "I have a good deal to do with signatures, cheques and disputed documents of various kinds. Now a skilled eye, aided by a pocket-lens, can make out very minute details on a cheque or bank-note, but it is not possible to lend one's skilled eye to a judge or juryman, so that it is often very convenient to be able to hand them a photograph in which the magnification is already done, which they can compare with the original. Small things, when magnified, develop quite unexpected characters. For instance, you have handled a good many postage stamps, I suppose, but have you ever noticed the little white spots in the upper corner of a penny stamp, or even the difference in the foliage on the two sides of the wreath?"

Miss Gibson admitted that she had not.

"Very few people have, I suppose, excepting stamp-collectors," continued Thorndyke, "but now just glance at this and you will find these unnoticed details forced upon your attention." As he spoke, he handed her a photograph, which he had taken from a drawer, showing a penny stamp enlarged to a length of eight inches.

While the ladies were marvelling over this production, Polton proceeded with his work. The "Thumbograph" having been fixed in position, the light from a powerful incandescent gas lamp, fitted with a parabolic reflector, was concentrated on it, and the camera racked out to its proper distance.

"What are those figures intended to show?" inquired Miss Gibson, indicating the graduation on the side of one of the guides.

"They show the amount of magnification or reduction," Thorndyke explained. "When the pointer is opposite 0, the photograph is the same size as the object photographed. When it points to, say, *times four*, the photograph will be four times the width and length of the object, while if it should point to, say, *divide four*, the photograph will be one-fourth the length of the object. It is now, you see, pointing to *times eight*, so the photograph will be eight times the diameter of the original thumb-mark."

By this time Polton had brought the camera to an accurate focus and, when we had all been gratified by a glimpse of the enlarged image on the focussing screen, we withdrew to a smaller room which was devoted to bacteriology and microscopical research, while the exposure was made and the plate developed. Here, after an interval, we were joined by Polton, who bore with infinite tenderness the dripping negative on which could be seen the grotesque transparency of a colossal thumb-mark.

This Thorndyke scrutinised eagerly, and having pronounced it satisfactory, informed Mrs. Hornby that the object of her visit was attained, and thanked her for the trouble she had taken.

"I am very glad we came," said Miss Gibson to me, as a little later we walked slowly up Mitre Court in the wake of Mrs. Hornby and Thorndyke, "and I am glad to have seen these wonderful instruments, too. It has made me realise that something is being done and that Dr. Thorndyke really has some object in view. It has really encouraged me immensely."

"And very properly so," I replied. "I, too, although I really know nothing of what my colleague is doing, feel very strongly that he would not take all this trouble and give up so much valuable time if he had not some very definite purpose and some substantial reasons for taking a hopeful view."

"Thank you for saying that," she rejoined warmly, "and you will let me have a crumb of comfort when you can, won't you?" She looked in my face so wistfully as she made this appeal that I was quite moved, and, indeed, I am not sure that my state of mind at that moment did not fully justify my colleague's reticence towards me.

However, I, fortunately, had nothing to tell, and so, when we emerged into Fleet Street to find Mrs. Hornby already ensconced in a hansom, I could only promise, as I grasped the hand that she offered to me, to see her again at the earliest opportunity – a promise which my inner consciousness assured me would be strictly fulfilled.

"You seem to be on quite confidential terms with our fair friend," Thorndyke remarked, as we strolled back towards his chambers. "You are an insinuating dog, Jervis."

"She is very frank and easy to get on with," I replied.

"Yes. A good girl and a clever girl, and comely to look upon withal. I suppose it would be superfluous for me to suggest that you mind your eye?"

"I shouldn't, in any case, try to cut out a man who is under a cloud," I replied sulkily.

"Of course you wouldn't. Hence the need of attention to the ophthalmic member. Have you ascertained what Miss Gibson's actual relation is to Reuben Hornby?"

"No," I answered.

"It might be worth while to find out," said Thorndyke, and then he relapsed into silence.

Chapter VI
Committed for Trial

Thorndyke's hint as to the possible danger foreshadowed by my growing intimacy with Juliet Gibson had come upon me as a complete surprise, and had, indeed, been resented by me as somewhat of an impertinence. Nevertheless, it gave me considerable food for meditation, and I presently began to suspect that the watchful eyes of my observant friend might have detected something in my manner towards Miss Gibson suggestive of sentiments that had been unsuspected by myself.

Of course it would be absurd to suppose that any real feeling could have been engendered by so ridiculously brief an acquaintance. I had only met the girl three times, and even now, excepting for business relations, was hardly entitled to more than a bow of recognition. But yet, when I considered the matter impartially and examined my own consciousness, I could not but recognise that she had aroused in me an interest which bore no relation to the part that she had played in the drama that was so slowly unfolding. She was undeniably a very handsome girl, and her beauty was of a type that specially appealed to me – full of dignity and character that gave promise of a splendid middle age. And her personality was in other ways not less attractive, for she was frank and open, sprightly and intelligent, and though evidently quite self-reliant, was in nowise lacking in that womanly softness that so strongly engages a man's sympathy.

In short, I realised that, had there been no such person as Reuben Hornby, I should have viewed Miss Gibson with uncommon interest.

But, unfortunately, Reuben Hornby was a most palpable reality, and, moreover, the extraordinary difficulties of his position entitled him to very special consideration by any man of honour. It was true that Miss Gibson had repudiated any feelings towards Reuben other than those of old-time friendship, but young ladies are not always impartial judges of their own feelings, and, as a man of the world, I could not but have my own opinion on the matter – which opinion I believed to be shared by Thorndyke. The conclusions to which my cogitations at length brought me were: First, that I was an egotistical donkey, and, second, that my relations with Miss Gibson were of an exclusively business character and must in future be conducted on that basis, with the added consideration that I was the confidential agent, for the time being, of Reuben Hornby, and in honour bound to regard his interests as paramount.

"I am hoping," said Thorndyke, as he held out his hand for my teacup, "that these profound reflections of yours are connected with the Hornby affair. In which case I should expect to hear that the riddle is solved and the mystery made plain."

"Why should you expect that?" I demanded, reddening somewhat, I suspect, as I met his twinkling eye. There was something rather disturbing in the dry, quizzical smile that I encountered and the reflection that I had been under observation, and I felt as much embarrassed as I should suppose a self-conscious water-flea might feel on finding itself on the illuminated stage of a binocular microscope.

"My dear fellow," said Thorndyke, "you have not spoken a word for the last quarter-of-an-hour. You have devoured your food with the relentless regularity of a sausage-machine, and you have, from time to time, made the most damnable faces at the coffee-pot – though there I'll wager the coffee-pot was even with you, if I may judge by the presentment that it offers of my own countenance."

I roused myself from my reverie with a laugh at Thorndyke's quaint conceit and a glance at the grotesquely distorted reflection of my face in the polished silver.

"I am afraid I *have* been a rather dull companion this morning," I admitted apologetically.

"By no means," replied Thorndyke, with a grin. "On the contrary, I have found you both amusing and instructive, and I only spoke when I had exhausted your potentialities as a silent entertainer."

"You are pleased to be facetious at my expense," said I.

"Well, the expense was not a very heavy one," he retorted. "I have been merely consuming a by-product of your mental activity – Hallo! That's Anstey already."

A peculiar knock, apparently delivered with the handle of a walking-stick on the outer door, was the occasion of this exclamation, and as Thorndyke sprang up and flung the door open, a clear, musical voice was borne in, the measured cadences of which proclaimed at once the trained orator.

"Hail, learned brother!" it exclaimed. "Do I disturb you untimely at your studies?" Here our visitor entered the room and looked round critically. "'Tis even so," he declared. "Physiological chemistry and its practical applications appears to be the subject. A physico-chemical inquiry into the properties of streaky bacon and fried eggs. Do I see another learned brother?"

He peered keenly at me through his pince-nez, and I gazed at him in some embarrassment.

81

"This is my friend Jervis, of whom you have heard me speak," said Thorndyke. "He is with us in this case, you know."

"The echoes of your fame have reached me, sir," said Anstey, holding out his hand. "I am proud to know you. I should have recognised you instantly from the portrait of your lamented uncle in Greenwich Hospital."

"Anstey is a wag, you understand," explained Thorndyke, "but he has lucid intervals. He'll have one presently if we are patient."

"Patient!" snorted our eccentric visitor, "it is I who need to be patient when I am dragged into police courts and other sinks of iniquity to plead for common thieves and robbers like a Kennington Lane advocate."

"You've been talking to Lawley, I see," said Thorndyke.

"Yes, and he tells me that we haven't a leg to stand upon."

"No, we've got to stand on our heads, as men of intellect should. But Lawley knows nothing about the case."

"He thinks he knows it all," said Anstey.

"Most fools do," retorted Thorndyke. "They arrive at their knowledge by intuition – a deuced easy road and cheap travelling too. We reserve our defence – I suppose you agree to that?"

"I suppose so. The magistrate is sure to commit unless you have an unquestionable *alibi*."

"We shall put in an *alibi*, but we are not depending on it."

"Then we had better reserve our defence," said Anstey, "and it is time that we wended on our pilgrimage, for we are due at Lawley's at half-past ten. Is Jervis coming with us?"

"Yes, you'd better come," said Thorndyke. "It's the adjourned hearing of poor Hornby's case, you know. There won't be anything done on our side, but we may be able to glean some hint from the prosecution."

"I should like to hear what takes place, at any rate," I said, and we accordingly sallied forth together in the direction of Lincoln's Inn, on the north side of which Mr. Lawley's office was situated.

"Ah!" said the solicitor, as we entered, "I am glad you've come. I was getting anxious – it doesn't do to be late on these occasions, you know. Let me see, do you know Mr. Walter Hornby? I don't think you do." He presented Thorndyke and me to our client's cousin, and as we shook hands, we viewed one another with a good deal of mutual interest.

"I have heard about you from my aunt," said he, addressing himself more particularly to me. "She appears to regard you as a kind of legal Maskelyne and Cooke. I hope, for my cousin's sake, that you will be able to work the wonders that she anticipates. Poor old fellow! He looks pretty bad, doesn't he?"

I glanced at Reuben, who was at the moment talking to Thorndyke, and as he caught my eye he held out his hand with a warmth that I found very pathetic. He seemed to have aged since I had last seen him, and was pale and rather thinner, but he was composed in his manner and seemed to me to be taking his trouble very well on the whole.

"Cab's at the door, sir," a clerk announced.

"Cab," repeated Mr. Lawley, looking dubiously at me, "we want an omnibus."

"Dr. Jervis and I can walk," Walter Hornby suggested. "We shall probably get there as soon as you, and it doesn't matter if we don't."

"Yes, that will do," said Mr. Lawley, "you two walk down together. Now let us go."

We trooped out on to the pavement, beside which a four-wheeler was drawn up, and as the others were entering the cab, Thorndyke stood close beside me for a moment.

"Don't let him pump you," he said in a low voice, without looking at me. Then he sprang into the cab and slammed the door.

"What an extraordinary affair this is," Walter Hornby remarked, after we had been walking in silence for a minute or two, "a most ghastly business. I must confess that I can make neither head nor tail of it."

"How is that?" I asked.

"Why, do you see, there are apparently only two possible theories of the crime, and each of them seems to be unthinkable. On the one hand there is Reuben, a man of the most scrupulous honour, as far as my experience of him goes, committing a mean and sordid theft for which no motive can be discovered – for he is not poor, nor pecuniarily embarrassed nor in the smallest degree avaricious. On the other hand, there is this thumb-print, which, in the opinion of the experts, is tantamount to the evidence of an eye-witness that he did commit the theft. It is positively bewildering. Don't you think so?"

"As you put it," I answered, "the case is extraordinarily puzzling."

"But how else would you put it?" he demanded, with ill-concealed eagerness.

"I mean that, if Reuben is the man you believe him to be, the thing is incomprehensible."

"Quite so," he agreed, though he was evidently disappointed at my colourless answer.

He walked on silently for a few minutes and then said: "I suppose it would not be fair to ask if you see any way out of the difficulty? We are all, naturally anxious about the upshot of the affair, seeing what poor old Reuben's position is."

"Naturally. But the fact is that I know no more than you do, and as to Thorndyke, you might as well cross-examine a Whitstable native as put questions to him."

83

"Yes, so I gathered from Juliet. But I thought you might have gleaned some notion of the line of defence from your work in the laboratory – the microscopical and photographic work I mean."

"I was never in the laboratory until last night, when Thorndyke took me there with your aunt and Miss Gibson. The work there is done by the laboratory assistant, and his knowledge of the case, I should say, is about as great as a type-founder's knowledge of the books that he is helping to produce. No. Thorndyke is a man who plays a single-handed game and no one knows what cards he holds until he lays them on the table."

My companion considered this statement in silence while I congratulated myself on having parried, with great adroitness, a rather inconvenient question. But the time was not far distant when I should have occasion to reproach myself bitterly for having been so explicit and emphatic.

"My uncle's condition," Walter resumed after a pause, "is a pretty miserable one at present, with this horrible affair added to his own personal worries."

"Has he any special trouble besides this, then?" I asked.

"Why, haven't you heard? I thought you knew about it, or I shouldn't have spoken – not that it is in any way a secret, seeing that it is public property in the city. The fact is that his financial affairs are a little entangled just now."

"Indeed!" I exclaimed, considerably startled by this new development.

"Yes, things have taken a rather awkward turn, though I think he will pull through all right. It is the usual thing, you know – investments, or perhaps one should say speculations. He appears to have sunk a lot of capital in mines – thought he was 'in the know,' not unnaturally, but it seems he wasn't after all, and the things have gone wrong, leaving him with a deal more money than he can afford locked up and the possibility of a dead loss if they don't revive. Then there are these infernal diamonds. He is not morally responsible, we know, but it is a question if he is not legally responsible, though the lawyers think he is not. Anyhow, there is going to be a meeting of the creditors to-morrow."

"And what do you think they will do?"

"Oh, they will, most probably, let him go on for the present, but, of course, if he is made accountable for the diamonds there will be nothing for it but to 'go through the hoop,' as the sporting financier expresses it."

"The diamonds were of considerable value, then?"

"From twenty-five to thirty thousand pounds' worth vanished with that parcel."

I whistled. This was a much bigger affair than I had imagined, and I was wondering if Thorndyke had realised the magnitude of the robbery, when we arrived at the police court.

"I suppose our friends have gone inside," said Walter. "They must have got here before us."

This supposition was confirmed by a constable of whom we made inquiry, and who directed us to the entrance to the court. Passing down a passage and elbowing our way through the throng of idlers, we made for the solicitor's box, where we had barely taken our seats when the case was called.

Unspeakably dreary and depressing were the brief proceedings that followed, and dreadfully suggestive of the helplessness of even an innocent man on whom the law has laid its hand and in whose behalf its inexorable machinery has been set in motion.

The presiding magistrate, emotionless and dry, dipped his pen while Reuben, who had surrendered to his bail, was placed in the dock and the charge read over to him. The counsel representing the police gave an abstract of the case with the matter-of-fact air of a house-agent describing an eligible property. Then, when the plea of "not guilty" had been entered, the witnesses were called. There were only two, and when the name of the first, John Hornby, was called, I glanced towards the witness-box with no little curiosity.

I had not hitherto met Mr. Hornby, and as he now entered the box, I saw an elderly man, tall, florid, and well-preserved, but strained and wild in expression and displaying his uncontrollable agitation by continual nervous movements which contrasted curiously with the composed demeanour of the accused man. Nevertheless, he gave his evidence in a perfectly connected manner, recounting the events connected with the discovery of the crime in much the same words as I had heard Mr. Lawley use, though, indeed, he was a good deal more emphatic than that gentleman had been in regard to the excellent character borne by the prisoner.

After him came Mr. Singleton, of the finger-print department at Scotland Yard, to whose evidence I listened with close attention. He produced the paper which bore the thumb-print in blood (which had previously been identified by Mr. Hornby) and a paper bearing the print, taken by himself, of the prisoner's left thumb. These two thumb-prints, he stated, were identical in every respect.

"And you are of opinion that the mark on the paper that was found in Mr. Hornby's safe, was made by the prisoner's left thumb?" the magistrate asked in dry and business-like tones.

"I am certain of it."

"You are of opinion that no mistake is possible?"

"No mistake is possible, your worship. It is a certainty."

The magistrate looked at Anstey inquiringly, whereupon the barrister rose.

"We reserve our defence, your worship."

The magistrate then, in the same placid, business-like manner, committed the prisoner for trial at the Central Criminal Court, refusing to accept bail for his appearance, and, as Reuben was led forth from the dock, the next case was called.

By special favour of the authorities, Reuben was to be allowed to make his journey to Holloway in a cab, thus escaping the horrors of the filthy and verminous prison van, and while this was being procured, his friends were permitted to wish him farewell.

"This is a hard experience, Hornby," said Thorndyke, when we three were, for a few moments, left apart from the others, and as he spoke the warmth of a really sympathetic nature broke through his habitual impassivity. "But be of good cheer. I have convinced myself of your innocence and have good hopes of convincing the world – though this is for your private ear, you understand, to be mentioned to no one."

Reuben wrung the hand of this "friend in need," but was unable, for the moment, to speak, and, as his self-control was evidently strained to the breaking point, Thorndyke, with a man's natural instinct, wished him a hasty good-bye, and passing his hand through my arm, turned away.

"I wish it had been possible to save the poor fellow from this delay, and especially from the degradation of being locked up in a jail," he exclaimed regretfully as we walked down the street.

"There is surely no degradation in being merely accused of a crime," I answered, without much conviction, however. "It may happen to the best of us, and he is still an innocent man in the eyes of the law."

"That, my dear Jervis, you know, as well as I do, to be mere casuistry," he rejoined. "The law professes to regard the unconvicted man as innocent, but how does it treat him? You heard how the magistrate addressed our friend. Outside the court he would have called him *Mr.* Hornby. You know what will happen to Reuben at Holloway. He will be ordered about by warders, will have a number label fastened on to his coat, he will be locked in a cell with a spy-hole in the door, through which any passing stranger may watch him. His food will be handed to him in a tin pan with a tin knife and spoon, and he will be periodically called out of his cell and driven round the exercise yard with a mob composed, for the most part, of the sweepings of the London slums. If he is acquitted, he will be turned loose without a suggestion of compensation or apology for these indignities or the losses he may have sustained through his detention."

"Still I suppose these evils are unavoidable," I said.

"That may or may not be," he retorted. "My point is that the presumption of innocence is a pure fiction. That the treatment of an accused man, from the moment of his arrest, is that of a criminal. However," he concluded, hailing a passing hansom, "this discussion must be adjourned or I shall be late at the hospital. What are you going to do?"

"I shall get some lunch and then call on Miss Gibson to let her know the real position."

"Yes, that will be kind, I think – baldly stated, the news may seem rather alarming. I was tempted to thrash the case out in the police court, but it would not have been safe. He would almost certainly have been committed for trial after all, and then we should have shown our hand to the prosecution."

He sprang into the hansom and was speedily swallowed up in the traffic, while I turned back towards the police court to make certain inquiries concerning the regulations as to visitors at Holloway Prison. At the door I met the friendly inspector from Scotland Yard, who gave me the necessary information, whereupon with a certain homely little French restaurant in my mind I bent my steps in the direction of Soho.

Chapter VII
Shoals and Quicksands

When I arrived at Endsley Gardens, Miss Gibson was at home, and to my unspeakable relief, Mrs. Hornby was not. My veneration for that lady's moral qualities was excessive, but her conversation drove me to the verge of insanity – an insanity not entirely free from homicidal tendencies.

"It is good of you to come – though I thought you would," Miss Gibson said impulsively, as we shook hands. "You have been so sympathetic and human – both you and Dr. Thorndyke – so free from professional stiffness. My aunt went off to see Mr. Lawley directly we got Walter's telegram."

"I am sorry for her," I said (and was on the point of adding "and him," but fortunately a glimmer of sense restrained me), "she will find him dry enough."

"Yes. I dislike him extremely. Do you know that he had the impudence to advise Reuben to plead 'guilty'?"

"He told us he had done so, and got a well-deserved snubbing from Thorndyke for his pains."

"I am so glad," exclaimed Miss Gibson viciously. "But tell me what has happened. Walter simply said 'Transferred to higher court,' which we agreed was to mean, 'Committed for trial.' Has the defence failed? And where is Reuben?"

"The defence is reserved. Dr. Thorndyke considered it almost certain that the case would be sent for trial, and that being so, decided that it was essential to keep the prosecution in the dark as to the line of defence. You see, if the police knew what the defence was to be they could revise their own plans accordingly."

"I see that," said she dejectedly, "but I am dreadfully disappointed. I had hoped that Dr. Thorndyke would get the case dismissed. What has happened to Reuben?"

This was the question that I had dreaded, and now that I had to answer it I cleared my throat and bent my gaze nervously on the floor.

"The magistrate refused bail," I said after an uncomfortable pause.
"Well?"

"Consequently Reuben has been – er – detained in custody."

"You don't mean to say that they have sent him to prison?" she exclaimed breathlessly.

"Not as a convicted prisoner, you know. He is merely detained pending his trial."

"But in prison?"

"Yes," I was forced to admit, "in Holloway Prison."

She looked me stonily in the face for some seconds, pale and wide-eyed, but silent. Then, with a sudden catch in her breath, she turned away, and, grasping the edge of the mantel-shelf, laid her head upon her arm and burst into a passion of sobbing.

Now I am not, in general, an emotional man, nor even especially impulsive, but neither am I a stock or a stone or an effigy of wood, which I most surely must have been if I could have looked without being deeply moved on the grief, so natural and unselfish, of this strong, brave, loyal-hearted woman. In effect, I moved to her side and, gently taking in mine the hand that hung down, murmured some incoherent words of consolation in a particularly husky voice.

Presently she recovered herself somewhat and softly withdrew her hand, as she turned towards me drying her eyes.

"You must forgive me for distressing you, as I fear I have," she said, "for you are so kind, and I feel that you are really my friend and Reuben's."

"I am indeed, dear Miss Gibson," I replied, "and so, I assure you, is my colleague."

"I am sure of it," she rejoined. "But I was so unprepared for this – I cannot say why, excepting that I trusted so entirely in Dr. Thorndyke – and it is so horrible and, above all, so dreadfully suggestive of what may happen. Up to now the whole thing has seemed like a nightmare – terrifying, but yet unreal. But now that he is actually in prison, it has suddenly become a dreadful reality and I am overwhelmed with terror. Oh! Poor boy! What will become of him? For pity's sake, Dr. Jervis, tell me what is going to happen."

What could I do? I had heard Thorndyke's words of encouragement to Reuben and knew my colleague well enough to feel sure that he meant all he had said. Doubtless my proper course would have been to keep my own counsel and put Miss Gibson off with cautious ambiguities. But I could not – she was worthy of more confidence than that.

"You must not be unduly alarmed about the future," I said. "I have it from Dr. Thorndyke that he is convinced of Reuben's innocence, and is hopeful of being able to make it clear to the world. But I did not have this to repeat," I added, with a slight qualm of conscience.

"I know," she said softly, "and I thank you from my heart."

"And as to this present misfortune," I continued, "you must not let it distress you too much. Try to think of it as of a surgical operation, which is a dreadful thing in itself, but is accepted in lieu of something which is immeasurably more dreadful."

"I will try to do as you tell me," she answered meekly, "but it is so shocking to think of a cultivated gentleman like Reuben, herded with common thieves and murderers, and locked in a cage like some wild animal. Think of the ignominy and degradation!"

"There is no ignominy in being wrongfully accused," I said – a little guiltily, I must own, for Thorndyke's words came back to me with all their force. But regardless of this I went on. "An acquittal will restore him to his position with an unstained character, and nothing but the recollection of a passing inconvenience to look back upon."

She gave her eyes a final wipe, and resolutely put away her handkerchief.

"You have given me back my courage," she said, "and chased away my terror. I cannot tell you how I feel your goodness, nor have I any thank-offering to make, except the promise to be brave and patient henceforth, and trust in you entirely."

She said this with such a grateful smile, and looked withal so sweet and womanly that I was seized with an overpowering impulse to take her in my arms. Instead of this I said with conscious feebleness, "I am more than thankful to have been able to give you any encouragement – which you must remember comes from me second-hand, after all. It is to Dr. Thorndyke that we all look for ultimate deliverance."

"I know. But it is you who came to comfort me in my trouble, so, you see, the honours are divided – and not divided quite equally, I fear, for women are unreasoning creatures, as, no doubt, your experience has informed you. I think I hear my aunt's voice, so you had better escape before your retreat is cut off. But before you go, you must tell me how and when I can see Reuben. I want to see him at the earliest possible moment. Poor fellow! He must not be allowed to feel that his friends have forgotten him even for a single instant."

"You can see him to-morrow, if you like," I said, and, casting my good resolutions to the winds, I added, "I shall be going to see him myself, and perhaps Dr. Thorndyke will go."

"Would you let me call at the Temple and go with you? Should I be much in the way? It is rather an alarming thing to go to a prison alone."

"It is not to be thought of," I answered. "If you will call at the Temple – it is on the way – we can drive to Holloway together. I suppose you are resolved to go? It will be rather unpleasant, as you are probably aware."

"I am quite resolved. What time shall I come to the Temple?"

"About two o'clock, if that will suit you."

"Very well. I will be punctual, and now you must go or you will be caught."

She pushed me gently towards the door and, holding out her hand, said, "I haven't thanked you half enough and I never can. Good-bye!"

She was gone, and I stood alone in the street, up which yellowish wreaths of fog were beginning to roll. It had been quite clear and bright when I entered the house, but now the sky was settling down into a colourless grey, the light was failing and the houses dwindling into dim, unreal shapes that vanished at half their height. Nevertheless I stepped out briskly and strode along at a good pace, as a young man is apt to do when his mind is in somewhat of a ferment. In truth, I had a good deal to occupy my thoughts and, as will often happen both to young men and old, those matters that bore most directly upon my own life and prospects were the first to receive attention.

What sort of relations were growing up between Juliet Gibson and me? And what was my position? As to hers, it seemed plain enough – she was wrapped up in Reuben Hornby and I was her very good friend because I was his. But for myself, there was no disguising the fact that I was beginning to take an interest in her that boded ill for my peace of mind.

Never had I met a woman who so entirely realised my conception of what a woman should be, nor one who exercised so great a charm over me. Her strength and dignity, her softness and dependency, to say nothing of her beauty, fitted her with the necessary weapons for my complete and utter subjugation. And utterly subjugated I was – there was no use in denying the fact, even though I realised already that the time would presently come when she would want me no more and there would remain no remedy for me but to go away and try to forget her.

But was I acting as a man of honour? To this I felt I could fairly answer "yes," for I was but doing my duty, and could hardly act differently if I wished to. Besides, I was jeopardising no one's happiness but my own, and a man may do as he pleases with his own happiness. No, even Thorndyke could not accuse me of dishonourable conduct.

Presently my thoughts took a fresh turn and I began to reflect upon what I had heard concerning Mr. Hornby. Here was a startling development, indeed, and I wondered what difference it would make in Thorndyke's hypothesis of the crime. What his theory was I had never been able to guess, but as I walked along through the thickening fog I tried to fit this new fact into our collection of data and determine its bearings and significance.

In this, for a time, I failed utterly. The red thumb-mark filled my field of vision to the exclusion of all else. To me, as to everyone else but Thorndyke, this fact was final and pointed to a conclusion that was

91

unanswerable. But as I turned the story of the crime over and over, there came to me presently an idea that set in motion a new and very startling train of thought.

Could Mr. Hornby himself be the thief? His failure appeared sudden to the outside world, but he must have seen difficulties coming. There, indeed, was the thumb-mark on the leaf which he had torn from his pocket-block. Yes! But who had seen him tear it off? No one. The fact rested on his bare statement.

But the thumb-mark? Well, it was possible (though unlikely) – still possible – that the mark might have been made accidentally on some previous occasion and forgotten by Reuben, or even unnoticed. Mr. Hornby had seen the "Thumbograph," in fact his own mark was in it, and so would have had his attention directed to the importance of finger-prints in identification. He might have kept the marked paper for future use, and, on the occasion of the robbery, pencilled a dated inscription on it, and slipped it into the safe as a sure means of diverting suspicion. All this was improbable in the highest degree, but then so was every other explanation of the crime, and as to the unspeakable baseness of the deed, what action is too base for a gambler in difficulties?

I was so much excited and elated by my own ingenuity in having formed an intelligible and practicable theory of the crime, that I was now impatient to reach home that I might impart my news to Thorndyke and see how they affected him. But as I approached the centre of the town the fog grew so dense that all my attention was needed to enable me to thread my way safely through the traffic, while the strange, deceptive aspect that it lent to familiar objects and the obliteration of landmarks made my progress so slow that it was already past six o'clock when I felt my way down Middle Temple Lane and crept through Crown Office Row towards my colleague's chambers.

On the doorstep I found Polton peering with anxious face into the blank expanse of yellow vapour.

"The Doctor's late, sir," said he. "Detained by the fog, I expect. It must be pretty thick in the Borough."

(I may mention that, to Polton, Thorndyke was *The Doctor*. Other inferior creatures there were, indeed, to whom the title of "doctor" in a way, appertained, but they were of no account in Polton's eyes. Surnames were good enough for them.)

"Yes, it must be," I replied, "judging by the condition of the Strand."

I entered and ascended the stairs, glad enough of the prospect of a warm and well-lighted room after my comfortless groping in the murky streets, and Polton, with a final glance up and down the walk reluctantly followed.

"You would like some tea, sir, I expect?" said he, as he let me in (though I had a key of my own now).

I thought I should, and he accordingly set about the preparations in his deft methodical way, but with an air of abstraction that was unusual with him.

"The Doctor said he should be home by five," he remarked, as he laid the tea-pot on the tray.

"Then he is a defaulter," I answered. "We shall have to water his tea."

"A wonderful punctual man, sir, is the Doctor," pursued Polton. "Keeps his time to the minute, as a rule, he does."

"You can't keep your time to a minute in a 'London Particular,'" I said a little impatiently, for I wished to be alone that I might think over matters, and Polton's nervous flutterings irritated me somewhat. He was almost as bad as a female housekeeper.

The little man evidently perceived my state of mind, for he stole away silently, leaving me rather penitent and ashamed, and, as I presently discovered on looking out of the window, resumed his vigil on the doorstep. From this coign of vantage he returned after a time to take away the tea-things, and thereafter, though it was now dark as well as foggy, I could hear him softly flitting up and down the stairs with a gloomy stealthiness that at length reduced me to a condition as nervously apprehensive as his own.

93

Chapter VIII
A Suspicious Accident

The Temple clock had announced in soft and confidential tones that it was a quarter-to-seven, in which statement it was stoutly supported by its colleague on our mantelpiece, and still there was no sign of Thorndyke. It was really a little strange, for he was the soul of punctuality, and moreover, his engagements were of such a kind as rendered punctuality possible. I was burning with impatience to impart my news to him, and this fact, together with the ghostly proceedings of Polton, worked me up to a state of nervous tension that rendered either rest or thought equally impossible. I looked out of the window at the lamp below, glaring redly through the fog, and then, opening the door, went out on to the landing to listen.

At this moment Polton made a silent appearance on the stairs leading from the laboratory, giving me quite a start, and I was about to retire into the room when my ear caught the tinkle of a hansom approaching from Paper Buildings.

The vehicle drew nearer, and at length stopped opposite the house, on which Polton slid down the stairs with the agility of a harlequin. A few moments later I heard his voice ascending from the hall, "I do hope, sir, you're not much hurt?"

I ran down the stairs and met Thorndyke coming up slowly with his right hand on Polton's shoulder. His clothes were muddy, his left arm was in a sling, and a black handkerchief under his hat evidently concealed a bandage.

"I am not really hurt at all," Thorndyke replied cheerily, "though very disreputable to look at. Just came a cropper in the mud, Jervis," he added, as he noted my dismayed expression. "Dinner and a clothes-brush are what I chiefly need." Nevertheless, he looked very pale and shaken when he came into the light on the landing, and he sank into his easy-chair in the limp manner of a man either very weak or very fatigued.

"How did it happen?" I asked when Polton had crept away on tip-toe to make ready for dinner.

Thorndyke looked round to make sure that his henchman had departed, and said, "A queer affair, Jervis, a very odd affair indeed. I was coming up from the Borough, picking my way mighty carefully across the road on account of the greasy, slippery mud, and had just reached the foot of London Bridge when I heard a heavy lorry coming down the slope a good deal too fast, considering that it was impossible to see more than a

94

dozen yards ahead, and I stopped on the kerb to see it safely past. Just as the horses emerged from the fog, a man came up behind and lurched violently against me and, strangely enough, at the same moment passed his foot in front of mine. Of course I went sprawling into the road right in front of the lorry. The horses came stamping and sliding straight on to me, and, before I could wriggle out of the way, the hoof of one of them smashed in my hat – that was a new one that I came home in – and half-stunned me. Then the near wheel struck my head, making a dirty little scalp wound, and pinned down my sleeve so that I couldn't pull away my arm, which is consequently barked all the way down. It was a mighty near thing, Jervis – another inch or two and I should have been rolled out as flat as a starfish."

"What became of the man?" I asked, wishing I could have had a brief interview with him.

"Lost to sight though to memory dear, he was off like a lamplighter. An alcoholic apple-woman picked me up and escorted me back to the hospital. It must have been a touching spectacle," he added, with a dry smile at the recollection.

"And I suppose they kept you there for a time to recover?"

"Yes. I went into dry dock in the O. P. room, and then old Langdale insisted on my lying down for an hour or so in case any symptoms of concussion should appear. But I was only a trifle shaken and confused. Still, it was a queer affair."

"You mean the man pushing you down in that way?"

"Yes. I can't make out how his foot got in front of mine."

"You don't think it was intentional, surely?" I said.

"No, of course not," he replied, but without much conviction, as it seemed to me, and I was about to pursue the matter when Polton reappeared, and my friend abruptly changed the subject.

After dinner I recounted my conversation with Walter Hornby, watching my colleague's face with some eagerness to see what effect this new information would produce on him. The result was, on the whole, disappointing. He was interested, keenly interested, but showed no symptoms of excitement.

"So John Hornby has been plunging in mines, eh?" he said, when I had finished. "He ought to know better at his age. Did you learn how long he had been in difficulties?"

"No. But it can hardly have been quite sudden and unforeseen."

"I should think not," Thorndyke agreed. "A sudden slump often proves disastrous to the regular Stock Exchange gambler who is paying differences on large quantities of unpaid-for stock. But it looks as if Hornby had actually bought and paid for these mines, treating them as investments rather than speculations, in which case the depreciation would not have affected him in the same way. It would be interesting to know for certain."

"It might have a considerable bearing on the present case, might it not?"

"Undoubtedly," said Thorndyke. "It might bear on the case in more ways than one. But you have some special point in your mind, I think."

"Yes. I was thinking that if these embarrassments had been growing up gradually for some time, they might have already assumed an acute form at the time of the robbery."

"That is well considered," said my colleague. "But what is the special bearing on the case supposing it was so?"

"On the supposition," I replied, "that Mr. Hornby was in actual pecuniary difficulties at the date of the robbery, it seems to me possible to construct a hypothesis as to the identity of the robber."

"I should like to hear that hypothesis stated," said Thorndyke, rousing himself and regarding me with lively interest.

"It is a highly improbable one," I began with some natural shyness at the idea of airing my wits before this master of inductive method, "in fact, it is almost fantastic."

"Never mind that," said he. "A sound thinker gives equal consideration to the probable and the improbable."

Thus encouraged, I proceeded to set forth the theory of the crime as it had occurred to me on my way home in the fog, and I was gratified to observe the close attention with which Thorndyke listened, and his little nods of approval at each point that I made.

When I had finished, he remained silent for some time, looking thoughtfully into the fire and evidently considering how my theory and the new facts on which it was based would fit in with the rest of the data. At length he spoke, without, however, removing his eyes from the red embers, "This theory of yours, Jervis, does great credit to your ingenuity. We may disregard the improbability, seeing that the alternative theories are almost equally improbable, and the fact that emerges, and that gratifies me more than I can tell you, is that you are gifted with enough scientific imagination to construct a possible train of events. Indeed, the improbability – combined, of course, with possibility – really adds to the achievement, for the dullest mind can perceive the obvious – as, for instance, the importance of a finger-print. You have really done a great thing, and I congratulate you, for you have emancipated yourself, at least to some extent, from the great finger-print obsession, which has possessed the legal mind ever since Galton published his epoch-making monograph. In that work I remember he states that a finger-print affords evidence requiring no corroboration –

a most dangerous and misleading statement which has been fastened upon eagerly by the police, who have naturally been delighted at obtaining a sort of magic touchstone by which they are saved the labour of investigation. But there is no such thing as a single fact that 'affords evidence requiring no corroboration.' As well might one expect to make a syllogism with a single premise."

"I suppose they would hardly go so far as that," I said, laughing.

"No," he admitted. "But the kind of syllogism that they do make is this: "*The crime was committed by the person who made this finger-print.*'

"*But John Smith is the person who made the finger-print.*'

"*Therefore the crime was committed by John Smith.*'"

"Well, that is a perfectly good syllogism, isn't it?" I asked.

"Perfectly," he replied. "But, you see, it begs the whole question, which is, 'Was the crime committed by the person who made this finger-print?' That is where the corroboration is required."

"That practically leaves the case to be investigated without reference to the finger-print, which thus becomes of no importance."

"Not at all," rejoined Thorndyke, "the finger-print is a most valuable clue as long as its evidential value is not exaggerated. Take our present case, for instance. Without the thumb-print, the robbery might have been committed by anybody. There is no clue whatever. But the existence of the thumb-print narrows the inquiry down to Reuben or some person having access to his finger-prints."

"Yes, I see. Then you consider my theory of John Hornby as the perpetrator of the robbery as quite a tenable one?"

"Quite," replied Thorndyke. "I have entertained it from the first, and the new facts that you have gathered increase its probability. You remember I said that four hypotheses were possible: That the robbery was committed either by Reuben, by Walter, by John Hornby, or by some other person. Now, putting aside the 'some other person' for consideration only if the first three hypotheses fail, we have left, Reuben, Walter, and John. But if we leave the thumb-print out of the question, the probabilities evidently point to John Hornby, since he, admittedly, had access to the diamonds, whereas there is nothing to show that the others had. The thumb-print, however, transfers the suspicion to Reuben, but yet, as your theory makes evident, it does not completely clear John Hornby. As the case stands, the balance of probabilities may be stated thus: John Hornby undoubtedly had access to the diamonds, and therefore might have stolen them. But if the thumb-mark was made after he closed the safe and before he opened it again, some other person must have had access to them, and was probably the thief.

"The thumb-mark is that of Reuben Hornby, a fact that establishes a *prima facie* probability that he stole the diamonds. But there is no evidence that he had access to them, and if he had not, he could not have made the thumb-mark in the manner and at the time stated.

"But John Hornby may have had access to the previously-made thumb-mark of Reuben, and may possibly have obtained it. In which case he is almost certainly the thief.

"As to Walter Hornby, he may have had the means of obtaining Reuben's thumb-mark, but there is no evidence that he had access either to the diamonds or to Mr. Hornby's memorandum block. The *prima facie* probabilities in his case, therefore, are very slight."

"The actual points at issue, then," I said, "are, whether Reuben had any means of opening the safe, and whether Mr. Hornby ever did actually have the opportunity of obtaining Reuben's thumb-mark in blood on his memorandum block."

"Yes," replied Thorndyke. "Those are the points – with some others – and they are likely to remain unsettled. Reuben's rooms have been searched by the police, who failed to find any skeleton or duplicate keys, but this proves nothing, as he would probably have made away with them when he heard of the thumb-mark being found. As to the other matter, I have asked Reuben, and he has no recollection of ever having made a thumb-mark in blood. So there the matter rests."

"And what about Mr. Hornby's liability for the diamonds?"

"I think we may dismiss that," answered Thorndyke. "He had undertaken no liability and there was no negligence. He would not be liable at law."

After my colleague retired, which he did quite early, I sat for a long time pondering upon this singular case in which I found myself involved. And the more I thought about it the more puzzled I became. If Thorndyke had no more satisfactory explanation to offer than that which he had given me this evening, the defence was hopeless, for the court was not likely to accept his estimate of the evidential value of finger-prints. Yet he had given Reuben something like a positive assurance that there would be an adequate defence, and had expressed his own positive conviction of the accused man's innocence. But Thorndyke was not a man to reach such a conviction through merely sentimental considerations. The inevitable conclusion was that he had something up his sleeve – that he had gained possession of some facts that had escaped my observation, and when I had reached this point I knocked out my pipe and betook myself to bed.

Chapter IX
The Prisoner

On the following morning, as I emerged from my room, I met Polton coming up with a tray (our bedrooms were on the attic floor above the laboratory and workshop), and I accordingly followed him into my friend's chamber.

"I shan't go out to-day," said Thorndyke, "though I shall come down presently. It is very inconvenient, but one must accept the inevitable. I have had a knock on the head, and, although I feel none the worse, I must take the proper precautions – rest and a low diet – until I see that no results are going to follow. You can attend to the scalp wound and send round the necessary letters, can't you?"

I expressed my willingness to do all that was required and applauded my friend's self-control and good sense. Indeed, I could not help contrasting the conduct of this busy, indefatigable man, cheerfully resigning himself to most distasteful inaction, with the fussy behaviour of the ordinary patient who, with nothing of importance to do, can hardly be prevailed upon to rest, no matter how urgent the necessity. Accordingly, I breakfasted alone, and spent the morning in writing and despatching letters to the various persons who were expecting visits from my colleague.

Shortly after lunch (a very spare one, by the way, for Polton appeared to include me in the scheme of reduced diet) my expectant ear caught the tinkle of a hansom approaching down Crown Office Row.

"Here comes your fair companion," said Thorndyke, whom I had acquainted with my arrangements, "Tell Hornby, from me, to keep up his courage, and, for yourself, bear my warning in mind. I should be sorry indeed if you ever had cause to regret that you had rendered me the very valuable services for which I am now indebted to you. Good-bye. Don't keep her waiting."

I ran down the stairs and came out of the entry just as the cabman had pulled up and flung open the doors.

"Holloway Prison – main entrance," I said, as I stepped up on to the footboard.

"There ain't no back door there, sir," the man responded, with a grin, and I was glad that neither the answer nor the grin was conveyed to my fellow-passenger.

"You are very punctual, Miss Gibson," I said. "It is not half-past one yet."

"Yes. I thought I should like to get there by two, so as to have as long a time with him as is possible without shortening your interview."

I looked at my companion critically. She was dressed with rather more than her usual care, and looked, in fact, a very fine lady indeed. This circumstance, which I noted at first with surprise and then with decided approbation, caused me some inward discomfort, for I had in my mind a very distinct and highly disagreeable picture of the visiting arrangements at a local prison in one of the provinces, at which I had acted temporarily as medical officer.

"I suppose," I said at length, "it is of no use for me to re-open the question of the advisability of this visit on your part?"

"Not the least," she replied resolutely, "though I understand and appreciate your motive in wishing to do so."

"Then," said I, "if you are really decided, it will be as well for me to prepare you for the ordeal. I am afraid it will give you a terrible shock."

"Indeed?" said she. "Is it so bad? Tell me what it will be like."

"In the first place," I replied, "you must keep in your mind the purpose of a prison like Holloway. We are going to see an innocent man – a cultivated and honourable gentleman. But the ordinary inmates of Holloway are not innocent men. For the most part, the remand cases on the male side are professional criminals, while the women are either petty offenders or chronic inebriates. Most of them are regular customers at the prison – such is the idiotic state of the law – who come into the reception-room like travellers entering a familiar hostelry, address the prison officers by name and demand the usual privileges and extra comforts – the 'drunks,' for instance, generally ask for a dose of bromide to steady their nerves and a light in the cell to keep away the horrors. And such being the character of the inmates, their friends who visit them are naturally of the same type – the lowest outpourings of the slums, and it is not surprising to find that the arrangements of the prison are made to fit its ordinary inmates. The innocent man is a negligible quantity, and no arrangements are made for him or his visitors."

"But shall we not be taken to Reuben's cell?" asked Miss Gibson.

"Bless you! No," I answered, and, determined to give her every inducement to change her mind, I continued, "I will describe the procedure as I have seen it – and a very dreadful and shocking sight I found it, I can tell you. It was while I was acting as a prison doctor in the Midlands that I had this experience. I was going my round one morning when, passing along a passage, I became aware of a strange, muffled roar from the other side of the wall.

"'What is that noise?' I asked the warder who was with me.

"'Prisoners seeing their friends,' he answered. 'Like to have a look at them, sir?'

"He unlocked a small door and, as he threw it open, the distant, muffled sound swelled into a deafening roar. I passed through the door and found myself in a narrow alley at one end of which a warder was sitting. The sides of the alley were formed by two immense cages with stout wire bars, one for the prisoners and the other for the visitors, and each cage was lined with faces and hands, all in incessant movement, the faces mouthing and grimacing, and the hands clawing restlessly at the bars. The uproar was so terrific that no single voice could be distinguished, though everyone present was shouting his loudest to make himself heard above the universal din. The result was a very strange and horrid illusion, for it seemed as if no one was speaking at all, but that the noise came from outside, and that each one of the faces – low, vicious faces, mostly – was silently grimacing and gibbering, snapping its jaws and glaring furiously at the occupants of the opposite cage. It was a frightful spectacle. I could think of nothing but the monkey-house at the Zoo. It seemed as if one ought to walk up the alley and offer nuts and pieces of paper to be torn to pieces."

"Horrible!" exclaimed Miss Gibson. "And do you mean to say that we shall be turned loose into one of these cages with a herd of other visitors?"

"No. You are not turned loose anywhere in a prison. The arrangement is this: Each cage is divided by partitions into a number of small boxes or apartments, which are numbered. The prisoner is locked in one box and his visitor in the corresponding box opposite. They are thus confronted, with the width of the alley between them. They can see one another and talk but cannot pass any forbidden articles across – a very necessary precaution, I need hardly say."

"Yes, I suppose it is necessary, but it is horrible for decent people. Surely they ought to be able to discriminate."

"Why not give it up and let me take a message to Reuben? He would understand and be thankful to me for dissuading you."

"No, no," she said quickly, "the more repulsive it is the greater the necessity for me to go. He must not be allowed to think that a trifling inconvenience or indignity is enough to scare his friends away. What building is that ahead?"

We had just swung round from Caledonian Road into a quiet and prosperous-looking suburban street, at the end of which rose the tower of a castellated building.

101

"That is the prison," I replied. "We are looking at it from the most advantageous point of view – seen from the back, and especially from the inside, it is a good deal less attractive."

Nothing more was said until the cab drove into the courtyard and set us down outside the great front gates. Having directed the cabman to wait for us, I rang the bell and we were speedily admitted through a wicket (which was immediately closed and locked) into a covered court closed in by a second gate, through the bars of which we could see across an inner courtyard to the actual entrance to the prison. Here, while the necessary formalities were gone through, we found ourselves part of a numerous and very motley company, for a considerable assemblage of the prisoners' friends was awaiting the moment of admission. I noticed that my companion was observing our fellow-visitors with a kind of horrified curiosity, which she strove, however, and not unsuccessfully, to conceal, and certainly the appearance of the majority furnished eloquent testimony to the failure of crime as a means of worldly advancement. Their present position was productive of very varied emotions – some were silent and evidently stricken with grief. A larger number were voluble and excited, while a considerable proportion were quite cheerful and even inclined to be facetious.

At length the great iron gate was unlocked and our party taken in charge by a warder, who conducted us to that part of the building known as "the wing", and, in the course of our progress, I could not help observing the profound impression made upon my companion by the circumstance that every door had to be unlocked to admit us and was locked again as soon as we had passed through.

"It seems to me," I said, as we neared our destination, "that you had better let me see Reuben first. I have not much to say to him and shall not keep you waiting long."

"Why do you think so?" she asked, with a shade of suspicion.

"Well," I answered, "I think you may be a little upset by the interview, and I should like to see you into your cab as soon as possible afterwards."

"Yes," she said, "perhaps you are right, and it is kind of you to be so thoughtful on my account."

A minute later, accordingly, I found myself shut into a narrow box, like one of those which considerate pawnbrokers provide for their more diffident clients, and in a similar, but more intense, degree, pervaded by a subtle odour of uncleanness. The woodwork was polished to an unctuous smoothness by the friction of numberless dirty hands and soiled garments, and the general appearance – taken in at a glance as I entered – was such as to cause me to thrust my hands into my pockets and studiously avoid

102

contact with any part of the structure but the floor. The end of the box opposite the door was closed in by a strong grating of wire – excepting the lower three feet, which was of wood – and looking through this, I perceived, behind a second grating, Reuben Hornby, standing in a similar attitude to my own. He was dressed in his usual clothes and with his customary neatness, but his face was unshaven and he wore, suspended from a button-hole, a circular label bearing the characters "B.31", and these two changes in his exterior carried with them a suggestiveness as subtle as it was unpleasant, making me more than ever regretful that Miss Gibson had insisted on coming.

"It is exceedingly good of you, Dr. Jervis, to come and see me," he said heartily, making himself heard quite easily, to my surprise, above the hubbub of the adjoining boxes, "but I didn't expect you here. I was told I could see my legal advisers in the solicitor's box."

"So you could," I answered. "But I came here by choice because I have brought Miss Gibson with me."

"I am sorry for that," he rejoined, with evident disapproval, "she oughtn't to have come among these riff-raff."

"I told her so, and that you wouldn't like it, but she insisted."

"I know," said Reuben. "That's the worst of women – they will make a beastly fuss and sacrifice themselves when nobody wants them to. But I mustn't be ungrateful – she means it kindly, and she's a deuced good sort, is Juliet."

"She is indeed," I exclaimed, not a little disgusted at his cool, unappreciative tone, "a most noble-hearted girl, and her devotion to you is positively heroic."

The faintest suspicion of a smile appeared on the face seen through the double grating. On which I felt that I could have pulled his nose with pleasure – only that a pair of tongs of special construction would have been required for the purpose.

"Yes," he answered calmly, "we have always been very good friends."

A rejoinder of the most extreme acidity was on my lips. Damn the fellow! What did he mean by speaking in that supercilious tone of the loveliest and sweetest woman in the world? But, after all, one cannot trample on a poor devil locked up in a jail on a false charge, no matter how great may be the provocation. I drew a deep breath, and, having recovered myself, outwardly at least, said, "I hope you don't find the conditions here too intolerable?"

"Oh, no," he answered. "It's beastly unpleasant, of course, but it might easily be worse. I don't mind if it's only for a week or two, and I am

103

really encouraged by what Dr. Thorndyke said. I hope he wasn't being merely soothing."

"You may take it that he was not. What he said, I am sure he meant. Of course, you know I am not in his confidence – nobody is – but I gather that he is satisfied with the defence he is preparing."

"If he is satisfied, I am," said Reuben, "and, in any case, I shall owe him an immense debt of gratitude for having stood by me and believed in me when all the world – except my aunt and Juliet – had condemned me."

He then went on to give me a few particulars of his prison life, and when he had chatted for a quarter-of-an-hour or so, I took my leave to make way for Miss Gibson.

Her interview with him was not as long as I had expected, though, to be sure, the conditions were not very favourable either for the exchange of confidences or for utterances of a sentimental character. The consciousness that one's conversation could be overheard by the occupants of adjacent boxes destroyed all sense of privacy, to say nothing of the disturbing influence of the warder in the alley-way.

When she rejoined me, her manner was abstracted and very depressed, a circumstance that gave me considerable food for reflection as we made our way in silence towards the main entrance. Had she found Reuben as cool and matter-of-fact as I had? He was assuredly a very calm and self-possessed lover, and it was conceivable that his reception of the girl, strung up, as she was, to an acute pitch of emotion, might have been somewhat in the nature of an anticlimax. And then, was it possible that the feeling was on her side only? Could it be that the priceless pearl of her love was cast before – I was tempted to use the colloquial singular and call him an "unappreciative swine!" The thing was almost unthinkable to me, and yet I was tempted to dwell upon it, for when a man is in love – and I could no longer disguise my condition from myself – he is inclined to be humble and to gather up thankfully the treasure that is rejected of another.

I was brought up short in these reflections by the clank of the lock in the great iron gate. We entered together the gloomy vestibule, and a moment later were let out through the wicket into the courtyard, and as the lock clicked behind us, we gave a simultaneous sigh of relief to find ourselves outside the precincts of the prison, beyond the domain of bolts and bars.

I had settled Miss Gibson in the cab and given her address to the driver, when I noticed her looking at me, as I thought, somewhat wistfully.

"Can't I put you down somewhere?" she said, in response to a half-questioning glance from me.

I seized the opportunity with thankfulness and replied, "You might set me down at King's Cross if it is not delaying you." And giving the

104

word to the cabman, I took my place by her side as the cab started and a black-painted prison van turned into the courtyard with its freight of squalid misery.

"I don't think Reuben was very pleased to see me," Miss Gibson remarked presently, "but I shall come again all the same. It is a duty I owe both to him and to myself."

I felt that I ought to endeavour to dissuade her, but the reflection that her visits must almost of necessity involve my companionship, enfeebled my will. I was fast approaching a state of infatuation.

"I was so thankful," she continued, "that you prepared me. It was a horrible experience to see the poor fellow caged like a wild beast, with that dreadful label hanging from his coat, but it would have been overwhelming if I had not known what to expect."

As we proceeded, her spirits revived somewhat, a circumstance that she graciously ascribed to the enlivening influence of my society, and I then told her of the mishap that had befallen my colleague.

"What a terrible thing!" she exclaimed, with evidently unaffected concern. "It is the merest chance that he was not killed on the spot. Is he much hurt? And would he mind, do you think, if I called to inquire after him?"

I said that I was sure he would be delighted (being, as a matter of fact, entirely indifferent as to his sentiments on the subject in my delight at the proposal), and when I stepped down from the cab at King's Cross to pursue my way homewards, there already opened out before me the prospect of the renewal of this bitter-sweet and all too dangerous companionship on the morrow.

Chapter X
Polton is Mystified

A couple of days sufficed to prove that Thorndyke's mishap was not to be productive of any permanent ill consequences – his wounds progressed favourably and he was able to resume his ordinary avocations.

Miss Gibson's visit – but why should I speak of her in these formal terms? To me, when I thought of her, which I did only too often, she was Juliet, with perhaps an adjective thrown in, and as Juliet I shall henceforth speak of her (but without the adjective) in this narrative, wherein nothing has been kept back from the reader – Juliet's visit, then, had been a great success, for my colleague was really pleased by the attention, and displayed a quiet geniality that filled our visitor with delight.

He talked a good deal of Reuben, and I could see that he was endeavouring to settle in his own mind the vexed question of her relations with and sentiments towards our unfortunate client, but what conclusions he arrived at I was unable to discover, for he was by no means communicative after she had left. Nor was there any repetition of the visit – greatly to my regret – since, as I have said, he was able, in a day or two, to resume his ordinary mode of life.

The first evidence I had of his renewed activity appeared when I returned to the chambers at about eleven o'clock in the morning, to find Polton hovering dejectedly about the sitting-room, apparently perpetrating as near an approach to a "spring clean" as could be permitted in a bachelor establishment.

"Hallo, Polton!" I exclaimed, "have you contrived to tear yourself away from the laboratory for an hour or two?"

"No, sir," he answered gloomily. "The laboratory has torn itself away from me."

"What do you mean?" I asked.

"The Doctor has shut himself in and locked the door, and he says I am not to disturb him. It will be a cold lunch to-day."

"What is he doing in there?" I inquired.

"Ah!" said Polton, "that's just what I should like to know. I'm fair eaten up with curiosity. He is making some experiments in connection with some of his cases, and when The Doctor locks himself in to make experiments, something interesting generally follows. I should like to know what it is this time."

106

"I suppose there is a keyhole in the laboratory door?" I suggested, with a grin.

"Sir!" he exclaimed indignantly. "Dr. Jervis, I am surprised at you." Then, perceiving my facetious intent, he smiled also and added, "But there *is* a keyhole if you'd like to try it, though I'll wager The Doctor would see more of you than you would of him."

"You are mighty secret about your doings, you and The Doctor," I said.

"Yes," he answered. "You see, it's a queer trade this of The Doctor's, and there are some queer secrets in it. Now, for instance, what do you make of this?"

He produced from his pocket a leather case, whence he took a piece of paper which he handed to me. On it was a neatly executed drawing of what looked like one of a set of chessmen, with the dimensions written on the margin.

"It looks like a pawn – one of the Staunton pattern," I said.

"Just what I thought, but it isn't. I've got to make twenty-four of them, and what The Doctor is going to do with them fairly beats me."

"Perhaps he has invented some new game," I suggested facetiously.

"He is always inventing new games and playing them mostly in courts of law, and then the other players generally lose. But this is a puzzler, and no mistake. Twenty-four of these to be turned up in the best-seasoned boxwood! What can they be for? Something to do with the experiments he is carrying on upstairs at this very moment, I expect." He shook his head, and, having carefully returned the drawing to his pocket-book, said, in a solemn tone, 'Sir, there are times when The Doctor makes me fairly dance with curiosity. And this is one of them."

Although not afflicted with a curiosity so acute as that of Polton, I found myself speculating at intervals on the nature of my colleague's experiments and the purpose of the singular little objects which he had ordered to be made, but I was unacquainted with any of the cases on which he was engaged, excepting that of Reuben Hornby, and with the latter I was quite unable to connect a set of twenty-four boxwood chessmen. Moreover, on this day, I was to accompany Juliet on her second visit to Holloway, and that circumstance gave me abundant mental occupation of another kind.

At lunch, Thorndyke was animated and talkative but not communicative. He "had some work in the laboratory that he must do himself," he said, but gave no hint as to its nature, and as soon as our meal was finished, he returned to his labours, leaving me to pace up and down the walk, listening with ridiculous eagerness for the sound of the hansom that was to transport me to the regions of the blest, and – incidentally – to Holloway Prison.

When I returned to the Temple, the sitting-room was empty and hideously neat, as the result of Polton's spring-cleaning efforts. My colleague was evidently still at work in the laboratory, and, from the circumstance that the tea-things were set out on the table and a kettle of water placed in readiness on the gas-ring by the fireplace, I gathered that Polton also was full of business and anxious not to be disturbed.

Accordingly, I lit the gas and made my tea, enlivening my solitude by turning over in my mind the events of the afternoon.

Juliet had been charming – as she always was – frank, friendly and unaffectedly pleased to have my companionship. She evidently liked me and did not disguise the fact – why should she indeed? – but treated me with a freedom, almost affectionate, as though I had been a favourite brother, which was very delightful, and would have been more so if I could have accepted the relationship. As to her feelings towards me, I had not the slightest misgiving, and so my conscience was clear, for Juliet was as innocent as a child, with the innocence that belongs to the direct, straightforward nature that neither does evil itself nor looks for evil motives in others. For myself, I was past praying for. The thing was done and I must pay the price hereafter, content to reflect that I had trespassed against no one but myself. It was a miserable affair, and many a heartache did it promise me in the lonely days that were to come, when I should have said "good-bye" to the Temple and gone back to my old nomadic life, and yet I would not have had it changed if I could – would not have bartered the bitter-sweet memories for dull forgetfulness.

But other matters had transpired in the course of our drive than those that loomed so large to me in the egotism of my love. We had spoken of Mr. Hornby and his affairs, and from our talk there had emerged certain facts of no little moment to the inquiry on which I was engaged.

"Misfortunes are proverbially sociable," Juliet had remarked, in reference to her adopted uncle. "As if this trouble about Reuben were not enough, there are worries in the city. Perhaps you have heard of them."

I replied that Walter had mentioned the matter to me.

"Yes," said Juliet rather viciously, "I am not quite clear as to what part that good gentleman has played in the matter. It has come out, quite accidentally, that he had a large holding in the mines himself, but he seems to have 'cut his loss,' as the phrase goes, and got out of them. Though how he managed to pay such large differences is more than we can understand. We think he must have raised money somehow to do it."

"Do you know when the mines began to depreciate?" I asked.

108

"Yes, it was quite a sudden affair – what Walter calls 'a slump' – and it occurred only a few days before the robbery. Mr. Hornby was telling me about it only yesterday, and he recalled it to me by a ridiculous accident that happened on that day."

"What was that?" I inquired.

"Why, I cut my finger and nearly fainted," she answered, with a shamefaced little laugh. "It was rather a bad cut, you know, but I didn't notice it until I found my hand covered with blood. Then I turned suddenly faint, and had to lie down on the hearthrug – it was in Mr. Hornby's study, which I was tidying up at the time. Here I was found by Reuben, and a dreadful fright it gave him at first, and then he tore up his handkerchief to tie up the wounded finger, and you never saw such an awful mess as he got his hands in. He might have been arrested as a murderer, poor boy, from the condition he was in. It will make your professional gorge rise to learn that he fastened up the extemporised bandage with red tape, which he got from the writing table after rooting about among the sacred papers in the most ruthless fashion.

"When he had gone I tried to put the things on the table straight again, and really you might have thought some horrible crime had been committed. The envelopes and papers were all smeared with blood and marked with the print of gory fingers. I remembered it afterwards, when Reuben's thumb-mark was identified, and thought that perhaps one of the papers might have got into the safe by accident, but Mr. Hornby told me that was impossible. He tore the leaf off his memorandum block at the time when he put away the diamonds."

Such was the gist of our conversation as the cab rattled through the streets on the way to the prison, and certainly it contained matter sufficiently important to draw away my thoughts from other subjects, more agreeable, but less relevant to the case. With a sudden remembrance of my duty, I drew forth my notebook, and was in the act of committing the statements to writing, when Thorndyke entered the room.

"Don't let me interrupt you, Jervis," said he. "I will make myself a cup of tea while you finish your writing, and then you shall exhibit the day's catch and hang your nets out to dry."

I was not long in finishing my notes, for I was in a fever of impatience to hear Thorndyke's comments on my latest addition to our store of information. By the time the kettle was boiling my entries were completed, and I proceeded forthwith to retail to my colleague those extracts from my conversation with Juliet that I have just recorded.

He listened, as usual, with deep and critical attention.

"This is very interesting and important," he said, when I had finished, "really, Jervis, you are a most invaluable coadjutor. It seems that information, which would be strictly withheld from the forbidding Jorkins, trickles freely and unasked into the ear of the genial Spenlow. Now, I suppose you regard your hypothesis as having received very substantial confirmation?"

"Certainly, I do."

"And very justifiably. You see now how completely you were in the right when you allowed yourself to entertain this theory of the crime in spite of its apparent improbability. By the light of these new facts it has become quite a probable explanation of the whole affair, and if it could only be shown that Mr. Hornby's memorandum block was among the papers on the table, it would rise to a high degree of probability. The obvious moral is, never disregard the improbable. By the way, it is odd that Reuben failed to recall this occurrence when I questioned him. Of course, the bloody finger-marks were not discovered until he had gone, but one would have expected him to recall the circumstance when I asked him, pointedly, if he had never left bloody finger-prints on any papers."

"I must try to find out if Mr. Hornby's memorandum block was on the table and among the marked papers," I said.

"Yes, that would be wise," he answered, "though I don't suppose the information will be forthcoming."

My colleague's manner rather disappointed me. He had heard my report with the greatest attention, he had discussed it with animation, but yet he seemed to attach to the new and – as they appeared to me – highly important facts an interest that was academic rather than practical. Of course, his calmness might be assumed, but this did not seem likely, for John Thorndyke was far too sincere and dignified a character to cultivate in private life the artifices of the actor. To strangers, indeed, he presented habitually a calm and impassive exterior, but this was natural to him, and was but the outward sign of his even and judicial habit of mind.

No. There was no doubt that my startling news had left him unmoved, and this must be for one of two reasons: Either he already knew all that I had told him (which was perfectly possible), or he had some other and better means of explaining the crime. I was turning over these two alternatives, not unobserved by my watchful colleague, when Polton entered the room, a broad grin was on his face, and a drawing-board, that he carried like a tray, bore twenty-four neatly turned boxwood pieces.

Thorndyke at once entered into the unspoken jest that beamed from the countenance of his subordinate.

"Here is Polton with a problem for you, Jervis," he said. "He assumes that I have invented a new parlour game, and has been trying to work out the moves. Have you succeeded yet, Polton?"

110

"No, sir, I haven't, but I suspect that one of the players will be a man in a wig and gown."

"Perhaps you are right," said Thorndyke, "but that doesn't take you very far. Let us hear what Dr. Jervis has to say."

"I can make nothing of them," I answered. "Polton showed me the drawing this morning, and then was terrified lest he had committed a breach of confidence, and I have been trying ever since, without a glimmer of success, to guess what they can be for."

"H'm," grunted Thorndyke, as he sauntered up and down the room, teacup in hand, "to guess, eh? I like not that word 'guess' in the mouth of a man of science. What do you mean by a 'guess'?"

His manner was wholly facetious, but I professed to take his question seriously, and replied, "By a guess, I mean a conclusion arrived at without data."

"Impossible!" he exclaimed, with mock sternness. "Nobody but an utter fool arrives at a conclusion without data."

"Then I must revise my definition instantly," I rejoined. "Let us say that a guess is a conclusion drawn from insufficient facts."

"That is better," said he, "but perhaps it would be better still to say that a guess is a particular and definite conclusion deduced from facts which properly yield only a general and indefinite one. Let us take an instance," he continued. "Looking out of the window, I see a man walking round Paper Buildings. Now suppose I say, after the fashion of the inspired detective of the romances, 'That man is a stationmaster or inspector,' that would be a guess. The observed facts do not yield the conclusion, though they do warrant a conclusion less definite and more general."

"You'd have been right though, sir!" exclaimed Polton, who had stepped forward with me to examine the unconscious subject of the demonstration. "That gent used to be the stationmaster at Camberwell. I remember him well."

The little man was evidently greatly impressed.

"I happen to be right, you see," said Thorndyke, "but I might as easily have been wrong."

"You weren't though, sir," said Polton. "You spotted him at a glance."

In his admiration of the result he cared not a fig for the correctness of the means by which it had been attained.

"Now why do I suggest that he is a stationmaster?" pursued Thorndyke, disregarding his assistant's comment.

"I suppose you were looking at his feet," I answered. "I seem to have noticed that peculiar, splay-footed gait in stationmasters, now that you mention it."

"Quite so. The arch of the foot has given way. The plantar ligaments have become stretched and the deep calf muscles weakened. Then, since bending of the weakened arch causes discomfort, the feet have become turned outwards, by which the bending of the foot is reduced to a minimum, and as the left foot is the more flattened, so it is turned out more than the right. Then the turning out of the toes causes the legs to splay outward from the knees downwards – a very conspicuous condition in a tall man like this one – and you notice that the left leg splays out more than the other.

"But we know that depression of the arch of the foot is brought about by standing for long periods. Continuous pressure on a living structure weakens it, while intermittent pressure strengthens it. So the man who stands on his feet continuously develops a flat instep and a weak calf, while the professional dancer or runner acquires a high instep and a strong calf. Now there are many occupations which involve prolonged standing and so induce the condition of flat foot: Waiters, hall-porters, hawkers, policemen, shop-walkers, salesmen, and station officials are examples. But the waiter's gait is characteristic – a quick, shuffling walk which enables him to carry liquids without spilling them. This man walks with a long, swinging stride. He is obviously not a waiter. His dress and appearance in general exclude the idea of a hawker or even a hall-porter – he is a man of poor physique and so cannot be a policeman. The shop-walker or salesman is accustomed to move in relatively confined spaces, and so acquires a short, brisk step, and his dress tends to rather exuberant smartness. The station official patrols long platforms, often at a rapid pace, and so tends to take long strides, while his dress is dignified and neat rather than florid. The last-mentioned characteristics, you see, appear in the subject of our analysis. He agrees with the general description of a stationmaster. But if we therefore conclude that he *is* a stationmaster, we fall into the time-honoured fallacy of the undistributed middle term – the fallacy that haunts all brilliant guessers, including the detective, not only of romance, but too often also of real life. All that the observed facts justify us in inferring is that this man is engaged in some mode of life that necessitates a good deal of standing. The rest is mere guess-work."

"It's wonderful," said Polton, gazing at the now distant figure, "perfectly wonderful. I should never have known he was a stationmaster." With this and a glance of deep admiration at his employer, he took his departure.

"You will also observe," said Thorndyke, with a smile, "that a fortunate guess often brings more credit than a piece of sound reasoning with a less striking result."

"Yes, that is unfortunately the case, and it is certainly true in the present instance. Your reputation, as far as Polton is concerned, is now firmly established even if it was not before. In his eyes you are a wizard from whom nothing is hidden. But to return to these little pieces, as I must call them, for the lack of a better name. I can form no hypothesis as to their use. I seem to have no 'departure,' as the nautical phrase goes, from which to start an inquiry. I haven't even the material for guess-work. Ought I to be able to arrive at any opinion on the subject?"

Thorndyke picked up one of the pieces, fingering it delicately and inspecting with a critical eye the flat base on which it stood, and reflected for a few moments.

"It is easy to trace a connection when one knows all the facts," he said at length, "but it seems to me that you have the materials from which to form a conjecture. Perhaps I am wrong, but I think, when you have had more experience, you will find yourself able to work out a problem of this kind. What is required is constructive imagination and a rigorous exactness in reasoning. Now, you are a good reasoner, and you have recently shown me that you have the necessary imagination. You merely lack experience in the use of your faculties. When you learn my purpose in having these things made – as you will before long – you will probably be surprised that their use did not occur to you. And now let us go forth and take a brisk walk to refresh ourselves (or perhaps I should say myself) after the day's labour.

Chapter XI
The Ambush

"**I** am going to ask for your collaboration in another case," said Thorndyke, a day or two later. "It appears to be one of suicide, but the solicitors to the 'Griffin' office have asked me to go down to the place, which is in the neighbourhood of Barnet, and be present at the *post-mortem* and the inquest. They have managed to arrange that the inquest shall take place directly after the *post-mortem*, so that we shall be able to do the whole business in a single visit."

"Is the case one of any intricacy?" I asked.

"I don't think so," he answered. "It looks like a common suicide, but you can never tell. The importance of the case at present arises entirely from the heavy insurance – a verdict of suicide will mean a gain of ten thousand pounds to the 'Griffin,' so, naturally, the directors are anxious to get the case settled and not inclined to boggle over a little expense."

"Naturally. And when will the expedition take place?" I asked.

"The inquest is fixed for to-morrow – what is the matter? Does that fall foul of any arrangement of yours?"

"Oh, nothing of any importance," I replied hastily, deeply ashamed of the momentary change of countenance that my friend had been so quick to observe.

"Well, what is it?" persisted Thorndyke. "You have got something on."

"It is nothing, I tell you, but what can be quite easily arranged to suit your plans."

"*Cherchez la* – h'm?" queried Thorndyke, with an exasperating grin.

"Yes," I answered, turning as red as a pickled cabbage, "since you are so beastly inquisitive. Miss Gibson wrote, on behalf of Mrs. Hornby, asking me to dine with them *en famille* to-morrow evening, and I sent off an acceptance an hour ago."

"And you call that 'nothing of any importance'!" exclaimed Thorndyke. "Alas! And likewise alackaday (which is an approximately synonymous expression)! The age of chivalry is past, indeed. Of course you must keep your appointment. I can manage quite well alone."

"We shouldn't be back early enough for me to go to Kensington from the station, I suppose?"

"No, certainly not. I find that the trains are very awkward. We should not reach King's Cross until nearly one in the morning."

114

"Then, in that case, I shall write to Miss Gibson and excuse myself."

"Oh, I wouldn't do that," said Thorndyke, "it will disappoint them, and really it is not necessary."

"I shall write forthwith," I said firmly, "so please don't try to dissuade me. I have been feeling quite uncomfortable at the thought that, all the time I have been in your employ, I seem to have done nothing but idle about and amuse myself. The opportunity of doing something tangible for my wage is too precious to be allowed to slip."

Thorndyke chuckled indulgently. "You shall do as you please, my dear boy," he said, "but don't imagine that you have been eating the bread of idleness. When you see this Hornby case worked out in detail, you will be surprised to find how large a part you have taken in unravelling it. Your worth to me has been far beyond your poor little salary, I can assure you."

"It is very handsome of you to say that," I said, highly gratified to learn that I was really of use, and not, as I had begun to suspect, a mere object of charity.

"It is perfectly true," he answered, "and now, since you are going to help me in this case, I will set you your task. The case, as I have said, appears to be quite simple, but it never does to take the simplicity for granted. Here is the letter from the solicitors giving the facts as far as they are known at present. On the shelves there you will find Casper, Taylor, Guy and Ferrier, and the other authorities on medical jurisprudence, and I will put out one or two other books that you may find useful. I want you to extract and make classified notes of everything that may bear on such a case as the present one may turn out to be. We must go prepared to meet any contingency that may arise. This is my invariable practice, and even if the case turns out to be quite simple, the labour is never wasted, for it represents so much experience gained."

"Casper and Taylor are pretty old, aren't they?" I objected.

"So is suicide," he retorted drily. "It is a capital mistake to neglect the old authorities. 'There were strong men before Agamemnon,' and some of them were uncommonly strong, let me tell you. Give your best attention to the venerable Casper and the obsolete Taylor and you will not be without your reward."

As a result of these injunctions, I devoted the remainder of the day to the consideration of the various methods by which a man might contrive to effect his exit from the stage of human activities. And a very engrossing study I found it, and the more interesting in view of the problem that awaited solution on the morrow, but yet not so engrossing but that I was able to find time to write a long, rather intimate and minutely explanatory letter to Miss Gibson, in which I even mentioned the hour of our return as showing the impossibility of my keeping my engagement. Not that I had

115

the smallest fear of her taking offence, for it is an evidence of my respect and regard for her that I cancelled the appointment without a momentary doubt that she would approve of my action, but it was pleasant to write to her at length and to feel the intimacy of keeping her informed of the details of my life.

The case, when we came to inquire into it on the spot, turned out to be a suicide of the most transparent type, whereat both Thorndyke and I were, I think, a little disappointed – he at having apparently done so little for a very substantial fee, and I at having no opportunity for applying my recently augmented knowledge.

"Yes," said my colleague, as we rolled ourselves up in our rugs in adjacent corners of the railway carriage, "it has been a flat affair, and the whole thing could have been managed by the local solicitor. But it is not a waste of time after all, for, you see, I have to do many a day's work for which I get not a farthing of payment, nor even any recognition, so that I do not complain if I occasionally find myself receiving more payment than my actual services merit. And as to you, I take it that you have acquired a good deal of valuable knowledge on the subject of suicide, and knowledge, as the late Lord Bacon remarked with more truth than originality, is power."

To this I made no reply, having just lit my pipe and feeling uncommonly drowsy, and, my companion having followed my example, we smoked in silence, becoming more and more somnolent, until the train drew up in the terminus and we turned out, yawning and shivering, on to the platform.

"Bah!" exclaimed Thorndyke, drawing his rug round his shoulders, "this is a cheerless hour – a quarter-past-one. See how chilly and miserable all these poor devils of passengers look. Shall we cab it or walk?"

"I think a sharp walk would rouse our circulation after sitting huddled up in the carriage for so long," I answered.

"So do I," said Thorndyke, "so let us away – Hark forward! And also Tally Ho! In fact one might go so far as to say Yoicks! That gentleman appears to favour the strenuous life, if one may judge by the size of his sprocket-wheel."

He pointed to a bicycle that was drawn up by the kerb in the approach – a machine of the road-racer type, with an enormous sprocket-wheel, indicating a gear of, at least, ninety.

"Some scorcher or amateur racer, probably," I said, "who takes the opportunity of getting a spin on the wood pavement when the streets are empty." I looked round to see if I could identify the owner, but the machine appeared to be, for the moment, taking care of itself.

116

King's Cross is one of those districts of which the inhabitants are slow in settling down for the night, and even at a quarter-past-one in the morning its streets are not entirely deserted. Here and there the glimmer of a street lamp or the far-reaching ray from a tall electric light reveals the form of some nocturnal prowler creeping along with cat-like stealthiness, or bursting, cat-like, into unmelodious song. Not greatly desirous of the society of these roysterers, we crossed quickly from the station into the Gray's Inn Road, now silent and excessively dismal in aspect, and took our way along the western side. We had turned the curve and were crossing Manchester Street, when a series of yelps from ahead announced the presence of a party of merry-makers, whom we were not yet able to see, however, for the night was an exceptionally dark one, but the sounds of revelry continued to increase in volume as we proceeded, until, as we passed Sidmouth Street, we came in sight of the revellers. They were some half-dozen in number, all of them roughs of the hooligan type, and they were evidently in boisterous spirits, for, as they passed the entrance to the Royal Free Hospital, they halted and battered furiously at the gate. Shortly after this exploit they crossed the road on to our side, whereupon Thorndyke caught my arm and slackened his pace.

"Let them draw ahead," said he. "It is a wise precaution to give all hooligan gangs a very wide berth at this time of night. We had better turn down Heathcote Street and cross Mecklenburgh Square."

We continued to walk on at reduced speed until we reached Heathcote Street, into which we turned and so entered Mecklenburgh Square, where we mended our pace once more.

"The hooligan," pursued Thorndyke, as we walked briskly across the silent square, "covers a multitude of sins, ranging from highway robbery with violence and paid assassination (technically known as 'bashing') down to the criminal folly of the philanthropic magistrate, who seems to think that his function in the economy of nature is to secure the survival of the unfittest. There goes a cyclist along Guildford Street. I wonder if that is our strenuous friend from the station. If so, he has slipped past the hooligans."

We were just entering Doughty Street, and, as Thorndyke spoke, a man on a bicycle was visible for an instant at the crossing of the two streets. When we reached Guildford Street we both looked down the long, lamp-lighted vista, but the cyclist had vanished.

"We had better go straight on into Theobald's Road," said Thorndyke, and we accordingly pursued our way up the fine old-world street, from whose tall houses our footfalls echoed, so that we seemed to be accompanied by an invisible multitude, until we reached that part where it unaccountably changes its name and becomes John Street.

117

"There always seems to me something very pathetic about these old Bloomsbury streets," said Thorndyke, "with their faded grandeur and dignified seediness. They remind me of some prim and aged gentlewoman in reduced circumstances who – Hallo! What was that?"

A faint, sharp thud from behind had been followed instantly by the shattering of a ground-floor window in front.

We both stopped dead and remained, for a couple of seconds, staring into the gloom, from whence the first sound had come. Then Thorndyke darted diagonally across the road at a swift run and I immediately followed.

At the moment when the affair happened we had gone about forty yards up John Street, that is, from the place where it is crossed by Henry Street, and we now raced across the road to the further corner of the latter street. When we reached it, however, the little thoroughfare was empty, and, as we paused for a moment, no sound of retreating footsteps broke the silence.

"The shot certainly came from here!" said Thorndyke, "come on," and he again broke into a run. A few yards up the street a mews turns off to the left, and into this my companion plunged, motioning me to go straight on, which I accordingly did, and in a few paces reached the top of the street. Here a narrow thoroughfare, with a broad, smooth pavement, bears off to the left, parallel with the mews, and, as I arrived at the corner and glanced up the little street, I saw a man on a bicycle gliding swiftly and silently towards Little James' Street.

With a mighty shout of "Stop thief!" I started in hot pursuit, but, though the man's feet were moving in an apparently leisurely manner, he drew ahead at an astonishing pace, in spite of my efforts to overtake him, and it then dawned upon me that the slow revolutions of his feet were due, in reality, to the unusually high gear of the machine that he was riding. As I realised this, and at the same moment recalled the bicycle that we had seen in the station, the fugitive swung round into Little James' Street and vanished.

The speed at which the man was travelling made further pursuit utterly futile, so I turned and walked back, panting and perspiring from the unwonted exertion. As I re-entered Henry Street, Thorndyke emerged from the mews and halted on seeing me.

"Cyclist?" he asked laconically, as I came up.

"Yes," I answered, "riding a machine geared up to about ninety."

"Ah! He must have followed us from the station," said Thorndyke. "Did you notice if he was carrying anything?"

"He had a walking-stick in his hand. I didn't see anything else."

"What sort of walking-stick?"

118

"I couldn't see very distinctly. It was a stoutish stick – I should say a Malacca, probably – and it had what looked like a horn handle. I could see that as he passed a street lamp."

"What kind of lamp had he?"

"I couldn't see, but, as he turned the corner, I noticed that it seemed to burn very dimly."

"A little vaseline, or even oil, smeared on the outside of the glass will reduce the glare of a lamp very appreciably," my companion remarked, "especially on a dusty road. Ha! Here is the proprietor of the broken window. He wants to know, you know."

We had once more turned into John Street and now perceived a man, standing on the wide doorstep of the house with the shattered window, looking anxiously up and down the street.

"Do either of you gents know anything about this here?" he asked, pointing to the broken pane.

"Yes," said Thorndyke, "we happened to be passing when it was done. In fact," he added, "I rather suspect that the missile, whatever it was, was intended for our benefit."

"Oh!" said the man. "Who done it?"

"That I can't say," replied Thorndyke. "Whoever he was, he made off on a bicycle and we were unable to catch him."

"Oh!" said the man once more, regarding us with growing suspicion. "On a bicycle, hay! Dam funny, ain't it? What did he do it with?"

"That is what I should like to find out," said Thorndyke. "I see this house is empty."

"Yes, it's empty – leastways it's to let. I'm the caretaker. But what's that got to do with it?"

"Merely this," answered Thorndyke, "that the object – stone, bullet or whatever it may have been – was aimed, I believe, at me, and I should like to ascertain its nature. Would you do me the favour of permitting me to look for it?"

The caretaker was evidently inclined to refuse this request, for he glanced suspiciously from my companion to me once or twice before replying, but, at length, he turned towards the open door and gruffly invited us to enter.

A paraffin lamp was on the floor in a recess of the hall, and this our conductor took up when he had elosed the street door.

"This is the room," he said, turning the key and thrusting the door open, "the library they call it, but it's the front parlour in plain English." He entered and, holding the lamp above his head, stared balefully at the broken window.

119

Thorndyke glanced quickly along the floor in the direction that the missile would have taken, and then said, "Do you see any mark on the wall there?"

As he spoke, he indicated the wall opposite the window, which obviously could not have been struck by a projectile entering with such extreme obliquity, and I was about to point out this fact when I fortunately remembered the great virtue of silence.

Our friend approached the wall, still holding up the lamp, and scrutinised the surface with close attention, and while he was thus engaged, I observed Thorndyke stoop quickly and pick up something, which he deposited carefully, and without remark, in his waistcoat pocket.

"I don't see no bruise anywhere," said the caretaker, sweeping his hand over the wall.

"Perhaps the thing struck this wall," suggested Thorndyke, pointing to the one that was actually in the line of fire. "Yes, of course," he added, "it would be this one – the shot came from Henry Street."

The caretaker crossed the room and threw the light of his lamp on the wall thus indicated.

"Ah! Here we are!" he exclaimed, with gloomy satisfaction, pointing to a small dent in which the wall-paper was turned back and the plaster exposed, "looks almost like a bullet mark, but you say you didn't hear no report."

"No," said Thorndyke, "there was no report. It must have been a catapult."

The caretaker set the lamp down on the floor and proceeded to grope about for the projectile, in which operation we both assisted, and I could not suppress a faint smile as I noted the earnestness with which Thorndyke peered about the floor in search of the missile that was quietly reposing in his waistcoat pocket.

We were deep in our investigations when there was heard an uncompromising double knock at the street door, followed by the loud pealing of a bell in the basement.

"Bobby, I suppose," growled the caretaker. "Here's a blooming fuss about nothing." He caught up the lamp and went out, leaving us in the dark.

"I picked it up, you know," said Thorndyke, when we were alone.

"I saw you," I answered.

"Good. I applaud your discretion," he rejoined. The caretaker's supposition was correct. When he returned, he was accompanied by a burly constable, who saluted us with a cheerful smile and glanced facetiously round the empty room.

"Our boys," said he, nodding towards the broken window, "they're playful lads, that they are. You were passing when it happened, sir, I hear."

"Yes," answered Thorndyke, and he gave the constable a brief account of the occurrence, which the latter listened to, notebook in hand.

"Well," said he when the narrative was concluded, "if those hooligan boys are going to take to catapults they'll make things lively all round."

"You ought to run some of 'em in," said the caretaker.

"Run 'em in!" exclaimed the constable in a tone of disgust. "Yes! And then the magistrate will tell 'em to be good boys and give 'em five shillings out of the poor-box to buy illustrated Testaments. I'd Testament them, the worthless varmints!"

He rammed his notebook fiercely into his pocket and stalked out of the room into the street, whither we followed.

"You'll find that bullet or stone when you sweep up the room," he said, as he turned on to his beat, "and you'd better let us have it. Good night, sir."

He strolled off towards Henry Street, while Thorndyke and I resumed our journey southward.

"Why were you so secret about that projectile?" I asked my friend as we walked up the street.

"Partly to avoid discussion with the caretaker," he replied, "but principally because I thought it likely that a constable would pass the house and, seeing the light, come in to make inquiries."

"And then?"

"Then I should have had to hand over the object to him."

"And why not? Is the object a specially interesting one?"

"It is highly interesting to me at the present moment," replied Thorndyke, with a chuckle, "because I have not examined it. I have a theory as to its nature, which theory I should like to test before taking the police into my confidence."

"Are you going to take me into your confidence?" I asked.

"When we get home, if you are not too sleepy," he replied.

On our arrival at his chambers, Thorndyke desired me to light up and clear one end of the table while he went up to the workshop to fetch some tools. I turned back the table cover, and, having adjusted the gas so as to light this part of the table, waited in some impatience for my colleague's return. In a few minutes he re-entered bearing a small vice, a metal saw and a wide-mouthed bottle.

"What have you got in that bottle?" I asked, perceiving a metal object inside it.

"That is the projectile, which I have thought fit to rinse in distilled water, for reasons that will presently appear."

He agitated the bottle gently for a minute or so, and then, with a pair of dissecting forceps, lifted out the object and held it above the surface of the water to drain, after which he laid it carefully on a piece of blotting-paper.

I stooped over the projectile and examined it with great curiosity, while Thorndyke stood by regarding me with almost equal interest.

"Well," he said, after watching me in silence for some time, "what do you see?"

"I see a small brass cylinder," I answered, "about two inches long and rather thicker than an ordinary lead pencil. One end is conical, and there is a small hole at the apex which seems to contain a steel point. The other end is flat, but has in the centre a small square projection such as might fit a watch-key. I notice also a small hole in the side of the cylinder close to the flat end. The thing looks like a miniature shell, and appears to be hollow."

"It is hollow," said Thorndyke. "You must have observed that, when I held it up to drain, the water trickled out through the hole at the pointed end."

"Yes, I noticed that."

"Now take it up and shake it."

I did so and felt some heavy object rattle inside it.

"There is some loose body inside it," I said, "which fits it pretty closely, as it moves only in the long diameter."

"Quite so. Your description is excellent. And now, what is the nature of this projectile?"

"I should say it is a miniature shell or explosive bullet."

"Wrong!" said Thorndyke. "A very natural inference, but a wrong one."

"Then what is the thing?" I demanded, my curiosity still further aroused.

"I will show you," he replied. "It is something much more subtle than an explosive bullet – which would really be a rather crude appliance – admirably thought out and thoroughly well executed. We have to deal with a most ingenious and capable man."

I was fain to laugh at his enthusiastic appreciation of the methods of his would-be assassin, and the humour of the situation then appeared to dawn on him, for he said, with an apologetic smile, "I am not expressing approval, you must understand, but merely professional admiration. It is this class of criminal that creates the necessity for my services. He is my patron, so to speak, my ultimate employer. For the common crook can be dealt with quite efficiently by the common policeman!"

While he was speaking he had been fitting the little cylinder between two pads of tissue-paper in the vice, which he now screwed up tight. Then, with the fine metal saw, he began to cut the projectile, lengthwise, into two slightly unequal parts. This operation took some time, especially since he was careful not to cut the loose body inside, but at length the section was completed and the interior of the cylinder exposed, when he released it from the vice and held it up before me with an expression of triumph.

"Now, what do you make it?" he demanded.

I took the object in my fingers and looked at it closely, but was at first more puzzled than before. The loose body I now saw to be a cylinder of lead about half-an-inch long, accurately fitting the inside of the cylinder but capable of slipping freely backwards and forwards. The steel point which I had noticed in the hole at the apex of the conical end, was now seen to be the pointed termination of a slender steel rod which projected fully an inch into the cavity of the cylinder, and the conical end itself was a solid mass of lead.

"Well?" queried Thorndyke, seeing that I was still silent.

"You tell me it is not an explosive bullet," I replied, "otherwise I should have been confirmed in that opinion. I should have said that the percussion cap was carried by this lead plunger and struck on the end of that steel rod when the flight of the bullet was suddenly arrested."

"Very good indeed," said Thorndyke. "You are right so far that this is, in fact, the mechanism of a percussion shell.

"But look at this. You see this little rod was driven inside the bullet when the latter struck the wall. Let us replace it in its original position."

He laid the end of a small flat file against the end of the rod and pressed it firmly, when the rod slid through the hole until it projected an inch beyond the apex of the cone. Then he handed the projectile back to me.

A single glance at the point of the steel rod made the whole thing clear, and I gave a whistle of consternation, for the "rod" was a fine tube with a sharply pointed end.

"The infernal scoundrel!" I exclaimed, "it is a hypodermic needle."

"Yes. A veterinary hypodermic, of extra large bore. Now you see the subtlety and ingenuity of the whole thing. If he had had a reasonable chance he would certainly have succeeded."

"You speak quite regretfully," I said, laughing again at the oddity of his attitude towards the assassin.

"Not at all," he replied. "I have the character of a single-handed player, but even the most self-reliant man can hardly make a *post-mortem* on himself. I am merely appreciating an admirable piece of mechanical design most efficiently carried out. Observe the completeness of the thing,

123

and the way in which all the necessities of the case are foreseen and met. This projectile was discharged from a powerful air-gun – the walking-stick form – provided with a force-pump and key. The barrel of that gun was rifled."

"How do you know that?" I asked.

"Well, to begin with, it would be useless to fit a needle to the projectile unless the latter was made to travel with the point forwards, but there is direct evidence that the barrel was rifled. You notice the little square projection on the back surface of the cylinder. That was evidently made to fit a washer or wad – probably a thin plate of soft metal which would be driven by the pressure from behind into the grooves of the rifling and thus give a spinning motion to the bullet. When the latter left the barrel, the wad would drop off, leaving it free."

"I see. I was wondering what the square projection was for. It is, as you say, extremely ingenious."

"Highly ingenious," said Thorndyke, enthusiastically, "and so is the whole device. See how perfectly it would have worked but for a mere fluke and for the complication of your presence. Supposing that I had been alone, so that he could have approached to a shorter distance. In that case he would not have missed, and the thing would have been done. You see how it was intended to be done, I suppose?"

"I think so," I answered, "but I should like to hear your account of the process."

"Well, you see, he first finds out that I am returning by a late train – which he seems to have done – and he waits for me at the terminus. Meanwhile he fills the cylinder with a solution of a powerful alkaloidal poison, which is easily done by dipping the needle into the liquid and sucking at the small hole near the back end, when the piston will be drawn up and the liquid will follow it. You notice that the upper side of the piston is covered with vaseline – introduced through the hole, no doubt – which would prevent the poison from coming out into the mouth, and make the cylinder secure from leakage. On my arrival, he follows me on his bicycle until I pass through a sufficiently secluded neighbourhood. Then he approaches me, or passes me and waits round a corner, and shoots at pretty close range. It doesn't matter where he hits me. All parts are equally vital, so he can aim at the middle of my back. Then the bullet comes spinning through the air point foremost. The needle passes through the clothing and enters the flesh, and, as the bullet is suddenly stopped, the heavy piston flies down by its own great momentum and squirts out a jet of the poison into the tissues. The bullet then disengages itself and drops on to the ground.

"Meanwhile, our friend has mounted his bicycle and is off, and when I feel the prick of the needle, I turn, and, without stopping to look for the bullet, immediately give chase. I am, of course, not able to overtake a man on a racing machine, but still I follow him some distance. Then the poison begins to take effect – the more rapidly from the violent exercise – and presently I drop insensible. Later on, my body is found. There are no marks of violence, and probably the needle-puncture escapes observation at the *post-mortem,* in which case the verdict will be death from heart-failure. Even if the poison and the puncture are discovered, there is no clue. The bullet lies some streets away, and is probably picked up by some boy or passing stranger, who cannot conjecture its use, and who would never connect it with the man who was found dead. You will admit that the whole plan has been worked out with surprising completeness and foresight."

"Yes," I answered, "there is no doubt that the fellow is a most infernally clever scoundrel. May I ask if you have any idea who he is?"

"Well," Thorndyke replied, "seeing that, as Carlyle has unkindly pointed out, clever people are not in an overwhelming majority, and that, of the clever people whom I know, only a very few are interested in my immediate demise, I am able to form a fairly probable conjecture."

"And what do you mean to do?"

"For the present I shall maintain an attitude of masterly inactivity and avoid the night air."

"But, surely," I exclaimed, "you will take some measures to protect yourself against attempts of this kind. You can hardly doubt now that your accident in the fog was really an attempted murder."

"I never did doubt it, as a matter of fact, although I prevaricated at the time. But I have not enough evidence against this man at present, and, consequently, can do nothing but show that I suspect him, which would be foolish. Whereas, if I lie low, one of two things will happen: Either the occasion for my removal (which is only a temporary one) will pass, or he will commit himself – will put a definite clue into my hands. Then we shall find the air-cane, the bicycle, perhaps a little stock of poison, and certain other trifles that I have in my mind, which will be good confirmatory evidence, though insufficient in themselves. And now, I think, I must really adjourn this meeting, or we shall be good for nothing to-morrow."

Chapter XII
It Might Have Been

It was now only a week from the date on which the trial was to open. In eight days the mystery would almost certainly be solved (if it was capable of solution), for the trial promised to be quite a short one, and then Reuben Hornby would be either a convicted felon or a free man, clear of the stigma of the crime.

For several days past, Thorndyke had been in almost constant possession of the laboratory, while his own small room, devoted ordinarily to bacteriology and microscopical work was kept continually locked – a state of things that reduced Polton to a condition of the most extreme nervous irritation, especially when, as he told me indignantly, he met Mr. Anstey emerging from the holy of holies, grinning and rubbing his hands and giving utterance to genial but unparliamentary expressions of amused satisfaction.

I had met Anstey on several occasions lately, and each time liked him better than the last, for his whimsical, facetious manner covered a nature (as it often does) that was serious and thoughtful, and I found him, not only a man of considerable learning, but one also of a lofty standard of conduct. His admiration for Thorndyke was unbounded, and I could see that the two men collaborated with the utmost sympathy and mutual satisfaction.

But although I regarded Mr. Anstey with feelings of the liveliest friendship, I was far from gratified when, on the morning of which I am writing, I observed him from our sitting-room window crossing the gravelled space from Crown Office Row and evidently bearing down on our chambers. For the fact is that I was awaiting the arrival of Juliet, and should greatly have preferred to be alone at the moment, seeing that Thorndyke had already gone out. It is true that my fair enslaver was not due for nearly half-an-hour, but then, who could say how long Anstey would stay, or what embarrassments might arise from my efforts to escape? By all of which it may be perceived that my disease had reached a very advanced stage, and that I was unequal to those tactics of concealment that are commonly attributed to the ostrich.

A sharp rap of the knocker announced the arrival of the disturber of my peace, and when I opened the door Anstey walked in with the air of a man to whom an hour more or less is of no consequence whatever. He shook my hand with mock solemnity, and, seating himself upon the edge of the table, proceeded to roll a cigarette with exasperating deliberation.

"I infer," said he, "that our learned brother is practising parlour magic upstairs, or peradventure he has gone on a journey?"

"He has a consultation this morning," I answered. "Was he expecting you?"

"Evidently not, or he would have been here. No, I just looked in to ask a question about the case of your friend Hornby. You know it comes on for trial next week?"

"Yes. Thorndyke told me. What do you think of Hornby's prospects? Is he going to be convicted, or will he get an acquittal?"

"*He* will be entirely passive," replied Anstey, "but *we*" – here he slapped his chest impressively – "are going to secure an acquittal. You will be highly entertained, my learned friend, and Mr. The Enemy will be excessively surprised." He inspected the newly-made cigarette with a critical air and chuckled softly.

"You seem pretty confident," I remarked.

"I am," he answered, "though Thorndyke considers failure possible – which, of course, it is if the jury-box should chance to be filled with microcephalic idiots and the judge should prove incapable of understanding simple technical evidence. But we hope that neither of these things will happen, and, if they do not, we feel pretty safe. By the way, I hope I am not divulging your principal's secrets?"

"Well," I replied, with a smile, "you have been more explicit than Thorndyke ever has."

"Have I?" he exclaimed, with mock anxiety, "then I must swear you to secrecy. Thorndyke is so very close – and he is quite right too. I never cease admiring his tactics of allowing the enemy to fortify and barricade the entrance that he does *not* mean to attack. But I see you are wishing me at the devil, so give me a cigar and I will go – though not to that particular destination."

"Will you have one of Thorndyke's special brand?" I asked malignantly.

"What! Those foul Trichinopolies? Not while brown paper is to be obtained at every stationer's. I'd sooner smoke my own wig."

I tendered my own case, from which he selected a cigar with anxious care and much sniffing. Then he bade me a ceremonious adieu and departed down the stairs, blithely humming a melody from the latest comic opera.

He had not left more than five minutes when a soft and elaborate rat-tat from the little brass knocker brought my heart into my mouth. I ran to the door and flung it open, revealing Juliet standing on the threshold.

"May I come in?" she asked. "I want to have a few words with you before we start."

127

I looked at her with some anxiety, for she was manifestly agitated, and the hand that she held out to me trembled.

"I am greatly upset, Dr. Jervis," she said, ignoring the chair that I had placed for her. "Mr. Lawley has been giving us his views of poor Reuben's case, and his attitude fills me with dismay."

"Hang Mr. Lawley!" I muttered, and then apologised hastily. "What made you go to him, Miss Gibson?"

"I didn't go to him. He came to us. He dined with us last night – he and Walter – and his manner was gloomy in the extreme. After dinner Walter took him apart with me and asked him what he really thought of the case. He was most pessimistic. 'My dear sir,' he said, 'the only advice I can give you is that you prepare yourself to contemplate disaster as philosophically as you can. In my opinion your cousin is almost certain to be convicted.' 'But,' said Walter, 'what about the defence? I understood that there was at least a plausible case.' Mr. Lawley shrugged his shoulders. 'I have a sort of *alibi* that will go for nothing, but I have no evidence to offer in answer to that of the prosecution, and no case, and I may say, speaking in confidence, that I do not believe there is any case. I do not see how there can be any case, and I have heard nothing from Dr. Thorndyke to lead me to suppose that he has really done anything in the matter.' Is this true, Dr. Jervis? Oh! Do tell me the real truth about it! I have been so miserable and terrified since I heard this, and I was so full of hope before. Tell me, is it true? Will Reuben be sent to prison after all?"

In her agitation she laid her hands on my arm and looked up into my face with her grey eyes swimming with tears, and was so piteous, so trustful, and, withal, so bewitching that my reserve melted like snow before a July sun.

"It is not true," I answered, taking her hands in mine and speaking perforce in a low tone that I might not betray my emotion. "If it were, it would mean that I have wilfully deceived you, that I have been false to our friendship, and how much that friendship has been to me, no one but myself will ever know."

She crept a little closer to me with a manner at once penitent and wheedling.

"You are not going to be angry with me, are you? It was foolish of me to listen to Mr. Lawley after all you have told me, and it did look like a want of trust in you, I know. But you, who are so strong and wise, must make allowance for a woman who is neither. It is all so terrible that I am quite unstrung, but say you are not really displeased with me, for that would hurt me most of all."

Oh! Delilah! That concluding stroke of the shears severed the very last lock, and left me – morally speaking – as bald as a billiard ball.

Henceforth I was at her mercy and would have divulged, without a scruple, the uttermost secrets of my principal, but that that astute gentleman had placed me beyond the reach of temptation.

"As to being angry with you," I answered, "I am not, like Thorndyke, one to essay the impossible, and if I could be angry it would hurt me more than it would you. But, in fact, you are not to blame at all, and I am an egotistical brute. Of course you were alarmed and distressed – nothing could be more natural. So now let me try to chase away your fears and restore your confidence.

"I have told you what Thorndyke said to Reuben: That he had good hopes of making his innocence clear to everybody. That alone should have been enough."

"I know it should," murmured Juliet remorsefully, "please forgive me for my want of faith."

"But," I continued, "I can quote you the words of one to whose opinions you will attach more weight. Mr. Anstey was here less than half-an-hour ago – "

"Do you mean Reuben's counsel?"

"Yes."

"And what did he say? Oh, do tell me what he said."

"He said, in brief, that he was quite confident of obtaining an acquittal, and that the prosecution would receive a great surprise. He seemed highly pleased with his brief, and spoke with great admiration of Thorndyke."

"Did he really say that – that he was confident of an acquittal?" Her voice was breathless and unsteady, and she was clearly, as she had said, quite unstrung. "What a relief it is," she murmured incoherently, "and so very, very kind of you!" She wiped her eyes and laughed a queer, shaky little laugh. Then, quite suddenly, she burst into a passion of sobbing.

Hardly conscious of what I did, I drew her gently towards me, and rested her head on my shoulder whilst I whispered into her ear I know not what words of consolation, but I am sure that I called her "dear Juliet," and probably used other expressions equally improper and reprehensible. Presently she recovered herself, and, having dried her eyes, regarded me somewhat shamefacedly, blushing hotly, but smiling very sweetly nevertheless.

"I am ashamed of myself," she said, "coming here and weeping on your bosom like a great baby. It is to be hoped that your other clients do not behave in this way."

Whereat we both laughed heartily, and, our emotional equilibrium being thus restored, we began to think of the object of our meeting.

"I am afraid I have wasted a great deal of time," said Juliet, looking at her watch. "Shall we be too late, do you think?"

"I hope not," I replied, "for Reuben will be looking for us, but we must hurry."

I caught up my hat, and we went forth, closing the oak behind us, and took our way up King's Bench Walk in silence, but with a new and delightful sense of intimate comradeship. I glanced from time to time at my companion, and noted that her cheek still bore a rosy flush, and when she looked at me there was a sparkle in her eye, and a smiling softness in her glance, that stirred my heart until I trembled with the intensity of the passion that I must needs conceal. And even while I was feeling that I must tell her all, and have done with it, tell her that I was her abject slave, and she my goddess, my queen. That in the face of such a love as mine no man could have any claim upon her. Even then, there arose the still, small voice that began to call me an unfaithful steward and to remind me of a duty and trust that were sacred even beyond love.

In Fleet Street I hailed a cab, and, as I took my seat beside my fair companion, the voice began to wax and speak in bolder and sterner accents.

"Christopher Jervis," it said, "what is this that you are doing? Are you a man of honour or nought but a mean, pitiful blackguard? You, the trusted agent of this poor, misused gentleman, are you not planning in your black heart how you shall rob him of that which, if he is a man at all, must be more to him than his liberty, or even his honour? Shame on you for a miserable weakling! Have done with these philanderings and keep your covenants like a gentleman – or, at least, an honest man!"

At this point in my meditations Juliet turned towards me with a coaxing smile.

"My legal adviser seems to be revolving some deep and weighty matter," she said.

I pulled myself together and looked at her – at her sparkling eyes and rosy, dimpling cheeks, so winsome and lovely and lovable.

"Come," I thought, "I must put an end to this at once, or I am lost." But it cost me a very agony of effort to do it – which agony, I trust, may be duly set to my account by those who may sit in judgement on me.

"Your legal adviser, Miss Gibson," I said (and at that "Miss Gibson" I thought she looked at me a little queerly), "has been reflecting that he has acted considerably beyond his jurisdiction."

"In what respect?" she asked.

"In passing on to you information which was given to him in very strict confidence, and, in fact, with an implied promise of secrecy on his part."

"But the information was not of a very secret character, was it?"

"More so than it appeared. You see, Thorndyke thinks it so important not to let the prosecution suspect that he has anything up his sleeve, that he has kept even Mr. Lawley in the dark, and he has never said as much to me as Anstey did this morning."

"And now you are sorry you told me. You think I have led you into a breach of trust. Is it not so?" She spoke without a trace of petulance, and her tone of dignified self-accusation made me feel a veritable worm.

"My dear Miss Gibson," I expostulated, "you entirely misunderstand me. I am not in the least sorry that I told you. How could I have done otherwise under the circumstances? But I want you to understand that I have taken the responsibility of communicating to you what is really a professional secret, and that you are to consider it as such."

"That was how I understood it," replied Juliet, "and you may rely upon me not to utter a syllable on the subject to anyone."

I thanked her for this promise, and then, by way of making conversation, gave her an account in detail of Anstey's visit, not even omitting the incident of the cigar.

"And are Dr. Thorndyke's cigars so extraordinarily bad?" she asked.

"Not at all," I replied, "only they are not to every man's taste. The Trichinopoly cheroot is Thorndyke's one dissipation, and, I must say, he takes it very temperately. Under ordinary circumstances he smokes a pipe, but after a specially heavy day's work, or on any occasion of festivity or rejoicing, he indulges in a Trichinopoly, and he smokes the very best that can be got."

"So even the greatest men have their weaknesses," Juliet moralised, "but I wish I had known Dr. Thorndyke's sooner, for Mr. Hornby had a large box of Trichinopoly cheroots given to him, and I believe they were exceptionally fine ones. However, he tried one and didn't like it, so he transferred the whole consignment to Walter, who smokes all sorts and conditions of cigars."

So we talked on from one commonplace to another, and each more conventional than the last. In my nervousness, I overdid my part, and having broken the ice, proceeded to smash it to impalpable fragments. Endeavouring merely to be unemotional and to avoid undue intimacy of manner, I swung to the opposite extreme and became almost stiff, and perhaps the more so since I was writhing with the agony of repression.

Meanwhile a corresponding change took place in my companion. At first her manner seemed doubtful and bewildered. Then she, too, grew more distant and polite and less disposed for conversation. Perhaps her conscience began to rebuke her, or it may be that my coolness suggested to her that her conduct had not been quite of the kind that would have

131

commended itself to Reuben. But however that may have been, we continued to draw farther and farther apart, and in that short half-hour we retraced the steps of our growing friendship to such purpose that, when we descended from the cab at the prison gate, we seemed more like strangers than on the first day that we met. It was a miserable ending to all our delightful comradeship, and yet what other end could one expect in this world of cross purposes and things that might have been? In the extremity of my wretchedness I could have wept on the bosom of the portly warder who opened the wicket, even as Juliet had wept upon mine, and it was almost a relief to me, when our brief visit was over, to find that we should not return together to King's Cross as was our wont, but that Juliet would go back by omnibus that she might do some shopping in Oxford Street, leaving me to walk home alone.

I saw her into her omnibus, and stood on the pavement looking wistfully at the lumbering vehicle as it dwindled in the distance. At last, with a sigh of deepest despondency, I turned my face homeward, and, walking like one in a dream, retraced the route over which I had journeyed so often of late and with such different sensations.

Chapter XIII
Murder by Post

The next few days were perhaps the most unhappy that I have known. My life, indeed, since I had left the hospital had been one of many disappointments and much privation. Unfulfilled desires and ambitions unrealised had combined with distaste for the daily drudgery that had fallen to my lot to embitter my poverty and cause me to look with gloomy distrust upon the unpromising future. But no sorrow that I had hitherto experienced could compare with the grief that I now felt in contemplating the irretrievable ruin of what I knew to be the great passion of my life. For to a man like myself, of few friends and deep affections, one great emotional upheaval exhausts the possibilities of nature, leaving only the capacity for feeble and ineffective echoes. The edifice of love that is raised upon the ruins of a great passion can compare with the original no more than can the paltry mosque that perches upon the mound of Jonah with the glories of the palace that lies entombed beneath.

I had made a pretext to write to Juliet and had received a reply quite frank and friendly in tone, by which I knew that she had not – as some women would have done – set the blame upon me for our temporary outburst of emotion. And yet there was a subtle difference from her previous manner of writing that only emphasised the finality of our separation.

I think Thorndyke perceived that something had gone awry, though I was at great pains to maintain a cheerful exterior and keep myself occupied, and he probably formed a pretty shrewd guess at the nature of the trouble, but he said nothing, and I only judged that he had observed some change in my manner by the fact that there was blended with his usual quiet geniality an almost insensible note of sympathy and affection.

A couple of days after my last interview with Juliet, an event occurred which served, certainly, to relieve the tension and distract my thoughts, though not in a very agreeable manner.

It was the pleasant, reposeful hour after dinner when it was our custom to sit in our respective easy chairs and, as we smoked our pipes, discuss some of the many topics in which we had a common interest. The postman had just discharged into the capacious letter-box an avalanche of letters and circulars, and as I sat glancing through the solitary letter that had fallen to my share, I looked from time to time at Thorndyke and noticed, as I had often done before, with some surprise, a curious habit that

133

he had of turning over and closely scrutinising every letter and package before he opened it.

"I observe, Thorndyke," I now ventured to remark, "that you always examine the outside of a letter before looking at the inside. I have seen other people do the same, and it has always appeared to me a singularly foolish proceeding. Why speculate over an unopened letter when a glance at the contents will tell you all there is to know?"

"You are perfectly right," he answered, "if the object of the inspection is to discover who is the sender of the letter. But that is not my object. In my case the habit is one that has been deliberately cultivated – not in reference to letters only, but to everything that comes into my hands – the habit of allowing nothing to pass without a certain amount of conscious attention. The observant man is, in reality, the attentive man, and the so-called power of observation is simply the capacity for continuous attention. As a matter of fact, I have found in practice, that the habit is a useful one even in reference to letters. More than once I have gleaned a hint from the outside of a letter that has proved valuable when applied to the contents. Here, for instance, is a letter which has been opened after being fastened up – apparently by the aid of steam. The envelope is soiled and rubbed, and smells faintly of stale tobacco, and has evidently been carried in a pocket along with a well-used pipe. Why should it have been opened? On reading it I perceive that it should have reached me two days ago, and that the date has been skilfully altered from the thirteenth to the fifteenth. The inference is that my correspondent has a highly untrustworthy clerk."

"But the correspondent may have carried the letter in his own pocket," I objected.

"Hardly," replied Thorndyke. "He would not have troubled to steam his own letter open and close it again. He would have cut the envelope and addressed a fresh one. This the clerk could not do, because the letter was confidential and was addressed in the principal's handwriting. And the principal would have almost certainly added a postscript, and, moreover, he does not smoke. This, however, is all very obvious, but here is something rather more subtle which I have put aside for more detailed examination. What do you make of it?"

He handed me a small parcel to which was attached by string a typewritten address label, the back of which bore the printed inscription, "James Bartlett and Sons, Cigar Manufacturers, London and Havana."

"I am afraid," said I, after turning the little packet over and examining every part of it minutely, "that this is rather too subtle for me. The only thing that I observe is that the typewriter has bungled the address considerably. Otherwise this seems to me a very ordinary packet indeed."

134

"Well, you have observed one point of interest, at any rate," said Thorndyke, taking the packet from me. "But let us examine the thing systematically and note down what we see. In the first place, you will notice that the label is an ordinary luggage label such as you may buy at any stationer's, with its own string attached. Now, manufacturers commonly use a different and more substantial pattern, which is attached by the string of the parcel. But that is a small matter. What is much more striking is the address on the label. It is typewritten and, as you say, typed very badly. Do you know anything about typewriters?"

"Very little."

"Then you do not recognise the machine? Well, this label was typed with a Blickensderfer – an excellent machine, but not the form most commonly selected for the rough work of a manufacturer's office, but we will let that pass. The important point is this: The Blickensderfer Company make several forms of machine, the smallest and lightest of which is the literary, specially designed for the use of journalists and men of letters. Now this label was typed with the literary machine, or, at least, with the literary typewheel, which is really a very remarkable circumstance indeed."

"How do you know that?" I asked.

"By this asterisk, which has been written by mistake, the inexpert operator having pressed down the figure lever instead of the one for capitals. The literary typewheel is the only one that has an asterisk, as I noticed when I was thinking of purchasing a machine. Here, then, we have a very striking fact, for even if a manufacturer chose to use a 'Blick' in his factory, it is inconceivable that he should select the literary form in preference to the more suitable 'commercial' machine."

"Yes," I agreed, "it is certainly very singular."

"And now," pursued Thorndyke, "to consider the writing itself. It has been done by an absolute beginner. He has failed to space in two places, he has written five wrong letters, and he has written figures instead of capitals in two instances."

"Yes. He has made a shocking muddle of it. I wonder he didn't throw the label away and type another."

"Precisely," said Thorndyke. "And if we wish to find out why he did not, we have only to look at the back of the label. You see that the name of the firm, instead of being printed on the label itself in the usual manner, is printed on a separate slip of paper which is pasted on the label – a most foolish and clumsy arrangement, involving an immense waste of time. But if we look closely at the printed slip itself we perceive something still more remarkable, for that slip has been cut down to fit the label, and has been cut with a pair of scissors. The edges are not quite straight, and in one

135

place the 'overlap,' which is so characteristic of the cut made with scissors, can be seen quite plainly."

He handed the packet to me with a reading-lens, through which I could distinctly make out the points he had mentioned.

"Now I need not point out to you," he continued, "that these slips would, ordinarily, have been trimmed by the printer to the correct size in his machine, which would leave an absolutely true edge. Nor need I say that no sane business man would adopt such a device as this. The slip of paper has been cut with scissors to fit the label, and it has then been pasted on to the surface that it has been made to fit, when all this waste of time and trouble – which, in practice, means money – could have been saved by printing the name on the label itself."

"Yes, that is so, but I still do not see why the fellow should not have thrown away this label and typed another."

"Look at the slip again," said Thorndyke. "It is faintly but evenly discoloured and, to me, has the appearance of having been soaked in water. Let us, for the moment, assume that it has been. That would look as if it had been removed from some other package, which again would suggest that the person using it had only the one slip, which he had soaked off the original package, dried, cut down and pasted on the present label. If he pasted it on before typing the address – which he would most probably have done – he might well be unwilling to risk destroying it by soaking it a second time."

"You think, then, there is a suspicion that the package may have been tampered with?"

"There is no need to jump to conclusions," replied Thorndyke. "I merely gave this case as an instance showing that careful examination of the outside of a package or letter may lead us to bestow a little extra attention on the contents. Now let us open it and see what those contents are."

With a sharp knife he divided the outside cover, revealing a stout cardboard box wrapped in a number of advertisement sheets. The box, when the lid was raised, was seen to contain a single cigar – a large cheroot – packed in cotton wool.

"A 'Trichy,' by Jove!" I exclaimed. "Your own special fancy, Thorndyke."

"Yes, and another anomaly, at once, you see, which might have escaped our notice if we had not been on the *qui vive*."

"As a matter of fact, I *don't* see," said I. "You will think me an awful blockhead, but I don't perceive anything singular in a cigar manufacturer sending a sample cigar."

"You read the label, I think?" replied Thorndyke. "However, let us look at one of these leaflets and see what they say. Ah! Here we are: 'Messrs. Bartlett and Sons, who own extensive plantations on the island of Cuba, manufacture their cigars exclusively from selected leaves grown by themselves.' They would hardly make a Trichinopoly cheroot from leaf grown in the West Indies, so we have here a striking anomaly of an East Indian cigar sent to us by a West Indian grower."

"And what do you infer from that?"

"Principally that this cigar – which, by the way, is an uncommonly fine specimen and which I would not smoke for ten thousand pounds – is deserving of very attentive examination." He produced from his pocket a powerful doublet lens, with the aid of which he examined every part of the surface of the cigar, and finally, both ends.

"Look at the small end," he said, handing me the cigar and the lens, "and tell me if you notice anything."

I focussed the lens on the flush-cut surface of closely-rolled leaf, and explored every part of it minutely.

"It seems to me," I said, "that the leaf is opened slightly in the centre, as if a fine wire had been passed up it."

"So it appeared to me," replied Thorndyke, "and, as we are in agreement so far, we will carry our investigations a step further."

He laid the cigar down on the table, and, with the keen, thin-bladed penknife, neatly divided it lengthwise into two halves.

"*Ecce signum!*" exclaimed Thorndyke, as the two parts fell asunder, and for a few moments we stood silently regarding the dismembered cheroot. For, about half-an-inch from the small end, there appeared a little circular patch of white, chalky material which, by the even manner in which it was diffused among the leaf, had evidently been deposited from a solution.

"Our ingenious friend again, I surmise," said Thorndyke at length, taking up one of the halves and examining the white patch through his lens. "A thoughtful soul, Jervis, and original too. I wish his talents could be applied in some other direction. I shall have to remonstrate with him if he becomes troublesome."

"It is your duty to society, Thorndyke," I exclaimed passionately, "to have this infernal, cold-blooded scoundrel arrested instantly. Such a man is a standing menace to the community. Do you really know who sent this thing?"

"I can form a pretty shrewd guess, which, however, is not quite the same thing. But, you see, he has not been quite so clever this time, for he has left one or two traces by which his identity might be ascertained."

"Indeed! What traces has he left?"

137

"Ah! Now there is a nice little problem for us to consider." He settled himself in his easy chair and proceeded to fill his pipe with the air of a man who is about to discuss a matter of merely general interest.

"Let us consider what information this ingenious person has given us about himself. In the first place, he evidently has a strong interest in my immediate decease. Now, why should he feel so urgent a desire for my death? Can it be a question of property? Hardly, for I am far from a rich man, and the provisions of my will are known to me alone. Can it then be a question of private enmity or revenge? I think not. To the best of my belief I have no private enemies whatever. There remains only my vocation as an investigator in the fields of legal and criminal research. His interest in my death must, therefore, be connected with my professional activities. Now, I am at present conducting an exhumation which may lead to a charge of murder, but if I were to die to-night the inquiry would be carried out with equal efficiency by Professor Spicer or some other toxicologist. My death would not affect the prospects of the accused. And so in one or two other cases that I have in hand. They could be equally well conducted by someone else. The inference is that our friend is not connected with any of these cases, but that he believes me to possess some exclusive information concerning him – believes me to be the one person in the world who suspects and can convict him. Let us assume the existence of such a person – a person of whose guilt I alone have evidence. Now this person, being unaware that I have communicated my knowledge to a third party, would reasonably suppose that by making away with me he had put himself in a position of security.

"Here, then, is our first point. The sender of this offering is probably a person concerning whom I hold certain exclusive information.

"But see, now, the interesting corollary that follows from this. I, alone, suspect this person. Therefore I have not published my suspicions, or others would suspect him too. Why, then, does he suspect me of suspecting him, since I have not spoken? Evidently, he too must be in possession of exclusive information. In other words, my suspicions are correct, for if they were not, he could not be aware of their existence.

"The next point is the selection of this rather unusual type of cigar. Why should he have sent a Trichinopoly instead of an ordinary Havana such as Bartletts actually manufacture? It looks as if he were aware of my peculiar predilection, and, by thus consulting my personal tastes, had guarded against the chance of my giving the cigar to some other person. We may, therefore, infer that our friend probably has some knowledge of my habits.

"The third point is: What is the social standing of this gentle stranger, whom we will call X? Now, Bartletts do not send their advertisements and samples to Thomas, Richard, and Henry. They send, chiefly, to members of the professions and men of means and position. It is true that the original package might have been annexed by a clerk, office boy, or domestic servant, but the probabilities are that X received the package himself, and this is borne out by the fact that he was able to obtain access to a powerful alkaloidal poison – such as this undoubtedly is."

"In that case he would probably be a medical man or a chemist," I suggested.

"Not necessarily," replied Thorndyke. "The laws relating to poisons are so badly framed and administered that any well-to-do person, who has the necessary knowledge, can obtain almost any poison that he wants. But social position is an important factor, whence we may conclude that X belongs, at least, to the middle class.

"The fourth point relates to the personal qualities of X. Now it is evident, from this instance alone, that he is a man of exceptional intelligence, of considerable general information, and both ingenious and resourceful. This cigar device is not only clever and original, but it has been adapted to the special circumstances with remarkable forethought. Thus the cheroot was selected, apparently, for two excellent reasons: First, that it was the most likely form to be smoked by the person intended, and second, that it did not require to have the end cut off – which might have led to a discovery of the poison. The plan also shows a certain knowledge of chemistry. The poison was not intended merely to be dissolved in the moisture of the mouth. The idea evidently was that the steam generated by the combustion of the leaf at the distal end, would condense in the cooler part of the cigar and dissolve the poison, and the solution would then be drawn into the mouth. Then the nature of the poison and certain similarities of procedure seem to identify X with the cyclist who used that ingenious bullet. The poison in this case is a white, non-crystalline solid. The poison contained in the bullet was a solution of a white, non-crystalline solid, which analysis showed to be the most poisonous of all akaloids.

"The bullet was virtually a hypodermic syringe. The poison in this cigar has been introduced, in the form of an alcoholic or ethereal solution, by a hypodermic syringe. We shall thus be justified in assuming that the bullet and the cigar came from the same person, and, if this be so, we may say that X *is* a person of considerable knowledge, of great ingenuity and no mean skill as a mechanician – as shown by the manufacture of the bullet.

"These are our principal facts – to which we may add the surmise that he has recently purchased a second-hand Blickensderfer of the literary form or, at least, fitted with a literary typewheel."

"I don't quite see how you arrive at that," I said, in some surprise.

139

"It is merely a guess, you know," he replied, "though a probable one. In the first place he is obviously unused to typing, as the numerous mistakes show. Therefore he has not had the machine very long. The type is that which is peculiar to the Blickensderfer, and, in one of the mistakes, an asterisk has been printed in place of a letter. But the literary typewheel is the only one that has the asterisk. As to the age of the machine, there are evident signs of wear, for some of the letters have lost their sharpness, and this is most evident in the case of those letters which are the most used – the '*e*,' you will notice, for instance, is much worn, and '*e*' occurs more frequently than any other letter of the alphabet. Hence the machine, if recently purchased, was bought second-hand."

"But," I objected, "it may not have been his own machine at all."

"That is quite possible," answered Thorndyke, "though, considering the secrecy that would be necessary, the probabilities are in favour of his having bought it. But, in any case, we have here a means of identifying the machine, should we ever meet with it."

He picked up the label and handed it to me, together with his pocket lens.

"Look closely at the '*e*' that we have been discussing. It occurs five times. In '*Thorndyke*,' in '*Bench*,' in '*Inner*,' and in '*Temple*.' Now in each case you will notice a minute break in the loop, just at the summit. That break corresponds to a tiny dent in the type – caused, probably, by its striking some small, hard object."

"I can make it out quite distinctly," I said, "and it should be a most valuable point for identification."

"It should be almost conclusive," Thorndyke replied, "especially when joined to other facts that would be elicited by a search of his premises. And now let us just recapitulate the facts which our friend X has placed at our disposal.

"First: X is a person concerning whom I possess certain exclusive information.

"Second: He has some knowledge of my personal habits.

"Third: He is a man of some means and social position.

"Fourth: He is a man of considerable knowledge, ingenuity, and mechanical skill.

"Fifth: He has probably purchased, quite recently, a second-hand 'Blick' fitted with a literary typewheel.

"Sixth: That machine, whether his own or some other person's property, can be identified by a characteristic mark on the small '*e*.'

"If you will note down those six points and add that X is probably an expert cyclist and a fairly good shot with a rifle, you may possibly be able, presently, to complete the equation, $X = ?$"

"I am afraid," I said, "I do not possess the necessary data, but I suspect you do, and if it is so, I repeat that it is your duty to society – to say nothing of your clients, whose interests would suffer by your death – to have this fellow laid by the heels before he does any mischief."

"Yes. I shall have to interfere if he becomes really troublesome, but I have reasons for wishing to leave him alone at present."

"You do really know who he is, then?"

"Well, I think I can solve the equation that I have just offered to you for solution. You see, I have certain data, as you suggest, which you do not possess. There is, for instance, a certain ingenious gentleman concerning whom I hold what I believe to be exclusive information, and my knowledge of him does not make it appear unlikely that he might be the author of these neat little plans."

"I am much impressed," I said, as I put away my notebook, after having jotted down the points that Thorndyke had advised me to consider,"I am much impressed by your powers of observation and your capacity for reasoning from apparently trivial data, but I do not see, even now, why you viewed that cigar with such immediate and decided suspicion. There was nothing actually to suggest the existence of poison in it, and yet you seemed to form the suspicion at once and to search for it as though you expected to find it."

"Yes," replied Thorndyke, "to a certain extent you are right. The idea of a poisoned cigar was not new to me – and thereby hangs a tale."

He laughed softly and gazed into the fire with eyes that twinkled with quiet amusement. "You have heard me say," he resumed, after a short pause, "that when I first took these chambers I had practically nothing to do. I had invented a new variety of medico-legal practice and had to build it up by slow degrees, and the natural consequence was that, for a long time, it yielded nothing but almost unlimited leisure. Now, that leisure was by no means wasted, for I employed it in considering the class of cases in which I was likely to be employed, and in working out theoretical examples, and seeing that crimes against the person have nearly always a strong medical interest, I gave them special attention. For instance, I planned a series of murders, selecting royal personages and great ministers as the victims, and on each murder I brought to bear all the special knowledge, skill and ingenuity at my command. I inquired minutely into the habits of my hypothetical victims – ascertained who were their associates, friends, enemies and servants, considered their diet, their residences, their modes of conveyance, the source of their clothing and, in fact, everything which it was necessary to know in order to achieve their deaths with certainty and with absolute safety to the murderer."

"How deeply gratified and flattered those great personages would have felt," I remarked, "if they had known how much attention they were receiving."

"Yes. I suppose it would have been somewhat startling, to the Prime Minister, for instance, to have learned that he was being watched and studied by an attentive observer and that the arrangements for his decease had been completed down to the minutest detail. But, of course, the application of the method to a particular case was the essential thing, for it brought into view all the incidental difficulties, in meeting which all the really interesting and instructive details were involved. Well, the particulars of these crimes I wrote out at length, in my private shorthand, in a journal which I kept for the purpose – and which, I need not say, I locked up securely in my safe when I was not using it. After completing each case, it was my custom to change sides and play the game over again from the opposite side of the board. That is to say, I added, as an appendix to each case, an analysis with a complete scheme for the detection of the crime. I have in my safe at the present moment six volumes of cases, fully indexed, and I can assure you that they are not only highly instructive reading, but are really valuable as works of reference."

"That I can readily believe," I replied, laughing heartily, nevertheless, at the grotesqueness of the whole proceeding, "though they might have proved rather incriminating documents if they had passed out of your possession."

"They would never have been read," rejoined Thorndyke. "My shorthand is, I think, quite undecipherable. It has been so made intentionally with a view to secrecy."

"And have any of your theoretical cases ever turned up in real life?"

"Several of them have, though very imperfectly planned and carried out as a rule. The poisoned cigar is one of them, though, of course I should never have adopted such a conspicuous device for presenting it, and the incident of the other night is a modification – for the worse – of another. In fact, most of the intricate and artistic crimes with which I have had to deal professionally have had their more complete and elaborate prototypes in my journals."

I was silent for some time, reflecting on the strange personality of my gifted friend and the singular fitness that he presented for the part he had chosen to play in the drama of social life, but presently my thoughts returned to the peril that overshadowed him, and I came back, once more, to my original question.

"And now, Thorndyke," I said, "that you have penetrated both the motives and the disguise of this villain, what are you going to do? Is he to be put safely under lock and key, or is he to be left in peace and security to plan some other, and perhaps more successful, scheme for your destruction?"

"For the present," replied Thorndyke, "I am going to put these things in a place of safety. To-morrow you shall come with me to the hospital and see me place the ends of the cigar in the custody of Dr. Chandler, who will make an analysis and report on the nature of the poison. After that we shall act in whatever way seems best."

Unsatisfactory as this conclusion appeared, I knew it was useless to raise further objections, and, accordingly, when the cigar with its accompanying papers and wrappings had been deposited in a drawer, we dismissed it, if not from our thoughts, at least from our conversation.

Chapter XIV
A Startling Discovery

The morning of the trial, so long looked forward to, had at length arrived, and the train of events which it has been my business to chronicle in this narrative was now fast drawing to an end. To me those events had been in many ways of the deepest moment. Not only had they transported me from a life of monotonous drudgery into one charged with novelty and dramatic interest – not only had they introduced me to a renascence of scientific culture and revived under new conditions my intimacy with the comrade of my student days, but, far more momentous than any of these, they had given me the vision – all too fleeting – of happiness untold, with the reality of sorrow and bitter regret that promised to be all too enduring.

Whence it happened that on this morning my thoughts were tinged with a certain greyness. A chapter in my life that had been both bitter and sweet was closing, and already I saw myself once more an Ishmaelite and a wanderer among strangers.

This rather egotistical frame of mind, however, was soon dispelled when I encountered Polton, for the little man was in a veritable twitter of excitement at the prospect of witnessing the clearing up of the mysteries that had so severely tried his curiosity, and even Thorndyke, beneath his habitual calm, showed a trace of expectancy and pleasurable anticipation.

"I have taken the liberty of making certain little arrangements on your behalf," he said, as we sat at breakfast, "of which I hope you will not disapprove. I have written to Mrs. Hornby, who is one of the witnesses, to say that you will meet her at Mr. Lawley's office and escort her and Miss Gibson to the court. Walter Hornby may be with them, and, if he is, you had better leave him, if possible, to come on with Lawley."

"You will not come to the office, then?"

"No. I shall go straight to the court with Anstey. Besides, I am expecting Superintendent Miller from Scotland Yard, who will probably walk down with us."

"I am glad to hear that," I said, "for I have been rather uneasy at the thought of your mixing in the crowd without some kind of protection."

"Well, you see that I am taking precautions against the assaults of the too-ingenious X, and, to tell the truth – and also to commit a flagrant bull – I should never forgive myself if I allowed him to kill me before I had completed Reuben Hornby's defence. Ah, here is Polton – that man is on wires this morning. He has been wandering in and out of the rooms ever since he came, like a cat in a new house."

"It's quite true, sir," said Polton, smiling and unabashed, "so it's no use denying it. I have come to ask what we are going to take with us to the court."

"You will find a box and a portfolio on the table in my room," replied Thorndyke. "We had better also take a microscope and the micrometers, though we are not likely to want them. That is all, I think."

"A box and a portfolio," repeated Polton in a speculative tone. "Yes, sir, I will take them with me." He opened the door and was about to pass out, when, perceiving a visitor ascending the stairs, he turned back.

"Here's Mr. Miller, from Scotland Yard, sir. Shall I show him in?"

"Yes, do." He rose from his chair as a tall, military-looking man entered the room and saluted, casting, at the same time, an inquiring glance in my direction.

"Good morning, Doctor," he said briskly. "I got your letter and couldn't make such of it, but I have brought down a couple of plain-clothes men and a uniform man, as you suggested. I understand you want a house watched?"

"Yes, and a man, too. I will give you the particulars presently – that is, if you think you can agree to my conditions."

"That I act entirely on my own account and make no communication to anybody? Well, of course, I would rather you gave me all the facts and let me proceed in the regular way, but if you make conditions I have no choice but to accept them, seeing that you hold the cards."

Perceiving that the matter in hand was of a confidential nature, I thought it best to take my departure, which I accordingly did, as soon as I had ascertained that it wanted yet half-an-hour to the time at which Mrs. Hornby and Juliet were due at the lawyer's office.

Mr. Lawley received me with stiffness that bordered on hostility. He was evidently deeply offended at the subordinate part that he had been compelled to play in the case, and was at no great pains to conceal the fact.

"I am informed," said he, in a frosty tone, when I had explained my mission, "that Mrs. Hornby and Miss Gibson are to meet you here. The arrangement is none of my making. None of the arrangements in this case are of my making. I have been treated throughout with a lack of ceremony and confidence that is positively scandalous. Even now, I – the solicitor for the defence – am completely in the dark as to what defence is contemplated, though I fully expect to be involved in some ridiculous fiasco. I only trust that I may never again be associated with any of your hybrid practitioners. *Ne sutor ultra crepidam*, sir, is an excellent motto. Let the medical cobbler stick to his medical last."

145

"It remains to be seen what kind of boot he can turn out on the legal last," I retorted.

"That is so," he rejoined, "but I hear Mrs. Hornby's voice in the outer office, and as neither you nor I have any time to waste in idle talk, I suggest that you make your way to the court without delay. I wish you good morning!"

Acting on this very plain hint, I retired to the clerks' office, where I found Mrs. Hornby and Juliet, the former undisguisedly tearful and terrified, and the latter calm, though pale and agitated.

"We had better start at once," I said, when we had exchanged greetings. "Shall we take a cab, or walk?"

"I think we will walk, if you don't mind," said Juliet. "Mrs. Hornby wants to have a few words with you before we go into court. You see, she is one of the witnesses, and she is terrified lest she should say something damaging to Reuben."

"By whom was the subpoena served?" I asked.

"Mr. Lawley sent it," replied Mrs. Hornby, "and I went to see him about it the very next day, but he wouldn't tell me anything – he didn't seem to know what I was wanted for, and he wasn't at all nice – not at all."

"I expect your evidence will relate to the 'Thumbograph,'" I said. "There is really nothing else in connection with the case that you have any knowledge of."

"That is just what Walter said," exclaimed Mrs. Hornby. "I went to his rooms to talk the matter over with him. He is very upset about the whole affair, and I am afraid he thinks very badly of poor Reuben's prospects. I only trust he may be wrong! Oh dear! What a dreadful thing it is, to be sure!" Here the poor lady halted to mop her eyes elaborately, to the surprise and manifest scorn of a passing errand boy.

"He was very thoughtful and sympathetic – Walter, I mean, you know," pursued Mrs. Hornby, "and most helpful. He asked me all I knew about that horrid little book, and took down my answers in writing. Then he wrote out the questions I was likely to be asked, with my answers, so that I could read them over and get them well into my head. Wasn't it good of him! And I made him print them with his machine so that I could read them without my glasses, and he did it beautifully. I have the paper in my pocket now."

"I didn't know Mr. Walter went in for printing," I said. "Has he a regular printing press?"

"It isn't a printing press exactly," replied Mrs. Hornby, "it is a small thing with a lot of round keys that you press down – Dickensblerfer, I think it is called – ridiculous name, isn't it? Walter bought it from one of his literary friends about a week ago, but he is getting quite clever with it already, though he does make a few mistakes still, as you can see."

She halted again, and began to search for the opening of a pocket which was hidden away in some occult recess of her clothing, all unconscious of the effect that her explanation had produced on me. For, instantly, as she spoke, there flashed into my mind one of the points that Thorndyke had given me for the identification of the mysterious *X*. *"He has probably purchased, quite recently, a second-hand Blickensderfer, fitted with a literary typewheel."* The coincidence was striking and even startling, though a moment's reflection convinced me that it was nothing more than a coincidence, for there must be hundreds of second-hand "Blicks" on the market, and, as to Walter Hornby, he certainly could have no quarrel with Thorndyke, but would rather be interested in his preservation on Reuben's account.

These thoughts passed through my mind so rapidly that by the time Mrs. Hornby had run her pocket to earth I had quite recovered from the momentary shock.

"Ah! Here it is," she exclaimed triumphantly, producing an obese Morocco purse. "I put it in here for safety, knowing how liable one is to get one's pocket picked in these crowded London streets." She opened the bulky receptacle and drew it out after the manner of a concertina, exhibiting multitudinous partitions, all stuffed with pieces of paper, coils of tape and sewing silk, buttons, samples of dress materials and miscellaneous rubbish, mingled indiscriminately with gold, silver, and copper coins.

"Now just run your eye through that, Dr. Jervis," she said, handing me a folded paper, "and give me your advice on my answers."

I opened the paper and read: *"The Committee of the Society for the Protection of Paralysed Idiots, in submitting this – "*

"Oh! That isn't it. I have given you the wrong paper. How silly of me! That is the appeal of – you remember, Juliet, dear, that troublesome person – I had, really, to be quite rude, you know, Dr. Jervis. I had to tell him that charity begins at home, although, thank Heaven! None of us are paralysed, but we must consider our own, mustn't we? And then – "

"Do you think this is the one, dear?" interposed Juliet, in whose pale cheek the ghost of a dimple had appeared. "It looks cleaner than most of the others."

She selected a folded paper from the purse which Mrs. Hornby was holding with both hands extended to its utmost, as though she were about to produce a burst of music, and, opening it, glanced at its contents.

"Yes, this is your evidence," she said, and passed the paper to me.

147

I took the document from her hand and, in spite of the conclusion at which I had arrived, examined it with eager curiosity. And at the very first glance I felt my head swim and my heart throb violently. For the paper was headed: "*Evidence respecting the Thumbograph*," and in every one of the five small "*e's*" that occurred in that sentence I could see plainly by the strong out-door light a small break or interval in the summit of the loop.

I was thunderstruck.

One coincidence was quite possible and even probable, but the two together, and the second one of so remarkable a character, were beyond all reasonable limits of probability. The identification did not seem to admit of a doubt, and yet –

"Our legal adviser appears to be somewhat preoccupied," remarked Juliet, with something of her old gaiety of manner, and, in fact, though I held the paper in my hand, my gaze was fixed unmeaningly on an adjacent lamp-post. As she spoke, I pulled myself together, and, scanning the paper hastily, was fortunate enough to find in the first paragraph matter requiring comment.

"I observe, Mrs. Hornby," I said, "that in answer to the first question, '*Whence did you obtain the "Thumbograph"*?' you say, '*I do not remember clearly. I think I must have bought it at a railway bookstall.*' Now I understood that it was brought home and given to you by Walter himself."

"That was what I thought," replied Mrs. Hornby, "but Walter tells me that it was not so, and, of course, he would remember better than I should."

"But, my dear aunt, I am sure he gave it to you," interposed Juliet. "Don't you remember? It was the night the Colleys came to dinner, and we were so hard pressed to find amusement for them, when Walter came in and produced the 'Thumbograph.'"

"Yes, I remember quite well now," said Mrs. Hornby. "How fortunate that you reminded me. We must alter that answer at once."

"If I were you, Mrs. Hornby," I said, "I would disregard this paper altogether. It will only confuse you and get you into difficulties. Answer the questions that are put, as well as you can, and if you don't remember, say so."

"Yes, that will be much the wisest plan," said Juliet. "Let Dr. Jervis take charge of the paper and rely on your own memory."

"Very well, my dear," replied Mrs. Hornby, "I will do what you think best, and you can keep the paper, Dr. Jervis, or throw it away."

I slipped the document into my pocket without remark, and we proceeded on our way, Mrs. Hornby babbling inconsequently, with occasional outbursts of emotion, and Juliet silent and abstracted. I struggled to concentrate my attention on the elder lady's conversation, but my thoughts continually reverted to the paper in my pocket, and the startling solution that it seemed to offer of the mystery of the poisoned cigar.

Could it be that Walter Hornby was in reality the miscreant X? The thing seemed incredible, for, hitherto, no shadow of suspicion had appeared to fall on him. And yet there was no denying that his description tallied in a very remarkable manner with that of the hypothetical X. He was a man of some means and social position. He was a man of considerable knowledge and mechanical skill, though as to his ingenuity I could not judge. He had recently bought a second-hand Blickensderfer which probably had a literary typewheel, since it was purchased from a literary man, and that machine showed the characteristic mark on the small "e." The two remaining points, indeed, were not so clear. Obviously I could form no opinion as to whether or not Thorndyke held any exclusive information concerning him, and, with reference to his knowledge of my friend's habits, I was at first inclined to be doubtful until I suddenly recalled, with a pang of remorse and self-accusation, the various details that I had communicated to Juliet and that she might easily, in all innocence, have handed on to Walter. I had, for instance, told her of Thorndyke's preference for the Trichinopoly cheroot, and of this she might very naturally have spoken to Walter, who possessed a supply of them. Again, with regard to the time of our arrival at King's Cross, I had informed her of this in a letter which was in no way confidential, and again there was no reason why the information should not have been passed on to Walter, who was to have been one of the party at the family dinner. The coincidence seemed complete enough, in all truth. Yet it was incredible that Reuben's cousin could be so blackhearted a villain or could have any motive for these dastardly crimes.

Suddenly a new idea struck me. Mrs Hornby had obtained access to this typewriting machine, and if Mrs. Hornby could do so, why not John Hornby? The description would, for the most part, fit the elder man as well as the younger, though I had no evidence of his possessing any special mechanical skill, but my suspicions had already fastened upon him, and I remembered that Thorndyke had by no means rejected my theory which connected him with the crime.

At this point, my reflections were broken in upon by Mrs. Hornby, who grasped my arm and uttered a deep groan. We had reached the corner of the Old Bailey, and before us were the frowning walls of Newgate. Within those walls, I knew – though I did not mention the fact – that Reuben Hornby was confined with the other prisoners who were awaiting their trial, and a glance at the massive masonry, stained to a dingy grey by

149

the grime of the city, put an end to my speculations and brought me back to the drama that was so nearly approaching its climax.

Down the old thoroughfare, crowded with so many memories of hideous tragedy – By the side of the gloomy prison. Past the debtors' door with its forbidding spiked wicket. Past the gallows gate with its festoons of fetters. We walked in silence until we reached the entrance to the Sessions House.

Here I was not a little relieved to find Thorndyke on the look-out for us, for Mrs. Hornby, in spite of really heroic efforts to control her emotion, was in a state of impending hysteria, while Juliet, though outwardly calm and composed, showed by the waxen pallor of her cheeks and a certain wildness of her eyes that all her terror was reviving, and I was glad that they were spared the unpleasantness of contact with the policemen who guarded the various entrances.

"We must be brave," said Thorndyke gently, as he took Mrs. Hornby's hand, "and show a cheerful face to our friend who has so much to bear and who bears it so patiently. A few more hours, and I hope we shall see restored, not only his liberty, but his honour. Here is Mr. Anstey, who, we trust, will be able to make his innocence apparent."

Anstey, who, unlike Thorndyke, had already donned his wig and gown, bowed gravely, and, together, we passed through the mean and grimy portals into a dark hall. Policemen in uniform and unmistakable detectives stood about the various entries, and little knots of people, evil-looking and unclean for the most part, lurked in the background or sat on benches and diffused through the stale, musty air that distinctive but indescribable odour that clings to police vans and prison reception rooms, an odour that, in the present case, was pleasantly mingled with the suggestive aroma of disinfectants. Through the unsavoury throng we hurried, and up a staircase to a landing from which several passages diverged. Into one of these passages – a sort of "dark entry," furnished with a cage-like gate of iron bars – we passed to a black door, on which was painted the inscription, "Old Court. Counsel and clerks."

Anstey held the door open for us, and we passed through into the court, which at once struck me with a sense of disappointment. It was smaller than I had expected, and plain and mean to the point of sordidness. The woodwork was poor, thinly disguised by yellow graining, and slimy with dirt wherever a dirty hand could reach it. The walls were distempered a pale, greenish grey. The floor was of bare and dirty planking, and the only suggestions of dignity or display were those offered by the canopy over the judge's seat – lined with scarlet baize and surmounted by the royal arms – the scarlet cushions of the bench, and the large, circular clock in the gallery, which was embellished with a gilded border and asserted its importance by a loud, aggressive tick.

Following Anstey and Thorndyke into the well of the court, we were ushered into one of the seats reserved for counsel – the third from the front – where we sat down and looked about us, while our two friends seated themselves in the front bench next to the central table. Here, at the extreme right, a barrister – presumably the counsel for the prosecution – was already in his place and absorbed in the brief that lay on the desk before him. Straight before us were the seats for the jury, rising one above the other, and at their side the witness-box. Above us on the right was the judge's seat, and immediately below it a structure somewhat resembling a large pew or a counting-house desk, surmounted by a brass rail, in which a person in a grey wig – the clerk of the court – was mending a quill pen. On our left rose the dock – suggestively large and roomy – enclosed at the sides with high glazed frames, and above it, near the ceiling, was the spectators' gallery.

"What a hideous place!" exclaimed Juliet, who separated me from Mrs. Hornby. "And how sordid and dirty everything looks!"

"Yes," I answered. "The uncleanness of the criminal is not confined to his moral being – wherever he goes, he leaves a trail of actual, physical dirt. It is not so long ago that the dock and the bench alike used to be strewn with medicinal herbs, and I believe the custom still survives of furnishing the judge with a nosegay as a preventive of jail-fever."

"And to think that Reuben should be brought to a place like this!" Juliet continued bitterly, "to be herded with such people as we saw downstairs!"

She sighed and looked round at the benches that rose behind us, where a half-dozen reporters were already seated and apparently in high spirits at the prospect of a sensational case.

Our conversation was now interrupted by the clatter of feet on the gallery stairs, and heads began to appear over the wooden parapet. Several junior counsel filed into the seats in front of us. Mr. Lawley and his clerk entered the attorney's bench. The ushers took their stand below the jury-box. A police officer seated himself at a desk in the dock, and inspectors, detectives and miscellaneous officers began to gather in the entries or peer into the court through the small glazed openings in the doors.

Chapter XV
The Finger-Print Experts

The hum of conversation that had been gradually increasing as the court filled suddenly ceased. A door at the back of the dais was flung open. Counsel, solicitors, and spectators alike rose to their feet, and the judge entered, closely followed by the Lord Mayor, the sheriff, and various civic magnates, all picturesque and gorgeous in their robes and chains of office. The Clerk of Arraigns took his place behind his table under the dais. The counsel suspended their conversation and fingered their briefs, and, as the judge took his seat, lawyers, officials, and spectators took their seats, and all eyes were turned towards the dock.

A few moments later Reuben Hornby appeared in the enclosure in company with a warder, the two rising, apparently, from the bowels of the earth, and, stepping forward to the bar, stood with a calm and self-possessed demeanour, glancing somewhat curiously around the court. For an instant his eye rested upon the group of friends and well-wishers seated behind the counsel, and the faintest trace of a smile appeared on his face, but immediately he turned his eyes away and never again throughout the trial looked in our direction.

The Clerk of Arraigns now rose and, reading from the indictment which lay before him on the table, addressed the prisoner, "Reuben Hornby, you stand indicted for that you did, on the ninth or tenth day of March, feloniously steal a parcel of diamonds of the goods and chattels of John Hornby. Are you guilty or not guilty?"

"Not guilty," replied Reuben.

The Clerk of Arraigns, having noted the prisoner's reply, then proceeded, "The gentlemen whose names are about to be called will form the jury who are to try you. If you wish to object to any of them, you must do so as each comes to the book to be sworn, and before he is sworn. You will then be heard."

In acknowledgment of this address, which was delivered in clear, ringing tones, and with remarkable distinctness, Reuben bowed to the clerk, and the process of swearing-in the jury was commenced, while the counsel opened their briefs and the judge conversed facetiously with an official in a fur robe and a massive neck chain.

Very strange, to unaccustomed eyes and ears, was the effect of this function – half-solemn and half-grotesque, with an effect intermediate between that of a religious rite and that of a comic opera. Above the half-suppressed hum of conversation the clerk's voice arose at regular intervals, calling out the name of one of the jurymen, and, as its owner stood up, the court usher, black-gowned and sacerdotal of aspect, advanced and proffered the book. Then, as the juryman took the volume in his hand, the voice of the usher resounded through the court like that of a priest intoning some refrain or antiphon – an effect that was increased by the rhythmical and archaic character of the formula, "Samuel Seppings!"

A stolid-looking working-man rose and, taking the Testament in his hand, stood regarding the usher while that official sang out in a solemn monotone, "You shall well and truly try and true deliverance make between our Sovereign Lord the King and the prisoner at the bar, whom you shall have in charge, and a true verdict give according to the evidence. So help you God!"

"James Piper!" Another juryman rose and was given the Book to hold, and again the monotonous sing-song arose, "You shall well and truly try and true deliverance make, etc."

"I shall scream aloud if that horrible chant goes on much longer," Juliet whispered. "Why don't they all swear at once and have done with it?"

"That would not meet the requirements," I answered. "However, there are only two more, so you must have patience."

"And you will have patience with me, too, won't you? I am horribly frightened. It is all so solemn and dreadful."

"You must try to keep up your courage until Dr. Thorndyke has given his evidence," I said. "Remember that, until he has spoken, everything is against Reuben, so be prepared."

"I will try," she answered meekly, "but I can't help being terrified."

The last of the jurymen was at length sworn, and when the clerk had once more called out the names one by one, the usher counting loudly as each man answered to his name, the latter officer turned to the Court and spectators, and proclaimed in solemn tones, "If anyone can inform my Lords the King's justices, the King's attorney-general, or the King's serjeant, ere this inquest be now taken between our Sovereign Lord the King and the prisoner at the bar, of any treason, murder, felony, or misdemeanour, committed or done by him, let him come forth and he shall be heard, for the prisoner stands at the bar upon his deliverance."

This proclamation was followed by a profound silence, and after a brief interval the Clerk of Arraigns turned towards the jury and addressed them collectively, "Gentlemen of the jury, the prisoner at the bar stands indicted by the name of Reuben Hornby, for that he, on the ninth or tenth of March, feloniously did steal, take and carry away a parcel of diamonds of the goods of John Hornby. To this indictment he has pleaded that he is

153

not guilty, and your charge is to inquire whether he be guilty or not and to hearken to the evidence."

When he had finished his address the clerk sat down, and the judge, a thin-faced, hollow-eyed elderly man, with bushy grey eyebrows and a very large nose, looked attentively at Reuben for some moments over the tops of his gold-rimmed pince-nez. Then he turned towards the counsel nearest the bench and bowed slightly.

The barrister bowed in return and rose, and for the first time I obtained a complete view of Sir Hector Trumpler, K.C., the counsel for the prosecution. His appearance was not prepossessing nor – though he was a large man and somewhat florid as to his countenance – particularly striking, except for a general air of untidiness. His gown was slipping off one shoulder, his wig was perceptibly awry, and his pince-nez threatened every moment to drop from his nose.

"The case that I have to present to you, my Lord and gentlemen of the jury," he began in a clear, though unmusical voice, "is one the like of which is but too often met with in this court. It is one in which we shall see unbounded trust met by treacherous deceit, in which we shall see countless benefactions rewarded by the basest ingratitude, and in which we shall witness the deliberate renunciation of a life of honourable effort in favour of the tortuous and precarious ways of the criminal. The facts of the case are briefly as follows: The prosecutor in this case – most unwilling prosecutor, gentlemen – is Mr. John Hornby, who is a metallurgist and dealer in precious metals. Mr. Hornby has two nephews, the orphan sons of his two elder brothers, and I may tell you that since the decease of their parents he has acted the part of a father to both of them. One of these nephews is Mr. Walter Hornby, and the other is Reuben Hornby, the prisoner at the bar. Both of these nephews were received by Mr. Hornby into his business with a view to their succeeding him when he should retire, and both, I need not say, occupied positions of trust and responsibility.

"Now, on the evening of the ninth of March there was delivered to Mr. Hornby a parcel of rough diamonds of which one of his clients asked him to take charge pending their transfer to the brokers. I need not burden you with irrelevant details concerning this transaction. It will suffice to say that the diamonds, which were of the aggregate value of about thirty thousand pounds, were delivered to him, and the unopened package deposited by him in his safe, together with a slip of paper on which he had written in pencil a memorandum of the circumstances. This was on the evening of the ninth of March, as I have said. Having deposited the parcel, Mr. Hornby locked the safe, and shortly afterwards left the premises and went home, taking the keys with him.

154

"On the following morning, when he unlocked the safe, he perceived with astonishment and dismay that the parcel of diamonds had vanished. The slip of paper, however, lay at the bottom of the safe, and on picking it up Mr. Hornby perceived that it bore a smear of blood, and in addition, the distinct impression of a human thumb. On this he closed and locked the safe and sent a note to the police station, in response to which a very intelligent officer – Inspector Sanderson – came and made a preliminary examination. I need not follow the case further, since the details will appear in the evidence, but I may tell you that, in effect, it has been made clear, beyond all doubt, that the thumb-print on that paper was the thumb-print of the prisoner, Reuben Hornby."

He paused to adjust his glasses, which were in the very act of falling from his nose, and hitch up his gown, while he took a leisurely survey of the jury, as though he were estimating their impressionability. At this moment I observed Walter Hornby enter the court and take up a position at the end of our bench nearest the door, and, immediately after, Superintendent Miller came in and seated himself on one of the benches opposite.

"The first witness whom I shall call," said Sir Hector Trumpler, "is John Hornby."

Mr. Hornby, looking wild and agitated, stepped into the witness-box, and the usher, having handed him the Testament, sang out, "The evidence you shall give to the court and jury sworn, between our Sovereign Lord the King and the prisoner at the bar shall be the truth, the whole truth, and nothing but the truth, so help you God!"

Mr. Hornby kissed the Book, and, casting a glance of unutterable misery at his nephew, turned towards the counsel.

"Your name is John Hornby, is it not?" asked Sir Hector.

"It is."

"And you occupy premises in St. Mary Axe?"

"Yes. I am a dealer in precious metals, but my business consists principally in the assaying of samples of ore and quartz and bars of silver and gold."

"Do you remember what happened on the ninth of March last?"

"Perfectly. My nephew Reuben – the prisoner – delivered to me a parcel of diamonds which he had received from the purser of the *Elmina Castle*, to whom I had sent him as my confidential agent. I had intended to deposit the diamonds with my banker, but when the prisoner arrived at my office, the banks were already closed, so I had to put the parcel, for the night, in my own safe. I may say that the prisoner was not in any way responsible for the delay."

"You are not here to defend the prisoner," said Sir Hector. "Answer my questions and make no comments, if you please. Was anyone present when you placed the diamonds in the safe?"

"No one was present but myself."

"I did not ask if you were present when you put them in," said Sir Hector (whereupon the spectators sniggered and the judge smiled indulgently). "What else did you do?"

"I wrote in pencil on a leaf of my pocket memorandum block, '*Handed in by Reuben at 7.3 p.m., 9.3.01*,' and initialled it. Then I tore the leaf from the block and laid it on the parcel, after which I closed the safe and locked it."

"How soon did you leave the premises after this?"

"Almost immediately. The prisoner was waiting for me in the outer office – "

"Never mind where the prisoner was. Confine your answers to what is asked. Did you take the keys with you?"

"Yes."

"When did you next open the safe?"

"On the following morning at ten o'clock."

"Was the safe locked or unlocked when you arrived?"

"It was locked. I unlocked it."

"Did you notice anything unusual about the safe?"

"No."

"Had the keys left your custody in the interval?"

"No. They were attached to a key-chain, which I always wear."

"Are there any duplicates of those keys? – the keys of the safe, I mean."

"No, there are no duplicates."

"Have the keys ever gone out of your possession?"

"Yes. If I have had to be absent from the office for a considerable time, it has been my custom to hand the keys to one of my nephews, whichever has happened to be in charge at the time."

"And never to any other person?"

"Never to any other person."

"What did you observe when you opened the safe?"

"I observed that the parcel of diamonds had disappeared."

"Did you notice anything else?"

"Yes. I found the leaf from my memorandum block lying at the bottom of the safe. I picked it up and turned it over, and then saw that there were smears of blood on it and what looked like the print of a thumb in blood. The thumb-mark was on the under-surface, as the paper lay at the bottom of the safe."

156

"What did you do next?"

"I closed and locked the safe, and sent a note to the police station saying that a robbery had been committed on my premises."

"You have known the prisoner several years, I believe?"

"Yes. I have known him all his life. He is my eldest brother's son."

"Then you can tell us, no doubt, whether he is left-handed or right-handed?"

"I should say he was ambidextrous, but he uses his left hand by preference."

"A fine distinction, Mr. Hornby, a very fine distinction. Now tell me, did you ascertain beyond all doubt that the diamonds were really gone?"

"Yes. I examined the safe thoroughly, first by myself and afterwards with the police. There was no doubt that the diamonds had really gone."

"When the detective suggested that you should have the thumb-prints of your two nephews taken, did you refuse?"

"I refused."

"Why did you refuse?"

"Because I did not choose to subject my nephews to the indignity. Besides, I had no power to make them submit to the proceeding."

"Had you any suspicions of either of them?"

"I had no suspicions of anyone."

"Kindly examine this piece of paper, Mr. Hornby," said Sir Hector, passing across a small oblong slip, "and tell us if you recognise it."

Mr. Hornby glanced at the paper for a moment, and then said, "This is the memorandum slip that I found lying at the bottom of the safe."

"How do you identify it?"

"By the writing on it, which is in my own hand, and bears my initials."

"Is it the memorandum that you placed on the parcel of diamonds?"

"Yes."

"Was there any thumb-mark or blood-smear on it when you placed it in the safe?"

"No."

"Was it possible that there could have been any such marks?"

"Quite impossible. I tore it from my memorandum block at the time I wrote upon it."

"Very well." Sir Hector Trumpler sat down, and Mr. Anstey stood up to cross-examine the witness.

"You have told us, Mr. Hornby," said he, "that you have known the prisoner all his life. Now what estimate have you formed of his character?"

"I have always regarded him as a young man of the highest character – honourable, truthful, and in every way trustworthy. I have never, in all my experience of him, known him to deviate a hair's-breadth from the strictest honour and honesty of conduct."

"You regarded him as a man of irreproachable character. Is that so?"

"That is so, and my opinion of him is unchanged."

"Has he, to your knowledge, any expensive or extravagant habits?"

"No. His habits are simple and rather thrifty."

"Have you ever known him to bet, gamble, or speculate?"

"Never."

"Has he ever seemed to be in want of money?"

"No. He has a small private income, apart from his salary, which I know he does not spend, since I have occasionally employed my broker to invest his savings."

"Apart from the thumb-print which was found in the safe, are you aware of any circumstances that would lead you to suspect the prisoner of having stolen the diamonds?"

"None whatever."

Mr. Anstey sat down, and as Mr. Hornby left the witness-box, mopping the perspiration from his forehead, the next witness was called.

"Inspector Sanderson!"

The dapper police officer stepped briskly into the box, and having been duly sworn, faced the prosecuting counsel with the air of a man who was prepared for any contingency.

"Do you remember," said Sir Hector, after the usual preliminaries had been gone through, "what occurred on the morning of the tenth of March?"

"Yes. A note was handed to me at the station at 10:23 a.m. It was from Mr. John Hornby, and stated that a robbery had occurred at his premises in St. Mary Axe. I went to the premises and arrived there at 10:31 a.m. There I saw the prosecutor, Mr. John Hornby, who told me that a parcel of diamonds had been stolen from the safe. At his request I examined the safe. There were no signs of its having been forced open. The locks seemed to be quite uninjured and in good order. Inside the safe, on the bottom, I found two good-sized drops of blood, and a slip of paper with pencil-writing on it. The paper bore two blood-smears and a print of a human thumb in blood."

"Is this the paper?" asked the counsel, passing a small slip across to the witness.

"Yes," replied the inspector, after a brief glance at the document.

"What did you do next?"

"I sent a message to Scotland Yard acquainting the Chief of the Criminal Investigation Department with the facts, and then went back to the station. I had no further connection with the case."

Sir Hector sat down, and the judge glanced at Anstey.

"You tell us," said the latter, rising, "that you observed two good-sized drops of blood on the bottom of the safe. Did you notice the condition of the blood, whether moist or dry?"

"The blood looked moist, but I did not touch it. I left it undisturbed for the detective officers to examine."

The next witness called was Sergeant Bates, of the Criminal Investigation Department. He stepped into the box with the same ready, business-like air as the other officer, and, having been sworn, proceeded to give his evidence with a fluency that suggested careful preparation, holding an open notebook in his hand but making no references to it.

"On the tenth of March, at 12:08 p.m., I received instructions to proceed to St. Mary Axe to inquire into a robbery that had taken place there. Inspector Sanderson's report was handed to me, and I read it in the cab on my way to the premises. On arriving at the premises at 12:30 p.m., I examined the safe carefully. It was quite uninjured, and there were no marks of any kind upon it. I tested the locks and found them perfect. There were no marks or indications of any picklock having been used. On the bottom of the inside I observed two rather large drops of a dark fluid. I took up some of the fluid on a piece of paper and found it to be blood. I also found, in the bottom of the safe, the burnt head of a wax match, and, on searching the floor of the office, I found, close by the safe, a used wax match from which the head had fallen. I also found a slip of paper which appeared to have been torn from a perforated block. On it was written in pencil, '*Handed in by Reuben at 7.3 p.m. 9.3.01. J.H.*' There were two smears of blood on the paper and the impression of a human thumb in blood. I took possession of the paper in order that it might be examined by the experts. I inspected the office doors and the outer door of the premises, but found no signs of forcible entrance on any of them. I questioned the housekeeper, but obtained no information from him. I then returned to headquarters, made my report, and handed the paper with the marks on it to the Superintendent."

"Is this the paper that you found in the safe?" asked the counsel, once more handing the leaflet across.

"Yes. This is the paper."

"What happened next?"

"The following afternoon I was sent for by Mr. Singleton, of the Finger-print Department. He informed me that he had gone through the files and had not been able to find any thumb-print resembling the one on the paper, and recommended me to endeavour to obtain prints of the thumbs of any persons who might have been concerned in the robbery. He also gave me an enlarged photograph of the thumb-print for reference if necessary. I accordingly went to St. Mary Axe and had an interview with

Mr. Hornby, when I requested him to allow me to take prints of the thumbs of all the persons employed on the premises, including his two nephews. This he refused, saying that he distrusted finger-prints and that there was no suspicion of anyone on the premises. I asked if he would allow his nephews to furnish their thumb-prints privately, to which he replied, 'Certainly not.'"

"Had you then any suspicion of either of the nephews?"

"I thought they were both open to some suspicion. The safe had certainly been opened with false keys, and as they had both had the real keys in their possession it was possible that one of them might have taken impressions in wax and made counterfeit keys."

"Yes."

"I called on Mr. Hornby several times and urged him, for the sake of his nephews' reputations, to sanction the taking of the thumb-prints, but he refused very positively and forbade them to submit, although I understood that they were both willing. It then occurred to me to try if I could get any help from Mrs. Hornby, and on the fifteenth of March I called at Mr. Hornby's private house and saw her. I explained to her what was wanted to clear her nephews from the suspicion that rested on them, and she then said that she could dispose of those suspicions at once, for she could show me the thumb-prints of the whole family: She had them all in a 'Thumbograph.'"

"A 'Thumbograph'?" repeated the judge. "What is a 'Thumbograph'?"

Anstey rose with the little red-covered volume in his hand.

"A 'Thumbograph,' my Lord," said he, "is a book, like this, in which foolish people collect the thumb-prints of their more foolish acquaintances."

He passed the volume up to the judge, who turned over the leaves curiously and then nodded to the witness.

"Yes. She said she had them all in a 'Thumbograph.'"

"Then she fetched from a drawer a small red-covered book which she showed to me. It contained the thumb-prints of all the family and some of her friends."

"Is this the book?" asked the judge, passing the volume down to the witness.

The sergeant turned over the leaves until he came to one which he apparently recognised, and said, "Yes, m'Lord. This is the book. Mrs. Hornby showed me the thumb-prints of various members of the family, and then found those of the two nephews. I compared them with the photograph that I had with me and discovered that the print of the left

160

thumb of Reuben Hornby was in every respect identical with the thumb-print shown in the photograph."

"What did you do then?"

"I asked Mrs. Hornby to lend me the 'Thumbograph' so that I might show it to the Chief of the Finger-print Department, to which she consented. I had not intended to tell her of my discovery, but, as I was leaving, Mr. Hornby arrived home, and when he heard of what had taken place, he asked me why I wanted the book, and then I told him. He was greatly astonished and horrified, and wished me to return the book at once. He proposed to let the whole matter drop and take the loss of the diamonds on himself, but I pointed out that this was impossible as it would practically amount to compounding a felony. Seeing that Mrs. Hornby was so distressed at the idea of her book being used in evidence against her nephew, I promised her that I would return it to her if I could obtain a thumb-print in any other way.

"I then took the 'Thumbograph' to Scotland Yard and showed it to Mr. Singleton, who agreed that the print of the left thumb of Reuben Hornby was in every respect identical with the thumb-print on the paper found in the safe. On this I applied for a warrant for the arrest of Reuben Hornby, which I executed on the following morning. I told the prisoner what I had promised Mrs. Hornby, and he then offered to allow me to take a print of his left thumb so that his aunt's book should not have to be used in evidence."

"How is it, then," asked the judge, "that it has been put in evidence?"

"It has been put in by the defence, my Lord," said Sir Hector Trumpler.

"I see," said the judge. "'A hair of the dog that bit him.' The 'Thumbograph' is to be applied as a remedy on the principle that *similia similibus curantur*. Well?"

"When I arrested him, I administered the usual caution, and the prisoner then said, 'I am innocent. I know nothing about the robbery.'"

The counsel for the prosecution sat down, and Anstey rose to cross-examine.

"You have told us," said he, in his clear musical voice, "that you found at the bottom of the safe two rather large drops of a dark fluid which you considered to be blood. Now, what led you to believe that fluid to be blood?"

"I took some of the fluid up on a piece of white paper, and it had the appearance and colour of blood."

"Was it examined microscopically or otherwise?"

"Not to my knowledge."

"Was it quite liquid?"

161

"Yes, I should say quite liquid."

"What appearance had it on paper?"

"It looked like a clear red liquid of the colour of blood, and was rather thick and sticky."

Anstey sat down, and the next witness, an elderly man, answering to the name of Francis Simmons, was called.

"You are the housekeeper at Mr. Hornby's premises in St. Mary Axe?" asked Sir Hector Trumpler.

"I am."

"Did you notice anything unusual on the night of the ninth of March?"

"I did not."

"Did you make your usual rounds on that occasion?"

"Yes. I went all over the premises several times during the night, and the rest of the time I was in a room over the private office."

"Who arrived first on the morning of the tenth?"

"Mr. Reuben. He arrived about twenty minutes before anybody else."

"What part of the building did he go to?"

"He went into the private office, which I opened for him. He remained there until a few minutes before Mr. Hornby arrived, when he went up to the laboratory."

"Who came next?"

"Mr. Hornby, and Mr. Walter came in just after him."

The counsel sat down, and Anstey proceeded to cross-examine the witness.

"Who was the last to leave the premises on the evening of the ninth?"

"I am not sure."

"Why are you not sure?"

"I had to take a note and a parcel to a firm in Shoreditch. When I started, a clerk named Thomas Holker was in the outer office and Mr. Walter Hornby was in the private office. When I returned they had both gone."

"Was the outer door locked?"

"Yes."

"Had Holker a key of the outer door?"

"No. Mr. Hornby and his two nephews had each a key, and I have one. No one else had a key."

"How long were you absent?"

"About three-quarters of an hour."

"Who gave you the note and the parcel?"

"Mr. Walter Hornby."

"When did he give them to you?"

162

"He gave them to me just before I started, and told me to go at once for fear the place should be closed before I got there."

"And was the place closed?"

"Yes. It was all shut up, and everybody had gone."

Anstey resumed his seat, the witness shuffled out of the box with an air of evident relief, and the usher called out, "Henry James Singleton."

Mr. Singleton rose from his seat at the table by the solicitors for the prosecution and entered the box. Sir Hector adjusted his glasses, turned over a page of his brief, and cast a steady and impressive glance at the jury.

"I believe, Mr. Singleton," he said at length, "that you are connected with the Finger-print Department at Scotland Yard?"

"Yes. I am one of the chief assistants in that department."

"What are your official duties?"

"My principal occupation consists in the examination and comparison of the finger-prints of criminals and suspected persons. These finger-prints are classified by me according to their characters and arranged in files for reference."

"I take it that you have examined a great number of finger-prints?"

"I have examined many thousands of finger-prints, and have studied them closely for purposes of identification."

"Kindly examine this paper, Mr. Singleton" (here the fatal leaflet was handed to him by the usher), "have you ever seen it before?"

"Yes. It was handed to me for examination at my office on the tenth of March."

"There is a mark upon it – the print of a finger or thumb. Can you tell us anything about that mark?"

"It is the print of the left thumb of Reuben Hornby, the prisoner at the bar."

"You are quite sure of that?"

"I am quite sure."

"Do you swear that the mark upon that paper was made by the thumb of the prisoner?"

"I do."

"Could it not have been made by the thumb of some other person?"

"No. It is impossible that it could have been made by any other person."

At this moment I felt Juliet lay a trembling hand on mine, and, glancing at her, I saw that she was deathly pale. I took her hand in mine and, pressing it gently, whispered to her, "Have courage. There is nothing unexpected in this."

"Thank you," she whispered in reply, with a faint smile, "I will try, but it is all so horribly unnerving."

"You consider," Sir Hector proceeded, "that the identity of this thumb-print admits of no doubt?"

"It admits of no doubt whatever," replied Mr. Singleton.

"Can you explain to us, without being too technical, how you have arrived at such complete certainty?"

"I myself took a print of the prisoner's thumb – having first obtained the prisoner's consent after warning him that the print would be used in evidence against him – and I compared that print with the mark on this paper. The comparison was made with the greatest care and by the most approved method, point by point and detail by detail, and the two prints were found to be identical in every respect.

"Now it has been proved by exact calculations – which calculations I have personally verified – that the chance that the print of a single finger of any given person will be exactly like the print of the same finger of any other given person is as one to sixty-four-thousand-millions. That is to say that, since the number of the entire human race is about sixteen-thousand-millions, the chance is about one-to-four that the print of a single finger of any one person will be identical with that of the same finger of any other member of the human race.

"It has been said by a great authority – and I entirely agree with the statement – that a complete, or nearly complete, accordance between two prints of a single finger affords evidence requiring no corroboration that the persons from whom they were made are the same.

"Now, these calculations apply to the prints of ordinary and normal fingers or thumbs. But the thumb from which these prints were taken is not ordinary or normal. There is upon it a deep but clean linear scar – the scar of an old incised wound – and this scar passes across the pattern of the ridges, intersecting the latter at certain places and disturbing their continuity at others. Now this very characteristic scar is an additional feature, having a set of chances of its own. So that we have to consider not only the chance that the print of the prisoner's left thumb should be identical with the print of some other person's left thumb – which is as one to sixty-four-thousand-millions – but the further chance that these two identical thumb-prints should be traversed by the impression of a scar identical in size and appearance, and intersecting the ridges at exactly the same places and producing failures of continuity in the ridges of exactly the same character. But these two chances, multiplied into one another, yield an ultimate chance of about one to four-thousand-trillions that the prisoner's left thumb will exactly resemble the print of some other person's thumb, both as to the pattern and the scar which crosses the pattern. In other words such a coincidence is an utter impossibility."

Sir Hector Trumpler took off his glasses and looked long and steadily at the jury as though he should say, "Come, my friends. What do you think of that?" Then he sat down with a jerk and turned towards Anstey and Thorndyke with a look of triumph.

"Do you propose to cross-examine the witness?" inquired the judge, seeing that the counsel for the defence made no sign.

"No, my Lord," replied Anstey.

Thereupon Sir Hector Trumpler turned once more towards the defending counsel, and his broad, red face was illumined by a smile of deep satisfaction. That smile was reflected on the face of Mr. Singleton as he stepped from the box, and, as I glanced at Thorndyke, I seemed to detect, for a single instant, on his calm and immovable countenance, the faintest shadow of a smile.

"Herbert John Nash!"

A plump, middle-aged man, of keen, though studious, aspect, stepped into the box, and Sir Hector rose once more.

"You are one of the chief assistants in the Finger-print Department, I believe, Mr. Nash?"

"I am."

"Have you heard the evidence of the last witness?"

"I have."

"Do you agree with the statements made by that witness?"

"Entirely. I am prepared to swear that the print on the paper found in the safe is that of the left thumb of the prisoner, Reuben Hornby."

"And you are certain that no mistake is possible?"

"I am certain that no mistake is possible."

Again Sir Hector glanced significantly at the jury as he resumed his seat, and again Anstey made no sign beyond the entry of a few notes on the margin of his brief.

"Are you calling any more witnesses?" asked the judge, dipping his pen in the ink.

"No, my Lord," replied Sir Hector. "That is our case."

Upon this Anstey rose and, addressing the judge, said, "I call witnesses, my Lord."

The judge nodded and made an entry in his notes while Anstey delivered his brief introductory speech, "My Lord and gentlemen of the jury, I shall not occupy the time of the Court with unnecessary appeals at this stage, but shall proceed to take the evidence of my witnesses without delay."

There was a pause of a minute or more, during which the silence was broken only by the rustle of papers and the squeaking of the judge's quill pen. Juliet turned a white, scared face to me and said in a hushed whisper,

165

"This is terrible. That last man's evidence is perfectly crushing. What can possibly be said in reply? I am in despair. Oh! Poor Reuben! He is lost, Dr. Jervis! He hasn't a chance now."

"Do you believe that he is guilty?" I asked.

"Certainly not!" she replied indignantly. "I am as certain of his innocence as ever."

"Then," said I, "if he is innocent, there must be some means of proving his innocence."

"Yes. I suppose so," she rejoined in a dejected whisper. "At any rate we shall soon know now."

At this moment the usher's voice was heard calling out the name of the first witness for the defence.

"Edmund Horford Rowe!"

A keen-looking, grey-haired man, with a shaven face and close-cut side-whiskers, stepped into the box and was sworn in due form.

"You are a Doctor of Medicine, I believe," said Anstey, addressing the witness, "and Lecturer on Medical Jurisprudence at the South London Hospital?"

"I am."

"Have you had occasion to study the properties of blood?"

"Yes. The properties of blood are of great importance from a medico-legal point of view."

"Can you tell us what happens when a drop of blood – say from a cut finger – falls upon a surface such as the bottom of an iron safe?"

"A drop of blood from a living body falling upon any non-absorbent surface will, in the course of a few minutes, solidify into a jelly which will, at first, have the same bulk and colour as the liquid blood."

"Will it undergo any further change?"

"Yes. In a few minutes more the jelly will begin to shrink and become more solid so that the blood will become separated into two parts, the solid and the liquid. The solid part will consist of a firm, tough jelly of a deep red colour, and the liquid part will consist of a pale yellow, clear, watery liquid."

"At the end, say, of two hours, what will be the condition of the drop of blood?"

"It will consist of a drop of clear, nearly colourless liquid, in the middle of which will be a small, tough, red clot."

"Supposing such a drop to be taken up on a piece of white paper, what would be its appearance?"

"The paper would be wetted by the colourless liquid, and the solid clot would probably adhere to the paper in a mass."

"Would the blood on the paper appear as a clear, red liquid?"

"Certainly not. The liquid would appear like water, and the clot would appear as a solid mass sticking to the paper."

"Does blood always behave in the way you have described?"

"Always, unless some artificial means are taken to prevent it from clotting."

"By what means can blood be prevented from clotting or solidifying?"

"There are two principal methods. One is to stir or whip the fresh blood rapidly with a bundle of fine twigs. When this is done, the fibrin – the part of the blood that causes solidification – adheres to the twigs, and the blood that remains, though it is unchanged in appearance, will remain liquid for an indefinite time. The other method is to dissolve a certain proportion of some alkaline salt in the fresh blood, after which it no longer has any tendency to solidify."

"You have heard the evidence of Inspector Sanderson and Sergeant Bates?"

"Yes."

"Inspector Sanderson has told us that he examined the safe at 10:31 a.m. and found two good-sized drops of blood on the bottom. Sergeant Bates has told us that he examined the safe two hours later, and that he took up one of the drops of blood on a piece of white paper. The blood was then quite liquid, and, on the paper, it looked like a clear, red liquid of the colour of blood. What should you consider the condition and nature of that blood to have been?"

"If it was really blood at all, I should say that it was either defibrinated blood – that is, blood from which the fibrin has been extracted by whipping – or that it had been treated with an alkaline salt."

"You are of opinion that the blood found in the safe could not have been ordinary blood shed from a cut or wound?"

"I am sure it could not have been."

"Now, Dr. Rowe, I am going to ask you a few questions on another subject. Have you given any attention to finger-prints made by bloody fingers?"

"Yes. I have recently made some experiments on the subject."

"Will you give us the results of those experiments?"

"My object was to ascertain whether fingers wet with fresh blood would yield distinct and characteristic prints. I made a great number of trials, and as a result found that it is extremely difficult to obtain a clear print when the finger is wetted with fresh blood. The usual result is a mere red blot showing no ridge pattern at all, owing to the blood filling the furrows between the ridges. But if the blood is allowed to dry almost completely on the finger, a very clear print is obtained."

167

"Is it possible to recognise a print that has been made by a nearly dry finger?"

"Yes, quite easily. The half-dried blood is nearly solid and adheres to the paper in a different way from the liquid, and it shows minute details, such as the mouths of the sweat glands, which are always obliterated by the liquid."

"Look carefully at this paper, which was found in the safe, and tell me what you see."

The witness took the paper and examined it attentively, first with the naked eye and then with a pocket-lens.

"I see," said he, "two blood-marks and a print, apparently of a thumb. Of the two marks, one is a blot, smeared slightly by a finger or thumb. The other is a smear only. Both were evidently produced with quite liquid blood. The thumb-print was also made with liquid blood."

"You are quite sure that the thumb-print was made with liquid blood?"

"Quite sure."

"Is there anything unusual about the thumb-print?"

"Yes. It is extraordinarily clear and distinct. I have made a great number of trials and have endeavoured to obtain the clearest prints possible with fresh blood, but none of my prints are nearly as distinct as this one."

Here the witness produced a number of sheets of paper, each of which was covered with the prints of bloody fingers, and compared them with the memorandum slip.

The papers were handed to the judge for his inspection, and Anstey sat down, when Sir Hector Trumpler rose, with a somewhat puzzled expression on his face, to cross-examine.

"You say that the blood found in the safe was defibrinated or artificially treated. What inference do you draw from that fact?"

"I infer that it was not dropped from a bleeding wound."

"Can you form any idea how such blood should have got into the safe?"

"None whatever."

"You say that the thumb-print is a remarkably distinct one. What conclusion do you draw from that?"

"I do not draw any conclusion. I cannot account for its distinctness at all."

The learned counsel sat down with rather a baffled air, and I observed a faint smile spread over the countenance of my colleague.

"Arabella Hornby."

168

A muffled whimpering from my neighbour on the left hand was accompanied by a wild rustling of silk. Glancing at Mrs. Hornby, I saw her stagger from the bench, shaking like a jelly, mopping her eyes with her handkerchief and grasping her open purse. She entered the witness-box, and, having gazed wildly round the court, began to search the multitudinous compartments of her purse.

"The evidence you shall give," sang out the usher – whereat Mrs. Hornby paused in her search and stared at him apprehensively – "to the court and jury sworn, between our Sovereign Lord the King and the prisoner at the bar shall be the truth, – "

"Certainly," said Mrs. Hornby stiffly, "I – "

" – the whole truth, and nothing but the truth, so help you God!"

He held out the Testament, which she took from him with a trembling hand and forthwith dropped with a resounding bang on to the floor of the witness-box, diving after it with such precipitancy that her bonnet jammed violently against the rail of the box.

She disappeared from view for a moment, and then rose from the depths with a purple face and her bonnet flattened and cocked over one ear like an artillery-man's forage cap.

"Kiss the Book, if you please," said the usher, suppressing a grin by an heroic effort, as Mrs. Hornby, encumbered by her purse, her handkerchief and the Testament, struggled to unfasten her bonnet-strings. She clawed frantically at her bonnet, and, having dusted the Testament with her handkerchief, kissed it tenderly and laid it on the rail of the box, whence it fell instantly on to the floor of the court.

"I am really very sorry!" exclaimed Mrs. Hornby, leaning over the rail to address the usher as he stooped to pick up the Book, and discharging on to his back a stream of coins, buttons and folded bills from her open purse, "you will think me very awkward, I'm afraid."

She mopped her face and replaced her bonnet rakishly on one side, as Anstey rose and passed a small red book across to her.

"Kindly look at that book, Mrs. Hornby."

"I'd rather not," said she, with a gesture of repugnance. "It is associated with matters of so extremely disagreeable a character – "

"Do you recognise it?"

"Do I recognise it! How can you ask me such a question when you must know – "

"Answer the question," interposed the judge. "Do you or do you not recognise the book in your hand?"

"Of course I recognise it. How could I fail to – "

"Then say so," said the judge.

"I have said so," retorted Mrs. Hornby indignantly.

The judge nodded to Anstey, who then continued,"It is called a 'Thumbograph,' I believe."

"Yes, the name 'Thumbograph' is printed on the cover, so I suppose that is what it is called."

"Will you tell us, Mrs. Hornby, how the 'Thumbograph' came into your possession?"

For one moment Mrs. Hornby stared wildly at her interrogator. Then she snatched a paper from her purse, unfolded it, gazed at it with an expression of dismay, and crumpled it up in the palm of her hand.

"You are asked a question," said the judge.

"Oh! Yes," said Mrs. Hornby. "The Committee of the Society – no, that is the wrong one – I mean Walter, you know – at least – "

"I beg your pardon," said Anstey, with polite gravity.

"You were speaking of the committee of some society," interposed the judge. "What society were you referring to?"

Mrs. Hornby spread out the paper and, after a glance at it, replied, "The Society of Paralysed Idiots, your worship," whereat a rumble of suppressed laughter arose from the gallery.

"But what has that society to do with the 'Thumbograph'?" inquired the judge.

"Nothing, your worship. Nothing at all."

"Then why did you refer to it?"

"I am sure I don't know," said Mrs. Hornby, wiping her eyes with the paper and then hastily exchanging it for her handkerchief.

The judge took off his glasses and gazed at Mrs. Hornby with an expression of bewilderment. Then he turned to the counsel and said in a weary voice,"Proceed, if you please, Mr. Anstey."

"Can you tell us, Mrs. Hornby, how the 'Thumbograph' came into your possession?" said the latter in persuasive accents.

"I thought it was Walter, and so did my niece, but Walter says it was not, and he ought to know, being young and having a most excellent memory, as I had myself when I was his age, and really, you know, it can't possibly matter where I got the thing – "

"But it does matter," interrupted Anstey. "We wish particularly to know."

"If you mean that you wish to get one like it – "

"We do not," said Anstey. "We wish to know how that particular 'Thumbograph' came into your possession. Did you, for instance, buy it yourself, or was it given to you by someone?"

"Walter says I bought it myself, but I thought he gave it to me, but he says he did not, and you see – "

"Never mind what Walter says. What is your own impression?"

170

"Why I still think that he gave it to me, though, of course, seeing that my memory is not what it was – "

"You think that Walter gave it to you?"

"Yes, in fact I feel sure he did, and so does my niece."

"Walter is your nephew, Walter Hornby?"

"Yes, of course. I thought you knew."

"Can you recall the occasion on which the 'Thumbograph' was given to you?"

"Oh yes, quite distinctly. We had some people to dinner – some people named Colley – not the Dorsetshire Colleys, you know, although they are exceedingly nice people, as I have no doubt the other Colleys are, too, when you know them, but we don't. Well, after dinner we were a little dull and rather at a loss, because Juliet, my niece, you know, had cut her finger and couldn't play the piano excepting with the left hand, and that is so monotonous as well as fatiguing, and the Colleys are not musical, excepting Adolphus, who plays the trombone, but he hadn't got it with him, and then, fortunately, Walter came in and brought the 'Thumbograph' and took all our thumb-prints and his own as well, and we were very much amused, and Matilda Colley – that is the eldest daughter but one – said that Reuben jogged her elbow, but that was only an excuse – "

"Exactly," interrupted Anstey. "And you recollect quite clearly that your nephew Walter gave you the 'Thumbograph' on that occasion?"

"Oh, distinctly. Though, you know, he is really my husband's nephew – "

"Yes. And you are sure that he took the thumb-prints?"

"Quite sure."

"And you are sure that you never saw the 'Thumbograph' before that?"

"Never. How could I? He hadn't brought it."

"Have you ever lent the 'Thumbograph' to anyone?"

"No, never. No one has ever wanted to borrow it, because, you see – "

"Has it never, at any time, gone out of your possession?"

"Oh, I wouldn't say that. In fact, I have often thought, though I hate suspecting people, and I really don't suspect anybody in particular, you know, but it certainly was very peculiar and I can't explain it in any other way. You see, I kept the 'Thumbograph' in a drawer in my writing table, and in the same drawer I used to keep my handkerchief-bag – in fact I do still, and it is there at this very moment, for in my hurry and agitation, I forgot about it until we were in the cab, and then it was too late, because Mr. Lawley – "

"Yes. You kept it in a drawer with your handkerchief-bag."

171

"That was what I said. Well, when Mr. Hornby was staying at Brighton he wrote to ask me to go down for a week and bring Juliet – Miss Gibson, you know – with me. So we went, and, just as we were starting, I sent Juliet to fetch my handkerchief-bag from the drawer, and I said to her, 'Perhaps we might take the thumb-book with us. It might come in useful on a wet day.' So she went, and presently she came back and said that the 'Thumbograph' was not in the drawer. Well, I was so surprised that I went back with her and looked myself, and sure enough the drawer was empty. Well, I didn't think much of it at the time, but when we came home again, as soon as we got out of the cab, I gave Juliet my handkerchief-bag to put away, and presently she came running to me in a great state of excitement. 'Why, Auntie,' she said, 'the "Thumbograph" is in the drawer. Somebody must have been meddling with your writing table.' I went with her to the drawer, and there, sure enough, was the 'Thumbograph.' Somebody must have taken it out and put it back while we were away."

"Who could have had access to your writing table?"

"Oh, anybody, because, you see, the drawers were never locked. We thought it must have been one of the servants."

"Had anyone been to the house during your absence?"

"No. Nobody, except, of course, my two nephews, and neither of them had touched it, because we asked them, and they both said they had not."

"Thank you." Anstey sat down, and Mrs. Hornby having given another correcting twist to her bonnet, was about to step down from the box when Sir Hector rose and bestowed upon her an intimidating stare.

"You made some reference," said he, "to a society – the Society of Paralysed Idiots, I think, whatever that may be. Now what caused you to make that reference?"

"It was a mistake. I was thinking of something else."

"I know it was a mistake. You referred to a paper that was in your hand."

"I did not refer to it, I merely looked at it. It is a letter from the Society of Paralysed Idiots. It is nothing to do with me really, you know. I don't belong to the society, or anything of that sort."

"Did you mistake that paper for some other paper?"

"Yes, I took it for a paper with some notes on it to assist my memory."

"What kind of notes?"

"Oh, just the questions I was likely to be asked."

"Were the answers that you were to give to those questions also written on the paper?"

"Of course they were. The questions would not have been any use without the answers."

"Have you been asked the questions that were written on the paper?"

"Yes. At least, some of them."

"Have you given the answers that were written down?"

"I don't think I have – in fact, I am sure I haven't, because, you see – "

"Ah! You don't think you have." Sir Hector Trumpler smiled significantly at the jury, and continued, "Now who wrote down those questions and answers?"

"My nephew, Walter Hornby. He thought, you know – "

"Never mind what he thought. Who advised or instructed him to write them down?"

"Nobody. It was entirely his own idea, and very thoughtful of him, too, though Dr. Jervis took the paper away from me and said I must rely on my memory."

Sir Hector was evidently rather taken aback by this answer, and sat down suddenly, with a distinctly chapfallen air.

"Where is this paper on which the questions and answers are written?" asked the judge. In anticipation of this inquiry I had already handed it to Thorndyke, and had noted by the significant glance that he bestowed on me that he had not failed to observe the peculiarity in the type. Indeed the matter was presently put beyond all doubt, for he hastily passed to me a scrap of paper, on which I found, when I opened it out, that he had written "$X = W.H.$"

As Anstey handed the rather questionable document up to the judge, I glanced at Walter Hornby and observed him to flush angrily, though he strove to appear calm and unconcerned, and the look that he directed at his aunt was very much the reverse of benevolent.

"Is this the paper?" asked the judge, passing it down to the witness.

"Yes, your worship," answered Mrs. Hornby, in a tremulous voice, whereupon the document was returned to the judge, who proceeded to compare it with his notes.

"I shall order this document to be impounded," said he sternly, after making a brief comparison. "There has been a distinct attempt to tamper with witnesses. Proceed with your case, Mr. Anstey."

There was a brief pause, during which Mrs. Hornby tottered across the court and resumed her seat, gasping with excitement and relief. Then the usher called out, "John Evelyn Thorndyke!"

"Thank God!" exclaimed Juliet, clasping her hands. "Oh! Will he be able to save Reuben? Do you think he will, Dr. Jervis?"

"There is someone who thinks he will," I replied, glancing towards Polton, who, clasping in his arms the mysterious box and holding on to the microscope case, gazed at his master with a smile of ecstasy. "Polton has more faith than you have, Miss Gibson."

"Yes, the dear, faithful little man!" she rejoined. "Well, we shall know the worst very soon now, at any rate."

"The worst or the best," I said. "We are now going to hear what the defence really is."

"God grant that it may be a good defence," she exclaimed in a low voice, and I – though not ordinarily a religious man – murmured "Amen!"

Chapter XVI
Thorndyke Plays His Card

As Thorndyke took his place in the box I looked at him with a sense of unreasonable surprise, feeling that I had never before fully realised what manner of man my friend was as to his externals. I had often noted the quiet strength of his face, its infinite intelligence, its attractiveness and magnetism, but I had never before appreciated what now impressed me most – that Thorndyke was actually the handsomest man I had ever seen. He was dressed simply, his appearance unaided by the flowing gown or awe-inspiring wig, and yet his presence dominated the court. Even the judge, despite his scarlet robe and trappings of office, looked commonplace by comparison, while the jurymen, who turned to look at him, seemed like beings of an inferior order. It was not alone the distinction of the tall figure, erect and dignified, nor the power and massive composure of his face, but the actual symmetry and comeliness of the face itself that now arrested my attention – a comeliness that made it akin rather to some classic mask, wrought in the ivory-toned marble of Pentelicus, than to the eager faces that move around us in the hurry and bustle of a life at once strenuous and trivial.

"You are attached to the medical school at St. Margaret's Hospital, I believe, Dr. Thorndyke?" said Anstey.

"Yes. I am the lecturer on Medical Jurisprudence and Toxicology."

"Have you had much experience of medico-legal inquiries?"

"A great deal. I am engaged exclusively in medico-legal work."

"You heard the evidence relating to the two drops of blood found in the safe?"

"I did."

"What is your opinion as to the condition of that blood?"

"I should say there is no doubt that it had been artificially treated – probably by defibrination."

"Can you suggest any explanation of the condition of that blood?"

"I can."

"Is your explanation connected with any peculiarities in the thumb-print on the paper that was found in the safe?"

"It is."

"Have you given any attention to the subject of finger-prints?"

"Yes. A great deal of attention."

"Be good enough to examine that paper." (Here the usher handed to Thorndyke the memorandum slip). "Have you seen it before?"

"Yes. I saw it at Scotland Yard."

"Did you examine it thoroughly?"

"Very thoroughly. The police officials gave me every facility and, with their permission, I took several photographs of it."

"There is a mark on that paper resembling the print of a human thumb?"

"There is."

"You have heard two expert witnesses swear that that mark was made by the left thumb of the prisoner, Reuben Hornby?"

"I have."

"Do you agree to that statement?"

"I do not."

"In your opinion, was the mark upon that paper made by the thumb of the prisoner?"

"No. I am convinced that it was not made by the thumb of Reuben Hornby."

"Do you think that it was made by the thumb of some other person?"

"No. I am of opinion that it was not made by a human thumb at all."

At this statement the judge paused for a moment, pen in hand, and stared at Thorndyke with his mouth slightly open, while the two experts looked at one another with raised eyebrows.

"By what means do you consider that the mark was produced?"

"By means of a stamp, either of india rubber or, more probably, of chromicized gelatine."

Here Polton, who had been, by degrees, rising to an erect posture, smote his thigh a resounding thwack and chuckled aloud, a proceeding that caused all eyes, including those of the judge, to be turned on him.

"If that noise is repeated," said the judge, with a stony stare at the horrified offender – who had shrunk into the very smallest space that I have ever seen a human being occupy – "I shall cause the person who made it to be removed from the court."

"I understand, then," pursued Anstey, "that you consider the thumb-print, which has been sworn to as the prisoner's, to be a forgery?"

"Yes. It is a forgery."

"But is it possible to forge a thumb-print or a finger-print?"

"It is not only possible, but quite easy to do."

"As easy as to forge a signature, for instance?"

"Much more so, and infinitely more secure. A signature, being written with a pen, requires that the forgery should also be written with a pen, a process demanding very special skill and, after all, never resulting in an absolute *facsimile*. But a finger-print is a stamped impression – the finger-tip being the stamp, and it is only necessary to obtain a stamp identical in character with the finger-tip, in order to produce an impression which is an absolute *facsimile*, in every respect, of the original, and totally indistinguishable from it."

"Would there be no means at all of detecting the difference between a forged finger-print and the genuine original?"

"None whatever, for the reason that there would be no difference to detect."

"But you have stated, quite positively, that the thumb-print on this paper is a forgery. Now, if the forged print is indistinguishable from the original, how are you able to be certain that this particular print is a forgery?"

"I was speaking of what is possible with due care, but, obviously, a forger might, through inadvertence, fail to produce an absolute *facsimile* and then detection would be possible. That is what has happened in the present case. The forged print is not an absolute *facsimile* of the true print. There is a slight discrepancy. But, in addition to this, the paper bears intrinsic evidence that the thumb-print on it is a forgery."

"We will consider that evidence presently, Dr. Thorndyke. To return to the possibility of forging a finger-print, can you explain to us, without being too technical, by what methods it would be possible to produce such a stamp as you have referred to?"

"There are two principal methods that suggest themselves to me. The first, which is rather crude though easy to carry out, consists in taking an actual cast of the end of the finger. A mould would be made by pressing the finger into some plastic material, such as fine modelling clay or hot sealing wax, and then, by pouring a warm solution of gelatine into the mould, and allowing it to cool and solidify, a cast would be produced which would yield very perfect finger-prints. But this method would, as a rule, be useless for the purpose of the forger, as it could not, ordinarily, be carried out without the knowledge of the victim. Though in the case of dead bodies and persons asleep or unconscious or under an anaesthetic, it could be practised with success, and would offer the advantage of requiring practically no technical skill or knowledge and no special appliances. The second method, which is much more efficient, and is the one, I have no doubt, that has been used in the present instance, requires more knowledge and skill.

"In the first place it is necessary to obtain possession of, or access to, a genuine finger-print. Of this finger-print a photograph is taken, or rather, a photographic negative, which for this purpose requires to be taken on a reversed plate, and the negative is put into a special printing frame, with a

177

plate of gelatine which has been treated with potassium bichromate, and the frame is exposed to light.

"Now gelatine treated in this way – chromicized gelatine, as it is called – has a very peculiar property. Ordinary gelatine, as is well known, is easily dissolved in hot water, and chromicized gelatine is also soluble in hot water as long as it is not exposed to light, but on being exposed to light, it undergoes a change and is no longer capable of being dissolved in hot water. Now the plate of chromicized gelatine under the negative is protected from the light by the opaque parts of the negative, whereas the light passes freely through the transparent parts, but the transparent parts of the negative correspond to the black marks on the finger-print, and these correspond to the ridges on the finger. Hence it follows that the gelatine plate is acted upon by light only on the parts corresponding to the ridges, and in these parts the gelatine is rendered insoluble, while all the rest of the gelatine is soluble. The gelatine plate, which is cemented to a thin plate of metal for support, is now carefully washed with hot water, by which the soluble part of the gelatine is dissolved away leaving the insoluble part (corresponding to the ridges) standing up from the surface. Thus there is produced a *facsimile* in relief of the finger-print having actual ridges and furrows identical in character with the ridges and furrows of the finger-tip. If an inked roller is passed over this relief, or if the relief is pressed lightly on an inked slab, and then pressed on a sheet of paper, a finger-print will be produced which will be absolutely identical with the original, even to the little white spots which mark the orifices of the sweat glands. It will be impossible to discover any difference between the real finger-print and the counterfeit because, in fact, no difference exists."

"But surely the process you have described is a very difficult and intricate one?"

"Not at all. It is very little more difficult than ordinary carbon printing, which is practised successfully by numbers of amateurs. Moreover, such a relief as I have described – which is practically nothing more than an ordinary process block – could be produced by any photo-engraver. The process that I have described is, in all essentials, that which is used in the reproduction of pen-and-ink drawings, and any of the hundreds of workmen who are employed in that industry could make a relief-block of a finger-print, with which an undetectable forgery could be executed."

"You have asserted that the counterfeit finger-print could not be distinguished from the original. Are you prepared to furnish proof that this is the case?"

"Yes. I am prepared to execute a counterfeit of the prisoner's thumb-print in the presence of the Court."

178

"And do you say that such a counterfeit would be indistinguishable from the original, even by the experts?"

"I do."

Anstey turned towards the judge. "Would your Lordship give your permission for a demonstration such as the witness proposes?"

"Certainly," replied the judge. "The evidence is highly material. How do you propose that the comparison should be made?" he added, addressing Thorndyke.

"I have brought, for the purpose, my Lord," answered Thorndyke, "some sheets of paper, each of which is ruled into twenty numbered squares. I propose to make on ten of the squares counterfeits of the prisoner's thumb-mark, and to fill the remaining ten with real thumb-marks. I propose that the experts should then examine the paper and tell the Court which are the real thumb-prints and which are the false."

"That seems a fair and efficient test," said his Lordship. "Have you any objection to offer, Sir Hector?"

Sir Hector Trumpler hastily consulted with the two experts, who were sitting in the attorney's bench, and then replied, without much enthusiasm, "We have no objection to offer, my Lord."

"Then, in that case, I shall direct the expert witnesses to withdraw from the court while the prints are being made."

In obedience to the judge's order, Mr. Singleton and his colleague rose and left the court with evident reluctance, while Thorndyke took from a small portfolio three sheets of paper which he handed up to the judge.

"If your Lordship," said he, "will make marks in ten of the squares on two of these sheets, one can be given to the jury and one retained by your Lordship to check the third sheet when the prints are made on it."

"That is an excellent plan," said the judge, "and, as the information is for myself and the jury, it would be better if you came up and performed the actual stamping on my table in the presence of the foreman of the jury and the counsel for the prosecution and defence."

In accordance with the judge's direction Thorndyke stepped up on the dais, and Anstey, as he rose to follow, leaned over towards me.

"You and Polton had better go up too," said he. "Thorndyke will want your assistance, and you may as well see the fun. I will explain to his Lordship."

He ascended the stairs leading to the dais and addressed a few words to the judge, who glanced in our direction and nodded, whereupon we both gleefully followed our counsel, Polton carrying the box and beaming with delight.

The judge's table was provided with a shallow drawer which pulled out at the side and which accommodated the box comfortably, leaving the small table-top free for the papers. When the lid of the box was raised, there were displayed a copper inking-slab, a small roller and the twenty-four "pawns" which had so puzzled Polton, and on which he now gazed with a twinkle of amusement and triumph.

"Are those all stamps?" inquired the judge, glancing curiously at the array of turned-wood handles.

"They are all stamps, my Lord," replied Thorndyke, "and each is taken from a different impression of the prisoner's thumb."

"But why so many?" asked the judge.

"I have multiplied them," answered Thorndyke, as he squeezed out a drop of finger-print ink on to the slab and proceeded to roll it out into a thin film, "to avoid the tell-tale uniformity of a single stamp. And I may say," he added, "that it is highly important that the experts should not be informed that more than one stamp has been used."

"Yes, I see that," said the judge. "You understand that, Sir Hector," he added, addressing the counsel, who bowed stiffly, clearly regarding the entire proceeding with extreme disfavour.

Thorndyke now inked one of the stamps and handed it to the judge, who examined it curiously and then pressed it on a piece of waste paper, on which there immediately appeared a very distinct impression of a human thumb.

"Marvellous!" he exclaimed. "Most ingenious! Too ingenious!" He chuckled softly and added, as he handed the stamp and the paper to the foreman of the jury. "It is well, Dr. Thorndyke, that you are on the side of law and order, for I am afraid that, if you were on the other side, you would be one too many for the police. Now, if you are ready, we will proceed. Will you, please, stamp an impression in square number three."

Thorndyke drew a stamp from its compartment, inked it on the slab, and pressed it neatly on the square indicated, leaving there a sharp, clear thumb-print.

The process was repeated on nine other squares, a different stamp being used for each impression. The judge then marked the ten corresponding squares of the other two sheets of paper, and having checked them, directed the foreman to exhibit the sheet bearing the false thumb-prints to the jury, together with the marked sheet which they were to retain, to enable them to check the statements of the expert witnesses. When this was done, the prisoner was brought from the dock and stood beside the table. The judge looked with a curious and not unkindly interest at the handsome, manly fellow who stood charged with a crime so sordid and out of character with his appearance, and I felt, as I noted the look, that Reuben would, at least, be tried fairly on the evidence, without prejudice or even with some prepossession in his favour.

With the remaining part of the operation Thorndyke proceeded carefully and deliberately. The inking-slab was rolled afresh for each impression, and, after each, the thumb was cleansed with petrol and thoroughly dried, and when the process was completed and the prisoner led back to the dock, the twenty squares on the paper were occupied by twenty thumb-prints, which, to my eye, at any rate, were identical in character.

The judge sat for near upon a minute poring over this singular document with an expression halfway between a frown and a smile. At length, when we had all returned to our places, he directed the usher to bring in the witnesses.

I was amused to observe the change that had come over the experts in the short interval. The confident smile, the triumphant air of laying down a trump card, had vanished, and the expression of both was one of anxiety, not unmixed with apprehension. As Mr. Singleton advanced hesitatingly to the table, I recalled the words that he had uttered in his room at Scotland Yard. Evidently his scheme of the game that was to end in an easy checkmate, had not included the move that had just been made.

"Mr. Singleton," said the judge, "here is a paper on which there are twenty thumb-prints. Ten of them are genuine prints of the prisoner's left thumb and ten are forgeries. Please examine them and note down in writing which are the true prints and which are the forgeries. When you have made your notes the paper will be handed to Mr. Nash."

"Is there any objection to my using the photograph that I have with me for comparison, my Lord?" asked Mr. Singleton.

"I think not," replied the judge. "What do you say, Mr. Anstey?"

"No objection whatever, my Lord," answered Anstey.

Mr. Singleton accordingly drew from his pocket an enlarged photograph of the thumb-print and a magnifying glass, with the aid of which he explored the bewildering array of prints on the paper before him, and as he proceeded I remarked with satisfaction that his expression became more and more dubious and worried. From time to time he made an entry on a memorandum slip beside him, and, as the entries accumulated, his frown grew deeper and his aspect more puzzled and gloomy.

At length he sat up, and taking the memorandum slip in his hand, addressed the judge.

"I have finished my examination, my Lord."

"Very well. Mr. Nash, will you kindly examine the paper and write down the results of your examination?"

"Oh! I wish they would make haste," whispered Juliet. "Do you think they will be able to tell the real from the false thumb-prints?"

"I can't say," I replied, "but we shall soon know. They looked all alike to me."

Mr. Nash made his examination with exasperating deliberateness, and preserved throughout an air of stolid attention, but at length he, too, completed his notes and handed the paper back to the usher.

"Now, Mr. Singleton," said the judge, "let us hear your conclusions. You have been sworn."

Mr. Singleton stepped into the witness-box, and, laying his notes on the ledge, faced the judge.

"Have you examined the paper that was handed to you?" asked Sir Hector Trumpler.

"I have."

"What did you see on the paper?"

"I saw twenty thumb-prints, of which some were evident forgeries, some were evidently genuine, and some were doubtful."

"Taking the thumb-prints *seriatim*, what have you noted about them?"

Mr. Singleton examined his notes and replied, "The thumb-print on square one is evidently a forgery, as is also number two, though it is a passable imitation. Three and four are genuine. Five is an obvious forgery. Six is a genuine thumb-print. Seven is a forgery, though a good one. Eight is genuine. Nine is, I think, a forgery, though it is a remarkably good imitation. Ten and eleven are genuine thumb-marks. Twelve and thirteen are forgeries, but as to fourteen I am very doubtful, though I am inclined to regard it as a forgery. Fifteen is genuine, and I think sixteen is also, but I will not swear to it. Seventeen is certainly genuine. Eighteen and nineteen I am rather doubtful about, but I am disposed to consider them both forgeries. Twenty is certainly a genuine thumb-print."

As Mr. Singleton's evidence proceeded, a look of surprise began to make its appearance on the judge's face, while the jury glanced from the witness to the notes before them and from their notes to one another in undisguised astonishment.

As to Sir Hector Trumpler, that luminary of British jurisprudence was evidently completely fogged, for, as statement followed statement, he pursed up his lips and his broad, red face became overshadowed by an expression of utter bewilderment.

For a few seconds he stared blankly at his witness and then dropped on to his seat with a thump that shook the court.

"You have no doubt," said Anstey, "as to the correctness of your conclusions? For instance, you are quite sure that the prints one and two are forgeries?"

"I have no doubt."

"You swear that those two prints are forgeries?"

Mr. Singleton hesitated for a moment. He had been watching the judge and the jury and had apparently misinterpreted their surprise, assuming it to be due to his own remarkable powers of discrimination, and his confidence had revived accordingly.

"Yes," he answered, "I swear that they are forgeries."

Anstey sat down, and Mr. Singleton, having passed his notes up to the judge, retired from the box, giving place to his colleague.

Mr. Nash, who had listened with manifest satisfaction to the evidence, stepped into the box with all his original confidence restored. His selection of the true and the false thumb-prints was practically identical with that of Mr. Singleton, and his knowledge of this fact led him to state his conclusions with an air that was authoritative and even dogmatic.

"I am quite satisfied of the correctness of my statements," he said, in reply to Anstey's question, "and I am prepared to swear, and do swear, that those thumb-prints which I have stated to be forgeries, are forgeries, and that their detection presents no difficulty to an observer who has an expert acquaintance with finger-prints."

"There is one question that I should like to ask," said the judge, when the expert had left the box and Thorndyke had re-entered it to continue his evidence. "The conclusions of the expert witnesses – manifestly *bona fide* conclusions, arrived at by individual judgement, without collusion or comparison of results – are practically identical. They are virtually in complete agreement. Now, the strange thing is this: Their conclusions are wrong in every instance" (here I nearly laughed aloud, for, as I glanced at the two experts, the expression of smug satisfaction on their countenances changed with lightning rapidity to a ludicrous spasm of consternation), "not sometimes wrong and sometimes right, as would have been the case if they had made mere guesses, but wrong every time. When they are quite certain, they are quite wrong, and when they are doubtful, they incline to the wrong conclusion. This is a very strange coincidence, Dr. Thorndyke. Can you explain it?"

Thorndyke's face, which throughout the proceedings had been as expressionless as that of a wooden figurehead, now relaxed into a dry smile.

"I think I can, my Lord," he replied. "The object of a forger in executing a forgery is to produce deception on those who shall examine the forgery."

"Ah!" said the judge, and *his* face relaxed into a dry smile, while the jury broke out into unconcealed grins.

183

"It was evident to me," continued Thorndyke, "that the experts would be unable to distinguish the real from the forged thumb-prints, and, that being so, that they would look for some collateral evidence to guide them. I, therefore, supplied that collateral evidence. Now, if ten prints are taken, without special precautions, from a single finger, it will probably happen that no two of them are exactly alike, for the finger being a rounded object of which only a small part touches the paper, the impressions produced will show little variations according to the part of the finger by which the print is made. But a stamp such as I have used has a flat surface like that of a printer's type, and, like a type, it always prints the same impression. It does not reproduce the finger-tip, but a particular print of the finger, and so, if ten prints are made with a single stamp, each print will be a mechanical repetition of the other nine. Thus, on a sheet bearing twenty finger-prints, of which ten were forgeries made with a single stamp, it would be easy to pick out the ten forged prints by the fact that they would all be mechanical repetitions of one another, while the genuine prints could be distinguished by the fact of their presenting trifling variations in the position of the finger.

"Anticipating this line of reasoning, I was careful to make each print with a different stamp and each stamp was made from a different thumb-print, and I further selected thumb-prints which varied as widely as possible when I made the stamps. Moreover, when I made the real thumb-prints, I was careful to put the thumb down in the same position each time as far as I was able, and so it happened that, on the sheet submitted to the experts, the real thumb-prints were nearly all alike, while the forgeries presented considerable variations. The instances in which the witnesses were quite certain were those in which I succeeded in making the genuine prints repeat one another, and the doubtful cases were those in which I partially failed."

"Thank you, that is quite clear," said the judge, with a smile of deep content, such as is apt to appear on the judicial countenance when an expert witness is knocked off his pedestal. "We may now proceed, Mr. Anstey."

"You have told us," resumed Anstey, "and have submitted proofs, that it is possible to forge a thumb-print so that detection is impossible. You have also stated that the thumb-print on the paper found in Mr. Hornby's safe is a forgery. Do you mean that it *may* be a forgery, or that it actually is one?"

"I mean that it actually is a forgery."

"When did you first come to the conclusion that it was a forgery?"

"When I saw it at Scotland Yard. There are three facts which suggested this conclusion. In the first place the print was obviously produced with liquid blood, and yet it was a beautifully clear and distinct impression. But such an impression could not be produced with liquid blood without the use of a slab and roller, even if great care were used, and still less could it have been produced by an accidental smear.

"In the second place, on measuring the print with a micrometer, I found that it did not agree in dimensions with a genuine thumb-print of Reuben Hornby. It was appreciably larger. I photographed the print with the micrometer in contact and on comparing this with a genuine thumb-print, also photographed with the same micrometer in contact, I found that the suspected print was larger by the fortieth-of-an-inch, from one given point on the ridge-pattern to another given point. I have here enlargements of the two photographs in which the disagreement in size is clearly shown by the lines of the micrometer. I have also the micrometer itself and a portable microscope, if the Court wishes to verify the photographs."

"Thank you," said the judge, with a bland smile, "we will accept your sworn testimony unless the learned counsel for the prosecution demands verification."

He received the photographs which Thorndyke handed up and, having examined them with close attention, passed them on to the jury.

"The third fact," resumed Thorndyke, "is of much more importance, since it not only proves the print to be a forgery, but also furnishes a very distinct clue to the origin of the forgery, and so to the identity of the forger." (Here the court became hushed until the silence was so profound that the ticking of the clock seemed a sensible interruption. I glanced at Walter, who sat motionless and rigid at the end of the bench, and perceived that a horrible pallor had spread over his face, while his forehead was covered with beads of perspiration.) "On looking at the print closely, I noticed at one part a minute white mark or space. It was of the shape of a capital S and had evidently been produced by a defect in the paper – a loose fibre which had stuck to the thumb and been detached by it from the paper, leaving a blank space where it had been. But, on examining the paper under a low power of the microscope, I found the surface to be perfect and intact. No loose fibre had been detached from it, for if it had, the broken end or, at least, the groove in which it had lain, would have been visible. The inference seemed to be that the loose fibre had existed, not in the paper which was found in the safe, but in the paper on which the original thumb-mark had been made. Now, as far as I knew, there was only one undoubted thumb-print of Reuben Hornby's in existence – the one in the 'Thumbograph.' At my request, the 'Thumbograph' was brought to my chambers by Mrs. Hornby, and, on examining the print of Reuben Hornby's left thumb, I perceived on it a minute, S-shaped white space occupying a similar position to that in the red thumb-mark, and when I looked at it through a powerful lens, I could clearly see the little groove in the paper in which the fibre had lain and from which it had been lifted by the inked thumb. I subsequently made a systematic comparison of the marks in the two thumb-prints. I found that the dimensions of the mark were proportionally the same in each – that is to say, the mark in the 'Thumbograph' print had an extreme length of 26/1000th's-of-an-inch and an extreme breadth of 14.5/1000th's-of-an-inch, while that in the red thumb-mark was one-fortieth larger in each dimension, having an extreme length of 26.65/1000th's-of-an-inch and an extreme breadth of 14.86/1000th's-of-an-inch. That the shape was identical, as was shown by superimposing tracings of greatly enlarged photographs of each mark on similar enlargements of the other, and that the mark intersected the ridges of the thumb-print in the same manner and at exactly the same parts in the two prints."

"Do you say that – having regard to the facts which you have stated – it is certain that the red thumb-mark is a forgery?"

"I do, and I also say that it is certain that the forgery was executed by means of the 'Thumbograph.'"

"Might not the resemblances be merely a coincidence?"

"No. By the law of probabilities which Mr. Singleton explained so clearly in his evidence, the adverse chances would run into untold millions. Here are two thumb-prints made in different places and at different times – an interval of many weeks intervening. Each of them bears an accidental mark which is due not to any peculiarity of the thumb, but to a peculiarity of the paper. On the theory of coincidences it is necessary to suppose that each piece of paper had a loose fibre of exactly identical shape and size and that this fibre came, by accident, in contact with the thumb at exactly the same spot. But such a supposition would be more opposed to probabilities even than the supposition that two exactly similar thumb-prints should have been made by different persons. And then there is the further fact that the paper found in the safe had no loose fibre to account for the mark."

"What is your explanation of the presence of defibrinated blood in the safe?"

"It was probably used by the forger in making the thumb-print, for which purpose fresh blood would be less suitable by reason of its clotting. He would probably have carried a small quantity in a bottle, together with the pocket slab and roller invented by Mr. Galton. It would thus be possible for him to put a drop on the slab, roll it out into a thin film and take a clean impression with his stamp. It must be remembered that these precautions were quite necessary, since he had to make a recognisable print at the first attempt. A failure and a second trial would have destroyed the accidental appearance, and might have aroused suspicion."

186

"You have made some enlarged photographs of the thumb-prints, have you not?"

"Yes. I have here two enlarged photographs, one of the 'Thumbograph' print and one of the red thumb-print. They both show the white mark very clearly and will assist comparison of the originals, in which the mark is plainly visible through a lens."

He handed the two photographs up to the judge, together with the 'Thumbograph,' the memorandum slip, and a powerful doublet lens with which to examine them.

The judge inspected the two original documents with the aid of the lens and compared them with the photographs, nodding approvingly as he made out the points of agreement. Then he passed them on to the jury and made an entry in his notes.

While this was going on my attention was attracted by Walter Hornby. An expression of terror and wild despair had settled on his face, which was ghastly in its pallor and bedewed with sweat. He looked furtively at Thorndyke and, as I noted the murderous hate in his eyes, I recalled our midnight adventure in John Street and the mysterious cigar.

Suddenly he rose to his feet, wiping his brow and steadying himself against the bench with a shaking hand. Then he walked quietly to the door and went out. Apparently, I was not the only onlooker who had been interested in his doings, for, as the door swung to after him, Superintendent Miller rose from his seat and went out by the other door.

"Are you cross-examining this witness?" the judge inquired, glancing at Sir Hector Trumpler.

"No, my Lord," was the reply.

"Are you calling any more witnesses, Mr. Anstey?"

"Only one, my Lord," replied Anstey, "the prisoner, whom I shall put in the witness-box, as a matter of form, in order that he may make a statement on oath."

Reuben was accordingly conducted from the dock to the witness-box, and, having been sworn, made a solemn declaration of his innocence. A brief cross-examination followed, in which nothing was elicited, but that Reuben had spent the evening at his club and gone home to his rooms about half-past eleven and had let himself in with his latchkey. Sir Hector at length sat down. The prisoner was led back to the dock, and the Court settled itself to listen to the speeches of the counsel.

"My Lord and gentlemen of the jury," Anstey commenced in his clear, mellow tones, "I do not propose to occupy your time with a long speech. The evidence that has been laid before you is at once so intelligible, so lucid, and so conclusive, that you will, no doubt, arrive at

187

your verdict uninfluenced by any display of rhetoric either on my part or on the part of the learned counsel for the prosecution.

"Nevertheless, it is desirable to disentangle from the mass of evidence those facts which are really vital and crucial.

"Now the one fact which stands out and dominates the whole case is this: The prisoner's connection with this case rests solely upon the police theory of the infallibility of finger-prints. Apart from the evidence of the thumb-print there is not, and there never was, the faintest breath of suspicion against him. You have heard him described as a man of unsullied honour, as a man whose character is above reproach – a man who is trusted implicitly by those who have had dealings with him. And this character was not given by a casual stranger, but by one who has known him from childhood. His record is an unbroken record of honourable conduct. His life has been that of a clean-living, straightforward gentleman. And now he stands before you charged with a miserable, paltry theft – charged with having robbed that generous friend, the brother of his own father, the guardian of his childhood and the benefactor who has planned and striven for his well-being. Charged, in short, gentlemen, with a crime which every circumstance connected with him and every trait of his known character renders utterly inconceivable. Now upon what grounds has this gentleman of irreproachable character been charged with this mean and sordid crime? Baldly stated, the grounds of the accusation are these: A certain learned and eminent man of science has made a statement, which the police have not merely accepted but have, in practice, extended beyond its original meaning. That statement is as follows: 'A complete, or nearly complete, accordance between two prints of a single finger . . . affords evidence requiring no corroboration, that the persons from whom they were made are the same.'

"That statement, gentlemen, is in the highest degree misleading, and ought not to have been made without due warning and qualification. So far is it from being true, in practice, that its exact contrary is the fact. The evidence of a finger-print, in the absence of corroboration, is absolutely worthless. Of all forms of forgery, the forgery of a finger-print is the easiest and most secure, as you have seen in this court to-day. Consider the character of the high-class forger – his skill, his ingenuity, his resource. Think of the forged banknotes, of which not only the engraving, the design and the signature, but even the very paper with its private watermarks, is imitated with a perfection that is at once the admiration and the despair of those who have to distinguish the true from the false. Think of the forged cheque, in which actual perforations are filled up, of which portions are cut out bodily and replaced by indistinguishable patches. Think of these, and then of a finger-print, of which any photo-engraver's apprentice can make you a forgery that the greatest experts cannot distinguish from the original, which any capable amateur can imitate beyond detection after a month's practice, and then ask yourselves if this is the kind of evidence on which, without any support or corroboration, a gentleman of honour and position should be dragged before a criminal court and charged with having committed a crime of the basest and most sordid type.

"But I must not detain you with unnecessary appeals. I will remind you briefly of the salient facts. The case for the prosecution rests upon the assertion that the thumb-print found in the safe was made by the thumb of the prisoner. If that thumb-print was not made by the prisoner, there is not only no case against him but no suspicion of any kind.

"Now, was that thumb-print made by the prisoner's thumb? You have had conclusive evidence that it was not. That thumb-print differed in the size, or scale, of the pattern from a genuine thumb-print of the prisoner's. The difference was small, but it was fatal to the police theory. The two prints were not identical.

"But, if not the prisoner's thumb-print, what was it? The resemblance of the pattern was too exact for it to be the thumb-print of another person, for it reproduced not only the pattern of the ridges on the prisoner's thumb, but also the scar of an old wound. The answer that I propose to this question is, that it was an intentional imitation of the prisoner's thumb-print, made with the purpose of fixing suspicion on the prisoner, and so ensuring the safety of the actual criminal. Are there any facts which support this theory? Yes, there are several facts which support it very strongly.

"First, there are the facts that I have just mentioned. The red thumb-print disagreed with the genuine print in its scale or dimensions. It was not the prisoner's thumb-print, but neither was it that of any other person. The only alternative is that it was a forgery.

"In the second place, that print was evidently made with the aid of certain appliances and materials, and one of those materials, namely defibrinated blood, was found in the safe.

"In the third place, there is the coincidence that the print was one which it was possible to forge. The prisoner has ten digits – eight fingers and two thumbs. But there were in existence actual prints of the two thumbs, whereas no prints of the fingers were in existence. Hence it would have been impossible to forge a print of any of the fingers. So it happens that the red thumb-print resembled one of the two prints of which forgery was possible.

"In the fourth place, the red thumb-print reproduces an accidental peculiarity of the 'Thumbograph' print. Now, if the red thumb-print is a forgery, it must have been made from the 'Thumbograph' print, since there

189

exists no other print from which it could have been made. Hence we have the striking fact that the red thumb-print is an exact replica – including accidental peculiarities – of the only print from which a forgery could have been made. The accidental S-shaped mark in the 'Thumbograph' print is accounted for by the condition of the paper. The occurrence of this mark in the red thumb-print is not accounted for by any peculiarity of the paper, and can be accounted for in no way, excepting by assuming the one to be a copy of the other. The conclusion is thus inevitable that the red thumb-print is a photo-mechanical reproduction of the 'Thumbograph' print.

"But there is yet another point. If the red thumb-print is a forgery reproduced from the 'Thumbograph' print, the forger must at some time have had access to the 'Thumbograph.' Now, you have heard Mrs. Hornby's remarkable story of the mysterious disappearance of the 'Thumbograph' and its still more mysterious reappearance. That story can have left no doubt in your minds that some person had surreptitiously removed the 'Thumbograph' and, after an unknown interval, secretly replaced it. Thus the theory of forgery receives confirmation at every point, and is in agreement with every known fact, whereas the theory that the red thumb-print was a genuine thumb-print, is based upon a gratuitous assumption, and has not had a single fact advanced in its support.

"Accordingly, gentlemen, I assert that the prisoner's innocence has been proved in the most complete and convincing manner, and I ask you for a verdict in accordance with that proof."

As Anstey resumed his seat, a low rumble of applause was heard from the gallery. It subsided instantly on a gesture of disapproval from the judge, and a silence fell upon the court, in which the clock, with cynical indifference, continued to record in its brusque monotone the passage of the fleeting seconds.

"He is saved, Dr. Jervis! Oh! Surely he is saved!" Juliet exclaimed in an agitated whisper. "They must see that he is innocent now."

"Have patience a little longer," I answered. "It will soon be over now."

Sir Hector Trumpler was already on his feet and, after bestowing on the jury a stern hypnotic stare, he plunged into his reply with a really admirable air of conviction and sincerity.

"My Lord and gentlemen of the jury: The case which is now before this Court is one, as I have already remarked, in which human nature is presented in a highly unfavourable light. But I need not insist upon this aspect of the case, which will already, no doubt, have impressed you sufficiently. It is necessary merely for me, as my learned friend has aptly expressed it, to disentangle the actual facts of the case from the web of casuistry that has been woven around them.

190

"Those facts are of extreme simplicity. A safe has been opened and property of great value abstracted from it. It has been opened by means of false keys. Now there are two men who have, from time to time, had possession of the true keys, and thus had the opportunity of making copies of them. When the safe is opened by its rightful owner, the property is gone, and there is found the print of the thumb of one of these two men. That thumb-print was not there when the safe was closed. The man whose thumb-print is found is a left-handed man. The print is the print of a left thumb. It would seem, gentlemen, as if the conclusion were so obvious that no sane person could be found to contest it, and I submit that the conclusion which any sane person would arrive at – the only possible conclusion – is, that the person whose thumb-print was found in the safe is the person who stole the property from the safe. But the thumb-print was, admittedly, that of the prisoner at the bar, and therefore the prisoner at the bar is the person who stole the diamonds from the safe.

"It is true that certain fantastic attempts have been made to explain away these obvious facts. Certain far-fetched scientific theories have been propounded and an exhibition of legerdemain has taken place which, I venture to think, would have been more appropriate to some place of public entertainment than to a court of justice. That exhibition has, no doubt, afforded you considerable amusement. It has furnished a pleasing relaxation from the serious business of the court. It has even been instructive, as showing to what extent it is possible for plain facts to be perverted by misdirected ingenuity. But unless you are prepared to consider this crime as an elaborate hoax – as a practical joke carried out by a facetious criminal of extraordinary knowledge, skill and general attainments – you must, after all, come to the only conclusion that the facts justify: That the safe was opened and the property abstracted by the prisoner. Accordingly, gentlemen, I ask you, having regard to your important position as the guardians of the well-being and security of your fellow-citizens, to give your verdict in accordance with the evidence, as you have solemnly sworn to do, which verdict, I submit, can be no other than that the prisoner is guilty of the crime with which he is charged."

Sir Hector sat down, and the jury, who had listened to his speech with solid attention, gazed expectantly at the judge, as though they should say: "Now, which of these two are we to believe?"

The judge turned over his notes with an air of quiet composure, writing down a word here and there as he compared the various points in the evidence. Then he turned to the jury with a manner at once persuasive and confidential.

"It is not necessary, gentlemen," he commenced, "for me to occupy your time with an exhaustive analysis of the evidence. That evidence you

191

yourselves have heard, and it has been given, for the most part, with admirable clearness. Moreover, the learned counsel for the defence has collated and compared that evidence so lucidly, and, I may say, so impartially, that a detailed repetition on my part would be superfluous. I shall therefore confine myself to a few comments which may help you in the consideration of your verdict.

"I need hardly point out to you that the reference made by the learned counsel for the prosecution to far-fetched scientific theories is somewhat misleading. The only evidence of a theoretical character was that of the finger-print experts. The evidence of Dr. Rowe and of Dr. Thorndyke dealt exclusively with matters of fact. Such inferences as were drawn by them were accompanied by statements of the facts which yielded such inferences.

"Now, an examination of the evidence which you have heard shows, as the learned counsel for the defence has justly observed, that the entire case resolves itself into a single question, which is this: 'Was the thumb-print that was found in Mr. Hornby's safe made by the thumb of the prisoner, or was it not?' If that thumb-print was made by the prisoner's thumb, then the prisoner must, at least, have been present when the safe was unlawfully opened. If that thumb-print was not made by the prisoner's thumb, there is nothing to connect him with the crime. The question is one of fact upon which it will be your duty to decide, and I must remind you, gentlemen, that you are the sole judges of the facts of the case, and that you are to consider any remarks of mine as merely suggestions which you are to entertain or to disregard according to your judgement.

"Now let us consider this question by the light of the evidence. This thumb-print was either made by the prisoner or it was not. What evidence has been brought forward to show that it was made by the prisoner? Well, there is the evidence of the ridge-pattern. That pattern is identical with the pattern of the prisoner's thumb-print, and even has the impression of a scar which crosses the pattern in a particular manner in the prisoner's thumb-print. There is no need to enter into the elaborate calculations as to the chances of agreement. The practical fact, which is not disputed, is that if this red thumb-print is a genuine thumb-print at all, it was made by the prisoner's thumb. But it is contended that it is not a genuine thumb-print. That it is a mechanical imitation – in fact a forgery.

"The more general question thus becomes narrowed down to the more particular question: 'Is this a genuine thumb-print or is it a forgery?' Let us consider the evidence. First, what evidence is there that it is a genuine thumb-print? There is none. The identity of the pattern is no evidence on this point, because a forgery would also exhibit identity of pattern. The genuineness of the thumb-print was assumed by the prosecution, and no evidence has been offered.

"But now what evidence is there that the red thumb-print is a forgery?

"First, there is the question of size. Two different-sized prints could hardly be made by the same thumb. Then there is the evidence of the use of appliances. Safe-robbers do not ordinarily provide themselves with inking-slabs and rollers with which to make distinct impressions of their own fingers. Then there is the accidental mark on the print which also exists on the only genuine print that could have been used for the purpose of forgery, which is easily explained on the theory of a forgery, but which is otherwise totally incomprehensible. Finally, there is the strange disappearance of the 'Thumbograph' and its strange reappearance. All this is striking and weighty evidence, to which must be added that adduced by Dr. Thorndyke as showing how perfectly it is possible to imitate a finger-print.

"These are the main facts of the case, and it is for you to consider them. If, on careful consideration, you decide that the red thumb-print was actually made by the prisoner's thumb, then it will be your duty to pronounce the prisoner guilty, but if, on weighing the evidence, you decide that the thumb-print is a forgery, then it will be your duty to pronounce the prisoner not guilty. It is now past the usual luncheon hour, and, if you desire it, you can retire to consider your verdict while the Court adjourns."

The jurymen whispered together for a few moments and then the foreman stood up.

"We have agreed on our verdict, my Lord," he said.

The prisoner, who had just been led to the back of the dock, was now brought back to the bar. The grey-wigged clerk of the court stood up and addressed the jury.

"Are you all agreed upon your verdict, gentlemen?"

"We are," replied the foreman.

"What do you say, gentlemen? Is the prisoner guilty or not guilty?"

"Not guilty," replied the foreman, raising his voice and glancing at Reuben.

A storm of applause burst from the gallery and was, for the moment, disregarded by the judge. Mrs. Hornby laughed aloud – a strange, unnatural laugh – and then crammed her handkerchief into her mouth, and so sat gazing at Reuben with the tears coursing down her face, while Juliet laid her head upon the desk and sobbed silently.

After a brief space the judge raised an admonitory hand, and, when the commotion had subsided, addressed the prisoner, who stood at the bar, calm and self-possessed, though his face bore a slight flush.

"Reuben Hornby, the jury, after duly weighing the evidence in this case, have found you to be not guilty of the crime with which you were charged. With that verdict I most heartily agree. In view of the evidence which has been given, I consider that no other verdict was possible, and I venture to say that you leave this court with your innocence fully established, and without a stain upon your character. In the distress which you have recently suffered, as well as in your rejoicing at the verdict of the jury, you have the sympathy of the Court, and of everyone present, and that sympathy will not be diminished by the consideration that, with a less capable defence, the result might have been very different.

"I desire to express my admiration at the manner in which that defence was conducted, and I desire especially to observe that not you alone, but the public at large, are deeply indebted to Dr. Thorndyke, who, by his insight, his knowledge, and his ingenuity, has probably averted a very serious miscarriage of justice. The Court will now adjourn until half-past two."

The judge rose from his seat and everyone present stood up, and, amidst the clamour of many feet upon the gallery stairs, the door of the dock was thrown open by a smiling police officer and Reuben came down the stairs into the body of the court.

Chapter XVII
At Last

"We had better let the people clear off," said Thorndyke, when the first greetings were over and we stood around Reuben in the fast-emptying court. "We don't want a demonstration as we go out."

"No, anything but that, just now," replied Reuben. He still held Mrs. Hornby's hand, and one arm was passed through that of his uncle, who wiped his eyes at intervals, though his face glowed with delight.

"I should like you to come and have a little quiet luncheon with me at my chambers – all of us friends together," continued Thorndyke.

"I should be delighted," said Reuben, "if the programme would include a satisfactory wash."

"You will come, Anstey?" asked Thorndyke.

"What have you got for lunch?" demanded Anstey, who was now disrobed and in his right mind – that is to say, in his usual whimsical, pseudo-frivolous character.

"That question savours of gluttony," answered Thorndyke. "Come and see."

"I will come and eat, which is better," answered Anstey, "and I must run off now, as I have to look in at my chambers."

"How shall we go?" asked Thorndyke, as his colleague vanished through the doorway. "Polton has gone for a four-wheeler, but it won't hold us all."

"It will hold four of us," said Reuben, "and Dr. Jervis will bring Juliet. Won't you, Jervis?"

The request rather took me aback, considering the circumstances, but I was conscious, nevertheless, of an unreasonable thrill of pleasure and answered with alacrity. "If Miss Gibson will allow me, I shall be very delighted." My delight was, apparently, not shared by Juliet, to judge by the uncomfortable blush that spread over her face. She made no objection, however, but merely replied rather coldly, "Well, as we can't sit on the roof of the cab, we had better go by ourselves."

The crowd having by this time presumably cleared off, we all took our way downstairs. The cab was waiting at the kerb, surrounded by a group of spectators, who cheered Reuben as he appeared at the doorway, and we saw our friends enter and drive away. Then we turned and walked quickly down the Old Bailey towards Ludgate Hill.

"Shall we take a hansom?" I asked.

"No, let us walk," replied Juliet. "A little fresh air will do us good after that musty, horrible court. It all seems like a dream, and yet what a relief – Oh! What a relief it is."

"It is rather like the awakening from a nightmare to find the morning sun shining," I rejoined.

"Yes. That is just what it is like," she agreed, "but I still feel dazed and shaken."

We turned presently down New Bridge Street, towards the Embankment, walking side by side without speaking, and I could not help comparing, with some bitterness, our present stiff and distant relations with the intimacy and comradeship that had existed before the miserable incident of our last meeting.

"You don't look so jubilant over your success as I should have expected," she said at length, with a critical glance at me, "but I expect you are really very proud and delighted, aren't you?"

"Delighted, yes. Not proud. Why should I be proud? I have only played jackal, and even that I have done very badly."

"That is hardly a fair statement of the facts," she rejoined, with another quick, inquisitive look at me, "but you are in low spirits to-day – which is not at all like you. Is it not so?"

"I am afraid I am a selfish, egotistical brute," was my gloomy reply. "I ought to be as gay and joyful as everyone else to-day, whereas the fact is that I am chafing over my own petty troubles. You see, now that this case is finished, my engagement with Dr. Thorndyke terminates automatically, and I relapse into my old life – a dreary repetition of journeying amongst strangers – and the prospect is not inspiriting. This has been a time of bitter trial to you, but to me it has been a green oasis in the desert of a colourless, monotonous life. I have enjoyed the companionship of a most lovable man, whom I admire and respect above all other men, and with him have moved in scenes full of colour and interest. And I have made one other friend whom I am loth to see fade out of my life, as she seems likely to do."

"If you mean me," said Juliet, "I may say that it will be your own fault if I fade out of your life. I can never forget all that you have done for us, your loyalty to Reuben, your enthusiasm in his cause, to say nothing of your many kindnesses to me. And, as to your having done your work badly, you wrong yourself grievously. I recognised in the evidence by which Reuben was cleared to-day how much you had done, in filling in the details, towards making the case complete and convincing. I shall always feel that we owe you a debt of the deepest gratitude, and so will Reuben, and so, perhaps, more than either of us, will someone else."

196

"And who is that?" I asked, though with no great interest. The gratitude of the family was a matter of little consequence to me.

"Well, it is no secret now," replied Juliet. "I mean the girl whom Reuben is going to marry. What is the matter, Dr. Jervis?" she added, in a tone of surprise.

We were passing through the gate that leads from the Embankment to Middle Temple Lane, and I had stopped dead under the archway, laying a detaining hand upon her arm and gazing at her in utter amazement.

"The girl that Reuben is going to marry!" I repeated. "Why, I had always taken it for granted that he was going to marry you."

"But I told you, most explicitly, that was not so!" she exclaimed with some impatience.

"I know you did," I admitted ruefully, "but I thought – well, I imagined that things had, perhaps, not gone quite smoothly and – "

"Did you suppose that if I had cared for a man, and that man had been under a cloud, I should have denied the relation or pretended that we were merely friends?" she demanded indignantly.

"I am sure you wouldn't," I replied hastily. "I was a fool, an idiot – by Jove, what an idiot I have been!"

"It was certainly very silly of you," she admitted, but there was a gentleness in her tone that took away all bitterness from the reproach.

"The reason of the secrecy was this," she continued, "they became engaged the very night before Reuben was arrested, and, when he heard of the charge against him, he insisted that no one should be told unless, and until, he was fully acquitted. I was the only person who was in their confidence, and as I was sworn to secrecy, of course I couldn't tell you, nor did I suppose that the matter would interest you. Why should it?"

"Imbecile that I am," I murmured. "If I had only known!"

"Well, if you *had* known," said she, "what difference could it have made to you?"

This question she asked without looking at me, but I noted that her cheek had grown a shade paler.

"Only this," I answered. "That I should have been spared many a day and night of needless self-reproach and misery."

"But why?" she asked, still keeping her face averted. "What had you to reproach yourself with?"

"A great deal," I answered, "if you consider my supposed position. If you think of me as the trusted agent of a man, helpless and deeply wronged – a man whose undeserved misfortunes made every demand upon chivalry and generosity. If you think of me as being called upon to protect and carry comfort to the woman whom I regarded as, virtually, that man's betrothed wife, and then if you think of me as proceeding straightway, before I had

197

known her twenty-four hours, to fall hopelessly in love with her myself, you will admit that I had something to reproach myself with."

She was still silent, rather pale and very thoughtful, and she seemed to breathe more quickly than usual.

"Of course," I continued, "you may say that it was my own look-out, that I had only to keep my own counsel, and no one would be any the worse. But there's the mischief of it. How can a man who is thinking of a woman morning, noon, and night, whose heart leaps at the sound of her coming, whose existence is a blank when she is away from him – a blank which he tries to fill by recalling, again and again, all that she has said and the tones of her voice, and the look that was in her eyes when she spoke – how can he help letting her see, sooner or later, that he cares for her? And if he does, when he has no right to, there is an end of duty and chivalry and even common honesty."

"Yes, I understand now," said Juliet softly. "Is this the way?" She tripped up the steps leading to Fountain Court and I followed cheerfully. Of course it was not the way, and we both knew it, but the place was silent and peaceful, and the plane-trees cast a pleasant shade on the gravelled court. I glanced at her as we walked slowly towards the fountain. The roses were mantling in her cheeks now and her eyes were cast down, but when she lifted them to me for an instant, I saw that they were shining and moist.

"Did you never guess?" I asked.

"Yes," she replied in a low voice, "I guessed, but – but then," she added shyly, "I thought I had guessed wrong."

We walked on for some little time without speaking again until we came to the further side of the fountain, where we stood listening to the quiet trickle of the water, and watching the sparrows as they took their bath on the rim of the basin. A little way off another group of sparrows had gathered with greedy joy around some fragments of bread that had been scattered abroad by the benevolent Templars, and hard by a more sentimentally-minded pigeon, unmindful of the crumbs and the marauding sparrows, puffed out his breast and strutted and curtsied before his mate with endearing gurgles.

Juliet had rested her hand on one of the little posts that support the chain by which the fountain is enclosed and I had laid my hand on hers. Presently she turned her hand over so that mine lay in its palm, and so we were standing hand-in-hand when an elderly gentleman, of dry and legal aspect, came up the steps and passed by the fountain. He looked at the pigeons and then he looked at us, and went his way smiling and shaking his head.

"Juliet," said I.

She looked up quickly with sparkling eyes and a frank smile that was yet a little shy, too.

"Yes."

"Why did he smile – that old gentleman – when he looked at us?"

"I can't imagine," she replied mendaciously.

"It was an approving smile," I said. "I think he was remembering his own spring-time and giving us his blessing."

"Perhaps he was," she agreed. "He looked a nice old thing." She gazed fondly at the retreating figure and then turned again to me. Her cheeks had grown pink enough by now, and in one of them a dimple displayed itself to great advantage in its rosy setting.

"Can you forgive me, dear, for my unutterable folly?" I asked presently, as she glanced up at me again.

"I am not sure," she answered. "It was dreadfully silly of you."

"But remember, Juliet, that I loved you with my whole heart – as I love you now and shall love you always."

"I can forgive you anything when you say that," she answered softly.

Here the voice of the distant Temple clock was heard uttering a polite protest. With infinite reluctance we turned away from the fountain, which sprinkled us with a parting benediction, and slowly retraced our steps to Middle Temple Lane and thence into Pump Court.

"You haven't said it, Juliet," I whispered, as we came through the archway into the silent, deserted court.

"Haven't I, dear?" she answered, "but you know it, don't you? You know I do."

"Yes, I know," I said, "and that knowledge is all my heart's desire."

She laid her hand in mine for a moment with a gentle pressure and then drew it away, and so we passed through into the cloisters.

The End

THE EYE OF
: OSIRIS :
BY R. AUSTIN FREEMAN

*A most dramatic and
surprising detective story
by the Author of · ·*
THE RED THUMB MARK

1911 Hodder & Stoughton Cover

also known as
The Vanishing Man

201

Some photographs of Nevill's Court
at the time of this narrative . . . .

Chapter I
The Vanishing Man

The school of St. Margaret's Hospital was fortunate in its lecturer on Medical Jurisprudence, or Forensic Medicine, as it is sometimes described. At some schools the lecturer on this subject is appointed apparently for the reason that he lacks the qualifications to lecture on any other. But with us it was very different – John Thorndyke was not only an enthusiast, a man of profound learning and great reputation, but he was an exceptional teacher, lively and fascinating in style and of endless resources. Every remarkable case that had ever been reported he appeared to have at his fingers' ends. Every fact – chemical, physical, biological, or even historical – that could in any way be twisted into a medico-legal significance, was pressed into his service, and his own varied and curious experiences seemed as inexhaustible as the widow's curse. One of his favorite devices for giving life and interest to a rather dry subject was that of analyzing and commenting upon contemporary cases as reported in the papers (always, of course, with a due regard to the legal and social proprieties), and it was in this way that I first became introduced to the astonishing series of events that was destined to exercise so great an influence on my own life.

The lecture which had just been concluded had dealt with the rather unsatisfactory subject of survivorship. Most of the students had left the theater, and the remainder had gathered round the lecturer's table to listen to the informal comments that Dr. Thorndyke was wont to deliver on these occasions in an easy, conversational manner, leaning against the edge of the table and apparently addressing his remarks to a stick of blackboard chalk that he held in his fingers.

"The problem of survivorship," he was saying, in reply to a question put by one of the students, "ordinarily occurs in cases where the bodies of the parties are producible, or where, at any rate, the occurrence of death and its approximate time are actually known. But an analogous difficulty may arise in a case where the body of one of the parties is not forthcoming, and the fact of death may have to be assumed on collateral evidence.

"Here, of course, the vital question to be settled is, what is the latest instant at which it is certain that this person was alive? And the settlement of that question may turn on some circumstance of the most trivial and insignificant kind. There is a case in this morning's paper which illustrates this. A gentleman has disappeared rather mysteriously. He was last seen by the servant of a relative at whose house he had called. Now, if this gentleman should never reappear, dead or alive, the question as to what was the latest moment at which he was certainly alive will turn upon the further question: 'Was he or was he not wearing a particular article of jewelry when he called at the relative's house?'"

He paused with a reflective eye bent upon the stump of chalk he still held. Then, noting the expectant interest with which we were regarding him, he resumed, "The circumstances in this case are very curious. In fact, they are highly mysterious, and if any legal issues should arise in respect of them, they are likely to yield some very remarkable complications. The gentleman who has disappeared, Mr. John Bellingham, is a man well known in archeological circles. He recently returned from Egypt, bringing with him a very fine collection of antiquities – some of which, by the way, he has presented to the British Museum, where they are now on view – and having made this presentation, he appears to have gone to Paris on business. I may mention that the gift consisted of a very fine mummy and a complete set of tomb-furniture. The latter, however, had not arrived from Egypt at the time when the missing man left for Paris, but the mummy was inspected on the fourteenth of October at Mr. Bellingham's house by Dr. Norbury of the British Museum, in the presence of the donor and his solicitor, and the latter was authorized to hand over the complete collection to the British Museum authorities when the tomb-furniture arrived, which he has since done.

"From Paris he seems to have returned on the twenty-third of November, and to have gone direct to Charing Cross to the house of a relative, a Mr. Hurst, who is a bachelor and lives at Eltham. He appeared at the house at twenty-minutes-past-five, and as Mr. Hurst had not yet come down from town and was not expected until a quarter-to-six, he explained who he was and said he would wait in the study and write some letters. The housemaid accordingly showed him into the study, furnished him with writing materials, and left him.

"At a quarter-to-six Mr. Hurst let himself in with his latchkey, and before the housemaid had time to speak to him he had passed through into the study and shut the door.

"At six o'clock, when the dinner bell was rung, Mr. Hurst entered the dining-room alone, and observing that the table was laid for two, asked the reason.

"'I thought Mr. Bellingham was staying to dinner, sir,' was the housemaid's reply.

"'Mr. Bellingham!' exclaimed the astonished host. 'I didn't know he was here. Why was I not told?'

"'I thought he was in the study with you, sir,' said the housemaid.

"On this a search was made for the visitor, with the result that he was nowhere to be found. He had disappeared without leaving a trace, and what made the incident more odd was that the housemaid was certain that he had not gone out by the front door. For since neither she nor the cook was acquainted with Mr. John Bellingham, she had remained the whole time either in the kitchen, which commanded a view of the front gate, or in the dining-room, which opened into the hall opposite the study door. The study itself has a French window opening on a narrow grass plot, across which is a side-gate that opens into an alley, and it appears that Mr. Bellingham must have made his exit by this rather eccentric route. At any rate – and this is the important fact – he was not in the house, and no one had seen him leave it.

"After a hasty meal Mr. Hurst returned to town and called at the office of Mr. Bellingham's solicitor and confidential agent, a Mr. Jellicoe, and mentioned the matter to him. Mr. Jellicoe knew nothing of his client's return from Paris, and the two men at once took the train down to Woodford, where the missing man's brother, Mr. Godfrey Bellingham, lives. The servant who admitted them said that Mr. Godfrey was not at home, but that his daughter was in the library, which is a detached building situated in a shrubbery beyond the garden at the back of the house. Here the two men found, not only Miss Bellingham, but also her father, who had come in by the back gate.

"Mr. Godfrey and his daughter listened to Mr. Hurst's story with the greatest surprise, and assured him that they had neither seen nor heard anything of John Bellingham.

"Presently the party left the library to walk up to the house, but only a few feet from the library door Mr. Jellicoe noticed an object lying in the grass and pointed it out to Mr. Godfrey.

"The latter picked it up, and they all recognized it as a scarab which Mr. John Bellingham had been accustomed to wear suspended from his watch-chain. There was no mistaking it. It was a very fine scarab of the eighteenth dynasty fashioned of lapis lazuli and engraved with the cartouche of Amenhotep III. It had been suspended by a gold ring fastened to a wire which passed through the suspension hole, and the ring, though broken, was still in position.

"This discovery of course only added to the mystery, which was still further increased when, on inquiry, a suit-case bearing the initials *J.B.* was found to be unclaimed in the cloak-room at Charing Cross. Reference to the counterfoil of the ticket-book showed that it had been deposited about the time of the arrival of the Continental Express on the twenty-third of November, so that its owner must have gone straight on to Eltham.

209

"That is how the affair stands at present, and, should the missing man never reappear or should his body never be found, the question, as you see, which will be required to be settled is, 'What is the exact time and place, when and where, he was last known to be alive!' As to the place, the importance of the issues involved in that question is obvious and we need not consider it. But the question of time has another kind of significance. Cases have occurred, as I pointed out in the lecture, in which proof of survivorship by less than a minute has secured succession to property. Now, the missing man was last seen alive at Mr. Hurst's house at twenty-minutes-past-five on the twenty-third of November. But he appears to have visited his brother's house at Woodford, and, since nobody saw him at that house, it is at present uncertain whether he went there before calling on Mr. Hurst. If he went there first, then twenty-minutes-past-five on the evening of the twenty-third is the latest moment at which he is known to have been alive, but if he went there after, there would have to be added to this time the shortest time possible in which he could travel from the one house to the other.

"But the question as to which house he visited first hinges on the scarab. If he was wearing the scarab when he arrived at Mr. Hurst's house, it would be certain that he went there first, but if it was not then on his watch-chain, a probability would be established that he went first to Woodford. Thus, you see, a question which may conceivably become of the most vital moment in determining the succession of property turns on the observation or non-observation by this housemaid of an apparently trivial and insignificant fact."

"Has the servant made any statement on this subject, sir?" I ventured to inquire.

"Apparently not," replied Dr. Thorndyke. "At any rate, there is no reference to any such statement in the newspaper report, though otherwise, the case is reported in great detail. Indeed, the wealth of detail, including plans of the two houses, is quite remarkable and well worth noting as being in itself a fact of considerable interest."

"In what respect, sir, is it of interest?" one of the students asked.

"Ah," replied Dr. Thorndyke, "I think I must leave you to consider that question yourself. This is an untried case, and we mustn't make free with the actions and motives of individuals."

"Does the paper give any description of the missing man, sir?" I asked.

"Yes, quite an exhaustive description. Indeed, it is exhaustive to the verge of impropriety, considering that the man may turn up alive and well at any moment. It seems that he has an old Pott's fracture of the left ankle, a linear, longitudinal scar on each knee – origin not stated, but easily guessed at – and that he has tattooed on his chest in vermilion a very finely and distinctly executed representation of the symbolical Eye of Osiris – or Horus or Ra, as the different authorities have it. There certainly ought to be no difficulty in identifying the body. But we hope that it will not come to that.

"And now I must really be running away, and so must you, but I would advise you all to get copies of the paper and file them when you have read the remarkably full details. It is a most curious case, and it is highly probable that we shall hear of it again. Good afternoon, gentlemen."

Dr. Thorndyke's advice appealed to all who heard it, for medical jurisprudence was a live subject at St. Margaret's, and all of us were keenly interested in it. As a result, we sallied forth in a body to the nearest news-vendor's, and, having each provided himself with a copy of *The Daily Telegraph*, adjourned together to the Common room to devour the report and thereafter to discuss the bearings of the case, unhampered by those considerations of delicacy that afflicted our more squeamish and scrupulous teacher.

211

Chapter II
The Eavesdropper

It is one of the canons of correct conduct, scrupulously adhered to (when convenient) by all well-bred persons, that an acquaintance should be initiated by a proper introduction. To this salutary rule, which I have disregarded to the extent of an entire chapter, I now hasten to conform, and the more so inasmuch as nearly two years have passed since my first informal appearance.

Permit me then, to introduce Paul Berkeley, M.B., etc., recently – very recently – qualified, faultlessly attired in the professional frock-coat and tall hat, and, at the moment of introduction, navigating with anxious care a perilous strait between a row of well-filled coal-sacks and a colossal tray piled high with kidney potatoes.

The passage of this strait landed me on the terra firma of Fleur-de-Lys Court, where I halted for a moment to consult my visiting list. There was only one more patient for me to see this morning, and he lived at 49, Nevill's Court, wherever that might be. I turned for information to the presiding deity of the coal shop.

"Can you direct me, Mrs. Jablett, to Nevill's Court?"

She could and she did, grasping me confidentially by the arm (the mark remained on my sleeve for weeks) and pointing a shaking forefinger at the dead wall ahead. "Nevill's Court," said Mrs. Jablett, "is a alley, and you goes into it through a archway. It turns out on Fetter Lane on the right 'and as you goes up, oppersight Bream's Buildings."

I thanked Mrs. Jablett and went on my way, glad that the morning round was nearly finished, and vaguely conscious of a growing appetite and of a desire to wash in hot water.

The practice which I was conducting was not my own. It belonged to poor Dick Barnard, an old St. Margaret's man of irrepressible spirits and indifferent physique, who had started only the day before for a trip down the Mediterranean on board a tramp engaged in the currant trade, and this, my second morning's round, was in some sort a voyage of geographical discovery.

I walked on briskly up Fetter Lane until a narrow arched opening, bearing the superscription "Nevill's Court," arrested my steps, and here I turned to encounter one of those surprises that lie in wait for the traveler in London by-ways. Expecting to find the gray squalor of the ordinary London court, I looked out from under the shadow of the arch past a row of decent little shops through a vista full of light and color – a vista of ancient, warm-toned roofs and walls relieved by sunlit foliage. In the heart of London a tree is always a delightful surprise, but here were not only trees, but bushes and even flowers. The narrow footway was bordered by little gardens, which, with their wooden palings and well-kept shrubs, gave to the place an air of quaint and sober rusticity, and even as I entered, a bevy of workgirls, with gaily-colored blouses and hair aflame in the sunlight, brightened up the quiet background like the wild flowers that spangle a summer hedgerow.

In one of the gardens I noticed that the little paths were paved with what looked like circular tiles, but which, on inspection, I found to be old-fashioned stone ink-bottles, buried bottom upwards, and I was meditating upon the quaint conceit of the forgotten scrivener who had thus adorned his habitation – a law-writer perhaps or an author, or perchance even a poet – when I perceived the number that I was seeking inscribed on a shabby door in a high wall. There was no bell or knocker, so, lifting the latch, I pushed the door open and entered.

But if the court itself had been a surprise, this was a positive wonder, a dream. Here, within earshot of the rumble of Fleet Street, I was in an old-fashioned garden enclosed by high walls and, now that the gate was shut, cut off from all sight and knowledge of the urban world that seethed without. I stood and gazed in delighted astonishment. Sun-gilded trees and flower beds gay with blossoms. Lupins, snapdragons, nasturtiums, spiry foxgloves, and mighty hollyhocks formed the foreground, over which a pair of sulphur-tinted butterflies flitted, unmindful of a buxom and miraculously clean white cat which pursued them, dancing across the borders and clapping her snowy paws fruitlessly in mid-air. And the background was no less wonderful, a grand old house, dark-eaved and venerable, that must have looked down on this garden when ruffled dandies were borne in sedan chairs through the court, and gentle Izaak Walton, stealing forth from his shop in Fleet Street, strolled up Fetter Lane to "go a-angling" at Temple Mills.

So overpowered was I by this unexpected vision that my hand was on the bottom knob of a row of bell-pulls before I recollected myself, and it was not until a most infernal jangling from within recalled me to my business that I observed underneath it a small brass plate inscribed "Miss Oman."

The door opened with some suddenness and a short, middle-aged woman surveyed me hungrily.

"Have I rung the wrong bell?" I asked – foolishly enough, I must admit.

"How can I tell?" she demanded. "I expect you have. It's the sort of thing a man would do – ring the wrong bell and then say he's sorry."

"I didn't go as far as that," I retorted. "It seems to have had the desired effect, and I've made your acquaintance into the bargain."

"Whom do you want to see?" she asked.

"Mr. Bellingham."

"Are you the doctor?"

"I'm *a* doctor."

"Follow me upstairs," said Miss Oman, "and don't tread on the paint."

I crossed the spacious hall, and preceded by my conductress, ascended a noble oak staircase, treading carefully on a ribbon of matting that ran up the middle. On the first-floor landing Miss Oman opened a door and, pointing to the room, said, "Go in there and wait. I'll tell her you're here."

"I said *Mr.* Bellingham – " I began, but the door slammed on me, and Miss Oman's footsteps retreated rapidly down the stairs.

It was at once obvious to me that I was in a very awkward position. The room into which I had been shown communicated with another, and though the door of communication was shut, I was unpleasantly aware of a conversation that was taking place in the adjoining room. At first, indeed, only a vague mutter, with a few disjointed phrases, came through the door, but suddenly an angry voice rang out clear and painfully distinct.

"Yes, I did! And I say it again. Bribery! Collusion! That's what it amounts to. You want to square me!"

"Nothing of the kind, Godfrey," was the reply in a lower tone, but at this point I coughed emphatically and moved a chair, and the voices subsided once more into an indistinct murmur.

To distract my attention from my unseen neighbors I glanced curiously about the room and speculated upon the personalities of its occupants. A very curious room it was, with its pathetic suggestion of decayed splendor and old-world dignity, a room full of interest and character and of contrasts and perplexing contradictions. For the most part it spoke of unmistakable though decent poverty. It was nearly bare of furniture, and what little there was was of the cheapest – a small kitchen table and three Windsor chairs (two of them with arms), a threadbare string carpet on the floor, and a cheap cotton cloth on the table. These, with a set of bookshelves, frankly constructed of grocer's boxes, formed the entire suite. And yet, despite its poverty, the place exhaled an air of homely if rather ascetic comfort, and the taste was irreproachable. The quiet russet of the table-cloth struck a pleasant harmony with the subdued bluish green of the worn carpet. The Windsor chairs and the legs of the table had been

214

carefully denuded of their glaring varnish and stained a sober brown, and the austerity of the whole was relieved by a ginger jar filled with fresh-cut flowers and set in the middle of the table.

But the contrasts of which I have spoken were most singular and puzzling. There were the bookshelves, for instance, home made and stained at the cost of a few pence, but filled with recent and costly new works on archeology and ancient art. There were the objects on the mantelpiece: A facsimile in bronze – not bronze plaster – of the beautiful head of Hypnos and a pair of fine Ushabti figures. There were the decorations of the walls, a number of etchings – signed proofs, every one of them – of Oriental subjects, and a splendid facsimile reproduction of an Egyptian papyrus. It was incongruous in the extreme, this mingling of costly refinements with the barest and shabbiest necessaries of life, of fastidious culture with manifest poverty. I could make nothing of it. What manner of man, I wondered, was this new patient of mine? Was he a miser, hiding himself and his wealth in this obscure court? An eccentric *savant*? A philosopher? Or – more probably – a crank? But at this point my meditations were interrupted by the voice from the adjoining room, once more raised in anger.

"But I say that you *are* making an accusation! You are implying that I made away with him."

"Not at all," was the reply, "but I repeat that it is your business to ascertain what has become of him. The responsibility rests upon you."

"Upon me!" rejoined the first voice. "And what about you? Your position is a pretty fishy one if it comes to that."

"What!" roared the other. "Do you insinuate that I murdered my own brother?"

During this amazing colloquy I had stood gaping with sheer astonishment. Suddenly I recollected myself, and dropping into a chair, set my elbows on my knees and clapped my hands over my ears, and thus I must have remained for a full minute when I became aware of the closing of a door behind me.

I sprang to my feet and turned in some embarrassment (for I must have looked unspeakably ridiculous) to confront the somber figure of a rather tall and strikingly handsome girl, who, as she stood with her hand on the knob of the door, saluted me with a formal bow. In an instantaneous glance I noted how perfectly she matched her strange surroundings. Black-robed, black-haired, with black-gray eyes and a grave sad face of ivory pallor, she stood, like one of old Terborch's portraits, a harmony in tones so low as to be but one step removed from monochrome. Obviously a lady in spite of the worn and rusty dress, and something in the poise of the head

215

and the set of the straight brows hinted at a spirit that adversity had hardened rather than broken.

"I must ask you to forgive me for keeping you waiting," she said, and as she spoke a certain softening at the corners of the austere mouth reminded me of the absurd position in which she had found me.

I murmured that the trifling delay was of no consequence whatever. That I had, in fact, been rather glad of the rest, and I was beginning somewhat vaguely to approach the subject of the invalid when the voice from the adjoining room again broke forth with hideous distinctness.

"I tell you I'll do nothing of the kind! Why, confound you, it's nothing less than a conspiracy that you're proposing!"

Miss Bellingham – as I assumed her to be – stepped quickly across the floor, flushing angrily, as well she might, but, as she reached the door, it flew open and a small, spruce, middle-aged man burst into the room.

"Your father is mad, Ruth!" he exclaimed, "absolutely stark mad! And I refuse to hold any further communication with him."

"The present interview was not of his seeking," Miss Bellingham replied coldly.

"No, it was not," was the wrathful rejoinder, "it was my mistaken generosity. But there – what is the use of talking? I've done my best for you and I'll do no more. Don't trouble to let me out. I can find my way. Good-morning." With a stiff bow and a quick glance at me, the speaker strode out of the room, banging the door after him.

"I must apologize for this extraordinary reception," said Miss Bellingham, "but I believe medical men are not easily astonished. I will introduce you to your patient now." She opened the door and, as I followed her into the adjoining room, she said, "Here is another visitor for you, dear. Doctor – "

"Berkeley," said I. "I am acting for my friend Doctor Barnard."

The invalid, a fine-looking man of about fifty-five, who sat propped up in bed with a pile of pillows, held out an excessively shaky hand, which I grasped cordially, making a mental note of the tremor.

"How do you do, sir?" said Mr. Bellingham. "I hope Doctor Barnard is not ill."

"Oh, no," I answered, "he has gone for a trip down the Mediterranean on a currant ship. The chance occurred rather suddenly, and I bustled him off before he had time to change his mind. Hence my rather unceremonious appearance, which I hope you will forgive."

"Not at all," was the hearty response. "I'm delighted to hear that you sent him off. He wanted a holiday, poor man. And I am delighted to make your acquaintance, too."

"It is very good of you," I said, whereupon he bowed as gracefully as a man may who is propped up in bed with a heap of pillows, and having thus exchanged broadsides of civility, so to speak, we – or, at least, I – proceeded to business.

"How long have you been laid up?" I asked cautiously, not wishing to make too evident the fact that my principal had given me no information respecting his case.

"A week to-day," he replied. "The *fons et origo mali* was a hansom-cab which upset me opposite the Law Courts – sent me sprawling in the middle of the road. My own fault, of course – at least, the cabby said so, and I suppose he knew. But that was no consolation to me."

"Were you hurt much?"

"No, not really, but the fall bruised my knee rather badly and gave me a deuce of a shake up. I'm too old for that sort of thing, you know."

"Most people are," said I.

"True, but you can take a cropper more gracefully at twenty than at fifty-five. However, the knee is getting on quite well – you shall see it presently – and you observe that I am giving it complete rest. But that isn't the whole of the trouble or the worst of it. It's my confounded nerves. I'm as irritable as the devil and as nervous as a cat. And I can't get a decent night's rest."

I recalled the tremulous hand that he had offered me. He did not look like a drinker, but still –

"Do you smoke much?" I inquired diplomatically.

He looked at me slyly and chuckled. "That's a very delicate way to approach the subject, Doctor," he said. "No, I don't smoke much, and I don't crook my little finger. I saw you look at my shaky hand just now – oh, it's all right, I'm not offended. It's a doctor's business to keep his eyelids lifting. But my hand is steady enough as a rule, when I'm not upset, but the least excitement sets me shaking like a jelly. And the fact is that I have just had a deucedly unpleasant interview – "

"I think," Miss Bellingham interrupted, "Doctor Berkeley and, indeed, the neighborhood at large, are aware of the fact."

Mr. Bellingham laughed rather shamefacedly. "I'm afraid I did lose my temper," he said, "but I am an impulsive old fellow, Doctor, and when I'm put out I'm apt to speak my mind – a little too bluntly perhaps."

"And audibly," his daughter added. "Do you know that Doctor Berkeley was reduced to the necessity of stopping his ears?" She glanced at me as she spoke, with something like a twinkle in her solemn gray eyes.

"Did I shout?" Mr. Bellingham asked, not very contritely, I thought, though he added, "I'm very sorry, my dear, but it won't happen again. I think we've seen the last of that good gentleman."

"I am sure I hope so," she rejoined, adding, "And now I will leave you to your talk. I shall be in the next room if you should want me."

I opened the door for her, and when she had passed out with a stiff little bow I seated myself by the bedside and resumed the consultation. It was evidently a case of nervous breakdown, to which the cab accident had, no doubt, contributed. As to the other antecedents, they were of no concern of mine, though Mr. Bellingham seemed to think otherwise, for he resumed, "That cab business was the last straw, you know, and it finished me off, but I have been going down the hill for a long time. I've had a lot of trouble during the last two years. But I suppose I oughtn't to pester you with the details of my personal affairs."

"Anything that bears on your present state of health is of interest to me if you don't mind telling it," I said.

"Mind!" he exclaimed. "Did you ever meet an invalid who didn't enjoy talking about his own health? It's the listener who minds, as a rule."

"Well, the present listener doesn't," I said.

"Then," said Mr. Bellingham, "I'll treat myself to the luxury of telling you all my troubles. I don't often get the chance of a confidential grumble to a responsible man of my own class. And I really have some excuses for railing at Fortune, as you will agree when I tell you that, a couple of years ago, I went to bed one night a gentleman of independent means and excellent prospects and woke up in the morning to find myself practically a beggar. Not a cheerful experience that, you know, at my time of life, eh?"

"No," I agreed, "nor at any other."

"And that was not all," he continued, "for at the same moment I lost my brother, my dearest, kindest friend. He disappeared – vanished off the face of the earth, but perhaps you have heard of the affair. The confounded papers were full of it at the time."

He paused abruptly, noticing, no doubt, a sudden change in my face. Of course I recollected the case now. Indeed, ever since I had entered the house some chord of memory had been faintly vibrating, and now his last words had struck out the full note.

"Yes," I said, "I remember the incident, though I don't suppose I should but for the fact that our lecturer on medical jurisprudence drew my attention to it."

"Indeed," said Mr. Bellingham, rather uneasily, as I fancied. "What did he say about it?"

"He referred to it as a case that was calculated to give rise to some very pretty legal complications."

"By Jove!" exclaimed Bellingham, "that man was a prophet! Legal complications, indeed! But I'll be bound he never guessed at the sort of infernal tangle that has actually gathered round the affair. By the way, what was his name?"

"Thorndyke," I replied. "Doctor John Thorndyke."

"Thorndyke," Mr. Bellingham repeated in a musing, retrospective tone. "I seem to remember the name. Yes, of course. I have heard a legal friend of mine, a Mr. Marchmont, speak of him in reference to the case of a man whom I knew slightly years ago – a certain Jeffrey Blackmore, who also disappeared very mysteriously. I remember now that Dr. Thorndyke unraveled that case with most remarkable ingenuity."

"I daresay he would be very much interested to hear about your case," I suggested.

"I daresay he would," was the reply, "but one can't take up a professional man's time for nothing, and I couldn't afford to pay him. And that reminds me that I'm taking up your time by gossiping about purely personal affairs."

"My morning round is finished," said I, "and, moreover, your personal affairs are highly interesting. I suppose I mustn't ask what is the nature of the legal entanglement?"

"Not unless you are prepared to stay here for the rest of the day and go home a raving lunatic. But I'll tell you this much: The trouble is about my poor brother's will. In the first place it can't be administered because there is not sufficient evidence that my brother is dead, and in the second place, if it could, all the property would go to people who were never intended to benefit. The will itself is the most diabolically exasperating document that was ever produced by the perverted ingenuity of a wrongheaded man. That's all. Will you have a look at my knee?"

As Mr. Bellingham's explanation (delivered in a rapid *crescendo* and ending almost in a shout) had left him purple-faced and trembling, I thought it best to bring our talk to an end. Accordingly I proceeded to inspect the injured knee, which was now nearly well, and to overhaul my patient generally, and having given him detailed instructions as to his general conduct, I rose and took my leave.

"And remember," I said as I shook his hand, "No tobacco, no coffee, no excitement of any kind. Lead a quiet, bovine life."

"That's all very well," he grumbled, "but supposing people come here and excite me?"

"Disregard them," said I, "and read *Whitaker's Almanack*." And with this parting advice I passed out into the other room.

Miss Bellingham was seated at the table with a pile of blue-covered notebooks before her, two of which were open, displaying pages closely written in a small, neat handwriting. She rose as I entered and looked at me inquiringly.

"I heard you advising my father to read *Whitaker's Almanack*," she said. "Was that a curative measure?"

"Entirely," I replied. "I recommended it for its medicinal virtues, as an antidote to mental excitement."

She smiled faintly. "It certainly is not a highly emotional book," she said, and then asked, "Have you any other instructions to give?"

"Well, I might give the conventional advice – to maintain a cheerful outlook and avoid worry, but I don't suppose you would find it very helpful."

"No," she answered bitterly, "it is a counsel of perfection. People in our position are not a very cheerful class, I'm afraid, but still they don't seek out worries from sheer perverseness. The worries come unsought. But, of course, you can't enter into that."

"I can't give any practical help, I fear, though I do sincerely hope that you father's affairs will straighten themselves out soon."

She thanked me for my good wishes and accompanied me down to the street door, where, with a bow and a rather stiff handshake, she gave me my *congé*.

Very ungratefully the noise of Fetter Lane smote on my ears as I came out through the archway, and very squalid and unrestful the little street looked when contrasted with the dignity and monastic quiet of the old garden. As to the surgery, with its oilcloth floor and walls made hideous with gaudy insurance show-cards in sham gilt frames, its aspect was so revolting that I flew to the day-book for distraction, and was still busily entering the morning's visits when the bottle-boy, Adolphus, entered stealthily to announce lunch.

Chapter III
John Thorndyke

That the character of an individual tends to be reflected in his dress is a fact familiar to the least observant. That the observation is equally applicable to aggregates of men is less familiar, but equally true. Do not the members of fighting professions, even to this day, deck themselves in feathers, in gaudy colors and gilded ornaments, after the manner of the African war-chief or the Redskin "brave," and thereby indicate the place of war in modern civilization? Does not the Church of Rome send her priests to the altar in habiliments that were fashionable before the fall of the Roman Empire, in token of her immovable conservatism? And, lastly, does not the Law, lumbering on in the wake of progress, symbolize its subjection to precedent by head-gear reminiscent of the good days of Queen Anne?

I should apologize for intruding upon the reader these somewhat trite reflections, which were set going by the quaint stock-in-trade of the wig-maker's shop in the cloisters of the Inner Temple, whither I strayed on a sultry afternoon in quest of shade and quiet. I had halted opposite the little shop window, and, with my eyes bent dreamily on the row of wigs, was pursuing the above train of thought when I was startled by a deep voice saying softly in my ear, "I'd have the full-bottomed one if I were you."

I turned swiftly and rather fiercely, and looked into the face of my old friend and fellow student, Jervis, behind whom, regarding us with a sedate smile, stood my former teacher, Dr. John Thorndyke. Both men greeted me with a warmth that I felt to be very flattering, for Thorndyke was quite a great personage, and even Jervis was several years my academic senior.

"You are coming in to have a cup of tea with us, I hope," said Thorndyke, and as I assented gladly, he took my arm and led me across the court in the direction of the Treasury.

"But why that hungry gaze at those forensic vanities, Berkeley?" he asked. "Are you thinking of following my example and Jervis's – deserting the bedside for the Bar?"

"What! Has Jervis gone in for the law?" I exclaimed.

"Bless you, yes!" replied Jervis. "I have become parasitical on Thorndyke! 'The big fleas have little fleas,' you know. I am the additional fraction trailing after the whole number in the rear of a decimal point."

"Don't you believe him, Berkeley," interposed Thorndyke. "He is the brains of the firm. I supply the respectability and moral worth. But you haven't answered my question. What are you doing here on a summer afternoon staring into a wig-maker's window?"

"I am Barnard's *locum*. He is in practise in Fetter Lane."

"I know," said Thorndyke, "we meet him occasionally, and very pale and peaky he has been looking of late. Is he taking a holiday?"

"Yes. He has gone for a trip to the Isles of Greece in a currant ship."

"Then," said Jervis, "you are actually a local G.P. I thought you were looking beastly respectable."

"And judging from your leisured manner when we encountered you," added Thorndyke, "the practise is not a strenuous one. I suppose it is entirely local?"

"Yes," I replied. "The patients mostly live in the small streets and courts within a half-mile radius of the surgery, and the abodes of some of them are pretty squalid. Oh! And that reminds me of a very strange coincidence. It will interest you, I think."

"Life is made up of strange coincidences," said Thorndyke. "Nobody but a reviewer of novels is ever really surprised at a coincidence. But what is yours?"

"It is connected with a case that you mentioned to us at the hospital about two years ago, the case of a man who disappeared under rather mysterious circumstances. Do you remember it? The man's name was Bellingham."

"The Egyptologist? Yes, I remember the case quite well. What about it?"

"The brother is a patient of mine. He is living in Nevill's Court with his daughter, and they seem to be as poor as church mice."

"Really," said Thorndyke, "this is quite interesting. They must have come down in the world rather suddenly. If I remember rightly, the brother was living in a house of some pretentions standing in its own grounds."

"Yes, that is so. I see you recollect all about the case."

"My dear fellow," said Jervis, "Thorndyke never forgets a likely case. He is a sort of medico-legal camel. He gulps down the raw facts from the newspapers or elsewhere, and then, in his leisure moments, he calmly regurgitates them and has a quiet chew at them. It is a quaint habit. A case crops up in the papers or in one of the courts, and Thorndyke swallows it whole. Then it lapses and every one forgets it. A year or two later it crops up in a new form, and, to your astonishment, you find that Thorndyke has got it all cut and dried. He has been ruminating on it periodically in the interval.

"You notice," said Thorndyke, "that my learned friend is pleased to indulge in mixed metaphors. But his statement is substantially true, though obscurely worded. You must tell us more about the Bellinghams when we have fortified you with a cup of tea."

Our talk had brought us to Thorndyke's chambers, which were on the first floor of No. 5A, King's Bench Walk, and as we entered the fine, spacious, paneled room we found a small, elderly man, neatly dressed in black, setting out the tea-service on the table. I glanced at him with some curiosity. He hardly looked like a servant, in spite of his neat, black clothes. In fact, his appearance was rather puzzling, for while his quiet dignity and his serious intelligent face suggested some kind of professional man, his neat, capable hands were those of a skilled mechanic.

Thorndyke surveyed the tea-tray thoughtfully and then looked at his retainer. "I see you have put three teacups, Polton," he said. "Now, how did you know I was bringing someone in to tea?"

The little man smiled a quaint, crinkly smile of gratification as he explained, "I happened to look out of the laboratory window as you turned the corner, sir."

"How disappointingly simple," said Jervis. "We were hoping for something abstruse and telepathic."

"Simplicity is the soul of efficiency, sir," replied Polton as he checked the tea-service to make sure that nothing was forgotten, and with this remarkable aphorism he silently evaporated.

"To return to the Bellingham case," said Thorndyke, when he had poured out the tea. "Have you picked up any facts relating to the parties – and facts, I mean, of course, that it would be proper for you to mention?"

"I have learned one or two things that there is no harm in repeating. For instance, I gather that Godfrey Bellingham – my patient – lost all his property quite suddenly about the time of the disappearance."

"That is really odd," said Thorndyke. "The opposite condition would be quite understandable, but one doesn't see exactly how this can have happened, unless there was an allowance of some sort."

"No, that was what struck me. But there seem to be some queer features in the case, and the legal position is evidently getting complicated. There is a will, for example, which is giving trouble."

"They will hardly be able to administer the will without either proof or presumption of death," Thorndyke remarked.

"Exactly. That's one of the difficulties. Another is that there seems to be some fatal defect in the drafting of the will itself. I don't know what it is, but I expect I shall hear sooner or later. By the way, I mentioned the interest that you have taken in the case, and I think Bellingham would have liked to consult you, but, of course, the poor devil has no money."

"That is awkward for him if the other interested parties have. There will probably be legal proceedings of some kind, and as the law takes no account of poverty, he is likely to go to the wall. He ought to have advice of some sort."

"I don't see how he is to get it," said I.

"Neither do I," Thorndyke admitted. "There are no hospitals for impecunious litigants. It is assumed that only persons of means have a right to go to law. Of course, if we knew the man and the circumstances we might be able to help him, but for all we know to the contrary, he may be an arrant scoundrel."

I had recalled the strange conversation that I had overheard, and wondered what Thorndyke would have thought of it if it had been allowable for me to repeat it. Obviously it was not, however, and I could only give my own impressions.

"He doesn't strike me as that," I said, "but of course, one never knows. Personally, he impressed me rather favorably, which is more than the other man did."

"What other man?" asked Thorndyke.

"There was another man in the case, wasn't there? I forget his name. I saw him at the house and didn't much like the look of him. I suspect he's putting some sort of pressure on Bellingham."

"Berkeley knows more about this than he's telling us," said Jervis. "Let us look up the report and see who this stranger is." He took down from a shelf a large volume of newspaper cuttings and laid it on the table.

"You see," said he, as he ran his finger down the index. "Thorndyke files all the cases that are likely to come to something, and I know he had expectations regarding this one. I fancy he had some ghoulish hope that the missing gentleman's head might turn up in somebody's dust-bin. Here we are. The other man's name is Hurst. He is apparently a cousin, and it was at his house the missing man was last seen alive."

"So you think Mr. Hurst is moving in the matter?" said Thorndyke, when he had glanced over the report.

"That is my impression," I replied, "though I really know nothing about it."

"Well," said Thorndyke, "if you should learn what is being done and should have permission to speak of it, I shall be very interested to hear how the case progresses and if an unofficial opinion on any point would be of service, I think there would be no harm in giving it."

"It would certainly be of great value if the other parties are taking professional advice," I said, and then, after a pause, I asked, "Have you given this case much consideration?"

Thorndyke reflected. "No," he said, "I can't say that I have. I turned it over rather carefully when the report first appeared, and I have speculated on it occasionally since. It is my habit, as Jervis was telling you, to utilize odd moments of leisure (such as a railway journey, for instance) by constructing theories to account for the facts of such obscure cases as have come to my notice. It is a useful habit, I think, for, apart from the mental exercise and experience that one gains from it, an appreciable portion of these cases ultimately comes into my hands, and then the previous consideration of them is so much time gained."

"Have you formed any theory to account for the facts in this case?" I asked.

"Yes, I have several theories, one of which I especially favor, and I am awaiting with great interest such new facts as may indicate to me which of these theories is probably the correct one."

"It's no use your trying to pump him, Berkeley," said Jervis. "He is fitted with an information valve that opens inward. You can pour in as much as you like, but you can't get any out."

Thorndyke chuckled. "My learned friend is, in the main, correct," he said. "You see, I may be called upon any day to advise on this case, in which event I should feel remarkably foolish if I had already expounded my views in detail. But I should like to hear what you and Jervis make of the case as reported in the newspapers."

"There now," exclaimed Jervis, "what did I tell you? He wants to suck our brains."

"As far as my brain is concerned," I said, "the process of suction isn't likely to yield much except a vacuum, so I will resign in favor of you. You are a full-blown lawyer, whereas I am only a simple G.P."

Jervis filled his pipe with deliberate care and lighted it. Then, blowing a slender stream of smoke into the air, he said, "If you want to know what I make of the case from that report, I can tell you in one word – nothing. Every road seems to end in a cul-de-sac."

"Oh, come!" said Thorndyke, "this is mere laziness. Berkeley wants to witness a display of your forensic wisdom. A learned counsel may be in a fog – he very often is – but he doesn't state the fact baldly. He wraps it up in a decent verbal disguise. Tell us how you arrive at your conclusion. Show us that you have really weighed the facts."

"Very well," said Jervis, "I will give you a masterly analysis of the case – leading to nothing." He continued to puff at his pipe for a time with slight embarrassment, as I thought – and I fully sympathized with him. Finally he blew a little cloud and commenced, "The position appears to be this, Here is a man seen to enter a certain house, who is shown into a certain room, and shut in. He is not seen to come out, and yet, when the room is next entered, it is found to be empty, and that man is never seen again, alive or dead. That is a pretty tough beginning.

226

"Now, it is evident that one of three things must have happened. Either he must have remained in that room, or at least in that house, alive, or he must have died, naturally or otherwise, and his body have been concealed, or he must have left the house unobserved. Let us take the first case. This affair happened nearly two years ago. Now, he couldn't have remained alive in the house for two years. He would have been noticed. The servants, for instance, when cleaning out the rooms, would have observed him."

Here Thorndyke interposed with an indulgent smile at his junior, "My learned friend is treating the inquiry with unbecoming levity. We accept the conclusion that the man did not remain in the house alive."

"Very well. Then did he remain in it dead? Apparently not. The report says that as soon as the man was missed, Hurst and the servants together searched the house thoroughly. But there had been no time or opportunity to dispose of the body, whence the only possible conclusion is that the body was not there. Moreover, if we admit the possibility of his having been murdered – for that is what concealment of the body would imply – there is the question: 'Who could have murdered him?' Not the servants, obviously, and as to Hurst – well, of course, we don't know what his relations with the missing man may have been – at least, I don't."

"Neither do I," said Thorndyke. "I know nothing beyond what is in the newspaper report and what Berkeley has told us."

"Then we know nothing. He may have had a motive for murdering the man or he may not. The point is that he doesn't seem to have had the opportunity. Even if we suppose that he managed to conceal the body temporarily, still there was the final disposal of it. He couldn't have buried it in the garden with the servants about. Neither could he have burned it. The only conceivable method by which he could have got rid of it would have been that of cutting it up into fragments and burying the dismembered parts in some secluded spots or dropping them into ponds or rivers. But no remains of the kind have been found, as some of them probably would have been by now, so that there is nothing to support this suggestion. Indeed, the idea of murder, in this house at least, seems to be excluded by the search that was made the instant the man was missed.

"Then to take the third alternative: Did he leave the house unobserved? Well, it is not impossible, but it would be a queer thing to do. He may have been an impulsive or eccentric man. We can't say. We know nothing about him. But two years have elapsed and he has never turned up, so that if he left the house secretly he must have gone into hiding and be hiding still. Of course, he may have been the sort of lunatic who would behave in that manner or he may not. We have no information as to his personal character.

227

"Then there is the complication of the scarab that was picked up in the grounds of his brother's house at Woodford. That seems to show that he visited that house at some time. But no one admits having seen him there, and it is uncertain, therefore, whether he went first to his brother's house or to Hurst's. If he was wearing the scarab when he arrived at the Eltham house, he must have left that house unobserved and gone to Woodford, but if he was not wearing it he probably went from Woodford to Eltham, and there finally disappeared. As to whether he was or was not wearing the scarab when he was last seen alive by Hurst's housemaid, there is at present no evidence.

"If he went to his brother's house *after* his visit to Hurst, the disappearance is more understandable if we don't mind flinging accusations of murder about rather casually, for the disposal of the body would be much less difficult in that case. Apparently no one saw him enter the house, and, if he did enter, it was by a back gate which communicated with the library – a separate building some distance from the house. In that case it would have been physically possible for the Bellinghams to have made away with him. There was plenty of time to dispose of the body unobserved – temporarily, at any rate. Nobody had seen him come to the house, and nobody knew that he was there – if he was there, and apparently no search was made either at the time or afterward. In fact, if it could be shown that the missing man left Hurst's house alive, or that he was wearing the scarab when he arrived there, things would look rather fishy for the Bellinghams – for, of course, the girl must have been in it if the father was. But there's the crux: There is no proof that the man ever did leave Hurst's house alive. And if he didn't – but there! As I said at first, whichever turning you take, you find that it ends in a blind alley."

"A lame ending to a masterly exposition," was Thorndyke's comment.

"I know," said Jervis. "But what would you have? There are quite a number of possible solutions, and one of them must be the true one. But how are we to judge which it is? I maintain that until we know something of the parties and the financial and other interests involved we have no data."

"There," said Thorndyke, "I disagree with you entirely. I maintain that we have ample data. You say that we have no means of judging which of the various possible solutions is the true one, but I think that if you read the report carefully and thoughtfully you will find that the facts now known point to one explanation, and one only. It may not be the true explanation, and I don't suppose it is. But we are now dealing with the matter speculatively, academically, and I contend that our data yield a definite conclusion. What do you say, Berkeley?"

"I say that it is time for me to be off. The evening consultations begin at half-past six."

"Well," said Thorndyke, "don't let us keep you from your duties, with poor Barnard currant picking in the Grecian Isles. But come in and see us again. Drop in when you like after your work is done. You won't be in our way even if we are busy, which we very seldom are after eight o'clock."

I thanked Dr. Thorndyke most heartily for making me free of his chambers in this hospitable fashion and took my leave, setting forth homeward by way of Middle Temple Lane and the Embankment – not a very direct route for Fetter Lane, it must be confessed, but our talk had revived my interest in the Bellingham household and put me in a reflective vein.

From the remarkable conversation that I had overheard it was evident that the plot was thickening. Not that I supposed that these two respectable gentlemen really suspected one another of having made away with the missing man, but still, their unguarded words, spoken in anger, made it clear that each had allowed the thought of sinister possibilities to enter his mind – a dangerous condition that might easily grow into actual suspicion. And then the circumstances really were highly mysterious, as I realized with especial vividness now after listening to my friend's analysis of the evidence.

From the problem itself my mind traveled, not for the first time during the last few days, to the handsome girl, who had seemed in my eyes the high-priestess of this temple of mystery in the quaint little court. What a strange figure she had made against this strange background, with her quiet, chilly, self-contained manner, her pale face, so sad and worn, her black, straight brows and solemn gray eyes, so inscrutable, mysterious, Sibylline. A striking, even impressive, personality this, I reflected, with something in it somber and enigmatic that attracted and yet repelled.

And here I recalled Jervis's words: "The girl must have been in it if the father was." It was a dreadful thought, even though only speculatively uttered, and my heart rejected it, rejected it with indignation that rather surprised me. And this notwithstanding that the somber black-robed figure that my memory conjured up was one that associated itself with the idea of mystery and tragedy.

229

Chapter IV
Legal Complications and a Jackal

My meditations brought me by a circuitous route, and ten minutes late, to the end of Fetter Lane, where, exchanging my rather abstracted air for the alert manner of a busy practitioner, I strode briskly forward and darted into the surgery with knitted brows, as though just released from an anxious case. But there was only one patient waiting, and she saluted me as I entered with a snort of defiance.

"Here you are, then?" said she.

"You are perfectly correct, Miss Oman," I replied. "In fact, you have put the case in a nutshell. What can I have the pleasure of doing for you?"

"Nothing," was the answer. "My medical adviser is a lady, but I've brought a note from Mr. Bellingham. Here it is," and she thrust the envelope into my hand.

I glanced through the note and learned that my patient had had a couple of bad nights and a very harassing day. "Could I have something to give me a night's rest?" it concluded.

I reflected for a few moments. One is not very ready to prescribe sleeping draughts for unknown patients, but still, insomnia is a very distressing condition. In the end I temporized with a moderate dose of bromide, deciding to call and see if more energetic measures were necessary.

"He had better take a dose of this at once, Miss Oman," said I, as I handed her the bottle, "and I will look in later and see how he is."

"I expect he will be glad to see you," she answered, "for he is all alone to-night and very dumpy. Miss Bellingham is out. But I must remind you that he's a poor man and pays his way. You must excuse my mentioning it."

"I am much obliged to you for the hint, Miss Oman," I rejoined. "It isn't necessary for me to see him, but I should like just to look in and have a chat."

"Yes, it will do him good. You have your points, though punctuality doesn't seem to be one of them," and with this parting shot Miss Oman bustled away.

Half-past eight found me ascending the great, dim staircase of the house in Nevill's Court preceded by Miss Oman, by whom I was ushered into the room. Mr. Bellingham, who had just finished some sort of meal, was sitting hunched up in his chair gazing gloomily into the empty grate. He brightened up as I entered, but was evidently in very low spirits.

"I didn't mean to drag you out after your day's work was finished," he said, "though I am very glad to see you."

"You haven't dragged me out. I heard you were alone, so I just dropped in for a few minutes' gossip."

"That is really kind of you," he said heartily. "But I'm afraid you'll find me rather poor company. A man who is full of his own highly disagreeable affairs is not a desirable companion."

"You mustn't let me disturb you if you'd rather be alone," said I, with a sudden fear that I was intruding.

"Oh, you won't disturb me," he replied, adding, with a laugh, "It's more likely to be the other way about. In fact, if I were not afraid of boring you to death I would ask you to let me talk my difficulties over with you."

"You won't bore me," I said. "It is generally interesting to share another man's experiences without their inconveniences. 'The proper study of mankind is – man,' you know, especially to a doctor."

Mr. Bellingham chuckled grimly. "You make me feel like a microbe," he said. "However, if you would care to take a peep at me through your microscope, I will crawl on to the stage for your inspection, though it is not *my* actions that furnish the materials for your psychological studies. It is my poor brother who is the *Deus ex machina*, who, from his unknown grave, as I fear, pulls the strings of this infernal puppet-show."

He paused and for a space gazed thoughtfully into the grate as if he had forgotten my presence. At length he looked up and resumed. "It is a curious story, Doctor – a very curious story. Part of it you know – the middle part. I will tell you it from the beginning, and then you will know as much as I do, for, as to the end, that is known to no one. It is written, no doubt, in the book of destiny, but the page has yet to be turned.

"The mischief began with my father's death. He was a country clergyman of very moderate means, a widower with two children, my brother John and me. He managed to send us both to Oxford, after which John went into the Foreign Office and I was to have gone into the Church. But I suddenly discovered that my views on religion had undergone a change that made this impossible, and just about this time my father came into quite considerable property. Now, as it was his expressed intention to leave the estate equally divided between my brother and me, there was no need for me to take up any profession for a livelihood. Archeology was already the passion of my life, and I determined to devote myself henceforth to my favorite study, in which, by the way, I was following a family tendency, for my father was an enthusiastic student of ancient Oriental history, and John was, as you know, an ardent Egyptologist.

231

"Then my father died quite suddenly, and left no will. He had intended to have one drawn up, but had put it off until it was too late. And since nearly all the property was in the form of real estate, my brother inherited practically the whole of it. However, in deference to the known wishes of my father, he made me an allowance of five-hundred a year, which was about a quarter of the annual income. I urged him to assign me a lump sum, but he refused to do this. Instead, he instructed his solicitor to pay me an allowance in quarterly instalments during the rest of his life, and it was understood that, on his death, the entire estate should devolve on me, or if I died first, on my daughter, Ruth. Then, as you know, he disappeared suddenly, and as the circumstances suggested that he was dead, and there was no evidence that he was alive, his solicitor – a Mr. Jellicoe – found himself unable to continue the payment of the allowance. On the other hand, as there was no positive evidence that my brother was dead, it was impossible to administer the will."

"You say the circumstances suggested that your brother was dead. What circumstances were they?"

"Principally the suddenness and completeness of the disappearance. His luggage, as you may remember, was found lying unclaimed at the railway station, and there was another circumstance even more suggestive. My brother drew a pension from the Foreign Office, for which he had to apply in person, or, if abroad, produce proof that he was alive on the date when the payment became due. Now, he was exceedingly regular in this respect. In fact, he had never been known to fail, either to appear in person or to transmit the necessary documents to his agent, Mr. Jellicoe. But from the moment when he vanished so mysteriously to the present day, nothing whatever has been heard of him."

"It's a very awkward position for you," I said, "but I should think there will not be much difficulty in obtaining the permission of the Court to presume death and to proceed to prove the will."

Mr. Bellingham made a wry face. "I expect you are right," he said, "but that doesn't help me much. You see, Mr. Jellicoe, having waited a reasonable time for my brother to reappear, took a very unusual but, I think, in the special circumstances, a very proper step. He summoned me and the other interested party to his office and communicated to us the provisions of the will. And very extraordinary provisions they turned out to be. I was thunderstruck when I heard them. And the exasperating thing is that I feel sure my poor brother imagined that he had made everything perfectly safe and simple."

"They generally do," I said, rather vaguely.

"I suppose they do," said Mr. Bellingham, "but poor John has made the most infernal hash of his will, and I am certain that he has utterly defeated his own intentions. You see, we are an old London family. The house in Queen Square where my brother nominally lived, but actually kept his collection, has been occupied by us for generations, and most of the Bellinghams are buried in St. George's burial-ground close by, though some members of the family are buried in other churchyards in the neighborhood. Now, my brother – who, by the way, was a bachelor – had a strong feeling for the family traditions, and he stipulated, not unnaturally, in his will that he should be buried in St. George's burial-ground among his ancestors, or, at least, in one of the places of burial appertaining to his native parish. But instead of simply expressing the wish and directing his executors to carry it out, he made it a condition affecting the operation of the will."

"Affecting it in what respect?" I asked.

"In a very vital respect," answered Mr. Bellingham. "The bulk of the property he bequeathed to me, or if I predeceased him, to my daughter Ruth. But the bequest was subject to the condition I have mentioned – that he should be buried in a certain place – and if that condition was not fulfilled, the bulk of the property was to go to my cousin, George Hurst."

"But in that case," said I, "as you can't produce the body, neither of you can get the property."

"I am not so sure of that," he replied. "If my brother is dead, it is pretty certain that he is not buried in St. George's or any of the other places mentioned, and the fact can easily be proved by production of the registers. So that a permission to presume death would result in the handing over to Hurst of almost the entire estate."

"Who is the executor?" I asked.

"Ah!" he exclaimed, "there is another muddle. There are two executors: Jellicoe is one, and the other is the principal beneficiary – Hurst or myself, as the case may be. But, you see, neither of us can become an executor until the Court has decided which of us is the principal beneficiary."

"But who is to apply to the Court? I thought that was the business of the executors."

"Exactly, that is Hurst's difficulty. We were discussing it when you called the other day, and a very animated discussion it was," he added, with a grim smile. "You see, Jellicoe naturally refuses to move in the matter alone. He says he must have the support of the other executor. But Hurst is not at present the other executor. Neither am I. But the two of us together are the co-executor, since the duty devolves upon one or other of us, in any case."

"It's a complicated position," I said.

233

"It is, and the complication has elicited a very curious proposal from Hurst. He points out – quite correctly, I am afraid – that as the conditions as to burial have not been complied with, the property must come to him, and he proposes a very neat little arrangement, which is this: That I shall support him and Jellicoe in their application for permission to presume death and to administer the will, and that he shall pay me four-hundred a year for life. The arrangement to hold good *in all eventualities*."

"What does he mean by that?"

"He means," said Bellingham, fixing me with a ferocious scowl, "that if the body should turn up at any future time, so that the conditions as to burial should be able to be carried out, he should still retain the property and pay me the four-hundred a year."

"The deuce!" said I. "He seems to know how to drive a bargain."

"His position is that he stands to lose four-hundred a year for the term of my life if the body is never found, and he ought to stand to win if it is."

"And I gather that you have refused this offer?"

"Yes, very emphatically, and my daughter agrees with me, but I am not sure that I have done the right thing. A man should think twice, I suppose, before he burns his boats."

"Have you spoken to Mr. Jellicoe about the matter?"

"Yes, I have been to see him to-day. He is a cautious man, and he doesn't advise me one way or the other. But I think he disapproves of my refusal. In fact, he remarked that a bird in the hand is worth two in the bush, especially when the whereabouts of the bush is unknown."

"Do you think he will apply to the Court without your sanction?"

"He doesn't want to, but I suppose, if Hurst puts pressure on him, he will have to. Besides, Hurst, as an interested party, could apply on his own account, and after my refusal he probably will – at least, that is Jellicoe's opinion."

"The whole thing is a most astonishing muddle," I said, "especially when one remembers that your brother had a lawyer to advise him. Didn't Mr. Jellicoe point out to him how absurd the provisions were?"

"Yes, he did. He tells me that he implored my brother to let him draw up a will embodying the matter in a reasonable form. But John wouldn't listen to him. Poor old fellow! He could be very pig-headed when he chose."

"And is Hurst's proposal still open?"

"No, thanks to my peppery temper. I refused it very definitely, and sent him off with a flea in his ear. I hope I have not made a false step. I was quite taken by surprise when Hurst made the proposal and got rather angry. You remember, my brother was last seen alive at Hurst's house – but there, I oughtn't to talk like that, and I oughtn't to pester you with my confounded affairs when you come in for a friendly chat, though I gave you fair warning, you remember."

"Oh, but you have been highly entertaining. You don't realize what an interest I take in your case."

Mr. Bellingham laughed somewhat grimly. "My case!" he repeated. "You speak as if I were some rare and curious sort of criminal lunatic. However, I'm glad you find me amusing. It's more than I find myself."

"I didn't say amusing. I said interesting. I view you with deep respect as the central figure of a stirring drama. And I am not the only person who regards you in that light. Do you remember my speaking to you of Doctor Thorndyke?"

"Yes, of course I do."

"Well, oddly enough, I met him this afternoon and we had a long talk at his chambers. I took the liberty of mentioning that I had made your acquaintance. Did I do wrong?"

"No. Certainly not. Why shouldn't you tell him? Did he remember my infernal case, as you call it?"

"Perfectly, in all its details. He is quite an enthusiast, you know, and uncommonly keen to hear how the case develops."

"So am I, for that matter," said Mr. Bellingham.

"I wonder," said I, "if you would mind my telling him what you have told me to-night? It would interest him enormously."

Mr. Bellingham reflected for a while with his eyes fixed on the empty grate. Presently he looked up, and said slowly, "I don't know why I should. It's no secret, and if it were, I hold no monopoly in it. No, tell him, if you think he'd care to hear about it."

"You needn't be afraid of his talking," I said. "He's as close as an oyster, and the facts may mean more to him than they do to us. He may be able to give a useful hint or two."

"Oh, I'm not going to pick his brains," Mr. Bellingham said quickly and with some wrath. "I'm not the sort of man who goes round cadging for free professional advice. Understand that, Doctor."

"I do," I answered hastily. "That wasn't what I meant at all. Is that Miss Bellingham coming in? I heard the front door shut."

"Yes, that will be my girl, I expect, but don't run away. You're not afraid of her, are you?" he added as I hurriedly picked up my hat.

"I'm not sure that I'm not," I answered. "She is rather a majestic young lady."

Mr. Bellingham chuckled and smothered a yawn, and at that moment his daughter entered the room, and, in spite of her shabby black dress and a shabbier handbag that she carried, I thought her appearance and manner fully justified my description.

"You come in, Miss Bellingham," I said as she shook my hand with cool civility, "to find your father yawning and me taking my departure. So I have my uses, you see. My conversation is the infallible cure for insomnia."

Miss Bellingham smiled. "I believe I am driving you away," she said.

"Not at all," I replied hastily. "My mission was accomplished, that was all."

"Sit down for a few moments, Doctor," urged Mr. Bellingham, "and let Ruth sample the remedy. She will be affronted if you run away as soon as she comes in."

"Well, you mustn't let me keep you up," I said.

"Oh, I'll let you know when I fall asleep," he replied, with a chuckle, and with this understanding I sat down again – not at all unwillingly.

At this moment Miss Oman entered with a small tray and a smile of which
I should not have supposed her capable.

"You'll take your toast and cocoa while they're hot, dear, won't you?" she said coaxingly.

"Yes, I will, Phyllis, thank you," Miss Bellingham answered. "I am only just going to take off my hat," and she left the room, followed by the astonishingly transfigured spinster.

She returned almost immediately as Mr. Bellingham was in the midst of a profound yawn, and sat down to her frugal meal, when her father mystified me considerably by remarking, "You're late to-night, chick. Have the Shepherd Kings been giving trouble?"

"No," she replied, "but I thought I might as well get them done. So I dropped in at the Ormond Street Library on my way home and finished them."

"Then they are ready for stuffing now?"

"Yes." As she answered she caught my astonished eye (for a stuffed Shepherd King is undoubtedly a somewhat surprising phenomenon) and laughed softly.

"We mustn't talk in riddles like this," she said, "before Doctor Berkeley, or he will turn us both into pillars of salt. My father is referring to my work," she explained to me.

"Are you a taxidermist, then?" I asked.

She hastily set down the cup that she was raising to her lips and broke into a ripple of quiet laughter.

"I am afraid my father has misled you with his irreverent expressions. He will have to atone by explaining."

"You see, Doctor," said Mr. Bellingham, "Ruth is a literary searcher
– "

236

"Oh, don't call me a searcher!" Miss Bellingham protested. "It suggests the female searcher at a police station. Say investigator."

"Very well, investigator, or *investigatrix*, if you like. She hunts up references and bibliographies at the Museum for people who are writing books. She looks up everything that has been written on a given subject, and then, when she has crammed herself to a bursting-point with facts, she goes to her client and disgorges and crams him or her, and he or she finally disgorges into the Press."

"What a disgusting way to put it!" said his daughter. "However, that is what it amounts to. I am a literary jackal, a collector of provender for the literary lions. Is that quite clear?"

"Perfectly. But I don't think that, even now, I quite understand about the stuffed Shepherd Kings."

"Oh, it was not the Shepherd Kings who were to be stuffed. It was the author! That was mere obscurity of speech on the part of my father. The position is this: A venerable Archdeacon wrote an article on the patriarch Joseph – "

"And didn't know anything about him," interrupted Mr. Bellingham, "and got tripped up by a specialist who did, and then got shirty – "

"Nothing of the kind," said Miss Bellingham. "He knew as much as venerable archdeacons ought to know, but the expert knew more. So the archdeacon commissioned me to collect the literature on the state of Egypt at the end of the seventeenth dynasty, which I have done, and to-morrow I shall go and stuff him, as my father expresses it, and then – "

"And then," Mr. Bellingham interrupted, "the archdeacon will rush forth and pelt that expert with Shepherd Kings and Sequenen-Ra and the whole tag-rag and bobtail of the seventeenth dynasty. Oh, there'll be wigs on the green, I can tell you."

"Yes, I expect there will be quite a skirmish," said Miss Bellingham. And thus dismissing the subject she made an energetic attack on the toast while her father refreshed himself with a colossal yawn.

I watched her with furtive admiration and deep and growing interest. In spite of her pallor, her weary eyes, and her drawn and almost haggard face, she was an exceedingly handsome girl, and there was in her aspect a suggestion of purpose, of strength and character that marked her off from the rank and file of womanhood. I noted this as I stole an occasional glance at her or turned to answer some remark addressed to me, and I noted, too, that her speech, despite a general undertone of depression, was yet not without a certain caustic, ironical humor. She was certainly a rather enigmatical young person, but very decidedly interesting.

237

When she had finished her repast she put aside the tray and, opening the shabby handbag, asked, "Do you take any interest in Egyptian history? We are as mad as hatters on the subject. It seems to be a family complaint."

"I don't know much about it," I answered. "Medical studies are rather engrossing and don't leave much time for general reading."

"Naturally," she said. "You can't specialize in everything. But if you would care to see how the business of a literary jackal is conducted, I will show you my notes."

I accepted the offer eagerly (not, I fear, from pure enthusiasm for the subject), and she brought forth from the bag four blue-covered, quarto notebooks, each dealing with one of the four dynasties from the fourteenth to the seventeenth. As I glanced through the neat and orderly extracts with which they were filled we discussed the intricacies of the peculiarly difficult and confused period that they covered, gradually lowering our voices as Mr. Bellingham's eyes closed and his head fell against the back of his chair. We had just reached the critical reign of Apepa II when a resounding snore broke in upon the studious quiet of the room and sent us both into a fit of silent laughter.

"Your conversation has done its work," she whispered as I stealthily picked up my hat, and together we stole on tiptoe to the door, which she opened without a sound. Once outside, she suddenly dropped her bantering manner and said quite earnestly, "How kind it was of you to come and see him tonight. You have done him a world of good, and I am most grateful. Good-night!"

She shook hands with me really cordially, and I took my way down the creaking stairs in a whirl of happiness that I was quite at a loss to account for.

Chapter V
The Watercress Bed

Barnard's practise, like most others, was subject to those fluctuations that fill the struggling practitioner alternately with hope and despair. The work came in paroxysms with intervals of almost complete stagnation. One of these intermissions occurred on the day after my visit to Nevill's Court, with the result that by half-past eleven I found myself wondering what I should do with the remainder of the day. The better to consider this weighty problem, I strolled down to the Embankment, and, leaning on the parapet, contemplated the view across the river. The gray stone bridge with its perspective of arches, the picturesque pile of the shot-towers, and beyond, the shadowy shapes of the Abbey and St. Stephen's.

It was a pleasant scene, restful and quiet, with a touch of life and a hint of sober romance, when a barge swept down through the middle arch of the bridge with a lugsail hoisted to a jury mast and a white-aproned woman at the tiller. Dreamily I watched the craft creep by upon the moving tide, noted the low freeboard, almost awash, the careful helmswoman, and the dog on the forecastle yapping at the distant shore – and thought of Ruth Bellingham.

What was there about this strange girl that had made so deep an impression on me? That was the question that I propounded to myself, and not for the first time. Of the fact itself there was no doubt. But what was the explanation? Was it her unusual surroundings? Her occupation and rather recondite learning? Her striking personality and exceptional good looks? Or her connection with the dramatic mystery of her lost uncle?

I concluded that it was all of these. Everything connected with her was unusual and arresting, but over and above these circumstances there was a certain sympathy and personal affinity of which I was strongly conscious and of which I dimly hoped that she, perhaps, was a little conscious too. At any rate, I was deeply interested in her. Of that there was no doubt whatever. Short as our acquaintance had been, she held a place in my thoughts that had never been held by any other woman.

From Ruth Bellingham my reflections passed by a natural transition to the curious story that her father had told me. It was a queer affair, that ill-drawn will, with the baffled lawyer protesting in the background. It almost seemed as if there must be something behind it all, especially when I remembered Mr. Hurst's very singular proposal. But it was out of my depth. It was a case for a lawyer, and to a lawyer it should go. This very night, I resolved, I would go to Thorndyke and give him the whole story as it had been told to me.

And then there happened one of those coincidences at which we all wonder when they occur, but which are so frequent as to have become enshrined in a proverb. For even as I formed the resolution, I observed two men approaching from the direction of Blackfriars, and recognized in them my quondam teacher and his junior.

"I was just thinking about you," I said as they came up.

"Very flattering," replied Jervis, "but I thought you had to talk of the devil."

"Perhaps," suggested Thorndyke, "he was talking to himself. But why were you thinking of us, and what was the nature of your thoughts?"

"My thoughts had reference to the Bellingham case. I spent the whole of last evening at Nevill's Court."

"Ha! And are there any fresh developments?"

"Yes, by Jove! There are. Bellingham gave me a full detailed description of the will, and a pretty document it seems to be."

"Did he give you permission to repeat the details to me?"

"Yes. I asked specifically if I might, and he had no objection whatever."

"Good. We are lunching at Soho to-day as Polton has his hands full. Come with us and share our table and tell us your story as we go. Will that suit you?"

It suited me admirably in the present state of the practise, and I accepted the invitation with undissembled glee.

"Very well," said Thorndyke, "then let us walk slowly and finish with matters confidential before we plunge into the maddening crowd."

We set forth at a leisurely pace along the broad pavement and I commenced my narration. As well as I could remember, I related the circumstances that had led up to the present disposition of the property and then proceeded to the actual provisions of the will, to all of which my two friends listened with rapt interest, Thorndyke occasionally stopping me to jot down a memorandum in his pocket-book.

"Why, the fellow must have been a stark lunatic!" Jervis exclaimed, when I had finished. "He seems to have laid himself out with the most devilish ingenuity to defeat his own ends."

"That is not an uncommon peculiarity with testators," Thorndyke remarked. "A direct and perfectly intelligible will is rather the exception. But we can hardly judge until we have seen the actual document. I suppose Bellingham hasn't a copy?"

"I don't know," said I, "but I will ask him."

"If he has one, I should like to look through it," said Thorndyke. "The provisions are very peculiar, and, as Jervis says, admirably calculated to defeat the testator's wishes if they have been correctly reported. And, apart from that, they have a remarkable bearing on the circumstances of the disappearance. I daresay you noticed that."

"I noticed that it is very much to Hurst's advantage that the body has not been found."

"Yes, of course. But there are some other points that are very significant. However, it would be premature to discuss the terms of the will until we have seen the actual document or a certified copy."

"If there is a copy extant," I said, "I will try to get hold of it. But Bellingham is terribly afraid of being suspected of a desire to get professional advice *gratis*."

"That," said Thorndyke, "is natural enough, and not discreditable. But you must overcome his scruples somehow. I expect you will be able to. You are a plausible young gentleman, as I remember of old, and you seem to have established yourself as quite the friend of the family."

"They are rather interesting people," I explained, "very cultivated and with a strong leaning toward archeology. It seems to be in the blood."

"Yes," said Thorndyke, "a family tendency, probably due to contact and common surroundings rather than heredity. So you like Godfrey Bellingham?"

"Yes. He is a trifle peppery and impulsive but quite an agreeable, genial old buffer."

"And the daughter," said Jervis, "what is she like?"

"Oh, she is a learned lady – works up bibliographies and references at the Museum."

"Ah!" Jervis exclaimed, with disfavor, "I know the breed. Inky fingers. No chest to speak of. All side and spectacles."

I rose artlessly at the gross and palpable bait.

"You're quite wrong," I exclaimed indignantly, contrasting Jervis's hideous presentment with the comely original. "She is an exceedingly good-looking girl, and her manners all that a lady's should be. A little stiff, perhaps, but then I am only an acquaintance – almost a stranger."

"But," Jervis persisted, "what is she like, in appearance I mean. Short? Fat? Sandy? Give us intelligible details."

I made a rapid mental inventory, assisted by my recent cogitations.

"She is about five-feet-seven, slim but rather plump, very erect in carriage and graceful in movements: Black hair, loosely parted in the middle and falling very prettily away from the forehead. Pale, clear complexion, dark gray eyes, straight eyebrows, straight, well-shaped nose, short mouth, rather full. Round chin – what the deuce are you grinning at,

241

Jervis?" For my friend had suddenly unmasked his batteries and now threatened, like the Cheshire cat, to dissolve into a mere abstraction of amusement.

"If there is a copy of that will, Thorndyke," he said, "we shall get it. I think you agree with me, reverend senior?"

"I have already said," was the reply, "that I put my trust in Berkeley. And now let us dismiss professional topics. This is our hostelry."

He pushed open an unpretentious glazed door, and we followed him into the restaurant, whereof the atmosphere was pervaded by an appetizing meatiness mingled with less agreeable suggestions of the destructive distillation of fat.

It was some two hours later when I wished my friends *adieu* under the golden-leaved plane trees of King's Bench Walk.

"I won't ask you to come in now," said Thorndyke, "as we have some consultations this afternoon. But come in and see us soon. Don't wait for that copy of the will."

"No," said Jervis. "Drop in in the evening when your work is done – unless, of course, there is more attractive society elsewhere. Oh, you needn't turn that color, my dear child. We have all been young once. There is even a tradition that Thorndyke was young some time back in the pre-dynastic period."

"Don't take any notice of him, Berkeley," said Thorndyke. "The egg-shell is sticking to his head still. He'll know better when he is my age."

"Methuselah!" exclaimed Jervis. "I hope I shan't have to wait as long as that!"

Thorndyke smiled benevolently at his irrepressible junior, and, shaking my hand cordially, turned into the entry.

From the Temple I wended northward, to the adjacent College of Surgeons, where I spent a couple of profitable hours examining the "pickles" and refreshing my memory on the subjects of pathology and anatomy, marveling afresh (as every practical anatomist must marvel) at the incredibly perfect technique of the dissections, and inwardly paying tribute to the founder of the collection. At length the warning of the clock, combined with an increasing craving for tea, drove me forth and bore me toward the scene of my not very strenuous labors. My mind was still occupied with the contents of the cases and the great glass jars, so that I found myself at the corner of Fetter Lane without a very clear idea of how I had got there. But at that point I was aroused from my reflections rather abruptly by a raucous voice in my ear.

"'Orrible discovery at Sidcup!"

I turned wrathfully – for a London street-boy's yell, let off at point-blank range, is, in effect, like the smack of an open hand – but the inscription on the staring yellow poster that was held up for my inspection changed my anger to curiosity.

"Horrible discovery in a watercress-bed!"

Now, let prigs deny it if they will, but there is something very attractive in a "horrible discovery". It hints at tragedy, at mystery, at romance. It promises to bring into our gray and commonplace life that element of the dramatic which is the salt that our existence is savored withal. "In a watercress-bed", too! The rusticity of the background seemed to emphasize the horror of the discovery, whatever it might be.

I bought a copy of the paper, and, tucking it under my arm, hurried on to the surgery, promising myself a mental feast of watercress, but as I opened the door I found myself confronted by a corpulent woman of piebald and pimply aspect who saluted me with a deep groan. It was the lady from the coal shop in Fleur-de-Lys Court.

"Good evening, Mrs. Jablett," I said briskly. "Not come about yourself, I hope."

"Yes, I have," she answered, rising and following me gloomily into the consulting-room, and then, when I had seated her in the patient's chair and myself at the writing table, she continued, "It's my inside, you know, Doctor."

The statement lacked anatomical precision and merely excluded the domain of the skin specialist. I accordingly waited for enlightenment and speculated on the watercress-beds, while Mrs. Jablett regarded me expectantly with a dim and watery eye.

"Ah!" I said at length, "it's your – your inside, is it, Mrs. Jablett?"

"Yus. *And* my 'ead," she added, with a voluminous sigh that filled the apartment with odorous reminiscences of "unsweetened".

"Your head aches, does it?"

"Somethink chronic!" said Mrs. Jablett. "Feels as if it was a-opening and a-shutting, a-opening and a-shutting, and when I sit down I feel as if I should *bust*."

This picturesque description of her sensations – not wholly inconsistent with her figure – gave the clue to Mrs. Jablett's sufferings. Resisting a frivolous impulse to reassure her as to the elasticity of the human integument, I considered her case in exhaustive detail, coasting delicately round the subject of "unsweetened" and finally sent her away, revived in spirits and grasping a bottle of Mist. *Sodae cum Bismutho* from Barnard's big stock-jar. Then I went back to investigate the Horrible Discovery, but before I could open the paper, another patient arrived (*Impetigo contagiosa*, this time, affecting the "wide and arched-front sublime" of a juvenile Fetter Laner), and then yet another, and so on through the evening until at last I forgot the watercress-beds altogether. It was only when I had purified myself from the evening consultations with hot water and a nail-brush and was about to sit down to a frugal supper, that I remembered the newspaper and fetched it from the drawer of the consulting-room table, where it had been hastily thrust out of sight. I folded it into a convenient form, and, standing it upright against the water-jug, read the report at my ease as I supped.

There was plenty of it. Evidently the reporter had regarded it as a "scoop", and the editor had backed him up with ample space and hair-raising head-lines.

Horrible Discovery in a Watercress Bed at Sidcup!

A startling discovery was made yesterday afternoon in the course of clearing out a watercress-bed near the erstwhile rural village of Sidcup in Kent – a discovery that will occasion many a disagreeable qualm to those persons who have been in the habit of regaling themselves with this refreshing esculent. But before proceeding to a description of the circumstances of the actual discovery or of the objects found – which, however, it may be stated at once, are nothing more or less than the fragments of a dismembered human body – it will be interesting to trace the remarkable chain of coincidences by virtue of which the discovery was made.

"The beds in question have been laid out in a small artificial lake fed by a tiny streamlet which forms one of the numerous tributaries of the River Cray. Its depth is greater than usual in the watercress-beds, otherwise the gruesome relics could never have been concealed beneath its surface, and the flow of water through it, though continuous is slow. The tributary streamlet meanders through a succession of pasture meadows, in one of which the beds themselves are situated, and here throughout most of the year the fleecy victims of the human carnivore carry on the industry of converting grass into mutton. Now it happened some years ago that the sheep frequenting these pastures became affected with the disease known as "liver-rot", and here we must make a short digression into the domain of pathology.

"Liver-rot" is a disease of quite romantic antecedents. Its cause is a small, flat worm – the liver-fluke – which infests the liver and bile-ducts of the affected sheep.

Now how does the worm get into the sheep's liver? That is where the romance comes in. Let us see.

244

The cycle of transformation begins with the deposit of the eggs of the fluke in some shallow stream or ditch running through pasture lands. Now each egg has a sort of lid, which presently opens and lets out a minute, hairy creature who swims away in search of a particular kind of water-snail – the kind called by naturalists Limnoea truncatula*. If he finds a snail, he bores his way into its flesh and soon begins to grow and wax fat. Then he brings forth a family – of tiny worms quite unlike himself, little creatures called* rediae, *which soon give birth to families of young* rediae. *So they go on for several generations, but at last there comes a generation of* rediae *which, instead of giving birth to fresh* rediae, *produce families of totally different offspring: Big-headed, long-tailed creatures like miniature tadpoles, called by the learned* cercariae. *The* cercariae *soon wriggle their way out of the body of the snail, and then complications arise, for it is the habit of this particular snail to leave the water occasionally and take a stroll in the fields. Thus the* cercariae, *escaping from the snail find themselves on the grass whereupon they promptly drop their tails and stick themselves to the grass-blades. Then comes the unsuspecting sheep to take his frugal meal, and, cropping the grass swallows it,* cercariae *and all. But the latter, when they find themselves in the sheep's stomach, make their way straight to the bile-ducts, up which they travel to the liver. Here, in a few weeks, they grow up into full-blown flukes and begin the important business of producing eggs.*

Such is the pathological romance of the "liver-rot", and now what is its connection with this mysterious discovery? It is this. After the outbreak of "liver-rot" above referred to, the ground landlord, a Mr. John Bellingham, instructed his solicitor to insert a clause in the lease of the beds directing that the latter should be periodically cleared and examined by an expert to make sure that they were free from the noxious water-snails. The last lease expired about two years ago, and since then the beds have been out of cultivation, but, for the safety of the adjacent pastures, it was considered necessary to make the customary periodical inspection, and it was in the course of cleaning the beds for this purpose that the present discovery was made.

The operation began two days ago. A gang of three men proceeded systematically to grub up the plants and collect the multitudes of water-snails that they might be examined by the

245

expert to see if any obnoxious species were present. They had cleared nearly half of the beds when, yesterday afternoon, one of the men working in the deepest part came upon some bones, the appearance of which excited his suspicion. Thereupon he called his mates, and they carefully picked away the plants piece-meal, a process that soon laid bare an unmistakable human hand lying on the mud amongst the roots. Fortunately they had the wisdom not to disturb the remains, but at once sent off a message to the police. Very soon, an inspector and a sergeant, accompanied by the divisional surgeon, arrived on the scene, and were able to view the remains lying as they had been found. And now another very strange fact came to light, for it was seen that the hand – a left one – lying on the mud was minus its third finger. This is regarded by the police as a very important fact as bearing on the question of identification, seeing that the number of persons having the third finger of the left hand missing must be quite small. After a thorough examination on the spot, the bones were carefully collected and conveyed to the mortuary, where they now lie awaiting further inquiries.

The divisional surgeon, Dr. Brandon, in an interview with our representative, made the following statements, "The bones are those of the left arm of a middle-aged or elderly man about five-feet-eight inches in height. All the bones of the arm are present, including the scapula, or shoulder-blade, and the clavicle, or collar-bone, but the three bones of the third finger are missing."

"Is this a deformity or has the finger been cut off?" our correspondent asked.

"The finger has been amputated," was the reply. "If it had been absent from birth, the corresponding hand bone, or metacarpal, would have been wanting or deformed, whereas it is present and quite normal."

"How long have the bones been in the water?" was the next question.

"More than a year, I should say. They are quite clean. There is not a vestige of the soft structures left."

"Have you any theory as to how the arm came to be deposited where it was found?"

"I should rather not answer that question," was the guarded response.

246

"One more question," our correspondent urged. "The ground landlord, Mr. John Bellingham. Is he not the gentleman who disappeared so mysteriously some time ago?"

"So I understand," Dr. Brandon replied.

"Can you tell me if Mr. Bellingham had lost the third finger of his left hand?"

"I cannot say," said Dr. Brandon, and he added with a smile, "You had better ask the police."

That is how the matter stands at present. But we understand that the police are making active inquiries for any missing man who has lost the third finger of his left hand, and if any of our readers know of such a person, they are earnestly requested to communicate at once, either with us or the authorities.

Also we believe that a systematic search is to be made for further remains.

I laid the newspaper down and fell into a train of reflection. It was certainly a most mysterious affair. The thought that had evidently come to the reporter's mind stole naturally into mine. Could these remains be those of John Bellingham? It was obviously possible, though I could not but see that the fact of the bones having been found on his land, while it undoubtedly furnished the suggestion, did not in any way add to its probability. The connection was accidental and in nowise relevant.

Then, too, there was the missing finger. No reference to any such deformity had been made in the original report of the disappearance, though it could hardly have been overlooked. But it was useless to speculate without facts. I should be seeing Thorndyke in the course of the next few days, and, undoubtedly, if the discovery had any bearing upon the disappearance of John Bellingham, I should hear of it. With such a reflection I rose from the table, and, adopting the advice contained in the spurious Johnsonian quotation, proceeded to "take a walk in Fleet Street" before settling down for the evening.

Chapter VII
Sidelights

The association of coal with potatoes is one upon which I have frequently speculated, without arriving at any more satisfactory explanation than that both products are of the earth, earthy. Of the connection itself Barnard's practise furnished several instances besides Mrs. Jablett's establishment in Fleur-de-Lys Court, one of which was a dark and mysterious cavern a foot below the level of the street, that burrowed under an ancient house on the west side of Fetter Lane – a crinkly, timber house of the three-decker type that leaned back drunkenly from the road as if about to sit down in its own back yard.

Passing this repository of the associated products about ten o'clock in the morning, I perceived in the shadows of the cavern no less a person than Miss Oman. She saw me at the same moment, and beckoned peremptorily with a hand that held a large Spanish onion. I approached with a deferential smile.

"What a magnificent onion, Miss Oman! And how generous of you to offer it to me – "

"I wasn't offering it to you. But there! Isn't it just like a man – "

"Isn't what just like a man?" I interrupted. "If you mean the onion – "

"I don't!" she snapped, "and I wish you wouldn't talk such a parcel of nonsense. A grown man and a member of a serious profession, too! You ought to know better."

"I suppose I ought," I said reflectively.

And she continued, "I called in at the surgery just now."

"To see me?"

"What else should I come for? Do you suppose that I called to consult the bottle-boy?"

"Certainly not, Miss Oman. So you find the lady doctor no use, after all?"

Miss Oman gnashed her teeth at me (and very fine teeth they were too).

"I called," she said majestically, "on behalf of Miss Bellingham."

My facetiousness evaporated instantly. "I hope Miss Bellingham is not ill," I said with a sudden anxiety that elicited a sardonic smile from Miss Oman.

"No," was the reply, "she is not ill, but she has cut her hand rather badly. It's her right hand too, and she can't afford to lose the use of it, not being a great, bulky, lazy, lolloping man. So you had better go and put some stuff on it."

With this advice, Miss Oman whisked to the right-about and vanished into the depths of the cavern like the witch of Wokey, while I hurried on to the surgery to provide myself with the necessary instruments and materials, and thence proceeded to Nevill's Court.

Miss Oman's juvenile maidservant, who opened the door to me, stated the existing conditions with epigrammatic conciseness.

"Mr. Bellingham is *hout*, sir, but Miss Bellingham is *hin*."

Having thus delivered herself she retreated toward the kitchen and I ascended the stairs, at the head of which I found Miss Bellingham awaiting me with her right hand encased in what looked like a white boxing-glove.

"I'm glad you have come," she said. "Phyllis – Miss Oman, you know – has kindly bound up my hand, but I should like you to see that it is all right."

We went into the sitting-room, where I laid out my paraphernalia on the table while I inquired into the particulars of the accident.

"It is most unfortunate that it should have happened just now," she said, as I wrestled with one of those remarkable feminine knots that, while they seem to defy the utmost efforts of human ingenuity to untie, yet have a singular habit of untying themselves at inopportune moments.

"Why just now in particular?" I asked.

"Because I have some specially important work to do. A very learned lady who is writing an historical book has commissioned me to collect all the literature relating to the Tell-el-Amarna Letters – the cuneiform tablets, you know, of Amenhotep the Fourth."

"Well," I said soothingly, "I expect your hand will soon be well."

"Yes, but that won't do. The work has to be done immediately. I have to send in completed notes not later than this day week, and it will be quite impossible. I am dreadfully disappointed."

By this time I had unwound the voluminous wrappings and exposed the injury – a deep gash in the palm that must have narrowly missed a good-sized artery. Obviously the hand would be useless for fully a week.

"I suppose," she said, "you couldn't patch it up so that I could write with it?"

I shook my head.

"No, Miss Bellingham. I shall have to put it on a splint. We can't run any risks with a deep wound like this."

"Then I shall have to give up the commission, and I don't know how my client will get the work done in time. You see, I am pretty well up in

249

the literature of Ancient Egypt. In fact, I was to receive special payment on that account. And it would have been such an interesting task, too. However, it can't be helped."

I proceeded methodically with the application of the dressings, and meanwhile reflected. It was evident that she was deeply disappointed. Loss of work meant loss of money, and it needed but a glance at her rusty black dress to see that there was little margin for that. Possibly, too, there was some special need to be met. Her manner seemed almost to imply that there was. And at this point I had a brilliant idea.

"I'm not sure that it can't be helped," said I.

She looked at me inquiringly, and I continued, "I am going to make a proposition, and I shall ask you to consider it with an open mind."

"That sounds rather portentous," said she, "but I promise. What is it?"

"It is this: When I was a student I acquired the useful art of writing shorthand. I am not a lightning reporter, you understand, but I can take matter down from dictation at quite respectable speed."

"Yes."

"Well, I have several hours free every day – usually the whole afternoon up to six or half-past – and it occurs to me that if you were to go to the Museum in the mornings you could get out your books, look up passages (you could do that without using your right hand), and put in bookmarks. Then I could come along in the afternoon and you could read out the selected passages to me, and I could take them down in shorthand. We should get through as much in a couple of hours as you could in a day using long-hand."

"Oh, but how kind of you, Dr. Berkeley!" she exclaimed. "How very kind! Of course, I couldn't think of taking up all your leisure in that way, but I do appreciate your kindness very much."

I was rather chapfallen at this very definite refusal, but persisted feebly, "I wish you would. It may seem rather a cheek for a comparative stranger like me to make such a proposal to a lady, but if you'd been a man – in those special circumstances – I should have made it all the same, and you would have accepted as a matter of course."

"I doubt that. At any rate, I am not a man. I sometimes wish I were."

"Oh, I am sure you are much better as you are!" I exclaimed, with such earnestness that we both laughed. And at this moment Mr. Bellingham entered the room carrying several large brand-new books in a strap.

"Well, I'm sure!" he exclaimed genially, "here are pretty goings on. Doctor and patient giggling like a pair of schoolgirls! What's the joke?"

He thumped his parcel of books down on the table and listened smilingly while my unconscious witticism was expounded.

"The doctor's quite right," he said. "You'll do as you are, chick, but the Lord knows what sort of man you would make. You take his advice and let well alone."

Finding him in this genial frame of mind, I ventured to explain my proposition to him and to enlist his support. He considered it with attentive approval, and when I had finished turned to his daughter.

"What is your objection, chick?" he asked.

"It would give Doctor Berkeley such a fearful lot of work," she answered.

"It would give him a fearful lot of pleasure," I said. "It would really."

"Then why not?" said Mr. Bellingham. "We don't mind being under an obligation to the Doctor, do we?"

"Oh, it isn't that!" she exclaimed hastily.

"Then take him at his word. He means it. It is a kind action and he'll like doing it, I'm sure. That's all right, Doctor. She accepts, don't you, chick?"

"Yes, if you say so, I do, and most thankfully."

She accompanied the acceptance with a gracious smile that was in itself a large repayment on account, and when we had made the necessary arrangements, I hurried away in a state of the most perfect satisfaction to finish my morning's work and order an early lunch.

When I called for her a couple of hours later I found her waiting in the garden with the shabby handbag, of which I relieved her, and we set forth together, watched jealously by Miss Oman, who had accompanied her to the gate.

As I walked up the court with this wonderful maid by my side I could hardly believe in my good fortune. By her presence and my own resulting happiness the mean surroundings became glorified and the commonest objects transfigured into things of beauty. What a delightful thoroughfare, for instance, was Fetter Lane, with its quaint charm and medieval grace! I snuffed the cabbage-laden atmosphere and seemed to breathe the scent of the asphodel. Holborn was even as the Elysian Fields. The omnibus that bore us westward was a chariot of glory, and the people who swarmed verminously on the pavements bore the semblance of the children of light.

Love is a foolish thing judged by workaday standards, and the thoughts and actions of lovers foolish beyond measure. But the workaday standard is the wrong one, after all, for the utilitarian mind does but busy itself with the trivial and transitory interests of life, behind which looms the great and everlasting reality of the love of man and woman. There is more significance in a nightingale's song in the hush of a summer night than in all the wisdom of Solomon (who, by the way, was not without his little experiences of the tender passion).

251

The janitor in the little glass box by the entrance to the library inspected us and passed us on, with a silent benediction, to the lobby, whence (when I had handed my stick to a bald-headed demigod and received a talismanic disc in exchange) we entered the enormous rotunda of the reading-room.

I have often thought that, if some lethal vapor of highly preservative properties – such as formaldehyde, for instance – could be shed into the atmosphere of this apartment, the entire and complete collection of books and book-worms would be well worth preserving, for the enlightenment of posterity, as a sort of anthropological appendix to the main collection of the Museum. For, surely, nowhere else in the world are so many strange and abnormal human beings gathered together in one place. And a curious question that must have occurred to many observers is: Whence do these singular creatures come, and whither do they go when the very distinct-faced clock (adjusted to literary eyesight) proclaims closing time? The tragic-faced gentleman, for instance, with the corkscrew ringlets that bob up and down like spiral springs as he walks? Or the short, elderly gentleman in the black cassock and bowler hat, who shatters your nerves by turning suddenly and revealing himself as a middle-aged woman? Whither do they go? One never sees them elsewhere. Do they steal away at closing time into the depths of the Museum and hide themselves until morning in sarcophagi or mummy cases? Or do they creep through spaces in the book-shelves and spend the night behind the volumes in a congenial atmosphere of leather and antique paper? Who can say? What I do know is that when Ruth Bellingham entered the reading-room she appeared in comparison with these like a creature of another order – even as the head of Antinous, which formerly stood (it has since been moved) amidst the portrait-busts of the Roman Emperors, seemed like the head of a god set in a portrait gallery of illustrious baboons.

"What have we got to do?" I asked when we had found a vacant seat. "Do you want to look up the catalogue?"

"No, I have the tickets in my bag. The books are waiting in the 'Kept Books' department."

I placed my hat on the leather-covered shelf, dropped her gloves into it – how delightfully intimate and companionable it seemed! – altered the numbers on the tickets, and then we proceeded together to the "kept books" desk to collect the volumes that contained the material for our day's work.

It was a blissful afternoon. Two-and-a-half hours of happiness unalloyed did I spend at that shiny, leather-clad desk, guiding my nimble pen across the pages of the notebook. It introduced me to a new world – a world in which love and learning, sweet intimacy and crusted archeology,

252

were mingled into the oddest, most whimsical and most delicious confection that the mind of man can conceive. Hitherto, these recondite histories had been far beyond my ken. Of the wonderful heretic, Amenhotep the Fourth, I had already heard – at the most he had been a mere name. The Hittites a mythical race of undetermined habitat, while cuneiform tablets had presented themselves to my mind merely as an uncouth kind of fossil biscuit suited to the digestion of a prehistoric ostrich.

Now all this was changed. As we sat with our chairs creaking together and she whispered the story of those stirring times into my receptive ear – talking is strictly forbidden in the reading-room – the disjointed fragments arranged themselves into a romance of supreme fascination. Egyptian, Babylonian, Aramean, Hittite, Memphis, Babylon, Hamath, Megiddo – I swallowed them all thankfully, wrote them down, and asked for more. Only once did I disgrace myself. An elderly clergyman of ascetic and acidulous aspect had passed us with a glance of evident disapproval, clearly setting us down as intruding philanderers, and when I contrasted the parson's probable conception of the whispered communications that were being poured into my ear so tenderly and confidentially with the dry reality, I chuckled aloud. But my fair taskmistress only paused, with her finger on the page, smilingly to rebuke me, and then went on with the dictation. She was certainly a Tartar for work.

It was a proud moment for me when, in response to my interrogative "Yes?" my companion said "That is all" and closed the book. We had extracted the pith and marrow of six considerable volumes in two-and-half hours.

"You have been better than your word," she said. "It would have taken me two full days of really hard work to make the notes that you have written down since we commenced. I don't know how to thank you."

"There's no need to. I've enjoyed myself and polished up my shorthand. What is the next thing? We shall want some books for to-morrow, shan't we?"

"Yes. I have made out a list, so if you will come with me to the catalogue desk I will look up the numbers and ask you to write the tickets."

The selection of a fresh batch of authorities occupied us for another quarter-of-an-hour, and then, having handed in the volumes that we had squeezed dry, we took our way out of the reading-room.

"Which way shall we go?" she asked as we passed out of the gate, where stood a massive policeman, like the guardian angel at the gate of Paradise (only – thank Heaven! – he bore no flaming sword forbidding re-entry).

"We are going," I replied, "to Museum Street, where is a milkshop in which one can get an excellent cup of tea."

She looked as if she would have demurred, but eventually followed obediently, and we were soon settled side by side at the little marble-topped table, retracing the ground we had covered in the afternoon's work and discussing various points of interest over a joint teapot.

"Have you been doing this sort of work long?" I asked, as she handed me my second cup of tea.

"Professionally," she answered, "only about two years – since we broke up our home, in fact. But long before that I used to come to the Museum with my Uncle John – the one who disappeared, you know, in that dreadfully mysterious way – and help him to look up references. We were good friends, he and I."

"I suppose he was a very learned man?" I suggested.

"Yes, in a certain way. In the way of the better-class collector he was very learned indeed. He knew the contents of every museum in the world, in so far as they were connected with Egyptian antiquities, and had studied them specimen by specimen. Consequently, as Egyptology is largely a museum science, he was a learned Egyptologist. But his real interest was in things rather than events. Of course, he knew a great deal – a very great deal – about Egyptian history, but still he was, before all, a collector."

"And what will happen to his collection if he is really dead?"

"The greater part of it goes to the British Museum by his will, and the remainder he has left to his solicitor, Mr. Jellicoe."

"To Mr. Jellicoe! Why, what will Mr. Jellicoe do with Egyptian antiquities?"

"Oh, he is an Egyptologist too, and quite an enthusiast. He has really a fine collection of scarabs and other small objects such as it is possible to keep in a private house. I have always thought that it was his enthusiasm for everything Egyptian that brought him and my uncle together on terms of such intimacy. Though I believe he is an excellent lawyer, and he is certainly a very discreet, cautious man."

"Is he? I shouldn't have thought so, judging by your uncle's will."

"Oh, but that is not Mr. Jellicoe's fault. He assures us that he entreated my uncle to let him draw up a fresh document with more reasonable provisions. But he says Uncle John was immovable, and he really was a rather obstinate man. Mr. Jellicoe repudiates any responsibility in the matter. He washes his hands of the whole affair, and says that it is the will of a lunatic. And so it is, I was glancing through it only a night or two ago, and really I cannot conceive how a sane man could have written such nonsense."

"You have a copy then?" I asked eagerly, remembering Thorndyke's parting instructions.

"Yes. Would you like to see it? I know my father has told you about it, and it is worth reading as a curiosity of perverseness."

"I should very much like to show it to my friend, Doctor Thorndyke," I replied. "He said he would be interested to read it and learn the exact provisions, and it might be well to let him, and hear what he has to say about it."

"I see no objection," she rejoined, "but you know what my father is: His horror, I mean, of what he calls 'cadging for advice *gratis*'."

"Oh, but he need have no scruples on that score. Doctor Thorndyke wants to see the will because the case interests him. He is an enthusiast, you know, and he put the request as a personal favor to himself."

"That is very nice and delicate of him, and I will explain the position to my father. If he is willing for Doctor Thorndyke to see the copy, I will send or bring it over this evening. Have we finished?"

I regretfully admitted that we had, and, when I had paid the modest reckoning, we sallied forth, turning back with one accord into Great Russell Street to avoid the noise and bustle of the larger thoroughfares.

"What sort of man was your uncle?" I asked presently, as we walked along the quiet, dignified street. And then I added hastily, "I hope you don't think me inquisitive, but, to my mind, he presents himself as a kind of mysterious abstraction. The unknown quantity of a legal problem."

"My Uncle John," she answered reflectively, "was a very peculiar man, rather obstinate, very self-willed, what people call 'masterful', and decidedly wrong-headed and unreasonable."

"That is certainly the impression that the terms of his will convey," I said.

"Yes, and not the will only. There was the absurd allowance that he made to my father. That was a ridiculous arrangement, and very unfair too. He ought to have divided the property up as my grandfather intended. And yet he was by no means ungenerous, only he would have his own way, and his own way was very commonly the wrong way."

"I remember," she continued, after a short pause, "a very odd instance of his wrong-headedness and obstinacy. It was a small matter, but very typical of him. He had in his collection a beautiful little ring of the eighteenth dynasty. It was said to have belonged to Queen Ti, the mother of our friend Amenhotep the Fourth, but I don't think that could have been so, because the device on it was the Eye of Osiris, and Ti, as you know, was an Aten-worshiper. However, it was a very charming ring, and Uncle John, who had a queer sort of devotion to the mystical eye of Osiris, commissioned a very clever goldsmith to make two exact copies of it, one

255

for himself and one for me. The goldsmith naturally wanted to take the measurements of our fingers, but this Uncle John would not hear of. The rings were to be exact copies, and an exact copy must be the same size as the original. You can imagine the result. My ring was so loose that I couldn't keep it in my finger, and Uncle John's was so tight that though he did manage to get it on, he was never able to get it off. And it was only the circumstance that his left hand was decidedly smaller than his right that made it possible for him to wear it all."

"So you never wore your copy?"

"No. I wanted to have it altered to make it fit, but he objected strongly, so I put it away, and have it in a box still."

"He must have been an extraordinarily pig-headed old fellow," I remarked.

"Yes. He was very tenacious. He annoyed my father a good deal, too, by making unnecessary alterations in the house in Queen Square when he fitted up his museum. We have a certain sentiment with regard to that house. Our people have lived in it ever since it was built, when the square was first laid out in the reign of Queen Anne, after whom it was named. It is a dear old house. Would you like to see it? We are quite near it now."

I assented eagerly. If it had been a coal-shed or a fried-fish shop I would still have visited it with pleasure, for the sake of prolonging our walk, but I was also really interested in this old house as a part of the background of the mystery of the vanished John Bellingham.

We crossed into Cosmo Place, with its quaint row of the now rare, cannon-shaped iron posts, and passing through stood for a few moments looking into the peaceful, stately old square. A party of boys disported themselves noisily on the range of stone posts that form a bodyguard round the ancient lamp-surmounted pump, but otherwise the place was wrapped in dignified repose suited to its age and station. And very pleasant it looked on this summer afternoon with the sunlight gilding the foliage of its widespreading plane trees and lighting up the warm-toned brick of the house-fronts. We walked slowly down the shady west side, near the middle of which my companion halted.

"This is the house," she said. "It looks gloomy and forsaken now, but it must have been a delightful house in the days when my ancestors could look out of the windows through the open end of the square across the fields of meadows to the heights of Hampstead and Highgate."

She stood at the edge of the pavement looking up with a curious wistfulness at the old house – a very pathetic figure I thought, with her handsome face and proud carriage, her threadbare dress and shabby gloves, standing at the threshold of the home that had been her family's

256

for generations, that should now have been hers, and that was shortly to pass away into the hands of strangers.

I, too, looked up at it with a strange interest, impressed by something gloomy and forbidding in its aspect. The windows were shuttered from basement to attic, and no sign of life was visible. Silent, neglected, desolate, it breathed an air of tragedy. It seemed to mourn in sackcloth and ashes for its lost master. The massive door within the splendid carven portico was crusted with grime, and seemed to have passed out of use as completely as the ancient lamp-irons or the rusted extinguishers wherein the footmen were wont to quench their torches when some Bellingham dame was borne up the steps in her gilded chair, in the days of good Queen Anne.

It was in a somewhat sobered frame of mind that we presently turned away and started homeward by way of Great Ormond Street. My companion was deeply thoughtful, relapsing for a while into that somberness of manner that had so impressed me when I first met her. Nor was I without a certain sympathetic pensiveness – as if, from the great, silent house, the spirit of the vanished man had issued forth to bear us company.

But still it was a delightful walk, and I was sorry when at last we arrived at the entrance to Nevill's Court, and Miss Bellingham halted and held out her hand.

"Good-by," she said, "and many, many thanks for your invaluable help. Shall I take the bag?"

"If you want it. But I must take out the notebooks."

"Why must you take them?" she asked.

"Why, haven't I got to copy the notes out into long-hand?"

An expression of utter consternation spread over her face. In fact, she was so completely taken aback that she forgot to release my hand.

"Heavens!" she exclaimed. "How idiotic of me! But it is impossible, Doctor Berkeley! It will take you hours!"

"It is perfectly possible, and it is going to be done. Otherwise the notes would be useless. Do you want the bag?"

"No, of course not. But I am positively appalled. Hadn't you better give up the idea?"

"And this is the end of our collaboration?" I exclaimed tragically, giving her hand a final squeeze (whereby she became suddenly aware of its position, and withdrew it rather hastily). "Would you throw away a whole afternoon's work? I won't certainly. So, good-by until to-morrow. I shall turn up in the reading-room as early as I can. You had better take the tickets. Oh, and you won't forget about the copy of the will for Doctor Thorndyke, will you?"

257

"No. If my father agrees, you shall have it this evening."

She took the tickets from me, and, thanking me yet again, retired into the court.

Chapter VII
John Bellingham's Will

The task upon which I had embarked so light-heartedly, when considered in cold blood, did certainly appear, as Miss Bellingham had said, rather appalling. The result of two and a half hours' pretty steady work at an average speed of nearly a hundred words a minute, would take some time to transcribe into longhand, and if the notes were to be delivered punctually on the morrow, the sooner I got to work the better.

Recognizing this truth, I lost no time, but, within five minutes of my arrival at the surgery, was seated at the writing-table with my copy before me busily converting the sprawling, inexpressive characters into good, legible round-hand.

The occupation was by no means unpleasant, apart from the fact that it was a labor of love, for the sentences, as I picked them up, were fragrant with the reminiscences of the gracious whisper in which they had first come to me. And then the matter itself was full of interest. I was gaining a fresh outlook on life, was crossing the threshold of a new world (which was her world), and so the occasional interruptions from the patients, while they gave me intervals of enforced rest, were far from welcome.

The evening wore on without any sign from Nevill's Court, and I began to fear that Mr. Bellingham's scruples had proved insurmountable. Not, I am afraid, that I was so much concerned for the copy of the will as for the possibility of a visit, no matter howsoever brief, from my fair employer, and when, on the stroke of half-past-seven, the surgery door flew open with startling abruptness, my fears were allayed and my hopes shattered simultaneously. For it was Miss Oman who stalked in, holding out a blue foolscap envelope with a warlike air as if it were an ultimatum.

"I've brought you this from Mr. Bellingham," she said. "There's a note inside."

"May I read the note, Miss Oman?" I asked.

"Bless the man!" she exclaimed. "What else would you do with it? Isn't that what it's brought for?"

I supposed it was, and, thanking her for her gracious permission, I glanced through the note – a few lines authorizing me to show the copy of the will to Dr. Thorndyke. When I looked up from the paper I found her eyes fixed on me with an expression critical and rather disapproving.

"You seem to be making yourself mighty agreeable in a certain quarter," she remarked.

"I make myself universally agreeable. It is my nature to."

"Ha!" she snorted.

"Don't you find me rather agreeable?" I asked.

"Oily," said Miss Oman. And then with a sour smile at the open notebooks, she remarked, "You've got some work to do now – quite a change for you."

"A delightful change, Miss Oman. '*For Satan findeth*' – but no doubt you are acquainted with the philosophical works of Dr. Watts?"

"If you are referring to '*idle hands*'," she replied, "I'll give you a bit of advice. Don't you keep that hand idle any longer than is really necessary. I have my suspicions about that splint – oh, you know what I mean," and before I had time to reply, she had taken advantage of the entrance of a couple of patients to whisk out of the surgery with the abruptness that had distinguished her arrival.

The evening consultations were considered to be over by half-past eight, at which time Adolphus was wont with exemplary punctuality to close the outer door of the surgery. To-night he was not less prompt than usual, and having performed this, his last daily office, and turned down the surgery gas, he reported the fact and took his departure.

As his retreating footsteps died away and the slamming of the outer door announced his final disappearance, I sat up and stretched myself. The envelope containing the copy of the will lay on the table, and I considered it thoughtfully. It ought to be conveyed to Thorndyke with as little delay as possible, and, as it certainly could not be trusted out of my hands, it ought to be conveyed by me.

I looked at the notebooks. Nearly two hours' work had made a considerable impression on the matter that I had to transcribe, but still, a great deal of the task yet remained to be done. However, I reflected, I could put in a couple of hours or more before going to bed and there would be an hour or two to spare in the morning. Finally I locked the notebooks, open as they were, in the writing-table drawer, and slipping the envelope into my pocket, set out for the Temple.

The soft chime of the Treasury clock was telling out, in confidential tones, the third quarter as I rapped with my stick on the forbidding "oak" of my friends' chambers. There was no response, nor had I perceived any gleam of light from the windows as I approached, and I was considering the advisability of trying the laboratory on the next floor, when footsteps on the stone stairs and familiar voices gladdened my ear.

"Hallo, Berkeley!" said Thorndyke, "do we find you waiting like a Peri at the gates of Paradise? Polton is upstairs, you know, tinkering at one of his inventions. If you ever find the nest empty, you had better go up and bang at the laboratory door. He's always there in the evenings."

"I haven't been waiting long," said I, "and I was just thinking of rousing him up when you came."

"That was right," said Thorndyke, turning up the gas. "And what news do you bring? Do I see a blue envelope sticking out of your pocket?"

"You do."

"Is it a copy of the will?" he asked.

I answered "Yes," and added that I had full permission to show it to him.

"What did I tell you?" exclaimed Jervis. "Didn't I say that he would get the copy for us if it existed?"

"We admit the excellence of your prognosis," said Thorndyke, "but there is no need to be boastful. Have you read through the document, Berkeley?"

"No, I haven't taken it out of the envelope."

"Then it will be equally new to us all, and we shall see if it tallies with your description."

He placed three easy-chairs at a convenient distance from the light, and Jervis, watching him with a smile, remarked, "Now Thorndyke is going to enjoy himself. To him, a perfectly unintelligible will is a thing of beauty and a joy forever – especially if associated with some kind of recondite knavery."

"I don't know," said I, "that this will is particularly unintelligible. The mischief seems to be that it is rather too intelligible. However, here it is," and I handed it over to Thorndyke.

"I suppose that we can depend on this copy," said the latter, as he drew out the document and glanced at it. "Oh, yes," he added, "I see it is copied by Godfrey Bellingham, compared with the original and certified correct. In that case I will get you to read it out slowly, Jervis, and I will make a rough copy for reference. Let us make ourselves comfortable and light our pipes before we begin."

He provided himself with a writing-pad, and, when we had seated ourselves and got our pipes well alight, Jervis opened the document, and with a premonitory "Hem!" commenced the reading:

> In the name of God Amen. This is the last will and testament of me John Bellingham of number 141 Queen Square in the parish of St. George Bloomsbury London in the county of Middlesex Gentleman made this twenty-first day of September in the year of our Lord One-thousand-eight-hundred-and-ninety-two.
>
> 1. I give and bequeath unto Arthur Jellicoe of number 184 New Square Lincoln's Inn London in the county of

261

Middlesex Attorney-at-law the whole of my collection of seals and scarabs and those in my cabinets marked A, B, and D together with the contents thereof and the sum of two-thousand pounds sterling free of legacy duty.

Unto the trustees of the British Museum the residue of my collection of antiquities.

Unto my cousin George Hurst of the Poplars Eltham in the county of Kent the sum of five-thousand pounds free of legacy duty and unto my brother Godfrey Bellingham or if he should die before the occurrence of my death unto his daughter Ruth Bellingham the residue of my estate and effects real and personal subject to the conditions set forth hereinafter namely:

2. That my body shall be deposited with those of my ancestors in the churchyard appertaining to the church and parish of St. George the Martyr or if that shall not be possible in some other churchyard cemetery burial ground church or chapel or other authorized place for the reception of the bodies of the dead situate within or appertaining to the parishes of St. Andrew above the Bars and St. George the Martyr or St. George Bloomsbury and St. Giles in the Fields. But if the conditions in this clause be not carried out then

3. I give and devise the said residue of my estate and effects unto my cousin George Hurst aforesaid and I hereby revoke all wills and codicils made by me at any time heretofore and I appoint Arthur Jellicoe aforesaid to be the executor of this my will jointly with the principal beneficiary and residuary legatee that is to say with the aforesaid Godfrey Bellingham if the conditions set forth hereinbefore in Clause 2 shall be duly carried out but with the aforesaid George Hurst if the said conditions in the said Clause 2 be not carried out.

JOHN BELLINGHAM

Signed by the said testator John Bellingham in the presence of us present at the same time who at his request and in his presence and in the presence of each other have subscribed our names as witnesses:

Frederick Wilton, 16 Medford Road, London, N., clerk.

262

James Barber, 32 Wadbury Crescent, London, S.W., clerk.

"Well," said Jervis, laying down the document as Thorndyke detached the last sheet from his writing-pad, "I have met with a good many idiotic wills, but this one can give them all points. I don't see how it is ever going to be administered. One of the two executors is a mere abstraction – a sort of algebraical problem with no answer."

"I think that difficulty could be overcome," said Thorndyke.

"I don't see how," retorted Jervis. "If the body is deposited in a certain place, *A* is executor. If it is somewhere else, *B* is the executor. But as you cannot produce the body, and no one has the least idea where it is, it is impossible to prove either that it is or that it is not in any specified place."

"You are magnifying the difficulty, Jervis," said Thorndyke. "The body may, of course, be anywhere in the entire world, but the place where it is lying is either inside or outside the general boundary of those two parishes. If it has been deposited within the boundary of those two parishes, the fact must be ascertainable by examining the burial certificates issued since the date when the missing man was last seen alive and by consulting the registers of those specified places of burial. I think that if no record can be found of any such interment within the boundary of those two parishes, that fact will be taken by the Court as proof that no such interment has taken place, and that therefore the body must have been deposited somewhere else. Such a decision would constitute George Hurst the co-executor and residuary legatee."

"That is cheerful for your friends, Berkeley," Jervis remarked, "for we may take it as pretty certain that the body has not been deposited in any of the places named."

"Yes," I agreed gloomily, "I'm afraid there is very little doubt of that. But what an ass that fellow must have been to make such a to-do about his beastly carcass! What the deuce could it have mattered to him where it was dumped, when he had done with it?"

Thorndyke chuckled softly. "Thus the irreverent youth of to-day," said he. "But yours is hardly a fair comment, Berkeley. Our training makes us materialists, and puts us a little out of sympathy with those in whom primitive beliefs and emotions survive. A worthy priest who came to look at our dissecting-room expressed surprise to me that the students, thus constantly in the presence of relics of mortality, should be able to think of anything but the resurrection and the life hereafter. He was a bad psychologist. There is nothing so dead as a dissecting-room 'subject', and the contemplation of the human body in the process of being quietly taken to pieces – being resolved into its structural units like a worn-out clock or an old engine in the scrapper's yard – is certainly not conducive to a vivid realization of the doctrine of the resurrection."

"No, but this absurd anxiety to be buried in some particular place has nothing to do with religious belief. It is merely silly sentiment."

"It is sentiment, I admit," said Thorndyke, "but I wouldn't call it silly. The feeling is so widespread in time and space that we must look on it with respect as something inherent in human nature. Think – as doubtless John Bellingham did – of the ancient Egyptians, whose chief aspiration was that of everlasting repose for the dead. See the trouble they took to achieve it. Think of the great Pyramid, or that of Amenhotep the Fourth with its labyrinth of false passages and its sealed and hidden sepulchral chambers. Think of Jacob, borne after death all those hundreds of weary miles in order that he might sleep with his fathers and then remember Shakespeare and his solemn adjuration to posterity to let him rest undisturbed in his grave. No, Berkeley, it is not a silly sentiment. I am as indifferent as you as to what becomes of my body 'when I have done with it', to use your irreverent phrase, but I recognize the solicitude that some other men display on the subject as a natural feeling that has to be taken seriously."

"But even so," I said, "if this man had a hankering for a freehold residence in some particular bone-yard, he might have gone about the business in a more reasonable way."

"There I am entirely with you," Thorndyke replied. "It is the absurd way in which this provision is worded that not only creates all the trouble but also makes the whole document so curiously significant in view of the testator's disappearance."

"How significant?" Jervis demanded eagerly.

"Let us consider the provisions of the will point by point," said Thorndyke, "and first note that the testator commanded the services of a very capable lawyer."

"But Mr. Jellicoe disapproved of the will," said I, "in fact, he protested strongly against the form of it."

"We will bear that in mind too," Thorndyke replied. "And now with reference to what we may call the contentious clauses. The first thing that strikes us is their preposterous injustice. Godfrey's inheritance is made conditional on a particular disposal of the testator's body. But this is a matter not necessarily under Godfrey's control. The testator might have been lost at sea, or killed in a fire or explosion, or have died abroad and been buried where his grave could not have been identified. There are numerous probable contingencies besides the improbable one that has happened that might prevent the body from being recovered.

"But even if the body had been recovered, there is another difficulty. The places of burial in the parishes have all been closed for many years. It would be impossible to reopen any of them without a special faculty, and I doubt whether such a faculty would be granted. Possibly cremation might meet the difficulty, but even that is doubtful, and, in any case, the matter would not be in the control of Godfrey Bellingham. Yet, if the required interment should prove impossible, he is to be deprived of his legacy."

"It is a monstrous and absurd injustice," I exclaimed.

"It is," Thorndyke agreed, "but this is nothing to the absurdity that comes to light when we consider Clauses Two and Three in detail. Observe that the testator presumably wished to be buried in a certain place. Also he wished his brother should benefit under the will. Let us take the first point and see how he has set about securing the accomplishment of what he desired. Now if we read Clauses Two and Three carefully, we shall see that he has rendered it virtually impossible that his wishes can be carried out. He desires to be buried in a certain place and makes Godfrey responsible for his being so buried. But he gives Godfrey no power or authority to carry out the provision, and places insuperable obstacles in his way. For until Godfrey is an executor, he has no power or authority to carry out the provision, and until the provisions are carried out, he does not become an executor."

"It is a preposterous muddle," exclaimed Jervis.

"Yes, but that is not the worst of it," Thorndyke continued. "The moment John Bellingham dies, his dead body has come into existence, and it is 'deposited,' for the time being, wherever he happens to have died. But unless he should happen to have died in one of the places of burial mentioned – which is in the highest degree unlikely – his body will be, for the time being, 'deposited' in some place other than those specified. In that case Clause Two is – for the time being – not complied with, and consequently George Hurst becomes, automatically, the co-executor.

"But will George Hurst carry out the provisions of Clause Two? Probably not. Why should he? The will contains no instructions to that effect. It throws the whole duty on Godfrey. On the other hand, if he should carry out Clause Two, what happens? He ceases to be an executor and he loses some seventy-thousand pounds. We may be pretty certain that he will do nothing of the kind. So that, on considering the two clauses, we see that the wishes of the testator could only be carried out in the unlikely event of his dying in one of the burial-places mentioned, or his body being conveyed immediately after death to a public mortuary in one of the said parishes. In any other event, it is virtually certain that he will be buried in some place other than that which he desired, and that his brother will be left absolutely without provision or recognition."

"John Bellingham could never have intended that," I said.

"Clearly not," agreed Thorndyke. "The provisions of the will furnish internal evidence that he did not. You note that he bequeathed five-thousand pounds to George Hurst, in the event of Clause Two being carried out, but he has made no bequest to his brother in the event of its not being carried out. Obviously, he had not entertained the possibility of this contingency at all. He assumed, as a matter of course, that the conditions of Clause Two would be fulfilled, and regarded the conditions themselves as a mere formality."

"But," Jervis objected, "Jellicoe must have seen the danger of a miscarriage and pointed it out to his client."

"Exactly," said Thorndyke. "There is the mystery. We understand that he objected strenuously, and that John Bellingham was obdurate. Now it is perfectly understandable that a man should adhere obstinately to the most stupid and perverse disposition of his property, but that a man should persist in retaining a particular form of words after it has been proved to him that the use of such form will almost certainly result in the defeat of his own wishes. That, I say, is a mystery that calls for very careful consideration."

"If Jellicoe had been an interested party," said Jervis, "one would have suspected him of lying low. But the form of Clause Two doesn't affect him at all."

"No," said Thorndyke, "the person who stands to profit by the muddle is George Hurst. But we understand that he was unacquainted with the terms of the will, and there is certainly nothing to suggest that he is in any way responsible for it."

"The practical question is," said I, "what is going to happen? And what can be done for the Bellinghams?"

"The probability is," Thorndyke replied, "that the next move will be made by Hurst. He is the party immediately interested. He will probably apply to the Court for permission to presume death and administer the will."

"And what will the Court do?"

Thorndyke smiled dryly. "Now you are asking a very pretty conundrum. The decisions of Courts depend on idiosyncrasies of temperament that no one can foresee. But one may say that a Court does not lightly grant permission to presume death. There will be a rigorous inquiry – and a decidedly unpleasant one, I suspect – and the evidence will be reviewed by the judge with a strong predisposition to regard the testator as being still alive. On the other hand, the known facts point very distinctly to the probability that he is dead, and, if the will were less complicated and all the parties interested were unanimous in supporting the application, I don't see why it might not be granted. But it will clearly be to the interest

266

of Godfrey to oppose the application, unless he can show that the conditions of Clause Two have been complied with – which it is virtually certain he cannot, and he may be able to bring forward reasons for believing John to be still alive. But even if he is unable to do this, inasmuch as it is pretty clear that he was intended to be the chief beneficiary, his opposition is likely to have considerable weight with the Court."

"Oh, is it?" I exclaimed eagerly. "Then that accounts for a very peculiar proceeding on the part of Hurst. I have stupidly forgotten to tell you about it. He has been trying to come to a private agreement with Godfrey Bellingham."

"Indeed!" said Thorndyke. "What sort of agreement?"

"His proposal was this: That Godfrey should support him and Jellicoe in an application to the Court for permission to presume death and to administer the will, that if it was successful, Hurst should pay him four-hundred pounds a year for life. The arrangement to hold good in all eventualities."

"By which he means?"

"That if the body should be discovered at any future time, so that the conditions of Clause Two could be carried out, Hurst should still retain the property and continue to pay Godfrey the four-hundred a year for life."

"Hey, ho!" exclaimed Thorndyke, "that is a queer proposal – a very queer proposal indeed."

"Not to say fishy," added Jervis. "I don't fancy the Court would look with approval on that little arrangement."

"The law does not look with much favor on any little arrangements that aim at getting behind the provisions of a will," Thorndyke replied, "though there would be nothing to complain of in this proposal if it were not for the reference to 'all eventualities'. If a will is hopelessly impracticable, it is not unreasonable or improper for the various beneficiaries to make such private arrangements among themselves as may seem necessary to avoid useless litigation and delay in administering the will. If, for instance, Hurst had proposed to pay four-hundred a year to Godfrey so long as the body remained undiscovered on condition that, in the event of its discovery, Godfrey should pay him a like sum for life, there would have been nothing to comment upon. It would have been an ordinary sporting chance. But the reference to 'all eventualities' is an entirely different matter. Of course, it may be mere greediness, but all the same it suggests some very curious reflections."

"Yes, it does," said Jervis. "I wonder if he has any reason to expect that the body will be found? Of course it doesn't follow that he has. He may be merely taking the opportunity offered by the other man's poverty to make sure of the bulk of the property whatever happens. But it is uncommonly sharp practice, to say the least."

"Do I understand that Godfrey declined the proposal?" Thorndyke asked.

"Yes, he did, very emphatically, and I fancy the two gentlemen proceeded to exchange opinions on the circumstances of the disappearance with more frankness than delicacy."

"Ah," said Thorndyke, "that is a pity. If the case comes into Court, there is bound to be a good deal of unpleasant discussion and still more unpleasant comment in the newspapers. But if the parties themselves begin to express suspicions of one another there is no telling where the matter will end."

"No, by Jove!" said Jervis. "If they begin flinging accusations of murder about, the fat will be in the fire with a vengeance. That way lies the Old Bailey."

"We must try to prevent them from making an unnecessary scandal," said Thorndyke. "It may be that an exposure will be unavoidable, and that must be ascertained in advance. But to return to your question, Berkeley, as to what is to be done. Hurst will probably make some move pretty soon. Do you know if Jellicoe will act with him?"

"No, he won't. He declines to take any steps without Godfrey's assent – at least, that is what he says at present. His attitude is one of correct neutrality."

"That is satisfactory so far," said Thorndyke, "though he may alter his tone when the case comes into Court. From what you said just now I gathered that Jellicoe would prefer to have the will administered and be quit of the whole business, which is natural enough, especially as he benefits under the will to the extent of two-thousand pounds and a valuable collection. Consequently, we may fairly assume that, even if he maintains an apparent neutrality, his influence will be exerted in favor of Hurst rather than of Bellingham, from which it follows that Bellingham ought certainly to be properly advised, and, when the case goes into Court, properly represented."

"He can't afford either the one or the other," said I. "He's as poor as an insolvent church mouse and as proud as the devil. He wouldn't accept professional aid that he couldn't pay for."

"Hmm," grunted Thorndyke, "that's awkward. But we can't allow the case to go 'by default', so to speak – to fail for the mere lack of technical assistance. Besides, it is one of the most interesting cases that I have ever met with, and I am not going to see it bungled. He couldn't object to a little general advice in a friendly, informal way – *amicus curiae*, as old Brodribb is so fond of saying, and there is nothing to prevent us from pushing forward the preliminary inquiries."

"Of what nature would they be?"

"Well, to begin with, we have to satisfy ourselves that the conditions of Clause Two have not been complied with: That John Bellingham has not been buried within the parish boundaries mentioned. Of course he has not, but we must not take anything for granted. Then we have to satisfy ourselves that he is not still alive and accessible. It is perfectly possible that he is, after all, and it is our business to trace him, if he is still in the land of the living. Jervis and I can carry out these investigations without saying anything to Bellingham. My learned brother will look through the Register of Burials – not forgetting the cremations – in the metropolitan area, and I will take the other matter in hand."

"You really think that John Bellingham may still be alive?" said I.

"Since his body has not been found, it is obviously a possibility. I think it in the highest degree improbable, but the improbable has to be investigated before it can be excluded."

"It sounds a rather hopeless quest," I remarked. "How do you propose to begin?"

"I think of beginning at the British Museum. The people there may be able to throw some light on his movements. I know that there are some important excavations in progress at Heliopolis – in fact, the Director of the Egyptian Department is out there at the present moment, and Doctor Norbury, who is taking his place temporarily, is an old friend of Bellingham's. I shall call on him and try to discover if there is anything that might have induced Bellingham suddenly to go abroad to Heliopolis, for instance. Also he may be able to tell me what it was that took the missing man to Paris on that last, rather mysterious journey. That might turn out to be an important clue. And meanwhile, Berkeley, you must endeavor tactfully to reconcile your friend to the idea of letting us give an eye to the case. Make it clear to him that I am doing this entirely for the enlargement of my own knowledge."

"But won't you have to be instructed by a solicitor?" I asked.

"Yes, nominally, but only as a matter of etiquette. We shall do all the actual work. Why do you ask?"

"I was thinking of the solicitor's costs, and I was going to mention that I have a little money of my own – "

"Then you keep it, my dear fellow. You'll want it when you go into practice. There will be no difficulty about the solicitor. I shall ask one of my friends to act nominally as a personal favor to me – Marchmont would take the case for us, Jervis, I am sure."

"Yes," said Jervis. "Or old Brodribb, if we put it to him *amicus curia*."

"It is excessively kind of both of you to take this benevolent interest in the case of my friends," I said, "and it is to be hoped that they won't be foolishly proud and stiff-necked about it. It's rather the way with poor gentlefolk."

"I'll tell you what!" exclaimed Jervis. "I have a most brilliant idea. You shall give us a little supper at your rooms and invite the Bellinghams to meet us. Then you and I will attack the old gentleman, and Thorndyke shall exercise his persuasive powers on the lady. These chronic incurable old bachelors, you know, are quite irresistible."

"You observe that my respected junior condemns me to lifelong celibacy," Thorndyke remarked. "But," he added, "his suggestion is quite a good one. Of course, we mustn't put any sort of pressure on Bellingham to employ us – for that is what it amounts to, even if we accept no payment – but a friendly talk over the supper-table would enable us to put the matter delicately and yet convincingly."

"Yes," said I, "I see that, and I like the idea immensely. But it won't be possible for several days, because I've got a job that takes up all my spare time – and that I ought to be at work on now," I added, with a sudden qualm at the way in which I had forgotten the passage of time in the interest of Thorndyke's analysis.

My two friends looked at me inquiringly, and I felt it necessary to explain about the injured hand and the Tell-el-Amarna tablets, which I accordingly did rather shyly and with a nervous eye upon Jervis. The slow grin, however, for which I was watching, never came. On the contrary, he not only heard me through quite gravely, but when I had finished said with some warmth, and using my old hospital pet name, "I'll say one thing for you, Polly: You're a good chum, and you always were. I hope your Nevill's Court friends appreciate the fact."

"They are far more appreciative than the occasion warrants," I answered. "But to return to this question: How will this day week suit you?"

"It will suit me," Thorndyke answered, with a glance at his junior.

"And me too," said the latter, "so, if it will do for the Bellinghams, we will consider it settled, but if they can't come, you must fix another night."

"Very well," I said, rising and knocking out my pipe. "I will issue the invitation to-morrow. And now I must be off to have another slog at those notes."

As I walked homeward I speculated cheerfully on the prospect of entertaining my friends under my own (or rather Barnard's) roof, if they could be lured out of their eremitical retirement. The idea had, in fact, occurred to me already, but I had been deterred by the peculiarities of Barnard's housekeeper. For Mrs. Gummer was one of those housewives who make up for an archaic simplicity of production by preparations on the most portentous and alarming scale. But this time I would not be deterred. If only the guests could be enticed into my humble lair it would be easy to furnish the raw materials of the feast from outside, and the consideration of ways and means occupied me pleasantly until I found myself once more at my writing-table, confronted by my voluminous notes on the incidents of the North Syrian War.

Chapter VIII
A Museum Idyll

W hether it was that practise revived a forgotten skill on my part, or that Miss Bellingham had over-estimated the amount of work to be done, I am unable to say. But whichever may have been the explanation, the fact is that the fourth afternoon saw our task so nearly completed that I was fain to plead that a small remainder might be left over to form an excuse for yet one more visit to the reading-room.

Short, however, as had been the period of our collaboration, it had been long enough to produce a great change in our relations to one another. For there is no friendship so intimate and satisfying as that engendered by community of work, and none – between man and woman, at any rate – so frank and wholesome.

Every day had arrived to find a pile of books with the places duly marked and the blue-covered quarto notebooks in readiness. Every day we had worked steadily at the allotted task, had then handed in the books and gone forth together to enjoy a most companionable tea in the milkshop. Thereafter to walk home by way of Queen Square, talking over the day's work and discussing the state of the world in the far-off days when Ahkhenaten was king and the Tell-el-Amarna tablets were a-writing.

It had been a pleasant time, so pleasant, that as I handed in the books for the last time, I sighed to think that it was over. That not only was the task finished, but that the recovery of my fair patient's hand, from which I had that morning removed the splint, had put an end to the need of my help.

"What shall we do?" I asked, as we came out into the central hall. "It is too early for tea. Shall we go and look at some of the galleries?"

"Why not?" she answered. "We might look over some of the things connected with what we have been doing. For instance, there is a relief of Ahkhenaten upstairs in the Third Egyptian Room. We might go and look at it."

I fell in eagerly with the suggestion, placing myself under her experienced guidance, and we started by way of the Roman Gallery, past the long row of extremely commonplace and modern-looking Roman Emperors.

"I don't know," she said, pausing for a moment opposite a bust labelled "Trajan" (but obviously a portrait of Phil May), "how I am ever even to thank you for all that you have done, to say nothing of repayment."

"There is no need to do either," I replied. "I have enjoyed working with you so I have had my reward. But still," I added, "if you want to do me a great kindness, you have it in your power."

"How?"

"In connection with my friend, Doctor Thorndyke. I told you he was an enthusiast. Now he is, for some reason, most keenly interested in everything relating to your uncle, and I happen to know that, if any legal proceedings should take place, he would very much like to keep a friendly eye on the case."

"And what do you want me to do?"

"I want you, if an opportunity should occur for him to give your father advice or help of any kind, to use your influence with your father in favor of, rather than in opposition to, his accepting it – always assuming that you have no real feeling against his doing so."

Miss Bellingham looked at me thoughtfully for a few moments, and then laughed softly.

"So the great kindness that I am to do you is to let you do me a further kindness through your friend?"

"No," I protested, "that is where you are mistaken. It isn't benevolence on Doctor Thorndyke's part. It's professional enthusiasm."

She smiled sceptically.

"You don't believe in it," I said, "but consider other cases. Why does a surgeon get out of bed on a winter's night to do an emergency operation at a hospital? He doesn't get paid for it. Do you think it is altruism?"

"Yes, of course. Isn't it?"

"Certainly not. He does it because it is his job, because it is his business to fight with disease – and win."

"I don't see much difference," she said. "It's work done for love instead of for payment. However, I will do as you ask if the opportunity arises, but I shan't suppose that I am repaying your kindness to me."

"I don't mind so long as you do it," I said, and we walked on for some time in silence.

"Isn't it odd," she said presently, "how our talk always seems to come back to my uncle? Oh, and that reminds me that the things he gave to the Museum are in the same room as the Ahkhenaten relief. Would you like to see them?"

"Of course I should."

"Then we will go and look at them first." She paused, and then, rather shyly and with a rising color, she continued. "And I think I should like to introduce you to a very dear friend of mine – with your permission, of course."

273

This last addition she made hastily, seeing, I suppose, that I looked rather glum at the suggestion. Inwardly I consigned her friend to the devil, especially if of the masculine gender. Outwardly I expressed my felicity at making the acquaintance of any person whom she should honor with her friendship. Whereat, to my discomfiture, she laughed enigmatically – a very soft laugh, low-pitched and musical, like the cooing of a glorified pigeon.

I strolled on by her side, speculating a little anxiously on the coming introduction. Was I being conducted to the lair of one of the *savants* attached to the establishment? And would he add a superfluous third to our little party of two, so complete and companionable, *solus cum sola*, in this populated wilderness? Above all, would he turn out to be a young man, and bring my aerial castles tumbling about my ears? The shy look and the blush with which she had suggested the introduction were ominous indications, upon which I mused gloomily as we ascended the stairs and passed through the wide doorway. I glanced apprehensively at my companion, and met a quiet, inscrutable smile, and at that moment she halted opposite a wall-case and faced me.

"This is my friend," she said. "Let me present you to Artemidorus, late of the Fayyum. Oh, don't smile!" she pleaded. "I am quite serious. Have you never heard of pious Catholics who cherish a devotion to some long-departed saint? That is my feeling toward Artemidorus, and if you only knew what comfort he has shed into the heart of a lonely woman – what a quiet, unobtrusive friend he has been to me in my solitary, friendless days, always ready with a kindly greeting on his gentle, thoughtful face, you would like him for that alone. And I want you to like him and to share our silent friendship. Am I very silly, very sentimental?"

A wave of relief swept over me, and the mercury of my emotional thermometer, which had shrunk almost into the bulb, leaped up to summer heat. How charming it was of her and how sweetly intimate, to wish to share this mystical friendship with me! And what a pretty conceit it was, too, and how like this strange, inscrutable maiden, to come here and hold silent converse with this long-departed Greek. And the pathos of it all touched me deeply amidst the joy of this new-born intimacy.

"Are you scornful?" she asked, with a shade of disappointment, as I made no reply.

"No, indeed I am not," I answered earnestly. "I want to make you aware of my sympathy and my appreciation without offending you by seeming to exaggerate, and I don't know how to express it."

"Oh, never mind about the expression, so long as you feel it. I thought you would understand," and she gave me a smile that made me tingle to my fingertips.

We stood awhile gazing in silence at the mummy – for such, indeed, was her friend Artemidorus. But not an ordinary mummy. Egyptian in form, it was entirely Greek in feeling, and brightly colored as it was, in accordance with the racial love of color, the tasteful refinement with which the decoration of the case was treated made those around look garish and barbaric. But the most striking feature was a charming panel picture which occupied the place of the usual mask. This painting was a revelation to me. Except that it was executed in tempera instead of oil, it differed in no respect from modern work. There was nothing archaic or ancient about it. With its freedom of handling and its correct rendering of light and shade, it might have been painted yesterday. Indeed, enclosed in an ordinary gilt frame, it might have passed without remark in an exhibition of modern portraits.

Miss Bellingham observed my admiration and smiled approvingly.

"It is a charming little portrait, isn't it?" she said, "and such a sweet face too. So thoughtful and human, with just a shade of melancholy. But the whole thing is full of charm. I fell in love with it the first time I saw it. And it is so Greek!"

"Yes, it is, in spite of the Egyptian gods and symbols."

"Rather because of them, I think," said she. "There we have the typical Greek attitude, the genial, cultivated eclecticism that appreciated the fitness of even the most alien forms of art. There is Anubis standing beside the bier. There are Isis and Nephthys, and there below Horus and Tahuti. But we can't suppose Artemidorus worshiped or believed in those gods. They are there because they are splendid decoration and perfectly appropriate in character. The real feeling of those who loved the dead man breaks out in the inscription." She pointed to a band below the pectoral, where, in gilt capital letters, was written the two words, "*ARTEMIDORE EYPSYCHI.*"

"Yes," I said, "it is very dignified and very human."

"And so sincere and full of real emotion," she added. "I find it unspeakably touching. '*O Artemidorus, farewell!*' There is the real note of human grief, the sorrow of eternal parting. How much finer it is than the vulgar boastfulness of the Semitic epitaphs, or our own miserable, insincere make-believe of the '*Not lost but gone before*' type. He was gone from them forever. They would look on his face and hear his voice no more. They realized that this was their last farewell. Oh, there is a world of love and sorrow in those two simple words!"

For some time neither of us spoke. The glamour of this touching memorial of a long-buried grief had stolen over me, and I was content to stand silent by my beloved companion and revive, with a certain pensive pleasure, the ghosts of human emotions over which so many centuries had

275

rolled. Presently she turned to me with a frank smile. "You have been weighed in the balance of friendship," she said, "and not found wanting. You have the gift of sympathy, even with a woman's sentimental fancies."

I suspected that a good many men would have developed this precious quality under the circumstances, but I refrained from saying so. There is no use in crying down one's own wares. I was glad enough to have earned her good opinion so easily, and when she at length turned away from the case and passed through into the adjoining room, it was a very complacent young man who bore her company.

"Here is Ahkhenaten – or Khu-en-aten, as the authorities here render the hieroglyphics. She indicated a fragment of a colored relief labeled: *'Portion of a painted stone tablet with a portrait figure of Amen-hotep IV,'* and we stopped to look at the frail, effeminate figure of the great king, with his large cranium, his queer, pointed chin, and the Aten rays stretching out their weird hands as if caressing him.

"We mustn't stay here if you want to see my uncle's gift, because this room closes at four to-day." With this admonition she moved on to the other end of the room, where she halted before a large floor-case containing a mummy and a large number of other objects. A black label with white lettering set forth the various contents with a brief explanation as follows: *"Mummy of Sebek-hotep, a scribe of the twenty-second dynasty, together with the objects found in the tomb. These include the four Canopic jars, in which the internal organs were deposited, the Ushabti figures, tomb provisions and various articles that had belonged to the deceased: His favorite chair, his head-rest, his ink-palette, inscribed with his name and the name of the king, Osorkon I, in whose reign he lived, and other smaller articles. Presented by John Bellingham, Esq."*

"They have put all the objects together in one case," Miss Bellingham explained, "to show the contents of an ordinary tomb of the better class. You see that the dead man was provided with all his ordinary comforts: Provisions, furniture, the ink-palette that he had been accustomed to use in writing on papyri, and a staff of servants to wait on him."

"Where are the servants?" I asked.

"The little Ushabti figures," she answered, "they were the attendants of the dead, you know, his servants in the under-world. It was a quaint idea, wasn't it? But it was all very complete and consistent, and quite reasonable, too, if one once accepts the belief in the persistence of the individual apart from the body."

"Yes," I agreed, "and that is the only fair way to judge a religious system, by taking the main beliefs for granted. But what a business it must have been, bringing all these things from Egypt to London."

276

"It is worth the trouble, though, for it is a fine and instructive collection. And the work is all very good of its kind. You notice that the Ushabti figures and the heads that form the stoppers of the Canopic jars are quite finely modeled. The mummy itself, too, is rather handsome, though that coat of bitumen on the back doesn't improve it. But Sebek-hotep must have been a fine-looking man."

"The mask on the face is a portrait, I suppose?"

"Yes. In fact, it's rather more. To some extent it is the actual face of the man himself. This mummy is enclosed in what is called a cartonnage, that is a case molded on the figure. The cartonnage was formed of a number of layers of linen or papyrus united by glue or cement, and when the case had been fitted to a mummy it was molded to the body, so that the general form of the features and limbs was often apparent. After the cement was dry the case was covered with a thin layer of stucco and the face modeled more completely, and then decorations and inscriptions were painted on. So that, you see, in a cartonnage, the body was sealed up like a nut in its shell, unlike the more ancient forms in which the mummy was merely rolled up and enclosed in a wooden coffin."

At this moment there smote upon our ears a politely protesting voice announcing in sing-song tones that it was closing time, and simultaneously a desire for tea suggested the hospitable milk-shop. With leisurely dignity that ignored the official who shepherded us along the galleries, we made our way to the entrance, still immersed in conversation on matters sepulchral.

It was rather earlier than our usual hour for leaving the Museum and, moreover, it was our last day – for the present. Wherefore we lingered over our tea to an extent that caused the milk-shop lady to view us with some disfavor, and when at length we started homeward, we took so many short cuts that six o'clock found us no nearer our destination than Lincoln's Inn Fields, whither we had journeyed by a slightly indirect route that traversed (among other places) Russell Square, Red Lion Square, with the quaint passage of the same name, Bedford Row, Jockey's Fields, Hand Court, and Great Turnstile.

It was in the last thoroughfare that our attention was attracted by a flaring poster outside a newsvendor's bearing the startling inscription:

MORE MEMENTOES OF MURDERED MAN

Miss Bellingham glanced at the poster and shuddered.

"Horrible, isn't it?" she said. "Have you read about them?"

"I haven't been noticing the papers the last few days," I replied.

277

"No, of course you haven't. You've been slaving at those wretched notes. We don't very often see the papers, at least we don't take them in, but Miss Oman has kept us supplied during the last day or two. She is a perfect little ghoul. She delights in horrors of every kind, and the more horrible the better."

"But," I asked, "what is it they have found?"

"Oh, they are the remains of some poor creature who seems to have been murdered and cut into pieces. It is dreadful. It made me shudder to read of it, for I couldn't help thinking of poor Uncle John, and, as for my father, he was really quite upset."

"Are these the bones that were found in a watercress-bed at Sidcup?"

"Yes, but they have found several more. The police have been most energetic. They seem to have been making a systematic search, and the result has been that they have discovered several portions of the body, scattered about in very widely separated places – Sidcup, Lee, St. Mary Cray, and yesterday it was reported that an arm had been found in one of the ponds called 'the Cuckoo Pits,' close to our old home."

"What! In Essex?" I exclaimed.

"Yes, in Epping Forest, quite near Woodford. Isn't it dreadful to think of it? They were probably hidden when we were living there. I think it was that that horrified my father so much. When he read it he was so upset that he gathered up the whole bundle of newspapers and tossed them out of the window, and they blew over the wall, and poor Miss Oman had to rush and pursue them up the court."

"Do you think he suspects that these remains may be those of your uncle?"

"I think so, though he has said nothing to that effect and, of course, I have not made any suggestion to him. We always preserve the fiction between ourselves of believing that Uncle John is still alive."

"But you don't think he is, do you?"

"No, I'm afraid I don't, and I feel pretty sure that my father doesn't think so either, but he doesn't like to admit it to me."

"Do you happen to remember what bones have been found?"

"No, I don't. I know that an arm was found in the Cuckoo Pits, and I think a thigh-bone was dredged up out of a pond near St. Mary Cray. But Miss Oman will be able to tell you all about it, if you are interested. She will be delighted to meet a kindred spirit," Miss Bellingham added, with a smile.

"I don't know that I claim spiritual kinship with a ghoul," said I, "especially such a very sharp-tempered ghoul."

"Oh, don't disparage her, Doctor Berkeley!" Miss Bellingham pleaded. "She isn't really bad-tempered. Only a little prickly on the surface. I oughtn't to have called her a ghoul. She is just the sweetest, most affectionate, most unselfish little angelic human hedgehog that you could find if you traveled the wide world through. Do you know that she has been working her fingers to the bone making an old dress of mine presentable because she is so anxious that I shall look nice at your little supper party."

"You are sure to do that, in any case," I said, "but I withdraw my remark as to her temper unreservedly. And I really didn't mean it, you know. I have always liked the little lady."

"That's right, and now won't you come in and have a few minutes' chat with my father? We are quite early in spite of the short cuts."

I accepted readily, and the more so inasmuch as I wanted a few words with Miss Oman on the subject of catering and did not want to discuss it before my friends. Accordingly I went in and gossiped with Mr. Bellingham, chiefly about the work we had done at the Museum, until it was time for me to return to the surgery.

Having taken my leave, I walked down the stairs with reflective slowness and as much creaking of my boots as I could manage, with the result, hopefully anticipated, that as I approached the door of Miss Oman's room it opened and the lady's head protruded.

"I'd change my cobbler if I were you," she said.

I thought of the "angelic human hedgehog," and nearly sniggered in her face.

"I am sure you would, Miss Oman, instantly. Though, mind you, the poor fellow can't help his looks."

"You are a very flippant young man," she said severely. Whereat I grinned, and she regarded me silently with a baleful glare. Suddenly I remembered my mission and became serious and sober.

"Miss Oman," I said. "I very much want to take your advice on a matter of some importance – to me, at least." (That ought to fetch her, I thought. The "advice fly" – strangely neglected by Izaak Walton – is guaranteed to kill in any weather.) And it did fetch her. She rose in a flash and gorged it, cock's feathers, worsted body and all.

"What is it about?" she asked eagerly. "But don't stand out there where everybody can hear but me. Come in and sit down."

Now I didn't want to discuss the matter here, and, besides, there was not time. I therefore assumed an air of mystery.

"I can't, Miss Oman. I'm due at the surgery now. But if you should be passing and should have a few minutes to spare, I should be greatly obliged if you would look in. I really don't quite know how to act."

"No, I expect not. Men very seldom do. But you're better than most, for you know when you are in difficulties and have the sense to consult a woman. But what is it about? Perhaps I might be thinking it over."

"Well, you know," I began evasively, "it's a simple matter, but I can't very well – no, by Jove!" I added, looking at my watch, "I must run, or I shall keep the multitude waiting." And with this I bustled away, leaving her literally dancing with curiosity.

Chapter IX
The Sphinx of Lincoln's Inn

At the age of twenty-six one cannot claim to have attained to the position of a person of experience. Nevertheless, the knowledge of human nature accumulated in that brief period sufficed to make me feel confident that, at some time during the evening, I should receive a visit from Miss Oman. And circumstances justified my confidence, for the clock yet stood at two-minutes-to-seven when a premonitory tap at the surgery door heralded her arrival.

"I happened to be passing," she explained, and I forbore to smile at the coincidence, "so I thought I might as well drop in and hear what you wanted to ask me about."

She seated herself in the patients' chair and, laying a bundle of newspapers on the table, glared at me expectantly.

"Thank you, Miss Oman," said I. "It is very good of you to look in on me. I am ashamed to give you all this trouble about such a trifling matter."

She rapped her knuckles impatiently on the table.

"Never mind about the trouble," she exclaimed tartly. "What – is – it – that – you – want – to – *ask* – me about?"

I stated my difficulties in respect of the supper-party, and, as I proceeded, an expression of disgust and disappointment spread over her countenance.

"I don't see why you need have been so mysterious about it," she said glumly.

"I didn't mean to be mysterious. I was only anxious not to make a mess of the affair. It's all very fine to assume a lofty scorn of the pleasures of the table, but there is great virtue in a really good feed, especially when low-living and high-thinking have been the order of the day."

"Coarsely put," said Miss Oman, "but perfectly true."

"Very well. Now, if I leave the management to Mrs. Gummer, she will probably provide a tepid Irish stew with flakes of congealed fat on it, and a plastic suet-pudding or something of that kind, and turn the house upside down in getting it ready. So I thought of having a cold spread and getting the things from outside. But I don't want it to look as if I had been making enormous preparations."

"They won't think the things came down from heaven," said Miss Oman.

"No, I suppose they won't. But you know what I mean. Now, where do you advise me to go for the raw materials of conviviality?"

Miss Oman reflected. "You had better let me do your shopping and manage the whole business," was her final verdict.

This was precisely what I wanted, and I accepted thankfully, regardless of the feelings of Mrs. Gummer. I handed her two pounds, and, after some protests at my extravagance, she bestowed them in her purse – a process that occupied time, since that receptacle, besides being a sort of miniature Record Office of frayed and time-stained bills, already bulged with a lading of draper's samples, ends of tape, a card of linen buttons, another of hooks and eyes, a lump of beeswax, a rat-eaten stump of leadpencil, and other trifles that I have forgotten. As she closed the purse at the imminent risk of wrenching off its fastenings she looked at me severely and pursed her lips.

"You're a very plausible young man," she remarked.

"What makes you say that?" I asked.

"Philandering about museums," she continued, "with handsome young ladies on the pretense of work. Work, indeed! Oh, I heard her telling her father about it. She thinks you were perfectly enthralled by the mummies and dried cats and chunks of stone and all the other trash. She doesn't know what humbugs men are."

"Really, Miss Oman," I began.

"Oh, don't talk to me!" she snapped. "I can see it all. You can't impose upon me. I can see you staring into those glass cases, egging her on to talk and listening open-mouthed and bulging-eyed and sitting at her feet – now, didn't you?"

"I don't know about sitting at her feet," I said, "though it might easily have come to that with those infernal slippery floors, but I had a very jolly time, and I mean to go again if I can. Miss Bellingham is the cleverest and most accomplished woman I have ever spoken to."

This was a poser for Miss Oman, whose admiration and loyalty, I knew, were only equaled by my own. She would have liked to contradict me, but the thing was impossible. To cover her defeat she snatched up the bundle of newspapers and began to open them out.

"What sort of stuff is 'hibernation'?" she demanded suddenly.

"Hibernation!" I exclaimed.

"Yes. They found a patch of it on a bone that was discovered in a pond at St. Mary Cray, and a similar patch on one that was found at some other place in Essex. Now, I want to know what 'hibernation' is."

"You must mean 'eburnation'," I said, after a moment's reflection.

"The newspapers say 'hibernation,' and I suppose they know what they are talking about. If you don't know what it is, don't be ashamed to say so."

"Well, then, I don't."

"In that case you had better read the papers and find out," she said, a little illogically. And then, "Are you fond of murders? I am, awfully."

"What a shocking little ghoul you must be!" I exclaimed.

She stuck out her chin at me. "I'll trouble you," she said, "to be a little more respectful in your language. Do you realize that I am old enough to be your mother?"

"Impossible!" I ejaculated.

"Fact," said Miss Oman.

"Well, anyhow," said I, "age is not the only qualification. And besides, you are too late for the billet. The vacancy's filled."

Miss Oman slapped the papers down on the table and rose abruptly.

"You had better read the papers and see if you can learn a little sense," she said severely as she turned to go. "Oh, and don't forget the finger!" she added eagerly. "That is really thrilling."

"The finger?" I repeated.

"Yes. They found a hand with one missing. The police think it is an important clue. I don't know what they mean, but you read the account and tell me what you think."

With this parting injunction she bustled out through the surgery, and I followed to bid her a ceremonious *adieu* on the doorstep. I watched her little figure tripping with quick, bird-like steps down Fetter Lane, and was about to turn back into the surgery when my attention was attracted by the evolutions of an elderly gentleman on the opposite side of the street. He was a somewhat peculiar-looking man, tall, gaunt, and bony, and the way in which he carried his head suggested to the medical mind a pronounced degree of near sight and a pair of "deep" spectacle glasses. Suddenly he espied me and crossed the road with his chin thrust forward and a pair of keen blue eyes directed at me through the centers of his spectacles.

"I wonder if you can and will help me," said he, with a courteous salute. "I wish to call on an acquaintance, and I have forgotten his address. It is in some court, but the name of that court has escaped me for the moment. My friend's name is Bellingham. I suppose you don't chance to know it? Doctors know a great many people, as a rule."

"Do you mean Mr. Godfrey Bellingham?"

"Ah! Then you do know him. I have not consulted the oracle in vain. He is a patient of yours, no doubt?"

"A patient and a personal friend. His address is Forty-nine Nevill's Court."

"Thank you, thank you. Oh, and as you are a friend, perhaps you can inform me as to the customs of the household. I am not expected, and I do not wish to make an untimely visit. What are Mr. Bellingham's habits as to his evening meal? Would this be a convenient time to call?"

"I generally make my evening visits a little later than this – say about half-past eight. They have finished their meal by then."

"Ah! Half-past eight, then? Then I suppose I had better take a walk until that time. I don't want to disturb them."

"Would you care to come in and smoke a cigar until it is time to make your call? If you would, I could walk over with you and show you the house."

"That is very kind of you," said my new acquaintance, with an inquisitive glance at me through his spectacles. "I think I should like to sit down. It's a dull affair, mooning about the streets, and there isn't time to go back to my chambers – in Lincoln's Inn."

"I wonder," said I, as I ushered him into the room lately vacated by Miss Oman, "if you happen to be Mr. Jellicoe."

He turned his spectacles full on me with a keen, suspicious glance. "What makes you think I am Mr. Jellicoe?" he asked.

"Oh, only that you live in Lincoln's Inn."

"Ha! I see. I live in Lincoln's Inn. Mr. Jellicoe lives in Lincoln's Inn. Therefore I am Mr. Jellicoe. Ha! Ha! Bad logic, but a correct conclusion. Yes, I am Mr. Jellicoe. What do you know about me?"

"Mighty little, excepting that you were the late John Bellingham's man of business."

"The '*late* John Bellingham,' hey! How do you know he is the late John Bellingham?"

"As a matter of fact, I don't. Only I rather understood that that was your own belief."

"You understood! Now from whom did you 'understand' that? From Godfrey Bellingham? Hmm! And how did he know what I believe? I never told him. It is a very unsafe thing, my dear sir, to expound another man's beliefs."

"Then you think that John Bellingham is alive?"

"Do I? Who said so? I did not, you know."

"But he must be either dead or alive."

"There," said Mr. Jellicoe, "I am entirely with you. You have stated an undeniable truth."

"It is not a very illuminating one, however," I replied, laughing.

"Undeniable truths often are not," he retorted. "They are apt to be extremely general. In fact, I would affirm that the certainty of the truth of a given proposition is directly proportional to its generality."

"I suppose that is so," said I.

"Undoubtedly. Take an instance from your own profession. Given a million normal human beings under twenty, and you can say with certainty that a majority of them will die before reaching a certain age, that they will die in certain circumstances and of certain diseases. Then take a single unit from that million, and what can you predict concerning him? Nothing. He may die to-morrow. He may live to be a couple of hundred. He may die of a cold in the head or a cut finger, or from falling off the cross of St. Paul's. In a particular case you can predict nothing."

"That is perfectly true," said I. And then realizing that I had been led away from the topic of John Bellingham, I ventured to return to it.

"That was a very mysterious affair – the disappearance of John Bellingham, I mean."

"Why mysterious?" asked Mr. Jellicoe. "Men disappear from time to time, and when they reappear, the explanations that they give (when they give any) seem more or less adequate."

"But the circumstances were surely rather mysterious."

"What circumstances?" asked Mr. Jellicoe.

"I mean the way in which he vanished from Mr. Hurst's house."

"In what way did he vanish from it?"

"Well, of course, I don't know."

"Precisely. Neither do I. Therefore I can't say whether that way was a mysterious one or not."

"It is not even certain that he did leave it," I remarked, rather recklessly.

"Exactly," said Mr. Jellicoe. "And if he did not, he is there still. And if he is there still, he has not disappeared – in the sense understood. And if he has not disappeared, there is no mystery."

I laughed heartily, but Mr. Jellicoe preserved a wooden solemnity and continued to examine me through his spectacles (which I, in my turn, inspected and estimated at about minus five dioptres). There was something highly diverting about this grim lawyer, with his dry contentiousness and almost farcical caution. His ostentatious reserve encouraged me to ply him with fresh questions, the more indiscreet the better.

"I suppose," said I, "that, under these circumstances, you would hardly favor Mr. Hurst's proposal to apply for permission to presume death?"

"Under what circumstances?" he inquired.

"I was referring to the doubt you have expressed as to whether John Bellingham is, after all, really dead."

"My dear sir," said he, "I fail to see your point. If it were certain that the man was alive, it would be impossible to presume that he was dead, and if it were certain that he was dead, presumption of death would still be impossible. You do not presume a certainty. The uncertainty is of the essence of the transaction."

"But," I persisted, "if you really believe that he may be alive, I should hardly have thought that you would take the responsibility of presuming his death and dispersing his property."

"I don't," said Mr. Jellicoe. "I take no responsibility. I act in accordance with the decision of the Court and have no choice in the matter."

"But the Court may decide that he is dead and he may nevertheless be alive."

"Not at all. If the Court decides that he is presumably dead, then he is presumably dead. As a mere irrelevant, physical circumstance he may, it is true, be alive. But legally speaking, and for testamentary purposes, he is dead. You fail to perceive the distinction, no doubt?"

"I am afraid I do," I admitted.

"Yes. The members of your profession usually do. That is what makes them such bad witnesses in a court of law. The scientific outlook is radically different from the legal. The man of science relies on his own knowledge and observation and judgment, and disregards testimony. A man comes to you and tells you he is blind in one eye. Do you accept his statement? Not in the least. You proceed to test his eyesight with some infernal apparatus of colored glasses, and you find that he can see perfectly well with both eyes. Then you decide that he is not blind in one eye. That is to say, you reject his testimony in favor of facts of your own ascertaining."

"But surely that is the rational method of coming to a conclusion?"

"In science, no doubt. Not in law. A court of law must decide according to the evidence which is before it, and that evidence is of the nature of sworn testimony. If a witness is prepared to swear that black is white and no evidence to the contrary is offered, the evidence before the Court is that black is white, and the Court must decide accordingly. The judge and the jury may think otherwise – they may even have private knowledge to the contrary – but they have to decide according to the evidence."

"Do you mean to say that a judge would be justified in giving a decision which he knew to be contrary to the facts? Or that he might sentence a man whom he knew to be innocent?"

"Certainly. It has been done. There is a case of a judge who sentenced a man to death and allowed the execution to take place, notwithstanding that he – the judge – had actually seen the murder committed by another man. But that was carrying correctness of procedure to the verge of pedantry."

"It was, with a vengeance," I agreed. "But to return to the case of John Bellingham. Supposing that after the Court has decided that he is dead he should return alive? What then?"

"Ah! It would then be his turn to make an application, and the Court, having fresh evidence laid before it, would probably decide that he was alive."

"And meantime his property would have been dispersed?"

"Probably. But you will observe that the presumption of death would have arisen out of his own proceedings. If a man acts in such a way as to create a belief that he is dead, he must put up with the consequences."

"Yes, that is reasonable enough," said I. And then, after a pause, I asked, "Is there any immediate likelihood of proceedings of the kind being commenced?"

"I understood from what you said just now that Mr. Hurst was contemplating some action of the kind. No doubt you had your information from a reliable quarter." This answer Mr. Jellicoe delivered without moving a muscle, regarding me with the fixity of a spectacled figurehead.

I smiled feebly. The operation of pumping Mr. Jellicoe was rather like the sport of boxing with a porcupine, being chiefly remarkable as a demonstration of the power of passive resistance. I determined, however, to make one more effort, rather, I think, for the pleasure of witnessing his defensive maneuvers than with the expectation of getting anything out of him. I accordingly "opened out" on the subject of the "remains".

"Have you been following these remarkable discoveries of human bones that have been appearing in the papers?" I asked.

He looked at me stonily for some moments, and then replied, "Human bones are rather more within your province than mine, but, now that you mention it, I think I recall having read of some such discoveries. They were disconnected bones, I believe."

"Yes. Evidently parts of a dismembered body."

"So I should suppose. No, I have not followed the accounts. As we get on in life our interests tend to settle into grooves, and my groove is chiefly connected with conveyancing. These discoveries would be of more interest to a criminal lawyer."

"I thought you might, perhaps, have connected them with the disappearance of your client?"

"Why should I? What could be the nature of the connection?"

"Well," I said, "these are the bones of a man – "

"Yes, and my client was a man with bones. That is a connection, certainly, though not a very specific or distinctive one. But perhaps you had something more particular in your mind?"

"I had," I replied. "The fact that some of the bones were actually found on land belonging to your client seemed to me rather significant."

"Did it, indeed?" said Mr. Jellicoe. He reflected for a few moments, gazing steadily at me the while, and then continued, "In that I am unable to follow you. It would have seemed to me that the finding of human remains upon a certain piece of land might conceivably throw a *prima facie* suspicion upon the owner or occupant of the land as being the person who deposited them. But the case that you suggest is the one case in which this would be impossible. A man cannot deposit his own dismembered remains."

"No, of course not. I was not suggesting that he deposited them himself, but merely that the fact of their being deposited on his land, in a way, connected these remains with him."

"Again," said Mr. Jellicoe, "I fail to follow you, unless you are suggesting that it is customary for murderers who mutilate bodies to be punctilious in depositing the dismembered remains upon land belonging to their victims. In which case I am skeptical as to your facts. I am not aware of the existence of any such custom. Moreover, it appears that only a portion of the body was deposited on Mr. Bellingham's land, the remaining portions having been scattered broadcast over a wide area. How does that agree with your suggestion?"

"It doesn't, of course," I admitted. "But there is another fact that I think you will admit to be more significant. The first remains that were discovered were found at Sidcup. Now, Sidcup is close to Eltham, and Eltham is the place where Mr. Bellingham was last seen alive."

"And what is the significance of this? Why do you connect the remains with one locality rather than the various other localities in which other portions of the body were found?"

"Well," I replied, rather graveled by this very pertinent question, "the appearances seem to suggest that the person who deposited these remains started from the neighborhood of Eltham, where the missing man was last seen."

Mr. Jellicoe shook his head. "You appear," said he, "to be confusing the order of deposition with the order of discovery. What evidence is there that the remains found at Sidcup were deposited before those found elsewhere?"

"I don't know that there is any," I admitted.

"Then," said he, "I don't see how you support your suggestion that the person started from the neighborhood of Eltham."

On consideration, I had to admit that I had nothing to offer in support of my theory, and having thus shot my last arrow in this very unequal contest, I thought it time to change the subject.

"I called in at the British Museum the other day," said I, "and had a look at Mr. Bellingham's last gift to the nation. The things are very well shown in that central case."

"Yes. I was very pleased with the position they have given to the exhibit, and so would my poor old friend have been. I wished, as I looked at the case, that he could have seen it. But perhaps he may, after all."

"I am sure I hope he will," said I, with more sincerity, perhaps, than the lawyer gave me credit for. For the return of John Bellingham would most effectually have cut the Gordian knot of my friend Godfrey's difficulties. "You are a good deal interested in Egyptology yourself, aren't you?" I added.

"Greatly interested," replied Mr. Jellicoe, with more animation than I had thought possible in his wooden face. "It is a fascinating subject, the study of this venerable civilization, extending back to the childhood of the human race, preserved forever for our instruction in its own unchanging monuments like a fly in a block of amber. Everything connected with Egypt is full of an impressive solemnity. A feeling of permanence, of stability, defying time and change, pervades it. The place, the people, and the monuments alike breathe of eternity."

I was mightily surprised at this rhetorical outburst on the part of this dry, taciturn lawyer. But I liked him the better for the touch of enthusiasm that made him human, and determined to keep him astride of his hobby.

"Yet," said I, "the people must have changed in the course of centuries."

"Yes, that is so. The people who fought against Cambyses were not the race who marched into Egypt five-thousand years before – the dynastic people whose portraits we see on the early monuments. In those fifty centuries the blood of Hyksos and Syrians and Ethiopians and Hittites, and who can say how many more races, must have mingled with that of the old Egyptians. But still the national life went on without a break. The old culture leavened the new peoples, and the immigrant strangers ended by becoming Egyptians. It is a wonderful phenomenon. Looking back on it from our own time, it seems more like a geological period than the life history of a single nation. Are you at all interested in the subject?"

"Yes, decidedly, though I am completely ignorant of it. The fact is that my interest is of quite recent growth. It is only of late that I have been sensible of the glamor of things Egyptian."

"Since you made Miss Bellingham's acquaintance, perhaps?" suggested Mr. Jellicoe, himself as unchanging in aspect as an Egyptian effigy.

I suppose I must have reddened – I certainly resented the remark – for he continued in the same even tone, "I made the suggestion because I know that she takes an intelligent interest in the subject and is, in fact, quite well informed on it."

"Yes. She seems to know a great deal about the antiquities of Egypt, and I may as well admit that your surmise was correct. It was she who showed me her uncle's collection."

"So I had supposed," said Mr. Jellicoe. "And a very instructive collection it is, in a popular sense – very suitable for exhibition in a public museum, though there is nothing in it of unusual interest to the expert. The tomb furniture is excellent of its kind and the cartonnage case of the mummy is well made and rather finely decorated."

"Yes, I thought it quite handsome. But can you explain to me why, after taking all that trouble to decorate it, they should have disfigured it with those great smears of bitumen?"

"Ah!" said Mr. Jellicoe, "that is quite an interesting question. It is not unusual to find mummy cases smeared with bitumen. There is a mummy of a priestess in the next gallery which is completely coated with bitumen except the gilded face. Now, this bitumen was put on for a purpose – for the purpose of obliterating the inscriptions and thus concealing the identity of the deceased from the robbers and desecrators of tombs. And there is the oddity of this mummy of Sebek-hotep. Evidently there was an intention of obliterating the inscriptions. The whole of the back is covered thickly with bitumen, and so are the feet. Then the workers seem to have changed their minds and left the inscriptions and decoration untouched. Why they intended to cover it, and why, having commenced, they left it partially covered only, is a mystery. The mummy was found in its original tomb and quite undisturbed, so far as tomb-robbers are concerned. Poor Bellingham was greatly puzzled as to what the explanation could be."

"Speaking of bitumen," said I, "reminds me of a question that has occurred to me. You know that this substance has been used a good deal by modern painters and that it has a very dangerous peculiarity. I mean its tendency to liquefy, without any obvious reason, long after it has dried."

"Yes, I know. Isn't there some story about a picture of Reynolds's in which bitumen had been used? A portrait of a lady, I think. The bitumen softened, and one of the lady's eyes slipped down on to her cheek, and they had to hang the portrait upside down and keep it warm until the eye slipped back again into its place. But what was your question?"

"I was wondering whether the bitumen used by the Egyptian artists has ever been known to soften after this great lapse of time."

"Yes, I think it has. I have heard of instances in which the bitumen coatings have softened under certain circumstances and become quite 'tacky.' But, bless my soul! Here am I gossiping with you and wasting your time, and it is nearly a quarter to nine!"

My guest rose hastily, and I, with many apologies for having detained him, proceeded to fulfil my promise to guide him to his destination. As we sallied forth together the glamour of Egypt faded by degrees, and when he shook my hand stiffly at the gate of the Bellinghams' house, all his vivacity and enthusiasm had vanished, leaving the taciturn lawyer, dry, uncommunicative, and not a little suspicious.

Chapter X
The New Alliance

The "Great Lexicographer" – tutelary deity of my adopted habitat – has handed down to shuddering posterity a definition of the act of eating which might have been framed by a dyspeptic ghoul. "Eat, to devour with the mouth." It is a shocking view to take of so genial a function, cynical, indelicate, and finally unforgivable by reason of its very accuracy. For, after all, that is what eating amounts to, if one must needs express it with such crude brutality. But if "the ingestion of alimentary substances" – to ring a modern change upon the older formula – is in itself a process material even unto carnality, it is undeniable that it forms a highly agreeable accompaniment to more psychic manifestations.

And so, as the lamplight, reinforced by accessory candles, falls on the little table in the first-floor room looking on Fetter Lane – only now the curtains are drawn – the conversation is not the less friendly and bright for a running accompaniment executed with knives and forks, for clink of goblet, and jovial gurgle of wine-flask. On the contrary, to one of us, at least – to wit, Godfrey Bellingham – the occasion is one of uncommon festivity, and his boyish enjoyment of the simple feast makes pathetic suggestions of hard times, faced uncomplainingly, but keenly felt nevertheless.

The talk flitted from topic to topic, mainly concerning itself with matters artistic, and never for one moment approaching the critical subject of John Bellingham's will. From the stepped pyramid of Sakkara with its encaustic tiles to medieval church floors – from Elizabethan woodwork to Mycenean pottery, and thence to the industrial arts of the Stone Age and the civilization of the Aztecs. I began to suspect that my two legal friends were so carried away by the interest of the conversation that they had forgotten the secret purpose of the meeting, for the dessert had been placed on the table (by Mrs. Gummer with the manner of a bereaved dependent dispensing funeral bakemeats), and still no reference had been made to the "case." But it seemed that Thorndyke was but playing a waiting game – was only allowing the intimacy to ripen while he watched for the opportunity. And that opportunity came, even as Mrs. Gummer vanished spectrally with a tray of plates and glasses.

"So you had a visitor last night, Doctor," said Mr. Bellingham. "I mean my friend Jellicoe. He told us he had seen you, and mighty curious he was about you. I have never known Jellicoe to be so inquisitive before. What did you think of him?"

"A quaint old cock. I found him highly amusing. We entertained one another for quite a long time with cross-questions and crooked answers. I affecting eager curiosity, he replying with a defensive attitude of universal ignorance. It was a most diverting encounter."

"He needn't have been so close," Miss Bellingham remarked, "seeing that all the world will be regaled with our affairs before long."

"They are proposing to take the case into Court, then?" said Thorndyke.

"Yes," said Mr. Bellingham. "Jellicoe came to tell me that my cousin, Hurst, has instructed his solicitors to make the application and to invite me to join him. Actually he came to deliver an ultimatum from Hurst – but I mustn't disturb the harmony of this festive gathering with litigious discords."

"Now, why mustn't you?" asked Thorndyke. "Why is a subject in which we are all keenly interested to be taboo? You don't mind telling us about it, do you?"

"No, of course not. But what do you think of a man who button-holes a doctor at a dinner-party to retail a list of ailments?"

"It depends on what his ailments are," replied Thorndyke. "If he is a chronic dyspeptic and wishes to expound the virtues of Doctor Snaffler's Purple Pills for Pimply People, he is merely a bore. But if he chances to suffer from some rare and choice disease such as Trypanosomiasis or Acromegaly, the doctor will be delighted to listen."

"Then are we to understand," Miss Bellingham asked, "that we are rare and choice products, in a legal sense?"

"Undoubtedly," replied Thorndyke. "The case of John Bellingham is, in many respects, unique. It will be followed with the deepest interest by the profession at large, and especially by medical jurists."

"How gratifying that should be to us!" said Miss Bellingham. "We may even attain undying fame in textbooks and treatises, and yet we are not so very much puffed up with our importance."

"No," said her father, "we could do without the fame quite well, and so, I think, could Hurst. Did Berkeley tell you of the proposal that he made?"

"Yes," said Thorndyke, "and I gather from what you say that he has repeated it."

"Yes. He sent Jellicoe to give me another chance, and I was tempted to take it, but my daughter was strongly against any compromise, and probably she is right. At any rate, she is more concerned than I am."

"What view did Mr. Jellicoe take?" Thorndyke asked.

"Oh, he was very cautious and reserved, but he didn't disguise his feeling that I should be wise to take a certainty in lieu of a very problematical fortune. He would certainly like me to agree, for he naturally wishes to get the affair settled and pocket his legacy."

"And have you definitely refused?"

"Yes, quite definitely. So Hurst will apply for permission to presume death and prove the will, and Jellicoe will support him. He says he has no choice."

"And you?"

"I suppose I shall oppose the application, though I don't quite know on what grounds."

"Before you take definite steps," said Thorndyke, "you ought to give the matter very careful consideration. I take it that you have very little doubt that your brother is dead. And if he is dead, any benefit that you may receive under the will must be conditional on the previous presumption or proof of death. But perhaps you have taken advice?"

"No, I have not. As our friend the Doctor has probably told you, my means – or rather, the lack of them – do not admit of my getting professional advice. Hence my delicacy about discussing the case with you."

"Then do you propose to conduct your case in person?"

"Yes. If it is necessary for me to appear in Court, as I suppose it will be, if I oppose the application."

Thorndyke reflected for a few moments and then said gravely, "You had much better not appear in person to conduct your case, Mr. Bellingham, for several reasons. To begin with, Mr. Hurst is sure to be represented by a capable counsel, and you will find yourself quite unable to meet the sudden exigencies of a contest in Court. You will be out-maneuvered. Then there is the judge to be considered."

"But surely one can rely on the judge dealing fairly with a man who is unable to afford a solicitor and counsel?"

"Undoubtedly, as a rule, a judge will give an unrepresented litigant every assistance and consideration. English judges in general are high-minded men with a deep sense of their great responsibilities. But you cannot afford to take any chances. You must consider the exceptions. A judge has been a counsel, and he may carry to the bench some of the professional prejudices of the bar. Indeed, if you consider the absurd license permitted to counsel in their treatment of witnesses, and the hostile attitude adopted by some judges toward medical and other scientific men who have to give their evidence, you will see that the judicial mind is not always quite as judicial as one would wish, especially when the privileges and immunities of the profession are concerned. Now, your appearance in person to conduct your case must, unavoidably, cause some inconvenience to the Court. Your ignorance of procedure and legal details must occasion some delay, and if the judge should happen to be an irritable man he might resent the inconvenience and delay. I don't say that would affect his decision – I don't think it would – but I am sure it would be wise to avoid giving offense to the judge. And, above all, it is most desirable to be able to detect and reply to any maneuvers on the part of the opposing counsel, which you certainly would not be able to do."

"This is excellent advice, Doctor Thorndyke," said Bellingham, with a grim smile, "but I'm afraid I shall have to take my chance."

"Not necessarily," said Thorndyke. "I am going to make a little proposal, which I will ask you to consider without prejudice as a mutual accommodation. You see, your case is one of exceptional interest – it will become a textbook case, as Miss Bellingham prophesied, and, since it lies within my specialty, it will be necessary for me to follow it in the closest detail. Now, it would be much more satisfactory to me to study it from within than from without, to say nothing of the credit which would accrue to me if I should be able to conduct it to a successful issue. I am therefore going to ask you to put your case in my hands and let me see what can be done with it. I know this is an unusual course for a professional man to take, but I think it is not improper under the circumstances."

Mr. Bellingham pondered in silence for a few moments, and then, after a glance at his daughter, began rather hesitatingly, "It's very generous of you, Doctor Thorndyke – "

"Pardon me," interrupted Thorndyke, "it is not. My motives, as I have explained, are purely egoistic."

Mr. Bellingham laughed uneasily and again glanced at his daughter, who, however, pursued her occupation of peeling a pear with calm deliberation and without lifting her eyes. Getting no help from her he asked, "Do you think that there is any possibility whatever of a successful issue?"

"Yes, a remote possibility – very remote, I fear, as things look at present, but if I thought the case absolutely hopeless I should advise you to stand aside and let events take their course."

"Supposing the case should come to a favorable termination, would you allow me to settle your fees in the ordinary way?"

"If the choice lay with me," replied Thorndyke, "I should say 'yes' with pleasure. But it does not. The attitude of the profession is very definitely unfavorable to 'speculative' practise. You may remember the well-known firm of Dodson and Fogg, who gained thereby much profit, but little credit. But why discuss contingencies of this kind? If I bring your case to a successful issue I shall have done very well for myself. We shall have benefited one another mutually. Come now, Miss Bellingham, I appeal to you. We have eaten salt together, to say nothing of pigeon pie and other cakes. Won't you back me up, and at the same time do a kindness to Doctor Berkeley?"

"Why, is Doctor Berkeley interested in our decision?"

"Certainly he is, as you will appreciate when I tell you that he actually tried to bribe me secretly out of his own pocket."

"Did you?" she asked, looking at me with an expression that rather alarmed me.

"Well, not exactly," I replied, mighty hot and uncomfortable, and wishing Thorndyke at the devil with his confidences. "I merely mentioned that the – the – solicitor's costs, you know, and that sort of thing – but you needn't jump on me, Miss Bellingham. Doctor Thorndyke did all that was necessary in that way."

She continued to look at me thoughtfully as I stammered out my excuses, and then said, "I wasn't going to. I was only thinking that poverty has its compensations. You are all so very good to us, and, for my part, I should accept Doctor Thorndyke's generous offer most gratefully, and thank him for making it so easy for us."

"Very well, my dear," said Mr. Bellingham, "we will enjoy the sweets of poverty, as you say – we have sampled the other kind of thing pretty freely – and do ourselves the pleasure of accepting a great kindness, most delicately offered."

"Thank you," said Thorndyke. "You have justified my faith in you, Miss Bellingham, and in the power of Dr. Berkeley's salt. I understand that you place your affairs in my hands?"

"Entirely and thankfully," replied Mr. Bellingham. "Whatever you think best to be done we agree to beforehand."

"Then," said I, "let us drink success to the cause. Port, if you please, Miss Bellingham. The vintage is not recorded, but it is quite wholesome, and a suitable medium for the sodium chloride of friendship." I filled her glass, and when the bottle had made its circuit, we stood up and solemnly pledged the new alliance.

"There is just one thing I would say before we dismiss the subject for the present," said Thorndyke. "It is a good thing to keep one's own counsel. When you get formal notice from Mr. Hurst's solicitors that proceedings are being commenced, you may refer them to Mr. Marchmont of Gray's Inn, who will nominally act for you. He will actually have nothing to do, but we must preserve the fiction that I am instructed by a solicitor. Meanwhile, and until the case goes into court, I think it very necessary that neither Mr. Jellicoe nor anyone else should know that I am connected with it. We must keep the other side in the dark, if we can."

"We will be as secret as the grave," said Mr. Bellingham, "and, as a matter of fact, it will be quite easy, since it happens, by a curious coincidence, that I am already acquainted with Mr. Marchmont. He acted for Stephen Blackmore, you remember, in that case that you unraveled so wonderfully. I knew the Blackmores."

"Did you?" said Thorndyke. "What a small world it is. And what a remarkable affair that was! The intricacies and cross-issues made it quite absorbingly interesting, and it is noteworthy for me in another respect, for it was one of the first cases in which I was associated with Doctor Jervis."

"Yes, and a mighty useful associate I was," remarked Jervis, "though I did pick up one or two facts by accident. And, by the way, the Blackmore case had certain points in common with your case, Mr. Bellingham. There was a disappearance and a disputed will, and the man who vanished was a scholar and an antiquarian."

"Cases in our specialty are apt to have certain general resemblances," Thorndyke said, and as he spoke he directed a keen glance at his junior, the significance of which I partly understood when he abruptly changed the subject.

"The newspaper reports of your brother's disappearance, Mr. Bellingham, were remarkably full of detail. There were even plans of your house and that of Mr. Hurst. Do you know who supplied the information?"

"No, I don't," replied Mr. Bellingham. "I know that I didn't. Some newspaper men came to me for information, but I sent them packing. So, I understand, did Hurst, and as for Jellicoe, you might as well cross-examine an oyster."

"Well," said Thorndyke, "the pressmen have queer methods of getting 'copy', but still, someone must have given them that description of your brother and those plans. It would be interesting to know who it was. However, we don't know, and now let us dismiss these legal topics, with suitable apologies for having introduced them."

"And perhaps," said I, "we may as well adjourn to what we call the drawing-room – it is really Barnard's den – and leave the housekeeper to wrestle with the debris."

We migrated to the cheerfully shabby little apartment, and, when Mrs. Gummer had served coffee, with gloomy resignation (as who should say: "If you will drink this sort of stuff I suppose you must, but don't blame me for the consequences"), I settled Mr. Bellingham in Barnard's favorite lop-sided easy chair – the depressed seat of which suggested its customary use by an elephant of sedentary habits – and opened the diminutive piano.

"I wonder if Miss Bellingham would give us a little music?" I said.

"I wonder if she could?" was the smiling response. "Do you know," she continued, "I have not touched a piano for nearly two years? It will be quite an interesting experiment – to me, but if it fails, you will be the sufferers. So you must choose."

"My verdict," said Mr. Bellingham, "is *fiat experimentum*, though I won't complete the quotation, as that would seem to disparage Doctor Barnard's piano. But before you begin, Ruth, there is one rather disagreeable matter that I want to dispose of, so that I may not disturb the harmony with it later."

He paused and we all looked at him expectantly.

"I suppose, Doctor Thorndyke," he said, "you read the newspapers?"

"I don't," replied Dr. Thorndyke. "But I ascertain, for purely business purposes, what they contain."

"Then," said Mr. Bellingham, "you have probably met with some accounts of the finding of certain human remains, apparently portions of a mutilated body."

"Yes, I have seen those reports and filed them for future reference."

"Exactly. Well, now, it can hardly be necessary for me to tell you that those remains – the mutilated remains of some poor murdered creature, as there can be no doubt they are – have seemed to have a very dreadful significance for me. You will understand what I mean, and I want to ask you if – if they have made a similar suggestion to you?"

Thorndyke paused before replying, with his eyes bent thoughtfully on the floor, and we all looked at him anxiously.

"It's very natural," he said at length, "that you should associate these remains with the mystery of your brother's disappearance. I should like to say that you are wrong in doing so, but if I did I should be uncandid. There are certain facts that do, undoubtedly, seem to suggest a connection, and, up to the present, there are no definite facts of a contrary significance."

Mr. Bellingham sighed deeply and shifted uncomfortably in his chair.

"It is a horrible affair!" he said huskily, "horrible! Would you mind, Doctor Thorndyke, telling us just how the matter stands in your opinion – what the probabilities are, for and against?"

Again Thorndyke reflected awhile, and it seemed to me that he was not very willing to discuss the subject. However, the question had been asked pointedly, and eventually he answered, "At the present stage of the investigation it is not very easy to state the balance of probabilities. The matter is still quite speculative. The bones which have been found hitherto (for we are dealing with a skeleton, not with a body) have been exclusively those which are useless for personal identification, which is, in itself, a rather curious and striking fact. The general character and dimensions of the bones seem to suggest a middle-aged man of about your brother's height, and the date of deposition appears to be in agreement with the date of his disappearance."

"Is it known, then, when they were deposited?" asked Mr. Bellingham.

"In the case of those found at Sidcup it seems possible to deduce an approximate date. The watercress-bed was cleaned out about two years ago, so they could not have been lying there longer than that, and their condition suggests that they could not have been there much less than two years, as there is apparently no vestige of the soft structures left. Of course, I am speaking from the newspaper reports only. I have no direct knowledge of the matter."

"Have they found any considerable part of the body yet? I haven't been reading the papers myself. My little friend, Miss Oman, brought a great bundle of 'em for me to read, but I couldn't stand it. I pitched the whole boiling of 'em out of the window."

I thought I detected a slight twinkle in Thorndyke's eye, but he answered quite gravely, "I think I can give you the particulars from memory, though I won't guarantee the dates. The original discovery was made, apparently quite accidentally, at Sidcup on the fifteenth of July. It consisted of a complete left arm, minus the third finger and including the bones of the shoulder – the shoulder-blade and collar-bone. This discovery seems to have set the local population, especially the juvenile part of it, searching all the ponds and streams of the neighborhood – "

"Cannibals!" interjected Mr. Bellingham.

"With the result that there was dredged up out of a pond near St. Mary Cray, in Kent, a right thigh-bone. There is a slight clue to identity in respect of this bone, since the head of it has a small patch of 'eburnation' – that is a sort of porcelain-like polish that occurs on the parts of bones that form a joint when the natural covering of cartilage is destroyed by disease. It is produced by the unprotected surface of the bone grinding against the similarly unprotected surface of another."

"And how," Mr. Bellingham asked, "would that help the identification?"

"It would indicate," Thorndyke replied, "that the deceased had probably suffered from rheumatoid arthritis – what is commonly known as rheumatic gout – and he would probably have limped slightly and complained of some pain in the right hip."

"I'm afraid that doesn't help us very much," said Mr. Bellingham, "for, you see, John had a pretty pronounced limp from another cause, an old injury to his left ankle, and as to complaining of pain – well, he was a hardy old fellow and not much given to making complaints of any kind. But don't let me interrupt you."

"The next discovery," continued Thorndyke, "was made near Lee, by the police this time. They seem to have developed sudden activity in the

299

matter, and in searching the neighborhood of West Kent they dragged out of a pond near Lee the bones of a right foot. Now, if it had been the left instead of the right we might have a clue, as I understand your brother had fractured his left ankle, and there might have been some traces of the injury on the foot itself."

"Yes," said Mr. Bellingham. "I suppose there might. The injury was described as a Pott's fracture."

"Exactly. Well, now, after this discovery at Lee it seems that the police set on foot a systematic search of all the ponds and small pieces of water around London, and, on the twenty-third, they found in the Cuckoo Pits in Epping Forest, not far from Woodford, the bones of a right arm (including those of the shoulder, as before), which seem to be part of the same body."

"Yes," said Mr. Bellingham, "I heard of that. Quite close to my old house. Horrible! Horrible! It gave me the shudders to think of it – to think that poor old John may have been waylaid and murdered when he was actually coming to see me. He may even have got into the grounds by the back gate, if it was left unfastened, and been followed in there and murdered. You remember that a scarab from his watch-chain was found there? But is it clear that this arm was the fellow of the arm that was found at Sidcup?"

"It seems to agree in character and dimensions," said Thorndyke, "and the agreement is strongly supported by a discovery made two days later."

"What is that?" Mr. Bellingham demanded.

"It is the lower half of a trunk which the police dragged out of a rather deep pond on the skirts of the forest at Loughton – Staple's Pond, it is called. The bones found were the pelvis – that is, the two hip-bones – and six vertebrae, or joints of the backbone. Having discovered these, the police dammed the stream and pumped the pond dry, but no other bones were found, which is rather odd, as there should have been a pair of ribs belonging to the upper vertebra – the twelfth dorsal vertebra. It suggests some curious questions as to the method of dismemberment, but I mustn't go into unpleasant details. The point is that the cavity of the right hip-joint showed a patch of eburnation corresponding to that on the head of the right thigh-bone that was found at St. Mary Cray. So there can be very little doubt that these bones are all part of the same body."

"I see," grunted Mr. Bellingham, and he added, after a moment's thought, "Now, the question is, Are these bones the remains of my brother John? What do you say, Doctor Thorndyke?"

"I say that the question cannot be answered on the facts at present known to us. It can only be said that they may be, and that some of the circumstances suggest that they are. But we can only wait for further discoveries. At any moment the police may light upon some portion of the skeleton which will settle the question definitely one way or the other."

"I suppose," said Mr. Bellingham, "I can't be of any service to you in the matter of identification?"

"Indeed you can," said Thorndyke, "and I was going to ask you to assist me. What I want you to do is this: Write down a full description of your brother, including every detail known to you, together with an account of every illness or injury from which you know him to have suffered. Also the names and, if possible, the addresses of any doctors, surgeons, or dentists who may have attended him at any time. The dentists are particularly important, as their information would be invaluable if the skull belonging to these bones should be discovered."

Mr. Bellingham shuddered.

"It's a shocking idea," he said, "but, of course you are right. You must have the facts if you are to form an opinion. I will write out what you want and send it to you without delay. And now, for God's sake, let us throw off this nightmare, for a little while, at least! What is there, Ruth, among Doctor Barnard's music that you can manage?"

Barnard's collection in general inclined to the severely classical, but we disinterred from the heap a few lighter works of an old-fashioned kind, including a volume of Mendelssohn's *Lieder ohne Worte*, and with one of these Miss Bellingham made trial of her skill, playing it with excellent taste and quite adequate execution. That, at least, was her father's verdict, for, as to me, I found it the perfection of happiness merely to sit and look at her – a state of mind that would have been in no wise disturbed even by "Silvery Waves" or "The Maiden's Prayer."

Thus, with simple, homely music, and conversation always cheerful and sometimes brilliant, slipped away one of the pleasantest evenings of my life, and slipped away all too soon. St. Dunstan's clock was the fly in the ointment, for it boomed out intrusively the hour of eleven just as my guests were beginning thoroughly to appreciate one another, and thereby carried the sun (with a minor paternal satellite) out of the firmament of my heaven. For I had, in my professional capacity, given strict injunctions that Mr. Bellingham should on no account sit up late, and now, in my social capacity, I had smilingly to hear "the doctor's orders" quoted. It was a scurvy return for all my care.

When Mr. and Miss Bellingham departed, Thorndyke and Jervis would have gone too, but noting my bereaved condition, and being withal compassionate and tender of heart, they were persuaded to stay awhile and bear me company in a consolatory pipe.

301

Chapter XI
The Evidence Reviewed

"So the game has opened," observed Thorndyke, as he struck a match. "The play has begun with a cautious lead off by the other side. Very cautious and not very confident."

"Why do you say 'not very confident'?" I asked.

"Well, it is evident that Hurst – and, I fancy, Jellicoe too – is anxious to buy off Bellingham's opposition, and at a pretty long price, under the circumstances. And when we consider how very little Bellingham has to offer against the presumption of his brother's death, it looks as if Hurst hadn't much to say on his side."

"No," said Jervis, "he can't hold many trumps or he wouldn't be willing to pay four-hundred a year for his opponent's chance, and that is just as well, for it seems to me that our own hand is a pretty poor one."

"We must look through our hand and see what we do hold," said Thorndyke. "Our trump card at present – a rather small one, I'm afraid – is the obvious intention of the testator that the bulk of the property should go to his brother."

"I suppose you will begin your inquiries now?" I said.

"We began them some time ago – the day after you brought us the will, in fact. Jervis has been through the registers and has ascertained that no interment under the name of John Bellingham has taken place since the disappearance, which was just what we expected. He has also discovered that some other person has been making similar inquiries, which, again, is what we expected."

"And your own investigations?"

"Have given negative results for the most part. I found Doctor Norbury, at the British Museum, very friendly and helpful. So friendly, in fact, that I am thinking whether I may not be able to enlist his help in certain private researches of my own, with reference to the change effected by time in the physical properties of certain substances."

"Oh, you haven't told me about that," said Jervis.

"No. I haven't really commenced to plan my experiments yet, and they will probably lead to nothing when I do. It occurred to me that, possibly, in the course of time, certain molecular changes might take place in substances such as wood, bone, pottery, stucco, and other common materials, and that these changes might alter their power of conducting or transmitting molecular vibrations. Now, if this should turn out to be the case, it would be a fact of considerable importance, medico-legally and otherwise, for it would be possible to determine approximately the age of any object of known composition by testing its reactions to electricity, heat, light, and other molecular vibrations. I thought of seeking Doctor Norbury's assistance because he can furnish me with materials for experiment of such great age that the reactions, if any, should be extremely easy to demonstrate. But to return to our case. I learned from him that John Bellingham had certain friends in Paris – collectors and museum officials – whom he was in the habit of visiting for the purpose of study and exchange of specimens. I have made inquiries of all these, and none of them had seen him during his last visit. In fact, I have not yet discovered anyone who had seen Bellingham in Paris on this occasion. So his visit there remains a mystery for the present."

"It doesn't seem to be of much importance, since he undoubtedly came back," I remarked, but to this Thorndyke demurred.

"It is impossible to estimate the importance of the unknown," said he.

"Well, how does the matter stand," asked Jervis, "on the evidence that we have? John Bellingham disappeared on a certain date. Is there anything to show what was the manner of his disappearance?"

"The facts in our possession," said Thorndyke, "which are mainly those set forth in the newspaper report, suggest several alternative possibilities, and in view of the coming inquiry – for they will, no doubt, have to be gone into in Court, to some extent – it may be worth while to consider them. There are five conceivable hypotheses" – here Thorndyke checked them on his fingers as he proceeded – "First, he may still be alive. Second, he may have died and been buried without identification. Third, he may have been murdered by some unknown person. Fourth, he may have been murdered by Hurst and his body concealed. Fifth, he may have been murdered by his brother. Let us examine these possibilities seriatim.

"First, he may still be alive. If he is, he must either have disappeared voluntarily, have lost his memory suddenly and not been identified, or have been imprisoned – on a false charge or otherwise. Let us take the first case – that of voluntary disappearance. Obviously, its improbability is extreme."

"Jellicoe doesn't think so," said I. "He thinks it quite on the cards that John Bellingham is alive. He says that it is not a very unusual thing for a man to disappear for a time."

"Then why is he applying for a presumption of death?"

"Just what I asked him. He says that it is the correct thing to do. That the entire responsibility rests on the Court."

"That is all nonsense," said Thorndyke. "Jellicoe is the trustee for his absent client, and, if he thinks that client is alive, it is his duty to keep the

303

estate intact, and he knows that perfectly well. We may take it that Jellicoe is of the same opinion as I am: That John Bellingham is dead."

"Still," I urged, "men do disappear from time to time, and turn up again after years of absence."

"Yes, but for a definite reason. Either they are irresponsible vagabounds who take this way of shuffling off their responsibilities, or they are men who have been caught in a net of distasteful circumstances. For instance, a civil servant or a solicitor or a tradesman finds himself bound for life to a locality and an occupation of intolerable monotony. Perhaps he has an ill-tempered wife, who after the amiable fashion of a certain type of woman, thinking that her husband is pinned down without a chance of escape, gives a free rein to her temper. The man puts up with it for years, but at last it becomes unbearable. Then he suddenly disappears, and small blame to him. But this was not Bellingham's case. He was a wealthy bachelor with an engrossing interest in life, free to go whither he would and to do whatsoever he wished. Why should he disappear? The thing is incredible.

"As to his having lost his memory and remained unidentified, that, also, is incredible in the case of a man who had visiting-cards and letters in his pocket, whose linen was marked, and who was being inquired for everywhere by the police. As to his being in prison, we may dismiss that possibility, inasmuch as a prisoner, both before and after conviction, would have full opportunity of communicating with his friends.

"The second possibility, that he may have died suddenly and been buried without identification, is highly improbable, but, as it is conceivable that the body might have been robbed and the means of identification thus lost, it remains as a possibility that has to be considered, remote as it is.

"The third hypothesis, that he may have been murdered by some unknown person, is, under the circumstances, not wildly improbable, but, as the police were on the lookout and a detailed description of the missing man's person was published in the papers, it would involve the complete concealment of the body. But this would exclude the most probable form of crime – the casual robbery with violence. It is therefore possible, but highly improbable.

"The fourth hypothesis is that Bellingham was murdered by Hurst. Now the one fact which militates against this view is that Hurst apparently had no motive for committing the murder. We are assured by Jellicoe that no one but himself knew the contents of the will, and if this is so – but mind, we have no evidence that it is so – Hurst would have no reason to suppose that he had anything material to gain by his cousin's death. Otherwise the hypothesis presents no inherent improbabilities. The man was last seen alive at Hurst's house. He was seen to enter it and he was never seen to leave it – we are still taking the facts as stated in the newspapers, remember – and it now appears that he stands to benefit enormously by that man's death."

"But," I objected, "you are forgetting that, directly the man was missed Hurst and the servants together searched the entire house."

"Yes. What did they search for?"

"Why, for Mr. Bellingham, of course."

"Exactly, for Mr. Bellingham. That is, for a living man. Now how do you search a house for a living man? You look in all the rooms. When you look in a room if he is there, you see him. If you do not see him, you assume that he is not there. You don't look under the sofa or behind the piano, you don't pull out large drawers or open cupboards. You just look into the rooms. That is what these people seem to have done. And they did not see Mr. Bellingham. Mr. Bellingham's corpse might have been stowed away out of sight in any one of the rooms that they looked into."

"That is a grim thought," said Jervis, "but it is perfectly true. There is no evidence that the man was not lying dead in the house at the very time of the search."

"But even so," said I, "there was the body to be disposed of somehow. Now how could he possibly have got rid of the body without being observed?"

"Ah!" said Thorndyke, "now we are touching on a point of crucial importance. If anyone should ever write a treatise on the art of murder – not an exhibition of literary fireworks like De Quincey's, but a genuine working treatise – he might leave all other technical details to take care of themselves if he could describe some really practicable plan for disposing of the body. That is, and always has been, the great stumbling-block to the murderer: To get rid of the body. The human body," he continued, thoughtfully regarding his pipe, just as, in the days of my pupilage, he was wont to regard the black-board chalk, "is a very remarkable object. It presents a combination of properties, that make it singularly difficult to conceal permanently. It is bulky and of an awkward shape, it is heavy, it is completely incombustible, it is chemically unstable, and its decomposition yields great volumes of highly odorous gases, and it nevertheless contains identifiable structures of the highest degree of permanence. It is extremely difficult to preserve unchanged, and it is still more difficult completely to destroy. The essential permanence of the human body is well shown in the classical case of Eugene Aram, but a still more striking instance is that of Sekenen-Ra the Third, one of the last kings of the seventeenth Egyptian dynasty. Here, after a lapse of four-thousand years, it has been possible to determine not only the cause of death and the manner of its occurrence, but the way in which the king fell, the nature of the weapon with which the fatal wound was inflicted, and even the position of the assailant. And the permanence of the body under other conditions is admirably shown in the case of Doctor Parkman, of Boston, U. S. A., in which identification was actually effected by means of remains collected from the ashes of a furnace."

"Then we may take it," said Jervis, "that the world has not yet seen the last of John Bellingham."

"I think we may regard that as almost a certainty," replied Thorndyke. "The only question – and a very important one – is as to when the reappearance may take place. It may be to-morrow or it may be centuries hence, when all the issues involved have been forgotten."

"Assuming," said I, "for the sake of argument, that Hurst did murder him and that the body was concealed in the study at the time the search was made. How could it have been disposed of? If you had been in Hurst's place, how would you have gone to work?"

Thorndyke smiled at the bluntness of my question.

"You are asking me for an incriminating statement," said he, "delivered in the presence of a witness too. But, as a matter of fact, there is no use in speculating *a priori*. We should have to reconstruct a purely imaginary situation, the circumstances of which are unknown to us, and we should almost certainly reconstruct it wrong. What we may fairly assume is that no reasonable person, no matter how immoral, would find himself in the position that you suggest. Murder is usually a crime of impulse, and the murderer a person of feeble self-control. Such persons are most unlikely to make elaborate and ingenious arrangements for the disposal of the bodies of their victims. Even the cold-blooded perpetrators of the most carefully planned murders appear as I have said, to break down at this point. The almost insuperable difficulty of getting rid of the human body is not appreciated until the murderer suddenly finds himself face to face with it.

"In the case you are suggesting, the choice would seem to lie between burial on the premises or dismemberment and dispersal of the fragments, and either method would be pretty certain to lead to discovery."

"As illustrated by the remains of which you were speaking to Mr. Bellingham," Jervis remarked.

"Exactly," Thorndyke answered, "though we could hardly imagine a reasonably intelligent criminal adopting a watercress-bed as a hiding place.

"No. That was certainly an error of judgment. By the way, I thought it best to say nothing while you were talking to Bellingham, but I noticed that, in discussing the possibility of those being the bones of his brother, you made no comment on the absence of the third finger of the left hand. I am sure you didn't overlook it, but isn't it a point of some importance?"

"As to identification? Under the present circumstances, I think not. If there were a man missing who had lost that finger it would, of course, be an important fact. But I have not heard of any such man. Or, again, if there were any evidence that the finger had been removed before death, it would be highly important. But there is no such evidence. It may have been cut off after death, and that is where the real significance of its absence lies."

"I don't see quite what you mean," said Jervis.

"I mean that, if there is no report of any missing man who had lost that particular finger, the probability is that the finger was removed after death. And then arises the interesting question of motive. Why should it have been removed? It could hardly have become detached accidentally. What do you suggest?"

"Well," said Jervis, "it might have been a peculiar finger – a finger, for instance, with some characteristic deformity such as an ankylosed joint, which would be easy to identify."

"Yes, but that explanation introduces the same difficulty. No person with a deformed or ankylosed finger has been reported as missing."

Jervis puckered up his brows, and looked at me.

"I'm hanged if I see any other explanation," he said. "Do you, Berkeley?"

I shook my head.

"Don't forget which finger it is that is missing," said Thorndyke. "The third finger of the left hand."

"Oh, I see!" said Jervis. "The ring-finger. You mean that it may have been removed for the sake of a ring that wouldn't come off."

"Yes. It would not be the first instance of the kind. Fingers have been severed from dead hands – and even from living ones – for the sake of rings that were too tight to be drawn off. And the fact that it is the left hand supports the suggestion, for a ring that was inconveniently tight would be worn by preference on the left hand, as that is usually slightly smaller than the right. What is the matter, Berkeley?"

A sudden light had burst upon me, and I suppose my countenance betrayed the fact.

"I am a confounded fool!" I exclaimed.

"Oh, don't say that," said Jervis. "Give your friends a chance."

"I ought to have seen this long ago and told you about it. John Bellingham did wear a ring, and it was so tight that, when once he had got it on, he could never get it off again."

"Do you happen to know on which hand he wore it?" Thorndyke asked.

307

"Yes. It was on the left hand. Because Miss Bellingham, who told me about it, said that he would never have been able to get the ring on at all but for the fact that his left hand was slightly smaller than his right."

"There it is, then," said Thorndyke. "With this new fact in our possession, the absence of the finger furnishes the starting-point of some very curious speculations."

"As, for instance," said Jervis.

"Ah, under the circumstances, I must leave you to pursue those speculations independently. I am now acting for Mr. Bellingham."

Jervis grinned and was silent for a-while, refilling his pipe thoughtfully, but when he had got it alight he resumed.

"To return to the question of the disappearance. You don't consider it highly improbable that Bellingham might have been murdered by Hurst?"

"Oh, don't imagine I am making an accusation. I am considering the various probabilities merely in the abstract. The same reasoning applies to the Bellinghams. As to whether any of them did commit the murder, that is a question of personal character. I certainly do not suspect the Bellinghams after having seen them, and with regard to Hurst, I know nothing, or at least very little, to his disadvantage."

"Do you know anything?" asked Jervis.

"Well," Thorndyke said, with some hesitation, "it seems a thought unkind to rake up the little details of a man's past, and yet it has to be done. I have, of course, made the usual routine inquiries concerning the parties to this affair, and this is what they have brought to light.

"Hurst, as you know, is a stockbroker – a man of good position and reputation, but, about ten years ago, he seems to have committed an indiscretion, to put it mildly, which nearly got him into rather serious difficulties. He appears to have speculated rather heavily and considerably beyond his means, for when a sudden spasm of the markets upset his calculations, it turned out that he had been employing his clients' capital and securities. For a time it looked as if there was going to be serious trouble. Then, quite unexpectedly, he managed to raise the necessary amount in some way and settle all claims. Whence he got the money has never been discovered to this day, which is a curious circumstance, seeing that the deficiency was rather over five-thousand pounds, but the important fact is that he did get it and that he paid up all that he owed. So that he was only a potential defaulter, so to speak, and discreditable as the affair undoubtedly was, it does not seem to have any direct bearing on this present case."

"No," Jervis agreed, "though it makes one consider his position with more attention than one would otherwise."

308

"Undoubtedly," said Thorndyke. "A reckless gambler is a man whose conduct cannot be relied on. He is subject to vicissitudes of fortune which may force him into other kinds of wrong-doing. Many an embezzlement has been preceded by an unlucky plunge on the turf."

"Assuming the responsibility for this disappearance to lie between Hurst and – and the Bellinghams," said I, with an uncomfortable gulp as I mentioned the names of my friends, "to which side does the balance of probability incline?"

"To the side of Hurst, I should say, without doubt," replied Thorndyke. "The case stands thus – on the facts presented to us: Hurst appears to have had no motive for killing the deceased (as we will call him), but the man was seen to enter the house, was never seen to leave it, and was never again seen alive. Bellingham, on the other hand, had a motive, as he had believed himself to be the principal beneficiary under the will. But the deceased was not seen at his house, and there is no evidence that he went to the house or to the neighborhood, excepting the scarab that was found there. But the evidence of the scarab is vitiated by the fact that Hurst was present when it was picked up, and that it was found on a spot over which Hurst had passed only a few minutes previously. Until Hurst is cleared, it seems to me that the presence of the scarab proves nothing against the Bellinghams."

"Then your opinions on the case," said I, "are based entirely on the facts that have been made public?"

"Yes, mainly. I do not necessarily accept those facts just as they are presented, and I may have certain views of my own on the case. But if I have, I do not feel in a position to discuss them. For the present, discussion has to be limited to the facts and inferences offered by the parties concerned."

"There!" exclaimed Jervis, rising to knock his pipe out, "that is where Thorndyke has you. He lets you think you're in the thick of the 'know' until one fine morning you wake up and discover that you have only been a gaping outsider, and then you are mightily astonished – and so are the other side, too, for that matter. But we must really be off now, mustn't we, reverend senior?"

"I suppose we must," replied Thorndyke, and, as he drew on his gloves, he asked, "Have you heard from Barnard lately?"

"Oh, yes," I answered. "I wrote to him at Smyrna to say that the practise was flourishing and that I was quite happy and contented, and that he might stay away as long as he liked. He writes by return that he will prolong his holiday if an opportunity offers, but will let me know later."

"Gad," said Jervis, "it was a stroke of luck for Barnard that Bellingham happened to have such a magnificent daughter – there! Don't mind me, old man. You go in and win – she's worth it, isn't she, Thorndyke?"

"Miss Bellingham's a very charming young lady," replied Thorndyke. "I am most favorably impressed by both the father and the daughter, and I only trust that we may be able to be of some service to them." With this sedate little speech Thorndyke shook my hand, and I watched my two friends go on their way until their fading shapes were swallowed up in the darkness of Fetter Lane.

Chapter XII
A Voyage of Discovery

It was two or three mornings after my little supper party that, as I stood in the consulting-room brushing my hat preparatory to starting on my morning round, Adolphus appeared at the door to announce two gentlemen waiting in the surgery. I told him to bring them in, and a moment later Thorndyke entered, accompanied by Jervis. I noted that they looked uncommonly large in that little apartment, especially Thorndyke, but I had no time to consider this phenomenon, for the latter, when he had shaken my hand, proceeded at once to explain the object of their visit.

"We have come to ask a favor, Berkeley," he said, "to ask you to do us a very great service in the interests of your friends the Bellinghams."

"You know I shall be delighted," I said warmly. "What is it?"

"I will explain. You know – or perhaps you don't – that the police have collected all the bones that have been discovered and deposited them in the mortuary at Woodford, where they are to be viewed by the coroner's jury. Now, it has become imperative that I should have more definite and reliable information than I can get from the newspapers. The natural thing for me would be to go down and examine them myself, but there are circumstances that make it very desirable that my connection with the case should not leak out. Consequently, I can't go myself, and, for the same reason, I can't send Jervis. On the other hand, as it is now stated pretty openly that the police consider the bones to be almost certainly those of John Bellingham, it would seem perfectly natural that you, as Godfrey Bellingham's doctor, should go down to view them on his behalf."

"I should like to," I said. "I would give anything to go, but how is it to be managed? It would mean a whole day off and leaving the practise to look after itself."

"I think it could be managed," said Thorndyke, "and the matter is really important for two reasons. One is that the inquest opens to-morrow, and someone certainly ought to be there to watch the proceedings on Godfrey's behalf, and the other is that our client has received notice from Hurst's solicitors that the application will be heard in the Probate Court in a few days."

"Isn't that rather sudden?" I asked.

"It certainly suggests that there has been a good deal more activity than we were given to understand. But you see the importance of the affair. The inquest will be a sort of dress rehearsal for the Probate Court, and it is

311

quite essential that we should have a chance of estimating the management."

"Yes, I see that. But how are we to manage about the practise?"

"We shall find you a substitute."

"Through a medical agent?"

"Yes," said Jervis, "Turcival will find us a man. In fact, he has done it. I saw him this morning. He has a man who is waiting up in town to negotiate for the purchase of a practise and who would do the job for a couple of guineas. Quite a reliable man. Only say the word, and I will run off to Adam Street and engage him definitely."

"Very well. You engage the *locum tenens*, and I will be prepared to start for Woodford as soon as he turns up."

"Excellent!" said Thorndyke. "That is a great weight off my mind. And if you could manage to drop in this evening and smoke a pipe with us we could talk over the plan of campaign and let you know what items of information we are particularly in want of."

I promised to turn up at King's Bench Walk as soon after half-past eight as possible, and my two friends then took their departure, leaving me to set out in high spirits on my scanty round of visits.

It is surprising what different aspects things present from different points of view. How relative are our estimates of the conditions and circumstances of life. To the urban workman – the journeyman baker or tailor, for instance, laboring year in year out in a single building – a holiday ramble on Hampstead Heath is a veritable voyage of discovery – whereas to the sailor the shifting panorama of the whole wide world is but the commonplace of the day's work.

So I reflected as I took my place in the train at Liverpool Street on the following day. There had been a time when a trip by rail to the borders of Epping Forest would have been far from a thrilling experience. Now, after vegetating in the little world of Fetter Lane, it was quite an adventure.

The enforced inactivity of a railway journey is favorable to thought, and I had much to think about. The last few weeks had witnessed momentous changes in my outlook. New interests had arisen, new friendships had grown up, and above all, there had stolen into my life that supreme influence that, for good or for evil, according to my fortune, was to color and pervade it even to its close. Those few days of companionable labor in the reading-room, with the homely hospitalities of the milk-shop and the pleasant walks homeward through the friendly London streets, had called into existence a new world – a world in which the gracious personality of Ruth Bellingham was the one dominating reality. And thus, as I leaned back in the corner of the railway carriage with an unlighted pipe in my hand, the events of the immediate past, together with those

312

more problematical ones of the impending future, occupied me rather to the exclusion of the business of the moment, which was to review the remains collected in the Woodford mortuary, until, as the train approached Stratford, the odors of the soap and bone-manure factories poured in at the open window and (by a natural association of ideas) brought me back to the object of my quest.

As to the exact purpose of this expedition, I was not very clear, but I knew that I was acting as Thorndyke's proxy and thrilled with pride at the thought. But what particular light my investigations were to throw upon the intricate Bellingham case I had no very definite idea. With a view to fixing the procedure in my mind, I took Thorndyke's written instructions from my pocket and read them over carefully. They were very full and explicit, making ample allowance for my lack of experience in medico-legal matters:

> *1. Do not appear to make minute investigations or in any way excite remark.*
>
> *2. Ascertain if all the bones belonging to each region are present, and if not, which are missing.*
>
> *3. Measure the extreme length of the principal bones and compare those of opposite sides.*
>
> *4. Examine the bones with reference to age, sex, and muscular development of the deceased.*
>
> *5. Note the presence or absence of signs of constitutional disease, local disease of bone or adjacent structures, old or recent injuries, and any other departures from the normal or usual.*
>
> *6. Observe the presence or absence of adipocere and its position, if present.*
>
> *7. Note any remains of tendons, ligaments, or other soft structures.*
>
> *8. Examine the Sidcup hand with reference to the question as to whether the finger was separated before or after death.*
>
> *9. Estimate the probable period of submersion and note any changes (as e.g., mineral or organic staining) due to the character of the water or mud.*
>
> *10. Ascertain the circumstances (immediate and remote) that led to the discovery of the bones and the names of the persons concerned in those circumstances.*
>
> *11. Commit all information to writing as soon as possible, and make plans and diagrams on the spot, if circumstances permit.*

12. Preserve an impassive exterior. Listen attentively but without eagerness; ask as few questions as possible; pursue any inquiry that your observations on the spot may suggest.

These were my instructions, and, considering that I was going merely to inspect a few dry bones, they appeared rather formidable. In fact, the more I read them over the greater became my misgivings as to my qualifications for the task.

As I approached the mortuary it became evident that some, at least, of Thorndyke's admonitions were by no means unnecessary. The place was in charge of a police sergeant, who watched my approach suspiciously, and some half-dozen men, obviously newspaper reporters, hovered about the entrance like a pack of jackals. I presented the coroner's order which Mr. Marchmont had obtained, and which the sergeant read with his back against the wall, to prevent the newspaper men from looking over his shoulder.

My credentials being found satisfactory, the door was unlocked and I entered, accompanied by three enterprising reporters, whom, however, the sergeant summarily ejected and locked out, returning to usher me into the presence and to observe my proceedings with intelligent but highly embarrassing interest.

The bones were laid out on a large table and covered with a sheet, which the sergeant slowly turned back, watching my face intently as he did so to note the impression that the spectacle made upon me. I imagine that he must have been somewhat disappointed by my impassive demeanor, for the remains suggested to me nothing more than a rather shabby set of "student's osteology." The whole collection had been set out by the police surgeon (as the sergeant informed me) in their proper anatomical order – notwithstanding which I counted them over carefully to make sure that none were missing, checking them by the list with which Thorndyke had furnished me.

"I see you have found the left thigh-bone," I remarked, observing that this did not appear in the list.

"Yes," said the sergeant, "that turned up yesterday evening in a big pond called Baldwin's Pond in the Sandpit plain, near Little Monk Wood."

"Is that near here?" I asked.

"In the forest up Loughton way," was the reply.

I made a note of the fact (on which the sergeant looked as if he was sorry he had mentioned it), and then turned my attention to a general consideration of the bones before examining them in detail. Their appearance would have been improved and examination facilitated by a thorough scrubbing, for they were just as they had been taken from their

314

respective resting-places, and it was difficult to decide whether their reddish-yellow color was an actual stain or due to a deposit on the surface. In any case, as it affected them all alike, I thought it an interesting feature and made a note of it. They bore numerous traces of their sojourn in the various ponds from which they had been recovered, but these gave me little help in determining the length of time during which they had been submerged. They were, of course, encrusted with mud, and little wisps of pond-weed stuck to them in places, but these facts furnished only the vaguest measure of time.

Some of the traces were, indeed, more informing. To several of the bones, for instance, there adhered the dried egg-clusters of the common pond-snail, and in one of the hollows of the right shoulder-blade (the "infraspinous fossa") was a group of the mud-built tubes of the red river-worm. These remains gave proof of a considerable period of submersion, and since they could not have been deposited on the bones until all the flesh had disappeared they furnished evidence that some time – a month or two at any rate – had elapsed since this had happened. Incidentally, too, their distribution showed the position in which the bones had lain, and though this appeared to be of no importance in the existing circumstances, I made careful notes of the situation of each adherent body, illustrating their position by rough sketches.

The sergeant watched my proceedings with an indulgent smile.

"You're making a regular inventory, sir," he remarked, "as if you were going to put 'em up for auction. I shouldn't think those snails' eggs would be much help in identification. And all that has been done already," he added as I produced my measuring-tape.

"No doubt," I replied, "but my business is to make independent observations, to check the others, if necessary." And I proceeded to measure each of the principal bones separately and to compare those of the opposite sides. The agreement in dimensions and general characteristics of the pairs of bones left little doubt that all were parts of one skeleton, a conclusion that was confirmed by the eburnated patch on the head of the right thigh-bone and the corresponding patch in the socket of the right hip-bone. When I had finished my measurements I went over the entire series of bones in detail, examining each with the closest attention for any of those signs which Thorndyke had indicated, and eliciting nothing but a monotonously reiterated negative. They were distressingly and disappointingly normal.

"Well, sir, what do you make of 'em?" the sergeant asked cheerfully as I shut up my notebook and straightened my back. "Whose bones are they? Are they Mr. Bellingham's, think ye?"

"I should be very sorry to say whose bones they are," I replied. "One bone is very much like another, you know."

"I suppose it is," he agreed, "but I thought that, with all that measuring and all those notes, you might have arrived at something definite." Evidently he was disappointed in me, and I was somewhat disappointed in myself when I contrasted Thorndyke's elaborate instructions with the meager result of my investigations. For what did my discoveries amount to? And how much was the inquiry advanced by the few entries in my notebook?

The bones were apparently those of a man of fair though not remarkable muscular development. Over thirty years of age, but how much older I was unable to say. His height I judged roughly to be five-feet-eight inches, but my measurements would furnish data for a more exact estimate by Thorndyke. Beyond this the bones were quite uncharacteristic. There were no signs of disease either local or general, no indications of injuries either old or recent, no departures of any kind from the normal or usual, and the dismemberment had been effected with such care that there was not a single scratch on any of the separate surfaces. Of adipocere (the peculiar waxy or soapy substance that is commonly found in bodies that have slowly decayed in damp situations) there was not a trace, and the only remnant of the soft structures was a faint indication, like a spot of dried glue, of the tendon on the tip of the right elbow.

The sergeant was in the act of replacing the sheet, with the air of a showman who has just given an exhibition, when there came a sharp rapping on the mortuary door. The officer finished spreading the sheet with official precision, and having ushered me out into the lobby turned the key and admitted three persons, holding the door open after they had entered for me to go out. But the appearance of the newcomers inclined me to linger. One of them was a local constable, evidently in official charge. A second was a laboring man, very wet and muddy, who carried a small sack, while in the third I thought I scented a professional brother.

The sergeant continued to hold the door open.

"Nothing more I can do for you, sir?" he asked genially.

"Is that the divisional surgeon?" I inquired.

"Yes. I am the divisional surgeon," the newcomer answered. "Did you want anything of me?"

"This," said the sergeant, "is a medical gentleman who has got permission from the coroner to inspect the remains. He is acting for the family of the deceased – I mean, for the family of Mr. Bellingham," he added in answer to an inquiring glance from the surgeon.

"I see," said the latter. "Well, they have found the rest of the trunk, including, I understand, the ribs that were missing from the other part. Isn't that so, Davis?"

"Yes, sir," replied the constable. "Inspector Badger says all the ribs is here, and all the bones of the neck as well."

"The inspector seems to be an anatomist," I remarked.

The sergeant grinned. "He is a very knowing gentleman, is Mr. Badger. He came down here this morning quite early and spent a long time looking over the bones and checking them by some notes in his pocket-book. I fancy he's got something on, but he was precious close about it."

Here the sergeant shut up rather suddenly – perhaps contrasting his own conduct with that of his superior.

"Let us have these new bones out on the table," said the police surgeon. "Take the sheet off, and don't shoot them out as if they were coals. Hand them out carefully."

The laborer fished out the wet and muddy bones one by one from the sack, and as he laid them on the table the surgeon arranged them in their proper relative positions.

"This has been a neatly executed job," he remarked, "none of your clumsy hacking with a chopper or a saw. The bones have been cleanly separated at the joints. The fellow who did this must have had some anatomical knowledge, unless he was a butcher, which by the way, is not impossible. He has used his knife uncommonly skilfully, and you notice that each arm was taken off with the scapula attached, just as a butcher takes off a shoulder of mutton. Are there any more bones in that bag?"

"No, sir," replied the laborer, wiping his hands with an air of finality on the posterior aspect of his trousers, "that's the lot."

The surgeon looked thoughtfully at the bones as he gave a final touch to their arrangement, and remarked, "The inspector is right. All the bones of the neck are there. Very odd. Don't you think so?"

"You mean – "

"I mean that this very eccentric murderer seems to have given himself such an extraordinary amount of trouble for no reason that one can see. There are these neck vertebrae, for instance. He must have carefully separated the skull from the atlas instead of just cutting through the neck. Then there is the way he divided the trunk. The twelfth ribs have just come in with this lot, but the twelfth dorsal vertebra to which they belong was attached to the lower half. Imagine the trouble he must have taken to do that, and without cutting or hacking the bones about, either. It is extraordinary. This is rather interesting, by the way. Handle it carefully."

317

He picked up the breast-bone daintily – for it was covered with wet mud – and handed it to me with the remark, "That is the most definite piece of evidence we have."

"You mean," I said, "that the union of the two parts into a single mass fixes this as the skeleton of an elderly man?"

"Yes, that is the obvious suggestion, which is confirmed by the deposit of bone in the rib-cartilages. You can tell the inspector, Davis, that I have checked this lot of bones and that they are all here."

"Would you mind writing it down, sir?" said the constable. "Inspector Badger said I was to have everything in writing."

The surgeon took out his pocket-book, and, while he was selecting a suitable piece of paper, he asked, "Did you form any opinion as to the height of the deceased?"

"Yes, I thought he would be about five-feet-eight." (Here I caught the sergeant's eyes, fixed on me with a knowing leer).

"I made it five-eight-and-a-half," said the police surgeon, "but we shall know better when we have seen the lower leg-bones. Where was this lot found, Davis?"

"In the pond just off the road in Lord's Bushes, sir, and the inspector has gone off now to – "

"Never mind where he's gone," interrupted the sergeant. "You just answer questions and attend to your business."

The sergeant's reproof conveyed a hint to me on which I was not slow to act. Friendly as my professional colleague was, it was clear that the police were disposed to treat me as an interloper who was to be kept out of the "know" as far as possible. Accordingly I thanked my colleague and the sergeant for their courtesy, and bidding them *adieu* until we should meet at the inquest, took my departure and walked away quickly until I found an inconspicuous position from which I could keep the door of the mortuary in view. A few moments later I saw Constable Davis emerge and stride away up the road.

I watched his rapidly diminishing figure until he had gone as far as I considered desirable, and then I set forth in his wake. The road led straight away from the village, and in less than half-a-mile entered the outskirts of the forest. Here I quickened my pace to close up somewhat, and it was well that I did so, for suddenly he diverged from the road into a green lane, where for a while I lost sight of him. Still hurrying forward, I again caught sight of him just as he turned off into a narrow path that entered a beech wood with a thickish undergrowth of holly, along which I followed him for several minutes, gradually decreasing the distance between us, until suddenly there fell on my ear a rhythmical sound like the clank of a pump.

Soon after I caught the sound of men's voices, and then the constable struck off the path into the wood.

I now advanced more cautiously, endeavoring to locate the search party by the sound of the pump, and when I had done this I made a little detour so that I might approach from the opposite direction to that from which the constable had appeared.

Still guided by the noise of the pump, I at length came out into a small opening among the trees and halted to survey the scene. The center of the opening was occupied by a small pond, not more than a dozen yards across, by the side of which stood a builder's handcart. The little two-wheeled vehicle had evidently been used to convey the appliances which were deposited on the ground near it, and which consisted of a large tub – now filled with water – a shovel, a rake, a sieve, and a portable pump, the latter being fitted with a long delivery hose. There were three men besides the constable, one of whom was working the handle of the pump, while another was glancing at a paper that the constable had just delivered to him. He looked up sharply as I appeared, and viewed me with unconcealed disfavor.

"Hallo, sir!" said he. "You can't come here."

Now, seeing that I was actually here, this was clearly a mistake, and I ventured to point out the fallacy.

"Well, I can't allow you to stay here. Our business is of a private nature."

"I know exactly what your business is, Inspector Badger."

"Oh, do you?" said he, surveying me with a foxy smile. "And I expect I know what yours is, too. But we can't have any of you newspaper gentry spying on us just at present, so you just be off."

I thought it best to undeceive him at once, and accordingly, having explained who I was, I showed him the coroner's permit, which he read with manifest annoyance.

"This is all very well, sir," said he as he handed me back the paper, "but it doesn't authorize you to come spying on the proceedings of the police. Any remains that we discover will be deposited in the mortuary, where you can inspect them to your heart's content, but you can't stay here and watch us."

I had no defined object in keeping a watch on the inspector's proceedings, but the sergeant's indiscreet hint had aroused my curiosity, which was further excited by Mr. Badger's evident desire to get rid of me. Moreover, while we had been talking, the pump had stopped (the muddy floor of the pond being now pretty fully exposed), and the inspector's assistant was handling the shovel impatiently.

"Now I put it to you, Inspector," said I, persuasively, "is it politic of you to allow it to be said that you refused an authorized representative of the family facilities for verifying any statements that you may make hereafter?"

"What do you mean?" he asked.

"I mean that if you should happen to find some bone which could be identified as part of the body of Mr. Bellingham, that fact would be of more importance to his family than to anyone else. You know that there is a very valuable estate and a rather difficult will."

"I didn't know it, and I don't see the bearing of it now." (Neither did I for that matter.) "But if you make such a point of being present at the search, I can't very well refuse. Only you mustn't get in our way, that's all."

On hearing this conclusion, his assistant, who looked like a plain-clothes officer, took up his shovel and stepped into the mud that formed the bottom of the pond, stooping as he went and peering among the masses of weed that had been left stranded by the withdrawal of the water. The inspector watched him anxiously, cautioning him from time to time to "look out where he was treading". The laborer left the pump and craned forward from the margin of the mud, and the constable and I looked on from our respective points of vantage. For some time the search was fruitless. Once the searcher stooped and picked up what turned out to be a fragment of decayed wood. Then the remains of a long-deceased jay were discovered, examined, and rejected. Suddenly the man bent down by the side of a small pool that had been left in one of the deeper hollows, stared intently into the mud, and stood up.

"There's something here that looks like a bone, sir," he sang out.

"Don't grub about then," said the inspector. "Drive your shovel right into the mud where you saw it and bring it to the sieve."

The man followed out these instructions, and as he came shoreward with a great pile of the slimy mud on his shovel we all converged on the sieve, which the inspector took up and held over the tub, directing the constable and laborer to "lend a hand," meaning thereby that they were to crowd round the tub and exclude me as completely as possible. This, in fact, they did very effectively with his assistance, for, when the shovelful of mud had been deposited on the sieve, the four men leaned over it and so nearly hid it from view that it was only by craning over, first on one side and then on the other, that I was able to catch an occasional glimpse of it and to observe it gradually melting away as the sieve, immersed in the water, was shaken to and fro.

Presently the inspector raised the sieve from the water and stooped over it more closely to examine its contents. Apparently the examination yielded no very conclusive results, for it was accompanied by a series of rather dubious grunts.

At length the officer stood up, and turning to me with a genial but foxy smile, held out the sieve for my inspection.

"Like to see what we have found, Doctor?" said he.

I thanked him and stood over the sieve. It contained the sort of litter of twigs, skeleton leaves, weed, pond-snails, dead shells, and fresh-water mussels that one would expect to strain out from the mud of an ancient pond, but in addition to these there were three small bones which at first glance gave me quite a start until I saw what they were.

The inspector looked at me inquiringly. "H'm?" said he.

"Yes," I replied. "Very interesting."

"Those will be human bones, I fancy. Hmm?"

"I should say so undoubtedly," I answered.

"Now," said the inspector, "could you say, offhand, which finger those bones belong to?"

I smothered a grin (for I had been expecting this question), and answered, "I can say offhand that they don't belong to any finger. They are the bones of the left great toe."

The inspector's jaw dropped.

"The deuce they are!" he muttered. "H'm. I thought they looked a bit stout."

"I expect," said I, "that if you go through the mud close to where this came from you'll find the rest of the foot."

The plain-clothes man proceeded at once to act on my suggestion, taking the sieve with him to save time. And sure enough, after filling it twice with the mud from the bottom of the pool, the entire skeleton of the foot was brought to light.

"Now you're happy, I suppose," said the inspector when I had checked the bones and found them all present.

"I should be more happy," I replied, "if I knew what you were searching for in this pond. You weren't looking for the foot, were you?"

"I was looking for anything that I might find," he answered. "I shall go on searching until we have the whole body. I shall go through all the streams and ponds around here, excepting Connaught Water. That I shall leave to the last, as it will be a case of dredging from a boat and isn't so likely as the smaller ponds. Perhaps the head will be there. It's deeper than any of the others."

It now occurred to me that as I had learned all that I was likely to learn, which was little enough, I might as well leave the inspector to pursue his researches unembarrassed by my presence. Accordingly I thanked him for his assistance and departed by the way I had come.

But as I retraced my steps along the shady path I speculated profoundly on the officer's proceedings. My examinations of the mutilated hand had yielded the conclusion that the finger had been removed after death or shortly before, but more probably after. Someone else had evidently arrived at the same conclusion, and had communicated his opinion to Inspector Badger, for it was clear that that gentleman was in full cry after the missing finger. But why was he searching for it here when the hand had been found at Sidcup? And what did he expect to learn from it when he found it? There is nothing particularly characteristic about a finger, or, at least, the bones of one, and the object of the present researches was to determine the identity of the person of whom these bones were the remains. There was something mysterious about the affair, something suggesting that Inspector Badger was in possession of private information of some kind. But what information could he have? And whence could he have obtained it? These were questions to which I could find no answer, and I was still fruitlessly revolving them when I arrived at the modest inn where the inquest was to be held, and where I proposed to fortify myself with a correspondingly modest lunch as a preparation for my attendance at the inquiry.

Chapter XIII
The Coroner's Quest

The proceedings of that fine old institution, the coroner's court, are apt to have their dignity impaired by the somewhat unjudicial surroundings amidst which they are conducted. The present inquiry was to be held in a long room attached to the inn, ordinarily devoted, as its various appurtenances testified, to gatherings of a more convivial character.

Hither I betook myself after a protracted lunch and a meditative pipe, and being the first to arrive – the jury having already been sworn and conducted to the mortuary to view the remains – whiled away the time by considering the habits of the customary occupants of the room by the light of the objects contained in it. A wooden target with one or two darts sticking in it hung on the end wall and invited the Robin Hoods of the village to try their skill – a system of incised marks on the oaken table made sinister suggestions of shove-halfpenny, and a large open box filled with white wigs, gaudily colored robes and wooden spears, swords and regalia, crudely coated with gilded paper, obviously appertained to the puerile ceremonials of the Order of Druids.

I had exhausted the interest of these relics and had transferred my attentions to the picture gallery when the other spectators and the witnesses began to arrive. Hastily I seated myself in the only comfortable chair beside the one placed at the head of the table, presumably for the coroner, and I had hardly done so when the latter entered accompanied by the jury. Immediately after them came the sergeant, Inspector Badger, one or two plain-clothes men, and finally the divisional surgeon.

The coroner took his seat at the head of the table and opened his book, and the jury seated themselves on a couple of benches on one side of the long table.

I looked with some interest at the twelve "good men and true." They were a representative group of British tradesmen, quiet, attentive, and rather solemn, but my attention was particularly attracted by a small man with a very large head and a shock of upstanding hair whom I had diagnosed, after a glance at his intelligent but truculent countenance and the shiny knees of his trousers, as the village cobbler. He sat between the broad-shouldered foreman, who looked like a blacksmith, and a dogged, red-faced man whose general aspect of prosperous greasiness suggested the calling of a butcher.

"The inquiry, gentlemen," the coroner commenced, "upon which we are now entering concerns itself with two questions. The first is that of identity: Who was this person whose body we have just viewed? The second is: How, when, and by what means did he come by his death? We will take the identity first and begin with the circumstances under which the body was discovered."

Here the cobbler stood up and raised an excessively dirty hand.

"I rise, Mr. Chairman," said he, "to a point of order." The other jurymen looked at him curiously and some of them, I regret to say, grinned. "You have referred, sir," he continued, "to the body which we have just viewed. I wish to point out that we have not viewed a body. We have viewed a collection of bones."

"We will refer to them as the remains, if you prefer it," said the coroner.

"I do prefer it," was the reply, and the objector sat down.

"Very well," rejoined the coroner, and he proceeded to call the witnesses, of whom the first was a laborer who had discovered the bones in the watercress-bed.

"Do you happen to know how long it was since the watercress-beds had been cleaned out previously?" the coroner asked, when the witness had told the story of the discovery.

"They was cleaned out by Mr. Tapper's orders just before he gave them up. That will be a little better than two years ago. In May it were. I helped to clean 'em. I worked on this very same place and there wasn't no bones there then."

The coroner glanced at the jury. "Any questions, gentlemen," he asked.

The cobbler directed an intimidating scowl at the witness and demanded, "Were you searching for bones when you came on these remains?"

"Me!" exclaimed the witness. "What should I be searching for bones for?"

"Don't prevaricate," said the cobbler sternly, "answer the question: Yes or no."

"No, of course I wasn't."

The juryman shook his enormous head dubiously as though implying that he would let it pass this time but it mustn't happen again, and the examination of the witnesses continued, without eliciting anything that was new to me or giving rise to any incident, until the sergeant had described the finding of the right arm in the Cuckoo Pits.

"Was this an accidental discovery?" the coroner asked.

324

"No. We had instructions from Scotland Yard to search any likely ponds in this neighborhood."

The coroner discreetly forbore to press this matter any further, but my friend the cobbler was evidently on the *qui vive*, and I anticipated a brisk cross-examination for Mr. Badger when his turn came. The inspector was apparently of the same opinion, for I saw him cast a glance of the deepest malevolence at the too inquiring disciple of St. Crispin. In fact, his turn came next, and the cobbler's hair stood up with unholy joy.

The finding of the lower half of the trunk in Staple's Pond at Loughton was the inspector's own achievement, but he was not boastful about it. The discovery, he remarked, followed naturally on the previous one in the Cuckoo Pits.

"Had you any private information that led you to search this particular neighborhood?" the cobbler asked.

"We had no private information whatever," replied Badger.

"Now I put it to you," pursued the juryman, shaking a forensic, and very dirty, forefinger at the inspector, "here are certain remains found at Sidcup. He re are certain other remains found at St. Mary Cray, and certain others at Lee. All those places are in Kent. Now isn't it very remarkable that you should come straight down to Epping Forest, which is in Essex, and search for those bones and find 'em?"

"We were making a systematic search of all likely places," replied Badger.

"Exactly," said the cobbler, with a ferocious grin, "that's just my point. I say, isn't it very funny that, after finding the remains in Kent some twenty miles from here, with the River Thames between, you should come here to look for the bones and go straight to Staple's Pond, where they happen to be – and find 'em?"

"It would have been more funny," Badger replied sourly, "if we'd gone straight to a place where they happened *not* to be – and found them."

A gratified snigger arose from the other eleven good men and true, and the cobbler grinned savagely, but before he could think of a suitable rejoinder the coroner interposed.

"The question is not very material," he said, "and we mustn't embarrass the police by unnecessary inquiries."

"It's my belief," said the cobbler, "that he knew they were there all the time."

"The witness has stated that he had no private information," said the coroner, and he proceeded to take the rest of the inspector's evidence, watched closely by the critical juror.

The account of the finding of the remains having been given in full, the police surgeon was called and sworn. The jurymen straightened their backs with an air of expectancy, and I turned over a page of my notebook.

"You have examined the bones at present lying in the mortuary and forming the subject of this inquiry?" the coroner asked.

"I have."

"Will you kindly tell us what you have observed?"

"I find that the bones are human bones, and are, in my opinion, all parts of the same person. They form a skeleton which is complete with the exception of the skull, the third finger of the left hand, the knee-caps, and the leg-bones – I mean the bones between the knees and the ankles."

"Is there anything to account for the absence of the missing finger?"

"No. There is no deformity and no sign of its having been amputated during life. In my opinion it was removed after death."

"Can you give us any description of the deceased?"

"I should say that these are the bones of an elderly man, probably over sixty years of age, about five-eight-and-a-half inches in height, of rather stout build, fairly muscular, and well preserved. There are no signs of disease excepting some old-standing rheumatic gout of the right hip-joint."

"Can you form any opinion as to the cause of death?"

"No. There are no marks of violence or signs of injury. But it will be impossible to form any opinion as to the cause of death until we have seen the skull."

"Did you note anything else of importance?"

"Yes. I was struck by the appearance of anatomical knowledge and skill on the part of the person who dismembered the body. The knowledge of anatomy is proved by the fact that the corpse has been divided into definite anatomical regions. For instance, the bones of the neck are complete and include the top joint of the backbone known as the atlas, whereas a person without anatomical knowledge would probably take off the head by cutting through the neck. Then the arms have been separated with the scapula (or shoulder-blade) and clavicle (or collar-bone) attached, just as an arm would be removed for dissection.

"The skill is shown by the neat way in which the dismemberment has been carried out. The parts have not been rudely hacked asunder, but have been separated at the joints so skilfully that I have not discovered a single scratch or mark of the knife on any of the bones."

"Can you suggest any class of person who would be likely to possess the knowledge and skill to which you refer?"

"It would, of course, be possessed by a surgeon or medical student, and possibly by a butcher."

326

"You think that the person who dismembered this body may have been a surgeon or a medical student?"

"Yes. Or a butcher. Someone accustomed to the dismemberment of bodies and skilful with the knife."

Here the cobbler suddenly rose to his feet.

"I rise, Mr. Chairman," said he, "to protest against the statement that has just been made."

"What statement?" demanded the coroner.

"Against the aspersion," continued the cobbler, with an oratorical flourish, "that has been cast upon a honorable calling."

"I don't understand you," said the coroner.

"Doctor Summers has insinuated that this murder was committed by a butcher. Now a member of that honorable calling is sitting on this jury – "

"You let me alone," growled the butcher.

"I will not let you alone," persisted the cobbler. "I desire – "

"Oh, shut up, Pope!" This was from the foreman, who, at the same moment, reached out an enormous hairy hand with which he grabbed the cobbler's coat-tails and brought him into a sitting posture with a thump that shook the room.

But Mr. Pope, though seated, was not silenced. "I desire," he said, "to have my protest put on record."

"I can't do that," said the coroner, "and I can't allow you to interrupt the witnesses."

"I am acting," said Mr. Pope, "in the interests of my friend here and the members of a honorable – "

But here the butcher turned on him savagely, and, in a hoarse stage-whisper, exclaimed, "Look here, Pope. You've got too much of what the cat licks – "

"Gentlemen! Gentlemen!" the coroner protested sternly, "I cannot permit this unseemly conduct. You are forgetting the solemnity of the occasion and your own responsible positions. I must insist on more decent and decorous behavior."

There was profound silence, in the midst of which the butcher concluded in the same hoarse whisper, " – licks 'er paws with."

The coroner cast a withering glance at him, and, turning to the witness, resumed the examination.

"Can you tell us, Doctor, how long a time has elapsed since the death of the deceased?"

"I should say not less than eighteen months, but probably more. How much more it is impossible from inspection alone to say. The bones are perfectly clean – that is, clean of all soft structures – and will remain substantially in their present condition for many years."

"The evidence of the man who found the remains in the watercress-bed suggests that they could not have been there for more than two years. Do the appearances in your opinion agree with that view?"

"Yes, perfectly."

"There is one more point, Doctor, a very important one. Do you find anything in any of the bones, or all of them together, which would enable you to identify them as the bones of any particular individual?"

"No," replied Dr. Summers, "I found no peculiarity that could furnish the means of personal identification."

"The description of a missing individual has been given to us," said the coroner, "a man, fifty-nine years of age, five-feet-eight inches in height, healthy, well preserved, rather broad in build, and having an old Pott's fracture of the left ankle. Do the remains that you have examined agree with that description?"

"Yes, so far as agreement is possible. There is no disagreement."

"The remains might be those of that individual?"

"They might, but there is no positive evidence that they are. The description would apply to a large proportion of elderly men, except as to the fracture."

"You found no signs of such a fracture?"

"No. Pott's fracture affects the bone called the fibula. That is one of the bones that has not yet been found, so there is no evidence on that point. The left foot was quite normal, but then it would be in any case, unless the fracture had resulted in great deformity."

"You estimated the height of the deceased as half-an-inch greater than that of the missing person. Does that constitute a disagreement?"

"No, my estimate is only approximate. As the arms are complete and the legs are not, I have based my calculations on the width across the two arms. But measurement of the thigh-bones gives the same result. The length of the thigh-bones is one-foot-seven inches-and-five-eighths."

"So the deceased might not have been taller than five-feet-eight?"

"That is so – from five-feet-eight to five-feet-nine."

"Thank you. I think that is all we want to ask you, Doctor, unless the jury wish to put any questions."

He glanced uneasily at that august body, and instantly the irrepressible Pope rose to the occasion.

"About that finger that is missing," said the cobbler. "You say that it was cut off after death?"

"That is my opinion."

"Now can you tell us why it was cut off?"

328

"No, I cannot."

"Oh, come now, Doctor Summers, you must have formed some opinion on the subject."

Here the coroner interposed. "The doctor is only concerned with the evidence arising out of the actual examination of the remains. Any personal opinions or conjectures that he may have formed are not evidence, and he must not be asked about them."

"But, sir," objected Pope, "we want to know why that finger was cut off. It couldn't have been took off for no reason. May I ask, sir, if the person who is missing had anything peculiar about that finger?"

"Nothing is stated to that effect in the written description," replied the coroner.

"Perhaps," suggested Pope, "Inspector Badger can tell us."

"I think," said the coroner, "we had better not ask the police too many questions. They will tell us anything that they wish to be made public."

"Oh, very well," snapped the cobbler. "If it's a matter of hushing it up I've got no more to say. Only I don't see how we are to arrive at a verdict if we don't have the facts put before us."

All the witnesses having now been examined, the coroner proceeded to sum up and address the jury.

"You have heard the evidence, gentlemen, of the various witnesses, and you will have perceived that it does not enable us to answer either of the questions that form the subject of this inquiry. We now know that the deceased was an elderly man, about sixty years of age, and about five-feet-eight to nine in height, and that his death took place from eighteen months to two years ago. That is all we know. From the treatment to which the body has been subjected we may form conjectures as to the circumstances of his death. But we have no actual knowledge. We do not know who the deceased was or how he came by his death. Consequently, it will be necessary to adjourn this inquiry until fresh facts are available, and as soon as that is the case, you will receive due notice that your attendance is required."

The silence of the Court gave place to the confused noise of moving chairs and a general outbreak of eager talk amidst which I rose and made my way out into the street. At the door I encountered Dr. Summers, whose dog-cart was waiting close by.

"Are you going back to town now?" he asked.

"Yes," I answered, "as soon as I can catch a train."

"If you jump into my cart I'll run you down in time for the five-one. You'll miss it if you walk."

I accepted his offer thankfully, and a minute later was spinning briskly down the road to the station.

329

"Queer little devil, that man Pope," Dr. Summers remarked. "Quite a character: A socialist, laborite, agitator, general crank. Anything for a row."

"Yes," I answered, "that was what his appearance suggested. It must be trying for the coroner to get a truculent rascal like that on a jury."

Summers laughed. "I don't know. He supplies the comic relief. And then, you know, those fellows have their uses. Some of his questions were pretty pertinent."

"So Badger seemed to think."

"Yes, by Jove," chuckled Summers. "Badger didn't like him a bit, and I suspect the worthy inspector was sailing pretty close to the wind in his answers."

"You think he really has some private information?"

"Depends upon what you mean by 'information.' The police are not a speculative body. They wouldn't be taking all this trouble unless they had a pretty straight tip from somebody. How are Mr. and Miss Bellingham? I used to know them when they lived here."

I was considering a discreet answer to this question when we swept into the station yard. At the same moment the train drew up at the platform, and, with a hurried hand-shake and hastily spoken thanks, I sprang from the dog-cart and darted into the station.

During the rather slow journey homeward I read over my notes and endeavored to extract from the facts they set forth some significance other than that which lay on the surface, but without much success. Then I fell to speculating on what Thorndyke would think of the evidence at the inquest and whether he would be satisfied with the information that I had collected. These speculations lasted me, with occasional digressions, until I arrived at the Temple and ran up the stairs rather eagerly to my friends' chambers.

But here a disappointment awaited me. The nest was empty with the exception of Polton, who appeared at the laboratory door in his white apron, with a pair of flat-nosed pliers in his hands.

"The Doctor had to go down to Bristol to consult over an urgent case," he explained, "and Doctor Jervis has gone with him. They'll be away a day or two, I expect, but The Doctor left this note for you."

He took a letter from the shelf, where it had been stood conspicuously on edge, and handed it to me. It was a short note from Thorndyke apologizing for his sudden departure and asking me to give Polton my notes with any comments that I had to make.

"*You will be interested to learn,*" he added, "*that the application will be heard in the Probate Court the day after to-morrow. I shall not be present, of course, nor will Jervis, so I should like you to attend and keep*

330

your eyes open for anything that may happen during the hearing and that may not appear in the notes that Marchmont's clerk will be instructed to take. I have retained Dr. Payne to stand by and help you with the practise, so that you can attend the Court with a clear conscience."

This was highly flattering and quite atoned for the small disappointment. With deep gratification at the trust that Thorndyke had reposed in me, I pocketed the letter, handed my notes to Polton, wished him "Good-evening," and betook myself to Fetter Lane.

Chapter XIV
Which Carries the Reader
Into the Probate Court

The Probate Court wore an air of studious repose when I entered with Miss Bellingham and her father. Apparently the great and inquisitive public had not become aware of the proceedings that were about to take place, or had not realized their connection with the sensational "Mutilation Case", but barristers and Pressmen, better informed, had gathered in some strength, and the hum of their conversation filled the air like the droning of the voluntary that ushers in a cathedral service.

As we entered, a pleasant-faced, elderly gentleman rose and came forward to meet us, shaking Mr. Bellingham's hand cordially and saluting Miss Bellingham with a courtly bow.

"This is Mr. Marchmont, Doctor," said the former, introducing me, and the solicitor, having thanked me for the trouble I had taken in attending at the inquest, led us to a bench, at the farther end of which was seated a gentleman whom I recognized as Mr. Hurst.

Mr. Bellingham recognized him at the same moment and glared at him wrathfully.

"I see that scoundrel is here!" he exclaimed in a distinctly audible voice, "pretending that he doesn't see me, because he is ashamed to look me in the face, but – "

"Hush! Hush! My dear sir," exclaimed the horrified solicitor, "we mustn't talk like that, especially in this place. Let me beg you – let me entreat you to control your feelings, to make no indiscreet remarks. In fact, to make no remarks at all," he added, with the evident conviction that any remarks that Mr. Bellingham might make would be certain to be indiscreet.

"Forgive me, Marchmont," Mr. Bellingham replied contritely. "I will control myself. I will really be quite discreet. I won't even look at him again – because, if I do, I shall probably go over and pull his nose."

This form of discretion did not appear to be quite to Mr. Marchmont's liking, for he took the precaution of insisting that Miss Bellingham and I should sit on the farther side of his client, and thus effectually separate him from his enemy.

"Who's the long-nosed fellow talking to Jellicoe?" Mr. Bellingham asked.

"That is Mr. Loram, K.C., Mr. Hurst's counsel, and the convivial-looking gentleman next to him is our counsel, Mr. Heath, a most able man and" – here Mr. Marchmont whispered behind his hand – "fully instructed by Doctor Thorndyke."

At this juncture the judge entered and took his seat, the usher proceeded with great rapidity to swear in the jury, and the Court gradually settled down into that state of academic quiet which it maintained throughout the proceedings, excepting when the noisy swing-doors were set oscillating by some bustling clerk or reporter.

The judge was a somewhat singular-looking old gentleman, very short as to his face and very long as to his mouth, which peculiarities, together with a pair of large and bulging eyes (which he usually kept closed), suggested a certain resemblance to a frog. And he had a curious frog-like trick of flattening his eyelids – as if in the act of swallowing a large beetle – which was the only outward and visible sign of emotion that he ever displayed.

As soon as the swearing in of the jury was completed Mr. Loram rose to introduce the case, whereupon his Lordship leaned back in his chair and closed his eyes, as if bracing himself for a painful operation.

"The present proceedings," Mr. Loram explained, "are occasioned by the unaccountable disappearance of Mr. John Bellingham, of 141 Queen Square, Bloomsbury, which occurred about two years ago, or, to be more precise, on the twenty-third of November, Nineteen-hundred-and-two. Since that date nothing has been heard of Mr. Bellingham, and, as there are certain substantial reasons for believing him to be dead, the principal beneficiary under his will, Mr. George Hurst, is now applying to the Court for permission to presume the death of the testator and prove the will. As the time which has elapsed since the testator was last seen alive is only two years, the application is based upon the circumstances of the disappearance, which were, in many respects, very singular, the most remarkable feature of that disappearance being, perhaps, its suddenness and completeness."

Here the judge remarked in a still, small voice that "It would, perhaps, have been even more remarkable if the testator had disappeared gradually and incompletely."

"No doubt, my Lord," agreed Mr. Loram, "but the point is that the testator, whose habits had always been regular and orderly, disappeared on the date mentioned without having made any of the usual provisions for the conduct of his affairs, and has not since then been seen or heard of."

With this preamble Mr. Loram proceeded to give a narrative of the events connected with the disappearance of John Bellingham, which was substantially identical with that which I had read in the newspapers, and having laid the actual facts before the jury, he went on to discuss their probable import.

"Now, what conclusion," he asked, "will this strange, this most mysterious train of events suggest to an intelligent person who shall consider it impartially? Here is a man who steps forth from the house of his cousin or his brother, as the case may be, and forthwith, in the twinkling of an eye, vanishes from human ken. What is the explanation? Did he steal forth and, without notice or hint of his intention, take train to some seaport, thence to embark for some distant land, leaving his affairs to take care of themselves and his friends to speculate vainly as to his whereabouts? Is he now hiding abroad, or even at home, indifferent alike to the safety of his own considerable property and the peace of mind of his friends? Or is it that death has come upon him unawares by sickness, by accident, or, more probably, by the hand of some unknown criminal? Let us consider the probabilities.

"Can he have disappeared by his own deliberate act? Why not? It may be asked. Men undoubtedly do disappear from time to time, to be discovered by chance or to reappear voluntarily after intervals of years and find their names almost forgotten and their places filled by new-comers. Yes, but there is always some reason for a disappearance of this kind, even though it be a bad one. Family discords that make life a weariness: Pecuniary difficulties that make life a succession of anxieties. Distaste for particular circumstances and surroundings from which there seems no escape. Inherent restlessness and vagabond tendencies, and so on.

"Do any of these explanations apply to the present case? No, they do not. Family discords – at least those capable of producing chronic misery – appertain exclusively to a married state. But the testator was a bachelor with no encumbrances whatever. Pecuniary anxieties can be equally excluded. The testator was in easy, in fact, in affluent circumstances. His mode of life was apparently agreeable and full of interest and activity, and he had full liberty of change if he wished. He had been accustomed to travel, and could do so again without absconding. He had reached an age when radical changes do not seem desirable. He was a man of fixed and regular habits, and his regularity was of his own choice and not due to compulsion or necessity. When last seen by his friends, as I shall prove, he was proceeding to a definite destination with the expressed intention of returning for purposes of his own appointing. He did return and then vanished, leaving those purposes unachieved.

"If we conclude that he has voluntarily disappeared and is at present in hiding, we adopt an opinion that is entirely at variance with all these weighty facts. If, on the other hand, we conclude that he has died suddenly, or has been killed by an accident or otherwise, we are adopting a view that involves no inherent improbabilities and that is entirely congruous with the known facts – facts that will be proved by the testimony of the witnesses whom I shall call. The supposition that the testator is dead is not only more probable than that he is alive. I submit it is the only reasonable explanation of the circumstances of his disappearance.

"But this is not all. The presumption of death which arises so inevitably out of the mysterious and abrupt manner in which the testator disappeared has recently received most conclusive and dreadful confirmation. On the fifteenth of July last there were discovered at Sidcup the remains of a human arm – a left arm, gentlemen, from the hand of which the third, or ring, finger was missing. The doctor who has examined that arm will tell you that the finger was cut off either after death or immediately before, and his evidence will prove conclusively that that arm must have been deposited in the place where it was found just about the time when the testator disappeared. Since that first discovery, other portions of the same mutilated body have come to light, and it is a strange and significant fact that they have all been found in the immediate neighborhood of Eltham or Woodford. You will remember, gentlemen, that it was either at Eltham or Woodford that the testator was last seen alive.

"And now observe the completeness of the coincidence. These human remains, as you will be told presently by the experienced and learned medical gentleman who has examined them most exhaustively, are those of a man of about sixty years of age, about five-feet-eight inches in height, fairly muscular and well preserved, apparently healthy, and rather stoutly built. Another witness will tell you that the missing man was about sixty years of age, about five-feet-eight inches in height, fairly muscular and well preserved, apparently healthy, and rather stoutly built. And – another most significant and striking fact – the testator was accustomed to wear upon the third finger of his left hand – the very finger that is missing from the remains that were found – a most peculiar ring, which fitted so tightly that he was unable to get it off after once putting it on – a ring, gentlemen, of so peculiar a pattern that had it been found on the body must have instantly established the identity of the remains. In a word, gentlemen, the remains which have been found are those of a man exactly like the testator. They differ from him in no respects whatever. They display a mutilation which suggests an attempt to conceal an identifying peculiarity which he undoubtedly presented, and they were deposited in their various hiding-places about the time of the testator's disappearance. Accordingly, when you have heard these facts proved by the sworn testimony of competent witnesses, together with the facts relating to the disappearance, I shall ask you for a verdict in accordance with that evidence."

Mr. Loram sat down, and adjusting a pair of pince-nez, rapidly glanced over his brief while the usher was administering the oath to the first witness.

This was Mr. Jellicoe, who stepped into the box and directed a stony gaze at the (apparently) unconscious judge. The usual preliminaries having been gone through, Mr. Loram proceeded to examine him.

"You were the testator's solicitor and confidential agent, I believe?"

"I was – and am."

"How long have you known him?"

"Twenty-seven years."

"Judging from your experience of him, should you say that he was a person likely to disappear voluntarily and suddenly to cease to communicate with his friends?"

"No."

"Kindly give your reasons for that opinion."

"Such conduct on the part of the testator would be entirely opposed to his habits and character as they are known to me. He was exceedingly regular and business-like in his dealings with me. When traveling abroad he always kept me informed as to his whereabouts, or, if he was likely to be beyond reach of communication, he always advised me beforehand. One of my duties was to collect a pension which he drew from the Foreign Office, and on no occasion, previous to his disappearance, has he ever failed to furnish me punctually with the necessary documents."

"Had he, so far as you know, any reasons for wishing to disappear?"

"No."

"When and where did you last see him alive?"

"At six o'clock in the evening, on the fourteenth of October, Nineteen-hundred-and-two, at 141 Queen Square, Bloomsbury."

"Kindly tell us what happened on that occasion."

"The testator had called for me at my office at a quarter-past-three, and asked me to come with him to his house to meet Doctor Norbury. I accompanied him to 141 Queen Square, and shortly after we arrived Doctor Norbury came to look at some antiquities that the testator proposed to give to the British Museum. The gift consisted of a mummy with four Canopic jars and other tomb-furniture which the testator stipulated should be exhibited together in a single case and in the state in which they were then presented. Of these objects, the mummy only was ready for inspection. The tomb-furniture had not yet arrived in England, but was expected within a week. Doctor Norbury accepted the gift on behalf of the Museum, but could not take possession of the objects until he had communicated with the Director and obtained his formal authority. The testator accordingly gave me certain instructions concerning the delivery of the gift, as he was leaving England that evening."

"Are those instructions relevant to the subject of this inquiry?"

"I think they are. The testator was going to Paris, and perhaps from thence to Vienna. He instructed me to receive and unpack the tomb-furniture on its arrival, and to store it, with the mummy, in a particular room, where it was to remain for three weeks. If he returned within that time he was to hand it over in person to the Museum authorities. If he had not returned within that time, he desired me to notify the Museum authorities that they were at liberty to take possession of and remove the collection at their convenience. From these instructions I gathered that the testator was uncertain as to the length of his absence from England and the extent of his journey."

"Did he state precisely where he was going?"

"No. He said he was going to Paris and perhaps to Vienna, but he gave no particulars and I asked for none."

"Do you, in fact, know where he went?"

"No. He left the house at six o'clock wearing a long, heavy overcoat and carrying a suit-case and an umbrella. I wished him 'Good-by' at the door and watched him walk away as if going toward Southampton Row. I have no idea where he went, and I never saw him again."

"Had he no other luggage than the suit-case?"

"I do not know, but I believe not. He was accustomed to travel with the bare necessaries, and to buy anything further he wanted *en route*."

"Did he say nothing to the servants as to the probable date of his return?"

"There were no servants excepting the caretaker. The house was not used for residential purposes. The testator slept and took his meals at his club, though he kept his clothes at the house."

"Did you receive any communication from him after he left?"

"No. I never heard from him again in any way. I waited for three weeks as he had instructed me, and then notified the Museum authorities that the collection was ready for removal. Five days later Doctor Norbury came and took formal possession of it, and it was transferred to the Museum forthwith."

"When did you next hear of the testator?"

"On the twenty-third of November following at a quarter-past-seven in the evening. Mr. George Hurst came to my rooms, which are over my office, and informed me that the testator had called at his house during his absence and had been shown into the study to wait for him. That on his – Mr. Hurst's – arrival it was found that the testator had disappeared without acquainting the servants of his intended departure, and without being seen

337

by anyone to leave the house. Mr. Hurst thought this so remarkable that he had hastened up to town to inform me. I also thought it a remarkable circumstance, especially as I had received no communication from the testator, and we both decided that it was advisable to inform the testator's brother, Godfrey, of what had happened.

"Accordingly Mr. Hurst and I proceeded as quickly as possible to Liverpool Street and took the first train available to Woodford, where Mr. Godfrey Bellingham then resided. We arrived at his house at five minutes to nine, and were informed by the servant that he was not at home, but that his daughter was in the library, which was a detached building situated in the grounds. The servant lighted a lantern and conducted us through the grounds to the library, where we found Mr. Godfrey Bellingham and Miss Bellingham. Mr. Godfrey had only just come in and had entered by the back gate, which had a bell that rang in the library. Mr. Hurst informed Mr. Godfrey of what had occurred, and then we left the library to walk up to the house. A few paces from the library I noticed by the light of the lantern, which Mr. Godfrey was carrying, a small object lying on the lawn. I pointed it out to him and he picked it up, and then we all recognized it as a scarab that the testator was accustomed to wear on his watch-chain. It was fitted with a gold wire passed through the suspension hole and a gold ring. Both the wire and the ring were in position, but the ring was broken. We went to the house and questioned the servants as to visitors, but none of them had seen the testator, and they all agreed that no visitor whatsoever had come to the house during the afternoon or evening. Mr. Godfrey and Miss Bellingham both declared that they had neither seen nor heard anything of the testator, and were both unaware that he had returned to England. As the circumstances were somewhat disquieting, I communicated, on the following morning, with the police and requested them to make inquiries, which they did, with the result that a suit-case bearing the initials '*J.B.*' was found to be lying unclaimed in the cloakroom at Charing Cross Station. I was able to identify the suit-case as that which I had seen the testator carry away from Queen Square. I was also able to identify some of the contents. I interviewed the cloakroom attendant, who informed me that the suit-case had been deposited on the twenty-third about 4:15 p.m. He had no recollection of the person who deposited it. It remained unclaimed in the possession of the railway company for three months, and was then surrendered to me."

"Were there any marks or labels on it showing the route by which it had traveled?"

"There were no labels on it and no marks other than the initials '*J.B.*'"

"Do you happen to know the testator's age?"

"Yes. He was fifty-nine on the eleventh of October, Nineteen-hundred-and-two."

"Can you tell us what his height was?"

"Yes. He was exactly five-feet eight inches."

"What sort of health had he?"

"So far as I know his health was good. I am not aware that he suffered from any disease. I am only judging by his appearance, which was that of a healthy man."

"Should you describe him as well preserved or otherwise?"

"I should describe him as a well preserved man for his age."

"How should you describe his figure?"

"I should describe him as rather broad and stout in build, and fairly muscular, though not exceptionally so."

Mr. Loram made a rapid note of these answers and then said, "You have told us, Mr. Jellicoe, that you have known the testator intimately for twenty-seven years. Now, did you ever notice whether he was accustomed to wear any rings upon his fingers?"

"He wore upon the third finger of his left hand a copy of an antique ring which bore the device of the Eye of Osiris. That was the only ring he ever wore as far as I know."

"Did he wear it constantly?"

"Yes, necessarily, because it was too small for him, and having once squeezed it on he was never able to get it off again."

This was the sum of Mr. Jellicoe's evidence, and at its conclusion the witness glanced inquiringly at Mr. Bellingham's counsel. But Mr. Heath remained seated, attentively considering the notes that he had just made, and finding that there was to be no cross-examination, Mr. Jellicoe stepped down from the box. I leaned back on my bench, and, turning my head, observed Miss Bellingham deep in thought.

"What do you think of it?" I asked.

"It seems very complete and conclusive," she replied. And then, with a sigh, she murmured, "Poor old Uncle John! How horrid it sounds to talk of him in this cold-blooded, business-like way, as 'the testator', as if he were nothing but a sort of algebraical sign."

"There isn't much room for sentiment, I suppose, in the proceedings of the Probate Court," I replied. To which she assented, and then asked, "Who is this lady?"

"This lady" was a fashionably dressed young woman who had just bounced into the witness-box and was now being sworn. The preliminaries being finished, she answered Miss Bellingham's question and Mr. Loram's by stating that her name was Augustina Gwendoline Dobbs, and that she was housemaid to Mr. George Hurst, of "The Poplars", Eltham.

339

"Mr. Hurst lives alone, I believe?" said Mr. Loram.

"I don't know what you mean by that," Miss Dobbs began, but the barrister explained, "I mean that I believe he is unmarried?"

"Well, and what about it?" the witness demanded tartly.

"I am asking you a question."

"I know that," said the witness viciously, "and I say that you've no business to make any such insinuations to a respectable young lady when there's a cook-housekeeper and a kitchenmaid living in the house, and him old enough to be my father – "

Here his Lordship flattened his eyelids with startling effect, and Mr. Loram interrupted, "I make no insinuations. I merely ask, Is your employer, Mr. Hurst, an unmarried man, or is he not?"

"I never asked him," said the witness sulkily.

"Please answer my question – yes or no."

"How can I answer your question? He may be married or he may not. How do I know? I'm no private detective."

Mr. Loram directed a stupefied gaze at the witness, and in the ensuing silence a plaintive voice came from the bench. "Is that point material?"

"Certainly, my Lord," replied Mr. Loram.

"Then, as I see that you are calling Mr. Hurst, perhaps you had better put the question to him. He will probably know."

Mr. Loram bowed, and as the Judge subsided into his normal state of coma he turned to the triumphant witness.

"Do you remember anything remarkable occurring on the twenty-third of November the year before last?"

"Yes. Mr. John Bellingham called at our house."

"How did you know he was Mr. John Bellingham?"

"I didn't, but he said he was, and I supposed he knew."

"At what time did he arrive?"

"At twenty-minutes-past-five in the evening."

"What happened then?"

"I told him that Mr. Hurst had not come home yet, and he said he would wait for him in the study and write some letters, so I showed him into the study and shut the door."

"What happened next?"

"Nothing. Then Mr. Hurst came home at his usual time – a quarter-to-six – and let himself in with his key. He went straight into the study where I supposed Mr. Bellingham still was, so I took no notice, but laid the table for two. At six o'clock Mr. Hurst came into the dining-room – he has tea in the City and dines at six – and when he saw the table laid for two he asked the reason. I said I thought Mr. Bellingham was staying to dinner.

"'Mr. Bellingham!' says he. 'I didn't know he was here. Why didn't you tell me?' he says. 'I thought he was with you, sir,' I said. 'I showed him into the study,' I said. 'Well, he wasn't there when I came in,' he said, 'and he isn't there now,' he said. 'Perhaps he has gone to wait in the drawing-room,' he said. So he went and looked in the drawing-room, but he wasn't there. Then Mr. Hurst said he thought Mr. Bellingham must have got tired of waiting and gone away, but I told him I was quite sure he hadn't, because I had been watching all the time. Then he asked me if Mr. Bellingham was alone or whether his daughter was with him, and I said that it wasn't Mr. Bellingham at all, but Mr. John Bellingham, and then he was more surprised than ever. I said we had better search the house to make sure whether he was there or not, and Mr. Hurst said he would come with me, so we all went over the house and looked in all the rooms, but there was not a sign of Mr. Bellingham in any of them. Then Mr. Hurst got very nervous and upset, and when he had just snatched a little dinner he ran off to catch the six-thirty-one train up to town."

"You say that Mr. Bellingham could not have left the house because you were watching all the time. Where were you while you were watching?"

"I was in the kitchen. I could see the front gate from the kitchen window."

"You say that you laid the table for two. Where did you lay it?"

"In the dining-room, of course."

"Could you see the front gate from the dining-room?"

"No, but I could see the study door. The study is opposite the dining-room."

"Do you have to come upstairs to get from the kitchen to the dining-room?"

"Yes, of course you do!"

"Then, might not Mr. Bellingham have left the house while you were coming up the stairs?"

"No, he couldn't have done."

"Why not?"

"Because it would have been impossible."

"But why would it have been impossible?"

"Because he couldn't have done it."

"I suggest that Mr. Bellingham left the house quietly while you were on the stairs?"

"No, he didn't."

"How do you know he did not?"

"I am quite sure he didn't."

"But how can you be certain?"

"Because I should have seen him if he had."

"But I mean when you were on the stairs."

"He was in the study when I was on the stairs."

"How do you know he was in the study?"

"Because I showed him in there and he hadn't come out."

Mr. Loram paused and took a deep breath, and his Lordship flattened his eyelids.

"Is there a side gate to the premises?" the barrister resumed wearily.

"Yes. It opens into a narrow lane at the side of the house."

"And there is a French window in the study, is there not?"

"Yes. It opens on to the small grass plot opposite the side gate."

"The window and the gate both have catches on the inside. Could it have been possible for Mr. Bellingham to let himself out into the lane?"

"The window and gate both have catches on the inside. He could have got out that way, but, of course he didn't."

"Why not?"

"Well, no gentleman would go creeping out the back way like a thief."

"Did you look to see if the French window was shut and fastened after you missed Mr. Bellingham?"

"I looked at it when we shut the house up for the night. It was then shut and fastened on the inside."

"And the side gate?"

"That gate was shut and latched. You have to slam the gate to make the latch fasten, so no one could have gone out of the gate without being heard."

Here the examination-in-chief ended, and Mr. Loram sat down with an audible sigh of relief. Miss Dobbs was about to step down from the witness-box when Mr. Heath rose to cross-examine.

"Did you see Mr. Bellingham in a good light?" he asked.

"Pretty good. It was dark outside, but the hall-lamp was alight."

"Kindly look at this" – here a small object was passed across to the witness. "It is a trinket that Mr. Bellingham is stated to have carried suspended from his watch-guard. Can you remember if he was wearing it in that manner when he came to the house?"

"No, he was not."

"You are sure of that."

"Quite sure."

"Thank you. And now I want to ask you about the search that you have mentioned. You say that you went all over the house. Did you go into the study?"

"No – at least, not until Mr. Hurst had gone to London."

342

"When you did go in, was the window fastened?"

"Yes."

"Could it have been fastened from the outside?"

"No. There is no handle outside."

"What furniture is there in the study?"

"There is a writing-table, a revolving-chair, two easy chairs, two large book-cases, and a wardrobe that Mr. Hurst keeps his overcoats and hats in."

"Does the wardrobe lock?"

"Yes."

"Was it locked when you went in?"

"I'm sure I don't know. I don't go about trying the cupboards and drawers."

"What furniture is there in the drawing-room?"

"A cabinet, six or seven chairs, a Chesterfield sofa, a piano, a silver-table, and one or two occasional tables."

"Is the piano a grand or upright?"

"It is an upright grand."

"In what position is it placed?"

"It stands across a corner near the window."

"Is there sufficient room behind it for a man to conceal himself?"

Miss Dobbs was amused and did not dissemble. "Oh, yes," she sniggered, "there's plenty of room for a man to hide behind it."

"When you searched the drawing-room, did you look behind the piano?"

"No, I didn't," Miss Dobbs replied scornfully.

"Did you look under the sofa?"

"Certainly not!"

"What did you do then?"

"We opened the door and looked into the room. We were not looking for a cat or a monkey. We were looking for a middle-aged gentleman."

"And am I to take it that your search over the rest of the house was conducted in a similar manner?"

"Certainly. We looked into the rooms, but we did not search under the beds or in the cupboards."

"Are all the rooms in the house in use as living or sleeping rooms?"

"No. There is one room on the second floor that is used as a store and lumber-room, and one on the first floor that Mr. Hurst uses to store trunks and things that he is not using."

"Did you look in those rooms when you searched the house?"

"No."

"Have you looked in them since?"

343

"I have been in the lumber-room since, but not in the other. It is always kept locked."

At this point an ominous flattening became apparent in his Lordship's eyelids, but these symptoms passed when Mr. Heath sat down and indicated that he had no further questions to ask.

Miss Dobbs once more prepared to step down from the witness box, when Mr. Loram shot up like a jack-in-the-box.

"You have made certain statements," said he, "concerning the scarab which Mr. Bellingham was accustomed to wear suspended from his watch-guard. You say that he was not wearing it when he came to Mr. Hurst's house on the twenty-third of November, Nineteen-hundred-and-two. Are you quite sure of that?"

"Quite sure."

"I must ask you to be very careful in your statement on this point. The question is a highly important one. Do you swear that the scarab was not hanging from his watch-guard?"

"Yes, I do."

"Did you notice the watch-guard particularly?"

"No, not particularly."

"Then what makes you sure that the scarab was not attached to it?"

"It couldn't have been."

"Why could it not?"

"Because if it had been there I should have seen it."

"What kind of watch-guard was Mr. Bellingham wearing?"

"Oh, an ordinary sort of watch-guard."

"I mean was it a chain or a ribbon or a strap?"

"A chain, I think – or perhaps a ribbon – or it might have been a strap."

His Lordship flattened his eyelids, but made no further sign and Mr. Loram continued. "Did you or did you not notice what kind of watch-guard Mr. Bellingham was wearing?"

"I did not. Why should I? It was no business of mine."

"But yet you are quite sure about the scarab?"

"Yes, quite sure."

"You noticed that, then?"

"No, I didn't. How could I when it wasn't there?"

Mr. Loram paused and looked helplessly at the witness. A suppressed titter arose from the body of the Court, and a faint voice from the bench inquired. "Are you *quite* incapable of giving a straightforward answer?"

Miss Dobbs' only reply was to burst into tears, whereupon Mr. Loram abruptly sat down and abandoned his re-examination.

344

The witness-box vacated by Miss Dobbs was occupied successively by Dr. Norbury, Mr. Hurst, and the cloak-room attendant, none of whom contributed any new facts, but merely corroborated the statements made by Mr. Jellicoe and the housemaid. Then came the laborer who discovered the bones at Sidcup, and who repeated the evidence that he had given at the inquest, showing that the remains could not have been lying in the watercress-bed more than two years. Finally Dr. Summers was called, and, after he had given a brief description of the bones that he had examined, was asked by Mr. Loram, "You have heard the description that Mr. Jellicoe has given of the testator?"

"I have."

"Does that description apply to the person whose remains you examined."

"In a general way it does."

"I must ask you for a direct answer – yes or no. Does it apply?"

"Yes. But I ought to say that my estimate of the height of the deceased is only approximate."

"Quite so. Judging from your examination of those remains and from Mr. Jellicoe's description, might those remains be the remains of the testator, John Bellingham?"

"Yes, they might."

On receiving this admission Mr. Loram sat down, and Mr. Heath immediately rose to cross-examine.

"When you examined these remains, Doctor Summers, did you discover any personal peculiarities which would enable you to identify them as the remains of any one individual rather than any other individual of similar size, age, and proportions?"

"No. I found nothing that would identify the remains as those of any particular individual."

As Mr. Heath asked no further questions, the witness received his dismissal, and Mr. Loram informed the Court that that was his case. The judge bowed somnolently, and then Mr. Heath rose to address the Court on behalf of the respondent. It was not a long speech, nor was it enriched by any displays of florid rhetoric. It concerned itself exclusively with a rebutment of the arguments of the counsel for the petitioner.

Having briefly pointed out that the period of absence was too short to give rise of itself to the presumption of death, Mr. Heath continued. "The claim therefore rests upon evidence of a positive character. My learned friend asserts that the testator is presumably dead, and it is for him to prove what he has affirmed. Now, has he done this? I submit that he has not. He has argued with great force and ingenuity that the testator, being a bachelor, a solitary man without wife or child, dependant or master, public

345

or private office of duty, or any bond, responsibility, or any other condition limiting his freedom of action, had no reason or inducement for absconding. This is my learned friend's argument, and he has conducted it with so much skill and ingenuity that he has not only succeeded in proving his case. He has proved a great deal too much. For if it is true, as my learned friend so justly argues, that a man thus unfettered by obligations of any kind has no reason for disappearing, is it not even more true that he has no reason for not disappearing? My friend has urged that the testator was at liberty to go where he pleased, when he pleased, and how he pleased, and that therefore there was no need for him to abscond. I reply, if he was at liberty to go away, whither, when, and how he pleased, why do we express surprise that he has made use of his liberty? My learned friend points out that the testator notified nobody of his intention of going away and has acquainted no one with his whereabouts, but, I ask, whom should he have notified? He was responsible to nobody. There was no one dependent upon him. His presence or absence was the concern of nobody but himself. If circumstances suddenly arising made it desirable that he should go abroad, why should he not go? I say there was no reason whatever.

"My learned friend has said that the testator went away leaving his affairs to take care of themselves. Now, gentlemen, I ask you if this can fairly be said of a man whose affairs are, as they have been for many years, in the hands of a highly capable, completely trustworthy agent who is better acquainted with them than the testator himself? Clearly it cannot.

"To conclude this part of the argument, I submit that the circumstances of the so-called disappearance of the testator present nothing out of the ordinary. The testator is a man of ample means, without any responsibilities to fetter his movements, and has been in the constant habit of traveling, often into remote and distant regions. The mere fact that he has been absent somewhat longer than usual affords no ground whatever for the drastic proceeding of presumption of death and taking possession of his property.

"With reference to the human remains which have been mentioned in connection with the case I need say but little. The attempt to connect them with the testator has failed completely. You yourselves have heard Doctor Summers state on oath that they cannot be identified as the remains of any particular person. That would seem to dispose of them effectually. I must remark upon a very singular point that has been raised by the learned counsel for the petitioner, which is this:

"My learned friend points out that these remains were discovered near Eltham and near Woodford and that the testator was last seen alive at one of these two places. This he considers for some reason to be a highly significant fact. But I cannot agree with him. If the testator had been last seen alive at Woodford and the remains had been found at Woodford, or if he had disappeared from Eltham, and the remains had been found at Eltham, that would have had some significance. But he can only have been last seen at one of the places, whereas the remains have been found at both places. Here again my learned friend seems to have proved too much.

"But I need not occupy your time further. I repeat that, in order to justify us in presuming the death of the testator, clear and positive evidence would be necessary. That no such evidence has been brought forward. Accordingly, seeing that the testator may return at any time and is entitled to find his property intact, I shall ask you for a verdict that will secure to him this measure of ordinary justice."

At the conclusion of Mr. Heath's speech the judge, as if awakening from a refreshing nap, opened his eyes, and uncommonly shrewd, intelligent eyes they were when the expressive eyelids were duly tucked up out of the way. He commenced by reading over a part of the will and certain notes – which he appeared to have made in some miraculous fashion with his eyes shut – and then proceeded to review the evidence and the counsels' arguments for the instruction of the jury.

"Before considering the evidence which you have heard, gentlemen," he said, "it will be well for me to say a few words to you on the general aspects of the case which is occupying our attention.

"If a person goes abroad or disappears from his home and his ordinary places of resort and is absent for a long period of time, the presumption of death arises at the expiration of seven years from the date on which he was last heard of. That is to say, that the total disappearance of an individual for seven years constitutes presumptive evidence that the said individual is dead, and the presumption can be set aside only by the production of evidence that he was alive at some time within that period of seven years. But if, on the other hand, it is sought to presume the death of a person who has been absent for a shorter period than seven years, it is necessary to produce such evidence as shall make it highly probable that the said person is dead. Of course, presumption implies supposition as opposed to actual demonstration, but, nevertheless, the evidence in such a case must be of a kind that tends to create a very strong belief that death has occurred, and I need hardly say that the shorter the period of absence, the more convincing must be the evidence.

"In the present case, the testator, John Bellingham, has been absent somewhat under two years. This is a relatively short period, and in itself gives rise to no presumption of death. Nevertheless, death has been presumed in a case where the period of absence was even shorter and the insurance recovered, but here the evidence supporting the belief in the occurrence of death was exceedingly weighty.

"The testator in this case was a shipmaster, and his disappearance was accompanied by the disappearance of the ship and the entire ship's company in the course of a voyage from London to Marseilles. The loss of the ship and her crew was the only reasonable explanation of the disappearance, and, short of actual demonstration, the facts offered convincing evidence of the death of all persons on board. I mention this case as an illustration. You are not dealing with speculative probabilities. You are contemplating a very momentous proceeding, and you must be very sure of your ground. Consider what it is that you are asked to do.

"The petitioner asks permission to presume the death of the testator in order that the testator's property may be distributed among the beneficiaries under the will. The granting of such permission involves us in the gravest responsibility. An ill-considered decision might be productive of a serious injustice to the testator, an injustice that could never be remedied. Hence it is incumbent upon you to weigh the evidence with the greatest care, to come to no decision without the profoundest consideration of all the facts.

"The evidence that you have heard divides itself into two parts – that relating to the circumstances of the testator's disappearance, and that relating to certain human remains. In connection with the latter I can only express my surprise and regret that the application was not postponed until the completion of the coroner's inquest, and leave you to consider the evidence. You will bear in mind that Doctor Summers has stated explicitly that the remains cannot be identified as those of any particular individual, but that the testator and the unknown deceased had so many points of resemblance that they might possibly be one and the same person.

"With reference to the circumstances of the disappearance, you have heard the evidence of Mr. Jellicoe to the effect that the testator has on no previous occasion gone abroad without informing him as to his proposed destination. But in considering what weight you are to give to this statement you will bear in mind that when the testator set out for Paris after his interview with Doctor Norbury he left Mr. Jellicoe without any information as to his specific destination, his address in Paris, or the precise date when he should return, and that Mr. Jellicoe was unable to tell us where the testator went or what was his business. Mr. Jellicoe was, in fact, for a time without any means of tracing the testator or ascertaining his whereabouts.

"The evidence of the housemaid, Dobbs, and of Mr. Hurst is rather confusing. It appears that the testator came to the house, and when looked for later was not to be found. A search of the premises showed that he was not in the house, whence it seems to follow that he must have left it, but since no one was informed of his intention to leave, and he had expressed the intention of staying to see Mr. Hurst, his conduct in thus going away surreptitiously must appear somewhat eccentric. The point that you have to consider, therefore, is whether a person who is capable of thus departing in a surreptitious and eccentric manner from a house, without giving notice to the servants, is capable also of departing in a surreptitious and eccentric manner from his usual places of resort without giving notice to his friends or thereafter informing them of his whereabouts.

"The questions, then, gentlemen, that you have to ask yourselves before deciding on your verdict are two: First, Are the circumstances of the testator's disappearance and his continued absence incongruous with his habits and personal peculiarities as they are known to you? And second, Are there any facts which indicate in a positive manner that the testator is dead? Ask yourselves these questions, gentlemen, and the answers to them, furnished by the evidence that you have heard, will guide you to your decision."

Having delivered himself of the above instructions, the judge applied himself to the perusal of the will with professional gusto, in which occupation he was presently disturbed by the announcement of the foreman of the jury that a verdict had been agreed upon.

The judge sat up and glanced at the jury-box, and when the foreman proceeded to state that "We find no sufficient reason for presuming the testator, John Bellingham, to be dead," he nodded approvingly. Evidently that was his opinion, too, as he was careful to explain when he conveyed to Mr. Loram the refusal of the Court to grant the permission applied for.

The decision was a great relief to me, and also, I think, to Miss Bellingham, but most of all to her father, who, with instinctive good manners, since he could not suppress a smile of triumph, rose and hastily stumped out of the Court, so that the discomfited Hurst should not see him. His daughter and I followed, and as we left the Court she remarked, with a smile, "So our pauperism is not, after all, made absolute. There is still a chance for us in the Chapter of Accidents – and perhaps even for poor old Uncle John."

Chapter XV
Circumstantial Evidence

The morning after the hearing saw me setting forth on my round in more than usually good spirits. The round itself was but a short one, for my list contained only a couple of "chronics", and this, perhaps, contributed to my cheerful outlook on life. But there were other reasons. The decision of the Court had come as an unexpected reprieve and the ruin of my friends' prospects was at least postponed. Then, I had learned that Thorndyke was back from Bristol and wished me to look in on him, and, finally, Miss Bellingham had agreed to spend this very afternoon with me, browsing round the galleries at the British Museum.

I had disposed of my two patients by a quarter-to-eleven, and three minutes later was striding down Mitre Court, all agog to hear what Thorndyke had to say with reference to my notes on the inquest. The "oak" was open when I arrived at his chambers, and a modest flourish on the little brass knocker of the inner door was answered by my quondam teacher himself.

"How good of you, Berkeley," he said, shaking hands genially, "to look me up so early. I am alone, just looking through the report of the evidence of yesterday's proceedings."

He placed an easy chair for me, and, gathering up a bundle of typewritten papers, laid them aside on the table.

"Were you surprised at the decision?" I asked.

"No," he answered. "Two years is a short period of absence, but still, it might easily have gone the other way. I am greatly relieved. The respite gives us time to carry out our investigations without undue hurry."

"Did you find my notes of any use?" I asked.

"Heath did. Polton handed them to him, and they were invaluable to him for his cross-examination. I haven't seen them yet. In fact, I have only just got them back from him. Let us go through them together now."

He opened a drawer and taking from it my notebook, seated himself, and began to read through my notes with grave attention, while I stood and looked shyly over his shoulder. On the page that contained my sketches of the Sidcup arm, showing the distribution of the snails' eggs on the bones, he lingered with a faint smile that made me turn hot and red.

"Those sketches look rather footy," I said, "but I had to put something in my notebook."

"You did not attach any importance, then, to the facts that they illustrated?"

"No. The egg-patches were there, so I noted the fact. That's all."

"I congratulate you, Berkeley. There is not one man in twenty who would have had the sense to make a careful note of what he considers an unimportant or irrelevant fact, and the investigator who notes only those things that appear significant is perfectly useless. He gives himself no material for reconsideration. But you don't mean that these egg-patches and worm-tubes appeared to you to have no significance at all?"

"Oh, of course, they show the position in which the bones were lying."

"Exactly. The arm was lying, fully extended, with the dorsal side uppermost. But we also learn from these egg-patches that the hand had been separated from the arm before it was thrown into the pond, and there is something very remarkable in that."

I leaned over his shoulder and gazed at my sketches, amazed at the rapidity with which he had reconstructed the limb from my rough drawings of the individual bones.

"I don't quite see how you arrived at it, though," I said.

"Well, look at your drawings. The egg-patches are on the dorsal surface of the scapula, the humerus, and the bones of the fore-arm. But here you have shown six of the bones of the hand: Two metacarpals, the *os magnum*, and three phalanges, and they all have egg-patches on the palmar surface. Therefore the hand was lying palm upward."

"But the hand may have been pronated."

"If you mean pronated in relation to the arm, that is impossible, for the position of the egg-patches shows clearly that the bones of the arm were lying in the position of supination. Thus the dorsal surface of the arm and the palmar surface of the hand respectively were uppermost, which is an anatomical impossibility so long as the hand is attached to the arm."

"But might not the hand have become detached after lying in the pond for some time?"

"No. It could not have been detached until the ligaments had decayed, and if it had been separated after the decay of the soft parts, the bones would have been thrown into disorder. But the egg-patches are all on the palmar surface, showing that the bones were still in their normal relative positions. No, Berkeley, that hand was thrown into the pond separately from the arm."

"But why should it have been?" I asked.

"Ah, there is a very pretty little problem for you to consider. And, meantime, let me tell you that your expedition has been a brilliant success. You are an excellent observer. Your only fault is that when you have noted

351

certain facts you don't seem fully to appreciate their significance – which is merely a matter of inexperience. As to the facts that you have collected, several of them are of prime importance."

"I am glad you are satisfied," said I, "though I don't see that I have discovered much excepting those snail's eggs, and they don't seem to have advanced matters very much."

"A definite fact, Berkeley, is a definite asset. Perhaps we may presently find a little space in our Chinese puzzle which this fact of the detached hand will just drop into. But, tell me, did you find nothing unexpected or suggestive about those bones – as to their number and condition, for instance?"

"Well, I thought it a little queer that the scapula and clavicle should be there. I should have expected him to cut the arm off at the shoulder-joint."

"Yes," said Thorndyke, "so should I, and so it has been done in every case of dismemberment that I am acquainted with. To an ordinary person, the arm seems to join on to the trunk at the shoulder-joint, and that is where he would naturally sever it. What explanation do you suggest of this unusual mode of severing the arm?"

"Do you think the fellow could have been a butcher?" I asked, remembering Dr. Summers' remark. "This is the way a shoulder of mutton is taken off."

"No," replied Thorndyke. "A butcher includes the scapula in a shoulder of mutton for a specific purpose, namely, to take off a given quantity of meat. And also, as a sheep has no clavicle, it is the easiest way to detach the limb. But I imagine a butcher would find himself in difficulties if he attempted to take off a man's arm in that way. The clavicle would be a new and perplexing feature. Then, too, a butcher does not deal very delicately with his subject. If he has to divide a joint, he just cuts through it and does not trouble himself to avoid marking the bones. But you note here that there is not a single scratch or score on any one of the bones, not even where the finger was removed. Now, if you have ever prepared bones for a museum, as I have, you will remember the extreme care that is necessary in disarticulating joints to avoid disfiguring the articular ends of the bones with cuts and scratches."

"Then you think that the person who dismembered this body must have had some anatomical knowledge and skill?"

"That is what has been suggested. The suggestion is not mine."

"Then I infer that you don't agree?"

Thorndyke smiled. "I am sorry to be so cryptic, Berkeley, but you understand that I can't make statements. Still, I am trying to lead you to make certain inferences from the facts that are in your possession."

"If I make the right inference, will you tell me?" I asked.

"It won't be necessary," he answered, with the same quiet smile. "When you have fitted the puzzle together you don't need to be told you have done it."

It was most infernally tantalizing. I pondered on the problem with a scowl of such intense cogitation that Thorndyke laughed outright.

"It seems to me," I said, at length, "that the identity of the remains is the primary question and that it is a question of fact. It doesn't seem any use to speculate about it."

"Exactly. Either these bones are the remains of John Bellingham or they are not. There will be no doubt on the subject when all the bones are assembled – if ever they are. And the settlement of that question will probably throw light on the further question: Who deposited them in the places in which they were found? But to return to your observations: Did you gather nothing from the other bones? From the complete state of the neck vertebrae for instance?"

"Well, it did strike me as rather odd that the fellow should have gone to the trouble of separating the atlas from the skull. He must have been pretty handy with the scalpel to have done it as cleanly as he seems to have done, but I don't see why he should have gone about the business in the most inconvenient way."

"You notice the uniformity of method. He has separated the head from the spine, instead of cutting through the spine lower down, as most persons would have done, he removed the arms with the entire shoulder-girdle, instead of simply cutting them off at the shoulder-joints. Even in the thighs the same peculiarity appears, for in neither case was the knee-cap found with the thigh-bone, although it seems to have been searched for. Now the obvious way to divide the leg is to cut through the patellar ligament, leaving the knee-cap attached to the thigh. But in this case, the knee-cap appears to have been left attached to the shank. Can you explain why this person should have adopted this unusual and rather inconvenient method? Can you suggest a motive for this procedure, or can you think of any circumstances which might lead a person to adopt this method by preference?"

"It seems as if he wished, for some reason, to divide the body into definite anatomical regions."

Thorndyke chuckled. "You are not offering that suggestion as an explanation, are you? Because it would require more explaining than the original problem. And it is not even true. Anatomically speaking, the knee-cap appertains to the thigh rather than to the shank. It is a sesamoid bone belonging to the thigh muscles – yet in this case it has been left attached, apparently to the shank. No, Berkeley, that cat won't jump. Our unknown

353

operator was not preparing a skeleton as a museum specimen. He was dividing a body up into convenient sized portions for the purpose of conveying them to various ponds. Now what circumstances might have led him to divide it in this peculiar manner?"

"I am afraid I have no suggestion to offer. Have you?"

Thorndyke suddenly lapsed into ambiguity. "I think," he said, "it is possible to conceive such circumstances, and so, probably, will you if you think it over."

"Did you gather anything of importance from the evidence at the inquest?" I asked.

"It is difficult to say," he replied. "The whole of my conclusions in this case are based on what is virtually circumstantial evidence. I have not one single fact of which I can say that it admits only of a single interpretation. Still, it must be remembered that even the most inconclusive facts, if sufficiently multiplied, yield a highly conclusive total. And my little pile of evidence is growing, particle by particle, but we mustn't sit here gossiping at this hour of the day. I have to consult with Marchmont and you say that you have an early afternoon engagement. We can walk together as far as Fleet Street."

A minute or two later we went our respective ways, Thorndyke toward Lombard Street and I to Fetter Lane, not unmindful of those coming events that were casting so agreeable a shadow before them.

There was only one message awaiting me, and when Adolphus had delivered it (amidst mephitic fumes that rose from the basement, premonitory of fried plaice), I pocketed my stethoscope and betook myself to Gunpowder Alley, the aristocratic abode of my patient, joyfully threading the now familiar passages of Gough Square and Wine Office Court, and meditating pleasantly on the curious literary flavor that pervades these little-known regions. For the shade of the author of *Rasselas* still seems to haunt the scenes of his Titanic labors and his ponderous but homely and temperate rejoicings. Every court and alley whispers of books and of the making of books: Forms of type, trundled noisily on trolleys by ink-smeared boys, salute the wayfarer at odd corners – piles of strawboard, rolls or bales of paper, drums of printing-ink or roller composition stand on the pavement outside dark entries – basement windows give glimpses into Hadean caverns tenanted by legions of printer's devils, and the very air is charged with the hum of press and with odors of glue and paste and oil. The entire neighborhood is given up to the printer and binder, and even my patient turned out to be a guillotine-knife grinder – a ferocious and revolutionary calling strangely at variance with his harmless appearance and meek bearing.

354

I was in good time at my tryst, despite the hindrances of fried plaice and invalid guillotinists, but, early as I was, Miss Bellingham was already waiting in the garden – she had been filling a bowl with flowers – ready to sally forth.

"It is quite like old times," she said, as we turned into Fetter Lane, "to be going to the Museum together. It brings back the Tell-el-Amarna tablets and all your kindness and unselfish labor. I suppose we shall walk there to-day?"

"Certainly," I replied, "I am not going to share your society with the common mortals who ride in omnibuses. That would be sheer, sinful waste. Besides, it is more companionable to walk."

"Yes, it is, and the bustle of the streets makes one more appreciative of the quiet of the Museum. What are we going to look at when we get there?"

"You must decide that," I replied. "You know the collection much better than I do."

"Well, now," she mused, "I wonder what you would like to see. Or, in other words, what I should like you to see. The old English pottery is rather fascinating, especially the Fulham ware. I rather think I shall take you to see that."

She reflected a while, and then, just as we reached the gate of Staple Inn, she stopped and looked thoughtfully down the Gray's Inn Road.

"You have taken a great interest in our 'case' as Doctor Thorndyke calls it. Would you like to see the churchyard where Uncle John wished to be buried? It is a little out of our way, but we are not in a hurry, are we?"

I, certainly, was not. Any deviation that might prolong our walk was welcome, and as to the place – why, all places were alike to me if only she were by my side. Besides, the churchyard was really of some interest, since it was undoubtedly the "exciting cause" of the obnoxious paragraph two of the will. I accordingly expressed a desire to make its acquaintance, and we crossed to the entrance to Gray's Inn Road.

"Do you ever try," she asked, as we turned down the dingy thoroughfare, "to picture familiar places as they looked a couple of hundred years ago?"

"Yes," I answered, "and very difficult I find it. One has to manufacture the materials for reconstruction, and then the present aspect of the place will keep obtruding itself. But some places are easier to reconstitute than others."

"That is what I find," said she. "Now Holborn, for example, is quite easy to reconstruct, though I daresay the imaginary form isn't a bit like the original. But there are fragments left, like Staple Inn and the front of Gray's Inn, and then one has seen prints of the old Middle Row and some

355

of the taverns, so that one has some material with which to help out one's imagination. But this road we are walking in always baffles me. It looks so old and yet is, for the most part, so new that I find it impossible to make a satisfactory picture of its appearance, say, when Sir Roger de Coverley might have strolled in Gray's Inn Walks, or farther back, when Francis Bacon had chambers in the Inn."

"I imagine," said I, "that part of the difficulty is in the mixed character of the neighborhood. Here on the one side, is old Gray's Inn, not much changed since Bacon's time – his chambers are still to be seen, I think, over the gateway, and there, on the Clerkenwell side, is a dense and rather squalid neighborhood which has grown up over a region partly rural and wholly fugitive in character. Places like Bagnigge Wells and Hockley in the Hole would not have had many buildings that were likely to survive, and in the absence of surviving specimens the imagination hasn't much to work from."

"I daresay you are right," said she. "Certainly, the *purlieus* of old Clerkenwell present a very confused picture to me, whereas, in the case of an old street like, say, Great Ormond Street, one has only to sweep away the modern buildings and replace them with glorious old houses like the few that remain, dig up the roadway and pavements and lay down cobble-stones, plant a few wooden posts, hang up one or two oil-lamps, and the transformation is complete. And a very delightful transformation it is."

"Very delightful – which, by the way, is a melancholy thought. For we ought to be doing better work than our forefathers, whereas what we actually do is to pull down the old buildings, clap the doorways, porticoes, paneling, and mantels in our museums, and then run up something inexpensive and useful and deadly uninteresting in their place."

My companion looked at me and laughed softly. "For a naturally cheerful, and even gay young man," said she, "you are most amazingly pessimistic. The mantle of Jeremiah – if he ever wore one – seems to have fallen on you, but without in the least impairing your good spirits excepting in regard to matters architectural."

"I have much to be thankful for," said I. "Am I not taken to the Museum by a fair lady? And does she not stay me with mummy cases and comfort me with crockery?"

"Pottery," she corrected, and then as we met a party of grave-looking women emerging from a side-street, she said, "I suppose those are lady medical students."

"Yes, on their way to the Royal Free Hospital. Note the gravity of their demeanor and contrast it with the levity of the male student."

"I was doing so," she answered, "and wondering why professional women are usually so much more serious than men."

"Perhaps," I suggested, "it is a matter of selection. A peculiar type of woman is attracted to the professions, whereas every man has to earn his living as a matter of course."

"Yes, I daresay that is the explanation. This is our turning."

We passed into Heathcote Street, at the end of which was an open gate giving entrance to one of those disused and metamorphosed burial-grounds that are to be met with in the older districts of London. In which the dispossessed dead are jostled into corners to make room for the living. Many of the headstones were still standing, and others, displaced to make room for asphalted walks and seats, were ranged around by the walls exhibiting inscriptions made meaningless by their removal. It was a pleasant enough place on this summer afternoon, contrasted with the dingy streets whence we had come, though its grass was faded and yellow and the twitter of the birds in the trees mingled with the hideous Board-school drawls of the children who played around the seats and the few remaining tombs.

"So this is the last resting-place of the illustrious house of Bellingham," said I.

"Yes, and we are not the only distinguished people who repose in this place. The daughter of no less a person than Richard Cromwell is buried here. The tomb is still standing – but perhaps you have been here before, and know it."

"I don't think I have ever been here before, and yet there is something about the place that seems familiar." I looked around, cudgeling my brains for the key to the dimly reminiscent sensations that the place evoked, until, suddenly, I caught sight of a group of buildings away to the west, enclosed within a wall heightened by a wooden trellis.

"Yes, of course!" I exclaimed. "I remember the place now. I have never been in this part before, but in that enclosure beyond, which opens at the end of Henrietta Street, there used to be and may be still, for all I know, a school of anatomy, at which I attended in my first year. In fact, I did my first dissection there."

"There was a certain gruesome appropriateness in the position of the school," remarked Miss Bellingham. "It would have been really convenient in the days of the resurrection men. Your material would have been delivered at your very door. Was it a large school?"

"The attendance varied according to the time of the year. Sometimes I worked there quite alone. I used to let myself in with a key and hoist my subject out of a sort of sepulchral tank by means of a chain tackle. It was a ghoulish business. You have no idea how awful the body used to look to my unaccustomed eyes, as it rose slowly out of the tank. It was like the resurrection scene that you see on some old tombstones, where the

357

deceased is shown rising out of his coffin while the skeleton, Death, falls vanquished with his dart shattered and his crown toppling off.

"I remember, too, that the demonstrator used to wear a blue apron, which created a sort of impression of a cannibal butcher's shop. But I am afraid I am shocking you."

"No you are not. Every profession has its unpresentable aspects, which ought not to be seen by outsiders. Think of the sculptor's studio and of the sculptor himself when he is modeling a large figure or a group in clay. He might be a bricklayer or a roadsweeper if you judge by his appearance. This is the tomb I was telling you about."

We halted before the plain coffer of stone, weathered and wasted by age, but yet kept in decent repair by some pious hands, and read the inscription, setting forth with modest pride, that here reposed Anna, sixth daughter of Richard Cromwell, "The Protector", It was a simple monument and commonplace enough, with the crude severity of the ascetic age to which it belonged. But still, it carried the mind back to those stirring times when the leafy shades of Gray's Inn Lane must have resounded with the clank of weapons and the tramp of armed men – when this bald recreation-ground was a rustic churchyard, standing amidst green fields and hedgerows, and countrymen leading their pack-horses into London through the Lane would stop to look in over the wooden gate.

Miss Bellingham looked at me critically as I stood thus reflecting, and presently remarked, "I think you and I have a good many mental habits in common."

I looked up inquiringly, and she continued, "I notice that an old tombstone seems to set you meditating. So it does me. When I look at an ancient monument, and especially an old headstone, I find myself almost unconsciously retracing the years to the date that is written on the stone. Why do you think that is? Why should a monument be so stimulating to the imagination? And why should a common headstone be more so than any other?"

"I suppose it is," I answered reflectively, "that a churchyard monument is a peculiarly personal thing and appertains in a peculiar way to a particular time. And the circumstance that it has stood untouched by the passing years while everything around has changed, helps the imagination to span the interval. And the common headstone, the memorial of some dead and gone farmer or laborer who lived and died in the village hard by, is still more intimate and suggestive. The rustic, childish sculpture of the village mason and the artless doggerel of the village schoolmaster, bring back the time and place and the conditions of life more vividly than the more scholarly inscriptions and the more artistic enrichments of monuments of greater pretensions. But where are your own family tombstones?"

"They are over in that farther corner. There is an intelligent, but inopportune, person apparently copying the epitaphs. I wish he would go away. I want to show them to you."

I now noticed, for the first time, an individual engaged, notebook in hand, in making a careful survey of a group of old headstones. Evidently he was making a copy of the inscriptions, for not only was he poring attentively over the writing on the face of the stone, but now and again he helped out his vision by running his fingers over the worn lettering.

"That is my grandfather's tombstone that he is copying now," said Miss Bellingham, and even as she spoke, the man turned and directed a searching glance at us with a pair of keen, spectacled eyes.

Simultaneously we uttered an exclamation of surprise, for the investigator was Mr. Jellicoe.

Chapter XVI
O Artemidorus, Farewell!

Whether or not Mr. Jellicoe was surprised to see us, it is impossible to say. His countenance (which served the ordinary purposes of a face, inasmuch as it contained the principal organs of special sense, with inlets to the alimentary and respiratory tracts) was, as an apparatus for the expression of the emotions, a total failure. To a thought-reader it would have been about as helpful as the face carved upon the handle of an umbrella – a comparison suggested, perhaps, by a certain resemblance to such an object. He advanced, holding open his notebook and pencil, and having saluted us with a stiff bow and an old-fashioned flourish of his hat, shook hands rheumatically and waited for us to speak.

"This is an unexpected pleasure, Mr. Jellicoe," said Miss Bellingham.

"It is very good of you to say so," he replied.

"And quite a coincidence – that we should all happen to come here on the same day."

"A coincidence, certainly," he admitted, "and if we had all happened not to come – which must have occurred frequently – that also would have been a coincidence."

"I suppose it would," said she, "but I hope we are not interrupting you."

"Thank you, no. I had just finished when I had the pleasure of perceiving you."

"You were making some notes in reference to the case, I imagine," said I. It was an impertinent question, put with malice aforethought for the mere pleasure of hearing him evade it.

"The case?" he repeated. "You are referring, perhaps, to Stevens versus the Parish Council?"

"I think Doctor Berkeley was referring to the case of my uncle's will," Miss Bellingham said quite gravely, though with a suspicious dimpling about the corners of her mouth.

"Indeed," said Mr. Jellicoe. "There is a case, is there – a suit?"

"I mean the proceedings instituted by Mr. Hurst."

"Oh, but that was merely an application to the Court, and is, moreover, finished and done with. At least, so I understand. I speak, of course, subject to correction. I am not acting for Mr. Hurst, you will be pleased to remember. As a matter of fact," he continued, after a brief pause, "I was just refreshing my memory as to the wording of the inscriptions on these stones, especially that of your grandfather, Francis Bellingham. It has occurred to me that if it should appear by the finding of the coroner's jury that your uncle is deceased, it would be proper and decorous that some memorial should be placed here. But, as the burial ground is closed, there might be some difficulty about erecting a new monument, whereas there would probably be none in adding an inscription to one already existing. Hence these investigations. For if the inscriptions on your grandfather's stone had set forth that *'here rests the body of Francis Bellingham'*, it would have been manifestly improper to add *'also that of John Bellingham, son of the above'*. Fortunately the inscription was more discreetly drafted, merely recording the fact that this monument is *'sacred to the memory of the said Francis'*, and not committing itself as to the whereabouts of the remains. But perhaps I am interrupting you."

"No, not at all," replied Miss Bellingham (which was grossly untrue. He was interrupting *me* most intolerably.) "We were going to the British Museum and just looked in here on our way."

"Ha," said Mr. Jellicoe, "now, I happen to be going to the Museum too, to see Doctor Norbury. I suppose that is another coincidence?"

"Certainly it is," Miss Bellingham replied, and then she asked, "Shall we walk together?" and the old curmudgeon actually said, "Yes" – confound him!

We returned to the Gray's Inn Road, where, as there was now room for us to walk abreast, I proceeded to indemnify myself for the lawyer's unwelcome company by leading the conversation back to the subject of the missing man.

"Was there anything, Mr. Jellicoe, in Mr. John Bellingham's state of health that would make it probable that he might die suddenly?"

The lawyer looked at me suspiciously for a few moments and then remarked, "You seem to be greatly interested in John Bellingham and his affairs."

"I am. My friends are deeply concerned in them, and the case itself is of more than common interest from a professional point of view."

"And what is the bearing of this particular question?"

"Surely it is obvious," said I. "If a missing man is known to have suffered from some affliction, such as heart disease, aneurism, or arterial degeneration, likely to produce sudden death, that fact will surely be highly material to the question as to whether he is probably dead or alive."

"No doubt you are right," said Mr. Jellicoe. "I have little knowledge of medical affairs, but doubtless you are right. As to the question itself, I am Mr. Bellingham's lawyer, not his doctor. His health is a matter that lies outside my jurisdiction. But you heard my evidence in Court, to the effect that the testator appeared, to my untutored observation, to be a healthy man. I can say no more now."

"If the question is of any importance," said Miss Bellingham, "I wonder they did not call his doctor and settle it definitely. My own impression is that he was – or is – rather a strong and sound man. He certainly recovered very quickly and completely after his accident."

"What accident was that?" I asked.

"Oh, hasn't my father told you? It occurred while he was staying with us. He slipped from a curb and broke one of the bones of the left ankle – somebody's fracture – "

"Pott's?"

"Yes. That was the name – Pott's fracture, and he broke both his knee-caps as well. Sir Morgan Bennett had to perform an operation, or he would have been a cripple for life. As it was, he was about again in a few weeks, apparently none the worse excepting for a slight weakness of the left ankle."

"Could he walk upstairs?" I asked.

"Oh, yes, and play golf and ride a bicycle."

"You are sure he broke both knee-caps?"

"Quite sure. I remember that it was mentioned as an uncommon injury, and that Sir Morgan seemed quite pleased with him for doing it."

"That sounds rather libelous, but I expect he was pleased with the result of the operation. He might well be."

Here there was a brief lull in the conversation, and, even as I was trying to think of a poser for Mr. Jellicoe, that gentleman took the opportunity to change the subject.

"Are you going to the Egyptian rooms?" he asked.

"No," replied Miss Bellingham. "We are going to look at the pottery."

"Ancient or modern?"

"That old Fulham ware is what chiefly interests us at present. That of the seventeenth century. I don't know whether you call that ancient or modern."

"Neither do I," said Mr. Jellicoe. "Antiquity and modernity are terms that have no fixed connotation. They are purely relative and their application in a particular instance has to be determined by a sort of sliding scale. To a furniture collector, a Tudor chair or a Jacobean chest is ancient. To an architect, their period is modern, whereas an eleventh-century church is ancient, but to an Egyptologist, accustomed to remains of a vast antiquity, both are products of modern periods separated by an insignificant interval. And, I suppose," he added reflectively, "that to a geologist, the traces of the very earliest dawn of human history appertain only to the recent period. Conceptions of time, like all other conceptions, are relative."

"You would appear to be a disciple of Herbert Spencer," I remarked.

"I am a disciple of Arthur Jellicoe, sir," he retorted. And I believed him.

By the time we had reached the Museum he had become almost genial, and, if less amusing in this frame, he was so much more instructive and entertaining that I refrained from baiting him, and permitted him to discuss his favorite topic unhindered, especially since my companion listened with lively interest. Nor, when we entered the great hall, did he relinquish possession of us, and we followed submissively, as he led the way past the winged bulls of Nineveh and the great seated statues, until we found ourselves, almost without the exercise of our volition, in the upper room amidst the glaring mummy cases that had witnessed the birth of my friendship with Ruth Bellingham.

"Before I leave you," said Mr. Jellicoe, "I should like to show you that mummy that we were discussing the other evening. The one, you remember, that my friend, John Bellingham, presented to the Museum a little time before his disappearance. The point that I mentioned is only a trivial one, but it may become of interest hereafter if any plausible explanation should be forthcoming." He led us along the room until we arrived at the case containing John Bellingham's gift, where he halted and gazed in at the mummy with the affectionate reflectiveness of the connoisseur.

"The bitumen coating was what we were discussing, Miss Bellingham," said he. "You have seen it, of course."

"Yes," she answered. "It is a dreadful disfigurement, isn't it?"

"Esthetically it is to be deplored, but it adds a certain speculative interest to the specimen. You notice that the black coating leaves the principal decoration and the whole of the inscription untouched, which is precisely the part that one would expect to find covered up, whereas the feet and the back, which probably bore no writing, are quite thickly crusted. If you stoop down, you can see that the bitumen was daubed freely into the lacings of the back, where it served no purpose, so that even the strings are embedded." He stooped as he spoke, and peered up inquisitively at the back of the mummy, where it was visible between the supports.

"Has Doctor Norbury any explanation to offer?" asked Miss Bellingham.

"None whatever," replied Mr. Jellicoe. "He finds it as great a mystery as I do. But he thinks that we may get some suggestion from the Director when he comes back. He is a very great authority, as you know, and a practical excavator of great experience too. But I mustn't stay here talking of these things, and keeping you from your pottery. Perhaps I have stayed too long already. If I have I ask your pardon, and I will now wish you a very good afternoon." With a sudden return to his customary wooden impassivity, he shook hands with us, bowed stiffly, and took himself off toward the curator's office.

"What a strange man that is," said Miss Bellingham, as Mr. Jellicoe disappeared through the doorway at the end of the room, "or perhaps I should say, a strange being, for I can hardly think of him as a man. I have never met any other human creature at all like him."

"He is certainly a queer old fogey," I agreed.

"Yes, but there is something more than that. He is so emotionless, so remote and aloof from all mundane concerns. He moves among ordinary men and women, but as a mere presence, an unmoved spectator of their actions, quite dispassionate and impersonal."

"Yes. He is astonishingly self-contained. In fact, he seems, as you say, to go to and fro among men, enveloped in a sort of infernal atmosphere of his own, like Marley's ghost. But he is lively and human enough as soon as the subject of Egyptian antiquities is broached."

"Lively, but not human. He is always, to me, quite unhuman. Even when he is most interested, and even enthusiastic, he is a mere personification of knowledge. Nature ought to have furnished him with an ibis's head like Tahuti. Then he would have looked his part."

"He would have made a rare sensation in Lincoln's Inn if he had," said I, and we both laughed heartily at the imaginary picture of Tahuti Jellicoe, slender-beaked and top-hatted, going about his business in Lincoln's Inn and the Law Courts.

Insensibly, as we talked, we had drawn near to the mummy of Artemidorus, and now my companion halted before the case with her thoughtful gray eyes bent dreamily on the face that looked out at us. I watched her with reverent admiration. How charming she looked as she stood with her sweet, grave face turned so earnestly to the object of her mystical affection! How dainty and full of womanly dignity and grace! And then suddenly it was borne in upon me that a great change had come over her since the day of our first meeting. She had grown younger, more girlish, and more gentle. At first she had seemed much older than I – a sad-faced woman, weary, solemn, enigmatic, almost gloomy, with a bitter, ironic humor and a bearing distant and cold. Now she was only maidenly and sweet. Tinged, it is true, with a certain seriousness, but frank and gracious and wholly lovable.

Could the change be due to our friendship? As I asked myself the question, my heart leaped with a new hope. I yearned to tell her all that she was to me – all that I hoped we might be to one another in the years to come.

At length I ventured to break in upon her reverie.

"What are you thinking about so earnestly, fair lady?"

She turned quickly with a bright smile and sparkling eyes that looked frankly into mine. "I was wondering," said she, "if he was jealous of my new friend. But what a baby I am to talk such nonsense!"

She laughed softly and happily with just an adorable hint of shyness.

"Why should he be jealous?" I asked.

"Well, you see, before – we were friends, he had me all to himself. I have never had a man friend before – except my father – and no really intimate friend at all. And I was very lonely in those days, after our troubles had befallen. I am naturally solitary, but still, I am only a girl. I am not a philosopher. So when I felt very lonely, I used to come here and look at Artemidorus and make believe that he knew all the sadness of my life and sympathized with me. It was very silly, I know, but yet, somehow it was a real comfort to me."

"It was not silly of you at all. He must have been a good man, a gentle, sweet-faced man who had won the love of those who knew him, as this beautiful memorial tells, and it was wise and good of you to sweeten the bitterness of your life with the fragrance of this human love that blossoms in the dust after the lapse of centuries. No, you were not silly, and Artemidorus is not jealous of your new friend."

"Are you sure?" She still smiled as she asked the question, but her glance was soft – almost tender – and there was a note of whimsical anxiety in her voice.

"Quite sure. I give you my confident assurance."

She laughed gaily. "Then," said she, "I am satisfied, for I am sure you know. But here is a mighty telepathist who can read the thoughts even of a mummy. A most formidable companion. But tell me how you know."

"I know because it is he who gave you to me to be my friend. Don't you remember?"

"Yes, I remember," she answered softly. "It was when you were so sympathetic with my foolish whim that I felt we were really friends."

"And I, when you confided your pretty fancy to me, thanked you for the gift of your friendship, and treasured it, and do still treasure it, above everything on earth."

She looked at me quickly with a sort of nervousness in her manner, and cast down her eyes. Then, after a few moments' almost embarrassed silence, as if to bring back our talk to a less emotional plane, she said, "Do you notice the curious way in which this memorial divides itself up into two parts?"

365

"How do you mean?" I asked a little disconcerted by the sudden descent.

"I mean that there is a part of it that is purely decorative and a part that is expressive or emotional. You notice that the general design and scheme of decoration, although really Greek in feeling, follows rigidly the Egyptian conventions. But the portrait is entirely in the Greek manner, and when they came to that pathetic farewell, it had to be spoken in their own tongue, written in their own familiar characters."

"Yes. I have noticed that and admired the taste with which they have kept the inscription so inconspicuous as not to clash with the decoration. An obtrusive inscription in Greek characters would have spoiled the consistency of the whole scheme."

"Yes, it would." She assented absently as if she were thinking of something else, and once more gazed thoughtfully at the mummy. I watched her with deep content, noted the lovely contour of her cheek, the soft masses of hair that strayed away so gracefully from her brow, and thought her the most wonderful creature that had ever trod the earth. Suddenly she looked at me reflectively.

"I wonder," she said, "what made me tell you about Artemidorus. It was a rather silly, childish sort of make-believe, and I wouldn't have told anyone else for the world – not even my father. How did I know that you would sympathize and understand?"

She asked the question in all simplicity with her serious gray eyes looking inquiringly into mine. And the answer came to me in a flash, with the beating of my own heart.

"I will tell you how you know, Ruth," I whispered passionately. "It was because I loved you more than anyone else in the world has ever loved you, and you felt my love in your heart and called it sympathy."

I stopped short, for she had blushed scarlet and then turned deathly pale. And now she looked at me wildly, almost with terror.

"Have I shocked you, Ruth dearest?" I exclaimed penitently. "Have I spoken too soon? If I have, forgive me. But I had to tell you. I have been eating my heart out for love of you for I don't know how long. I think I have loved you from the first day we met. Perhaps I shouldn't have spoken yet, but, Ruth dear, if you only knew what a sweet girl you are, you wouldn't blame me."

"I don't blame you," she said, almost in a whisper, "I blame myself. I have been a bad friend to you, who have been so loyal and loving to me. I ought not to have let this happen. For it can't be, Paul. I can't say what you want me to say. We can never be anything more to one another than friends."

A cold hand seemed to grasp my heart – a horrible fear that I had lost all that I cared for – all that made life desirable.

"Why can't we?" I asked. "Do you mean that – that the gods have been gracious to some other man?"

"No, no," she answered hastily – almost indignantly, "of course I don't mean that."

"Then it is only that you don't love me yet. Of course you don't. Why should you? But you will, dear, some day. And I will wait patiently until that day comes and not trouble you with entreaties. I will wait for you as Jacob waited for Rachel, and as the long years seemed to him but as a few days because of the love he bore her, so it shall be with me, if only you will not send me away quite without hope."

She was looking down, white-faced, with a hardening of the lips as if she were in bodily pain. "You don't understand," she whispered. "It can't be – it can never be. There is something that makes it impossible, now and always. I can't tell you more than that."

"But, Ruth dearest," I pleaded despairingly, "may it not become possible some day? Can it not be made possible? I can wait, but I can't give you up. Is there no chance whatever that this obstacle may be removed?"

"Very little, I fear. Hardly any. No, Paul. It is hopeless, and I can't bear to talk about it. Let me go now. Let us say good-by here and see one another no more for a while. Perhaps we may be friends again some day – when you have forgiven me."

"Forgiven you, dearest!" I exclaimed. "There is nothing to forgive. And we are friends, Ruth. Whatever happens, you are the dearest friend I have on earth, or can ever have."

"Thank you, Paul," she said faintly. "You are very good to me. But let me go, please. I must be alone."

She held out a trembling hand, and, as I took it, I was shocked to see how terribly agitated and ill she looked.

"May I not come with you, dear?" I pleaded.

"No, no!" she exclaimed breathlessly, "I must go away by myself. I want to be alone. Good-by."

"Before I let you go, Ruth – if you must go – I must have a most solemn promise from you."

Her sad gray eyes met mine and her lips quivered with an unspoken question.

"You must promise me," I went on, "that if ever this barrier that parts us should be removed, you will let me know instantly. Remember that I love you always, and that I am waiting for you always on this side of the grave."

367

She caught her breath in a quick little sob, and pressed my hand.

"Yes," she whispered, "I promise. Good-by."

She pressed my hand again and was gone, and, as I gazed at the empty doorway through which she had passed, I caught a glimpse of her reflection in a glass on the landing, where she had paused for a moment to wipe her eyes. I felt it, in a manner, indelicate to have seen her, and turned away my head quickly, and yet I was conscious of a certain selfish satisfaction in the sweet sympathy that her grief bespoke.

But now that she was gone a horrible sense of desolation descended on me. Only now, by the consciousness of irreparable loss, did I begin to realize the meaning of this passion of love that had stolen unawares into my life. How it had glorified the present and spread a glamor of delight over the dimly considered future – how all pleasures and desires, hopes and ambitions, had converged upon it as a focus. How it had stood out as the one great reality behind which the other circumstances of life were as a background, shimmering, half seen, immaterial and unreal. And now it was gone – lost, as it seemed, beyond hope, and that which was left to me was but the empty frame from which the picture had vanished.

I have no idea how long I stood rooted to the spot where she had left me, wrapped in a dull consciousness of pain, immersed in a half-numb reverie. Recent events flitted, dream-like, through my mind. Our happy labors in the reading-room. Our first visit to the Museum, and this present day that had opened so brightly and with such joyous promise. One by one these phantoms of a vanished happiness came and went. Occasional visitors sauntered into the room – but the galleries were mostly empty that day – gazed inquisitively at my motionless figure, and went their way. And still the dull, intolerable ache in my breast went on, the only vivid consciousness that was left to me.

Presently I raised my eyes and met those of the portrait. The sweet, pensive face of the old Greek settler looked out at me wistfully as though he would offer comfort, as though he would tell me that he, too, had known sorrow when he lived his life in the sunny Fayyum. And a subtle consolation, like the faint scent of old rose leaves, seemed to exhale from that friendly face that had looked on the birth of my happiness and had seen it wither and fade. I turned away, at last, with a silent farewell, and when I looked back, he seemed to speed me on my way with gentle valediction.

368

Chapter XVII
The Accusing Finger

Of my wanderings after I left the Museum on that black and dismal *dies irae*, I have but a dim recollection. But I must have traveled a quite considerable distance, since it wanted an hour or two to the time for returning to the surgery, and I spent the interval walking swiftly through streets and squares, unmindful of the happenings around, intent only on my present misfortune, and driven by a natural impulse to seek relief in bodily exertion. For mental distress sets up, as it were, a sort of induced current of physical unrest – a beneficent arrangement, by which a dangerous excess of emotional excitement may be transformed into motor energy, and so safely got rid of. The motor apparatus acts as a safety-valve to the psychical, and if the engine races for a while, with the onset of a bodily fatigue the emotional pressure-gauge returns to a normal reading.

And so it was with me. At first I was conscious of nothing but a sense of utter bereavement, of the shipwreck of all my hopes. But, by degrees, as I threaded my way among the moving crowds, I came to a better and more worthy frame of mind. After all, I had lost nothing that I had ever had. Ruth was still all that she had ever been to me – perhaps even more, and if that had been a rich endowment yesterday, why not to-day also? And how unfair it would be to her if I should mope and grieve over a disappointment that was no fault of hers and for which there was no remedy? Thus I reasoned with myself, and to such purpose that, by the time I reached Fetter Lane, my dejection had come to quite manageable proportions and I had formed the resolution to get back to the *status quo ante bellum* as soon as possible.

About eight o'clock, as I was sitting alone in the consulting-room, gloomily persuading myself that I was now quite resigned to the inevitable, Adolphus brought me a registered packet, at the handwriting on which my heart gave such a bound that I had much ado to sign the receipt. As soon as Adolphus had retired (with undissembled contempt of the shaky signature) I tore open the packet, and as I drew out a letter a tiny box dropped on the table.

The letter was all too short, and I devoured it over and over again with the eagerness of a condemned man reading a reprieve:

369

My Dear Paul,

Forgive me for leaving you so abruptly this afternoon, and leaving you so unhappy, too. I am more sane and reasonable now, and so send you greeting and beg you not to grieve for that which can never be. It is quite impossible, dear friend, and I entreat you, as you care for me, never to speak of it again – never again to make me feel that I can give you so little when you have given so much. And do not try to see me for a little while. I shall miss your visits, and so will my father, who is very fond of you, but it is better that we should not meet, until we can take up our old relations – if that can ever be.

I am sending you a little keepsake in case we should drift apart on the eddies of life. It is the ring that I told you about – the one that my uncle gave me. Perhaps you may be able to wear it as you have a small hand, but in any case keep it in remembrance of our friendship. The device on it is the Eye of Osiris, a mystic symbol for which I have a sentimentally superstitious affection, as also had my poor uncle, who actually bore it tattooed in scarlet on his breast. It signifies that the great judge of the dead looks down on men to see that justice is done and that truth prevails. So I commend you to the good Osiris. May his eye be upon you, ever watchful over your welfare in the absence of

Your affectionate friend,

Ruth

It was a sweet letter, I thought, even if it carried little comfort – quiet and reticent like its writer, but with an undertone of affection. I laid it down at length, and, taking the ring from its box, examined it fondly. Though but a copy, it had all the quaintness and feeling of the antique original, and, above all, it was fragrant with the spirit of the giver. Dainty and delicate, wrought of silver and gold, with an inlay of copper, I would not have exchanged it for the Koh-i-noor, and when I had slipped it on my finger its tiny eye of blue enamel looked up at me so friendly and companionable that I felt the glamour of the old-world superstition stealing over me too.

Not a single patient came in this evening, which was well for me (and also for the patient), as I was able forthwith to write in reply a long letter, but this I shall spare the long-suffering reader excepting its concluding paragraph:

> *And now, dearest, I have said my say. Once for all I have said it, and I will not open my mouth on the subject again (I am not actually opening it now) 'until the times do alter.' And if the times do never alter – if it shall come to pass, in due course, that we two shall sit side by side, white-haired, and crinkly-nosed, and lean our poor old chins upon our sticks and mumble and gibber amicably over the things that might have been if the good Osiris had come up to the scratch – I will still be content, because your friendship, Ruth, is better than another woman's love. So you see, I have taken my gruel and come up to time smiling – if you will pardon the pugilistic metaphor – and I promise you loyally to do your bidding and never again to distress you.*

> *Your faithful and loving friend,*

> *Paul*

This letter I addressed and stamped, and then, with a wry grimace which I palmed off on myself (but not on Adolphus) as a cheerful smile, I went out and dropped it into the post-box, after which I further deluded myself by murmuring *Nunc dimittis* and assuring myself that the incident was now absolutely closed.

But despite this comfortable assurance I was, in the days that followed, an exceedingly miserable young man. It is all very well to write down troubles of this kind as trivial and sentimental. They are nothing of the kind. When a man of essentially serious nature has found the one woman of all the world who fulfils his highest ideals of womanhood, who is, in fact, a woman in ten-thousand, to whom he has given all that he has to give of love and worship, the sudden wreck of all his hopes is no small calamity. And so I found it. Resign myself as I would to the bitter reality, the ghost of the might-have-been haunted me night and day, so that I spent my leisure wandering abstractedly about the streets, always trying to banish thought and never for an instant succeeding. A great unrest was upon me, and when I received a letter from Dick Barnard announcing his arrival at Madeira, homeward bound, I breathed a sigh of relief. I had no plans for the future, but I longed to be rid of the now irksome, routine of the practise – to be free to come and go when and how I pleased.

371

One evening, as I sat consuming with little appetite my solitary supper, there fell on me a sudden sense of loneliness. The desire that I had hitherto felt to be alone with my own miserable reflections gave place to a yearning for human companionship. That, indeed, which I craved for most was forbidden, and I must abide by my lady's wishes, but there were my friends in the Temple. It was more than a week since I had seen them. In fact, we had not met since the morning of that unhappiest day of my life. They would be wondering what had become of me. I rose from the table, and having filled my pouch from a tin of tobacco, set forth for King's Bench Walk.

As I approached the entry of No. 5A in the gathering darkness I met Thorndyke himself emerging encumbered with two deck-chairs, a reading-lantern, and a book.

"Why, Berkeley!" he exclaimed. "Is it indeed thou? We have been wondering what had become of you."

"It *is* a long time since I looked you up," I admitted.

He scrutinized me attentively by the light of the entry lamp, and then remarked, "Fetter Lane doesn't seem to be agreeing with you very well, my son. You are looking quite thin and peaky."

"Well, I've nearly done with it. Barnard will be back in about ten days. His ship is putting in at Madeira to coal and take in some cargo, and then he is coming home. Where are you going with those chairs?"

"I am going to sit down at the end of the Walk by the railings. It's cooler there than indoors. If you will wait a moment I will go and fetch another chair for Jervis, though he won't be back for a little while." He ran up the stairs, and presently returned with a third chair, and we carried our impedimenta down to the quiet corner of the Walk.

"So your term of servitude is coming to an end," said he, when we had placed the chairs and hung the lantern on the railings. "Any other news?"

"No. Have you any?"

"I am afraid I have not. All my inquiries have yielded negative results. There is, of course, a considerable body of evidence, and it all seems to point one way. But I am unwilling to make a decisive move without something more definite. I am really waiting for confirmation or otherwise of my ideas on the subject, for some new item of evidence."

"I didn't know there was any evidence."

"Didn't you?" said Thorndyke. "But you know as much as I know. You have all the essential facts, but apparently you haven't collated them and extracted their meaning. If you had, you would have found them curiously significant."

"I suppose I mustn't ask what their significance is?"

"No, I think not. When I am conducting a case I mention my surmises to nobody – not even to Jervis. Then I can say confidently that there has been no leakage. Don't think I distrust you. Remember that my thoughts are my client's property, and that the essence of strategy is to keep the enemy in the dark."

"Yes, I see that. Of course I ought not to have asked."

"You ought not to need to ask," Thorndyke replied, with a smile. "You should put the facts together and reason from them yourself."

While we had been talking I had noticed Thorndyke glance at me inquisitively from time to time. Now after an interval of silence, he asked suddenly, "Is anything amiss, Berkeley? Are you worrying about your friends' affairs?"

"No, not particularly. Though their prospects don't look very rosy."

"Perhaps they are not quite so bad as they look," said he. "But I am afraid something is troubling you. All your gay spirits seem to have evaporated." He paused for a few moments, and then added, "I don't want to intrude on your private affairs, but if I can help you by advice or otherwise, remember that we are old friends and that you are my academic offspring."

Instinctively, with a man's natural reticence, I began to mumble a half-articulate disclaimer, and then I stopped. After all, why should I not confide in him? He was a good man and a wise man, full of human sympathy, as I knew, though so cryptic and secretive in his professional capacity. And I wanted a friend badly just now.

"I'm afraid," I began shyly, "it is not a matter that admits of much help, and it's hardly the sort of thing that I ought to worry you by talking about – "

"If it is enough to make you unhappy, my dear fellow, it is enough to merit serious consideration by your friend, so if you don't mind telling me – "

"Of course I don't, sir!" I exclaimed.

"Then fire away, and don't call me 'sir'. We are brother practitioners now."

Thus encouraged, I poured out the story of my little romance – bashfully at first and with halting phrases, but later, with more freedom and confidence. He listened with grave attention, and once or twice put a question when my narrative became a little disconnected. When I had finished he laid his hand softly on my arm.

"You have had rough luck, Berkeley. I don't wonder that you are miserable. I am more sorry than I can tell you."

373

"Thank you," I said. "It's exceedingly good of you to listen so patiently, but it's a shame for me to pester you with my sentimental troubles."

"Now, Berkeley, you don't think that, and I hope you don't think that I do. We should be bad biologists and worse physicians if we should underestimate the importance of that which is nature's chiefest care. The one salient biological truth is the paramount importance of sex, and we are deaf and blind if we do not hear and see it in everything that lives when we look abroad upon the world: When we listen to the spring song of the birds, or when we consider the lilies of the field. And as is man to the lower organisms, so is human love to their merely reflex manifestations of sex. I will maintain, and you will agree with me, I know, that the love of a serious and honorable man for a woman who is worthy of him is the most momentous of all human affairs. It is the foundation of social life, and its failure is a serious calamity, not only to those whose lives may be thereby spoilt, but to society at large."

"It's a serious enough matter for the parties concerned," I agreed, "but that is no reason why they should bore their friends."

"But they don't. Friends should help one another and think it a privilege."

"Oh, I shouldn't mind coming to you for help, knowing you as I do. But no one can help a poor devil in a case like this – and certainly not a medical jurist."

"Oh, come, Berkeley!" he protested. "Don't rate us too low. The humblest of creatures has its uses – 'even the little pismire', you know, as Izaak Walton tells us. Why, I have got substantial help from a stamp-collector. And then reflect upon the motor-scorcher and the earthworm and the blow-fly. All these lowly creatures play their parts in the scheme of nature, and shall we cast out the medical jurist as nothing worth?"

I laughed dejectedly at my teacher's genial irony.

"What I meant," said I, "was that there is nothing to be done but wait – perhaps forever. I don't know why she isn't able to marry me, and I mustn't ask her. She can't be married already."

"Certainly not. She told you explicitly that there was no man in the case."

"Exactly. And I can think of no other valid reason, excepting that she doesn't care enough for me. That would be a perfectly sound reason, but then it would only be a temporary one, not the insuperable obstacle that she assumes to exist, especially as we really got on excellently together. I hope it isn't some confounded perverse feminine scruple. I don't see how it could be, but women are most frightfully tortuous and wrong-headed at times."

"I don't see," said Thorndyke, "why we should cast about for perversely abnormal motives when there is a perfectly reasonable explanation staring us in the face."

"Is there?" I exclaimed. "I see none."

"You are, not unnaturally, overlooking some of the circumstances that affect Miss Bellingham, but I don't suppose she has failed to grasp their meaning. Do you realize what her position really is? I mean with regard to her uncle's disappearance?"

"I don't think I quite understand you."

"Well, there is no use in blinking the facts," said Thorndyke. "The position is this: If John Bellingham ever went to his brother's house at Woodford, it is nearly certain that he went there after his visit to Hurst. Mind, I say '*if* he went'. I don't say that I believe he did. But it is stated that he appears to have gone there, and if he did go, he was never seen alive afterward. Now, he did not go in at the front door. No one saw him enter the house. But there was a back gate, which John Bellingham knew, and which had a bell which rang in the library. And you will remember that, when Hurst and Jellicoe called, Mr. Bellingham had only just come in. Previous to that time Miss Bellingham had been alone in the library. That is to say, she was alone in the library at the very time when John Bellingham is said to have made his visit. That is the position, Berkeley. Nothing pointed has been said up to the present. But, sooner or later, if John Bellingham is not found, dead or alive, the question will be opened. Then it is certain that Hurst, in self-defense, will make the most of any facts that may transfer suspicion from him to someone else. And that someone else will be Miss Bellingham."

I sat for some moments literally paralyzed with horror. Then my dismay gave place to indignation. "But damn it!" I exclaimed, starting up – "I beg your pardon – but could anyone have the infernal audacity to insinuate that that gentle, refined lady murdered her uncle?"

"That is what will be hinted, if not plainly asserted, and she knows it. And that being so, is it difficult to understand why she should refuse to allow you to be publicly associated with her? To run the risk of dragging your honorable name into the sordid transactions of the police-court or the Old Bailey? To invest it, perhaps, with a dreadful notoriety?"

"Oh, don't! For God's sake! It is too horrible! Not that I would care for myself. I would be proud to share her martyrdom of ignominy, if it had to be, but it is the sacrilege, the blasphemy of even thinking of her in such terms that enrages me."

"Yes," said Thorndyke, "I understand and sympathize with you. Indeed, I share your righteous indignation at this dastardly affair. So you mustn't think me brutal for putting the case so plainly."

375

"I don't. You have only shown me the danger that I was fool enough not to see. But you seem to imply that this hideous position has been brought about deliberately."

"Certainly I do! This is no chance affair. Either the appearances indicate the real events – which I am sure they do not – or they have been created of a set purpose to lead to false conclusions. But the circumstances convince me that there has been a deliberate plot, and I am waiting – in no spirit of Christian patience, I can tell you – to lay my hand on the wretch who has done this."

"What are you waiting for?" I asked.

"I am waiting for the inevitable," he replied. "For the false move that the most artful criminal invariably makes. At present he is lying low, but presently he will make a move, and then I shall have him."

"But he may go on lying low. What will you do then?"

"Yes, that is the danger. We may have to deal with the perfect villain who knows when to leave well alone. I have never met him, but he may exist, nevertheless."

"And then we should have to stand by and see our friends go under."

"Perhaps," said Thorndyke, and we both subsided into gloomy and silent reflection.

The place was peaceful and quiet, as only a backwater of London can be. Occasional hoots from far-away tugs and steamers told of the busy life down below in the crowded Pool. A faint hum of traffic was borne in from the streets outside the precincts, and the shrill voices of newspaper boys came in unceasing chorus from the direction of Carmelite Street. They were too far away to be physically disturbing, but the excited yells, toned down as they were by distance, nevertheless stirred the very marrow in my bones, so dreadfully suggestive were they of those possibilities of the future at which Thorndyke had hinted. They seemed like the sinister shadows of coming misfortunes.

Perhaps they called up the same association of ideas in Thorndyke's mind, for he remarked presently, "The newsvendor is abroad to-night like a bird of ill-omen. Something unusual has happened – some public or private calamity, most likely, and these yelling ghouls are out to feast on the remains. The newspaper men have a good deal in common with the carrion-birds that hover over a battle-field."

Again we subsided into silence and reflection. Then, after an interval, I asked, "Would it be possible for me to help in any way in this investigation of yours?"

"That is exactly what I have been asking myself," replied Thorndyke. "It would be right and proper that you should, and I think you might."

"How?" I asked eagerly.

"I can't say offhand, but Jervis will be going away for his holiday almost at once – in fact, he will go off actual duty to-night. There is very little doing. The long vacation is close upon us, and I can do without him. But if you would care to come down here and take his place, you would be very useful to me, and if there should be anything to be done in the Bellinghams' case, I am sure you would make up in enthusiasm for any deficiency in experience."

"I couldn't really take Jervis's place," said I, "but if you would let me help you in any way it would be a great kindness. I would rather clean your boots than be out of it altogether."

"Very well. Let us leave it that you come here as soon as Barnard has done with you. You can have Jervis's room, which he doesn't often use nowadays, and you will be more happy here than elsewhere, I know. I may as well give you my latch-key now. I have a duplicate upstairs, and you understand that my chambers are yours too from this moment."

He handed me the latch-key and I thanked him warmly from my heart, for I felt sure that the suggestion was made, not for any use that I should be to him, but for my own peace of mind. I had hardly finished speaking when a quick step on the paved walk caught my ear.

"Here is Jervis," said Thorndyke. "We will let him know that there is a *locum tenens* ready to step into his shoes when he wants to be off." He flashed the lantern across the path, and a few moments later his junior stepped up briskly with a bundle of newspapers tucked under his arm.

It struck me that Jervis looked at me a little queerly when he recognized me in the dim light. Also he was a trifle constrained in his manner, as if my presence were an embarrassment. He listened to Thorndyke's announcement of our newly made arrangement without much enthusiasm and with none of his customary facetious comments. And again I noticed a quick glance at me, half-curious, half-uneasy, and wholly puzzling to me.

"That's all right," he said when Thorndyke had explained the situation. "I daresay you'll find Berkeley as useful as me, and, in any case, he'll be better here than staying on with Barnard." He spoke with unwonted gravity, and there was in his tone a solicitude for me that attracted my notice and that of Thorndyke as well, for the latter looked at him curiously, though he made no comment. After a short silence, however, he asked, "And what news does my learned brother bring? There is a mighty shouting among the outer barbarians and I see a bundle of newspapers under my learned friend's arm. Has anything in particular happened?"

Jervis looked more uncomfortable than ever. "Well – yes," he replied hesitatingly, "something has happened – there! It's no use beating about

377

the bush. Berkeley may as well learn it from me as from those yelling devils outside." He took a couple of papers from his bundle and silently handed one to me and the other to Thorndyke.

Jervis's ominous manner, naturally enough, alarmed me not a little. I opened the paper with a nameless dread. But whatever my vague fears, they fell far short of the occasion, and when I saw those yells from without crystallized into scare head-lines and flaming capitals I turned for a moment sick and dizzy with fear.

The paragraph was only a short one, and I read it through in less than a minute.

THE MISSING FINGER
DRAMATIC DISCOVERY AT WOODFORD

The mystery that has surrounded the remains of a mutilated human body, portions of which have been found in various places in Kent and Essex, has received a partial and very sinister solution. The police have, all along, suspected that those remains were those of a Mr. John Bellingham who disappeared under circumstances of some suspicion about two years ago. There is now no doubt upon the subject, for the finger which was missing from the hand that was found at Sidcup has been discovered at the bottom of a disused well together with a ring, which has been identified as one habitually worn by Mr. John Bellingham.

The house in the garden of which the well is situated was the property of the murdered man, and was occupied at the time of the disappearance by his brother, Mr. Godfrey Bellingham. But the latter left it very soon after, and it has been empty ever since. Just lately it has been put in repair, and it was in this way that the well came to be emptied and cleaned out. It seems that Detective-Inspector Badger, who was searching the neighborhood for further remains, heard of the emptying of the well and went down in the bucket to examine the bottom, where he found the three bones and the ring.

Thus the identity of the body is established beyond all doubt, and the question that remains is, Who killed John Bellingham? It may be remembered that a trinket, apparently broken from his watch-chain, was found in the grounds of this house on the day that he disappeared, and that he was never again seen alive. What may be the import of these facts time will show.

That was all, but it was enough. I dropped the paper to the ground and glanced round furtively at Jervis, who sat gazing gloomily at the toes of his boots. It was horrible! It was incredible! The blow was so crushing that it left my faculties numb, and for a while I seemed unable even to think intelligibly.

I was aroused by Thorndyke's voice – calm, business-like, composed. "Time will show, indeed! But meanwhile we must go warily. And don't be unduly alarmed, Berkeley. Go home, take a good dose of bromide with a little stimulant, and turn in. I am afraid this has been rather a shock to you."

I rose from my chair like one in a dream and held out my hand to Thorndyke, and even in the dim light and in my dazed condition I noticed that his face bore a look that I had never seen before. The look of a granite mask of Fate – grim, stern, inexorable.

My two friends walked with me as far as the gateway at the top of Inner Temple Lane, and as we reached the entry a stranger, coming quickly up the Lane, overtook and passed us. In the glare of the lamp outside the porter's lodge he looked at us quickly over his shoulder, and though he passed on without halt or greeting, I recognized him with a certain dull surprise which I did not understand then and do not understand now. It was Mr. Jellicoe.

I shook hands once more with my friends and strode out into Fleet Street, but as soon as I was outside the gate I made direct for Nevill's Court. What was in my mind I do not know. Only that some instinct of protection led me there, where my lady lay unconscious of the hideous menace that hung over her. At the entrance to the Court a tall, powerful man was lounging against the wall, and he seemed to look at me curiously as I passed, but I hardly noticed him and strode forward into the narrow passage. By the shabby gateway of the house I halted and looked up at such of the windows as I could see over the wall. They were all dark. All the inmates, then, were in bed. Vaguely comforted by this, I walked on to the New Street end of the Court and looked out. Here, too, a man – a tall, thick-set man – was loitering, and as he looked inquisitively into my face I turned and reëntered the Court, slowly retracing my steps. As I again reached the gate of the house I stopped to look once more at the windows, and turning I found the man whom I had last noticed close behind me. Then, in a flash of dreadful comprehension, I understood. These two were plainclothes policemen.

For a moment a blind fury possessed me. An insane impulse urged me to give battle to this intruder. To avenge upon this person the insult of his presence. Fortunately the impulse was but momentary, and I recovered myself without making any demonstration. But the appearance of those two policemen brought the peril into the immediate present, imparted to it a horrible actuality. A chilly sweat of terror stood on my forehead, and my ears were ringing when I walked with faltering steps out into Fetter Lane.

Chapter XVIII
John Bellingham

The next few days were a very nightmare of horror and gloom. Of course, I repudiated my acceptance of the decree of banishment that Ruth had passed upon me. I was her friend, at least, and in time of peril my place was at her side. Tacitly – though thankfully enough, poor girl! – she had recognized the fact and made me once more free of the house.

For there was no disguising the situation. Newspaper boys yelled the news up and down Fleet Street from morning to night – soul-shaking posters grinned on gaping crowds, and the newspapers fairly wallowed in the "*Shocking details*".

It is true that no direct accusations were made, but the original reports of the disappearance were reprinted with such comments as made me gnash my teeth with fury.

The wretchedness of those days will live in my memory until my dying day. Never can I forget the dread that weighed me down, the horrible suspense, the fear that clutched at my heart as I furtively scanned the posters in the streets. Even the wretched detectives who prowled about the entrances to Nevill's Court became grateful to my eyes, for, embodying as they did the hideous menace that hung over my dear lady, their presence at least told me that the blow had not yet fallen. Indeed, we came, after a time, to exchange glances of mutual recognition, and I thought that they seemed to be sorry for her and for me, and had no great liking for their task. Of course, I spent most of my leisure at the old house, though my heart ached more there than elsewhere, and I tried, with but poor success, I fear, to maintain a cheerful, confident manner, cracking my little jokes as of old, and even essaying to skirmish with Miss Oman. But this last experiment was a dead failure, and when she had suddenly broken down in a stream of brilliant repartee to weep hysterically on my breast, I abandoned the attempt and did not repeat it.

A dreadful gloom had settled down upon the old house. Poor Miss Oman crept silently but restlessly up and down the ancient stairs with dim eyes and a tremulous chin, or moped in her room with a parliamentary petition (demanding, if I remember rightly, the appointment of a female judge to deal with divorce and matrimonial causes) which lay on her table languidly awaiting signatures that never came. Mr. Bellingham, whose mental condition at first alternated between furious anger and absolute panic, was fast sinking into a state of nervous prostration that I viewed with no little alarm. In fact the only really self-possessed person in the entire household was Ruth herself, and even she could not conceal the ravages of sorrow and suspense and overshadowing peril. Her manner was almost unchanged. Or rather, I should say, she had gone back to that which I had first known – quiet, reserved, taciturn, with a certain bitter humor showing through her unvarying amiability. When she and I were alone, indeed, her reserve melted away and she was all sweetness and gentleness. But it wrung my heart to look at her, to see how, day by day, she grew ever more thin and haggard. To watch the growing pallor of her cheek. To look into her solemn gray eyes, so sad and tragic and yet so brave and defiant of fate.

It was a terrible time, and through it all the dreadful questions haunted me continually: When will the blow fall? What is it that the police are waiting for? And when they do strike, what will Thorndyke have to say?

So things went on for four dreadful days. But on the fourth day, just as the evening consultations were beginning and the surgery was filled with waiting patients, Polton appeared with a note, which he insisted, to the indignation of Adolphus, on delivering into my own hands. It was from Thorndyke, and was to the following effect:

> *I learn from Dr. Norbury that he has recently heard from* Herr *Lederbogen, of Berlin – a learned authority on Oriental antiquities – who makes some reference to an English Egyptologist whom he met in Vienna about a year ago. He cannot recall the Englishman's name, but there are certain expressions in the letter which make Dr. Norbury suspect that he is referring to John Bellingham.*
>
> *I want you to bring Mr. and Miss Bellingham to my chambers this evening at 8:30, to meet Dr. Norbury and talk over his letter, and in view of the importance of the matter, I look to you not to fail me.*

A wave of hope and relief swept over me. It was still possible that this Gordian Knot might be cut. That the deliverance might come before it was too late. I wrote a hasty note to Thorndyke and another to Ruth, making the appointment, and having given them both to the trusty Polton, returned somewhat feverishly to my professional duties. To my profound relief, the influx of patients ceased, and the practise sank into its accustomed torpor, whereby I was able without base and mendacious subterfuge to escape in good time to my tryst.

It was near upon eight o'clock when I passed through the archway into Nevill's Court. The warm afternoon light had died away, for the

382

summer was running out apace. The last red glow of the setting sun had faded from the ancient roofs and chimney stacks, and down in the narrow court the shades of evening had begun to gather in nooks and corners. I was due at eight, and, as it still wanted some minutes to the hour, I sauntered slowly down the court, looking reflectively on the familiar scene and the well-known friendly faces.

The day's work was drawing to a close. The little shops were putting up their shutters – lights were beginning to twinkle in parlor windows. A solemn hymn arose in the old Moravian chapel, and its echoes stole out through the dark entry that opens into the court under the archway.

Here was Mr. Finneymore (a man of versatile gifts, with a leaning toward paint and varnish) sitting, white-aproned and shirt-sleeved, on a chair in his garden, smoking his pipe with a complacent eye on his dahlias. There at an open window a young man, with a brush in his hand and another behind his ear, stood up and stretched himself while an older lady deftly rolled up a large map. The barber was turning out the gas in his little saloon. The greengrocer was emerging with a cigarette in his mouth and an aster in his buttonhole, and a group of children were escorting the lamplighter on his rounds.

All these good, homely folk were Nevill's Courtiers of the genuine breed: Born in the court, as had been their fathers before them for generations. And of such to a great extent was the population of the place. Miss Oman herself claimed aboriginal descent and so did the sweet-faced Moravian lady next door – a connection of the famous La Trobes of the old Conventicle, whose history went back to the Gordon Riots, and as to the gentleman who lived in the ancient timber-and-plaster house at the bottom of the court, it was reported that his ancestors had dwelt in that very house since the days of James the First.

On these facts I reflected as I sauntered down the court, on the strange phenomenon of an old-world hamlet with its ancient population lingering in the very heart of the noisy city – an island of peace set in an ocean of unrest, an oasis in a desert of change and ferment.

My meditations brought me to the shabby gate in the high wall, and as I raised the latch and pushed it open, I saw Ruth standing at the door of the house talking to Miss Oman. She was evidently waiting for me, for she wore her somber black coat and hat and a black veil, and when she saw me she came out, closing the door after her, and holding out her hand.

"You are punctual," said she. "St. Dunstan's clock is striking now."

"Yes," I answered. "But where is your father?"

"He has gone to bed, poor old dear. He didn't feel well enough to come, and I did not urge him. He is really very ill. This dreadful suspense will kill him if it goes on much longer."

383

"Let us hope it won't," I said, but with little conviction, I fear, in my tone.

It was harrowing to see her torn by anxiety for her father, and I yearned to comfort her. But what was there to say? Mr. Bellingham was breaking up visibly under the stress of the terrible menace that hung over his daughter, and no words of mine could make the fact less manifest.

We walked silently up the court. The lady at the window greeted us with a smiling salutation, Mr. Finneymore removed his pipe and raised his cap, receiving a gracious bow from Ruth in return, and then we passed through the covered way into Fetter Lane, where my companion paused and looked about her.

"What are you looking for?" I asked.

"The detective," she answered quietly. "It would be a pity if the poor man should miss me after waiting so long. However, I don't see him." And she turned away toward Fleet Street. It was an unpleasant surprise to me that her sharp eyes detected the secret spy upon her movements, and the dry, sardonic tone of her remark pained me too, recalling, as it did, the frigid self-possession that had so repelled me in the early days of our acquaintance. And yet I could not but admire the cool unconcern with which she faced her horrible peril.

"Tell me a little more about this conference," she said, as we walked down Fetter Lane. "Your note was rather more concise than lucid, but I suppose you wrote it in a hurry."

"Yes, I did. And I can't give you any details now. All I know is that Doctor Norbury has had a letter from a friend of his in Berlin, an Egyptologist, as I understand, named Lederbogen, who refers to an English acquaintance of his and Norbury's whom he saw in Vienna about a year ago. He cannot remember the Englishman's name, but from some of the circumstances Norbury seems to think that he is referring to your Uncle John. Of course, if this should turn out to be really the case, it would set everything straight, so Thorndyke was anxious that you and your father should meet Norbury and talk it over."

"I see," said Ruth. Her tone was thoughtful but by no means enthusiastic.

"You don't seem to attach much importance to the matter," I remarked.

"No. It doesn't seem to fit the circumstances. What is the use of suggesting that poor Uncle John is alive – and behaving like an imbecile, which he certainly was not – when his dead body has actually been found?"

"But," I suggested lamely, "there may be some mistake. It may not be his body after all."

"And the ring?" she asked, with a bitter smile.

"That may be just a coincidence. It was a copy of a well-known form of antique ring. Other people may have had copies made as well as your uncle. Besides," I added with more conviction, "we haven't seen the ring. It may not be his at all."

She shook her head. "My dear Paul," she said quietly, "it is useless to delude ourselves. Every known fact points to the certainty that it is his body. John Bellingham is dead – There can be no doubt of that. And to every one except his unknown murderer and one or two of my own loyal friends, it must seem that his death lies at my door. I realized from the beginning that the suspicion lay between George Hurst and me, and the finding of the ring fixes it definitely on me. I am only surprised that the police have made no move yet."

The quiet conviction of her tone left me for a while speechless with horror and despair. Then I recalled Thorndyke's calm, even confident, attitude, and I hastened to remind her of it.

"There is one of your friends," I said, "who is still undismayed. Thorndyke seems to anticipate no difficulties."

"And yet," she replied, "he is ready to consider a forlorn hope like this. However, we shall see."

I could think of nothing more to say, and it was in gloomy silence that we pursued our way down Inner Temple Lane and through the dark entries and tunnel-like passages that brought us out, at length, by the Treasury.

"I don't see any light in Thorndyke's chambers," I said, as we crossed King's Bench Walk, and I pointed out the row of windows all dark and blank.

"No, and yet the shutters are not closed. He must be out."

"He can't be after making an appointment with you and your father. It is most mysterious. Thorndyke is so very punctilious about his engagements."

The mystery was solved, when we reached the landing, by a slip of paper fixed by a tack on the iron-bound "oak."

"*A note for P. B. is on the table*", was the laconic message, on reading which I inserted my key, swung the heavy door outward, and opened the lighter inner door. The note was lying on the table and I brought it out to the landing to read by the light of the staircase lamp.

Apologize to our friends, it ran, *for the slight change of programme. Norbury is anxious that I should get my experiments over before the Director returns, so as to save discussion. He has asked me to begin to-night and says he will see Mr. and Miss Bellingham here, at the Museum. Please*

385

bring them along at once. I think some matters of importance
may transpire at the interview – J. E. T.

"I hope you don't mind," I said apologetically, when I had read the note to Ruth.

"Of course I don't," she replied. "I am rather pleased. We have so many associations with the dear old Museum, haven't we?" She looked at me for a moment with a strange and touching wistfulness and then turned to descend the stone stairs.

At the Temple gate I hailed a hansom, and we were soon speeding westward and north to the soft twinkle of the horse's bell.

"What are these experiments that Doctor Thorndyke refers to?" she asked presently.

"I can only answer you vaguely," I replied. "Their object, I believe, is to ascertain whether the penetrability of organic substances by the X-rays becomes altered by age – whether, for instance, an ancient block of wood is more or less transparent to the rays than a new block of the same size."

"And of what use would the knowledge be, if it were obtained?"

"I can't say. Experiments are made to obtain knowledge without regard to its utility. The use appears when the knowledge has been acquired. But in this case, if it should be possible to determine the age of any organic substance by its reaction to X-rays, the discovery might be found of some value in legal practise – as in demonstrating a new seal on an old document, for instance. But I don't know whether Thorndyke has anything definite in view. I only know that the preparations have been on a most portentous scale."

"How do you mean?"

"In regard to size. When I went into the workshop yesterday morning, I found Polton erecting a kind of portable gallows about nine-feet high, and he had just finished varnishing a pair of enormous wooden trays each over six-feet long. It looked as if he and Thorndyke were contemplating a few private executions with subsequent post-mortems on the victims."

"What a horrible suggestion!"

"So Polton said, with his quaint, crinkly smile. But he was mighty close about the use of the apparatus all the same. I wonder if we shall see anything of the experiments, when we get there. This is Museum Street, isn't it?"

"Yes." As she spoke, she lifted the flap of one of the little windows in the back of the cab and peered out. Then, closing it with a quiet, ironic smile, she said, "It is all right. He hasn't missed us. It will be quite a nice little change for him."

The cab swung round into Great Russell Street, and, glancing out as it turned, I saw another hansom following, but before I had time to inspect its solitary passenger, we drew up at the Museum gates.

The gate porter, who seemed to expect us, ushered us up the drive to the great portico and into the Central Hall, where he handed us over to another official.

"Doctor Norbury is in one of the rooms adjoining the Fourth Egyptian Room," the latter stated in answer to our inquiries, and, providing himself with a wire-guarded lantern, he prepared to escort us thither.

Up the great staircase, now wrapped in mysterious gloom, we passed in silence with bitter-sweet memories of that day of days when we had first trodden its steps together. Through the Central Saloon, the Medieval Room and the Asiatic Saloon, and so into the long range of the Ethnographical Galleries.

It was a weird journey. The swaying lantern shot its beams abroad into the darkness of the great, dim galleries, casting instantaneous flashes on the objects in the cases, so that they leaped into being and vanished in the twinkling of an eye. Hideous idols with round, staring eyes started forth from the darkness, glared at us for an instant and were gone. Grotesque masks, suddenly revealed by the shimmering light, took on the semblance of demon faces that seemed to mow and gibber at us as we passed. As for the life-sized models – realistic enough by daylight – their aspect was positively alarming, for the moving light and shadow endowed them with life and movement, so that they seemed to watch us furtively, to lie in wait and to hold themselves in readiness to steal out and follow us. The illusion evidently affected Ruth as well as me, for she drew nearer to me and whispered, "These figures are quite startling. Did you see that Polynesian? I really felt as if he were going to spring out on us."

"They are rather uncanny," I admitted, "but the danger is over now. We are passing out of their sphere of influence."

We came out on a landing as I spoke and then turned sharply to the left along the North Gallery, from the center of which we entered the Fourth Egyptian Room.

Almost immediately, a door in the opposite wall opened, a peculiar, high-pitched humming sound became audible, and Jervis came out on tiptoe with his hand raised.

"Tread as lightly as you can," he said. "We are just making an exposure."

The attendant turned back with his lantern, and we followed Jervis into the room from whence he had come. It was a large room, and little lighter than the galleries, for the single glow-lamp that burned at the end where we entered left the rest of the apartment in almost complete obscurity. We seated ourselves at once on the chairs that had been placed for us, and, when the mutual salutations had been exchanged, I looked about me. There were three people in the room besides Jervis: Thorndyke, who sat with his watch in his hand, a gray-headed gentleman whom I took to be Dr. Norbury, and a smaller person at the dim farther end – undistinguishable, but probably Polton. At our end of the room were the two large trays that I had seen in the workshop, now mounted on trestles and each fitted with a rubber drain-tube leading down to a bucket. At the farther end of the room the sinister shape of the gallows reared itself aloft in the gloom. Only now I could see that it was not a gallows at all. For affixed to the top cross-bar was a large, bottomless glass basin, inside which was a glass bulb that glowed with a strange green light, and in the heart of the bulb a bright spot of red.

It was all clear enough so far. The peculiar sound that filled the air was the hum of the interrupter. The bulb was, of course, a Crookes tube, and the red spot inside it, the glowing red-hot disc of the anti-cathode. Clearly an X-ray photograph was being made, but of what? I strained my eyes, peering into the gloom at the foot of the gallows, but though I could make out an elongated object lying on the floor directly under the bulb, I could not resolve the dimly seen shape into anything recognizable. Presently, however, Dr. Norbury supplied the clue.

"I am rather surprised," said he, "that you chose so composite an object as a mummy to begin on. I should have thought that a simpler object, such as a coffin or a wooden figure, would have been more instructive."

"In some ways it would," replied Thorndyke, "but the variety of materials that the mummy gives us has its advantages. I hope your father is not ill, Miss Bellingham."

"He is not at all well," said Ruth, "and we agreed that it was better for me to come alone. I knew *Herr* Lederbogen quite well. He stayed with us for a time when he was in England."

"I trust," said Dr. Norbury, "that I have not troubled you for nothing. *Herr* Lederbogen speaks of 'our erratic English friend with the long name that I can never remember', and it seemed to me that he might be referring to your uncle."

"I should hardly have called my uncle erratic," said Ruth.

"No, no. Certainly not," Dr. Norbury agreed hastily. "However, you shall see the letter presently and judge for yourself. We mustn't introduce irrelevant topics while the experiment is in progress, must we, Doctor?"

"You had better wait until we have finished," said Thorndyke, "because I am going to turn out the light. Switch off the current, Polton."

The green light vanished from the bulb, the hum of the interrupter swept down an octave or two and died away. Then Thorndyke and Dr. Norbury rose from their chairs and went toward the mummy, which they lifted tenderly while Polton drew from beneath it what presently turned out to be a huge black paper envelope. The single glow-lamp was switched off, leaving the room in total darkness until there burst out suddenly a bright orange red light immediately above one of the trays.

We all gathered round to watch, as Polton – the high priest of these mysteries – drew from the black envelope a colossal sheet of bromide paper, laid it carefully in the tray and proceeded to wet it with a large brush which he had dipped in a pail of water.

"I thought you always used plates for this kind of work," said Dr. Norbury.

"We do, by preference, but a six-foot plate would be impossible, so I had a special paper made to the size."

There is something singularly fascinating in the appearance of a developing photograph – in the gradual, mysterious emergence of the picture from the blank, white surface of plate or paper. But a skiagraph, or X-ray photograph, has a fascination all its own. Unlike the ordinary photograph, which yields a picture of things already seen, it gives a presentment of objects hitherto invisible, and hence, when Polton poured the developer on the already wet paper, we all craned over the tray with the keenest curiosity.

The developer was evidently a very slow one. For fully half-a-minute no change could be seen in the uniform surface. Then, gradually, almost insensibly, the marginal portion began to darken, leaving the outline of the mummy in pale relief. The change, once started, proceeded apace. Darker and darker grew the margin of the paper until from slaty gray it had turned to black, and still the shape of the mummy, now in strong relief, remained an enlongated patch of bald white. But not for long. Presently the white shape began to be tinged with gray, and, as the color deepened, there grew out of it a paler form that seemed to steal out of the enshrouding gray like an apparition, spectral, awesome, mysterious. The skeleton was coming into view.

"It is rather uncanny," said Dr. Norbury. "I feel as if I were assisting at some unholy rite. Just look at it now!"

The gray shadow of the cartonnage, the wrappings and the flesh was fading away into the background and the white skeleton stood out in sharp contrast. And it certainly was rather a weird spectacle.

"You'll lose the bones if you develop much farther," said Dr. Norbury.

"I must let the bones darken," Thorndyke replied, "in case there are any metallic objects. I have three more papers in the envelope."

The white shape of the skeleton now began to gray over and, as Dr. Norbury had said, its distinctness became less and yet less. Thorndyke leaned over the tray with his eyes fixed on a point in the middle of the breast and we all watched him in silence. Suddenly he rose. "Now, Polton," he said sharply, "get the hypo on as quickly as you can."

Polton, who had been waiting with his hand on the stop-cock of the drain-tube, rapidly ran off the developer into the bucket and flooded the paper with the fixing solution.

"Now we can look at it at our leisure," said Thorndyke. After waiting a few seconds, he switched on one of the glow-lamps, and as the flood of light fell on the photograph, he added, "You see we haven't quite lost the skeleton."

"No." Dr. Norbury put on a pair of spectacles and bent down over the tray, and at this moment I felt Ruth's hand touch my arm, lightly at first, and then with a strong nervous grasp, and I could feel that her hand was trembling. I looked round at her anxiously and saw that she had turned deathly pale.

"Would you rather go out into the gallery?" I asked, for the room with its tightly shut windows was close and hot.

"No," she replied quietly. "I will stay here. I am quite well." But still she kept hold of my arm.

Thorndyke glanced at her keenly and then looked away as Dr. Norbury turned to ask him a question.

"Why is it, think you, that some of the teeth show so much whiter than others?"

"I think the whiteness of the shadows is due to the presence of metal," Thorndyke replied.

"Do you mean that the teeth have metal fillings?" asked Dr. Norbury.

"Yes."

"Really! This is very interesting. The use of gold stoppings – and artificial teeth, too – by the ancient Egyptians is well known, but we have no examples in this Museum. This mummy ought to be unrolled. Do you think all those teeth are filled with the same metal? They are not equally white."

"No," replied Thorndyke. "Those teeth that are perfectly white are undoubtedly filled with gold, but that grayish one is probably filled with tin."

"Very interesting," said Dr. Norbury. "*Very* interesting! And what do you make of that faint mark across the chest, near the top of the sternum?"

It was Ruth who answered his question.

"It is the Eye of Osiris!" she exclaimed in a hushed voice.

"Dear me!" exclaimed Dr. Norbury, "so it is. You are quite right. It is the Utchat – the Eye of Horus – or Osiris, if you prefer to call it so. That, I presume, will be a gilded device on some of the wrappings."

"No. I should say it is a tattoo mark. It is too indefinite for a gilded device. And I should say further that the tattooing is done in vermilion, as carbon tattooing could cast no visible shadow."

"I think you must be mistaken about that," said Dr. Norbury, "but we shall see, if the Director allows us to unroll the mummy. By the way, those little objects in front of the knees are metallic, I suppose?"

"Yes, they are metallic. But they are not in front of the knees. They are in the knees. They are pieces of silver wire which have been used to repair fractured kneecaps."

"Are you sure of that?" exclaimed Dr. Norbury, peering at the little white marks with ecstasy, "because if you are, and if these objects are what you say they are, the mummy of Sebek-hotep is an absolutely unique specimen."

"I am quite certain of it," said Thorndyke.

"Then," said Dr. Norbury, "we have made a discovery, thanks to your inquiring spirit. Poor John Bellingham! He little knew what a treasure he was giving us! How I wish he could have known! How I wish he could have been here with us to-night!"

He paused once more to gaze in rapture at the photograph. And then Thorndyke, in his quiet, impassive way, said, "John Bellingham is here, Doctor Norbury. *This* is John Bellingham."

Dr. Norbury started back and stared at Thorndyke in speechless amazement.

"You don't mean," he exclaimed, after a long pause, "that this mummy is the body of John Bellingham!"

"I do indeed. There is no doubt of it."

"But it is impossible! The mummy was here in the gallery a full three weeks before he disappeared."

"Not so," said Thorndyke. "John Bellingham was last seen alive by you and Mr. Jellicoe on the fourteenth of October, more than three weeks before the mummy left Queen Square. After that date he was never seen alive or dead by any person who knew him and could identify him."

Dr. Norbury reflected a while in silence. Then, in a faint voice, he asked, "How do you suggest that John Bellingham's body came to be inside that cartonnage?"

"I think Mr. Jellicoe is the most likely person to be able to answer that question," Thorndyke replied dryly.

There was another interval of silence, and then Dr. Norbury asked suddenly, "But what do you suppose has become of Sebek-hotep? The real Sebek-hotep, I mean?"

"I take it," said Thorndyke, "that the remains of Sebek-hotep, or at least a portion of them, are at present lying in the Woodford mortuary awaiting an adjourned inquest."

As Thorndyke made this statement a flash of belated intelligence, mingled with self-contempt, fell on me. Now that the explanation was given, how obvious it was! And yet I, a competent anatomist and physiologist and actually a pupil of Thorndyke's, had mistaken those ancient bones for the remains of a recent body!

Dr. Norbury considered the last statement for some time in evident perplexity. "It is all consistent enough, I must admit," said he, at length, "and yet – are you quite sure there is no mistake? It seems so incredible."

"There is no mistake, I assure you," Thorndyke answered. "To convince you, I will give you the facts in detail. First, as to the teeth. I have seen John Bellingham's dentist and obtained particulars from his case-book. There were in all five teeth that had been filled. The right upper wisdom tooth, the molar next to it, and the second lower molar on the left side, had all extensive gold fillings. You can see them all quite plainly in the skiagraph. The lower left lateral incisor had a very small gold filling, which you can see as a nearly circular white dot. In addition to these, a filling of tin amalgam had been inserted while the deceased was abroad, in the second left upper bicuspid, the rather gray spot that we have already noticed. These would, by themselves, furnish ample means of identification. But in addition, there is the tattooed device of the Eye of Osiris – "

"Horus," murmured Dr. Norbury.

"Horus, then – in the exact locality in which it was borne by the deceased and tattooed, apparently, with the same pigment. There are, further, the suture wires in the knee-caps. Sir Morgan Bennett, having looked up the notes of the operation, informs me that he introduced three suture wires into the left patella and two into the right, which is what the skiagraph shows. Lastly, the deceased had an old Pott's fracture on the left side. It is not very apparent now, but I saw it quite distinctly just now when the shadows of the bones were whiter. I think that you may take it that the identification is beyond all doubt or question."

"Yes," agreed Dr. Norbury, with gloomy resignation, "it sounds, as you say, quite conclusive. Well, well, it is a most horrible affair. Poor old John Bellingham! It looks uncommonly as if he had met with foul play. Don't you think so?"

392

"I do," replied Thorndyke. "There was a mark on the right side of the skull that looked rather like a fracture. It was not very clear, being at the side, but we must develop the negative to show it."

Dr. Norbury drew his breath in sharply through his teeth. "This is a gruesome business, Doctor," said he. "A terrible business. Awkward for our people, too. By the way, what is our position in the matter? What steps ought we to take?"

"You should give notice to the coroner – I will manage the police – and you should communicate with one of the executors of the will."

"Mr. Jellicoe?"

"No, not Mr. Jellicoe, under the peculiar circumstances. You had better write to Mr. Godfrey Bellingham."

"But I rather understood that Mr. Hurst was the co-executor," said Dr. Norbury.

"He is, surely, as matters stand," said Jervis.

"Not at all," replied Thorndyke. "He *was* as matters *stood*, but he is not now. You are forgetting the condition of Clause Two. That clause sets forth the conditions under which Godfrey Bellingham shall inherit the bulk of the estate and become the co-executor and those conditions are, '*that the body of the testator shall be deposited in some authorized place for the reception of the bodies of the dead, situate within the boundaries of, or appertaining to some place of worship within, the parish of St. George, Bloomsbury, and St. Giles in the Fields, or St. Andrew above the Bars and St. George the Martyr.*' Now Egyptian mummies are bodies of the dead, and this Museum is an authorized place for their reception, and this building is situate within the boundaries of the parish of St. George, Bloomsbury. Therefore the provisions of Clause Two have been duly carried out and therefore Godfrey Bellingham is the principal beneficiary under the will, and the co-executor, in accordance with the wishes of the testator. Is that quite clear?"

"Perfectly," said Dr. Norbury, "and a most astonishing coincidence – but, my dear young lady, had you not better sit down? You are looking very ill."

He glanced anxiously at Ruth, who was pale to the lips and was now leaning heavily on my arm.

"I think, Berkeley," said Thorndyke, "you had better take Miss Bellingham out into the gallery, where there is more air. This has been a tremendous climax to all the trials she has borne so bravely. Go out with Berkeley," he added gently, laying his hand on her shoulder, "and sit down while we develop the other negatives. You mustn't break down now, you know, when the storm has passed and the sun is beginning to shine." He held the door open and as we passed out his face softened into a smile of

393

infinite kindness. "You won't mind my locking you out," said he. "This is a photographic dark-room at present."

The key grated in the lock and we turned away into the dim gallery. It was not quite dark, for a beam of moonlight filtered in here and there through the blinds that covered the skylights. We walked on slowly, her arm linked in mine, and for a while neither of us spoke. The great rooms were very silent and peaceful and solemn. The hush, the stillness, the mystery of the half-seen forms in the cases around, were all in harmony with the deeply-felt sense of a great deliverance that filled our hearts.

We had passed through into the next room before either of us broke the silence. Insensibly our hands had crept together, and as they met and clasped with mutual pressure, Ruth exclaimed, "How dreadful and tragic it is! Poor, poor Uncle John! It seems as if he had come back from the world of shadows to tell us of this awful thing. But, oh God! What a relief it is!"

She caught her breath in one or two quick sobs and pressed my hand passionately.

"It is over, dearest," I said. "It is gone forever. Nothing remains but the memory of your sorrow and your noble courage and patience."

"I can't realize it yet," she murmured. "It has been like a frightful, interminable dream."

"Let us put it away," said I, "and think only of the happy life that is opening."

She made no reply, and only a quick catch in her breath, now and again, told of the long agony that she had endured with such heroic calm.

We walked on slowly, scarcely disturbing the silence with our soft footfalls, through the wide doorway into the second room. The vague shapes of mummy-cases standing erect in the wall-cases, loomed out dim and gigantic, silent watchers keeping their vigil with the memories of untold centuries locked in their shadowy breasts. They were an awesome company. Reverend survivors from a vanished world, they looked out from the gloom of their abiding-place, but with no shade of menace or of malice in their silent presence – rather with a solemn benison on the fleeting creatures of to-day.

Halfway along the room a ghostly figure, somewhat aloof from its companions, showed a dim, pallid blotch where its face would have been. With one accord we halted before it.

"Do you know who this is, Ruth?" I asked.

"Of course I do," she answered. "It is Artemidorus."

We stood, hand in hand, facing the mummy, letting our memories fill in the vague silhouette with its well-remembered details. Presently I drew her nearer to me and whispered, "Ruth! Do you remember when we last stood here?"

"As if I could ever forget!" she answered passionately. "Oh, Paul! The sorrow of it! The misery! How it wrung my heart to tell you! Were you very unhappy when I left you?"

"Unhappy! I never knew, until then, what real heart-breaking sorrow was. It seemed as if the light had gone out of my life forever. But there was just one little spot of brightness left."

"What was that?"

"You made me a promise, dear – a solemn promise, and I felt – at least I hoped – that the day would come, if I only waited patiently, when you would be able to redeem it."

She crept closer to me and yet closer, until her head nestled on my shoulder and her soft cheek lay against mine.

"Dear heart," I whispered, "is it now? Is the time fulfilled?"

"Yes, dearest," she murmured softly. "It is now – and forever."

Reverently I folded her in my arms, gathered her to the heart that worshiped her utterly. Henceforth no sorrows could hurt us, no misfortune vex, for we should walk hand in hand on our earthly pilgrimage and find the way all too short.

Time, whose sands run out with such unequal swiftness for the just and the unjust, the happy and the wretched, lagged, no doubt, with the toilers in the room that we had left. But for us its golden grains trickled out apace, and left the glass empty before we had begun to mark their passage. The turning of a key and the opening of a door aroused us from our dream of perfect happiness. Ruth raised her head to listen, and our lips met for one brief moment. Then, with a silent greeting to the friend who had looked on our grief and witnessed our final happiness, we turned and retraced our steps quickly, filling the great empty rooms with chattering echoes.

"We won't go back into the dark-room – which isn't dark now," said Ruth.

"Why not?" I asked.

"Because – when I came out I was very pale, and I'm – well, I don't think I am very pale now. Besides, poor Uncle John is in there – and – I should be ashamed to look at him with my selfish heart overflowing with happiness."

"You needn't be," said I. "It is the day of our lives and we have a right to be happy. But you shan't go in, if you don't wish to," and I accordingly steered her adroitly past the beam of light that streamed from the open door.

"We have developed four negatives," said Thorndyke, as he emerged with the others, "and I am leaving them in the custody of Doctor Norbury, who will sign each when they are dry, as they may have to be put in evidence. What are you going to do?"

I looked at Ruth to see what she wished.

"If you won't think me ungrateful," said she, "I should rather be alone with my father to-night. He is very weak, and – "

"Yes, I understand," I said hastily. And I did. Mr. Bellingham was a man of strong emotions and would probably be somewhat overcome by the sudden change of fortune and the news of his brother's tragic death.

"In that case," said Thorndyke, "I will bespeak your services. Will you go on and wait for me at my chambers, when you have seen Miss Bellingham home?"

I agreed to this, and we set forth under the guidance of Dr. Norbury (who carried an electric lamp) to return by the way we had come – two of us, as least, in a vastly different frame of mind. The party broke up at the entrance gates, and as Thorndyke wished my companion "Good-night," she held his hand and looked up in his face with swimming eyes.

"I haven't thanked you, Doctor Thorndyke," she said, "and I don't feel that I ever can. What you have done for me and my father is beyond all thanks. You have saved his life and you have rescued me from the most horrible ignominy. Good-by! And God bless you!"

The hansom that bowled along eastward – at most unnecessary speed – bore two of the happiest human beings within the wide boundaries of the town. I looked at my companion as the lights of the street shone into the cab, and was astonished at the transformation. The pallor of her cheek had given place to a rosy pink, the hardness, the tension, the haggard self-repression that had aged her face, were all gone, and the girlish sweetness that had so bewitched me in the early days of our love had stolen back. Even the dimple was there when the sweeping lashes lifted and her eyes met mine in a smile of infinite tenderness.

Little was said on that brief journey. It was happiness enough to sit, hand clasped in hand, and know that our time of trial was past. That no cross of Fate could ever part us now.

The astonished cabman set us down, according to instructions, at the entrance to Nevill's Court, and watched us with open mouth as we vanished into the narrow passage. The court had settled down for the night, and no one marked our return, no curious eye looked down on us from the dark house-front as we said "Good-by," just inside the gate.

"You will come and see us to-morrow, dear, won't you?" she asked.

"Do you think it possible that I could stay away, then?"

"I hope not, but come as early as you can. My father will be positively frantic to see you, because I shall have told him, you know. And, remember, that it is you who have brought us this great deliverance. Good-night, Paul."

"Good-night, sweetheart."

She put up her face frankly to be kissed and then ran up to the ancient door, whence she waved me a last good-by. The shabby gate in the wall closed behind me and hid her from my sight, but the light of her love went with me and turned the dull street into a path of glory.

Chapter XIX
A Strange Symposium

It came upon me with something of a shock of surprise to find the scrap of paper still tacked to the oak of Thorndyke's chambers. So much had happened since I had last looked on it that it seemed to belong to another epoch of my life. I removed it thoughtfully and picked out the tack before entering, and then, closing the inner door, but leaving the oak open, I lit the gas and fell to pacing the room.

What a wonderful episode it had been! How the whole aspect of the world had been changed in a moment by Thorndyke's revelation! At another time, curiosity would have led me to endeavor to trace back the train of reasoning by which the subtle brain of my teacher had attained this astonishing conclusion. But now my own happiness held exclusive possession of my thoughts. The image of Ruth filled the field of my mental vision. I saw her again as I had seen her in the cab with her sweet, pensive face and downcast eyes – I felt again the touch of her soft cheek and the parting kiss by the gate, so frank and simple, so intimate and final.

I must have waited quite a long time, though the golden minutes sped unreckoned, for when my two colleagues arrived they tendered needless apologies.

"And I suppose," said Thorndyke, "you have been wondering what I wanted you for."

I had not, as a matter of fact, given the matter a moment's consideration.

"We are going to call on Mr. Jellicoe," Thorndyke explained. "There is something behind this affair, and until I have ascertained what it is, the case is not complete from my point of view."

"Wouldn't it have done as well to-morrow?" I asked.

"It might, and then it might not. There is an old saying as to catching a weasel asleep. Mr. Jellicoe is a somewhat wide-awake person, and I think it best to introduce him to Inspector Badger at the earliest possible moment."

"The meeting of a weasel and a badger suggests a sporting interview," remarked Jervis. "But you don't expect Jellicoe to give himself away, do you?"

"He can hardly do that, seeing that there is nothing to give away. But I think he may make a statement. There were some exceptional circumstances, I feel sure."

"How long have you known that the body was in the Museum?" I asked.

"About thirty or forty seconds longer than you have, I should say."

"Do you mean," I exclaimed, "that you did not know until the negative was developed?"

"My dear fellow," he replied, "do you suppose that, if I had had certain knowledge where the body was, I should have allowed that noble girl to go on dragging out a lingering agony of suspense that I could have cut short in a moment? Or that I should have made these humbugging pretenses of scientific experiments if a more dignified course had been open to me?"

"As to the experiments," said Jervis, "Norbury could hardly have refused if you had taken him into your confidence."

"Indeed he could, and probably would. My 'confidence' would have involved a charge of murder against a highly respectable gentleman who was well known to him. He would probably have referred me to the police, and then what could I have done? I had plenty of suspicions, but not a single solid fact."

Our discussion was here interrupted by hurried footsteps on the stairs and a thundering rat-tat on our knocker.

As Jervis opened the door, Inspector Badger burst into the room in a highly excited state.

"What is all this, Doctor Thorndyke?" he asked. "I see you've sworn an information against Mr. Jellicoe, and I have a warrant to arrest him, but before anything else is done I think it right to tell you that we have more evidence than is generally known pointing to quite a different quarter."

"Derived from Mr. Jellicoe's information," said Thorndyke. "But the fact is that I have just examined and identified the body at the British Museum, where it was deposited by Mr. Jellicoe. I don't say that he murdered John Bellingham – though that is what appearances suggest – but I do say that he will have to account for his secret disposal of the body."

Inspector Badger was thunderstruck. Also he was visibly annoyed. The salt which Mr. Jellicoe had so adroitly sprinkled on the constabulary tail appeared to develop irritating properties, for when Thorndyke had given him a brief outline of the facts he stuck his hands in his pockets and exclaimed gloomily, "Well, I'm hanged! And to think of all the time and trouble I've spent on those damned bones! I suppose they were just a plant?"

"Don't let us disparage them," said Thorndyke. "They have played a useful part. They represent the inevitable mistake that every criminal makes sooner or later. The murderer will always do a little too much. If he

399

would only lie low and let well alone, the detectives might whistle for a clue. But it is time we are starting."

"Are we all going?" asked the inspector, looking at me in particular with no very gracious recognition.

"We will all come with you," said Thorndyke, "but you will, naturally, make the arrest in the way that seems best to you."

"It's a regular procession," grumbled the inspector, but he made no more definite objection, and we started forth on our quest.

The distance from the Temple to Lincoln's Inn is not great. In five minutes we were at the gateway in Chancery Lane, and a couple of minutes later saw us gathered round the threshold of the stately old house in New Square.

"Seems to be a light in the first-floor front," said Badger. "You'd better move away before I ring the bell."

But the precaution was unnecessary. As the inspector advanced to the bell-pull a head was thrust out of the open window immediately above the street door.

"Who are you?" inquired the owner of the head in a voice which I recognized as that of Mr. Jellicoe.

"I am Inspector Badger of the Criminal Investigation Department. I wish to see Mr. Arthur Jellicoe."

"Then look at me. I am Mr. Arthur Jellicoe."

"I hold a warrant for your arrest, Mr. Jellicoe. You are charged with the murder of Mr. John Bellingham, whose body has been discovered in the British Museum."

"By whom?"

"By Doctor Thorndyke."

"Indeed," said Mr. Jellicoe. "Is he here?"

"Yes."

"Ha! And you wish to arrest me, I presume?"

"Yes. That is what I am here for."

"Well, I will agree to surrender myself subject to certain conditions."

"I can't make any conditions, Mr. Jellicoe."

"No, I will make them, and you will accept them. Otherwise you will not arrest me."

"It's no use for you to talk like that," said Badger. "If you don't let me in I shall have to break in. And I may as well tell you," he added mendaciously, "that the house is surrounded."

"You may accept my assurance," Mr. Jellicoe replied calmly, "that you will not arrest me if you do not accept my conditions."

"Well, what are you conditions?" demanded Badger.

"I desire to make a statement," said Mr. Jellicoe.

"You can do that, but I must caution you that anything you say may be used in evidence against you."

"Naturally. But I wish to make the statement in the presence of Doctor Thorndyke, and I desire to hear a statement from him of the method of investigation by which he discovered the whereabouts of the body. That is to say, if he is willing."

"If you mean that we should mutually enlighten one another, I am very willing indeed," said Thorndyke.

"Very well. Then my conditions, Inspector, are that I shall hear Doctor Thorndyke's statement and that I shall be permitted to make a statement myself, and that until those statements are completed, with any necessary interrogation and discussion, I shall remain at liberty and shall suffer no molestation or interference of any kind. And I agree that, on the conclusion of the said proceedings, I will submit without resistance to any course that you may adopt."

"I can't agree to that," said Badger.

"Can't you?" said Mr. Jellicoe coldly, and after a pause he added, "Don't be hasty. I have given you warning."

There was something in Mr. Jellicoe's passionless tone that disturbed the inspector exceedingly, for he turned to Thorndyke and said in a low tone, "I wonder what his game is? He can't get away, you know."

"There are several possibilities," said Thorndyke.

"M'yes," said Badger, stroking his chin perplexedly.

"After all, is there any objection? His statement might save trouble, and you'd be on the safe side. It would take you some time to break in."

"Well," said Mr. Jellicoe, with his hand on the window, "do you agree — yes or no?"

"All right," said Badger sulkily. "I agree."

"You promise not to molest me in any way until I have quite finished?"

"I promise."

Mr. Jellicoe's head disappeared and the window closed. After a short pause we heard the jar of massive bolts and the clank of a chain, and, as the heavy door swung open, Mr. Jellicoe stood revealed, calm and impassive, with an old-fashioned office candlestick in his hand.

"Who are the others?" he inquired, peering out sharply through his spectacles.

"Oh, they are nothing to do with me," replied Badger.

"They are Doctor Berkeley and Doctor Jervis," said Thorndyke.

"Ha!" said Mr. Jellicoe, "very kind and attentive of them to call. Pray, come in, gentlemen. I am sure you will be interested to hear our little discussion."

401

He held the door open with a certain stiff courtesy, and we all entered the hall led by Inspector Badger. He closed the door softly and preceded us up the stairs and into the apartment from the window of which he had dictated the terms of surrender. It was a fine old room, spacious, lofty, and dignified, with paneled walls and a carved mantelpiece, the central escutcheon of which bore the initials "*J. W. P.*" with the date "*1671*". A large writing-table stood at the farther end, and behind it was an iron safe.

"I have been expecting this visit," Mr. Jellicoe remarked tranquilly as he placed four chairs opposite the table.

"Since when?" asked Thorndyke.

"Since last Monday evening, when I had the pleasure of seeing you conversing with my friend Doctor Berkeley at the Inner Temple gate, and then inferred that you were retained in the case. That was a circumstance that had not been fully provided for. May I offer you gentlemen a glass of sherry?"

As he spoke he placed on the table a decanter and a tray of glasses, and looked at us interrogatively with his hand on the stopper.

"Well, I don't mind if I do, Mr. Jellicoe," said Badger, on whom the lawyer's glance had finally settled. Mr. Jellicoe filled a glass and handed it to him with a stiff bow. Then, with the decanter still in his hand, he said persuasively, "Doctor Thorndyke, pray allow me to fill you a glass?"

"No, thank you," said Thorndyke, in a tone so decided that the inspector looked round at him quickly. And as Badger caught his eye, the glass which he was about to raise to his lips became suddenly arrested and was slowly returned to the table untasted.

"I don't want to hurry you, Mr. Jellicoe," said the inspector, "but it's rather late, and I should like to get this business settled. What is it that you wish to do?"

"I desire," replied Mr. Jellicoe, "to make a detailed statement of the events that have happened, and I wish to hear from Doctor Thorndyke precisely how he arrived at his very remarkable conclusion. When this has been done I shall be entirely at your service, and I suggest that it would be more interesting if Doctor Thorndyke would give us his statement before I furnish you with the actual facts."

"I am entirely of your opinion," said Thorndyke.

"Then in that case," said Mr. Jellicoe, "I suggest that you disregard me, and address your remarks to your friends as if I were not present."

Thorndyke acquiesced with a bow, and Mr. Jellicoe, having seated himself in his elbow-chair behind the table, poured himself out a glass of water, selected a cigarette from a neat silver case, lighted it deliberately, and leaned back to listen at his ease.

"My first acquaintance with this case," Thorndyke began without preamble, "was made through the medium of the daily papers about two years ago, and I may say that, although I had no interest in it beyond the purely academic interest of a specialist in a case that lies in his particular specialty, I considered it with deep attention. The newspaper reports contained no particulars of the relations of the parties that could furnish any hints as to motives on the part of any of them, but merely a bare statement of the events. And this was a distinct advantage, inasmuch as it left one to consider the facts of the case without regard to motive – to balance the *prima facie* probabilities with an open mind. And it may surprize you to learn that those *prima facie* probabilities pointed from the very first to that solution which has been put to the test of experiment this evening. Hence it will be well for me to begin by giving the conclusions that I reached by reasoning from the facts set forth in the newspapers before any of the further facts came to my knowledge.

"From the facts as stated in the newspaper reports it is obvious that there were four possible explanations of the disappearance:

"1. The man might be alive and in hiding. This was highly improbable, for the reasons that were stated by Mr. Loram at the late hearing of the application, and for a further reason that I shall mention presently.

"2. He might have died by accident or disease, and his body failed to be identified. This was even more improbable, seeing that he carried on his person abundant means of identification, including visiting cards.

"3. He might have been murdered by some stranger for the sake of his portable property. This was highly improbable for the same reason: His body could hardly have failed to be identified.

"These three explanations are what we may call the outside explanations. They touched none of the parties mentioned. They were all obviously improbable on general grounds, and to all of them there was one conclusive answer – the scarab which was found in Godfrey Bellingham's garden. Hence I put them aside and gave my attention to the fourth explanation. This was that the missing man had been made away with by one of the parties mentioned in the report. But, since the reports mentioned three parties, it was evident that there was a choice of three hypotheses, namely:

"(*a*) That John Bellingham had been made away with by Hurst; or (*b*) by the Bellinghams; or (*c*) by Mr. Jellicoe.

403

"Now, I have constantly impressed on my pupils that the indispensable question that must be asked at the outset of such an inquiry as this is, 'When was the missing person last undoubtedly seen or known to be alive?' That is the question that I asked myself after reading the newspaper report, and the answer was, that he was last certainly seen alive on the fourteenth of October, Nineteen-hundred-and-two, at 141 Queen Square, Bloomsbury. Of the fact that he was alive at that time and place there could be no doubt whatever, for he was seen at the same moment by two persons, both of whom were intimately acquainted with him, and one of whom, Doctor Norbury, was apparently a disinterested witness. After that date he was never seen, alive or dead, by any person who knew him and was able to identify him. It was stated that he had been seen on the twenty-third of November following by the housemaid of Mr. Hurst, but as this person was unacquainted with him, it was uncertain whether the person whom she saw was or was not John Bellingham.

"Hence the disappearance dated, not from the twenty-third of November, as every one seems to have assumed, but from the fourteenth of October, and the question was not, 'What became of John Bellingham after he entered Mr. Hurst's house?' but, 'What became of him after his interview in Queen Square?'

"But as soon as I had decided that that interview must form the real starting point of the inquiry, a most striking set of circumstances came into view. It became obvious that if Mr. Jellicoe had had any reason for wishing to make away with John Bellingham, he had such an opportunity as seldom falls to the lot of an intending murderer.

"Just consider the conditions. John Bellingham was known to be setting out alone upon a journey beyond the sea. His exact destination was not stated. He was to be absent for an undetermined period, but at least three weeks. His disappearance would occasion no comment. His absence would lead to no inquiries, at least for several weeks, during which the murderer would have leisure quietly to dispose of the body and conceal all traces of the crime. The conditions were, from a murderer's point of view, ideal.

"But that was not all. During that very period of John Bellingham's absence Mr. Jellicoe was engaged to deliver to the British Museum what was admittedly a dead human body, and that body was to be enclosed in a sealed case. Could any more perfect or secure method of disposing of a body be devised by the most ingenious murderer? The plan would have had only one weak point: The mummy would be known to have left Queen Square *after* the disappearance of John Bellingham, and suspicion might in the end have arisen. To this point I shall return presently. Meanwhile

404

we will consider the second hypothesis – that the missing man was made away with by Mr. Hurst.

"Now, there seemed to be no doubt that some person, purporting to be John Bellingham, did actually visit Mr. Hurst's house, and he must either have left the house or remained in it. If he left, he did so surreptitiously. If he remained, there could be no reasonable doubt that he had been murdered and that his body had been concealed. Let us consider the probabilities in each case.

"Assuming – as every one seems to have done – that the visitor was really John Bellingham, we are dealing with a responsible, middle-aged gentleman, and the idea that such a person would enter a house, announce his intention of staying, and then steal away unobserved is very difficult to accept. Moreover, he would appear to have come down to Eltham by rail immediately on landing in England, leaving his luggage in the cloakroom at Charing Cross. This pointed to a definiteness of purpose quite inconsistent with his casual disappearance from the house.

"On the other hand, the idea that he might have been murdered by Hurst was not inconceivable. The thing was physically possible. If Bellingham had really been in the study when Hurst came home, the murder could have been committed – by appropriate means – and the body temporarily concealed in the cupboard or elsewhere. But although possible it was not at all probable. There was no real opportunity. The risk and the subsequent difficulties would be very great. There was not a particle of positive evidence that a murder had occurred, and the conduct of Hurst in immediately leaving the house in possession of the servants is quite inconsistent with the supposition that there was a body concealed in it. So that, while it is almost impossible to believe that John Bellingham left the house of his own accord, it is equally difficult to believe that he did not leave it.

"But there is a third possibility, which, strange to say, no one seems to have suggested. Supposing that the visitor was not John Bellingham at all, but someone who was impersonating him? That would dispose of the difficulties completely. The strange disappearance ceases to be strange, for a personator would necessarily make off before Mr. Hurst should arrive and discover the imposture. But if we accept this supposition, we raise two further questions: 'Who was the personator?' and 'What was the object of the personation?'

"Now, the personator was clearly not Hurst himself, for he would have been recognized by his housemaid. He was therefore either Godfrey Bellingham or Mr. Jellicoe or some other person, and as no other person was mentioned in the newspaper reports I confined my speculations to these two.

405

"And, first, as to Godfrey Bellingham. It did not appear whether he was or was not known to the housemaid, so I assumed – wrongly, as it turns out – that he was not. Then he might have been the personator. But why should he have personated his brother? He could not have already committed the murder. There had not been time enough. He would have had to leave Woodford before John Bellingham had set out for Charing Cross. And even if he had committed the murder, he would have no object in raising this commotion. His cue would have been to remain quiet and know nothing. The probabilities were all against the personator being Godfrey Bellingham.

"Then could it be Mr. Jellicoe? The answer to this question is contained in the answer to the further question: 'What could have been the object of the personation?'

"What motive could this unknown person have had in appearing, announcing himself as John Bellingham, and forthwith vanishing? There could only have been one motive: That, namely, of fixing the date of John Bellingham's disappearance – of furnishing a definite moment at which he was last seen alive.

"But who was likely to have had such a motive? Let us see.

"I said just now that if Mr. Jellicoe had murdered John Bellingham and disposed of the body in the mummy-case, he would have been absolutely safe for the time being. But there would be a weak spot in his armor. For a month or more the disappearance of his client would occasion no remark. But presently, when he failed to return, inquiries would be set on foot, and then it would appear that no one had seen him since he left Queen Square. Then it would be noted that the last person with whom he was seen was Mr. Jellicoe. It might, further, be remembered that the mummy had been delivered to the Museum some time *after* the missing man was last seen alive. And so suspicion might arise and be followed by disastrous investigations. But supposing it should be made to appear that John Bellingham had been seen alive more than a month after his interview with Mr. Jellicoe and some weeks after the mummy had been deposited in the Museum? Then Mr. Jellicoe would cease to be in any way connected with the disappearance and henceforth would be absolutely safe.

"Hence, after carefully considering this part of the newspaper report, I came to the conclusion that the mysterious occurrence at Mr. Hurst's house had only one reasonable explanation – namely, that the visitor was not John Bellingham, but someone personating him, and that that someone was Mr. Jellicoe.

"It remains to consider the case of Godfrey Bellingham and his daughter, though I cannot understand how any sane person can have seriously suspected either." (Here Inspector Badger smiled a sour smile).

406

"The evidence against them was negligible, for there was nothing to connect them with the affair save the finding of the scarab on their premises, and that event, which might have been highly suspicious under other circumstances, was robbed of any significance by the fact that the scarab was found on a spot which had been passed a few minutes previously by the other suspected party, Hurst. The finding of the scarab did, however, establish two important conclusions: Namely, that John Bellingham had probably met with foul play, and that of the four persons present when it was found, one at least had had possession of the body. As to which of the four was the one, the circumstances furnished only a hint, which was this: If the scarab had been purposely dropped, the most likely person to find it was the one who dropped it. And the person who discovered it was Mr. Jellicoe.

"Following up this hint, if we ask ourselves what motive Mr. Jellicoe could have had for dropping it – assuming him to be the murderer – the answer is obvious. It would not be his policy to fix the crime on any particular person, but rather to set up a complication of conflicting evidence which would occupy the attention of investigators and divert it from himself.

"Of course, if Hurst had been the murderer, he would have had a sufficient motive for dropping the scarab, so that the case against Mr. Jellicoe was not conclusive, but the fact that it was he who found it was highly significant.

"This completes the analysis of the evidence contained in the original newspaper report describing the circumstances of the disappearance. The conclusions that followed from it were, as you will have seen:

"1. That the missing man was almost certainly dead, as proved by the finding of the scarab after his disappearance.

"2. That he had probably been murdered by one or more of four persons, as proved by the finding of the scarab on the premises occupied by two of them and accessible to the others.

"3. That, of those four persons, one – Mr. Jellicoe – was the last person who was known to have been in the company of the missing man – had had an exceptional opportunity for committing the murder, and was known to have delivered a dead body to the Museum subsequently to the disappearance.

"4. That the supposition that Mr. Jellicoe had committed the murder rendered all the other circumstances of the disappearance clearly intelligible, whereas on any other supposition they were quite inexplicable."

407

"The evidence of the newspaper report, therefore, clearly pointed to the probability that John Bellingham had been murdered by Mr. Jellicoe and his body concealed in the mummy-case.

"I do not wish to give you the impression that I, then and there, believed that Mr. Jellicoe was the murderer. I did not. There was no reason to suppose that the report contained all the essential facts, and I merely considered it speculatively as a study in probabilities. But I did decide that that was the only probable conclusion from the facts that were given.

"Nearly two years had passed before I heard anything more of the case. Then it was brought to my notice by my friend, Doctor Berkeley, and I became acquainted with certain new facts, which I will consider in the order in which they became known to me.

"The first new light on the case came from the will. As soon as I had read the document I felt convinced that there was something wrong. The testator's evident intention was that his brother should inherit the property, whereas the construction of the will was such as almost certainly to defeat that intention. The devolution of the property depended on the burial clause – Clause Two, but the burial arrangement would ordinarily be decided by the executor, who happened to be Mr. Jellicoe. Thus the will left the disposition of the property under the control of Mr. Jellicoe, though his action could have been contested.

"Now, this will, although drawn up by John Bellingham, was executed in Mr. Jellicoe's office as is proved by the fact that it was witnessed by two of his clerks. He was the testator's lawyer, and it was his duty to insist on the will being properly drawn. Evidently he did nothing of the kind, and this fact strongly suggested some kind of collusion on his part with Hurst, who stood to benefit by the miscarriage of the will. And this was the odd feature in the case, for whereas the party responsible for the defective provisions was Mr. Jellicoe, the party who benefited was Hurst.

"But the most startling peculiarity of the will was the way in which it fitted the circumstances of the disappearance. It looked as if Clause Two had been drawn up with those very circumstances in view. Since, however, the will was ten years old, this was impossible. But if Clause Two could not have been devised to fit the disappearance, could the disappearance not have been devised to fit Clause Two? That was by no means impossible. Under the circumstances it looked rather probable. And if it had been so contrived, who was the agent in that contrivance? Hurst stood to benefit, but there was no evidence that he even knew the contents of the will. There only remained Mr. Jellicoe, who had certainly connived at the misdrawing of the will for some purpose of his own – some dishonest purpose.

"The evidence of the will, then, pointed to Mr. Jellicoe as the agent in the disappearance, and, after reading it, I definitely suspected him of the crime.

"Suspicion, however, is one thing and proof is another. I had not nearly enough evidence to justify me in laying an information, and I could not approach the Museum officials without making a definite accusation. The great difficulty of the case was that I could discover no motive. I could not see any way in which Mr. Jellicoe would benefit by the disappearance. His own legacy was secure, whenever and however the testator died. The murder and concealment apparently benefited Hurst alone, and, in the absence of any plausible motive, the facts required to be much more conclusive than they were."

"Did you form absolutely no opinion as to motive?" asked Mr. Jellicoe.

He put the question in a quiet, passionless tone, as if he were discussing some *cause célèbre* in which he had nothing more than a professional interest. Indeed, the calm, impersonal interest that he displayed in Thorndyke's analysis, his unmoved attention, punctuated by little nods of approval at each telling point in the argument, were the most surprising features of this astounding interview.

"I did form an opinion," replied Thorndyke, "but it was merely speculative, and I was never able to confirm it. I discovered that about ten years ago Mr. Hurst had been in difficulties and that he had suddenly raised a considerable sum of money, no one knew how or on what security. I observed that this even coincided with the execution of the will, and I surmised that there might be some connection between them. But that was only a surmise, and, as the proverb has it, '*He discovers who proves*'. I could prove nothing, so that I never discovered Mr. Jellicoe's motive, and I don't know it now."

"Don't you really?" said Mr. Jellicoe, in something approaching a tone of animation. He laid down the end of his cigarette, and, as he selected another from the silver case, he continued. "I think that is the most interesting feature of your really remarkable analysis. It does you great credit. The absence of motive would have appeared to most persons a fatal objection to the theory, of what I may call, the prosecution. Permit me to congratulate you on the consistency and tenacity with which you have pursued the actual, visible facts."

He bowed stiffly to Thorndyke (who returned his bow with equal stiffness), lighted a fresh cigarette, and once more leaned back in his chair with the calm, attentive manner of a man who is listening to a lecture or a musical performance.

"The evidence, then, being insufficient to act upon," Thorndyke resumed, "there was nothing for it but to wait for some new facts. Now, the study of a large series of carefully conducted murders brings into view an almost invariable phenomenon. The cautious murderer, in his anxiety to make himself secure, does too much, and it is this excess of precaution that leads to detection. It happens constantly. Indeed, I may say that it always happens – in those murders that are detected. Of those that are not we say nothing – and I had strong hopes that it would happen in this case. And it did.

"At the very moment when my client's case seemed almost hopeless, some human remains were discovered at Sidcup. I read the account of the discovery in the evening paper, and scanty as the report was, it recorded enough facts to convince me that the inevitable mistake had been made."

"Did it, indeed?" said Mr. Jellicoe. "A mere, inexpert, hearsay report! I should have supposed it to be quite valueless from a scientific point of view."

"So it was," said Thorndyke. "But it gave the date of the discovery and the locality, and it also mentioned what bones had been found. Which were all vital facts. Take the question of time. These remains, after lying *perdu* for two years, suddenly come to light just as the parties – who have also been lying *perdu* – have begun to take action in respect of the will. In fact, within a week or two of the hearing of the application. It was certainly a remarkable coincidence. And when the circumstances that occasioned the discovery were considered, the coincidence became more remarkable still. For these remains were found on land actually belonging to John Bellingham, and their discovery resulted from certain operations (the clearing of the watercress-beds) carried out on behalf of the absent landlord. But by whose orders were those works undertaken? Clearly by the orders of the landlord's agent. But the landlord's agent was known to be Mr. Jellicoe. Therefore these remains were brought to light at this peculiarly opportune moment by the action of Mr. Jellicoe. The coincidence, I say again, was very remarkable.

"But what instantly arrested my attention on reading the newspaper report was the unusual manner in which the arm had been separated, for, besides the bones of the arm proper, there were those of what anatomists call the 'shoulder-girdle' – the shoulder-blade and collar-bone. This was very remarkable. It seemed to suggest a knowledge of anatomy, and yet no murderer, even if he possessed such knowledge, would make a display of it on such an occasion. It seemed to me that there must be some other explanation. Accordingly, when other remains had come to light and all

410

had been collected at Woodford, I asked my friend Berkeley to go down there and inspect them. He did so, and this is what he found.

"Both arms had been detached in the same peculiar manner. Both were complete, and all the bones were from the same body. The bones were quite clean – of soft structures, I mean. There were no cuts, scratches or marks on them. There was not a trace of adipocere – the peculiar waxy soap that forms in bodies that decay in water or in a damp situation. The right hand had been detached at the time the arm was thrown into the pond, and the left ring finger had been separated and had vanished. This latter fact had attracted my attention from the first, but I will leave its consideration for the moment and return to it later."

"How did you discover that the hand had been detached?" Mr. Jellicoe asked.

"By the submersion marks," replied Thorndyke. "It was lying on the bottom of the pond in a position which would have been impossible if it had been attached to the arm."

"You interest me exceedingly," said Mr. Jellicoe. "It appears that a medico-legal expert finds *'books in the running brooks, sermons in bones, and evidence in everything'*. But don't let me interrupt you."

"Doctor Berkeley's observations," Thorndyke resumed, "together with the medical evidence at the inquest, led me to certain conclusions.

"Let me state the facts which were disclosed.

"The remains which had been assembled formed a complete human skeleton with the exception of the skull, one finger, and the legs from the knee to the ankle, including both knee-caps. This was a very impressive fact, for the bones that were missing included all those which could have been identified as belonging or not belonging to John Bellingham, and the bones that were present were the unidentifiable remainder.

"It had a suspicious appearance of selection.

"But the parts that were present were also curiously suggestive. In all cases the mode of dismemberment was peculiar, for an ordinary person would have divided the knee-joint leaving the knee-cap attached to the thigh, whereas it had evidently been left attached to the shinbone, and the head would most probably have been removed by cutting through the neck instead of being neatly detached from the spine. And all these bones were almost entirely free from marks or scratches such as would naturally occur in an ordinary dismemberment and all were quite free from adipocere. And now as to the conclusions which I drew from these facts. First, there was the peculiar grouping of the bones. What was the meaning of that? Well, the idea of a punctilious anatomist was obviously absurd, and I put it aside. But was there any other explanation? Yes, there was. The bones had appeared in the natural groups that are held together by ligaments, and they

411

had separated at points where they were attached principally by muscles. The knee-cap, for instance, which really belongs to the thigh, is attached to it by muscle, but to the shin-bone by a stout ligament. And so with the bones of the arm. They are connected to one another by ligaments, but to the trunk only by muscle, excepting at one end of the collar-bone.

"But this was a very significant fact. Ligament decays much more slowly than muscle, so that in a body of which the muscles had largely decayed the bones might still be held together by ligament. The peculiar grouping therefore suggested that the body had been partly reduced to a skeleton before it was dismembered. That it had then been merely pulled apart and not divided with a knife.

"This suggestion was remarkably confirmed by the total absence of knife-cuts or scratches.

"Then there was the fact that all the bones were quite free from adipocere. Now, if an arm or a thigh should be deposited in water and left undisturbed to decay, it is certain that large masses of adipocere would be formed. Probably more than half of the flesh would be converted into this substance. The absence of adipocere therefore proved that the bulk of the flesh had disappeared or been removed from the bones before they were deposited in the pond. That, in fact, it was not a body, but a skeleton, that had been deposited.

"But what kind of skeleton? If it was the recent skeleton of a murdered man, then the bones had been carefully stripped of flesh so as to leave the ligaments intact. But this was highly improbable, for there could be no object in preserving the ligaments. And the absence of scratches was against this view.

"Then they did not appear to be graveyard bones. The collection was too complete. It is very rare to find a graveyard skeleton of which many of the small bones are not missing. And such bones are usually more or less weathered and friable.

"They did not appear to be bones such as may be bought at an osteological dealer's, for these usually have perforations to admit the macerating fluid to the marrow cavities. Dealers' bones, too, are very seldom all from the same body, and the small bones of the hand are drilled with holes to enable them to be strung on catgut.

"They were not dissecting-room bones, as there was no trace of red lead in the openings for the nutrient arteries.

"What the appearances did suggest was that these were parts of a body which had decayed in a very dry atmosphere (in which no adipocere would be formed), and which had been pulled or broken apart. Also that the ligaments which held the body – or rather skeleton – together were brittle and friable as suggested by the detached hand, which had probably broken off accidentally. But the only kind of body that completely answered this description is an Egyptian mummy. A mummy, it is true, has been more or less preserved, but on exposure to the air of such a climate as ours it perishes rapidly, the ligaments being the last of the soft parts to disappear.

"The hypothesis that these bones were parts of a mummy naturally suggested Mr. Jellicoe. If he had murdered John Bellingham and concealed his body in the mummy-case, he would have a spare mummy on his hands, and that mummy would have been exposed to the air and to somewhat rough handling.

"A very interesting circumstance connected with these remains was that the ring finger was missing. Now, fingers have on sundry occasions been detached from dead hands for the sake of the rings on them. But in such cases the object has been to secure a valuable ring uninjured. If this hand was the hand of John Bellingham, there was no such object. The purpose was to prevent identification, and that purpose would have been more easily, and much more completely, achieved by sacrificing the ring, by filing through it or breaking it off the finger. The appearances, therefore, did not quite agree with the apparent purpose.

"Then, could there be any other purpose with which they agreed better? Yes, there could.

"If it had happened that John Bellingham were known to have worn a ring on that finger, and especially if that ring fitted tightly, the removal of the finger would serve a very useful purpose. It would create an impression that the finger had been removed on account of a ring, to prevent identification, which impression would, in turn, produce a suspicion that the hand was that of John Bellingham. And yet it would not be evidence that could be used to establish identity. Now, if Mr. Jellicoe were the murderer and had the body hidden elsewhere, vague suspicion would be precisely what he would desire, and positive evidence what he would wish to avoid.

"It transpired later that John Bellingham did wear a ring on that finger and that the ring fitted very tightly. Whence it followed that the absence of the finger was an additional point tending to implicate Mr. Jellicoe.

"And now let us briefly review this mass of evidence. You will see that it consists of a multitude of items, each either trivial or speculative. Up to the time of the actual discovery I had not a single crucial fact, nor any clue as to motive. But, slight as the individual points of evidence were, they pointed with impressive unanimity to one person – Mr. Jellicoe. Thus:

"The person who had the opportunity to commit murder and dispose of the body was Mr. Jellicoe.

"The deceased was last certainly seen alive with Mr. Jellicoe.

413

"An unidentified human body was delivered to the Museum by Mr. Jellicoe.

"The only person who could have a motive for personating the deceased was Mr. Jellicoe.

"The only known person who could possibly have done so was Mr. Jellicoe.

"One of the two persons who could have had a motive for dropping the scarab was Mr. Jellicoe. The person who found that scarab was Mr. Jellicoe, although, owing to his defective eyesight and his spectacles, he was the most unlikely person of those present to find it.

"The person who was responsible for the execution of the defective will was Mr. Jellicoe.

"Then as to the remains. They were apparently not those of John Bellingham, but parts of a particular kind of body. But the only person who was known to have had such a body in his possession was Mr. Jellicoe.

"The only person who could have had any motive for substituting those remains for the remains of the deceased was Mr. Jellicoe.

"Finally, the person who caused the discovery of those remains at that singularly opportune moment was Mr. Jellicoe.

"This was the sum of the evidence that was in my possession up to the time of the hearing and, indeed, for some time after, and it was not enough to act upon. But when the case had been heard in Court, it was evident either that the proceedings would be abandoned – which was unlikely – or that there would be new developments.

"I watched the progress of events with profound interest. An attempt had been made (by Mr. Jellicoe or some other person) to get the will administered without producing the body of John Bellingham, and that attempt had failed. The coroner's jury had refused to identify the remains, the Probate Court had refused to presume the death of the testator. As affairs stood the will could not be administered.

"What would be the next move?

"It was virtually certain that it would consist in the production of something which would identify the unrecognized remains as those of the testator.

"But what would that something be?

"The answer to that question would contain the answer to another question: 'Was my solution of the mystery the true solution?'

"If I was wrong, it was possible that some of the undoubtedly genuine bones of John Bellingham might presently be discovered, for instance, the skull, the knee-cap, or the left fibula, by any of which the remains could be positively identified.

414

"If I was right, only one thing could possibly happen. Mr. Jellicoe would have to play the trump card that he had been holding back in case the Court should refuse the application, a card that he was evidently reluctant to play.

"He would have to produce the bones of the mummy's finger, together with John Bellingham's ring. No other course was possible.

"But not only would the bones and the ring have to be found together. They would have to be found in a place which was accessible to Mr. Jellicoe, and so far under his control that he could determine the exact time when the discovery should be made.

"I waited patiently for the answer to my question. Was I right or was I wrong?

"And, in due course, the answer came.

"The bones and the ring were discovered in the well in the grounds of Godfrey Bellingham's late house. That house was the property of John Bellingham. Mr. Jellicoe was John Bellingham's agent. Hence it was practically certain that the date on which the well was emptied was settled by Mr. Jellicoe.

"The oracle had spoken.

"The discovery proved conclusively that the bones were not those of John Bellingham (for if they had been the ring would have been unnecessary for identification). But if the bones were not John Bellingham's, the ring was – from which followed the important corollary that whoever had deposited those bones in the well had had possession of the body of John Bellingham. And there could be no doubt that that person was Mr. Jellicoe.

"On receiving this final confirmation of my conclusions, I applied forthwith to Doctor Norbury for permission to examine the mummy of Sebek-hotep, with the result that you are already acquainted with."

As Thorndyke concluded, Mr. Jellicoe regarded him thoughtfully for a moment and then said, "You have given us a most complete and lucid exposition of your method of investigation, sir. I have enjoyed it exceedingly, and should have profited by it hereafter – under other circumstances. Are you sure you won't allow me to fill your glass?" He touched the stopper of the decanter, and Inspector Badger ostentatiously consulted his watch.

"Time is running on, I fear," said Mr. Jellicoe.

"It is, indeed," Badger assented emphatically.

"Well, I need not detain you long," said the lawyer. "My statement is a narration of events. But I desire to make it, and you, no doubt, will be interested to hear it."

He opened the silver case and selected a fresh cigarette, which, however, he did not light. Inspector Badger produced a funereal notebook, which he laid open on his knee, and the rest of us settled ourselves in our chairs with no little curiosity to hear Mr. Jellicoe's statement.

Chapter XX
The End of the Case

A profound silence had fallen on the room and its occupants. Mr. Jellicoe sat with his eyes fixed on the table as if deep in thought, the unlighted cigarette in one hand, the other grasping the tumbler of water. Presently Inspector Badger coughed impatiently and he looked up. "I beg your pardon, gentleman," he said. "I am keeping you waiting."

He took a sip from the tumbler, opened a match-box and took out a match, but apparently altering his mind, laid it down and commenced. "The unfortunate affair which has brought you here to-night, had its origin ten years ago. At that time my friend Hurst became suddenly involved in financial difficulties – am I speaking too fast for you, Mr. Badger?"

"No, not at all," replied Badger. "I am taking it down in shorthand."

"Thank you," said Mr. Jellicoe. "He became involved in serious difficulties and came to me for assistance. He wished to borrow five-thousand pounds to enable him to meet his engagements. I had a certain amount of money at my disposal, but I did not consider Hurst's security satisfactory. Accordingly I felt compelled to refuse. But on the very next day, John Bellingham called on me with a draft of his will which he wished me to look over before it was executed.

"It was an absurd will, and I nearly told him so, but then an idea occurred to me in connection with Hurst. It was obvious to me, as soon as I glanced through the will, that, if the burial clause was left as the testator had drafted it, Hurst had a very good chance of inheriting the property, and, as I was named as the executor I should be able to give full effect to that clause. Accordingly, I asked for a few days to consider the will, and then I called upon Hurst and made a proposal to him, which was this: That I should advance him five-thousand pounds without security. That I should ask for no repayment, but that he should assign to me any interest that he might have or acquire in the estate of John Bellingham up to ten-thousand pounds, or two-thirds of any sum that he might inherit if over that amount. He asked if John had yet made any will, and I replied, quite correctly, that he had not. He inquired if I knew what testamentary arrangements John intended to make, and again I answered, quite correctly, that I believed John proposed to devise the bulk of his property to his brother, Godfrey.

"Thereupon, Hurst accepted my proposal. I made him the advance and he executed the assignment. After a few days' delay, I passed the will as satisfactory. The actual document was written from the draft by the testator himself, and a fortnight after Hurst had executed the assignment, John signed the will in my office. By the provisions of that will I stood an excellent chance of becoming virtually the principal beneficiary, unless Godfrey should contest Hurst's claim and the Court should override the conditions of Clause Two.

"You will now understand the motives which governed my subsequent actions. You will also see, Doctor Thorndyke, how very near to the truth your reasoning carried you, and you will understand, as I wish you to do, that Mr. Hurst was no party to any of these proceedings which I am about to describe.

"Coming now to the interview in Queen Square in October, Nineteen-hundred-and-two, you are aware of the general circumstances from my evidence in Court, which was literally correct up to a certain point. The interview took place in a room on the third floor, in which were stored the cases which John had brought with him from Egypt. The mummy was unpacked, as were some other objects that he was not offering to the Museum, but several cases were still unopened. At the conclusion of the interview I accompanied Doctor Norbury down to the street door, and we stood on the doorstep conversing for perhaps a quarter-of-an-hour. Then Doctor Norbury went away and I returned upstairs.

"Now the house in Queen Square is virtually a museum. The upper part is separated from the lower by a massive door which opens from the hall and gives access to the staircase and which is fitted with a Chubb night-latch. There are two latch-keys, of which John used to keep one and I the other. You will find them both in the safe behind me. The caretaker had no key and no access to the upper part of the house unless admitted by one of us.

"At the time when I came in, after Doctor Norbury had left, the caretaker was in the cellar, where I could hear him breaking coke for the hot-water furnace. I had left John on the third floor opening some of the packing-cases by the light of a lamp with a tool somewhat like a plasterer's hammer. That is, a hammer with a small axe-blade at the reverse of the head. As I stood talking to Doctor Norbury, I could hear him knocking out the nails and wrenching up the lids, and when I entered the doorway leading to the stairs, I could still hear him. Just as I closed the staircase door behind me, I heard a rumbling noise from above. Then all was still.

"I went up the stairs to the second floor, where, as the staircase was all in darkness, I stopped to light the gas. As I turned to ascend the next flight, I saw a hand projecting over the edge of the halfway landing. I ran up the stairs, and there, on the landing, I saw John lying huddled up in a heap at the foot of the top flight. There was a wound at the side of his forehead from which a little blood was trickling. The case-opener lay on the floor close by him and there was blood on the axe-blade. When I looked up the stairs I saw a rag of torn matting over the top stair.

"It was quite easy to see what had happened. He had walked quickly out on the landing with the case-opener in his hand. His foot had caught in the torn matting and he had pitched head foremost down the stairs still holding the case-opener. He had fallen so that his head had come down on the upturned edge of the axe-blade. He had then rolled over and the case-opener had dropped from his hand.

"I lit a wax match and stooped down to look at him. His head was in a very peculiar position, which made me suspect that his neck was broken. There was extremely little bleeding from the wound. He was perfectly motionless. I could detect no sign of breathing, and I felt no doubt that he was dead.

"It was an exceedingly regrettable affair, and it placed me, as I perceived at once, in an extremely awkward position. My first impulse was to send the caretaker for a doctor and a policeman, but a moment's reflection convinced me that there were serious objections to this course.

"There was nothing to show that I had not, myself, knocked him down with the case-opener. Of course, there was nothing to show that I had, but we were alone in the house with the exception of the caretaker, who was down in the basement out of earshot.

"There would be an inquest. At the inquest inquiries would be made as to the will which was known to exist. But as soon as the will was produced, Hurst would become suspicious. He would probably make a statement to the coroner and I should be charged with the murder. Or, even if I were not charged, Hurst would suspect me and would probably repudiate the assignment, and, under the circumstances, it would be practically impossible for me to enforce it. He would refuse to pay and I could not take my claim into Court.

"I sat down on the stairs just above poor John's body and considered the matter in detail. At the worst, I stood a fair chance of hanging. At the best, I stood to lose close upon fifty-thousand pounds. These were not pleasant alternatives.

"Supposing, on the other hand, I concealed the body and gave out that John had gone to Paris. There was, of course, the risk of discovery, in which case I should certainly be convicted of the murder. But if no discovery occurred, I was not only safe from suspicion, but I secured the fifty-thousand pounds. In either case there was considerable risk, but in one there was the certainty of loss, whereas in the other there was a material advantage to justify the risk. The question was whether it would be possible to conceal the body. If it were, then the contingent profit was

419

worth the slight additional risk. But a human body is a very difficult thing to dispose of, especially by a person of so little scientific culture as myself.

"It is curious that I considered this question for a quite considerable time before the obvious solution presented itself. I turned over at least a dozen methods of disposing of the body, and rejected them all as impracticable. Then, suddenly, I remembered the mummy upstairs.

"At first it only occurred to me as a fantastic possibility that I could conceal the body in the mummy-case. But as I turned over the idea I began to see that it was really practicable, and not only practicable but easy, and not only easy but eminently safe. If once the mummy-case was in the Museum, I was rid of it forever.

"The circumstances were, as you, sir, have justly observed, singularly favorable. There would be no hue and cry, no hurry, no anxiety, but ample time for all the necessary preparations. Then the mummy-case itself was curiously suitable. Its length was ample, as I knew from having measured it. It was a cartonnage of rather flexible material and had an opening behind, secured with a lacing so that it could be opened without injury. Nothing need be cut but the lacing, which could be replaced. A little damage might be done in extracting the mummy and in introducing the deceased, but such cracks as might occur would be of no importance. For here again Fortune favored me. The whole of the back of the mummy-case was coated with bitumen, and it would be easy when once the deceased was safely inside to apply a fresh coat, which would cover up not only the cracks but also the new lacing.

"After careful consideration, I decided to adopt the plan. I went downstairs and sent the caretaker on an errand to the Law Courts. Then I returned and carried the deceased up to one of the third-floor rooms, where I removed his clothes and laid him out on a long packing-case in the position in which he would lie in the mummy-case. I folded his clothes neatly and packed them, with the exception of his boots, in a suit-case that he had been taking to Paris and which contained nothing but his nightclothes, toilet articles, and a change of linen. By the time I had done this and thoroughly washed the oilcloth on the stairs and landing, the caretaker had returned. I informed him that Mr. Bellingham had started for Paris and then I went home. The upper part of the house was, of course, secured by the Chubb lock, but I had also – *ex abundantiâ cautelae* – locked the door of the room in which I had deposited the deceased.

"I had, of course, some knowledge of the methods of embalming, but principally of those employed by the ancients. Hence, on the following day, I went to the British Museum library and consulted the most recent works on the subject, and exceedingly interesting they were, as showing the remarkable improvements that modern knowledge has effected in this

420

ancient art. I need not trouble you with details that are familiar to you. The process that I selected as the simplest for a beginner was that of formalin injection, and I went straight from the Museum to purchase the necessary materials. I did not, however, buy an embalming syringe: The book stated that an ordinary anatomical injecting syringe would answer the same purpose, and I thought it a more discreet purchase.

"I fear that I bungled the injection terribly, although I had carefully studied the plates in a treatise on anatomy – *Gray's*, I think. However, if my methods were clumsy, they were quite effectual. I carried out the process on the evening of the third day, and when I locked up the house that night, I had the satisfaction of knowing that poor John's remains were secure from corruption and decay.

"But this was not enough. The great weight of a fresh body as compared with that of a mummy would be immediately noticed by those who had the handling of the mummy-case. Moreover, the damp from the body would quickly ruin the cartonnage and would cause a steamy film on the inside of the glass case in which it would be exhibited. And this would probably lead to an examination. Clearly, then, it was necessary that the remains of the deceased should be thoroughly dried before they were enclosed in the cartonnage.

"Here my unfortunate deficiency in scientific knowledge was a great drawback. I had no idea how this result would be achieved and, in the end, was compelled to consult a taxidermist, to whom I represented that I wished to collect some small animals and reptiles and rapidly dry them for convenience of transport. By this person I was advised to immerse the dead animals in a jar of methylated spirit for a week and then expose them in a current of warm, dry air.

"But the plan of immersing the remains of the deceased in a jar of methylated spirit was obviously impracticable. However, I bethought me that we had in our collection a porphyry sarcophagus, the cavity of which had been shaped to receive a small mummy in its case. I tried the deceased in the sarcophagus and found that he just fitted the cavity loosely. I obtained a few gallons of methylated spirit, which I poured into the cavity, just covering the body, and then I put on the lid and luted it down air-tight with putty. I trust I do not weary you with these particulars?"

"I'll ask you to cut it as short as you can, Mr. Jellicoe," said Badger. "It has been a long yarn and time is running on."

"For my part," said Thorndyke, "I find these details deeply interesting and instructive. They fill in the outline that I had drawn by inference."

"Precisely," said Mr. Jellicoe. "Then I will proceed."

"I left the deceased soaking in the spirit for a fortnight and then took him out, wiped him dry, and laid him on four cane-bottomed chairs just over the hot-water pipes, and I let a free current of air pass through the room. The result interested me exceedingly. By the end of the third day the hands and feet had become quite dry and shriveled and horny – so that the ring actually dropped off the shrunken finger – the nose looked like a fold of parchment, and the skin of the body was so dry and smooth that you could have engrossed a lease on it. For the first day or two I turned the deceased at intervals so that he should dry evenly, and then I proceeded to get the case ready. I divided the lacing and extracted the mummy with great care – with great care as to the case, I mean, for the mummy suffered some injury in the extraction. It was very badly embalmed, and so brittle that it broke in several places while I was getting it out, and when I unrolled it the head separated and both the arms came off.

"On the sixth day after the removal from the sarcophagus, I took the bandages that I had removed from Sebek-hotep and very carefully wrapped the deceased in them, sprinkling powdered myrrh and gum benzoin freely on the body and between the folds of the wrappings to disguise the faint odor of the spirit and the formalin that still lingered about the body. When the wrappings had been applied, the deceased really had a most workmanlike appearance. He would have looked quite well in a glass case even without the cartonnage, and I felt almost regretful at having to put him out of sight forever.

"It was a difficult business getting him into the case without assistance, and I cracked the cartonnage badly in several places before he was safely enclosed. But I got him in at last, and then, when I had closed up the case with a new lacing, I applied a fresh layer of bitumen which effectually covered up the cracks and the new cord. A dusty cloth dabbed over the bitumen when it was dry disguised its newness, and the cartonnage with its tenant was ready for delivery. I notified Doctor Norbury of the fact, and five days later he came and removed it to the Museum.

"Now that the main difficulty was disposed of, I began to consider the further difficulty to which you, sir, have alluded with such admirable perspicuity. It was necessary that John Bellingham should make one more appearance in public before sinking into final oblivion.

"Accordingly, I devised the visit to Hurst's house, which was calculated to serve two purposes. It created a satisfactory date for the disappearance, eliminating me from any connection with it, and by throwing some suspicion on Hurst it would make him more amenable – less likely to dispute my claim when he learned the provisions of the will.

"The affair was quite simple. I knew that Hurst had changed his servants since I was last at his house, and I knew his habits. On that day I took the suitcase to Charing Cross and deposited it in the cloakroom, called at Hurst's office to make sure that he was there, and went from thence direct to Cannon Street and caught the train to Eltham. On arriving at the house, I took the precaution to remove my spectacles – the only distinctive feature of my exterior – and was duly shown into the study at my request. As soon as the housemaid had left the room I quietly let myself out by the French window, which I closed behind me but could not fasten, went out at the side gate and closed that also behind me, holding the bolt of the latch back with my pocket-knife so that I need not slam the gate to shut it.

"The other events of that day, including the dropping of the scarab, I need not describe, as they are known to you. But I may fitly make a few remarks on the unfortunate tactical error into which I fell in respect of the bones. That error arose, as you have doubtless perceived, from the lawyer's incurable habit of underestimating the scientific expert. I had no idea mere bones were capable of furnishing so much information to a man of science.

"The way in which the affair came about was this: The damaged mummy of Sebek-hotep, perishing gradually by exposure to the air, was not only an eyesore to me – it was a definite danger. It was the only remaining link between me and the disappearance. I resolved to be rid of it and cast about for some means of destroying it. And then, in an evil moment, the idea of utilizing it occurred to me.

"There was an undoubted danger that the Court might refuse to presume death after so short an interval, and if the permission should be postponed, the will might never be administered during my lifetime. Hence, if these bones of Sebek-hotep could be made to simulate the remains of the deceased testator, a definite good would be achieved. But I knew that the entire skeleton could never be mistaken for his. The deceased had broken his knee-caps and damaged his ankle, injuries which I assumed would leave some permanent trace. But if a judicious selection of the bones were deposited in a suitable place, together with some object clearly identifiable as appertaining to the deceased, it seemed to me that the difficulty would be met. I need not trouble you with details. The course which I adopted is known to you with the attendant circumstances, even the accidental detachment of the right hand – which broke off as I was packing the arm in my handbag. Erroneous as that course was, it would have been successful but for the unforeseen contingency of your being retained in the case.

"Thus, for nearly two years, I remained in complete security. From time to time I dropped in at the Museum to see if the deceased was keeping in good condition, and on those occasions I used to reflect with satisfaction on the gratifying circumstance – accidental though it was – that his wishes, as expressed (very imperfectly) in Clause Two, had been fully complied with, and that without prejudice to my interests.

"The awakening came on that evening when I saw you at the Temple gate talking with Doctor Berkeley. I suspected immediately that something was gone amiss and that it was too late to take any useful action. Since then, I have waited here in hourly expectation of this visit. And now the time has come. You have made the winning move and it remains only for me to pay my debts like an honest gambler."

He paused and quietly lit his cigarette. Inspector Badger yawned and put away his notebook.

"Have you done, Mr. Jellicoe?" the inspector asked. "I want to carry out my contract to the letter, you know, though it's getting devilish late."

Mr. Jellicoe took his cigarette from his mouth and drank a glass of water.

"I forgot to ask," he said, "whether you unrolled the mummy – if I may apply the term to the imperfectly treated remains of my deceased client."

"I did not open the mummy-case," replied Thorndyke.

"You did not!" exclaimed Mr. Jellicoe. "Then how did you verify your suspicions?"

"I took an X-ray photograph."

"Ah! Indeed!" Mr. Jellicoe pondered for some moments. "Astonishing!" he murmured, "and most ingenious. The resources of science at the present day are truly wonderful."

"Is there anything more that you want to say?" asked Badger, "because if you don't, time's up."

"Anything more?" Mr. Jellicoe repeated slowly, "anything more? No – I – think – think – the time – is – up. Yes – the – the – time – "

He broke off and sat with a strange look fixed on Thorndyke.

His face had suddenly undergone a curious change. It looked shrunken and cadaverous and his lips had assumed a peculiar cherry-red color.

"Is anything the matter, Mr. Jellicoe?" Badger asked uneasily. "Are you not feeling well, sir?"

Mr. Jellicoe did not appear to have heard the question, for he returned no answer, but sat motionless, leaning back in his chair, with his hands spread out on the table and his strangely intent gaze bent on Thorndyke.

Suddenly his head dropped on his breast and his body seemed to collapse, and as with one accord we sprang to our feet, he slid forward off his chair and disappeared under the table.

"Good Lord! The man's fainted!" exclaimed Badger. In a moment he was down on his hands and knees, trembling with excitement, groping under the table. He dragged the unconscious lawyer out into the light and knelt over him, staring into his face.

"What's the matter with him, Doctor?" he asked, looking up at Thorndyke. "Is it apoplexy? Or is it a heart attack, think you?"

Thorndyke shook his head, though he stooped and put his fingers on the unconscious man's wrist.

"Prussic acid or potassium cyanide is what the appearances suggest," he replied.

"But can't you do anything?" demanded the inspector.

Thorndyke dropped the arm, which fell limply to the floor.

"You can't do much for a dead man," he said.

"Dead! Then he has slipped through our fingers after all!"

"He has anticipated the sentence. That is all." Thorndyke spoke in an even, impassive tone which struck me as rather strange, considering the suddenness of the tragedy, as did also the complete absence of surprize in his manner. He seemed to treat the occurrence as a perfectly natural one.

Not so Inspector Badger, who rose to his feet and stood with his hands thrust into his pockets scowling sullenly down at the dead lawyer.

"I was an infernal fool to agree to his blasted conditions," he growled savagely.

"Nonsense," said Thorndyke. "If you had broken in you would have found a dead man. As it was you found a live man and obtained an important statement. You acted quite properly."

"How do you suppose he managed it?" asked Badger.

Thorndyke held out his hand.

"Let us look at his cigarette case," said he.

Badger extracted the little silver case from the dead man's pocket and opened it. There were five cigarettes in it, two of which were plain, while the other three were gold-tipped. Thorndyke took out one of each kind and gently pinched their ends. The gold-tipped one he returned. The plain one he tore through, about a quarter-of-an-inch from the end, when two little black tabloids dropped out on to the table. Badger eagerly picked one up and was about to smell it when Thorndyke grasped his wrist. "Be careful," said he, and when he had cautiously sniffed at the tabloid – held at a safe distance from his nose – he added, "Yes, potassium cyanide. I thought so when his lips turned that queer color. It was in that last cigarette. You can see that he has bitten the end off."

For some time we stood silently looking down at the still form stretched on the floor. Presently Badger looked up.

"As you pass the porter's lodge on your way out," said he, "you might just drop in and tell him to send a constable to me."

425

"Very well," said Thorndyke. "And by the way, Badger, you had better tip that sherry back into the decanter and put it under lock and key, or else pour it out of the window."

"Gad, yes!" exclaimed the inspector. "I'm glad you mentioned it. We might have had an inquest on a constable as well as a lawyer. Good-night, gentlemen, if you are off."

We went out and left him with his prisoner – passive enough, indeed, according to his ambiguously worded promise. As we passed through the gateway Thorndyke gave the inspector's message, curtly and without comment, to the gaping porter, and then we issued forth into Chancery Lane.

We were all silent and very grave, and I thought that Thorndyke seemed somewhat moved. Perhaps Mr. Jellicoe's last intent look – which I suspect he knew to be the look of a dying man – lingered in his memory as it did in mine. Halfway down Chancery Lane he spoke for the first time, and then it was only to ejaculate, "Poor devil!"

Jervis took him up. "He was a consummate villain, Thorndyke."

"Hardly that," was the reply. "I should rather say that he was non-moral. He acted without malice and without scruple or remorse. His conduct exhibited a passionateless expediency which was dreadful because utterly unhuman. But he was a strong man – a courageous, self-contained man, and I had been better pleased if it could have been ordained that some other hand than mine should let the axe fall."

Thorndyke's compunction may appear strange and inconsistent, but yet his feeling was also my own. Great as was the misery and suffering that this inscrutable man had brought into the lives of those I loved, I forgave him, and in his downfall forgot the callous relentlessness with which he had pursued his evil purpose. For it was he who had brought Ruth into my life, who had opened for me the Paradise of Love into which I had just entered. And so my thoughts turned away from the still shape that lay on the floor of the stately old room in Lincoln's Inn, away to the sunny vista of the future, where I should walk hand in hand with Ruth until my time, too, should come – until I, too, like the grim lawyer, should hear the solemn evening bell bidding me put out into the darkness of the silent sea.

426

1930 Dodd, Mead Reprint Cover

To my friend, Bernard E. Bishop

Editor's Note

The Mystery of 31 New Inn *(1912) – sometimes written as* 31, New Inn, *originally appeared as the similarly named novella* "31 New Inn" *in 1905. (The original shorter version appears in Volume II of these new editions.) The novella was actually the first Dr. Thorndyke adventure published, appearing two years before* The Red Thumb Mark *(1907).*

In spite of being published as the third Thorndyke novel, following The Eye of Osiris *(1911), this narrative actually takes place before* The Eye. *It occurs in the spring of 1902, about a year after the spring 1901 events of* The Red Thumb Mark. *In spite of the skewed chronology, the books are presented here in their publication order.*

Preface

C*ommenting upon one of my earlier novels, in respect of which I had claimed to have been careful to adhere to common probabilities and to have made use only of really practicable methods of investigation, a critic remarked that this was of no consequence whatever, so long as the story was amusing.*

Few people, I imagine, will agree with him. To most readers, and certainly to the kind of reader for whom an author is willing to take trouble, complete realism in respect of incidents and methods is an essential factor in maintaining the interest of a detective story. Hence it may be worthwhile to mention that Thorndyke's method of producing the track chart, described in Chapters II and III, has been actually used in practice. It is a modification of one devised by me many years ago when I was crossing Ashanti to the city of Bontuku, the whereabouts of which in the far interior was then only vaguely known. My instructions were to fix the positions of all towns, villages, rivers, and mountains as accurately as possible, but finding ordinary methods of surveying impracticable in the dense forest which covers the whole region, I adopted this simple and apparently rude method, checking the distances whenever possible by astronomical observation.

The resulting route-map was surprisingly accurate, as shown by the agreement of the outward and homeward tracks. It was published by the Royal Geographical Society, and incorporated in the map of this region compiled by the Intelligence Branch of the War Office, and it formed the basis of the map which accompanied my volume of Travels in Ashanti and Jaman. *So that Thorndyke's plan must be taken as quite a practicable one.*

New Inn, the background of this story, and one of the last surviving inns of Chancery, has recently passed away after upwards of four centuries of newness. Even now, however, a few of the old, dismantled houses (including perhaps, the mysterious 31) may be seen from the Strand peeping over the iron roof of the skating rink which has displaced the picturesque hall, the pension-room, and the garden. The postern gate, too, in Houghton Street still remains, though the arch is bricked up inside. Passing it lately, I made the rough sketch which appears on next page, and which shows all that is left of this pleasant old London backwater.

R. A. F., Gravesend

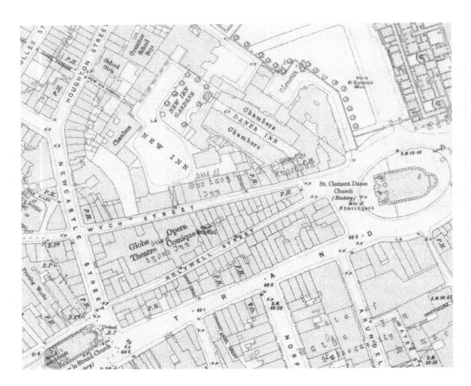

New Inn, London

Chapter I
The Mysterious Patient

As I look back through the years of my association with John Thorndyke, I am able to recall a wealth of adventures and strange experiences such as falls to the lot of very few men who pass their lives within hearing of Big Ben. Many of these experiences I have already placed on record, but it now occurs to me that I have hitherto left unrecorded one that is, perhaps, the most astonishing and incredible of the whole series, an adventure, too, that has for me the added interest that it inaugurated my permanent association with my learned and talented friend, and marked the close of a rather unhappy and unprosperous period of my life.

Memory, retracing the journey through the passing years to the starting-point of those strange events, lands me in a shabby little ground-floor room in a house near the Walworth end of Lower Kennington Lane. A couple of framed diplomas on the wall, a card of Snellen's test-types, and a stethoscope lying on the writing-table, proclaim it a doctor's consulting-room, and my own position in the round-backed chair at the said table, proclaims me the practitioner in charge.

It was nearly nine o'clock. The noisy little clock on the mantelpiece announced the fact, and, by its frantic ticking, seemed as anxious as I to get the consultation hours over. I glanced wistfully at my mud-splashed boots and wondered if I might yet venture to assume the slippers that peeped coyly from under the shabby sofa. I even allowed my thoughts to wander to the pipe that reposed in my coat pocket. Another minute and I could turn down the surgery gas and shut the outer door. The fussy little clock gave a sort of preliminary cough or hiccup, as if it should say: "Ahem! Ladies and gentlemen, I am about to strike." And at that moment, the bottle-boy opened the door and, thrusting in his head, uttered the one word: "Gentleman."

Extreme economy of words is apt to result in ambiguity. But I understood. In Kennington Lane, the race of mere men and women appeared to be extinct. They were all gentlemen – unless they were ladies or children – even as the Liberian army was said to consist entirely of generals. Sweeps, labourers, milkmen, costermongers – all were impartially invested by the democratic bottle-boy with the rank and title of *armigeri*. The present nobleman appeared to favour the aristocratic recreation of driving a cab or job-master's carriage, and, as he entered the room, he touched his hat, closed the door somewhat carefully, and then, without remark, handed me a note which bore the superscription "Dr. Stillbury."

"You understand," I said, as I prepared to open the envelope, "that I am not Dr. Stillbury. He is away at present and I am looking after his patients."

"It doesn't signify," the man replied. "You'll do as well."

On this, I opened the envelope and read the note, which was quite brief, and, at first sight, in no way remarkable.

Dear Sir, (it ran)

Would you kindly come and see a friend of mine who is staying with me? The bearer of this will give you further particulars and convey you to the house.

Yours truly,
H. Weiss

There was no address on the paper and no date, and the writer was unknown to me.

"This note," I said, "refers to some further particulars. What are they?"

The messenger passed his hand over his hair with a gesture of embarrassment. "It's a ridicklus affair," he said, with a contemptuous laugh. "If I had been Mr. Weiss, I wouldn't have had nothing to do with it. The sick gentleman, Mr. Graves, is one of them people what can't abear doctors. He's been ailing now for a week or two, but nothing would induce him to see a doctor. Mr. Weiss did everything he could to persuade him, but it was no go. He wouldn't. However, it seems Mr. Weiss threatened to send for a medical man on his own account, because, you see, he was getting a bit nervous, and then Mr. Graves gave way. But only on one condition. He said the doctor was to come from a distance and was not to be told who he was or where he lived or anything about him, and he made Mr. Weiss promise to keep to that condition before he'd let him send. So Mr. Weiss promised, and, of course, he's got to keep his word."

"But," I said, with a smile, "you've just told me his name – if his name really is Graves."

"You can form your own opinion on that," said the coachman.

"And," I added, "as to not being told where he lives, I can see that for myself. I'm not blind, you know."

"We'll take the risk of what you see," the man replied. "The question is, will you take the job on?"

Yes, that was the question, and I considered it for some time before replying. We medical men are pretty familiar with the kind of person who "can't abear doctors," and we like to have as little to do with him as possible. He is a thankless and unsatisfactory patient. Intercourse with him is unpleasant, he gives a great deal of trouble, and responds badly to treatment. If this had been my own practice, I should have declined the case off-hand. But it was not my practice. I was only a deputy. I could not lightly refuse work which would yield a profit to my principal, unpleasant though it might be.

As I turned the matter over in my mind, I half-unconsciously scrutinized my visitor – somewhat to his embarrassment – and I liked his appearance as little as I liked his mission. He kept his station near the door, where the light was dim – for the illumination was concentrated on the table and the patient's chair – but I could see that he had a somewhat sly, unprepossessing face and a greasy, red moustache that seemed out of character with his rather perfunctory livery, though this was mere prejudice. He wore a wig, too – not that there was anything discreditable in that – and the thumb-nail of the hand that held his hat bore disfiguring traces of some injury – which, again, though unsightly, in no wise reflected on his moral character. Lastly, he watched me keenly with a mixture of anxiety and sly complacency that I found distinctly unpleasant. In a general way, he impressed me disagreeably. I did not like the look of him at all, but nevertheless I decided to undertake the case.

"I suppose," I answered, at length, "it is no affair of mine who the patient is or where he lives. But how do you propose to manage the business? Am I to be led to the house blindfolded, like the visitor to the bandit's cave?"

The man grinned slightly and looked very decidedly relieved.

"No, sir," he answered, "we ain't going to blindfold you. I've got a carriage outside. I don't think you'll see much out of that."

"Very well," I rejoined, opening the door to let him out, "I'll be with you in a minute. I suppose you can't give me any idea as to what is the matter with the patient?"

"No, sir, I can't," he replied, and he went out to see to the carriage.

I slipped into a bag an assortment of emergency drugs and a few diagnostic instruments, turned down the gas and passed out through the surgery. The carriage was standing at the kerb, guarded by the coachman and watched with deep interest by the bottle-boy. I viewed it with mingled curiosity and disfavour. It was a kind of large brougham, such as is used by some commercial travellers, the usual glass windows being replaced by

439

wooden shutters intended to conceal the piles of sample-boxes, and the doors capable of being locked from outside with a railway key.

As I emerged from the house, the coachman unlocked the door and held it open.

"How long will the journey take?" I asked, pausing with my foot on the step.

The coachman considered a moment or two and replied, "It took me, I should say, nigh upon half-an-hour to get here."

This was pleasant hearing. A half-an-hour each way and a half-an-hour at the patient's house. At that rate it would be half-past ten before I was home again, and then it was quite probable that I should find some other untimely messenger waiting on the doorstep. With a muttered anathema on the unknown Mr. Graves and the unrestful life of a *locum tenens*, I stepped into the uninviting vehicle. Instantly the coachman slammed the door and turned the key, leaving me in total darkness.

One comfort was left to me – My pipe was in my pocket. I made shift to load it in the dark, and, having lit it with a wax match, took the opportunity to inspect the interior of my prison. It was a shabby affair. The moth-eaten state of the blue cloth cushions seemed to suggest that it had been long out of regular use, the oil-cloth floor-covering was worn into holes, ordinary internal fittings there were none. But the appearances suggested that the crazy vehicle had been prepared with considerable forethought for its present use. The inside handles of the doors had apparently been removed, the wooden shutters were permanently fixed in their places, and a paper label, stuck on the transom below each window, had a suspicious appearance of having been put there to cover the painted name and address of the job-master or livery-stable keeper who had originally owned the carriage.

These observations gave me abundant food for reflection. This Mr. Weiss must be an excessively conscientious man if he had considered that his promise to Mr. Graves committed him to such extraordinary precautions. Evidently no mere following of the letter of the law was enough to satisfy his sensitive conscience. Unless he had reasons for sharing Mr. Graves's unreasonable desire for secrecy – for one could not suppose that these measures of concealment had been taken by the patient himself.

The further suggestions that evolved themselves from this consideration were a little disquieting. Whither was I being carried and for what purpose? The idea that I was bound for some den of thieves where I might be robbed and possibly murdered, I dismissed with a smile. Thieves do not make elaborately concerted plans to rob poor devils like me. Poverty has its compensations in that respect. But there were other possibilities. Imagination backed by experience had no difficulty in conjuring up a number of situations in which a medical man might be called upon, with or without coercion, either to witness or actively to participate in the commission of some unlawful act.

Reflections of this kind occupied me pretty actively if not very agreeably during this strange journey. And the monotony was relieved, too, by other distractions. I was, for example, greatly interested to notice how, when one sense is in abeyance, the other senses rouse into a compensating intensity of perception. I sat smoking my pipe in darkness which was absolute save for the dim glow from the smouldering tobacco in the bowl, and seemed to be cut off from all knowledge of the world without. But yet I was not. The vibrations of the carriage, with its hard springs and iron-tired wheels, registered accurately and plainly the character of the roadway. The harsh rattle of granite setts, the soft bumpiness of macadam, the smooth rumble of wood-pavement, the jarring and swerving of crossed tram-lines, all were easily recognizable and together sketched the general features of the neighbourhood through which I was passing. And the sense of hearing filled in the details. Now the hoot of a tug's whistle told of proximity to the river. A sudden and brief hollow reverberation announced the passage under a railway arch (which, by the way, happened several times during the journey), and, when I heard the familiar whistle of a railway-guard followed by the quick snorts of a skidding locomotive, I had as clear a picture of a heavy passenger-train moving out of a station as if I had seen it in broad daylight.

I had just finished my pipe and knocked out the ashes on the heel of my boot, when the carriage slowed down and entered a covered way – as I could tell by the hollow echoes. Then I distinguished the clang of heavy wooden gates closed behind me, and a moment or two later the carriage door was unlocked and opened. I stepped out blinking into a covered passage paved with cobbles and apparently leading down to a mews, but it was all in darkness, and I had no time to make any detailed observations, as the carriage had drawn up opposite a side door which was open and in which stood a woman holding a lighted candle.

"Is that the doctor?" she asked, speaking with a rather pronounced German accent and shading the candle with her hand as she peered at me.

I answered in the affirmative, and she then exclaimed, "I am glad you have come. Mr. Weiss will be so relieved. Come in, please."

I followed her across a dark passage into a dark room, where she set the candle down on a chest of drawers and turned to depart. At the door, however, she paused and looked back.

441

"It is not a very nice room to ask you into," she said. "We are very untidy just now, but you must excuse us. We have had so much anxiety about poor Mr. Graves."

"He has been ill some time, then?"

"Yes. Some little time. At intervals, you know. Sometimes better, sometimes not so well."

As she spoke, she gradually backed out into the passage but did not go away at once. I accordingly pursued my inquiries.

"He has not been seen by any doctor, has he?"

"No," she answered, "he has always refused to see a doctor. That has been a great trouble to us. Mr. Weiss has been very anxious about him. He will be so glad to hear that you have come. I had better go and tell him. Perhaps you will kindly sit down until he is able to come to you," and with this she departed on her mission.

It struck me as a little odd that, considering his anxiety and the apparent urgency of the case, Mr. Weiss should not have been waiting to receive me. And when several minutes elapsed without his appearing, the oddness of the circumstance impressed me still more. Having no desire, after the journey in the carriage, to sit down, I whiled away the time by an inspection of the room. And a very curious room it was: Bare, dirty, neglected and, apparently, unused. A faded carpet had been flung untidily on the floor. A small, shabby table stood in the middle of the room, and beyond this, three horsehair-covered chairs and a chest of drawers formed the entire set of furniture. No pictures hung on the mouldy walls, no curtains covered the shuttered windows, and the dark drapery of cobwebs that hung from the ceiling to commemorate a long and illustrious dynasty of spiders hinted at months of neglect and disuse.

The chest of drawers – an incongruous article of furniture for what seemed to be a dining-room – as being the nearest and best lighted object received most of my attention. It was a fine old chest of nearly black mahogany, very battered and in the last stage of decay, but originally a piece of some pretensions. Regretful of its fallen estate, I looked it over with some interest and had just observed on its lower corner a little label bearing the printed inscription "Lot 201" when I heard footsteps descending the stairs. A moment later the door opened and a shadowy figure appeared standing close by the threshold.

"Good evening, Doctor," said the stranger, in a deep, quiet voice and with a distinct, though not strong, German accent. "I must apologize for keeping you waiting."

I acknowledged the apology somewhat stiffly and asked, "You are Mr. Weiss, I presume?"

"Yes, I am Mr. Weiss. It is very good of you to come so far and so late at night and to make no objection to the absurd conditions that my poor friend has imposed."

"Not at all," I replied. "It is my business to go when and where I am wanted, and it is not my business to inquire into the private affairs of my patients."

"That is very true, sir," he agreed cordially, "and I am much obliged to you for taking that very proper view of the case. I pointed that out to my friend, but he is not a very reasonable man. He is very secretive and rather suspicious by nature."

"So I inferred. And as to his condition, is he seriously ill?"

"Ah," said Mr. Weiss, "that is what I want you to tell me. I am very much puzzled about him."

"But what is the nature of his illness? What does he complain of?"

"He makes very few complaints of any kind although he is obviously ill. But the fact is that he is hardly ever more than half-awake. He lies in a kind of dreamy stupor from morning to night."

This struck me as excessively strange and by no means in agreement with the patient's energetic refusal to see a doctor.

"But," I asked, "does he never rouse completely?"

"Oh, yes," Mr. Weiss answered quickly, "he rouses from time to time and is then quite rational, and, as you may have gathered, rather obstinate. That is the peculiar and puzzling feature in the case, this alternation between a state of stupor and an almost normal and healthy condition. But perhaps you had better see him and judge for yourself. He had a rather severe attack just now. Follow me, please. The stairs are rather dark."

The stairs were very dark, and I noticed that they were without any covering of carpet, or even oil-cloth, so that our footsteps resounded dismally as if we were in an empty house. I stumbled up after my guide, feeling my way by the hand-rail, and on the first floor followed him into a room similar in size to the one below and very barely furnished, though less squalid than the other. A single candle at the farther end threw its feeble light on a figure in the bed, leaving the rest of the room in a dim twilight.

As Mr. Weiss tiptoed into the chamber, a woman – the one who had spoken to me below – rose from a chair by the bedside and quietly left the room by a second door. My conductor halted, and looking fixedly at the figure in the bed, called out, "Philip! Philip! Here is the doctor come to see you."

He paused for a moment or two, and, receiving no answer, said, "He seems to be dozing as usual. Will you go and see what you can make of him?"

I stepped forward to the bedside, leaving Mr. Weiss at the end of the room near the door by which we had entered, where he remained, slowly and noiselessly pacing backwards and forwards in the semi-obscurity. By the light of the candle I saw an elderly man with good features and a refined, intelligent and even attractive face, but dreadfully emaciated, bloodless and sallow. He lay quite motionless except for the scarcely perceptible rise and fall of his chest, his eyes were nearly closed, his features relaxed, and, though he was not actually asleep, he seemed to be in a dreamy, somnolent, lethargic state, as if under the influence of some narcotic.

I watched him for a minute or so, timing his slow breathing by my watch, and then suddenly and sharply addressed him by name, but the only response was a slight lifting of the eyelids, which, after a brief, drowsy glance at me, slowly subsided to their former position.

I now proceeded to make a physical examination. First, I felt his pulse, grasping his wrist with intentional brusqueness in the hope of rousing him from his stupor. The beats were slow, feeble, and slightly irregular, giving clear evidence, if any were needed, of his generally lowered vitality. I listened carefully to his heart, the sounds of which were very distinct through the thin walls of his emaciated chest, but found nothing abnormal beyond the feebleness and uncertainty of its action. Then I turned my attention to his eyes, which I examined closely with the aid of the candle and my ophthalmoscope lens, raising the lids somewhat roughly so as to expose the whole of the irises. He submitted without resistance to my rather ungentle handling of these sensitive structures, and showed no signs of discomfort even when I brought the candle-flame to within a couple of inches of his eyes.

But this extraordinary tolerance of light was easily explained by closer examination, for the pupils were contracted to such an extreme degree that only the very minutest point of black was visible at the centre of the grey iris. Nor was this the only abnormal peculiarity of the sick man's eyes. As he lay on his back, the right iris sagged down slightly towards its centre, showing a distinctly concave surface, and, when I contrived to produce a slight but quick movement of the eyeball, a perceptible undulatory movement could be detected. The patient had, in fact, what is known as a tremulous iris, a condition that is seen in cases where the crystalline lens has been extracted for the cure of cataract, or where it has become accidentally displaced, leaving the iris unsupported. In the present case, the complete condition of the iris made it clear that the ordinary extraction operation had not been performed, nor was I able, on the closest inspection with the aid of my lens, to find any trace of the less common "needle operation." The inference was that the patient had suffered from the accident known as "dislocation of the lens", and this led to the further inference that he was almost or completely blind in the right eye.

This conclusion was, indeed, to some extent negatived by a deep indentation on the bridge of the nose, evidently produced by spectacles, and by marks which I looked for and found behind the ears, corresponding to the hooks or "curl sides" of the glasses. For those spectacles which are fitted with curl sides to hook over the ears are usually intended to be worn habitually, and this agreed with the indentation on the nose, which was deeper than would have been accounted for by the merely occasional use of spectacles for reading. But if only one eye was useful, a single eye-glass would have answered the purpose, not that there was any weight in this objection, for a single eye-glass worn constantly would be much less convenient than a pair of hook-sided spectacles.

As to the nature of the patient's illness, only one opinion seemed possible. It was a clear and typical case of opium or morphine poisoning. To this conclusion all his symptoms seemed to point with absolute certainty. The coated tongue, which he protruded slowly and tremulously in response to a command bawled in his ear, his yellow skin and ghastly expression, his contracted pupils and the stupor from which he could hardly be roused by the roughest handling and which yet did not amount to actual insensibility, all these formed a distinct and coherent group of symptoms, not only pointing plainly to the nature of the drug, but also suggesting a very formidable dose.

But this conclusion in its turn raised a very awkward and difficult question. If a large – a poisonous – dose of the drug had been taken, how, and by whom had that dose been administered? The closest scrutiny of the patient's arms and legs failed to reveal a single mark such as would be made by a hypodermic needle. This man was clearly no common morphinomaniac, and in the absence of the usual sprinkling of needlemarks, there was nothing to show or suggest whether the drug had been taken voluntarily by the patient himself or administered by someone else.

And then there remained the possibility that I might, after all, be mistaken in my diagnosis. I felt pretty confident. But the wise man always holds a doubt in reserve. And, in the present case, having regard to the obviously serious condition of the patient, such a doubt was eminently disturbing. Indeed, as I pocketed my stethoscope and took a last look at the motionless, silent figure, I realized that my position was one of extraordinary difficulty and perplexity. On the one hand my suspicions – aroused, naturally enough, by the very unusual circumstances that surrounded my visit – inclined me to extreme reticence, while, on the

445

other, it was evidently my duty to give any information that might prove serviceable to the patient.

As I turned away from the bed Mr. Weiss stopped his slow pacing to and fro and faced me. The feeble light of the candle now fell on him, and I saw him distinctly for the first time. He did not impress me favourably. He was a thick-set, round-shouldered man, a typical fair German with tow-coloured hair, greased and brushed down smoothly, a large, ragged, sandy beard and coarse, sketchy features. His nose was large and thick with a bulbous end, and inclined to a reddish purple, a tint which extended to the adjacent parts of his face as if the colour had run. His eyebrows were large and beetling, overhanging deep-set eyes, and he wore a pair of spectacles which gave him a somewhat owlish expression. His exterior was unprepossessing, and I was in a state of mind that rendered me easily receptive of an unfavourable impression.

"Well," he said, "what do you make of him?"

I hesitated, still perplexed by the conflicting necessities of caution and frankness, but at length replied, "I think rather badly of him, Mr. Weiss. He is in a very low state."

"Yes, I can see that. But have you come to any decision as to the nature of his illness?"

There was a tone of anxiety and suppressed eagerness in the question which, while it was natural enough in the circumstances, by no means allayed my suspicions, but rather influenced me on the side of caution.

"I cannot give a very definite opinion at present," I replied guardedly. "The symptoms are rather obscure and might very well indicate several different conditions. They might be due to congestion of the brain, and, if no other explanation were possible, I should incline to that view. The alternative is some narcotic poison, such as opium or morphia."

"But that is quite impossible. There is no such drug in the house, and as he never leaves his room now, he could not get any from outside."

"What about the servants?" I asked.

"There are no servants excepting my housekeeper, and she is absolutely trustworthy."

"He might have some store of the drug that you are not aware of. Is he left alone much?"

"Very seldom indeed. I spend as much time with him as I can, and when I am not able to be in the room, Mrs Schallibaum, my housekeeper, sits with him."

"Is he often as drowsy as he is now?"

"Oh, very often, in fact, I should say that is his usual condition. He rouses up now and again, and then he is quite lucid and natural for, perhaps, an hour or so, but presently he becomes drowsy again and doses

446

off, and remains asleep, or half-asleep, for hours on end. Do you know of any disease that takes people in that way?"

"No," I answered. "The symptoms are not exactly like those of any disease that is known to me. But they are much very like those of opium poisoning."

"But, my dear sir," Mr. Weiss retorted impatiently, "since it is clearly impossible that it can be opium poisoning, it must be something else. Now, what else can it be? You were speaking of congestion of the brain."

"Yes. But the objection to that is the very complete recovery that seems to take place in the intervals."

"I would not say very complete," said Mr. Weiss. "The recovery is rather comparative. He is lucid and fairly natural in his manner, but he is still dull and lethargic. He does not, for instance, show any desire to go out, or even to leave his room."

I pondered uncomfortably on these rather contradictory statements. Clearly Mr. Weiss did not mean to entertain the theory of opium poisoning, which was natural enough if he had no knowledge of the drug having been used. But still –

"I suppose," said Mr. Weiss, "you have experience of sleeping sickness?"

The suggestion startled me. I had not. Very few people had. At that time practically nothing was known about the disease. It was a mere pathological curiosity, almost unheard of excepting by a few practitioners in remote parts of Africa, and hardly referred to in the text-books. Its connection with the trypanosome-bearing insects was as yet unsuspected, and, to me, its symptoms were absolutely unknown.

"No, I have not," I replied. "The disease is nothing more than a name to me. But why do you ask? Has Mr. Graves been abroad?"

"Yes. He has been travelling for the last three or four years, and I know that he spent some time recently in West Africa, where this disease occurs. In fact, it was from him that I first heard about it."

This was a new fact. It shook my confidence in my diagnosis very considerably, and inclined me to reconsider my suspicions. If Mr. Weiss was lying to me, he now had me at a decided disadvantage.

"What do you think?" he asked. "Is it possible that this can be sleeping sickness?"

"I should not like to say that it is impossible," I replied. "The disease is practically unknown to me. I have never practised out of England and have had no occasion to study it. Until I have looked the subject up, I should not be in a position to give an opinion. Of course, if I could see Mr. Graves in one of what we may call his 'lucid intervals' I should be able to form a better idea. Do you think that could be managed?"

"It might. I see the importance of it and will certainly do my best, but he is a difficult man, a very difficult man. I sincerely hope it is not sleeping sickness."

"Why?"

"Because – as I understood from him – that disease is invariably fatal, sooner or later. There seem to be no cure. Do you think you will be able to decide when you see him again?"

"I hope so," I replied. "I shall look up the authorities and see exactly what the symptoms are – that is, so far as they are known, but my impression is that there is very little information available."

"And in the meantime?"

"We will give him some medicine and attend to his general condition, and you had better let me see him again as soon as possible." I was about to say that the effect of the medicine itself might throw some light on the patient's condition, but, as I proposed to treat him for morphine poisoning, I thought it wiser to keep this item of information to myself. Accordingly, I confined myself to a few general directions as to the care of the patient, to which Mr. Weiss listened attentively. "And," I concluded, "we must not lose sight of the opium question. You had better search the room carefully and keep a close watch on the patient, especially during his intervals of wakefulness."

"Very well, Doctor," Mr. Weiss replied, "I will do all that you tell me and I will send for you again as soon as possible, if you do not object to poor Graves's ridiculous conditions. And now, if you will allow me to pay your fee, I will go and order the carriage while you are writing the prescription."

"There is no need for a prescription," I said. "I will make up some medicine and give it to the coachman."

Mr. Weiss seemed inclined to demur to this arrangement, but I had my own reasons for insisting on it. Modern prescriptions are not difficult to read, and I did not wish Mr. Weiss to know what treatment the patient was having.

As soon as I was left alone, I returned to the bedside and once more looked down at the impassive figure. And as I looked, my suspicions revived. It was very like morphine poisoning, and, if it was morphine, it was no common, medicinal dose that had been given. I opened my bag and took out my hypodermic case from which I extracted a little tube of atropine tabloids. Shaking out into my hand a couple of the tiny discs, I drew down the patient's under-lip and slipped the little tablets under his tongue. Then I quickly replaced the tube and dropped the case into my bag, and I had hardly done so when the door opened softly and the housekeeper entered the room.

448

"How do you find Mr. Graves?" she asked in what I thought a very unnecessarily low tone, considering the patient's lethargic state.

"He seems to be very ill," I answered.

"So!" she rejoined, and added, "I am sorry to hear that. We have been anxious about him."

She seated herself on the chair by the bedside, and, shading the candle from the patient's face – and her own, too – produced from a bag that hung from her waist a half-finished stocking and began to knit silently and with the skill characteristic of the German housewife. I looked at her attentively (though she was so much in the shadow that I could see her but indistinctly) and somehow her appearance prepossessed me as little as did that of the other members of the household. Yet she was not an ill-looking woman. She had an excellent figure, and the air of a person of good social position, her features were good enough and her colouring, although a little unusual, was not unpleasant. Like Mr. Weiss, she had very fair hair, greased, parted in the middle and brushed down as smoothly as the painted hair of a Dutch doll. She appeared to have no eyebrows at all – owing, no doubt, to the light colour of the hair – and the doll-like character was emphasized by her eyes, which were either brown or dark grey, I could not see which. A further peculiarity consisted in a "habit spasm," such as one often sees in nervous children, a periodical quick jerk of the head, as if a cap-string or dangling lock were being shaken off the cheek. Her age I judged to be about thirty-five.

The carriage, which one might have expected to be waiting, seemed to take some time in getting ready. I sat, with growing impatience, listening to the sick man's soft breathing and the click of the housekeeper's knitting-needles. I wanted to get home, not only for my own sake – the patient's condition made it highly desirable that the remedies should be given as quickly as possible. But the minutes dragged on, and I was on the point of expostulating when a bell rang on the landing.

"The carriage is ready," said Mrs. Schallibaum. "Let me light you down the stairs."

She rose, and, taking the candle, preceded me to the head of the stairs, where she stood holding the light over the baluster-rail as I descended and crossed the passage to the open side door. The carriage was drawn up in the covered way as I could see by the faint glimmer of the distant candle, which also enabled me dimly to discern the coachman standing close by in the shadow. I looked round, rather expecting to see Mr. Weiss, but, as he made no appearance, I entered the carriage. The door was immediately banged to and locked, and I then heard the heavy bolts of the gates withdrawn and the loud creaking of hinges. The carriage moved out slowly

449

and stopped, the gates slammed to behind me, I felt the lurch as the coachman climbed to his seat and we started forward.

My reflections during the return journey were the reverse of agreeable. I could not rid myself of the conviction that I was being involved in some very suspicious proceedings. It was possible, of course, that this feeling was due to the strange secrecy that surrounded my connection with this case, that, had I made my visit under ordinary conditions, I might have found in the patient's symptoms nothing to excite suspicion or alarm. It might be so, but that consideration did not comfort me.

Then, my diagnosis might be wrong. It might be that this was, in reality, a case of some brain affection accompanied by compression, such as slow haemorrhage, abscess, tumour, or simple congestion. These cases were very difficult at times. But the appearances in this one did not consistently agree with the symptoms accompanying any of these conditions. As to sleeping sickness, it was, perhaps a more hopeful suggestion, but I could not decide for or against it until I had more knowledge, and against this view was the weighty fact that the symptoms did exactly agree with the theory of morphine poisoning.

But even so, there was no conclusive evidence of any criminal act. The patient might be a confirmed opium-eater, and the symptoms heightened by deliberate deception. The cunning of these unfortunates is proverbial and is only equalled by their secretiveness and mendacity. It would be quite possible for this man to feign profound stupor so long as he was watched, and then, when left alone for a few minutes, to nip out of bed and help himself from some secret store of the drug. This would be quite in character with his objection to seeing a doctor and his desire for secrecy. But still, I did not believe it to be the true explanation. In spite of all the various alternative possibilities, my suspicions came back to Mr. Weiss and the strange, taciturn woman, and refused to budge.

For all the circumstances of the case were suspicious. The elaborate preparations implied by the state of the carriage in which I was travelling, the make-shift appearance of the house, the absence of ordinary domestic servants, although a coachman was kept, the evident desire of Mr. Weiss and the woman to avoid thorough inspection of their persons, and, above all, the fact that the former had told me a deliberate lie. For he had lied, beyond all doubt. His statement as to the almost continuous stupor was absolutely irreconcilable with his other statement as to the patient's wilfulness and obstinacy and even more irreconcilable with the deep and comparatively fresh marks of the spectacles on the patient's nose. That man had certainly worn spectacles within twenty-four hours, which he would hardly have done if he had been in a state bordering on coma.

450

My reflections were interrupted by the stopping of the carriage. The door was unlocked and thrown open, and I emerged from my dark and stuffy prison opposite my own house.

"I will let you have the medicine in a minute or two," I said to the coachman, and, as I let myself in with my latch-key, my mind came back swiftly from the general circumstances of the case to the very critical condition of the patient. Already I was regretting that I had not taken more energetic measures to rouse him and restore his flagging vitality, for it would be a terrible thing if he should take a turn for the worse and die before the coachman returned with the remedies. Spurred on by this alarming thought, I made up the medicines quickly and carried the hastily wrapped bottles out to the man, whom I found standing by the horse's head.

"Get back as quickly as you can," I said, "and tell Mr. Weiss to lose no time in giving the patient the draught in the small bottle. The directions are on the labels."

The coachman took the packages from me without reply, climbed to his seat, touched the horse with his whip and drove off at a rapid pace towards Newington Butts.

The little clock in the consulting-room showed that it was close on eleven, time for a tired G.P. to be thinking of bed. But I was not sleepy. Over my frugal supper I found myself taking up anew the thread of my meditations, and afterwards, as I smoked my last pipe by the expiring surgery fire, the strange and sinister features of the case continued to obtrude themselves on my notice. I looked up Stillbury's little reference library for information on the subject of sleeping sickness, but learned no more than that it was "a rare and obscure disease of which very little is known at present." I read up morphine poisoning and was only further confirmed in the belief that my diagnosis was correct, which would have been more satisfactory if the circumstances had been different.

For the interest of the case was not merely academic. I was in a position of great difficulty and responsibility and had to decide on a course of action. What ought I to do? Should I maintain the professional secrecy to which I was tacitly committed, or ought I to convey a hint to the police?

Suddenly, and with a singular feeling of relief, I bethought myself of my old friend and fellow-student, John Thorndyke, now an eminent authority on Medical Jurisprudence. I had been associated with him temporarily in one case as his assistant, and had then been deeply impressed by his versatile learning, his acuteness and his marvellous resourcefulness. Thorndyke was a barrister in extensive practice, and so would be able to tell me at once what was my duty from a legal point of view, and, as he was also a doctor of medicine, he would understand the

451

exigencies of medical practice. If I could find time to call at the Temple and lay the case before him, all my doubts and difficulties would be resolved.

Anxiously, I opened my visiting-list to see what kind of day's work was in store for me on the morrow. It was not a heavy day, even allowing for one or two extra calls in the morning, but yet I was doubtful whether it would allow of my going so far from my district, until my eye caught, near the foot of the page, the name of Burton. Now Mr. Burton lived in one of the old houses on the east side of Bouverie Street, less than five minutes' walk from Thorndyke's chambers in King's Bench Walk, and he was, moreover, a "chronic" who could safely be left for the last. When I had done with Mr. Burton I could look in on my friend with a very good chance of catching him on his return from the hospital. I could allow myself time for quite a long chat with him, and, by taking a hansom, still get back in good time for the evening's work.

This was a great comfort. At the prospect of sharing my responsibilities with a friend on whose judgment I could so entirely rely, my embarrassments seemed to drop from me in a moment. Having entered the engagement in my visiting-list, I rose, in greatly improved spirits, and knocked out my pipe just as the little clock banged out impatiently the hour of midnight.

Chapter II
Thorndyke Devises a Scheme

As I entered the Temple by the Tudor Street gate the aspect of the place smote my senses with an air of agreeable familiarity. Here had I spent many a delightful hour when working with Thorndyke at the remarkable Hornby case, which the newspapers had called "The Case of the Red Thumb Mark", and here had I met the romance of my life, the story whereof is told elsewhere. The place was thus endeared to me by pleasant recollections of a happy past, and its associations suggested hopes of happiness yet to come and in the not too far distant future.

My brisk tattoo on the little brass knocker brought to the door no less a person than Thorndyke himself, and the warmth of his greeting made me at once proud and ashamed. For I had not only been an absentee, I had been a very poor correspondent.

"The prodigal has returned, Polton," he exclaimed, looking into the room. "Here is Dr. Jervis."

I followed him into the room and found Polton – his confidential servant, laboratory assistant, artificer, and general "familiar" – setting out the tea-tray on a small table. The little man shook hands cordially with me, and his face crinkled up into the sort of smile that one might expect to see on a benevolent walnut.

"We've often talked about you, sir," said he. "The doctor was wondering only yesterday when you were coming back to us."

As I was not "coming back to them" quite in the sense intended I felt a little guilty, but reserved my confidences for Thorndyke's ear and replied in polite generalities. Then Polton fetched the tea-pot from the laboratory, made up the fire and departed, and Thorndyke and I subsided, as of old, into our respective arm-chairs.

"And whence do you spring from in this unexpected fashion?" my colleague asked. "You look as if you had been making professional visits."

"I have. The base of operations is in Lower Kennington Lane."

"Ah! Then you are 'back once more on the old trail'?"

"Yes," I answered, with a laugh, "'the old trail, the long trail, the trail that is always new'."

"And leads nowhere," Thorndyke added grimly.

I laughed again, not very heartily, for there was an uncomfortable element of truth in my friend's remark, to which my own experience bore only too complete testimony. The medical practitioner whose lack of

453

means forces him to subsist by taking temporary charge of other men's practices is apt to find that the passing years bring him little but grey hairs and a wealth of disagreeable experience.

"You will have to drop it, Jervis, you will, indeed," Thorndyke resumed after a pause. "This casual employment is preposterous for a man of your class and professional attainments. Besides, are you not engaged to be married and to a most charming girl?"

"Yes, I know. I have been a fool. But I will really amend my ways. If necessary, I will pocket my pride and let Juliet advance the money to buy a practice."

"That," said Thorndyke, "is a very proper resolution. Pride and reserve between people who are going to be husband and wife, is an absurdity. But why buy a practice? Have you forgotten my proposal?"

"I should be an ungrateful brute if I had."

"Very well. I repeat it now. Come to me as my junior, read for the Bar and work with me, and, with your abilities, you will have a chance of something like a career. I want you, Jervis," he added, earnestly. "I must have a junior, with my increasing practice, and you are the junior I want. We are old and tried friends, we have worked together, we like and trust one another, and you are the best man for the job that I know. Come, I am not going to take a refusal. This is an ultimatum."

"And what is the alternative?" I asked with a smile at his eagerness.

"There isn't any. You are going to say yes."

"I believe I am," I answered, not without emotion, "and I am more rejoiced at your offer and more grateful than I can tell you. But we must leave the final arrangements for our next meeting – in a week or so, I hope – for I have to be back in an hour, and I want to consult you on a matter of some importance."

"Very well," said Thorndyke, "we will leave the formal agreement for consideration at our next meeting. What is it that you want my opinion on?"

"The fact is," I said, "I am in a rather awkward dilemma, and I want you to tell me what you think I ought to do."

Thorndyke paused in the act of refilling my cup and glanced at me with unmistakable anxiety.

"Nothing of an unpleasant nature, I hope," said he.

"No, no, nothing of that kind," I answered with a smile as I interpreted the euphemism, for "something unpleasant", in the case of a young and reasonably presentable medical man is ordinarily the equivalent of trouble with the female of his species. "It is nothing that concerns me personally at all," I continued, "it is a question of professional responsibility. But I had better give you an account of the affair in a complete narrative, as I know that you like to have your data in a regular and consecutive order."

Thereupon I proceeded to relate the history of my visit to the mysterious Mr. Graves, not omitting any single circumstance or detail that I could recollect.

Thorndyke listened from the very beginning of my story with the closest attention. His face was the most impassive that I have ever seen, ordinarily as inscrutable as a bronze mask, but to me, who knew him intimately, there was a certain something – a change of colour, perhaps, or an additional sparkle of the eye – that told me when his curious passion for investigation was fully aroused. And now, as I told him of that weird journey and the strange, secret house to which it had brought me, I could see that it offered a problem after his very heart. During the whole of my narration he sat as motionless as a statue, evidently committing the whole story to memory, detail by detail, and even when I had finished he remained for an appreciable time without moving or speaking.

At length he looked up at me. "This is a very extraordinary affair, Jervis," he said.

"Very," I agreed, "and the question that is agitating me is, what is to be done?"

"Yes," he said, meditatively, "that is the question, and an uncommonly difficult question it is. It really involves the settlement of the antecedent question, What is it that is happening at that house?"

"What *do* you think is happening at that house?" I asked.

"We must go slow, Jervis," he replied. "We must carefully separate the legal tissues from the medical, and avoid confusing what we know with what we suspect. Now, with reference to the medical aspects of the case. The first question that confronts us is that of sleeping sickness, and here we are in a difficulty. We have not enough knowledge. Neither of us, I take it, has ever seen a case, and the extant descriptions are inadequate. From what I know of the disease, its symptoms agree with those in your case in respect of the alleged moroseness and in the gradually increasing periods of lethargy alternating with periods of apparent recovery. A more important fact is that, as far as I know, extreme contraction of the pupils is not a symptom of sleeping sickness. To sum up, the probabilities are against sleeping sickness, but with our insufficient knowledge, we cannot definitely exclude it."

"You think that it may really be sleeping sickness?"

"No, personally I do not entertain that theory for a moment. But I am considering the evidence apart from our opinions on the subject. We have to accept it as a conceivable hypothesis that it may be sleeping sickness because we cannot positively prove that it is not. That is all. But when we come to the hypothesis of morphine poisoning, the case is different. The symptoms agree with those of morphine poisoning in every respect. There is no exception or disagreement whatever. The common sense of the matter is therefore that we adopt morphine poisoning as our working diagnosis, which is what you seem to have done."

"Yes. For purposes of treatment."

"Exactly. For medical purposes you adopted the more probable view and dismissed the less probable. That was the reasonable thing to do. But for legal purposes you must entertain both possibilities, for the hypothesis of poisoning involves serious legal issues, whereas the hypothesis of disease involves no legal issues at all."

"That doesn't sound very helpful," I remarked.

"It indicates the necessity for caution," he retorted.

"Yes, I see that. But what is your own opinion of the case?"

"Well," he said, "let us consider the facts in order. Here is a man who, we assume, is under the influence of a poisonous dose of morphine. The question is, did he take that dose himself or was it administered to him by some other person? If he took it himself, with what object did he take it? The history that was given to you seems completely to exclude the idea of suicide. But the patient's condition seems equally to exclude the idea of morphinomania. Your opium-eater does not reduce himself to a state of coma. He usually keeps well within the limits of the tolerance that has been established. The conclusion that emerges is, I think, that the drug was administered by some other person, and the most likely person seems to be Mr. Weiss."

"Isn't morphine a very unusual poison?"

"Very, and most inconvenient except in a single, fatal dose, by reason of the rapidity with which tolerance of the drug is established. But we must not forget that slow morphine poisoning might be eminently suitable in certain cases. The manner in which it enfeebles the will, confuses the judgment, and debilitates the body might make it very useful to a poisoner whose aim was to get some instrument or document executed, such as a will, deed or assignment. And death could be produced afterwards by other means. You see the important bearing of this?"

"You mean in respect of a death certificate?"

"Yes. Suppose Mr. Weiss to have given a large dose of morphine. He then sends for you and throws out a suggestion of sleeping sickness. If you accept the suggestion he is pretty safe. He can repeat the process until he kills his victim and then get a certificate from you which will cover the murder. It was quite an ingenious scheme – which, by the way, is characteristic of intricate crimes, your subtle criminal often plans his crime like a genius, but he generally executes it like a fool – as this man seems to have done, if we are not doing him an injustice."

"How has he acted like a fool?"

"In several respects. In the first place, he should have chosen his doctor. A good, brisk, confident man who 'knows his own mind' is the sort of person who would have suited him, a man who would have jumped at a diagnosis and stuck to it, or else an ignorant weakling of alcoholic tendencies. It was shockingly bad luck to run against a cautious scientific practitioner like my learned friend. Then, of course, all this secrecy was sheer tomfoolery, exactly calculated to put a careful man on his guard, as it has actually done. If Mr. Weiss is really a criminal, he has mismanaged his affairs badly."

"And you apparently think that he is a criminal?"

"I suspect him deeply. But I should like to ask you one or two questions about him. You say he spoke with a German accent. What command of English had he? Was his vocabulary good? Did he use any German idioms?"

"No. I should say that his English was perfect, and I noticed that his phrases were quite well chosen even for an Englishman."

"Did he seem to you 'made up' in any way, disguised, I mean?"

"I couldn't say. The light was so very feeble."

"You couldn't see the colour of his eyes, for instance?"

"No. I think they were grey, but I couldn't be sure."

"And as to the coachman. He wore a wig, you said. Could you see the colour of his eyes? Or any peculiarity by which you could recognize him?"

"He had a malformed thumb-nail on his right hand. That is all I can say about him."

"He didn't strike you as resembling Weiss in any way, in voice or features?"

"Not at all, and he spoke, as I told you, with a distinct Scotch accent."

"The reason I ask is that if Weiss is attempting to poison this man, the coachman is almost certain to be a confederate and might be a relative. You had better examine him closely if you get another chance."

"I will. And that brings me back to the question, What am I to do? Ought I to report the case to the police?"

"I am inclined to think not. You have hardly enough facts. Of course, if Mr. Weiss has administered poison 'unlawfully and maliciously' he has committed a felony, and is liable under the Consolidation Acts of 1861 to ten years' penal servitude. But I do not see how you could swear an information. You don't know that he administered the poison – if poison has really been administered – and you cannot give any reliable name or any address whatever. Then there is the question of sleeping sickness. You

457

reject it for medical purposes, but you could not swear, in a court of law, that this is *not* a case of sleeping sickness."

"No," I admitted, "I could not."

"Then I think the police would decline to move in the matter, and you might find that you had raised a scandal in Dr. Stillbury's practice to no purpose."

"So you think I had better do nothing in the matter?"

"For the present. It is, of course, a medical man's duty to assist justice in any way that is possible. But a doctor is not a detective, he should not go out of his way to assume police functions. He should keep his eyes and ears open, and, though, in general, he should keep his own counsel, it is his duty to note very carefully anything that seems to him likely to bear on any important legal issues. It is not his business officiously to initiate criminal inquiries, but it is emphatically his business to be ready, if called upon, to assist justice with information that his special knowledge and opportunities have rendered accessible to him. You see the bearing of this?"

"You mean that I should note down what I have seen and heard and say nothing about it until I am asked."

"Yes, if nothing further happens. But if you should be sent for again, I think it is your duty to make further observations with a view, if necessary, to informing the police. It may be, for instance, of vital importance to identify the house, and it is your duty to secure the means of doing so."

"But, my dear Thorndyke," I expostulated, "I have told you how I was conveyed to the house. Now, will you kindly explain to me how a man, boxed up in a pitch-dark carriage, is going to identify any place to which he may be carried?"

"The problem doesn't appear to me to present any serious difficulties," he replied.

"Doesn't it?" said I. "To me it looks like a pretty solid impossibility. But what do you suggest? Should I break out of the house and run away up the street? Or should I bore a hole through the shutter of the carriage and peep out?"

Thorndyke smiled indulgently. "The methods proposed by my learned friend display a certain crudity inappropriate to the character of a man of science, to say nothing of the disadvantage of letting the enemy into our counsels. No, no, Jervis, we can do something better than that. Just excuse me for a minute while I run up to the laboratory."

He hurried away to Polton's sanctum on the upper floor, leaving me to speculate on the method by which he proposed that a man should be enabled, as Sam Weller would express it, "to see through a flight of stairs

458

and a deal door", or, what was equally opaque, the wooden shutters of a closed carriage.

"Now," he said, when he returned a couple of minutes later with a small, paper-covered notebook in his hand, "I have set Polton to work on a little appliance that will, I think, solve our difficulty, and I will show you how I propose that you should make your observations. First of all, we have to rule the pages of this book into columns."

He sat down at the table and began methodically to rule the pages each into three columns, two quite narrow and one broad. The process occupied some time, during which I sat and watched with impatient curiosity the unhurried, precise movements of Thorndyke's pencil, all agog to hear the promised explanation. He was just finishing the last page when there came a gentle tap at the door, and Polton entered with a satisfied smile on his dry, shrewd-looking face and a small board in his hand.

"Will this do, sir?" he asked.

As he spoke he handed the little board to Thorndyke, who looked at it and passed it to me.

"The very thing, Polton," my friend replied. "Where did you find it? It's of no use for you to pretend that you've made it in about two-minutes-and-a-half."

Polton smiled one of his queer crinkly smiles, and remarking that "it didn't take much making," departed much gratified by the compliment.

"What a wonderful old fellow that is, Jervis," Thorndyke observed as his factotum retired. "He took in the idea instantly and seems to have produced the finished article by magic, as the conjurers bring forth rabbits and bowls of goldfish at a moment's notice. I suppose you see what your *modus operandi* is to be?"

I had gathered a clue from the little appliance – a plate of white fret-wood about seven inches by five, to one corner of which a pocket-compass had been fixed with shellac – but was not quite clear as to the details of the method.

"You can read a compass pretty quickly, I think?" Thorndyke said.

"Of course I can. Used we not to sail a yacht together when we were students?"

"To be sure we did, and we will again before we die. And now as to your method of locating this house. Here is a pocket reading-lamp which you can hook on the carriage lining. This notebook can be fixed to the board with an india-rubber band – thus. You observe that the thoughtful Polton has stuck a piece of thread on the glass of the compass to serve as a lubber's line. This is how you will proceed. As soon as you are locked in the carriage, light your lamp – better have a book with you in case the light is noticed – take out your watch and put the board on your knee, keeping its long side exactly in a line with the axis of the carriage. Then enter in one narrow column of your notebook the time, in the other the direction shown by the compass, and in the broad column any particulars, including the number of steps the horse makes in a minute. Like this."

He took a loose sheet of paper and made one or two sample entries on it in pencil, thus –

9:40. S.E. Start from home.
9:41 S.W. Granite setts.
9:43. S.W. Wood pavement. Hoofs 104.
9:47. W. by S. Granite crossing. Macadam –

– and so on. Note every change of direction, with the time, and whenever you hear or feel anything from outside, note it, with the time and direction, and don't forget to note any variations in the horse's pace. You follow the process?"

"Perfectly. But do you think the method is accurate enough to fix the position of a house? Remember, this is only a pocket-compass with no dial, and it will jump frightfully. And the mode of estimating distance is very rough."

"That is all perfectly true," Thorndyke answered. "But you are overlooking certain important facts The track-chart that you will produce can be checked by other data. The house, for instance, has a covered way by which you could identify it if you knew approximately where to look for it. Then you must remember that your carriage is not travelling over a featureless plain. It is passing through streets which have a determined position and direction and which are accurately represented on the ordnance map. I think, Jervis, that, in spite of the apparent roughness of the method, if you make your observations carefully, we shall have no trouble in narrowing down the inquiry to a quite small area. If we get the chance, that is to say."

"Yes, if we do. I am doubtful whether Mr. Weiss will require my services again, but I sincerely hope he will. It would be rare sport to locate his secret burrow, all unsuspected. But now I must really be off."

"Good-bye, then," said Thorndyke, slipping a well-sharpened pencil through the rubber band that fixed the notebook to the board. "Let me know how the adventure progresses – if it progresses at all – and remember, I hold your promise to come and see me again quite soon in any case."

He handed me the board and the lamp, and, when I had slipped them into my pocket, we shook hands and I hurried away, a little uneasy at having left my charge so long.

Chapter III
"A Chiel's Amang Ye Takin' Notes"

The attitude of the suspicious man tends to generate in others the kind of conduct that seems to justify his suspicions. In most of us there lurks a certain strain of mischief which trustfulness disarms but distrust encourages. The inexperienced kitten which approaches us confidingly with arched back and upright tail, soliciting caresses, generally receives the gentle treatment that it expects, whereas the worldly-wise tom-cat, who, in response to friendly advances, scampers away and grins at us suspiciously from the fancied security of an adjacent wall, impels us to accelerate his retreat with a well-directed clod.

Now the proceedings of Mr. H. Weiss resembled those of the tom-cat aforesaid and invited an analogous reply. To a responsible professional man his extraordinary precautions were at once an affront and a challenge. Apart from graver considerations, I found myself dwelling with unholy pleasure on the prospect of locating the secret hiding-place from which he seemed to grin at me with such complacent defiance, and I lost no time and spared no trouble in preparing myself for the adventure. The very hansom which bore me from the Temple to Kennington Lane was utilized for a preliminary test of Thorndyke's little apparatus. During the whole of that brief journey I watched the compass closely, noted the feel and sound of the road-material and timed the trotting of the horse. And the result was quite encouraging. It is true that the compass-needle oscillated wildly to the vibration of the cab, but still its oscillations took place around a definite point which was the average direction, and it was evident to me that the data it furnished were very fairly reliable. I felt very little doubt, after the preliminary trial, as to my being able to produce a moderately intelligible track-chart if only I should get an opportunity to exercise my skill.

But it looked as if I should not. Mr. Weiss's promise to send for me again soon was not fulfilled. Three days passed and still he made no sign. I began to fear that I had been too outspoken, that the shuttered carriage had gone forth to seek some more confiding and easy-going practitioner, and that our elaborate preparations had been made in vain. When the fourth day drew towards a close and still no summons had come, I was disposed reluctantly to write the case off as a lost opportunity.

And at that moment, in the midst of my regrets, the bottle-boy thrust an uncomely head in at the door. His voice was coarse, his accent was hideous, and his grammatical construction beneath contempt, but I forgave him all when I gathered the import of his message.

"Mr. Weiss's carriage is waiting, and he says will you come as quickly as you can because he's took very bad to-night."

I sprang from my chair and hastily collected the necessaries for the journey. The little board and the lamp I put in my overcoat pocket, I overhauled the emergency bag and added to its usual contents a bottle of permanganate of potassium which I thought I might require. Then I tucked the evening paper under my arm and went out.

The coachman, who was standing at the horse's head as I emerged, touched his hat and came forward to open the door.

"I have fortified myself for the long drive, you see," I remarked, exhibiting the newspaper as I stepped into the carriage.

"But you can't read in the dark," said he.

"No, but I have provided myself with a lamp," I replied, producing it and striking a match.

He watched me as I lit the lamp and hooked it on the back cushion, and observed, "I suppose you found it rather a dull ride last time. It's a longish way. They might have fitted the carriage with an inside lamp. But we shall have to make it a quicker passage to-night. Governor says Mr. Graves is uncommon bad."

With this he slammed the door and locked it. I drew the board from my pocket, laid it on my knee, glanced at my watch, and, as the coachman climbed to his seat, I made the first entry in the little book.

"8:58. W. by S. Start from home. Horse 13 hands."

The first move of the carriage on starting was to turn round as if heading for Newington Butts, and the second entry accordingly read: *"8:58.30. E. by N."*

But this direction was not maintained long. Very soon we turned south and then west and then south again. I sat with my eyes riveted on the compass, following with some difficulty its rapid changes. The needle swung to and fro incessantly but always within a definite arc, the centre of which was the true direction. But this direction varied from minute to minute in the most astonishing manner. West, south, east, north, the carriage turned, "boxing" the compass until I lost all count of direction. It was an amazing performance. Considering that the man was driving against time on a mission of life and death urgency, his carelessness as to direction was astounding. The tortuousness of the route must have made the journey twice as long as it need have been with a little more careful selection. At least so it appeared to me, though, naturally, I was not in a position to offer an authoritative criticism.

463

As far as I could judge, we followed the same route as before. Once I heard a tug's whistle and knew that we were near the river, and we passed the railway station, apparently at the same time as on the previous occasion, for I heard a passenger train start and assumed that it was the same train. We crossed quite a number of thoroughfares with tram-lines – I had no idea there were so many – and it was a revelation to me to find how numerous the railway arches were in this part of London and how continually the nature of the road-metal varied.

It was by no means a dull journey this time. The incessant changes of direction and variations in the character of the road kept me most uncommonly busy, for I had hardly time to scribble down one entry before the compass-needle would swing round sharply, showing that we had once more turned a corner, and I was quite taken by surprise when the carriage slowed down and turned into the covered way. Very hastily I scribbled down the final entry ("*9:24. S.E. In covered way*"), and having closed the book and slipped it and the board into my pocket, had just opened out the newspaper when the carriage door was unlocked and opened, whereupon I unhooked and blew out the lamp and pocketed that too, reflecting that it might be useful later.

As on the last occasion, Mrs. Schallibaum stood in the open doorway with a lighted candle. But she was a good deal less self-possessed this time. In fact she looked rather wild and terrified. Even by the candle-light I could see that she was very pale and she seemed unable to keep still. As she gave me the few necessary words of explanation, she fidgeted incessantly and her hands and feet were in constant movement.

"You had better come up with me at once," she said. "Mr. Graves is much worse to-night. We will wait not for Mr. Weiss."

Without waiting for a reply she quickly ascended the stairs and I followed. The room was in much the same condition as before. But the patient was not. As soon as I entered the room, a soft, rhythmical gurgle from the bed gave me a very clear warning of danger. I stepped forward quickly and looked down at the prostrate figure, and the warning gathered emphasis. The sick man's ghastly face was yet more ghastly, his eyes were more sunken, his skin more livid, "his nose was as sharp as a pen," and if he did not "babble of green fields" it was because he seemed to be beyond even that. If it had been a case of disease, I should have said at once that he was dying. He had all the appearance of a man in *articulo mortis*. Even as it was, feeling convinced that the case was one of morphine poisoning, I was far from confident that I should be able to draw him back from the extreme edge of vitality on which he trembled so insecurely.

"He is very ill? He is dying?"

464

It was Mrs. Schallibaum's voice, very low, but eager and intense. I turned, with my finger on the patient's wrist, and looked into the face of the most thoroughly scared woman I have ever seen. She made no attempt now to avoid the light, but looked me squarely in the face, and I noticed, half-unconsciously, that her eyes were brown and had a curious strained expression.

"Yes," I answered, "he is very ill. He is in great danger."

She still stared at me fixedly for some seconds. And then a very odd thing occurred. Suddenly she squinted – squinted horribly, not with the familiar convergent squint which burlesque artists imitate, but with external or divergent squint of extreme near sight or unequal vision. The effect was quite startling. One moment both her eyes were looking straight into mine, the next, one of them rolled round until it looked out of the uttermost corner, leaving the other gazing steadily forward.

She was evidently conscious of the change, for she turned her head away quickly and reddened somewhat. But it was no time for thoughts of personal appearance.

"You can save him, Doctor! You will not let him die! He must not be allowed to die!"

She spoke with as much passion as if he had been the dearest friend that she had in the world, which I suspected was far from being the case. But her manifest terror had its uses.

"If anything is to be done to save him," I said, "it must be done quickly. I will give him some medicine at once, and meanwhile you must make some strong coffee."

"Coffee!" she exclaimed. "But we have none in the house. Will not tea do, if I make it very strong?"

"No, it will not. I must have coffee, and I must have it quickly."

"Then I suppose I must go and get some. But it is late. The shops will be shut. And I don't like leaving Mr. Graves."

"Can't you send the coachman?" I asked.

She shook her head impatiently. "No, that is no use. I must wait until Mr. Weiss comes."

"That won't do," I said, sharply. "He will slip through our fingers while you are waiting. You must go and get that coffee at once and bring it to me as soon as it is ready. And I want a tumbler and some water."

She brought me a water-bottle and glass from the wash-stand and then, with a groan of despair, hurried from the room.

I lost no time in applying the remedies that I had to hand. Shaking out into the tumbler a few crystals of potassium permanganate, I filled it up with water and approached the patient. His stupor was profound. I shook him as roughly as was safe in his depressed condition, but elicited no

465

resistance or responsive movement. As it seemed very doubtful whether he was capable of swallowing, I dared not take the risk of pouring the liquid into his mouth for fear of suffocating him. A stomach-tube would have solved the difficulty, but, of course, I had not one with me. I had, however, a mouth-speculum which also acted as a gag, and, having propped the patient's mouth open with this, I hastily slipped off one of the rubber tubes from my stethoscope and inserted into one end of it a vulcanite ear-speculum to serve as a funnel. Then, introducing the other end of the tube into the gullet as far as its length would permit, I cautiously poured a small quantity of the permanganate solution into the extemporized funnel. To my great relief a movement of the throat showed that the swallowing reflex still existed, and, thus encouraged, I poured down the tube as much of the fluid as I thought it wise to administer at one time.

The dose of permanganate that I had given was enough to neutralize any reasonable quantity of the poison that might yet remain in the stomach. I had next to deal with that portion of the drug which had already been absorbed and was exercising its poisonous effects. Taking my hypodermic case from my bag, I prepared in the syringe a full dose of atropine sulphate, which I injected forthwith into the unconscious man's arm. And that was all that I could do, so far as remedies were concerned, until the coffee arrived.

I cleaned and put away the syringe, washed the tube, and then, returning to the bedside, endeavoured to rouse the patient from his profound lethargy. But great care was necessary. A little injudicious roughness of handling, and that thready, flickering pulse might stop forever – and yet it was almost certain that if he were not speedily aroused, his stupor would gradually deepen until it shaded off imperceptibly into death. I went to work very cautiously, moving his limbs about, flicking his face and chest with the corner of a wet towel, tickling the soles of his feet, and otherwise applying stimuli that were strong without being violent.

So occupied was I with my efforts to resuscitate my mysterious patient that I did not notice the opening of the door, and it was with something of a start that, happening to glance round, I perceived at the farther end of the room the shadowy figure of a man relieved by two spots of light reflected from his spectacles. How long he had been watching me I cannot say, but, when he saw that I had observed him, he came forward – though not very far – and I saw that he was Mr. Weiss.

"I am afraid," he said, "that you do not find my friend so well to-night?"

"So well!" I exclaimed. "I don't find him well at all. I am exceedingly anxious about him."

"You don't – er – anticipate anything of a – er – anything serious, I hope?"

"There is no need to anticipate," said I. "It is already about as serious as it can be. I think he might die at any moment."

"Good God!" he gasped. "You horrify me!"

He was not exaggerating. In his agitation, he stepped forward into the lighter part of the room, and I could see that his face was pale to ghastliness – except his nose and the adjacent red patches on his cheeks, which stood out in grotesquely hideous contrast. Presently, however, he recovered a little and said, "I really think – at least I hope – that you take an unnecessarily serious view of his condition. He has been like this before, you know."

I felt pretty certain that he had not, but there was no use in discussing the question. I therefore replied, as I continued my efforts to rouse the patient, "That may or may not be. But in any case there comes a last time, and it may have come now."

"I hope not," he said, "although I understand that these cases always end fatally sooner or later."

"What cases?" I asked.

"I was referring to sleeping sickness, but perhaps you have formed some other opinion as to the nature of this dreadful complaint."

I hesitated for a moment, and he continued, "As to your suggestion that his symptoms might be due to drugs, I think we may consider that as disposed of. He has been watched, practically without cessation since you came last, and, moreover, I have myself turned out the room and examined the bed and have not found a trace of any drug. Have you gone into the question of sleeping sickness?"

I looked at the man narrowly before answering, and distrusted him more than ever. But this was no time for reticence. My concern was with the patient and his present needs. After all, I was, as Thorndyke had said, a doctor, not a detective, and the circumstances called for straightforward speech and action on my part.

"I have considered that question," I said, "and have come to a perfectly definite conclusion. His symptoms are not those of sleeping sickness. They are in my opinion undoubtedly due to morphine poisoning."

"But my dear sir!" he exclaimed, "the thing is impossible! Haven't I just told you that he has been watched continuously?"

"I can only judge by the appearances that I find," I answered, and, seeing that he was about to offer fresh objections, I continued, "Don't let us waste precious time in discussion, or Mr. Graves may be dead before we have reached a conclusion. If you will hurry them up about the coffee

467

that I asked for some time ago, I will take the other necessary measures, and perhaps we may manage to pull him round."

The rather brutal decision of my manner evidently daunted him. It must have been plain to him that I was not prepared to accept any explanation of the unconscious man's condition other than that of morphine poisoning, whence the inference was pretty plain that the alternatives were recovery or an inquest. Replying stiffly that I must do as I thought best, he hurried from the room, leaving me to continue my efforts without further interruption.

For some time these efforts seemed to make no impression. The man lay as still and impassive as a corpse excepting for the slow, shallow and rather irregular breathing with its ominous accompanying rattle. But presently, by imperceptible degrees, signs of returning life began to make their appearance. A sharp slap on the cheek with the wet towel produced a sensible flicker of the eyelids, a similar slap on the chest was followed by a slight gasp. A pencil, drawn over the sole of the foot, occasioned a visible shrinking movement, and, on looking once more at the eyes, I detected a slight change that told me that the atropine was beginning to take effect.

This was very encouraging, and, so far, quite satisfactory, though it would have been premature to rejoice. I kept the patient carefully covered and maintained the process of gentle irritation, moving his limbs and shoulders, brushing his hair and generally bombarding his deadened senses with small but repeated stimuli. And under this treatment, the improvement continued so far that on my bawling a question into his ear he actually opened his eyes for an instant, though in another moment, the lids had sunk back into their former position.

Soon after this, Mr. Weiss re-entered the room, followed by Mrs. Schallibaum, who carried a small tray, on which were a jug of coffee, a jug of milk, a cup and saucer and a sugar basin.

"How do you find him now?" Mr. Weiss asked anxiously.

"I am glad to say that there is a distinct improvement," I replied. "But we must persevere. He is by no means out of the wood yet."

I examined the coffee, which looked black and strong and had a very reassuring smell, and, pouring out half-a-cupful, approached the bed.

"Now, Mr. Graves," I shouted, "we want you to drink some of this."

The flaccid eyelids lifted for an instant but there was no other response. I gently opened the unresisting mouth and ladled in a couple of spoonfuls of coffee, which were immediately swallowed, whereupon I repeated the proceeding and continued at short intervals until the cup was empty. The effect of the new remedy soon became apparent. He began to mumble and mutter obscurely in response to the questions that I bellowed at him, and once or twice he opened his eyes and looked dreamily into my face. Then I sat him up and made him drink some coffee from the cup, and, all the time, kept up a running fire of questions, which made up in volume of sound for what they lacked of relevancy.

Of these proceedings Mr. Weiss and his housekeeper were highly interested spectators, and the former, contrary to his usual practice, came quite close up to the bed, to get a better view.

"It is really a most remarkable thing," he said, "but it almost looks as if you were right, after all. He is certainly much better. But tell me, would this treatment produce a similar improvement if the symptoms were due to disease?"

"No," I answered, "it certainly would not."

"Then that seems to settle it. But it is a most mysterious affair. Can you suggest any way in which he can have concealed a store of the drug?"

I stood up and looked him straight in the face, it was the first chance I had had of inspecting him by any but the feeblest light, and I looked at him very attentively. Now, it is a curious fact – though one that most persons must have observed – that there sometimes occurs a considerable interval between the reception of a visual impression and its complete transfer to the consciousness. A thing may be seen, as it were, unconsciously, and the impression consigned, apparently, to instant oblivion, and yet the picture may be subsequently revived by memory with such completeness that its details can be studied as though the object were still actually visible.

Something of this kind must have happened to me now. Preoccupied as I was by the condition of the patient, the professional habit of rapid and close observation caused me to direct a searching glance at the man before me. It was only a brief glance – for Mr. Weiss, perhaps embarrassed by my keen regard of him, almost immediately withdrew into the shadow – and my attention seemed principally to be occupied by the odd contrast between the pallor of his face and the redness of his nose and by the peculiar stiff, bristly character of his eyebrows. But there was another fact, and a very curious one, that was observed by me subconsciously and instantly forgotten, to be revived later when I reflected on the events of the night. It was this:

As Mr. Weiss stood, with his head slightly turned, I was able to look through one glass of his spectacles at the wall beyond. On the wall was a framed print, and the edge of the frame, seen through the spectacle-glass, appeared quite unaltered and free from distortion, magnification or reduction, as if seen through plain window-glass, and yet the reflections of the candle-flame in the spectacles showed the flame upside down, proving conclusively that the glasses were concave on one surface at least.

469

The strange phenomenon was visible only for a moment or two, and as it passed out of my sight it passed also out of my mind.

"No," I said, replying to the last question, "I can think of no way in which he could have effectually hidden a store of morphine. Judging by the symptoms, he has taken a large dose, and, if he has been in the habit of consuming large quantities, his stock would be pretty bulky. I can offer no suggestion whatever."

"I suppose you consider him quite out of danger now?"

"Oh, not at all. I think we can pull him round if we persevere, but he must not be allowed to sink back into a state of coma. We must keep him on the move until the effects of the drug have really passed off. If you will put him into his dressing-gown we will walk him up and down the room for a while."

"But is that safe?" Mr. Weiss asked anxiously.

"Quite safe," I answered. "I will watch his pulse carefully. The danger is in the possibility, or rather certainty, of a relapse if he is not kept moving."

With obvious unwillingness and disapproval, Mr. Weiss produced a dressing-gown and together we invested the patient in it. Then we dragged him, very limp, but not entirely unresisting, out of bed and stood him on his feet. He opened his eyes and blinked owlishly first at one and then at the other of us, and mumbled a few unintelligible words of protest, regardless of which, we thrust his feet into slippers and endeavoured to make him walk. At first he seemed unable to stand, and we had to support him by his arms as we urged him forward, but presently his trailing legs began to make definite walking movements, and, after one or two turns up and down the room, he was not only able partly to support his weight, but showed evidence of reviving consciousness in more energetic protests.

At this point Mr. Weiss astonished me by transferring the arm that he held to the housekeeper.

"If you will excuse me, Doctor," said he, "I will go now and attend to some rather important business that I have had to leave unfinished. Mrs. Schallibaum will be able to give you all the assistance that you require, and will order the carriage when you think it safe to leave the patient. In case I should not see you again I will say 'good night'. I hope you won't think me very unceremonious."

He shook hands with me and went out of the room, leaving me, as I have said, profoundly astonished that he should consider any business of more moment than the condition of his friend, whose life, even now, was but hanging by a thread. However, it was really no concern of mine. I could do without him, and the resuscitation of this unfortunate half-dead man gave me occupation enough to engross my whole attention.

470

The melancholy progress up and down the room re-commenced, and with it the mumbled protests from the patient. As we walked, and especially as we turned, I caught frequent glimpses of the housekeeper's face. But it was nearly always in profile. She appeared to avoid looking me in the face, though she did so once or twice, and on each of these occasions her eyes were directed at me in a normal manner without any sign of a squint. Nevertheless, I had the impression that when her face was turned away from me she squinted. The "swivel eye" – the left – was towards me as she held the patient's right arm, and it was almost continuously turned in my direction, whereas I felt convinced that she was really looking straight before her, though, of course, her right eye was invisible to me. It struck me, even at the time, as an odd affair, but I was too much concerned about my charge to give it much consideration.

Meanwhile the patient continued to revive apace. And the more he revived, the more energetically did he protest against this wearisome perambulation. But he was evidently a polite gentleman, for, muddled as his faculties were, he managed to clothe his objections in courteous and even gracious forms of speech singularly out of agreement with the character that Mr. Weiss had given him.

"I thangyou," he mumbled thickly. "Ver' good take s'much trouble. Think I will lie down now." He looked wistfully at the bed, but I wheeled him about and marched him once more down the room. He submitted unresistingly, but as we again approached the bed he reopened the matter.

"S'quite s'fficient, thang you. Gebback to bed now. Much 'bliged frall your kindness" – here I turned him round – "no, really, m'feeling rather tired. Sh'like to lie down now, f'you'd be s'good."

"You must walk about a little longer, Mr. Graves," I said. "It would be very bad for you to go to sleep again."

He looked at me with a curious, dull surprise, and reflected awhile as if in some perplexity. Then he looked at me again and said, "Thing, sir, you are mistake – mistaken me – mist – "

Here Mrs. Schallibaum interrupted sharply, "The doctor thinks it's good for you to walk about. You've been sleeping too much. He doesn't want you to sleep any more just now."

"Don't wanter sleep, wanter lie down," said the patient.

"But you mustn't lie down for a little while. You must walk about for a few minutes more. And you'd better not talk. Just walk up and down."

"There's no harm in his talking," said I, "in fact it's good for him. It will help to keep him awake."

"I should think it would tire him," said Mrs. Schallibaum, "and it worries me to hear him asking to lie down when we can't let him."

471

She spoke sharply and in an unnecessarily high tone so that the patient could not fail to hear. Apparently he took in the very broad hint contained in the concluding sentence, for he trudged wearily and unsteadily up and down the room for some time without speaking, though he continued to look at me from time to time as if something in my appearance puzzled him exceedingly. At length his intolerable longing for repose overcame his politeness and he returned to the attack.

"Surely v' walked enough now. Feeling very tired. Am really. Would you be s'kind 's t'let me lie down few minutes?"

"Don't you think he might lie down for a little while?" Mrs. Schallibaum asked.

I felt his pulse, and decided that he was really becoming fatigued, and that it would be wiser not to overdo the exercise while he was so weak. Accordingly, I consented to his returning to bed, and turned him round in that direction, whereupon he tottered gleefully towards his resting-place like a tired horse heading for its stable.

As soon as he was tucked in, I gave him a full cup of coffee, which he drank with some avidity as if thirsty. Then I sat down by the bedside, and, with a view to keeping him awake, began once more to ply him with questions.

"Does your head ache, Mr. Graves?" I asked.

"The doctor says 'does your head ache?'" Mrs. Schallibaum squalled, so loudly that the patient started perceptibly.

"I heard him, m'dear girl," he answered with a faint smile. "Not deaf you know. Yes. Head aches a good deal. But I thing this gennleman mistakes – "

"He says you are to keep awake. You mustn't go to sleep again, and you are not to close your eyes."

"All ri' Pol'n. Keep'm open," and he proceeded forthwith to shut them with an air of infinite peacefulness. I grasped his hand and shook it gently, on which he opened his eyes and looked at me sleepily. The housekeeper stroked his head, keeping her face half-turned from me – as she had done almost constantly, to conceal the squinting eye, as I assumed – and said, "Need we keep you any longer, Doctor? It is getting very late and you have a long way to go."

I looked doubtfully at the patient. I was loath to leave him, distrusting these people as I did. But I had my work to do on the morrow, with, perhaps, a night call or two in the interval, and the endurance even of a general practitioner has its limits.

"I think I heard the carriage some time ago," Mrs. Schallibaum added.

I rose hesitatingly and looked at my watch. It had turned half-past-eleven.

472

"You understand," I said in a low voice, "that the danger is not over? If he is left now he will fall asleep, and in all human probability will never wake. You clearly understand that?"

"Yes, quite clearly. I promise you he shall not be allowed to fall asleep again."

As she spoke, she looked me full in the face for a few moments, and I noted that her eyes had a perfectly normal appearance, without any trace whatever of a squint.

"Very well," I said. "On that understanding I will go now, and I shall hope to find our friend quite recovered at my next visit."

I turned to the patient, who was already dozing, and shook his hand heartily.

"Good-bye, Mr. Graves!" I said. "I am sorry to have to disturb your repose so much, but you must keep awake, you know. Won't do to go to sleep."

"Ver' well," he replied drowsily. "Sorry t' give you all this trouble. L' keep awake. But I think you're mistak'n – "

"He says it's very important that you shouldn't go to sleep, and that I am to see that you don't. Do you understand?"

"Yes, I un'stan'. But why does this gennlem'n – ?"

"Now it's of no use for you to ask a lot of questions," Mrs. Schallibaum said playfully. "We'll talk to you to-morrow. Good night, Doctor. I'll light you down the stairs, but I won't come down with you, or the patient will be falling asleep again."

Taking this definite dismissal, I retired, followed by a dreamily surprised glance from the sick man. The housekeeper held the candle over the balusters until I reached the bottom of the stairs, when I perceived through the open door along the passage a glimmer of light from the carriage lamps. The coachman was standing just outside, faintly illuminated by the very dim lamplight, and as I stepped into the carriage he remarked in his Scotch dialect that I "seemed to have been makin' a nicht of it." He did not wait for any reply – none being in fact needed – but shut the door and locked it.

I lit my little pocket-lamp and hung it on the back cushion. I even drew the board and notebook from my pocket. But it seemed rather unnecessary to take a fresh set of notes, and, to tell the truth, I rather shirked the labour, tired as I was after my late exertions. Besides, I wanted to think over the events of the evening, while they were fresh in my memory. Accordingly I put away the notebook, filled and lighted my pipe, and settled myself to review the incidents attending my second visit to this rather uncanny house.

473

Considered in leisurely retrospect, that visit offered quite a number of problems that called for elucidation. There was the patient's condition, for instance. Any doubt as to the cause of his symptoms was set at rest by the effect of the antidotes. Mr. Graves was certainly under the influence of morphine, and the only doubtful question was how he had become so. That he had taken the poison himself was incredible. No morphinomaniac would take such a knock-down dose. It was practically certain that the poison had been administered by someone else, and, on Mr. Weiss's own showing, there was no one but himself and the housekeeper who could have administered it. And to this conclusion all the other very queer circumstances pointed.

What were these circumstances? They were, as I have said, numerous, though many of them seemed trivial. To begin with, Mr. Weiss's habit of appearing some time after my arrival and disappearing some time before my departure was decidedly odd. But still more odd was his sudden departure this evening on what looked like a mere pretext. That departure coincided in time with the sick man's recovery of the power of speech. Could it be that Mr. Weiss was afraid that the half-conscious man might say something compromising to him in my presence? It looked rather like it. And yet he had gone away and left me with the patient and the housekeeper.

But when I came to think about it I remembered that Mrs. Schallibaum had shown some anxiety to prevent the patient from talking. She had interrupted him more than once, and had on two occasions broken in when he seemed to be about to ask me some question. I was "mistaken" about something. What was that something that he wanted to tell me?

It had struck me as singular that there should be no coffee in the house, but a sufficiency of tea. Germans are not usually tea-drinkers and they do take coffee. But perhaps there was nothing in this. Rather more remarkable was the invisibility of the coachman. Why could he not be sent to fetch the coffee, and why did not he, rather than the housekeeper, come to take the place of Mr. Weiss when the latter had to go away.

There were other points, too. I recalled the word that sounded like "Pol'n," which Mr. Graves had used in speaking to the housekeeper. Apparently it was a Christian name of some kind, but why did Mr. Graves call the woman by her Christian name when Mr. Weiss addressed her formally as Mrs. Schallibaum? And, as to the woman herself: What was the meaning of that curious disappearing squint? Physically it presented no mystery. The woman had an ordinary divergent squint, and, like many people, who suffer from this displacement, could, by a strong muscular effort, bring the eyes temporarily into their normal parallel position. I had detected the displacement when she had tried to maintain the effort too long, and the muscular control had given way. But why had she done it? Was it only feminine vanity – mere sensitiveness respecting a slight personal disfigurement? It might be so, or there might be some further motive. It was impossible to say.

Turning this question over, I suddenly remembered the peculiarity of Mr. Weiss's spectacles. And here I met with a real poser. I had certainly seen through those spectacles as clearly as if they had been plain window-glass, and they had certainly given an inverted reflection of the candle-flame like that thrown from the surface of a concave lens. Now they obviously could not be both flat and concave, but yet they had the properties peculiar to both flatness and concavity. And there was a further difficulty. If I could see objects unaltered through them, so could Mr. Weiss. But the function of spectacles is to alter the appearances of objects, by magnification, reduction, or compensating distortion. If they leave the appearances unchanged they are useless. I could make nothing of it. After puzzling over it for quite a long time, I had to give it up, which I did the less unwillingly inasmuch as the construction of Mr. Weiss's spectacles had no apparent bearing on the case.

On arriving home, I looked anxiously at the message-book, and was relieved to find that there were no further visits to be made. Having made up a mixture for Mr. Graves and handed it to the coachman, I raked the ashes of the surgery fire together and sat down to smoke a final pipe while I reflected once more on the singular and suspicious case in which I had become involved. But fatigue soon put an end to my meditations, and having come to the conclusion that the circumstances demanded a further consultation with Thorndyke, I turned down the gas to a microscopic blue spark and betook myself to bed.

Chapter IV
The Official View

I rose on the following morning still possessed by the determination to make some oportunity during the day to call on Thorndyke and take his advice on the now urgent question as to what I was to do. I use the word "urgent" advisedly, for the incidents of the preceding evening had left me with the firm conviction that poison was being administered for some purpose to my mysterious patient, and that no time must be lost if his life was to be saved. Last night he had escaped only by the narrowest margin – assuming him to be still alive – and it was only my unexpectedly firm attitude that had compelled Mr. Weiss to agree to restorative measures.

That I should be sent for again I had not the slightest expectation. If what I so strongly suspected was true, Weiss would call in some other doctor, in the hope of better luck, and it was imperative that he should be stopped before it was too late. This was my view, but I meant to have Thorndyke's opinion, and act under his direction, but *"The best laid plans of mice and men Gang aft agley"*.

When I came downstairs and took a preliminary glance at the rough memorandum-book, kept by the bottle-boy, or, in his absence, by the housemaid, I stood aghast. The morning's entries looked already like a sample page of the Post Office directory. The new calls alone were more than equal to an ordinary day's work, and the routine visits remained to be added. Gloomily wondering whether the Black Death had made a sudden reappearance in England, I hurried to the dining-room and made a hasty breakfast, interrupted at intervals by the apparition of the bottle-boy to announce new messages.

The first two or three visits solved the mystery. An epidemic of influenza had descended on the neighbourhood, and I was getting not only our own normal work but a certain amount of overflow from other practices. Further, it appeared that a strike in the building trade had been followed immediately by a widespread failure of health among the bricklayers who were members of a certain benefit club, which accounted for the remarkable suddenness of the outbreak.

Of course, my contemplated visit to Thorndyke was out of the question. I should have to act on my own responsibility. But in the hurry and rush and anxiety of the work – for some of the cases were severe and even critical – I had no opportunity to consider any course of action, nor time to carry it out. Even with the aid of a hansom which I chartered, as

476

Stillbury kept no carriage, I had not finished my last visit until near on midnight, and was then so spent with fatigue that I fell asleep over my postponed supper.

As the next day opened with a further increase of work, I sent a telegram to Dr. Stillbury at Hastings, whither he had gone, like a wise man, to recruit after a slight illness. I asked for authority to engage an assistant, but the reply informed me that Stillbury himself was on his way to town, and to my relief, when I dropped in at the surgery for a cup of tea, I found him rubbing his hands over the open day-book.

"It's an ill wind that blows nobody good," he remarked cheerfully as we shook hands. "This will pay the expenses of my holiday, including you. By the way, you are not anxious to be off, I suppose?"

As a matter of fact, I was, for I had decided to accept Thorndyke's offer, and was now eager to take up my duties with him. But it would have been shabby to leave Stillbury to battle alone with this rush of work or to seek the services of a strange assistant.

"I should like to get off as soon as you can spare me," I replied, "but I'm not going to leave you in the lurch."

"That's a good fellow," said Stillbury. "I knew you wouldn't. Let us have some tea and divide up the work. Anything of interest going?"

There were one or two unusual cases on the list, and, as we marked off our respective patients, I gave him the histories in brief synopsis. And then I opened the subject of my mysterious experiences at the house of Mr. Weiss.

"There's another affair that I want to tell you about, rather an unpleasant business."

"Oh, dear!" exclaimed Stillbury. He put down his cup and regarded me with quite painful anxiety.

"It looks to me like an undoubted case of criminal poisoning," I continued.

Stillbury's face cleared instantly. "Oh, I'm glad it's nothing more than that," he said with an air of relief. "I was afraid, it was some confounded woman. There's always that danger, you know, when a *locum* is young and happens – if I may say so, Jervis – to be a good-looking fellow. Let us hear about this case."

I gave him a condensed narrative of my connection with the mysterious patient, omitting any reference to Thorndyke, and passing lightly over my efforts to fix the position of the house, and wound up with the remark that the facts ought certainly to be communicated to the police.

"Yes," he admitted reluctantly, "I suppose you're right. Deuced unpleasant though. Police cases don't do a practice any good. They waste a lot of time, too – keep you hanging about to give evidence. Still, you are

477

quite right. We can't stand by and see the poor devil poisoned without making some effort. But I don't believe the police will do anything in the matter."

"Don't you really?"

"No, I don't. They like to have things pretty well cut-and-dried before they act. A prosecution is an expensive affair, so they don't care to prosecute unless they are fairly sure of a conviction. If they fail they get hauled over the coals."

"But don't you think they would get a conviction in this case?"

"Not on your evidence, Jervis. They might pick up something fresh, but, if they didn't they would fail. You haven't got enough hard-baked facts to upset a capable defence. Still, that isn't our affair. You want to put the responsibility on the police and I entirely agree with you."

"There ought not to be any delay," said I.

"There needn't be. I shall look in on Mrs. Wackford and you have to see the Rummel children, we shall pass the station on our way. Why shouldn't we drop in and see the inspector or superintendent?"

The suggestion met my views exactly. As soon as we had finished tea, we set forth, and in about ten minutes found ourselves in the bare and forbidding office attached to the station.

The presiding officer descended from a high stool, and, carefully laying down his pen, shook hands cordially.

"And what can I do for you gentlemen?" he asked, with an affable smile.

Stillbury proceeded to open our business.

"My friend here, Dr. Jervis, who has very kindly been looking after my work for a week or two, has had a most remarkable experience, and he wants to tell you about it."

"Something in my line of business?" the officer inquired.

"That," said I, "is for you to judge. I think it is, but you may think otherwise", and hereupon, without further preamble, I plunged into the history of the case, giving him a condensed statement similar to that which I had already made to Stillbury.

He listened with close attention, jotting down from time to time a brief note on a sheet of paper, and, when I had finished, he wrote out in a black-covered notebook a short *précis* of my statement.

"I have written down here," he said, "the substance of what you have told me. I will read the deposition over to you, and, if it is correct, I will ask you to sign it."

He did so, and, when I had signed the document, I asked him what was likely to be done in the matter.

"I am afraid," he replied, "that we can't take any active measures. You have put us on our guard and we shall keep our eyes open. But I think that is all we can do, unless we hear something further."

"But," I exclaimed, "don't you think that it is a very suspicious affair?"

"I do," he replied. "A very fishy business indeed, and you were quite right to come and tell us about it."

"It seems a pity not to take some measures," I said. "While you are waiting to hear something further, they may give the poor wretch a fresh dose and kill him."

"In which case we should hear something further, unless some fool of a doctor were to give a death certificate."

"But that is very unsatisfactory. The man ought not to be allowed to die."

"I quite agree with you, sir. But we've no evidence that he is going to die. His friends sent for you, and you treated him skilfully and left him in a fair way to recovery. That's all that we really know about it. Yes, I know," the officer continued as I made signs of disagreement, "you think that a crime is possibly going to be committed and that we ought to prevent it. But you overrate our powers. We can only act on evidence that a crime has actually been committed or is actually being attempted. Now we have no such evidence. Look at your statement, and tell me what you can swear to."

"I think I could swear that Mr. Graves had taken a poisonous dose of morphine."

"And who gave him that poisonous dose?"

"I very strongly suspect – "

"That's no good, sir," interrupted the officer. "Suspicion isn't evidence. We should want you to swear an information and give us enough facts to make out a *primâ facie* case against some definite person. And you couldn't do it. Your information amounts to this: That a certain person has taken a poisonous dose of morphine and apparently recovered. That's all. You can't swear that the names given to you are real names, and you can't give us any address or even any locality."

"I took some compass bearings in the carriage," I said. "You could locate the house, I think, without much difficulty."

The officer smiled faintly and fixed an abstracted gaze on the clock.

"You could, sir," he replied. "I have no doubt whatever that you could. I couldn't. But, in any case, we haven't enough to go upon. If you learn anything fresh, I hope you will let me know, and I am very much obliged to you for taking so much trouble in the matter. Good evening sir. Good evening, Dr. Stillbury."

479

He shook hands with us both genially, and, accepting perforce this very polite but unmistakable dismissal, we took our departure.

Outside the station, Stillbury heaved a comfortable sigh. He was evidently relieved to find that no upheavals were to take place in his domain.

"I thought that would be their attitude," he said, "and they are quite right, you know. The function of law is to prevent crime, it is true, but prophylaxis in the sense in which we understand it is not possible in legal practice."

I assented without enthusiasm. It was disappointing to find that no precautionary measures were to be taken. However, I had done all that I could in the matter. No further responsibility lay upon me, and, as it was practically certain that I had seen and heard the last of Mr. Graves and his mysterious household, I dismissed the case from my mind. At the next corner Stillbury and I parted to go our respective ways, and my attention was soon transferred from the romance of crime to the realities of epidemic influenza.

The plethora of work in Dr. Stillbury's practice continued longer than I had bargained for. Day after day went by and still found me tramping the dingy streets of Kennington or scrambling up and down narrow stairways, turning in at night dead tired, or turning out half-awake to the hideous jangle of the night bell.

It was very provoking. For months I had resisted Thorndyke's persuasion to give up general practice and join him. Not from lack of inclination, but from a deep suspicion that he was thinking of my wants rather than his own, that his was a charitable rather than a business proposal. Now that I knew this not to be the case, I was impatient to join him, and, as I trudged through the dreary thoroughfares of this superannuated suburb, with its once rustic villas and its faded gardens, my thoughts would turn enviously to the quiet dignity of the Temple and my friend's chambers in King's Bench Walk.

The closed carriage appeared no more, nor did any whisper either of good or evil reach me in connection with the mysterious house from which it had come. Mr. Graves had apparently gone out of my life for ever.

But if he had gone out of my life, he had not gone out of my memory. Often, as I walked my rounds, would the picture of that dimly-lit room rise unbidden. Often would I find myself looking once more into that ghastly face, so worn, so wasted and haggard, and yet so far from repellent. All the incidents of that last night would reconstitute themselves with a vividness that showed the intensity of the impression that they had made at the time. I would have gladly forgotten the whole affair, for every incident of it was fraught with discomfort. But it clung to my memory, it

480

haunted me, and ever as it returned it bore with it the disquieting questions: Was Mr. Graves still alive? And, if he was not, was there really nothing which could have been done to save him?

Nearly a month passed before the practice began to show signs of returning to its normal condition. Then the daily lists became more and more contracted and the day's work proportionately shorter. And thus the term of my servitude came to an end. One evening, as we were writing up the day-book, Stillbury remarked, "I almost think, Jervis, I could manage by myself now. I know you are only staying on for my sake."

"I am staying on to finish my engagement, but I shan't be sorry to clear out if you can do without me."

"I think I can. When would you like to be off?"

"As soon as possible. Say to-morrow morning, after I have made a few visits and transferred the patients to you."

"Very well," said Stillbury. "Then I will give you your cheque and settle up everything to-night, so that you shall be free to go off when you like to-morrow morning."

Thus ended my connection with Kennington Lane. On the following day at about noon, I found myself strolling across Waterloo Bridge with the sensations of a newly liberated convict and a cheque for twenty-five guineas in my pocket. My luggage was to follow when I sent for it. Now, unhampered even by a hand-bag, I joyfully descended the steps at the north end of the bridge and headed for King's Bench Walk by way of the Embankment and Middle Temple Lane.

Chapter V
Jeffrey Blackmore's Will

My arrival at Thorndyke's chambers was not unexpected, having been heralded by a premonitory post-card. The "oak" was open and an application of the little brass knocker of the inner door immediately produced my colleague himself and a very hearty welcome.

"At last," said Thorndyke, "you have come forth from the house of bondage. I began to think that you had taken up your abode in Kennington for good."

"I was beginning, myself, to wonder when I should escape. But here I am, and I may say at once that I am ready to shake the dust of general practice off my feet for ever – that is, if you are still willing to have me as your assistant."

"Willing!" exclaimed Thorndyke, "Barkis himself was not more willing than I. You will be invaluable to me. Let us settle the terms of our comradeship forthwith, and to-morrow we will take measures to enter you as a student of the Inner Temple. Shall we have our talk in the open air and the spring sunshine?"

I agreed readily to this proposal, for it was a bright, sunny day and warm for the time of year – the beginning of April. We descended to the Walk and thence slowly made our way to the quiet court behind the church, where poor old Oliver Goldsmith lies, as he would surely have wished to lie, in the midst of all that had been dear to him in his chequered life. I need not record the matter of our conversation. To Thorndyke's proposals I had no objections to offer but my own unworthiness and his excessive liberality. A few minutes saw our covenants fully agreed upon, and when Thorndyke had noted the points on a slip of paper, signed and dated it and handed it to me, the business was at an end.

"There," my colleague said with a smile as he put away his pocket-book, "if people would only settle their affairs in that way, a good part of the occupation of lawyers would be gone. Brevity is the soul of wit, and the fear of simplicity is the beginning of litigation."

"And now," I said, "I propose that we go and feed. I will invite you to lunch to celebrate our contract."

"My learned junior is premature," he replied. "I had already arranged a little festivity – or rather had modified one that was already arranged. You remember Mr. Marchmont, the solicitor?"

"Yes."

"He called this morning to ask me to lunch with him and a new client at the 'Cheshire Cheese'. I accepted and notified him that I should bring you."

"Why the 'Cheshire Cheese'?" I asked.

"Why not? Marchmont's reasons for the selection were, first, that his client has never seen an old-fashioned London tavern, and second, that this is Wednesday and he, Marchmont, has a gluttonous affection for a really fine beef-steak pudding. You don't object, I hope?"

"Oh, not at all. In fact, now that you mention it, my own sensations incline me to sympathize with Marchmont. I breakfasted rather early."

"Then come," said Thorndyke. "The assignation is for one o'clock, and, if we walk slowly, we shall just hit it off."

We sauntered up Inner Temple Lane, and, crossing Fleet Street, headed sedately for the tavern. As we entered the quaint old-world dining-room, Thorndyke looked round and a gentleman, who was seated with a companion at a table in one of the little boxes or compartments, rose and saluted us.

"Let me introduce you to my friend Mr. Stephen Blackmore," he said as we approached. Then, turning to his companion, he introduced us by our respective names.

"I engaged this box," he continued, "so that we might be private if we wished to have a little preliminary chat – not that beef-steak pudding is a great help to conversation. But when people have a certain business in view, their talk is sure to drift towards it, sooner or later."

Thorndyke and I sat down opposite the lawyer and his client, and we mutually inspected one another. Marchmont I already knew, an elderly, professional-looking man, a typical solicitor of the old school, fresh-faced, precise, rather irascible, and conveying a not unpleasant impression of taking a reasonable interest in his diet. The other man was quite young, not more than five-and-twenty, and was a fine athletic-looking fellow with a healthy, out-of-door complexion and an intelligent and highly prepossessing face. I took a liking to him at the first glance, and so, I saw, did Thorndyke.

"You two gentlemen," said Blackmore, addressing us, "seem to be quite old acquaintances. I have heard so much about you from my friend, Reuben Hornby."

"Ah!" exclaimed Marchmont, "that was a queer case – 'The Case of the Red Thumb Mark', as the papers called it. It was an eye-opener to old-fashioned lawyers like myself. We've had scientific witnesses before – and bullied 'em properly, by Jove! – when they wouldn't give the evidence that we wanted. But the scientific lawyer is something new. His appearance in court made us all sit up, I can assure you."

483

"I hope we shall make you sit up again," said Thorndyke.

"You won't this time," said Marchmont. "The issues in this case of my friend Blackmore's are purely legal, or rather, there are no issues at all. There is nothing in dispute. I tried to prevent Blackmore from consulting you, but he wouldn't listen to reason. Here! Waiter! How much longer are we to be waiters? We shall die of old age before we get our victuals!"

The waiter smiled apologetically. "Yessir!" said he. "Coming now, sir." And at this very moment there was borne into the room a Gargantuan pudding in a great bucket of a basin, which being placed on a three-legged stool was forthwith attacked ferociously by the white-clothed, white-capped carver. We watched the process – as did every one present – with an interest not entirely gluttonous, for it added a pleasant touch to the picturesque old room, with its sanded floor, its homely, pew-like boxes, its high-backed settles and the friendly portrait of the "great lexicographer" that beamed down on us from the wall.

"This is a very different affair from your great, glittering modern restaurant," Mr. Marchmont remarked.

"It is indeed," said Blackmore, "and if this is the way in which our ancestors lived, it would seem that they had a better idea of comfort than we have."

There was a short pause, during which Mr. Marchmont glared hungrily at the pudding, then Thorndyke said, "So you refused to listen to reason, Mr. Blackmore?"

"Yes. You see, Mr. Marchmont and his partner had gone into the matter and decided that there was nothing to be done. Then I happened to mention the affair to Reuben Hornby, and he urged me to ask your advice on the case."

"Like his impudence," growled Marchmont, "to meddle with my client."

"On which," continued Blackmore, "I spoke to Mr. Marchmont and he agreed that it was worth while to take your opinion on the case, though he warned me to cherish no hopes, as the affair was not really within your specialty."

"So you understand," said Marchmont, "that we expect nothing. This is quite a forlorn hope. We are taking your opinion as a mere formality, to be able to say that we have left nothing untried."

"That is an encouraging start," Thorndyke remarked. "It leaves me unembarrassed by the possibility of failure. But meanwhile you are arousing in me a devouring curiosity as to the nature of the case. Is it highly confidential? Because if not, I would mention that Jervis has now joined me as my permanent colleague."

484

"It isn't confidential at all," said Marchmont. "The public are in full possession of the facts, and we should be only too happy to put them in still fuller possession, through the medium of the Probate Court, if we could find a reasonable pretext. But we can't."

Here the waiter charged our table with the fussy rapidity of the overdue.

"Sorry to keep you waiting, sir. Rather early, sir. Wouldn't like it underdone, sir."

Marchmont inspected his plate critically and remarked, "I sometimes suspect these oysters of being mussels, and I'll swear the larks are sparrows."

"Let us hope so," said Thorndyke. "The lark is better employed 'at Heaven's gate singing' than garnishing a beef-steak pudding. But you were telling us about your case."

"So I was. Well it's just a matter of – ale or claret? Oh, claret, I know. You despise the good old British John Barleycorn."

"*He that drinks beer thinks beer*," retorted Thorndyke. "But you were saying that it is just a matter of – ?"

"A matter of a perverse testator and an ill-drawn will. A peculiarly irritating case, too, because the defective will replaces a perfectly sound one, and the intentions of the testator were – er – were – excellent ale, this. A little heady, perhaps, but sound. Better than your sour French wine, Thorndyke – were – er – were quite obvious. What he evidently desired was – mustard? Better have some mustard. No? Well, well! Even a Frenchman would take mustard. You can have no appreciation of flavour, Thorndyke, if you take your victuals in that crude, unseasoned state. And, talking of flavour, do you suppose that there is really any difference between that of a lark and that of a sparrow?"

Thorndyke smiled grimly. "I should suppose," said he, "that they were indistinguishable, but the question could easily be put to the test of experiment."

"That is true," agreed Marchmont, "and it would really be worth trying, for, as you say, sparrows are more easily obtainable than larks. But, about this will. I was saying – er – now, what was I saying?"

"I understood you to say," replied Thorndyke, "that the intentions of the testator were in some way connected with mustard. Isn't that so, Jervis?"

"That was what I gathered," said I.

Marchmont gazed at us for a moment with a surprised expression and then, laughing good-humouredly, fortified himself with a draught of ale.

"The moral of which is," Thorndyke added, "that testamentary dispositions should not be mixed up with beef-steak pudding."

485

"I believe you're right, Thorndyke," said the unabashed solicitor. "Business is business and eating is eating. We had better talk over our case in my office or your chambers after lunch."

"Yes," said Thorndyke, "come over to the Temple with me and I will give you a cup of coffee to clear your brain. Are there any documents?"

"I have all the papers here in my bag," replied Marchmont, and the conversation – such conversation as is possible "when beards wag all" over the festive board – drifted into other channels.

As soon as the meal was finished and the reckoning paid, we trooped out of Wine Office Court, and, insinuating ourselves through the line of empty hansoms that, in those days, crawled in a continuous procession on either side of Fleet Street, betook ourselves by way of Mitre Court to King's Bench Walk. There, when the coffee had been requisitioned and our chairs drawn up around the fire, Mr. Marchmont unloaded from his bag a portentous bundle of papers, and we addressed ourselves to the business in hand.

"Now," said Marchmont, "let me repeat what I said before. Legally speaking, we have no case – not the ghost of one. But my client wished to take your opinion, and I agreed on the bare chance that you might detect some point that we had overlooked. I don't think you will, for we have gone into the case very thoroughly, but still, there is the infinitesimal chance and we may as well take it. Would you like to read the two wills, or shall I first explain the circumstances?"

"I think," replied Thorndyke, "a narrative of the events in the order of their occurrence would be most helpful. I should like to know as much as possible about the testator before I examine the documents."

"Very well," said Marchmont. "Then I will begin with a recital of the circumstances, which, briefly stated, are these: My client, Stephen Blackmore, is the son of Mr. Edward Blackmore, deceased. Edward Blackmore had two brothers who survived him, John, the elder, and Jeffrey, the younger. Jeffrey is the testator in this case.

"Some two years ago, Jeffrey Blackmore executed a will by which he made his nephew Stephen his executor and sole legatee, and a few months later he added a codicil giving two-hundred-and-fifty pounds to his brother John."

"What was the value of the estate?" Thorndyke asked.

"About three-thousand-five-hundred pounds, all invested in Consols. The testator had a pension from the Foreign Office, on which he lived, leaving his capital untouched. Soon after having made his will, he left the rooms in Jermyn Street, where he had lived for some years, stored his furniture and went to Florence. From thence he moved on to Rome and then to Venice and other places in Italy, and so continued to travel about

486

until the end of last September, when it appears that he returned to England, for at the beginning of October he took a set of chambers in New Inn, which he furnished with some of the things from his old rooms. As far as we can make out, he never communicated with any of his friends, excepting his brother, and the fact of his being in residence at New Inn or of his being in England at all became known to them only when he died."

"Was this quite in accordance with his ordinary habits?" Thorndyke asked.

"I should say not quite," Blackmore answered. "My uncle was a studious, solitary man, but he was not formerly a recluse. He was not much of a correspondent but he kept up some sort of communication with his friends. He used, for instance, to write to me sometimes, and, when I came down from Cambridge for the vacations, he had me to stay with him at his rooms."

"Is there anything known that accounts for the change in his habits?"

"Yes, there is," replied Marchmont. "We shall come to that presently. To proceed with the narrative: On the fifteenth of last March he was found dead in his chambers, and a more recent will was then discovered, dated the twelfth of November of last year. Now no change had taken place in the circumstances of the testator to account for the new will, nor was there any appreciable alteration in the disposition of the property. As far as we can make out, the new will was drawn with the idea of stating the intentions of the testator with greater exactness and for the sake of doing away with the codicil. The entire property, with the exception of two-hundred-and-fifty pounds, was, as before, bequeathed to Stephen, but the separate items were specified, and the testator's brother, John Blackmore, was named as the executor and residuary legatee."

"I see," said Thorndyke. "So that your client's interest in the will would appear to be practically unaffected by the change."

"Yes. There it is," exclaimed the lawyer, slapping the table to add emphasis to his words. "That is the pity of it! If people who have no knowledge of law would only refrain from tinkering at their wills, what a world of trouble would be saved!"

"Oh, come!" said Thorndyke. "It is not for a lawyer to say that."

"No, I suppose not," Marchmont agreed. "Only, you see, we like the muddle to be made by the other side. But, in this case, the muddle is on our side. The change, as you say, seems to leave our friend Stephen's interests unaffected. That is, of course, what poor Jeffrey Blackmore thought. But he was mistaken. The effect of the change is absolutely disastrous."

"Indeed!"

487

"Yes. As I have said, no alteration in the testator's circumstances had taken place at the time the new will was executed. But only two days before his death, his sister, Mrs. Edmund Wilson, died, and on her will being proved it appeared that she had bequeathed to him her entire personalty, estimated at about thirty-thousand pounds."

"Heigho!" exclaimed Thorndyke. "What an unfortunate affair!"

"You are right," said Mr. Marchmont, "it was a disaster. By the original will this great sum would have accrued to our friend Mr. Stephen, whereas now, of course, it goes to the residuary legatee, Mr. John Blackmore. And what makes it even more exasperating is the fact that this is obviously not in accordance with the wishes and intentions of Mr. Jeffrey, who clearly desired his nephew to inherit his property."

"Yes," said Thorndyke, "I think you are justified in assuming that. But do you know whether Mr. Jeffrey was aware of his sister's intentions?"

"We think not. Her will was executed as recently as the third of September last, and it seems that there had been no communication between her and Mr. Jeffrey since that date. Besides, if you consider Mr. Jeffrey's actions, you will see that they suggest no knowledge or expectation of this very important bequest. A man does not make elaborate dispositions in regard to three-thousand pounds and then leave a sum of thirty-thousand to be disposed of casually as the residue of the estate."

"No," Thorndyke agreed. "And, as you have said, the manifest intention of the testator was to leave the bulk of his property to Mr. Stephen. So we may take it as virtually certain that Mr. Jeffrey had no knowledge of the fact that he was a beneficiary under his sister's will."

"Yes," said Mr. Marchmont, "I think we may take that as nearly certain."

"With reference to the second will," said Thorndyke, "I suppose there is no need to ask whether the document itself has been examined, I mean as to its being a genuine document and perfectly regular?"

Mr. Marchmont shook his head sadly.

"No," he said, "I am sorry to say that there can be no possible doubt as to the authenticity and regularity of the document. The circumstances under which it was executed establish its genuineness beyond any question."

"What were those circumstances?" Thorndyke asked.

"They were these: On the morning of the twelfth of November last, Mr. Jeffrey came to the porter's lodge with a document in his hand. 'This,' he said, 'is my will. I want you to witness my signature. Would you mind doing so, and can you find another respectable person to act as the second witness?' Now it happened that a nephew of the porter's, a painter by trade, was at work in the Inn. The porter went out and fetched him into the lodge and the two men agreed to witness the signature. 'You had better read the will,' said Mr. Jeffrey. 'It is not actually necessary, but it is an additional safeguard and there is nothing of a private nature in the document.' The two men accordingly read the document, and, when Mr. Jeffrey had signed it in their presence, they affixed their signatures, and I may add that the painter left the recognizable impressions of three greasy fingers."

"And these witnesses have been examined?"

"Yes. They have both sworn to the document and to their own signatures, and the painter recognized his finger-marks."

"That," said Thorndyke, "seems to dispose pretty effectually of any question as to the genuineness of the will, and if, as I gather, Mr. Jeffrey came to the lodge alone, the question of undue influence is disposed of too."

"Yes," said Mr. Marchmont. "I think we must pass the will as absolutely flawless."

"It strikes me as rather odd," said Thorndyke, "that Jeffrey should have known so little about his sister's intentions. Can you explain it, Mr. Blackmore?"

"I don't think that it is very remarkable," Stephen replied. "I knew very little of my aunt's affairs and I don't think my uncle Jeffrey knew much more, for he was under the impression that she had only a life interest in her husband's property. And he may have been right. It is not clear what money this was that she left to my uncle. She was a very taciturn woman and made few confidences to anyone."

"So that it is possible," said Thorndyke, "that she, herself, may have acquired this money recently by some bequest?"

"It is quite possible," Stephen answered.

"She died, I understand," said Thorndyke, glancing at the notes that he had jotted down, "two days before Mr. Jeffrey. What date would that be?"

"Jeffrey died on the fourteenth of March," said Marchmont.

"So that Mrs. Wilson died on the twelfth of March?"

"That is so," Marchmont replied, and Thorndyke then asked, "Did she die suddenly?"

"No," replied Stephen, "she died of cancer. I understand that it was cancer of the stomach."

"Do you happen to know," Thorndyke asked, "what sort of relations existed between Jeffrey and his brother John?"

489

"At one time," said Stephen, "I know they were not very cordial, but the breach may have been made up later, though I don't know that it actually was."

"I ask the question," said Thorndyke, "because, as I dare say you have noticed, there is, in the first will, some hint of improved relations. As it was originally drawn that will makes Mr. Stephen the sole legatee. Then, a little later, a codicil is added in favour of John, showing that Jeffrey had felt the necessity of making some recognition of his brother. This seems to point to some change in the relations, and the question arises: If such a change did actually occur, was it the beginning of a new and further improving state of feeling between the two brothers? Have you any facts bearing on that question?"

Marchmont pursed up his lips with the air of a man considering an unwelcome suggestion, and, after a few moments of reflection, answered, "I think we must say 'yes' to that. There is the undeniable fact that, of all Jeffrey's friends, John Blackmore was the only one who knew that he was living in New Inn."

"Oh, John knew that, did he?"

"Yes, he certainly did, for it came out in the evidence that he had called on Jeffrey at his chambers more than once. There is no denying that. But, mark you!" Mr. Marchmont added emphatically, "that does not cover the inconsistency of the will. There is nothing in the second will to suggest that Jeffrey intended materially to increase the bequest to his brother."

"I quite agree with you, Marchmont. I think that is a perfectly sound position. You have, I suppose, fully considered the question as to whether it would be possible to set aside the second will on the ground that it fails to carry out the evident wishes and intentions of the testator?"

"Yes. My partner, Winwood, and I went into that question very carefully, and we also took counsel's opinion – Sir Horace Barnaby – and he was of the same opinion as ourselves, that the court would certainly uphold the will."

"I think that would be my own view," said Thorndyke, "especially after what you have told me. Do I understand that John Blackmore was the only person who knew that Jeffrey was in residence at New Inn?"

"The only one of his private friends. His bankers knew and so did the officials from whom he drew his pension."

"Of course he would have to notify his bankers of his change of address."

"Yes, of course. And à propos of the bank, I may mention that the manager tells me that, of late, they had noticed a slight change in the character of Jeffrey's signature – I think you will see the reason of the change when you hear the rest of his story. It was very trifling, not more

490

than commonly occurs when a man begins to grow old, especially if there is some failure of eyesight."

"Was Mr. Jeffrey's eyesight failing?" asked Thorndyke.

"Yes, it was, undoubtedly," said Stephen. "He was practically blind in one eye and, in the very last letter that I ever had from him, he mentioned that there were signs of commencing cataract in the other."

"You spoke of his pension. He continued to draw that regularly?"

"Yes, he drew his allowance every month, or rather, his bankers drew it for him. They had been accustomed to do so when he was abroad, and the authorities seem to have allowed the practice to continue."

Thorndyke reflected a while, running his eye over the notes on the slips of paper in his hand, and Marchmont surveyed him with a malicious smile. Presently the latter remarked, "Methinks the learned counsel is floored."

Thorndyke laughed. "It seems to me," he retorted, "that your proceedings are rather like those of the amiable individual who offered the bear a flint pebble, that he might crack it and extract the kernel. Your confounded will seems to offer no soft spot on which one could commence an attack. But we won't give up. We seem to have sucked the will dry. Let us now have a few facts respecting the parties concerned in it, and, as Jeffrey is the central figure, let us begin with him and the tragedy at New Inn that formed the starting-point of all this trouble."

Chapter VI
Jeffrey Blackmore, Deceased

Having made the above proposition, Thorndyke placed a fresh slip of paper on the blotting pad on his knee and looked inquiringly at Mr. Marchmont, who, in his turn, sighed and looked at the bundle of documents on the table.

"What do you want to know?" he asked a little wearily.

"Everything," replied Thorndyke. "You have hinted at circumstances that would account for a change in Jeffrey's habits and that would explain an alteration in the character of his signature. Let us have those circumstances. And, if I might venture on a suggestion, it would be that we take the events in the order in which they occurred or in which they became known."

"That's the worst of you, Thorndyke," Marchmont grumbled. "When a case has been squeezed out to the last drop, in a legal sense, you want to begin all over again with the family history of every one concerned and a list of his effects and household furniture. But I suppose you will have to be humoured, and I imagine that the best way in which to give you the information you want will be to recite the circumstances surrounding the death of Jeffrey Blackmore. Will that suit you?"

"Perfectly," replied Thorndyke.

Thereupon Marchmont began. "The death of Jeffrey Blackmore was discovered at about eleven o'clock in the morning of the fifteenth of March. It seems that a builder's man was ascending a ladder to examine a gutter on Number 31 New Inn, when, on passing a second-floor window that was open at the top, he looked in and perceived a gentleman lying on a bed. The gentleman was fully clothed and had apparently lain down on the bed to rest, at least so the builder thought at the time, for he was merely passing the window on his way up, and, very properly, did not make a minute examination. But when, some ten minutes later, he came down and saw that the gentleman was still in the same position, he looked at him more attentively, and this is what he noticed – but perhaps we had better have it in his own words as he told the story at the inquest.

"'When I came to look at the gentleman a bit more closely, it struck me that he looked rather queer. His face looked very white, or rather pale yellow, like parchment, and his mouth was open. He did not seem to be breathing. On the bed by his side was a brass object of some kind – I could not make out what it was – and he seemed to be holding some small metal object in his hand. I thought it rather a queer affair, so, when I came down I went across to the lodge and told the porter about it. The porter came out across the square with me and I showed him the window. Then he told me to go up the stairs to Mr. Blackmore's chambers on the second pair and knock and keep on knocking until I got an answer. I went up and knocked and kept on knocking as loud as I could, but, though I fetched everybody out of all the other chambers in the house, I couldn't get any answer from Mr. Blackmore. So I went downstairs again and then Mr. Walker, the porter, sent me for a policeman.

"'I went out and met a policeman just by Dane's Inn and told him about the affair, and he came back with me. He and the porter consulted together, and then they told me to go up the ladder and get in at the window and open the door of the chambers from the inside. So I went up, and as soon as I got in at the window I saw that the gentleman was dead. I went through the other room and opened the outer door and let in the porter and the policeman.'

"That," said Mr. Marchmont, laying down the paper containing the depositions, "is the way in which poor Jeffrey Blackmore's death came to be discovered.

"The constable reported to his inspector and the inspector sent for the divisional surgeon, whom he accompanied to New Inn. I need not go into the evidence given by the police officers, as the surgeon saw all that they saw and his statement covers everything that is known about Jeffrey's death. This is what he says, after describing how he was sent for and arrived at the Inn:

"'In the bedroom I found the body of a man between fifty and sixty years of age, which has since been identified in my presence as that of Mr. Jeffrey Blackmore. It was fully dressed and wore boots on which was a moderate amount of dry mud. It was lying on its back on the bed, which did not appear to have been slept in, and showed no sign of any struggle or disturbance. The right hand loosely grasped a hypodermic syringe containing a few drops of clear liquid which I have since analysed and found to be a concentrated solution of strophanthin.

"'On the bed, close to the left side of the body, was a brass opium-pipe of a pattern which I believe is made in China. The bowl of the pipe contained a small quantity of charcoal, and a fragment of opium together with some ash, and there was on the bed a little ash which appeared to have dropped from the bowl when the pipe fell or was laid down. On the mantelshelf in the bedroom I found a small glass-stoppered jar containing about an ounce of solid opium, and another, larger jar containing wood charcoal broken up into small fragments. Also a bowl containing a quantity of ash with fragments of half-burned charcoal and a few minute particles of charred opium. By the side of the bowl were a knife, a kind of awl or pricker and a very small pair of tongs, which I believe to have been used for carrying a piece of lighted charcoal to the pipe.

"'On the dressing-table were two glass tubes labelled "*Hypodermic Tabloids: Strophanthin 1/500 grain*", and a minute glass mortar-and-pestle, of which the former contained a few crystals which have since been analysed by me and found to be strophanthin.

"'On examining the body, I found that it had been dead about twelve hours. There were no marks of violence or any abnormal condition excepting a single puncture in the right thigh, apparently made by the needle of the hypodermic syringe. The puncture was deep and vertical in direction as if the needle had been driven in through the clothing.

"'I made a post-mortem examination of the body and found that death was due to poisoning by strophanthin, which appeared to have been injected into the thigh. The two tubes which I found on the dressing-table would each have contained, if full, twenty tabloids, each tabloid representing one five-hundredth of a grain of strophanthin. Assuming that the whole of this quantity was injected the amount taken would be forty five-hundredths, or about one-twelfth of a grain. The ordinary medicinal dose of strophanthin is one five-hundredth of a grain.

"'I also found in the body appreciable traces of morphine – the principal alkaloid of opium – from which I infer that the deceased was a confirmed opium-smoker. This inference was supported by the general condition of the body, which was ill-nourished and emaciated and presented all the appearances usually met with in the bodies of persons addicted to the habitual use of opium.'

"That is the evidence of the surgeon. He was recalled later, as we shall see, but, meanwhile, I think you will agree with me that the facts testified to by him fully account, not only for the change in Jeffrey's habits – his solitary and secretive mode of life – but also for the alteration in his handwriting."

"Yes," agreed Thorndyke, "that seems to be so. By the way, what did the change in the handwriting amount to?"

"Very little," replied Marchmont. "It was hardly perceptible. Just a slight loss of firmness and distinctness, such a trifling change as you would expect to find in the handwriting of a man who had taken to drink or drugs, or anything that might impair the steadiness of his hand. I should not have noticed it, myself, but, of course, the people at the bank are experts, constantly scrutinizing signatures and scrutinizing them with a very critical eye."

"Is there any other evidence that bears on the case?" Thorndyke asked.

Marchmont turned over the bundle of papers and smiled grimly.

"My dear Thorndyke," he said, "none of this evidence has the slightest bearing on the case. It is all perfectly irrelevant as far as the will is concerned. But I know your little peculiarities and I am indulging you, as you see, to the top of your bent. The next evidence is that of the chief porter, a very worthy and intelligent man named Walker. This is what he says, after the usual preliminaries.

"'I have viewed the body which forms the subject of this inquiry. It is that of Mr. Jeffrey Blackmore, the tenant of a set of chambers on the second floor of Number Thirty-one, New Inn. I have known the deceased nearly six months, and during that time have seen and conversed with him frequently. He took the chambers on the second of last October and came into residence at once. Tenants at New Inn have to furnish two references. The references that the deceased gave were his bankers and his brother, Mr. John Blackmore. I may say that the deceased was very well known to me. He was a quiet, pleasant-mannered gentleman, and it was his habit to drop in occasionally at the lodge and have a chat with me. I went into his chambers with him once or twice on some small matters of business and I noticed that there were always a number of books and papers on the table. I understood from him that he spent most of his time indoors engaged in study and writing. I know very little about his way of living. He had no laundress to look after his rooms, so I suppose he did his own house-work and cooking, but he told me that he took most of his meals outside, at restaurants or his club.

"'Deceased impressed me as a rather melancholy, low-spirited gentleman. He was very much troubled about his eyesight and mentioned the matter to me on several occasions. He told me that he was practically blind in one eye and that the sight of the other was failing rapidly. He said that this afflicted him greatly, because his only pleasure in life was in the reading of books, and that if he could not read he should not wish to live. On another occasion he said that "to a blind man life was not worth living."'

"'On the twelfth of last November he came to the lodge with a paper in his hand which he said was his will' – But I needn't read that," said Marchmont, turning over the leaf, "I've told you how the will was signed and witnessed. We will pass on to the day of poor Jeffrey's death.

"'On the fourteenth of March,' the porter says, 'at about half-past six in the evening, the deceased came to the Inn in a four-wheeled cab. That was the day of the great fog. I do not know if there was anyone in the cab with the deceased, but I think not, because he came to the lodge just before eight o'clock and had a little talk with me. He said that he had been overtaken by the fog and could not see at all. He was quite blind and had been obliged to ask a stranger to call a cab for him as he could not find his

495

way through the streets. He then gave me a cheque for the rent. I reminded him that the rent was not due until the twenty-fifth, but he said he wished to pay it now. He also gave me some money to pay one or two small bills that were owing to some of the tradespeople – a milk-man, a baker and a stationer.

"'This struck me as very strange, because he had always managed his business and paid the tradespeople himself. He told me that the fog had irritated his eye so that he could hardly read, and he was afraid he should soon be quite blind. He was very depressed, so much so that I felt quite uneasy about him. When he left the lodge, he went back across the square as if returning to his chambers. There was then no gate open excepting the main gate where the lodge is situated. That was the last time that I saw the deceased alive'."

Mr. Marchmont laid the paper on the table. "That is the porter's evidence. The remaining depositions are those of Noble, the night porter, John Blackmore and our friend here, Mr. Stephen. The night porter had not much to tell. This is the substance of his evidence:

"'I have viewed the body of the deceased and identify it as that of Mr. Jeffrey Blackmore. I knew the deceased well by sight and occasionally had a few words with him. I know nothing of his habits excepting that he used to sit up rather late. It is one of my duties to go round the Inn at night and call out the hours until one o'clock in the morning. When calling out "one o'clock" I often saw a light in the sitting-room of the deceased's chambers. On the night of the fourteenth instant, the light was burning until past one o'clock, but it was in the bedroom. The light in the sitting-room was out by ten o'clock.'

"We now come to John Blackmore's evidence. He says:

"'I have viewed the body of the deceased and recognize it as that of my brother Jeffrey. I last saw him alive on the twenty-third of February, when I called at his chambers. He then seemed in a very despondent state of mind and told me that his eyesight was fast failing. I was aware that he occasionally smoked opium, but I did not know that it was a confirmed habit. I urged him, on several occasions, to abandon the practice. I have no reason to believe that his affairs were in any way embarrassed or that he had any reason for making away with himself other than his failing eyesight, but, having regard to his state of mind when I last saw him, I am not surprised at what has happened.'

"That is the substance of John Blackmore's evidence, and, as to Mr. Stephen, his statement merely sets forth the fact that he had identified the body as that of his uncle Jeffrey. And now I think you have all the facts. Is there anything more that you want to ask me before I go, for I must really run away now?"

"I should like," said Thorndyke, "to know a little more about the parties concerned in this affair. But perhaps Mr. Stephen can give me the information."

"I expect he can," said Marchmont. "At any rate, he knows more about them than I do, so I will be off. If you should happen to think of any way," he continued, with a sly smile, "of upsetting that will, just let me know, and I will lose no time in entering a *caveat*. Good-bye! Don't trouble to let me out."

As soon as he was gone, Thorndyke turned to Stephen Blackmore.

"I am going," he said, "to ask you a few questions which may appear rather trifling, but you must remember that my methods of inquiry concern themselves with persons and things rather than with documents. For instance, I have not gathered very completely what sort of person your uncle Jeffrey was. Could you tell me a little more about him?"

"What shall I tell you?" Stephen asked with a slightly embarrassed air.

"Well, begin with his personal appearance."

"That is rather difficult to describe," said Stephen. "He was a medium-sized man and about five-feet-seven – fair, slightly grey, clean-shaved, rather spare and slight, had grey eyes, wore spectacles, and stooped a little as he walked. He was quiet and gentle in manner, rather yielding and irresolute in character, and his health was not at all robust, though he had no infirmity or disease excepting his bad eyesight. His age was about fifty-five."

"How came he to be a civil-service pensioner at fifty-five?" asked Thorndyke.

"Oh, that was through an accident. He had a nasty fall from a horse, and, being a rather nervous man, the shock was very severe. For some time after he was a complete wreck. But the failure of his eyesight was the actual cause of his retirement. It seems that the fall damaged his eyes in some way – in fact he practically lost the sight of one – the right – from that moment, and, as that had been his good eye, the accident left his vision very much impaired, so that he was at first given sick leave and then allowed to retire on a pension."

Thorndyke noted these particulars and then said, "Your uncle has been more than once referred to as a man of studious habits. Does that mean that he pursued any particular branch of learning?"

"Yes. He was an enthusiastic Oriental scholar. His official duties had taken him at one time to Yokohama and Tokio and at another to Bagdad, and while at those places he gave a good deal of attention to the languages, literature, and arts of the countries. He was also greatly interested in

Babylonian and Assyrian archaeology, and I believe he assisted for some time in the excavations at Birs Nimroud."

"Indeed!" said Thorndyke. "This is very interesting. I had no idea that he was a man of such considerable attainments. The facts mentioned by Mr. Marchmont would hardly have led one to think of him as what he seems to have been: A scholar of some distinction."

"I don't know that Mr. Marchmont realized the fact himself," said Stephen, "or that he would have considered it of any moment if he had. Nor, as far as that goes, do I. But, of course, I have no experience of legal matters."

"You can never tell beforehand," said Thorndyke, "what facts may turn out to be of moment, so that it is best to collect all you can get. By the way, were you aware that your uncle was an opium-smoker?"

"No, I was not. I knew that he had an opium-pipe which he brought with him when he came home from Japan, but I thought it was only a curio. I remember him telling me that he once tried a few puffs at an opium-pipe and found it rather pleasant, though it gave him a headache. But I had no idea he had contracted the habit – in fact, I may say that I was utterly astonished when the fact came out at the inquest."

Thorndyke made a note of this answer, too, and said, "I think that is all I have to ask you about your uncle Jeffrey. And now as to Mr. John Blackmore. What sort of man is he?"

"I am afraid I can't tell you very much about him. Until I saw him at the inquest, I had not met him since I was a boy. But he is a very different kind of man from Uncle Jeffrey, different in appearance and different in character."

"You would say that the two brothers were physically quite unlike, then?"

"Well," said Stephen, "I don't know that I ought to say that. Perhaps I am exaggerating the difference. I am thinking of Uncle Jeffrey as he was when I saw him last and of uncle John as he appeared at the inquest. They were very different then. Jeffrey was thin, pale, clean shaven, wore spectacles and walked with a stoop. John is a shade taller, a shade greyer, has good eyesight, a healthy, florid complexion, a brisk, upright carriage, is distinctly stout and wears a beard and moustache which are black and only very slightly streaked with grey. To me they looked as unlike as two men could, though their features were really of the same type. Indeed, I have heard it said that, as young men, they were rather alike, and they both resembled their mother. But there is no doubt as to their difference in character. Jeffrey was quiet, serious, and studious, whereas John rather inclined to what is called a fast life, he used to frequent race meetings, and, I think, gambled a good deal at times."

498

"What is his profession?"

"That would be difficult to tell – he has so many, he is so very versatile. I believe he began life as an articled pupil in the laboratory of a large brewery, but he soon left that and went on the stage. He seems to have remained in 'the profession' for some years, touring about this country and making occasional visits to America. The life seemed to suit him and I believe he was decidedly successful as an actor. But suddenly he left the stage and blossomed out in connection with a bucket-shop in London."

"And what is he doing now?"

"At the inquest he described himself as a stockbroker, so I presume he is still connected with the bucket-shop."

Thorndyke rose, and taking down from the reference shelves a list of members of the Stock Exchange, turned over the leaves.

"Yes," he said, replacing the volume, "he must be an outside broker. His name is not in the list of members of 'the House'. From what you tell me, it is easy to understand that there should have been no great intimacy between the two brothers, without assuming any kind of ill-feeling. They simply had very little in common. Do you know of anything more?"

"No. I have never heard of any actual quarrel or disagreement. My impression that they did not get on very well may have been, I think, due to the terms of the will, especially the first will. And they certainly did not seek one another's society."

"That is not very conclusive," said Thorndyke. "As to the will, a thrifty man is not usually much inclined to bequeath his savings to a gentleman who may probably employ them in a merry little flutter on the turf or the Stock Exchange. And then there was yourself, clearly a more suitable subject for a legacy, as your life is all before you. But this is mere speculation and the matter is not of much importance, as far as we can see. And now, tell me what John Blackmore's relations were with Mrs. Wilson. I gather that she left the bulk of her property to Jeffrey, her younger brother. Is that so?"

"Yes. She left nothing to John. The fact is that they were hardly on speaking terms. I believe John had treated her rather badly, or, at any rate, she thought he had. Mr. Wilson, her late husband, dropped some money over an investment in connection with the bucket-shop that I spoke of, and I think she suspected John of having let him in. She may have been mistaken, but you know what ladies are when they get an idea into their heads."

"Did you know your aunt well?"

499

"No, very slightly. She lived down in Devonshire and saw very little of any of us. She was a taciturn, strong-minded woman, quite unlike her brothers. She seems to have resembled her father's family."

"You might give me her full name."

"Julia Elizabeth Wilson. Her husband's name was Edmund Wilson."

"Thank you. There is just one more point. What has happened to your uncle's chambers in New Inn since his death?"

"They have remained shut up. As all his effects were left to me, I have taken over the tenancy for the present to avoid having them disturbed. I thought of keeping them for my own use, but I don't think I could live in them after what I have seen."

"You have inspected them, then?"

"Yes, I have just looked through them. I went there on the day of the inquest."

"Now tell me – As you looked through those rooms, what kind of impression did they convey to you as to your uncle's habits and mode of life?"

Stephen smiled apologetically. "I am afraid," said he, "that they did not convey any particular impression in that respect. I looked into the sitting-room and saw all his old familiar household gods, and then I went into the bedroom and saw the impression on the bed where his corpse had lain, and that gave me such a sensation of horror that I came away at once."

"But the appearance of the rooms must have conveyed something to your mind," Thorndyke urged.

"I am afraid it did not. You see, I have not your analytical eye. But perhaps you would like to look through them yourself? If you would, pray do so. They are my chambers now."

"I think I should like to glance round them," Thorndyke replied.

"Very well," said Stephen. "I will give you my card now, and I will look in at the lodge presently and tell the porter to hand you the key whenever you like to look over the rooms."

He took a card from his case, and, having written a few lines on it, handed it to Thorndyke.

"It is very good of you," he said, "to take so much trouble. Like Mr. Marchmont, I have no expectation of any result from your efforts, but I am very grateful to you, all the same, for going into the case so thoroughly. I suppose you don't see any possibility of upsetting that will – if I may ask the question?"

"At present," replied Thorndyke, "I do not. But until I have carefully weighed every fact connected with the case – whether it seems to have any bearing or not – I shall refrain from expressing, or even entertaining, an opinion either way."

Stephen Blackmore now took his leave, and Thorndyke, having collected the papers containing his notes, neatly punched a couple of holes in their margins and inserted them into a small file, which he slipped into his pocket.

"That," said he, "is the nucleus of the body of data on which our investigations must be based, and I very much fear that it will not receive any great additions. What do you think, Jervis?"

"The case looks about as hopeless as a case could look," I replied.

"That is what I think," said he, "and for that reason I am more than ordinarily keen on making something of it. I have not much more hope than Marchmont has, but I shall squeeze the case as dry as a bone before I let go. What are you going to do? I have to attend a meeting of the board of directors of the Griffin Life Office."

"Shall I walk down with you?"

"It is very good of you to offer, Jervis, but I think I will go alone. I want to run over these notes and get the facts of the case arranged in my mind. When I have done that, I shall be ready to pick up new matter. Knowledge is of no use unless it is actually in your mind, so that it can be produced at a moment's notice. So you had better get a book and your pipe and spend a quiet hour by the fire while I assimilate the miscellaneous mental feast that we have just enjoyed. And you might do a little rumination yourself."

With this, Thorndyke took his departure, and I, adopting his advice, drew my chair closer to the fire and filled my pipe. But I did not discover any inclination to read. The curious history that I had just heard, and Thorndyke's evident determination to elucidate it further, disposed me to meditation. Moreover, as his subordinate, it was my business to occupy myself with his affairs. Wherefore, having stirred the fire and got my pipe well alight, I abandoned myself to the renewed consideration of the facts relating to Jeffrey Blackmore's will.

501

Chapter VII
The Cuneiform Inscription

The surprise which Thorndyke's proceedings usually occasioned, especially to lawyers, was principally due, I think, to my friend's habit of viewing occurrences from an unusual standpoint. He did not look at things quite as other men looked at them. He had no prejudices and he knew no conventions. When other men were cocksure, Thorndyke was doubtful. When other men despaired, he entertained hopes, and thus it happened that he would often undertake cases that had been rejected contemptuously by experienced lawyers, and, what is more, would bring them to a successful issue.

Thus it had been in the only other case in which I had been personally associated with him – the so-called "Red Thumb Mark" case. There he was presented with an apparent impossibility, but he had given it careful consideration. Then, from the category of the impossible he had brought it to that of the possible, from the merely possible to the actually probable, from the probable to the certain, and in the end had won the case triumphantly.

Was it conceivable that he could make anything of the present case? He had not declined it. He had certainly entertained it and was probably thinking it over at this moment. Yet could anything be more impossible? Here was the case of a man making his own will, probably writing it out himself, bringing it voluntarily to a certain place and executing it in the presence of competent witnesses. There was no suggestion of any compulsion or even influence or persuasion. The testator was admittedly sane and responsible, and if the will did not give effect to his wishes – which, however, could not be proved – that was due to his own carelessness in drafting the will and not to any unusual circumstances. And the problem – which Thorndyke seemed to be considering – was how to set aside that will.

I reviewed the statements that I had heard, but turn them about as I would, I could get nothing out of them but confirmation of Mr. Marchmont's estimate of the case. One fact that I had noted with some curiosity I again considered, that was Thorndyke's evident desire to inspect Jeffrey Blackmore's chambers. He had, it is true, shown no eagerness, but I had seen at the time that the questions which he put to Stephen were put, not with any expectation of eliciting information but for the purpose of getting an opportunity to look over the rooms himself.

I was still cogitating on the subject when my colleague returned, followed by the watchful Polton with the tea-tray, and I attacked him forthwith.

"Well, Thorndyke," I said, "I have been thinking about this Blackmore case while you have been gadding about."

"And may I take it that the problem is solved?"

"No, I'm hanged if you may. I can make nothing of it."

"Then you are in much the same position as I am."

"But, if you can make nothing of it, why did you undertake it?"

"I only undertook to think about it," said Thorndyke. "I never reject a case off-hand unless it is obviously fishy. It is surprising how difficulties, and even impossibilities, dwindle if you look at them attentively. My experience has taught me that the most unlikely case is, at least, worth thinking over."

"By the way, why do you want to look over Jeffrey's chambers? What do you expect to find there?"

"I have no expectations at all. I am simply looking for stray facts."

"And all those questions that you asked Stephen Blackmore, had you nothing in your mind – no definite purpose?"

"No purpose beyond getting to know as much about the case as I can."

"But," I exclaimed, "do you mean that you are going to examine those rooms without any definite object at all?"

"I wouldn't say that," replied Thorndyke. "This is a legal case. Let me put an analogous medical case as being more within your present sphere. Supposing that a man should consult you, say, about a progressive loss of weight. He can give no explanation. He has no pain, no discomfort, no symptoms of any kind – in short, he feels perfectly well in every respect, but he is losing weight continuously. What would you do?"

"I should overhaul him thoroughly," I answered.

"Why? What would you expect to find?"

"I don't know that I should start by expecting to find anything in particular. But I should overhaul him organ by organ and function by function, and if I could find nothing abnormal I should have to give it up."

"Exactly," said Thorndyke. "And that is just my position and my line of action. Here is a case which is perfectly regular and straightforward excepting in one respect. It has a single abnormal feature. And for that abnormality there is nothing to account.

"Jeffrey Blackmore made a will. It was a well-drawn will and it apparently gave full effect to his intentions. Then he revoked that will and made another. No change had occurred in his circumstances or in his intentions. The provisions of the new will were believed by him to be identical with those of the old one. The new will differed from the old one

503

only in having a defect in the drafting from which the first will was free, and of which he must have been unaware. Now why did he revoke the first will and replace it with another which he believed to be identical in its provisions? There is no answer to that question. It is an abnormal feature in the case. There must be some explanation of that abnormality and it is my business to discover it. But the facts in my possession yield no such explanation. Therefore it is my purpose to search for new facts which may give me a starting-point for an investigation."

This exposition of Thorndyke's proposed conduct of the case, reasonable as it was, did not impress me as very convincing. I found myself coming back to Marchmont's position, that there was really nothing in dispute. But other matters claimed our attention at the moment, and it was not until after dinner that my colleague reverted to the subject.

"How should you like to take a turn round to New Inn this evening?" he asked.

"I should have thought," said I, "that it would be better to go by daylight. Those old chambers are not usually very well illuminated."

"That is well thought of," said Thorndyke. "We had better take a lamp with us. Let us go up to the laboratory and get one from Polton."

"There is no need to do that," said I. "The pocket-lamp that you lent me is in my overcoat pocket. I put it there to return it to you."

"Did you have occasion to use it?" he asked.

"Yes. I paid another visit to the mysterious house and carried out your plan. I must tell you about it later."

"Do. I shall be keenly interested to hear all about your adventures. Is there plenty of candle left in the lamp?"

"Oh yes. I only used it for about an hour."

"Then let us be off," said Thorndyke, and we accordingly set forth on our quest, and, as we went, I reflected once more on the apparent vagueness of our proceedings. Presently I reopened the subject with Thorndyke.

"I can't imagine," said I, "that you have absolutely nothing in view. That you are going to this place with no defined purpose whatever."

"I did not say exactly that," replied Thorndyke. "I said that I was not going to look for any particular thing or fact. I am going in the hope that I may observe something that may start a new train of speculation. But that is not all. You know that an investigation follows a certain logical course. It begins with the observation of the conspicuous facts. We have done that. The facts were supplied by Marchmont. The next stage is to propose to oneself one or more provisional explanations or hypotheses. We have done that, too – or, at least I have, and I suppose you have."

"I haven't," said I. "There is Jeffrey's will, but why he should have made the change I cannot form the foggiest idea. But I should like to hear your provisional theories on the subject."

"You won't hear them at present. They are mere wild conjectures. But to resume: What do we do next?"

"Go to New Inn and rake over the deceased gentleman's apartments."

Thorndyke smilingly ignored my answer and continued, "We examine each explanation in turn and see what follows from it, whether it agrees with all the facts and leads to the discovery of new ones, or, on the other hand, disagrees with some facts or leads us to an absurdity. Let us take a simple example.

"Suppose we find scattered over a field a number of largish masses of stone, which are entirely different in character from the rocks found in the neighbourhood. The question arises, how did those stones get into that field? Three explanations are proposed. One: That they are the products of former volcanic action. Two: That they were brought from a distance by human agency. Three: That they were carried thither from some distant country by icebergs. Now each of those explanations involves certain consequences. If the stones are volcanic, then they were once in a state of fusion. But we find that they are unaltered limestone and contain fossils. Then they are not volcanic. If they were borne by icebergs, then they were once part of a glacier and some of them will probably show the flat surfaces with parallel scratches which are found on glacier-borne stones. We examine them and find the characteristic scratched surfaces. Then they have probably been brought to this place by icebergs. But this does not exclude human agency, for they might have been brought by men to this place from some other where the icebergs had deposited them. A further comparison with other facts would be needed.

"So we proceed in cases like this present one. Of the facts that are known to us we invent certain explanations. From each of those explanations we deduce consequences, and if those consequences agree with new facts, they confirm the explanation, whereas if they disagree they tend to disprove it. But here we are at our destination."

We turned out of Wych Street into the arched passage leading into New Inn, and, halting at the half-door of the lodge, perceived a stout, purple-faced man crouching over the fire, coughing violently. He held up his hand to intimate that he was fully occupied for the moment, and we accordingly waited for his paroxysm to subside. At length he turned towards us, wiping his eyes, and inquired our business.

"Mr. Stephen Blackmore," said Thorndyke, "has given me permission to look over his chambers. He said that he would mention the matter to you."

"So he has, sir," said the porter, "but he has just taken the key himself to go to the chambers. If you walk across the Inn you'll find him there, it's on the farther side - Number Thirty-one, second floor."

We made our way across to the house indicated, the ground floor of which was occupied by a solicitor's offices and was distinguished by a good-sized brass plate. Although it had now been dark some time there was no light on the lower stairs, but we encountered on the first-floor landing a man who had just lit the lamp there. Thorndyke halted to address him.

"Can you tell me who occupies the chambers on the third floor?"

"The third floor has been empty about three months," was the reply.

"We are going up to look at the chambers on the second floor," said Thorndyke. "Are they pretty quiet?"

"Quiet!" exclaimed the man. "Lord bless you, the place is like a cemetery for the deaf and dumb. There's the solicitors on the ground floor and the architects on the first floor. They both clear out about six, and when they're gone the house is as empty as a blown hegg. I don't wonder poor Mr. Blackmore made away with his-self. Livin' up there alone, it must have been like Robinson Crusoe without no man Friday and not even a blooming goat to talk to. Quiet! It's quiet enough, if that's what you want. Wouldn't be no good to me."

With a contemptuous shake of the head, he turned and retired down the next flight, and, as the echoes of his footsteps died away we resumed our ascent.

"So it would appear," Thorndyke commented, "that when Jeffrey Blackmore came home that last evening, the house was empty."

Arrived on the second-floor landing, we were confronted by a solid-looking door, on the lintel of which the deceased man's name was painted in white lettering which still looked new and fresh. Thorndyke knocked at the door, which was at once opened by Stephen Blackmore.

"I haven't wasted any time before taking advantage of your permission, you see," my colleague said as we entered.

"No, indeed," said Stephen, "you are very prompt. I have been rather wondering what kind of information you expect to gather from an inspection of these rooms."

Thorndyke smiled genially, amused, no doubt, by the similarity of Stephen's remarks to those of mine which he had so recently criticized.

"A man of science, Mr. Blackmore," he said, "expects nothing. He collects facts and keeps an open mind. As to me, I am a mere legal Autolycus, a snapper-up of unconsidered trifles of evidence. When I have accumulated a few facts, I arrange them, compare them, and think about them. Sometimes the comparison yields new matter and sometimes it

506

doesn't, but in any case, believe me, it is a capital error to decide beforehand what data are to be sought for."

"Yes, I suppose that is so," said Stephen, "though, to me, it almost looks as if Mr. Marchmont was right, that there is nothing to investigate."

"You should have thought of that before you consulted me," laughed Thorndyke. "As it is, I am engaged to look into the case and I shall do so, and, as I have said, I shall keep an open mind until I have all the facts in my possession."

He glanced round the sitting-room, which we had now entered, and continued.

"These are fine, dignified old rooms. It seems a sin to have covered up all this oak panelling and that carved cornice and mantel with paint. Think what it must have been like when the beautiful figured wood was exposed."

"It would be very dark," Stephen observed.

"Yes," Thorndyke agreed, "and I suppose we care more for light and less for beauty than our ancestors did. But now, tell me, looking round these rooms, do they convey to you a similar impression to that which the old rooms did? Have they the same general character?"

"Not quite, I think. Of course the rooms in Jermyn Street were in a different kind of house, but beyond that, I seem to feel a certain difference, which is rather odd, seeing that the furniture is the same. But the old rooms were more cosy, more homelike. I find something rather bare and cheerless, I was almost going to say squalid, in the look of these chambers."

"That is rather what I should have expected," said Thorndyke. "The opium habit alters a man's character profoundly, and, somehow, apart from the mere furnishing, a room reflects in some subtle way, but very distinctly, the personality of its occupant, especially when that occupant lives a solitary life. Do you see any evidences of the activities that used to occupy your uncle?"

"Not very much," replied Stephen. "But the place may not be quite as he left it. I found one or two of his books on the table and put them back in the shelves, but I found no manuscript or notes such as he used to make. I noticed, too, that his ink-slab which he used to keep so scrupulously clean is covered with dry smears and that the stick of ink is all cracked at the end, as if he had not used it for months. It seems to point to a great change in his habits."

"What used he to do with Chinese ink?" Thorndyke asked.

"He corresponded with some of his native friends in Japan, and he used to write in the Japanese character even if they understood English. That was what he chiefly used the Chinese ink for. But he also used to copy the inscriptions from these things." Here Stephen lifted from the mantelpiece what looked like a fossil Bath bun, but was actually a clay tablet covered with minute indented writing.

"Your uncle could read the cuneiform character, then?"

"Yes, he was something of an expert. These tablets are, I believe, leases and other legal documents from Eridu and other Babylonian cities. He used to copy the inscriptions in the cuneiform writing and then translate them into English. But I mustn't stay here any longer as I have an engagement for this evening. I just dropped in to get these two volumes – Thornton's *History of Babylonia*, which he once advised me to read. Shall I give you the key? You'd better have it and leave it with the porter as you go out."

He shook hands with us and we walked out with him to the landing and stood watching him as he ran down the stairs. Glancing at Thorndyke by the light of the gas lamp on the landing, I thought I detected in his impassive face that almost imperceptible change of expression to which I have already alluded as indicating pleasure or satisfaction.

"You are looking quite pleased with yourself," I remarked.

"I am not displeased," he replied calmly. "Autolycus has picked up a few crumbs, very small ones, but still crumbs. No doubt his learned junior has picked up a few likewise?"

I shook my head – and inwardly suspected it of being rather a thick head.

"I did not perceive anything in the least degree significant in what Stephen was telling you," said I. "It was all very interesting, but it did not seem to have any bearing on his uncle's will."

"I was not referring only to what Stephen has told us, although that was, as you say, very interesting. While he was talking I was looking about the room, and I have seen a very strange thing. Let me show it to you."

He linked his arm in mine and, walking me back into the room, halted opposite the fire-place.

"There," said he, "look at that. It is a most remarkable object."

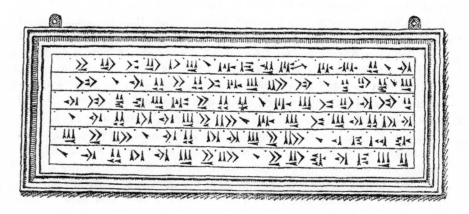

I followed the direction of his gaze and saw an oblong frame enclosing a large photograph of an inscription in the weird and cabalistic arrow-head character. I looked at it in silence for some seconds and then, somewhat disappointed, remarked, "I don't see anything very remarkable in it, under the circumstances. In any ordinary room it would be, I admit, but Stephen has just told us that his uncle was something of an expert in cuneiform writing."

"Exactly," said Thorndyke. "That is my point. That is what makes it so remarkable."

"I don't follow you at all," said I. "That a man should hang upon his wall an inscription that is legible to him does not seem to me at all out of the way. It would be much more singular if he should hang up an inscription that he could not read."

"No doubt," replied Thorndyke. "But you will agree with me that it would be still more singular if a man should hang upon his wall an inscription that he *could* read – and hang it upside down."

I stared at Thorndyke in amazement.

"Do you mean to tell me," I exclaimed, "that that photograph is really upside down?"

"I do indeed," he replied.

"But how do you know? Have we here yet another Oriental scholar?"

Thorndyke chuckled. "Some fool," he replied, "has said that 'a little knowledge is a dangerous thing'. Compared with much knowledge, it may be, but it is a vast deal better than *no* knowledge. Here is a case in point. I have read with very keen interest the wonderful history of the decipherment of the cuneiform writing, and I happen to recollect one or

509

two of the main facts that seemed to me to be worth remembering. This particular inscription is in the Persian cuneiform, a much more simple and open form of the script than the Babylonian or Assyrian. In fact, I suspect that this is the famous inscription from the gateway at Persepolis – the first to be deciphered, which would account for its presence here in a frame. Now this script consists, as you see, of two kinds of characters, the small, solid, acutely pointed characters which are known as *wedges*, and the larger, more obtuse characters, somewhat like our government broad arrows, and called *arrow-heads*. The names are rather unfortunate, as both forms are wedge-like and both resemble arrow-heads. The script reads from left to right, like our own writing, and unlike that of the Semitic peoples and the primitive Greeks, and the rule for the placing of the characters is that all the 'wedges' point to the right or downwards and the arrow-head forms are open towards the right. But if you look at this photograph you will see that all the wedges point upwards to the left and that the arrow-head characters are open towards the left. Obviously the photograph is upside down."

"But," I exclaimed, "this is really most mysterious. What do you suppose can be the explanation?"

"I think," replied Thorndyke, "that we may perhaps get a suggestion from the back of the frame. Let us see."

He disengaged the frame from the two nails on which it hung, and, turning it round, glanced at the back, which he then presented for my inspection. A label on the backing paper bore the words, "*J. Budge, Frame-maker and Gilder, 16, Gt. Anne Street, W.C.*"

"Well?" I said, when I had read the label without gathering from it anything fresh.

"The label, you observe, is the right way up as it hangs on the wall."

"So it is," I rejoined hastily, a little annoyed that I had not been quicker to observe so obvious a fact. "I see your point. You mean that the frame-maker hung the thing upside down and Jeffrey never noticed the mistake?"

"That is a perfectly sound explanation," said Thorndyke. "But I think there is something more. You will notice that the label is an old one. It must have been on some years, to judge by its dingy appearance, whereas the two mirror-plates look to me comparatively new. But we can soon put that matter to the test, for the label was evidently stuck on when the frame was new, and if the plates were screwed on at the same time, the wood that they cover will be clean and new-looking."

He drew from his pocket a "combination" knife containing, among other implements, a screw-driver, with which he carefully extracted the screws from one of the little brass plates by which the frame had been suspended from the nails.

"You see," he said, when he had removed the plate and carried the photograph over to the gasjet, "the wood covered by the plate is as dirty and time-stained as the rest of the frame. The plates have been put on recently."

"And what are we to infer from that?"

"Well, since there are no other marks of plates or rings upon the frame, we may safely infer that the photograph was never hung up until it came to these rooms."

"Yes, I suppose we may. But what then? What inference does that lead to?"

Thorndyke reflected for a few moments and I continued, "It is evident that this photograph suggests more to you than it does to me. I should like to hear your exposition of its bearing on the case, if it has any."

"Whether or no it has any real bearing on the case," Thorndyke answered, "it is impossible for me to say at this stage. I told you that I had proposed to myself one or two hypotheses to account for and explain Jeffrey Blackmore's will, and I may say that the curious misplacement of this photograph fits more than one of them. I won't say more than that, because I think it would be profitable to you to work at this case independently. You have all the facts that I have and you shall have a copy of my notes of Marchmont's statement of the case. With this material you ought to be able to reach some conclusion. Of course neither of us may be able to make anything of the case – it doesn't look very hopeful at present – but whatever happens, we can compare notes after the event and you will be the richer by so much experience of actual investigation. But I will start you off with one hint, which is this: That neither you nor Marchmont seem to appreciate in the least the very extraordinary nature of the facts that he communicated to us."

"I thought Marchmont seemed pretty much alive to the fact that it was a very queer will."

"So he did," agreed Thorndyke. "But that is not quite what I mean. The whole set of circumstances, taken together and in relation to one another, impressed me as most remarkable, and that is why I am giving so much attention to what looks at first sight like such a very unpromising case. Copy out my notes, Jervis, and examine the facts critically. I think you will see what I mean. And now let us proceed."

He replaced the brass plate and having reinserted the screws, hung up the frame, and proceeded to browse slowly round the room, stopping now and again to inspect the Japanese colour-prints and framed photographs of buildings and other objects of archaeological interest that formed the only attempts at wall-decoration. To one of the former he drew my attention.

"These things are of some value," he remarked. "Here is one by Utamaro – that little circle with the mark over it is his signature – and you notice that the paper is becoming spotted in places with mildew. The fact is worth noting in more than one connection."

I accordingly made a mental note and the perambulation continued.

"You observe that Jeffrey used a gas-stove, instead of a coal fire – no doubt to economize work, but perhaps for other reasons. Presumably he cooked by gas, too. Let us see."

We wandered into the little cupboard-like kitchen and glanced round. A ring-burner on a shelf, a kettle, a frying-pan, and a few pieces of crockery were its sole appointments. Apparently the porter was correct in his statement as to Jeffrey's habits.

Returning to the sitting-room, Thorndyke resumed his inspection, pulling out the table drawers, peering inquisitively into cupboards, and bestowing a passing glance on each of the comparatively few objects that the comfortless room contained.

"I have never seen a more characterless apartment," was his final comment. "There is nothing that seems to suggest any kind of habitual activity on the part of the occupant. Let us look at the bedroom."

We passed through into the chamber of tragic memories and, when Thorndyke had lit the gas, we stood awhile looking about us in silence. It was a bare, comfortless room, dirty, neglected, and squalid. The bed appeared not to have been remade since the catastrophe, for an indentation still marked the place where the corpse had lain, and even a slight powdering of ash could still be seen on the shabby counterpane. It looked to me a typical opium-smoker's bedroom.

"Well," Thorndyke remarked at length, "there is character enough here – of a kind. Jeffrey Blackmore would seem to have been a man of few needs. One could hardly imagine a bedroom in which less attention seemed to have been given to the comfort of the occupant."

He looked about him keenly and continued, "The syringe and the rest of the lethal appliances and material have been taken away, I see. Probably the analyst did not return them. But there are the opium-pipe and the jar and the ash-bowl, and I presume those are the clothes that the undertakers removed from the body. Shall we look them over?"

He took up the clothes which lay, roughly folded, on a chair and held them up, garment by garment.

"These are evidently the trousers," he remarked, spreading them out on the bed. "Here is a little white spot on the middle of the thigh which looks like a patch of small crystals from a drop of the solution. Just light the lamp, Jervis, and let us examine it with a lens."

I lit the lamp, and when we had examined the spot minutely and identified it as a mass of minute crystals, Thorndyke asked, "What do you make of those creases? You see there is one on each leg."

"It looks as if the trousers had been turned up. But if they have been, they must have been turned up about seven inches. Poor Jeffrey couldn't have had much regard for appearances, for they would have been right above his socks. But perhaps the creases were made in undressing the body."

"That is possible," said Thorndyke, "though I don't quite see how it would have happened. I notice that his pockets seem to have been emptied – no, wait, here is something in the waistcoat pocket."

He drew out a shabby, pigskin card-case and a stump of lead pencil, at which latter he looked with what seemed to me much more interest than was deserved by so commonplace an object.

"The cards, you observe," said he, "are printed from type, not from a plate. I would note that fact. And tell me what you make of that."

He handed me the pencil, which I examined with concentrated attention, helping myself even with the lamp and my pocket lens. But even with these aids I failed to discover anything unusual in its appearance. Thorndyke watched me with a mischievous smile, and, when I had finished, inquired, "Well, what is it?"

"Confound you!" I exclaimed. "It's a pencil. Any fool can see that, and this particular fool can't see any more. It's a wretched stump of a pencil, villainously cut to an abominably bad point. It is coloured dark red on the outside and was stamped with some name that began with $C - O -$ *Co-operative Stores*, perhaps."

"Now, my dear Jervis," Thorndyke protested, "don't begin by confusing speculation with fact. The letters which remain are $C - O$. Note that fact and find out what pencils there are which have inscriptions beginning with those letters. I am not going to help you, because you can easily do this for yourself. And it will be good discipline even if the fact turns out to mean nothing."

At this moment he stepped back suddenly, and, looking down at the floor, said, "Give me the lamp, Jervis, I've trodden on something that felt like glass."

I brought the lamp to the place where he had been standing, close by the bed, and we both knelt on the floor, throwing the light of the lamp on the bare and dusty boards. Under the bed, just within reach of the foot of a person standing close by, was a little patch of fragments of glass. Thorndyke produced a piece of paper from his pocket and delicately swept

513

the little fragments on to it, remarking, "By the look of things, I am not the first person who has trodden on that object, whatever it is. Do you mind holding the lamp while I inspect the remains?"

I took the lamp and held it over the paper while he examined the little heap of glass through his lens.

"Well," I asked. "What have you found?"

"That is what I am asking myself," he replied. "As far as I can judge by the appearance of these fragments, they appear to be portions of a small watch-glass. I wish there were some larger pieces."

"Perhaps there are," said I. "Let us look about the floor under the bed."

We resumed our groping about the dirty floor, throwing the light of the lamp on one spot after another. Presently, as we moved the lamp about, its light fell on a small glass bead, which I instantly picked up and exhibited to Thorndyke.

"Is this of any interest to you?" I asked.

Thorndyke took the bead and examined it curiously.

"It is certainly," he said, "a very odd thing to find in the bedroom of an old bachelor like Jeffrey, especially as we know that he employed no woman to look after his rooms. Of course, it may be a relic of the last tenant. Let us see if there are any more."

We renewed our search, crawling under the bed and throwing the light of the lamp in all directions over the floor. The result was the discovery of three more beads, one entire bugle, and the crushed remains of another, which had apparently been trodden on. All of these, including the fragments of the bugle that had been crushed, Thorndyke placed carefully on the paper, which he laid on the dressing-table the more conveniently to examine our find.

"I am sorry," said he, "that there are no more fragments of the watch-glass, or whatever it was. The broken pieces were evidently picked up, with the exception of the one that I trod on, which was an isolated fragment that had been overlooked. As to the beads, judging by their number and the position in which we found some of them – that crushed bugle, for instance – they must have been dropped during Jeffrey's tenancy and probably quite recently."

"What sort of garment do you suppose they came from?" I asked.

515

"They may have been part of a beaded veil or the trimming of a dress, but the grouping rather suggests to me a tag of bead fringe. The colour is rather unusual."

"I thought they looked like black beads."

"So they do by this light, but I think that by daylight we shall find them to be a dark, reddish-brown. You can see the colour now if you look at the smaller fragments of the one that is crushed."

He handed me his lens, and, when I had verified his statement, he produced from his pocket a small tin box with a closely-fitting lid in which he deposited the paper, having first folded it up into a small parcel.

"We will put the pencil in too," said he, and, as he returned the box to his pocket he added, "You had better get one of these little boxes from Polton. If is often useful to have a safe receptacle for small and fragile articles."

He folded up and replaced the dead man's clothes as we had found them. Then, observing a pair of shoes standing by the wall, he picked them up and looked them over thoughtfully, paying special attention to the backs of the soles and the fronts of the heels.

"I suppose we may take it," said he, "that these are the shoes that poor Jeffrey wore on the night of his death. At any rate there seem to be no others. He seems to have been a fairly clean walker. The streets were shockingly dirty that day, as I remember most distinctly. Do you see any slippers? I haven't noticed any."

He opened and peeped into a cupboard in which an overcoat surmounted by a felt hat hung from a peg like an attenuated suicide, he looked in all the corners and into the sitting-room, but no slippers were to be seen.

"Our friend seems to have had surprisingly little regard for comfort," Thorndyke remarked. "Think of spending the winter evenings in damp boots by a gas fire!"

"Perhaps the opium-pipe compensated," said I, "or he may have gone to bed early."

"But he did not. The night porter used to see the light in his rooms at one o'clock in the morning. In the sitting-room, too, you remember. But he seems to have been in the habit of reading in bed – or perhaps smoking – for here is a candlestick with the remains of a whole dynasty of candles in it. As there is gas in the room, he couldn't have wanted the candle to undress by. He used stearine candles, too, not the common paraffin variety. I wonder why he went to that expense."

"Perhaps the smell of the paraffin candle spoiled the aroma of the opium," I suggested, to which Thorndyke made no reply but continued his inspection of the room, pulling out the drawer of the washstand – which

516

contained a single, worn-out nail-brush – and even picking up and examining the dry and cracked cake of soap in the dish.

"He seems to have had a fair amount of clothing," said Thorndyke, who was now going through the chest of drawers, "though, by the look of it, he didn't change very often, and the shirts have a rather yellow and faded appearance. I wonder how he managed about his washing. Why, here are a couple of pairs of boots in the drawer with his clothes! And here is his stock of candles. Quite a large box – though nearly empty now – of stearine candles, six to the pound."

He closed the drawer and cast another inquiring look round the room.

"I think we have seen all now, Jervis," he said, "unless there is anything more that you would like to look into?"

"No," I replied. "I have seen all that I wanted to see and more than I am able to attach any meaning to. So we may as well go."

I blew out the lamp and put it in my overcoat pocket, and, when we had turned out the gas in both rooms, we took our departure.

As we approached the lodge, we found our stout friend in the act of retiring in favour of the night porter. Thorndyke handed him the key of the chambers, and, after a few sympathetic inquiries, about his health – which was obviously very indifferent – said, "Let me see, you were one of the witnesses to Mr. Blackmore's will, I think?"

"I was, sir," replied the porter.

"And I believe you read the document through before you witnessed the signature?"

"I did, sir."

"Did you read it aloud?"

"Aloud, sir! Lor' bless you, no, sir! Why should I? The other witness read it, and, of course, Mr. Blackmore knew what was in it, seeing that it was in his own handwriting. What should I want to read it aloud for?"

"No, of course you wouldn't want to. By the way, I have been wondering how Mr. Blackmore managed about his washing."

The porter evidently regarded this question with some disfavour, for he replied only with an interrogative grunt. It was, in fact, rather an odd question.

"Did you get it done for him," Thorndyke pursued.

"No, certainly not, sir. He got it done for himself. The laundry people used to deliver the basket here at the lodge, and Mr. Blackmore used to take it in with him when he happened to be passing."

"It was not delivered at his chambers, then?"

"No, sir. Mr. Blackmore was a very studious gentleman and he didn't like to be disturbed. A studious gentleman would naturally not like to be disturbed."

517

Thorndyke cordially agreed with these very proper sentiments and finally wished the porter "Good night." We passed out through the gateway into Wych Street, and, turning our faces eastward towards the Temple, set forth in silence, each thinking his own thoughts. What Thorndyke's were I cannot tell, though I have no doubt that he was busily engaged in piecing together all that he had seen and heard and considering its possible application to the case in hand.

As to me, my mind was in a whirl of confusion. All this searching and examining seemed to be the mere flogging of a dead horse. The will was obviously a perfectly valid and regular will and there was an end of the matter. At least, so it seemed to me. But clearly that was not Thorndyke's view. His investigations were certainly not purposeless, and, as I walked by his side trying to conceive some purpose in his actions, I only became more and more mystified as I recalled them one by one, and perhaps most of all by the cryptic questions that I had just heard him address to the equally mystified porter.

Chapter VIII
The Track Chart

As Thorndyke and I arrived at the main gateway of the Temple and he swung round into the narrow lane, it was suddenly borne in on me that I had made no arrangements for the night. Events had followed one another so continuously and each had been so engrossing that I had lost sight of what I may call my domestic affairs.

"We seem to be heading for your chambers, Thorndyke," I ventured to remark. "It is a little late to think of it, but I have not yet settled where I am to put up to-night."

"My dear fellow," he replied, "you are going to put up in your own bedroom which has been waiting in readiness for you ever since you left it. Polton went up and inspected it as soon as you arrived. I take it that you will consider my chambers yours until such time as you may join the benedictine majority and set up a home for yourself."

"That is very handsome of you," said I. "You didn't mention that the billet you offered was a resident appointment."

"Rooms and commons included," said Thorndyke, and when I protested that I should at least contribute to the costs of living he impatiently waved the suggestion away. We were still arguing the question when we reached our chambers – as I will now call them – and a diversion was occasioned by my taking the lamp from my pocket and placing it on the table.

"Ah," my colleague remarked, "that is a little reminder. We will put it on the mantelpiece for Polton to collect and you shall give me a full account of your further adventures in the wilds of Kennington. That was a very odd affair. I have often wondered how it ended."

He drew our two arm-chairs up to the fire, put on some more coal, placed the tobacco jar on the table exactly equidistant from the two chairs, and settled himself with the air of a man who is anticipating an agreeable entertainment.

I filled my pipe, and, taking up the thread of the story where I had broken off on the last occasion, began to outline my later experiences. But he brought me up short.

"Don't be sketchy, Jervis. To be sketchy is to be vague. Detail, my child, detail is the soul of induction. Let us have all the facts. We can sort them out afterwards."

I began afresh in a vein of the extremest circumstantiality. With deliberate malice I loaded a prolix narrative with every triviality that a fairly retentive memory could rake out of the half-forgotten past. I cudgelled my brains for irrelevant incidents. I described with the minutest accuracy things that had not the faintest significance. I drew a vivid picture of the carriage inside and out, I painted a lifelike portrait of the horse, even going into particulars of the harness – which I was surprised to find that I had noticed. I described the furniture of the dining-room and the cobwebs that had hung from the ceiling, the auction-ticket on the chest of drawers, the rickety table and the melancholy chairs. I gave the number-per-minute of the patient's respirations and the exact quantity of coffee consumed on each occasion, with an exhaustive description of the cup from which it was taken, and I left no personal details unconsidered, from the patient's finger-nails to the roseate pimples on Mr. Weiss's nose.

But my tactics of studied prolixity were a complete failure. The attempt to fatigue Thorndyke's brain with superabundant detail was like trying to surfeit a pelican with whitebait. He consumed it all with calm enjoyment and asked for more, and when, at last, I did really begin to think that I had bored him a little, he staggered me by reading over his notes and starting a brisk cross-examination to elicit fresh facts! And the most surprising thing of all was that when I had finished I seemed to know a great deal more about the case than I had ever known before.

"It was a very remarkable affair," he observed, when the cross-examination was over – leaving me somewhat in the condition of a cider-apple that has just been removed from a hydraulic press – "a very suspicious affair with a highly unsatisfactory end. I am not sure that I entirely agree with your police officer. Nor do I fancy that some of my acquaintances at Scotland Yard would have agreed with him."

"Do you think I ought to have taken any further measures?" I asked uneasily.

"No, I don't see how you could. You did all that was possible under the circumstances. You gave information, which is all that a private individual can do – especially if he is an overworked general practitioner. But still, an actual crime is the affair of every good citizen. I think we ought to take some action."

"You think there really was a crime, then?"

"What else can one think? What do you think about it yourself?"

"I don't like to think about it at all. The recollection of that corpse-like figure in that gloomy bedroom has haunted me ever since I left the house. What do you suppose has happened?"

Thorndyke did not answer for a few seconds. At length he said gravely, "I am afraid, Jervis, that the answer to that question can be given in one word."

"Murder?" I asked with a slight shudder.

He nodded, and we were both silent for a while.

"The probability," he resumed after a pause, "that Mr. Graves is alive at this moment seems to me infinitesimal. There was evidently a conspiracy to murder him, and the deliberate, persistent manner in which that object was being pursued points to a very strong and definite motive. Then the tactics adopted point to considerable forethought and judgment. They are not the tactics of a fool or an ignoramus. We may criticize the closed carriage as a tactical mistake, calculated to arouse suspicion, but we have to weigh it against its alternative."

"What is that?"

"Well, consider the circumstances. Suppose Weiss had called you in in the ordinary way. You would still have detected the use of poison. But now you could have located your man and made inquiries about him in the neighbourhood. You would probably have given the police a hint and they would almost certainly have taken action, as they would have had the means of identifying the parties. The result would have been fatal to Weiss. The closed carriage invited suspicion, but it was a great safeguard. Weiss's method's were not so unsound after all. He is a cautious man, but cunning and very persistent. And he could be bold on occasion. The use of the blinded carriage was a decidedly audacious proceeding. I should put him down as a gambler of a very discreet, courageous and resourceful type."

"Which all leads to the probability that he has pursued his scheme and brought it to a successful issue."

"I am afraid it does. But – have you got your notes of the compass-bearings?"

"The book is in my overcoat pocket with the board. I will fetch them."

I went into the office, where our coats hung, and brought back the notebook with the little board to which it was still attached by the rubber band. Thorndyke took them from me, and, opening the book, ran his eye quickly down one page after another. Suddenly he glanced at the clock.

"It is a little late to begin," said he, "but these notes look rather alluring. I am inclined to plot them out at once. I fancy, from their appearance, that they will enable us to locate the house without much difficulty. But don't let me keep you up if you are tired. I can work them out by myself."

"You won't do anything of the kind," I exclaimed. "I am as keen on plotting them as you are, and, besides, I want to see how it is done. It seems to be a rather useful accomplishment."

"It is," said Thorndyke. "In our work, the ability to make a rough but reliable sketch survey is often of great value. Have you ever looked over these notes?"

"No. I put the book away when I came in and have never looked at it since."

"It is a quaint document. You seem to be rich in railway bridges in those parts, and the route was certainly none of the most direct, as you noticed at the time. However, we will plot it out and then we shall see exactly what it looks like and whither it leads us."

He retired to the laboratory and presently returned with a T-square, a military protractor, a pair of dividers and a large drawing-board on which was pinned a sheet of cartridge paper.

"Now," said he, seating himself at the table with the board before him, "as to the method. You started from a known position and you arrived at a place the position of which is at present unknown. We shall fix the position of that spot by applying two factors, the distance that you travelled and the direction in which you were moving. The direction is given by the compass, and, as the horse seems to have kept up a remarkably even pace, we can take time as representing distance. You seem to have been travelling at about eight miles an hour, that is, roughly, a seventh of a mile in one minute. So if, on our chart, we take one inch as representing one minute, we shall be working with a scale of about seven inches to the mile."

"That doesn't sound very exact as to distance," I objected.

"It isn't. But that doesn't matter much. We have certain landmarks, such as these railway arches that you have noted, by which the actual distance can be settled after the route is plotted. You had better read out the entries, and, opposite each, write a number for reference, so that we need not confuse the chart by writing details on it. I shall start near the middle of the board, as neither you nor I seem to have the slightest notion what your general direction was."

I laid the open notebook before me and read out the first entry: "'Eight-fifty-eight. West-by-South. Start from home. Horse thirteen hands'."

"You turned round at once, I understand," said Thorndyke, "so we draw no line in that direction. The next is – ?"

"'Eight-fifty-eight minutes, thirty seconds, East-by-North', and the next is 'Eight-fifty-nine, North-east'."

"Then you travelled east-by-north about a fifteenth-of-a-mile and we shall put down half-an-inch on the chart. Then you turned north-east. How long did you go on?"

"Exactly a minute. The next entry is '*Nine. West-north-west*'."

"Then you travelled about the seventh-of-a-mile in a north-easterly direction and we draw a line an inch long at an angle of forty-five degrees to the right of the north-and-south line. From the end of that we carry a line at an angle of fifty-six-and-a-quarter degrees to the left of the north-and-south line, and so on. The method is perfectly simple, you see."

"Perfectly, I quite understand it now."

I went back to my chair and continued to read out the entries from the notebook while Thorndyke laid off the lines of direction with the protractor, taking out the distances with the dividers from a scale of equal parts on the back of the instrument. As the work proceeded, I noticed, from time to time, a smile of quiet amusement spread over my colleague's keen, attentive face, and at each new reference to a railway bridge he chuckled softly.

"What, again!" he laughed, as I recorded the passage of the fifth or sixth bridge. "It's like a game of croquet. Go on. What is the next?"

I went on reading out the notes until I came to the final one. "'*Nine-twenty-four. South-east. In covered way. Stop. Wooden gates closed*'."

Thorndyke ruled off the last line, remarking, "Then your covered way is on the south side of a street which bears north-east. So we complete our chart. Just look at your route, Jervis."

He held up the board with a quizzical smile and I stared in astonishment at the chart. The single line, which represented the route of the carriage, zigzagged in the most amazing manner, turning, re-turning and crossing itself repeatedly, evidently passing more than once down the same thoroughfares and terminating at a comparatively short distance from its commencement.

The Track Chart
Showing the Route Followed by Weiss's Carriage

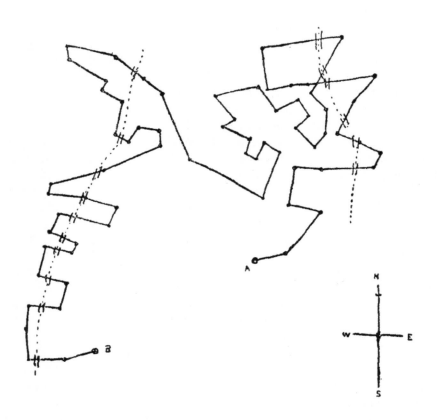

A. – Starting-point in Lower Kennington Lane.
B. – Position of Mr. Weiss's house.
The dotted lines connecting the bridges indicate probable railway lines.

"Why!" I exclaimed, the "rascal must have lived quite near to Stillbury's house!"

Thorndyke measured with the dividers the distance between the starting and arriving points of the route and took it off from the scale.

"Five-eighths of a mile, roughly," he said. "You could have walked it in less than ten minutes. And now let us get out the ordnance map and see if we can give to each of those marvellously erratic lines 'a local habitation and a name'."

He spread the map out on the table and placed our chart by its side. "I think," said he, "you started from Lower Kennington Lane?"

"Yes, from this point," I replied, indicating the spot with a pencil.

"Then," said Thorndyke, "if we swing the chart round twenty degrees to correct the deviation of the compass, we can compare it with the ordnance map."

He set off with the protractor an angle of twenty degrees from the north and south line and turned the chart round to that extent. After closely scrutinizing the map and the chart and comparing the one with the other, he said, "By mere inspection it seems fairly easy to identify the thoroughfares that correspond to the lines of the chart. Take the part that is near your destination. At nine-twenty-one you passed under a bridge, going westward. That would seem to be Glasshouse Street. Then you turned south, apparently along the Albert Embankment, where you heard the tug's whistle. Then you heard a passenger train start on your left, that would be Vauxhall Station. Next you turned round due east and passed under a large railway bridge, which suggests the bridge that carries the Station over Upper Kennington Lane. If that is so, your house should be on the south side of Upper Kennington Lane, some three-hundred yards from the bridge. But we may as well test our inferences by one or two measurements."

"How can you do that if you don't know the exact scale of the chart?"

"I will show you," said Thorndyke. "We shall establish the true scale and that will form part of the proof."

He rapidly constructed on the upper blank part of the paper, a proportional diagram consisting of two intersecting lines with a single cross-line.

"This long line," he explained, "is the distance from Stillbury's house to the Vauxhall railway bridge as it appears on the chart, the shorter cross-line is the same distance taken from the ordnance map. If our inference is correct and the chart is reasonably accurate, all the other distances will show a similar proportion. Let us try some of them. Take the distance from Vauxhall bridge to the Glasshouse Street bridge."

He made the two measurements carefully, and, as the point of the dividers came down almost precisely in the correct place on the diagram, he looked up at me.

"Considering the roughness of the method by which the chart was made, I think that is pretty conclusive, though, if you look at the various arches that you passed under and see how nearly they appear to follow the position of the South-Western Railway line, you hardly need further proof. But I will take a few more proportional measurements for the satisfaction of proving the case by scientific methods before we proceed to verify our conclusions by a visit to the spot."

He took off one or two more distances, and on comparing them with the proportional distances on the ordnance map, found them in every case as nearly correct as could be expected.

"Yes," said Thorndyke, laying down the dividers, "I think we have narrowed down the locality of Mr. Weiss's house to a few yards in a known street. We shall get further help from your note of nine-twenty-three thirty, which records a patch of newly laid macadam extending up to the house."

"That new macadam will be pretty well smoothed down by now," I objected.

"Not so very completely," answered Thorndyke. "It is only a little over a month ago, and there has been very little wet weather since. It may be smooth, but it will be easily distinguishable from the old."

"And do I understand that you propose to go and explore the neighbourhood?"

"Undoubtedly I do. That is to say, I intend to convert the locality of this house into a definite address, which, I think, will now be perfectly easy, unless we should have the bad luck to find more than one covered way. Even then, the difficulty would be trifling."

"And when you have ascertained where Mr. Weiss lives? What then?"

"That will depend on circumstances. I think we shall probably call at Scotland Yard and have a little talk with our friend Mr. Superintendent Miller – unless, for any reason, it seems better to look into the case ourselves."

"When is this voyage of exploration to take place?"

Thorndyke considered this question, and, taking out his pocket-book, glanced through his engagements.

"It seems to me," he said, "that to-morrow is a fairly free day. We could take the morning without neglecting other business. I suggest that we start immediately after breakfast. How will that suit my learned friend?"

"My time is yours," I replied, "and if you choose to waste it on matters that don't concern you, that's your affair."

"Then we will consider the arrangement to stand for to-morrow morning, or rather, for *this* morning, as I see that it is past twelve."

With this Thorndyke gathered up the chart and instruments and we separated for the night.

Chapter IX
The House of Mystery

Half-past nine on the following morning found us spinning along the Albert Embankment in a hansom to the pleasant tinkle of the horse's bell. Thorndyke appeared to be in high spirits, though the full enjoyment of the matutinal pipe precluded fluent conversation. As a precaution, he had put my notebook in his pocket before starting, and once or twice he took it out and looked over its pages, but he made no reference to the object of our quest, and the few remarks that he uttered would have indicated that his thoughts were occupied with other matters.

Arrived at Vauxhall Station, we alighted and forthwith made our way to the bridge that spans Upper Kennington Lane near its junction with Harleyford Road.

"Here is our starting point," said Thorndyke. "From this place to the house is about three-hundred yards – say four-hundred-and-twenty paces – and at about two-hundred paces we ought to reach our patch of new road-metal. Now, are you ready? If we keep step we shall average our stride."

We started together at a good pace, stepping out with military regularity and counting aloud as we went. As we told out the hundred-and-ninety-fourth pace I observed Thorndyke nod towards the roadway a little ahead, and, looking at it attentively as we approached, it was easy to see by the regularity of surface and lighter colour, that it had recently been re-metalled.

Having counted out the four-hundred-and-twenty paces, we halted, and Thorndyke turned to me with a smile of triumph.

"Not a bad estimate, Jervis," said he. "That will be your house if I am not much mistaken. There is no other mews or private roadway in sight."

He pointed to a narrow turning some dozen yards ahead, apparently the entrance to a mews or yard and closed by a pair of massive wooden gates.

"Yes," I answered, "there can be no doubt that this is the place, but, by Jove!" I added, as we drew nearer, "the nest is empty! Do you see?"

I pointed to a bill that was stuck on the gate, bearing, as I could see at this distance, the inscription "*To Let*".

"Here is a new and startling, if not altogether unexpected, development," said Thorndyke, as we stood gazing at the bill, which set forth that "*these premises, including stabling and workshops*" were "*to be let on lease or otherwise*" and referred inquiries to Messrs. Ryebody

527

Brothers, house-agents and valuers, Upper Kennington Lane. "The question is, should we make a few inquiries of the agent, or should we get the keys and have a look at the inside of the house? I am inclined to do both – and the latter first, if Messrs. Ryebody Brothers will trust us with the keys."

We proceeded up the lane to the address given and, entering the office, Thorndyke made his request – somewhat to the surprise of the clerk, for Thorndyke was not quite the kind of person whom one naturally associates with stabling and workshops. However, there was no difficulty, but as the clerk sorted out the keys from a bunch hanging from a hook, he remarked, "I expect you will find the place in a rather dirty and neglected condition. The house has not been cleaned yet. It is just as it was left when the brokers took away the furniture."

"Was the last tenant sold up, then?" Thorndyke asked.

"Oh, no. He had to leave rather unexpectedly to take up some business in Germany."

"I hope he paid his rent," said Thorndyke.

"Oh, yes. Trust us for that. But I should say that Mr. Weiss – that was his name – was a man of some means. He seemed to have plenty of money, though he always paid in notes. I don't fancy he had a banking account in this country. He hadn't been here more than about six or seven months and I imagine he didn't know many people in England, as he paid us a cash deposit in lieu of references when he first came."

"I think you said his name was Weiss. It wouldn't be *H.* Weiss by any chance?"

"I believe it was. But I can soon tell you." He opened a drawer and consulted what looked like a book of receipt forms. "Yes, H. Weiss. Do you know him, sir?"

"I knew a Mr. H. Weiss some years ago. He came from Bremen, I remember."

"This Mr. Weiss has gone back to Hamburg," the clerk observed.

"Ah," said Thorndyke, "then it would seem not to be the same. My acquaintance was a fair man with a beard and a decidedly red nose and he wore spectacles."

"That's the man. You've described him exactly," said the clerk, who was apparently rather easily satisfied in the matter of description.

"Dear me," said Thorndyke, "what a small world it is. Do you happen to have a note of his address in Hamburg?"

"I haven't," the clerk replied. "You see, we've done with him, having got the rent, though the house is not actually surrendered yet. Mr Weiss's housekeeper still has the front-door key. She doesn't start for Hamburg for a week or so, and meanwhile she keeps the key so that she can call every day and see if there are any letters."

"Indeed," said Thorndyke. "I wonder if he still has the same housekeeper."

"This lady is a German," replied the clerk, "with a regular jaw-twisting name. Sounded like Shallybang."

"Schallibaum. That is the lady. A fair woman with hardly any eyebrows and a pronounced cast in the left eye."

"Now that's very curious, sir," said the clerk. "It's the same name, and this is a fair woman with remarkably thin eyebrows, I remember, now that you mention it. But it can't be the same person. I have only seen her a few times and then only just for a minute or so, but I'm quite certain she had no cast in her eye. So, you see, sir, she can't be the same person. You can dye your hair or you can wear a wig or you can paint your face, but a squint is a squint. There's no faking a swivel eye."

Thorndyke laughed softly. "I suppose not – unless, perhaps, some one might invent an adjustable glass eye. Are these the keys?"

"Yes, sir. The large one belongs to the wicket in the front gate. The other is the latch-key belonging to the side door. Mrs. Shallybang has the key of the front door."

"Thank you," said Thorndyke. He took the keys, to which a wooden label was attached, and we made our way back towards the house of mystery, discussing the clerk's statements as we went.

"A very communicable young gentleman, that," Thorndyke remarked. "He seemed quite pleased to relieve the monotony of office work with a little conversation. And I am sure I was very delighted to indulge him."

"He hadn't much to tell, all the same," said I.

Thorndyke looked at me in surprise. "I don't know what you would have, Jervis, unless you expect casual strangers to present you with a ready-made body of evidence, fully classified, with all the inferences and implications stated. It seemed to me that he was a highly instructive young man."

"What did you learn from him?" I asked.

"Oh, come, Jervis," he protested. "Is that a fair question, under our present arrangement? However, I will mention a few points. We learn that about six or seven months ago, Mr. H. Weiss dropped from the clouds into Kennington Lane and that he has now ascended from Kennington Lane into the clouds. That is a useful piece of information. Then we learn that Mrs. Schallibaum has remained in England, which might be of little importance if it were not for a very interesting corollary that it suggests."

"What is that?"

"I must leave you to consider the facts at your leisure, but you will have noticed the ostensible reason for her remaining behind. She is engaged in puttying up the one gaping joint in their armour. One of them has been indiscreet enough to give this address to some correspondent – probably a foreign correspondent. Now, as they obviously wish to leave no tracks, they cannot give their new address to the Post Office to have their letters forwarded, and, on the other hand, a letter left in the box might establish such a connection as would enable them to be traced. Moreover, the letter might be of a kind that they would not wish to fall into the wrong hands. They would not have given this address excepting under some peculiar circumstances."

"No, I should think not, if they took this house for the express purpose of committing a crime in it."

"Exactly. And then there is one other fact that you may have gathered from our young friend's remarks."

"What is that?"

"That a controllable squint is a very valuable asset to a person who wishes to avoid identification."

"Yes, I did note that. The fellow seemed to think that it was absolutely conclusive."

"And so would most people, especially in the case of a squint of that kind. We can all squint towards our noses, but no normal person can turn his eyes away from one another. My impression is that the presence or absence, as the case might be, of a divergent squint would be accepted as absolute disproof of identity. But here we are."

He inserted the key into the wicket of the large gate, and, when we had stepped through into the covered way, he locked it from the inside.

"Why have you locked us in?" I asked, seeing that the wicket had a latch.

"Because," he replied, "if we now hear any one on the premises we shall know who it is. Only one person besides ourselves has a key."

His reply startled me somewhat. I stopped and looked at him.

"That is a quaint situation, Thorndyke. I hadn't thought of it. Why, she may actually come to the house while we are here. In fact, she may be in the house at this moment."

"I hope not," said he. "We don't particularly want Mr. Weiss to be put on his guard, for I take it, he is a pretty wide-awake gentleman under any circumstances. If she does come, we had better keep out of sight. I think we will look over the house first. That is of the most interest to us. If the lady does happen to come while we are here, she may stay to show us over the place and keep an eye on us. So we will leave the stables to the last."

530

We walked down the entry to the side door at which I had been admitted by Mrs. Schallibaum on the occasion of my previous visits. Thorndyke inserted the latch-key, and, as soon as we were inside, shut the door and walked quickly through into the hall, whither I followed him. He made straight for the front door, where, having slipped up the catch of the lock, he began very attentively to examine the letter-box. It was a somewhat massive wooden box, fitted with a lock of good quality and furnished with a wire grille through which one could inspect the interior.

"We are in luck, Jervis," Thorndyke remarked. "Our visit has been most happily timed. There is a letter in the box."

"Well," I said, "we can't get it out, and if we could, it would be hardly justifiable."

"I don't know," he replied, "that I am prepared to assent off-hand to either of those propositions, but I would rather not tamper with another person's letter, even if that person should happen to be a murderer. Perhaps we can get the information we want from the outside of the envelope."

He produced from his pocket a little electric lamp fitted with a bull's-eye, and, pressing the button, threw a beam of light in through the grille. The letter was lying on the bottom of the box face upwards, so that the address could easily be read.

"*Herrn Dr. H. Weiss,*" Thorndyke read aloud. "German stamp, postmark apparently Darmstadt. You notice that the '*Herrn* Dr.' is printed and the rest written. What do you make of that?"

"I don't quite know. Do you think he is really a medical man?"

"Perhaps we had better finish our investigation, in case we are disturbed, and discuss the bearings of the facts afterwards. The name of the sender may be on the flap of the envelope. If it is not, I shall pick the lock and take out the letter. Have you got a probe about you?"

"Yes. By force of habit I am still carrying my pocket case."

I took the little case from my pocket and extracting from it a jointed probe of thickish silver wire, screwed the two halves together and handed the completed instrument to Thorndyke, who passed the slender rod through the grille and adroitly turned the letter over.

"Ha!" he exclaimed with deep satisfaction, as the light fell on the reverse of the envelope, "we are saved from the necessity of theft – or rather, unauthorized borrowing – '*Johann Schnitzler, Darmstadt*'. That is all that we actually want. The German police can do the rest, if necessary."

He handed me back my probe, pocketed his lamp, released the catch of the lock on the door, and turned away along the dark, musty-smelling hall.

"Do you happen to know the name of Johann Schnitzler?" he asked.

531

I replied that I had no recollection of ever having heard the name before.

"Neither have I," said he, "but I think we may form a pretty shrewd guess as to his avocation. As you saw, the words '*Herrn* Dr.' were printed on the envelope, leaving the rest of the address to be written by hand. The plain inference is that he is a person who habitually addresses letters to medical men, and as the style of the envelope and the lettering – which is printed, not embossed – is commercial, we may assume that he is engaged in some sort of trade. Now, what is a likely trade?"

"He might be an instrument maker or a drug manufacturer – more probably the latter, as there is an extensive drug and chemical industry in Germany, and as Mr. Weiss seemed to have more use for drugs than instruments."

"Yes, I think you are right, but we will look him up when we get home. And now we had better take a glance at the bedroom – that is, if you can remember which room it was."

"It was on the first floor," said I, "and the door by which I entered was just at the head of the stairs."

We ascended the two flights, and, as we reached the landing, I halted.

"This was the door," I said, and was about to turn the handle when Thorndyke caught me by the arm.

"One moment, Jervis," said he. "What do you make of this?"

He pointed to a spot near the bottom of the door where, on close inspection, four good-sized screw-holes were distinguishable. They had been neatly stopped with putty and covered with knotting, and were so nearly the colour of the grained and varnished woodwork as to be hardly visible.

"Evidently," I answered, "there has been a bolt there, though it seems a queer place to fix one."

"Not at all," replied Thorndyke. "If you look up you will see that there was another at the top of the door, and, as the lock is in the middle, they must have been highly effective. But there are one or two other points that strike one. First, you will notice that the bolts have been fixed on quite recently, for the paint that they covered is of the same grimy tint as that on the rest of the door. Next, they have been taken off, which, seeing that they could hardly have been worth the trouble of removal, seems to suggest that the person who fixed them considered that their presence might appear remarkable, while the screw-holes, which have been so skilfully and carefully stopped, would be less conspicuous."

"Then, they are on the outside of the door – an unusual situation for bedroom bolts – and were of considerable size. They were long and thick."

"I can see, by the position of the screw-holes, that they were long, but how do you arrive at their thickness?"

"By the size of the counter-holes in the jamb of the door. These holes have been very carefully filled with wooden plugs covered with knotting, but you can make out their diameter, which is that of the bolts, and which is decidedly out of proportion for an ordinary bedroom door. Let me show you a light."

He flashed his lamp into the dark corner, and I was able to see distinctly the portentously large holes into which the bolts had fitted, and also to note the remarkable neatness with which they had been plugged.

"There was a second door, I remember," said I. "Let us see if that was guarded in a similar manner."

We strode through the empty room, awakening dismal echoes as we trod the bare boards, and flung open the other door. At top and bottom, similar groups of screw-holes showed that this also had been made secure, and that these bolts had been of the same very substantial character as the others.

Thorndyke turned away from the door with a slight frown.

"If we had any doubts," said he, "as to what has been going on in this house, these traces of massive fastenings would be almost enough to settle them."

"They might have been there before Weiss came," I suggested. "He only came about seven months ago and there is no date on the screw-holes."

"That is quite true. But when, with their recent fixture, you couple the facts that they have been removed, that very careful measures have been taken to obliterate the traces of their presence, and that they would have been indispensable for the commission of the crime that we are almost certain was being committed here, it looks like an excess of caution to seek other explanations."

"But," I objected, "if the man, Graves, was really imprisoned, could not he have smashed the window and called for help?"

"The window looks out on the yard, as you see, but I expect it was secured too."

He drew the massive, old-fashioned shutters out of their recess and closed them.

"Yes, here we are." He pointed to four groups of screw-holes at the corners of the shutters, and, once more producing his lamp, narrowly examined the insides of the recesses into which the shutters folded.

"The nature of the fastening is quite evident," said he. "An iron bar passed right across at the top and bottom and was secured by a staple and padlock. You can see the mark the bar made in the recess when the shutters were folded. When these bars were fixed and padlocked and the bolts were shot, this room was as secure, for a prisoner unprovided with tools, as a cell in Newgate."

We looked at one another for awhile without speaking, and I fancy that if Mr. H. Weiss could have seen our faces he might have thought it desirable to seek some retreat even more remote than Hamburg.

"It was a diabolical affair, Jervis," Thorndyke said at length, in an ominously quiet and even gentle tone. "A sordid, callous, cold-blooded crime of a type that is to me utterly unforgivable and incapable of extenuation. Of course, it may have failed. Mr. Graves may even now be alive. I shall make it my very especial business to ascertain whether he is or not. And if he is not, I shall take it to myself as a sacred duty to lay my hand on the man who has compassed his death."

I looked at Thorndyke with something akin to awe. In the quiet unemotional tone of his voice, in his unruffled manner and the stony calm of his face, there was something much more impressive, more fateful, than there could have been in the fiercest threats or the most passionate denunciations. I felt that in those softly spoken words he had pronounced the doom of the fugitive villain.

He turned away from the window and glanced round the empty room. It seemed that our discovery of the fastenings had exhausted the information that it had to offer.

"It is a thousand pities," I remarked, "that we were unable to look round before they moved out the furniture. We might have found some clue to the scoundrel's identity."

"Yes," replied Thorndyke, "there isn't much information to be gathered here, I am afraid. I see they have swept up the small litter from the floor and poked it under the grate. We will turn that over, as there seems to be nothing else, and then look at the other rooms."

He raked out the little heap of rubbish with his stick and spread it out on the hearth. It certainly looked unpromising enough, being just such a rubbish heap as may be swept up in any untidy room during a move. But Thorndyke went through it systematically, examining each item attentively, even to the local tradesmen's bills and empty paper bags, before laying them aside. Another rake of his stick scattered the bulky masses of crumpled paper and brought into view an object which he picked up with some eagerness. It was a portion of a pair of spectacles, which had apparently been trodden on, for the side-bar was twisted and bent and the glass was shattered into fragments.

"This ought to give us a hint," said he. "It will probably have belonged either to Weiss or Graves, as Mrs. Schallibaum apparently did not wear glasses. Let us see if we can find the remainder."

We both groped carefully with our sticks amongst the rubbish, spreading it out on the hearth and removing the numerous pieces of crumpled paper. Our search was rewarded by the discovery of the second eye-piece of the spectacles, of which the glass was badly cracked but less shattered than the other. I also picked up two tiny sticks at which Thorndyke looked with deep interest before laying them on the mantelshelf.

"We will consider them presently," said he. "Let us finish with the spectacles first. You see that the left eye-glass is a concave cylindrical lens of some sort. We can make out that much from the fragments that remain, and we can measure the curvature when we get them home, although that will be easier if we can collect some more fragments and stick them together. The right eye is plain glass, that is quite evident. Then these will have belonged to your patient, Jervis. You said that the tremulous iris was in the right eye, I think?"

"Yes," I replied. "These will be his spectacles, without doubt."

"They are peculiar frames," he continued. "If they were made in this country, we might be able to discover the maker. But we must collect as many fragments of glass as we can."

Once more we searched amongst the rubbish and succeeded, eventually, in recovering some seven or eight small fragments of the broken spectacle-glasses, which Thorndyke laid on the mantelshelf beside the little sticks.

"By the way, Thorndyke," I said, taking up the latter to examine them afresh, "what are these things? Can you make anything of them?"

He looked at them thoughtfully for a few moments and then replied, "I don't think I will tell you what they are. You should find that out for yourself, and it will be well worth your while to do so. They are rather suggestive objects under the circumstances. But notice their peculiarities carefully. Both are portions of some smooth, stout reed. There is a long, thin stick – about six inches long – and a thicker piece only three inches in length. The longer piece has a little scrap of red paper stuck on at the end, apparently a portion of a label of some kind with an ornamental border. The other end of the stick has been broken off. The shorter, stouter stick has had its central cavity artificially enlarged so that it fits over the other to form a cap or sheath. Make a careful note of those facts and try to think what they probably mean, what would be the most likely use for an object of this kind. When you have ascertained that, you will have learned something new about this case. And now, to resume our investigations. Here is a very suggestive thing." He picked up a small, wide-mouthed bottle and, holding it up for my inspection, continued, "Observe the fly sticking to the inside, and the name on the label, '*Fox, Russell Street, Covent Garden*'."

"I don't know Mr. Fox."

"Then I will inform you that he is a dealer in the materials for 'make-up', theatrical or otherwise, and will leave you to consider the bearing of this bottle on our present investigation. There doesn't seem to be anything else of interest in this El Dorado excepting that screw, which you notice is about the size of those with which the bolts were fastened on the doors. I don't think it is worth while to unstop any of the holes to try it – we should learn nothing fresh."

He rose, and, having kicked the discarded rubbish back under the grate, gathered up his gleanings from the mantelpiece, carefully bestowing the spectacles and the fragments of glass in the tin box that he appeared always to carry in his pocket, and wrapping the larger objects in his handkerchief.

"A poor collection," was his comment, as he returned the box and handkerchief to his pocket, "and yet not so poor as I had feared. Perhaps, if we question them closely enough, these unconsidered trifles may be made to tell us something worth learning after all. Shall we go into the other room?"

We passed out on to the landing and into the front room, where, guided by experience, we made straight for the fire-place. But the little heap of rubbish there contained nothing that even Thorndyke's inquisitive eye could view with interest. We wandered disconsolately round the room, peering into the empty cupboards and scanning the floor and the corners by the skirting, without discovering a single object or relic of the late occupants. In the course of my perambulations I halted by the window and was looking down into the street when Thorndyke called to me sharply, "Come away from the window, Jervis! Have you forgotten that Mrs. Schallibaum may be in the neighbourhood at this moment?"

As a matter of fact I had entirely forgotten the matter, nor did it now strike me as anything but the remotest of possibilities. I replied to that effect.

"I don't agree with you," Thorndyke rejoined. "We have heard that she comes here to look for letters. Probably she comes every day, or even oftener. There is a good deal at stake, remember, and they cannot feel quite as secure as they would wish. Weiss must have seen what view you took of the case and must have had some uneasy moments thinking of what you might do. In fact, we may take it that the fear of you drove them out of the neighbourhood, and that they are mighty anxious to get that letter and cut the last link that binds them to this house."

"I suppose that is so," I agreed, "and if the lady should happen to pass this way and should see me at the window and recognize me, she would certainly smell a rat."

"A rat!" exclaimed Thorndyke. "She would smell a whole pack of foxes, and Mr. H. Weiss would be more on his guard than ever. Let us have a look at the other rooms – there is nothing here."

We went up to the next floor and found traces of recent occupation in one room only. The garrets had evidently been unused, and the kitchen and ground-floor rooms offered nothing that appeared to Thorndyke worth noting. Then we went out by the side door and down the covered way into the yard at the back. The workshops were fastened with rusty padlocks that looked as if they had not been disturbed for months. The stables were empty and had been tentatively cleaned out, the coach-house was vacant, and presented no traces of recent use excepting a half-bald spoke-brush. We returned up the covered way and I was about to close the side door, which Thorndyke had left ajar, when he stopped me.

"We'll have another look at the hall before we go," said he, and, walking softly before me, he made his way to the front door, where, producing his lamp, he threw a beam of light into the letter-box.

"Any more letters?" I asked.

"Any more!" he repeated. "Look for yourself."

I stooped and peered through the grille into the lighted interior, and then I uttered an exclamation.

The box was empty.

Thorndyke regarded me with a grim smile. "We have been caught on the hop, Jervis, I suspect," said he.

"It is queer," I replied. "I didn't hear any sound of the opening or closing of the door, did you?"

"No, I didn't hear any sound, which makes me suspect that she did. She would have heard our voices and she is probably keeping a sharp look-out at this very moment. I wonder if she saw you at the window. But whether she did or not, we must go very warily. Neither of us must return to the Temple direct, and we had better separate when we have returned the keys and I will watch you out of sight and see if anyone is following you. What are you going to do?"

"If you don't want me, I shall run over to Kensington and drop in to lunch at the Hornbys'. I said I would call as soon as I had an hour or so free."

"Very well. Do so, and keep a look-out in case you are followed. I have to go down to Guildford this afternoon. Under the circumstances, I shall not go back home, but send Polton a telegram and take a train at Vauxhall and change at some small station where I can watch the platform.

Be as careful as you can. Remember that what you have to avoid is being followed to any place where you are known, and, above all, revealing your connection with Number 5A, King's Bench Walk."

Having thus considered our immediate movements, we emerged together from the wicket, and locking it behind us, walked quickly to the house-agents', where an opportune office-boy received the keys without remark. As we came out of the office, I halted irresolutely and we both looked up and down the lane.

"There is no suspicious looking person in sight at present," Thorndyke said, and then asked, "Which way do you think of going?"

"It seems to me," I replied, "that my best plan would be to take a cab or an omnibus so as to get out of the neighbourhood as quickly as possible. If I go through Ravensden Street into Kennington Park Road, I can pick up an omnibus that will take me to the Mansion House, where I can change for Kensington. I shall go on the top so that I can keep a look-out for any other omnibus or cab that may be following."

"Yes," said Thorndyke, "that seems a good plan. I will walk with you and see that you get a fair start."

We walked briskly along the lane and through Ravensden Street to the Kennington Park Road. An omnibus was approaching from the south at a steady jog-trot and we halted at the corner to wait for it. Several people passed us in different directions, but none seemed to take any particular notice of us, though we observed them rather narrowly, especially the women. Then the omnibus crawled up. I sprang on the foot-board and ascended to the roof, where I seated myself and surveyed the prospect to the rear. No one else got on the omnibus – which had not stopped – and no cab or other passenger vehicle was in sight. I continued to watch Thorndyke as he stood sentinel at the corner, and noted that no one appeared to be making any effort to overtake the omnibus. Presently my colleague waved his hand to me and turned back towards Vauxhall, and I, having satisfied myself once more that no pursuing cab or hurrying foot-passenger was in sight, decided that our precautions had been unnecessary and settled myself in a rather more comfortable position.

Chapter X
The Hunter Hunted

The omnibus of those days was a leisurely vehicle. Its ordinary pace was a rather sluggish trot, and in a thickly populated thoroughfare its speed was further reduced by frequent stoppages. Bearing these facts in mind, I gave an occasional backward glance as we jogged northward, though my attention soon began to wander from the rather remote possibility of pursuit to the incidents of our late exploration.

It had not been difficult to see that Thorndyke was very well pleased with the results of our search, but excepting the letter – which undoubtedly opened up a channel for further inquiry and possible identification – I could not perceive that any of the traces that we had found justified his satisfaction. There were the spectacles, for instance. They were almost certainly the pair worn by Mr. Graves. But what then? It was exceedingly improbable that we should be able to discover the maker of them, and if we were, it was still more improbable that he would be able to give us any information that would help us. Spectacle-makers are not usually on confidential terms with their customers.

As to the other objects, I could make nothing of them. The little sticks of reed evidently had some use that was known to Thorndyke and furnished, by inference, some kind of information about Weiss, Graves, or Mrs. Schallibaum. But I had never seen anything like them before and they conveyed nothing whatever to me. Then the bottle that had seemed so significant to Thorndyke was to me quite uninforming. It did, indeed, suggest that some member of the household might be connected with the stage, but it gave no hint as to which one. Certainly that person was not Mr. Weiss, whose appearance was as remote from that of an actor as could well be imagined. At any rate, the bottle and its label gave me no more useful hint than it might be worth while to call on Mr. Fox and make inquiries, and something told me very emphatically that this was not what it had conveyed to Thorndyke.

These reflections occupied me until the omnibus, having rumbled over London Bridge and up King William Street, joined the converging streams of traffic at the Mansion House. Here I got down and changed to an omnibus bound for Kensington, on which I travelled westward pleasantly enough, looking down into the teeming streets and whiling away the time by meditating upon the very agreeable afternoon that I promised myself, and considering how far my new arrangement with

Thorndyke would justify me in entering into certain domestic engagements of a highly interesting kind.

What might have happened under other circumstances it is impossible to tell and useless to speculate, the fact is that my journey ended in a disappointment. I arrived, all agog, at the familiar house in Endsley Gardens only to be told by a sympathetic housemaid that the family was out, that Mrs. Hornby had gone into the country and would not be home until night, and – which mattered a good deal more to me – that her niece, Miss Juliet Gibson, had accompanied her.

Now a man who drops into lunch without announcing his intention or previously ascertaining those of his friends has no right to quarrel with fate if he finds an empty house. Thus philosophically I reflected as I turned away from the house in profound discontent, demanding of the universe in general why Mrs. Hornby need have perversely chosen my first free day to go gadding into the country, and above all, why she must needs spirit away the fair Juliet. This was the crowning misfortune (for I could have endured the absence of the elder lady with commendable fortitude), and since I could not immediately return to the Temple it left me a mere waif and stray for the time being.

Instinct – of the kind that manifests itself especially about one o'clock in the afternoon – impelled me in the direction of Brompton Road, and finally landed me at a table in a large restaurant apparently adjusted to the needs of ladies who had come from a distance to engage in the feminine sport of shopping. Here, while waiting for my lunch, I sat idly scanning the morning paper and wondering what I should do with the rest of the day, and presently it chanced that my eye caught the announcement of a matinée at the theatre in Sloane Square. It was quite a long time since I had been at a theatre, and, as the play – light comedy – seemed likely to satisfy my not very critical taste, I decided to devote the afternoon to reviving my acquaintance with the drama. Accordingly as soon as my lunch was finished, I walked down the Brompton Road, stepped on to an omnibus, and was duly deposited at the door of the theatre. A couple of minutes later I found myself occupying an excellent seat in the second row of the pit, oblivious alike of my recent disappointment and of Thorndyke's words of warning.

I am not an enthusiastic play-goer. To dramatic performances I am disposed to assign nothing further than the modest function of furnishing entertainment. I do not go to a theatre to be instructed or to have my moral outlook elevated. But, by way of compensation, I am not difficult to please. To a simple play, adjusted to my primitive taste, I can bring a certain bucolic appreciation that enables me to extract from the performance the maximum of enjoyment, and when, on this occasion, the

540

final curtain fell and the audience rose, I rescued my hat from its insecure resting-place and turned to go with the feeling that I had spent a highly agreeable afternoon.

Emerging from the theatre, borne on the outgoing stream, I presently found myself opposite the door of a tea-shop. Instinct – the five o'clock instinct this time – guided me in, for we are creatures of habit, especially of the tea habit. The unoccupied table to which I drifted was in a shady corner not very far from the pay-desk, and here I had been seated less than a minute when a lady passed me on her way to the farther table. The glimpse that I caught of her as she approached – it was but a glimpse, since she passed behind me – showed that she was dressed in black, that she wore a beaded veil and hat, and in addition to the glass of milk and the bun that she carried, she was encumbered by an umbrella and a small basket, apparently containing some kind of needlework. I must confess that I gave her very little attention at the time, being occupied in anxious speculation as to how long it would be before the fact of my presence would impinge on the consciousness of the waitress.

The exact time by the clock on the wall was three-minutes-and-a-quarter, at the expiration of which an anaemic young woman sauntered up to the table and bestowed on me a glance of sullen interrogation, as if mutely demanding what the devil I wanted. I humbly requested that I might be provided with a pot of tea, whereupon she turned on her heel (which was a good deal worn down on the offside) and reported my conduct to a lady behind a marble-topped counter.

It seemed that the counter lady took a lenient view of the case, for in less than four minutes the waitress returned and gloomily deposited on the table before me a tea-pot, a milk-jug, a cup and saucer, a jug of hot water, and a small pool of milk. Then she once more departed in dudgeon.

I had just given the tea in the pot a preliminary stir and was about to pour out the first cup when I felt some one bump lightly against my chair and heard something rattle on the floor. I turned quickly and perceived the lady, whom I had seen enter, stooping just behind my chair. It seemed that having finished her frugal meal she was on her way out when she had dropped the little basket that I had noticed hanging from her wrist, which basket had promptly disgorged its entire contents on the floor.

Now every one must have noticed the demon of agility that seems to enter into an inanimate object when it is dropped, and the apparently intelligent malice with which it discovers, and rolls into, the most inaccessible places. Here was a case in point. This particular basket had contained materials for Oriental bead-work, and no sooner had it reached the floor than each item of its contents appeared to become possessed of a separate and particular devil impelling it to travel at headlong speed to

541

some remote and unapproachable corner as distant as possible from its fellows.

As the only man – and almost the only person – near, the duty of salvage-agent manifestly devolved upon me, and down I went, accordingly, on my hands and knees, regardless of a nearly new pair of trousers, to grope under tables, chairs and settles in reach of the scattered treasure. A ball of the thick thread or twine I recovered from a dark and dirty corner after a brief interview with the sharp corner of a settle, and a multitude of the large beads with which this infernal industry is carried on I gathered from all parts of the compass, coming forth at length (quadrupedally) with a double handful of the treasure-trove and a very lively appreciation of the resistant qualities of a cast-iron table-stand when applied to the human cranium.

The owner of the lost and found property was greatly distressed by the accident and the trouble it had caused me, in fact she was quite needlessly agitated about it. The hand which held the basket into which I poured the rescued trash trembled visibly, and the brief glance that I bestowed on her as she murmured her thanks and apologies – with a very slight foreign accent – showed me that she was excessively pale. That much I could see plainly in spite of the rather dim light in this part of the shop and the beaded veil that covered her face, and I could also see that she was a rather remarkable looking woman, with a great mass of harsh, black hair and very broad black eyebrows that nearly met above her nose and contrasted strikingly with the dead white of her skin. But, of course, I did not look at her intently. Having returned her property and received her acknowledgments, I resumed my seat and left her to go on her way.

I had once more grasped the handle of the tea-pot when I made a rather curious discovery. At the bottom of the tea-cup lay a single lump of sugar. To the majority of persons it would have meant nothing. They would have assumed that they had dropped it in and forgotten it and would have proceeded to pour out the tea. But it happened that, at this time, I did not take sugar in my tea, whence it followed that the lump had not been put in by me. Assuming, therefore, that it had been carelessly dropped in by the waitress, I turned it out on the table, filled the cup, added the milk, and took a tentative draught to test the temperature.

The cup was yet at my lips when I chanced to look into the mirror that faced my table. Of course it reflected the part of the shop that was behind me, including the cashier's desk, at which the owner of the basket now stood paying for her refreshment. Between her and me was a gas chandelier which cast its light on my back but full on her face, and her veil notwithstanding, I could see that she was looking at me steadily, was, in fact, watching me intently and with a very curious expression – an

542

expression of expectancy mingled with alarm. But this was not all. As I returned her intent look – which I could do unobserved, since my face, reflected in the mirror, was in deep shadow – I suddenly perceived that that steady gaze engaged her right eye only, the other eye was looking sharply towards her left shoulder. In short, she had a divergent squint of the left eye.

I put down my cup with a thrill of amazement and a sudden surging up of suspicion and alarm. An instant's reflection reminded me that when she had spoken to me a few moments before, both her eyes had looked into mine without the slightest trace of a squint. My thoughts flew back to the lump of sugar, to the unguarded milk-jug and the draught of tea that I had already swallowed, and, hardly knowing what I intended, I started to my feet and turned to confront her. But as I rose, she snatched up her change and darted from the shop. Through the glass door, I saw her spring on to the foot-board of a passing hansom and give the driver some direction. I saw the man whip up his horse, and, by the time I reached the door, the cab was moving off swiftly towards Sloane Street.

I stood irresolute. I had not paid and could not run out of the shop without making a fuss, and my hat and stick were still on the rail opposite my seat. The woman ought to be followed, but I had no fancy for the task. If the tea that I had swallowed was innocuous, no harm was done and I was rid of my pursuer. So far as I was concerned, the incident was closed. I went back to my seat, and picking up the lump of sugar which still lay on the table where I had dropped it, put it carefully in my pocket. But my appetite for tea was satisfied for the present. Moreover it was hardly advisable to stay in the shop lest some fresh spy should come to see how I fared. Accordingly I obtained my check, handed it in at the cashier's desk and took my departure.

All this time, it will be observed, I had been taking it for granted that the lady in black had followed me from Kensington to this shop, that, in fact, she was none other than Mrs. Schallibaum. And, indeed, the circumstances had rendered the conclusion inevitable. In the very instant when I had perceived the displacement of the left eye, complete recognition had come upon me. When I had stood facing the woman, the brief glance at her face had conveyed to me something dimly reminiscent of which I had been but half-conscious and had instantly forgotten. But the sight of that characteristic squint had at once revived and explained it. That the woman was Mrs. Schallibaum I now felt no doubt whatever.

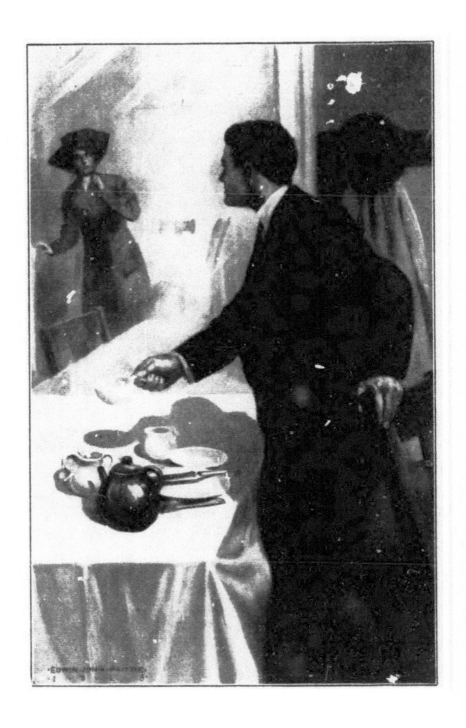

Nevertheless, the whole affair was profoundly mysterious. As to the change in the woman's appearance, there was little in that. The coarse, black hair might be her own, dyed, or it might be a wig. The eyebrows were made-up, it was a simple enough proceeding and made still more simple by the beaded veil. But how did she come to be there at all? How did she happen to be made-up in this fashion at this particular time? And, above all, how came she to be provided with a lump of what I had little doubt was poisoned sugar?

I turned over the events of the day, and the more I considered them the less comprehensible they appeared. No one had followed the omnibus either on foot or in a vehicle, as far as I could see, and I had kept a careful look-out, not only at starting but for some considerable time after. Yet, all the time, Mrs. Schallibaum must have been following. But how? If she had known that I was intending to travel by the omnibus she might have gone to meet it and entered before I did. But she could not have known, and moreover she did not meet the omnibus, for we watched its approach from some considerable distance. I considered whether she might not have been concealed in the house and overheard me mention my destination to Thorndyke. But this failed to explain the mystery, since I had mentioned no address beyond "Kensington." I had, indeed, mentioned the name of Mrs. Hornby, but the supposition that my friends might be known by name to Mrs. Schallibaum, or even that she might have looked the name up in the directory, presented a probability too remote to be worth entertaining.

But, if I reached no satisfactory conclusion, my cogitations had one useful effect, they occupied my mind to the exclusion of that unfortunate draught of tea. Not that I had been seriously uneasy after the first shock. The quantity that I had swallowed was not large – the tea being hotter than I cared for – and I remembered that, when I had thrown out the lump of sugar, I had turned the cup upside down on the table, so there could have been nothing solid left in it. And the lump of sugar was in itself reassuring, for it certainly would not have been used in conjunction with any less conspicuous but more incriminating form of poison. That lump of sugar was now in my pocket, reserved for careful examination at my leisure, and I reflected with a faint grin that it would be a little disconcerting if it should turn out to contain nothing but sugar after all.

On leaving the tea-shop, I walked up Sloane Street with the intention of doing what I ought to have done earlier in the day. I was going to make perfectly sure that no spy was dogging my footsteps. But for my ridiculous confidence I could have done so quite easily before going to Endsley Gardens, and now, made wiser by a startling experience, I proceeded with systematic care. It was still broad daylight – for the lamps in the tea-shop had been rendered necessary only by the faulty construction of the premises and the dullness of the afternoon – and in an open space I could see far enough for complete safety. Arriving at the top of Sloane Street, I crossed Knightsbridge, and, entering Hyde Park, struck out towards the Serpentine. Passing along the eastern shore, I entered one of the long paths that lead towards the Marble Arch and strode along it at such a pace as would make it necessary for any pursuer to hurry in order to keep me in sight. Halfway across the great stretch of turf, I halted for a few moments and noted the few people who were coming in my direction. Then I turned sharply to the left and headed straight for the Victoria Gate, but again, halfway, I turned off among a clump of trees, and, standing behind the trunk of one of them, took a fresh survey of the people who were moving along the paths. All were at a considerable distance and none appeared to be coming my way.

I now moved cautiously from one tree to another and passed through the wooded region to the south, crossed the Serpentine bridge at a rapid walk and hurrying along the south shore left the Park by Apsley House. From hence I walked at the same rapid pace along Piccadilly, insinuating myself among the crowd with the skill born of long acquaintance with the London streets, crossed amidst the seething traffic at the Circus, darted up Windmill Street and began to zigzag amongst the narrow streets and courts of Soho. Crossing the Seven Dials and Drury Lane I passed through the multitudinous back-streets and alleys that then filled the area south of Lincoln's Inn, came out by Newcastle Street, Holywell Street, and Half-Moon Alley into the Strand, which I crossed immediately, ultimately entering the Temple by Devereux Court.

Even then I did not relax my precautions. From one court to another I passed quickly, loitering in those dark entries and unexpected passages that are known to so few but the regular Templars, and coming out into the open only at the last where the wide passage of King's Bench Walk admits of no evasion. Halfway up the stairs, I stood for some time in the shadow, watching the approaches from the staircase window, and when, at length, I felt satisfied that I had taken every precaution that was possible, I inserted my key and let myself into our chambers.

Thorndyke had already arrived, and, as I entered, he rose to greet me with an expression of evident relief.

"I am glad to see you, Jervis," he said. "I have been rather anxious about you."

"Why?" I asked.

"For several reasons. One is that you are the sole danger that threatens these people – as far as they know. Another is that we made a most ridiculous mistake. We overlooked a fact that ought to have struck us instantly. But how have you fared?"

"Better than I deserved. That good lady stuck to me like a burr – at least I believe she did."

"I have no doubt she did. We have been caught napping finely, Jervis."

"How?"

"We'll go into that presently. Let us hear about your adventures first."

I gave him a full account of my movements from the time when we parted to that of my arrival home, omitting no incident that I was able to remember and, as far as I could, reconstituting my exceedingly devious homeward route.

"Your retreat was masterly," he remarked with a broad smile. "I should think that it would have utterly defeated any pursuer, and the only pity is that it was probably wasted on the desert air. Your pursuer had by that time become a fugitive. But you were wise to take these precautions, for, of course, Weiss might have followed you."

"But I thought he was in Hamburg?"

"Did you? You are a very confiding young gentleman, for a budding medical jurist. Of course we don't know that he is not, but the fact that he has given Hamburg as his present whereabouts establishes a strong presumption that he is somewhere else. I only hope that he has not located you, and, from what you tell me of your later methods, I fancy that you would have shaken him off even if he had started to follow you from the tea-shop."

"I hope so too. But how did that woman manage to stick to me in that way? What was the mistake we made?"

Thorndyke laughed grimly. "It was a perfectly asinine mistake, Jervis. You started up Kennington Park Road on a leisurely, jog-trotting omnibus, and neither you nor I remembered what there is underneath Kennington Park Road."

"Underneath!" I exclaimed, completely puzzled for the moment. Then, suddenly realizing what he meant, "Of course!" I exclaimed. "Idiot that I am! You mean the electric railway?"

"Yes. That explains everything. Mrs. Schallibaum must have watched us from some shop and quietly followed us up the lane. There were a good many women about and several were walking in our direction. There was nothing to distinguish her from the others unless you had recognized her, which you would hardly have been able to do if she had worn a veil and kept at a fair distance. At least I think not."

"No," I agreed, "I certainly should not. I had only seen her in a half-dark room. In outdoor clothes and with a veil, I should never have been able to identify her without very close inspection. Besides there was the disguise or make-up."

"Not at that time. She would hardly come disguised to her own house, for it might have led to her being challenged and asked who she was. I think we may take it that there was no actual disguise, although she would probably wear a shady hat and a veil, which would have prevented either of us from picking her out from the other women in the street."

"And what do you think happened next?"

"I think that she simply walked past us – probably on the other side of the road – as we stood waiting for the omnibus, and turned up Kennington Park Road. She probably guessed that we were waiting for the omnibus and walked up the road in the direction in which it was going. Presently the omnibus would pass her, and there were you in full view on top keeping a vigilant look-out in the wrong direction. Then she would quicken her pace a little and in a minute or two would arrive at the Kennington Station of the South London Railway. In a minute or two more she would be in one of the electric trains whirling along under the street on which your omnibus was crawling. She would get out at the Borough Station, or she might take a more risky chance and go on to the Monument, but in any case she would wait for your omnibus, hail it and get inside. I suppose you took up some passengers on the way?"

"Oh dear, yes. We were stopping every two or three minutes to take up or set down passengers, and most of them were women."

"Very well, then we may take it that when you arrived at the Mansion House, Mrs. Schallibaum was one of your inside passengers. It was a rather quaint situation, I think."

"Yes, confound her! What a couple of noodles she must have thought us!"

"No doubt. And that is the one consoling feature in the case. She will have taken us for a pair of absolute greenhorns. But to continue. Of course she travelled in your omnibus to Kensington – you ought to have gone inside on both occasions, so that you could see every one who entered and examine the inside passengers. She will have followed you to Endsley Gardens and probably noted the house you went to. Thence she will have followed you to the restaurant and may even have lunched there."

"It is quite possible," said I. "There were two rooms and they were filled principally with women."

"Then she will have followed you to Sloane Street, and, as you persisted in riding outside, she could easily take an inside place in your omnibus. As to the theatre, she must have taken it as a veritable gift of the gods, an arrangement made by you for her special convenience."

"Why?"

"My dear fellow! Consider. She had only to follow you in and see you safely into your seat and there you were, left till called for. She could then go home, make up for her part, draw out a plan of action, with the help, perhaps, of Mr. Weiss, provide herself with the necessary means and appliances and, at the appointed time, call and collect you."

"That is assuming a good deal," I objected. "It is assuming, for instance, that she lives within a moderate distance of Sloane Square. Otherwise it would have been impossible."

"Exactly. That is why I assume it. You don't suppose that she goes about habitually with lumps of prepared sugar in her pocket. And if not, then she must have got that lump from somewhere. Then the beads suggest a carefully prepared plan, and, as I said just now, she can hardly have been made-up when she met us in Kennington Lane. From all of which it seems likely that her present abode is not very far from Sloane Square."

"At any rate," said I, "it was taking a considerable risk. I might have left the theatre before she came back."

"Yes," Thorndyke agreed. "But it is like a woman to take chances. A man would probably have stuck to you when once he had got you off your guard. But she was ready to take chances. She chanced the railway, and it came off, she chanced your remaining in the theatre, and that came off too. She calculated on the probability of your getting tea when you came out, and she hit it off again. And then she took one chance too many, she assumed that you probably took sugar in your tea, and she was wrong."

"We are taking it for granted that the sugar was prepared," I remarked.

"Yes. Our explanation is entirely hypothetical and may be entirely wrong. But it all hangs together, and if we find any poisonous matter in the sugar, it will be reasonable to assume that we are right. The sugar is the *Experimentum Crucis*. If you will hand it over to me, we will go up to the laboratory and make a preliminary test or two."

I took the lump of sugar from my pocket and gave it to him, and he carried it to the gas-burner, by the light of which he examined it with a lens.

"I don't see any foreign crystals on the surface," said he, "but we had better make a solution and go to work systematically. If it contains any poison we may assume that it will be some alkaloid, though I will test for arsenic too. But a man of Weiss's type would almost certainly use an alkaloid, on account of its smaller bulk and more ready solubility. You ought not to have carried this loose in your pocket. For legal purposes that would seriously interfere with its value as evidence. Bodies that are suspected of containing poison should be carefully isolated and preserved from contact with anything that might lead to doubt in the analysis. It doesn't matter much to us, as this analysis is only for our own information and we can satisfy ourselves as to the state of your pocket. But bear the rule in mind another time."

We now ascended to the laboratory, where Thorndyke proceeded at once to dissolve the lump of sugar in a measured quantity of distilled water by the aid of gentle heat.

"Before we add any acid," said he, "or introduce any fresh matter, we will adopt the simple preliminary measure of tasting the solution. The sugar is a disturbing factor, but some of the alkaloids and most mineral poisons excepting arsenic have a very characteristic taste."

He dipped a glass rod in the warm solution and applied it gingerly to his tongue.

"Ha!" he exclaimed, as he carefully wiped his mouth with his handkerchief, "simple methods are often very valuable. There isn't much doubt as to what is in that sugar. Let me recommend my learned brother to try the flavour. But be careful. A little of this will go a long way."

He took a fresh rod from the rack, and, dipping it in the solution, handed it to me. I cautiously applied it to the tip of my tongue and was immediately aware of a peculiar tingling sensation accompanied by a feeling of numbness.

"Well," said Thorndyke, "what is it?"

"Aconite," I replied without hesitation.

"Yes," he agreed, "aconite it is, or more probably aconitine. And that, I think, gives us all the information we want. We need not trouble now to make a complete analysis, though I shall have a quantitative examination made later. You note the intensity of the taste and you see what the strength of the solution is. Evidently that lump of sugar contained a very large dose of the poison. If the sugar had been dissolved in your tea, the quantity that you drank would have contained enough aconitine to lay you out within a few minutes, which would account for Mrs. Schallibaum's anxiety to get clear of the premises. She saw you drink from the cup, but I imagine she had not seen you turn the sugar out."

"No, I should say not, to judge by her expression. She looked terrified. She is not as hardened as her rascally companion."

"Which is fortunate for you, Jervis. If she had not been in such a fluster, she would have waited until you had poured out your tea, which was what she probably meant to do, or have dropped the sugar into the milk-jug. In either case you would have got a poisonous dose before you noticed anything amiss."

"They are a pretty pair, Thorndyke," I exclaimed. "A human life seems to be no more to them than the life of a fly or a beetle."

"No, that is so. They are typical poisoners of the worst kind – of the intelligent, cautious, resourceful kind. They are a standing menace to society. As long as they are at large, human lives are in danger, and it is our business to see that they do not remain at large a moment longer than is unavoidable. And that brings us to another point. You had better keep indoors for the next few days."

"Oh, nonsense," I protested. "I can take care of myself."

"I won't dispute that," said Thorndyke, "although I might. But the matter is of vital importance and we can't be too careful. Yours is the only evidence that could convict these people. They know that and will stick at nothing to get rid of you – for by this time they will almost certainly have ascertained that the tea-shop plan has failed. Now your life is of some value to you and to another person whom I could mention, but apart from that, you are the indispensable instrument for ridding society of these dangerous vermin. Moreover, if you were seen abroad and connected with these chambers, they would get the information that their case was really being investigated in a businesslike manner. If Weiss has not already left the country he would do so immediately, and if he has, Mrs. Schallibaum would join him at once, and we might never be able to lay hands on them. You must stay indoors, out of sight, and you had better write to Miss Gibson and ask her to warn the servants to give no information about you to anyone."

"And how long," I asked, "am I to be held on parole?"

"Not long, I think. We have a very promising start. If I have any luck, I shall be able to collect all the evidence I want in about a week. But there is an element of chance in some of it which prevents me from giving a date. And it is just possible that I may have started on a false track. But that I shall be able to tell you better in a day or two."

"And I suppose," I said gloomily, "I shall be out of the hunt altogether?"

"Not at all," he replied. "You have got the Blackmore case to attend to. I shall hand you over all the documents and get you to make an orderly digest of the evidence. You will then have all the facts and can work out the case for yourself. Also I shall ask you to help Polton in some little operations which are designed to throw light into dark places and which you will find both entertaining and instructive."

"Supposing Mrs. Hornby should propose to call and take tea with us in the gardens?" I suggested.

"And bring Miss Gibson with her?" Thorndyke added dryly. "No, Jervis, it would never do. You must make that quite clear to her. It is more probable than not that Mrs. Schallibaum made a careful note of the house in Endsley Gardens, and as that would be the one place actually known to her, she and Weiss – if he is in England – would almost certainly keep a watch on it. If they should succeed in connecting that house with these

551

chambers, a few inquiries would show them the exact state of the case. No, we must keep them in the dark if we possibly can. We have shown too much of our hand already. It is hard on you, but it cannot be helped."

"Oh, don't think I am complaining," I exclaimed. "If it is a matter of business, I am as keen as you are. I thought at first that you were merely considering the safety of my vile body. When shall I start on my job?"

"To-morrow morning. I shall give you my notes on the Blackmore case and the copies of the will and the depositions, from which you had better draw up a digest of the evidence with remarks as to the conclusions that it suggests. Then there are our gleanings from New Inn to be looked over and considered, and with regard to this case, we have the fragments of a pair of spectacles which had better be put together into a rather more intelligible form in case we have to produce them in evidence. That will keep you occupied for a day or two, together with some work appertaining to other cases. And now let us dismiss professional topics. You have not dined and neither have I, but I dare say Polton has made arrangements for some sort of meal. We will go down and see."

We descended to the lower floor, where Thorndyke's anticipations were justified by a neatly laid table to which Polton was giving the finishing touches.

552

Chapter XI
The Blackmore Case Reviewed

One of the conditions of medical practice is the capability of transferring one's attention at a moment's notice from one set of circumstances to another equally important but entirely unrelated. At each visit on his round, the practitioner finds himself concerned with a particular, self-contained group of phenomena which he must consider at the moment with the utmost concentration, but which he must instantly dismiss from his mind as he moves on to the next case. It is a difficult habit to acquire, for an important, distressing or obscure case is apt to take possession of the consciousness and hinder the exercise of attention that succeeding cases demand, but experience shows the faculty to be indispensable, and the practitioner learns in time to forget everything but the patient with whose condition he is occupied at the moment.

My first morning's work on the Blackmore case showed me that the same faculty is demanded in legal practice, and it also showed me that I had yet to acquire it. For, as I looked over the depositions and the copy of the will, memories of the mysterious house in Kennington Lane continually intruded into my reflections, and the figure of Mrs. Schallibaum, white-faced, terrified, expectant, haunted me continually.

In truth, my interest in the Blackmore case was little more than academic, whereas in the Kennington case I was one of the parties and was personally concerned. To me, John Blackmore was but a name, Jeffrey but a shadowy figure to which I could assign no definite personality, and Stephen himself but a casual stranger. Mr. Graves, on the other hand, was a real person. I had seen him amidst the tragic circumstances that had probably heralded his death, and had brought away with me, not only a lively recollection of him, but a feeling of profound pity and concern as to his fate. The villain Weiss, too, and the terrible woman who aided, abetted and, perhaps, even directed him, lived in my memory as vivid and dreadful realities. Although I had uttered no hint to Thorndyke, I lamented inwardly that I had not been given some work – if there was any to do – connected with this case, in which I was so deeply interested, rather than with the dry, purely legal and utterly bewildering case of Jeffrey Blackmore's will.

Nevertheless, I stuck loyally to my task. I read through the depositions and the will – without getting a single glimmer of fresh light on the case – and I made a careful digest of all the facts. I compared my digest with Thorndyke's notes – of which I also made a copy – and found that, brief as they were, they contained several matters that I had overlooked. I also drew up a brief account of our visit to New Inn, with a list of the objects that we had observed or collected. And then I addressed myself to the second part of my task, the statement of my conclusions from the facts set forth.

It was only when I came to make the attempt that I realized how completely I was at sea. In spite of Thorndyke's recommendation to study Marchmont's statement as it was summarized in those notes which I had copied, and of his hint that I should find in that statement something highly significant, I was borne irresistibly to one conclusion, and one only – and the wrong one at that, as I suspected: That Jeffrey Blackmore's will was a perfectly regular, sound, and valid document.

I tried to attack the validity of the will from various directions, and failed every time. As to its genuineness, that was obviously not in question. There seemed to me only two conceivable respects in which any objection could be raised, *viz.* the competency of Jeffrey to execute a will and the possibility of undue influence having been brought to bear on him.

With reference to the first, there was the undoubted fact that Jeffrey was addicted to the opium habit, and this might, under some circumstances, interfere with a testator's competency to make a will. But had any such circumstances existed in this case? Had the drug habit produced such mental changes in the deceased as would destroy or weaken his judgment? There was not a particle of evidence in favour of any such belief. Up to the very end he had managed his own affairs, and, if his habits of life had undergone a change, they were still the habits of a perfectly sane and responsible man.

The question of undue influence was more difficult. If it applied to any person in particular, that person could be none other than John Blackmore. Now it was an undoubted fact that, of all Jeffrey's acquaintance, his brother John was the only one who knew that he was in residence at New Inn. Moreover, John had visited him there more than once. It was therefore possible that influence might have been brought to bear on the deceased. But there was no evidence that it had. The fact that the deceased man's only brother should be the one person who knew where he was living was not a remarkable one, and it had been satisfactorily explained by the necessity of Jeffrey's finding a reference on applying for the chambers. And against the theory of undue influence was the fact that the testator had voluntarily brought his will to the lodge and executed it in the presence of entirely disinterested witnesses.

In the end I had to give up the problem in despair, and, abandoning the documents, turned my attention to the facts elicited by our visit to New Inn.

554

What had we learned from our exploration? It was clear that Thorndyke had picked up some facts that had appeared to him important. But important in what respect? The only possible issue that could be raised was the validity or otherwise of Jeffrey Blackmore's will, and since the validity of that will was supported by positive evidence of the most incontestable kind, it seemed that nothing that we had observed could have any real bearing on the case at all.

But this, of course, could not be. Thorndyke was no dreamer nor was he addicted to wild speculation. If the facts observed by us seemed to him to be relevant to the case, I was prepared to assume that they were relevant, although I could not see their connection with it. And, on this assumption, I proceeded to examine them afresh.

Now, whatever Thorndyke might have observed on his own account, I had brought away from the dead man's chambers only a single fact, and a very extraordinary fact it was! The cuneiform inscription was upside down. That was the sum of the evidence that I had collected, and the question was, What did it prove? To Thorndyke it conveyed some deep significance. What could that significance be?

The inverted position was not a mere temporary accident, as it might have been if the frame had been stood on a shelf or support. It was hung on the wall, and the plates screwed on the frame showed that its position was permanent and that it had never hung in any other. That it could have been hung up by Jeffrey himself was clearly inconceivable. But allowing that it had been fixed in its present position by some workman when the new tenant moved in, the fact remained that there it had hung, presumably for months, and that Jeffrey Blackmore, with his expert knowledge of the cuneiform character, had never noticed that it was upside down, or, if he had noticed it, that he had never taken the trouble to have it altered.

What could this mean? If he had noticed the error but had not troubled to correct it, that would point to a very singular state of mind, an inertness and indifference remarkable even in an opium-smoker. But assuming such a state of mind, I could not see that it had any bearing on the will, excepting that it was rather inconsistent with the tendency to make fussy and needless alterations which the testator had actually shown. On the other hand, if he had not noticed the inverted position of the photograph he must have been nearly blind or quite idiotic, for the photograph was over two feet long and the characters large enough to be read easily by a person of ordinary eyesight at a distance of forty or fifty feet. Now he obviously was not in a state of dementia, whereas his eyesight was admittedly bad, and it seemed to me that the only conclusion deducible from the photograph was that it furnished a measure of the badness of the deceased man's vision – that it proved him to have been verging on total blindness.

555

But there was nothing startling new in this. He had, himself, declared that he was fast losing his sight. And again, what was the bearing of his partial blindness on the will? A totally blind man cannot draw up his will at all. But if he has eyesight sufficient to enable him to write out and sign a will, mere defective vision will not lead him to muddle the provisions. Yet something of this kind seemed to be in Thorndyke's mind, for now I recalled the question that he had put to the porter: "When you read the will over in Mr. Blackmore's presence, did you read it aloud?" That question could have but one significance. It implied a doubt as to whether the testator was fully aware of the exact nature of the document that he was signing. Yet, if he was able to write and sign it, surely he was able also to read it through, to say nothing of the fact that, unless he was demented, he must have remembered what he had written.

Thus, once more, my reasoning only led me into a blind alley at the end of which was the will, regular and valid and fulfilling all the requirements that the law imposed. Once again I had to confess myself beaten and in full agreement with Mr. Marchmont that "there was no case", that "there was nothing in dispute". Nevertheless, I carefully fixed in the pocket file that Thorndyke had given me the copy that I had made of his notes, together with the notes on our visit to New Inn, and the few and unsatisfactory conclusions at which I had arrived, and this brought me to the end of my first morning in my new capacity.

"And how," Thorndyke asked as we sat at lunch, "has my learned friend progressed? Does he propose that we advise Mr. Marchmont to enter a *caveat*?"

"I've read all the documents and boiled all the evidence down to a stiff jelly, and I am in a worse fog than ever."

"There seems to be a slight mixture of metaphors in my learned friend's remarks. But never mind the fog, Jervis. There is a certain virtue in fog. It serves, like a picture frame, to surround the essential with a neutral zone that separates it from the irrelevant."

"That is a very profound observation, Thorndyke," I remarked ironically.

"I was just thinking so myself," he rejoined.

"And if you could contrive to explain what it means – "

"Oh, but that is unreasonable. When one throws off a subtly philosophic *obiter dictum*, one looks to the discerning critic to supply the meaning. By the way, I am going to introduce you to the gentle art of photography this afternoon. I am getting the loan of all the cheques that were drawn by Jeffrey Blackmore during his residence at New Inn – there are only twenty-three of them, all told – and I am going to photograph them."

556

"I shouldn't have thought the bank people would have let them go out of their possession."

"They are not going to. One of the partners, a Mr. Britton, is bringing them here himself and will be present while the photographs are being taken, so they will not go out of his custody. But, all the same, it is a great concession, and I should not have obtained it but for the fact that I have done a good deal of work for the bank and that Mr. Britton is more or less a personal friend."

"By the way, how comes it that the cheques are at the bank? Why were they not returned to Jeffrey with the pass-book in the usual way?"

"I understand from Britton," replied Thorndyke, "that all Jeffrey's cheques were retained by the bank at his request. When he was travelling he used to leave his investment securities and other valuable documents in his bankers' custody, and, as he has never applied to have them returned, the bankers still have them and are retaining them until the will is proved, when they will, of course, hand over everything to the executors."

"What is the object of photographing these cheques?" I asked.

"There are several objects. First, since a good photograph is practically as good as the original, when we have the photographs we practically have the cheques for reference. Then, since a photograph can be duplicated indefinitely, it is possible to perform experiments on it which involve its destruction, which would, of course, be impossible in the case of original cheques."

"But the ultimate object, I mean. What are you going to prove?"

"You are incorrigible, Jervis," he exclaimed. "How should I know what I am going to prove? This is an investigation. If I knew the result beforehand, I shouldn't want to perform the experiment."

He looked at his watch, and, as we rose from the table, he said, "If we have finished, we had better go up to the laboratory and see that the apparatus is ready. Mr. Britton is a busy man, and, as he is doing us a great service, we mustn't keep him waiting when he comes."

We ascended to the laboratory, where Polton was already busy inspecting the massively built copying camera which – with the long, steel guides on which the easel or copy-holder travelled – took up the whole length of the room on the side opposite to that occupied by the chemical bench. As I was to be inducted into the photographic art, I looked at it with more attention than I had ever done before.

"We've made some improvements since you were here last, sir," said Polton, who was delicately lubricating the steel guides. "We've fitted these steel runners instead of the blackleaded wooden ones that we used to have. And we've made two scales instead of one. Hallo! That's the downstairs bell. Shall I go sir?"

"Perhaps you'd better," said Thorndyke. "It may not be Mr. Britton, and I don't want to be caught and delayed just now."

However, it was Mr. Britton, a breezy alert-looking middle-aged man, who came in escorted by Polton and shook our hands cordially, having been previously warned of my presence. He carried a small but solid hand-bag, to which he clung tenaciously up to the very moment when its contents were required for use.

"So that is the camera," said he, running an inquisitive eye over the instrument. "Very fine one, too, I am a bit of a photographer myself. What is that graduation on the side-bar?"

"Those are the scales," replied Thorndyke, "that shows the degree of magnification or reduction. The pointer is fixed to the easel and travels with it, of course, showing the exact size of the photograph. When the pointer is opposite *Zero* the photograph will be identical in size with the object photographed, when it points to, say, *Times six*, the photograph will be six times as long as the object, or magnified thirty-six times superficially, whereas if the pointer is at *Divide six*, the photograph will be a sixth of the length of the object, or one-thirty-sixth superficial."

"Why are there two scales?" Mr. Britton asked.

"There is a separate scale for each of the two lenses that we principally use. For great magnification or reduction a lens of comparatively short focus must be used, but, as a long-focus lens gives a more perfect image, we use one of very long focus – thirty-six inches – for copying the same size or for slight magnification or reduction."

"Are you going to magnify these cheques?" Mr. Britton asked.

"Not in the first place," replied Thorndyke. "For convenience and speed I am going to photograph them half-size, so that six cheques will go on one whole plate. Afterwards we can enlarge from the negatives as much as we like. But we should probably enlarge only the signatures in any case."

The precious bag was now opened and the twenty-three cheques brought out and laid on the bench in a consecutive series in the order of their dates. They were then fixed by tapes – to avoid making pin-holes in them – in batches of six to small drawing boards, each batch being so arranged that the signatures were towards the middle. The first board was clamped to the easel, the latter was slid along its guides until the pointer stood at *Divide two* on the long-focus scale, and Thorndyke proceeded to focus the camera with the aid of a little microscope that Polton had made for the purpose. When Mr. Britton and I had inspected the exquisitely sharp image on the focusing-screen through the microscope, Polton introduced the plate and made the first exposure, carrying the dark-slide off to develop the plate while the next batch of cheques was being fixed in position.

In his photographic technique, as in everything else, Polton followed as closely as he could the methods of his principal and instructor, methods characterized by that unhurried precision that leads to perfect accomplishment. When the first negative was brought forth, dripping, from the dark-room, it was without spot or stain, scratch or pin-hole, uniform in colour and of exactly the required density. The six cheques shown on it – ridiculously small in appearance, though only reduced to half-length – looked as clear and sharp as fine etchings, though, to be sure, my opportunity for examining them was rather limited, for Polton was uncommonly careful to keep the wet plate out of reach and so safe from injury.

"Well," said Mr. Britton, when, at the end of the séance, he returned his treasures to the bag, "you have now got twenty-three of our cheques, to all intents and purposes. I hope you are not going to make any unlawful use of them – must tell our cashiers to keep a bright look-out, and" – here he lowered his voice impressively and addressed himself to me and Polton – "you understand that this is a private matter between Dr. Thorndyke and me. Of course, as Mr. Blackmore is dead, there is no reason why his cheques should not be photographed for legal purposes, but we don't want it talked about, nor, I think, does Dr. Thorndyke."

"Certainly not," Thorndyke agreed emphatically, "but you need not be uneasy, Mr. Britton. We are very uncommunicative people in this establishment."

As my colleague and I escorted our visitor down the stairs, he returned to the subject of the cheques.

"I don't understand what you want them for," he remarked. "There is no question turning on signatures in the case of Blackmore deceased, is there?"

"I should say not," Thorndyke replied rather evasively.

"I should say very decidedly not," said Mr. Britton, "if I understood Marchmont aright. And, even if there were, let me tell you, these signatures that you have got wouldn't help you. I have looked them over very closely – and I have seen a few signatures in my time, you know. Marchmont asked me to glance over them as a matter of form, but I don't believe in matters of form, I examined them very carefully. There is an appreciable amount of variation, a very appreciable amount. But under the variation one can trace the personal character (which is what matters), the subtle, indescribable quality that makes it recognizable to the expert eye as Jeffrey Blackmore's writing. You understand me. There is such a quality, which remains when the coarser characteristics vary, just as a man may grow old, or fat, or bald, or may take to drink, and become quite changed, and yet, through it all, he preserves a certain something which makes him recognizable as a member of a particular family. Well, I find that quality in all those signatures, and so will you, if you have had enough experience of handwriting. I thought it best to mention it in case you might be giving yourself unnecessary trouble."

"It is very good of you," said Thorndyke, "and I need not say that the information is of great value, coming from such a highly expert source. As a matter of fact, your hint will be of great value to me."

He shook hands with Mr. Britton, and, as the latter disappeared down the stairs, he turned into the sitting-room and remarked, "There is a very weighty and significant observation, Jervis. I advise you to consider it attentively in all its bearings."

"You mean the fact that these signatures are undoubtedly genuine?"

"I meant, rather, the very interesting general truth that is contained in Britton's statement, that physiognomy is not a mere matter of facial character. A man carries his personal trademark – not in his face only, but in his nervous system and muscles – giving rise to characteristic movements and gait, in his larynx, producing an individual voice, and even in his mouth, as shown by individual peculiarities of speech and accent. And the individual nervous system, by means of these characteristic movements, transfers its peculiarities to inanimate objects that are the products of such movements, as we see in pictures, in carving, in musical execution, and in handwriting. No one has ever painted quite like Reynolds or Romney, no one has ever played exactly like Liszt or Paganini. The pictures or the sounds produced by them, were, so to speak, an extension of the physiognomy of the artist. And so with handwriting. A particular specimen is the product of a particular set of motor centres in an individual brain."

"These are very interesting considerations, Thorndyke," I remarked, "but I don't quite see their present application. Do you mean them to bear in any special way on the Blackmore case?"

"I think they do bear on it very directly. I thought so while Mr. Britton was making his very illuminating remarks."

"I don't see how. In fact I cannot see why you are going into the question of the signatures at all. The signature on the will is admittedly genuine, and that seems to me to dispose of the whole affair."

"My dear Jervis," said he, "you and Marchmont are allowing yourselves to be obsessed by a particular fact – a very striking and weighty fact, I will admit, but still, only an isolated fact. Jeffrey Blackmore executed his will in a regular manner, complying with all the necessary formalities and conditions. In the face of that single circumstance you and

Marchmont would 'chuck up the sponge', as the old pugilists expressed it. Now that is a great mistake. You should never allow yourself to be bullied and browbeaten by a single fact."

"But, my dear Thorndyke!" I protested, "this fact seems to be final. It covers all possibilities – unless you can suggest any other that would cancel it."

"I could suggest a dozen," he replied. "Let us take an instance. Supposing Jeffrey executed this will for a wager, that he immediately revoked it and made a fresh will, that he placed the latter in the custody of some person and that that person has suppressed it."

"Surely you do not make this suggestion seriously!" I exclaimed.

"Certainly I do not," he replied with a smile. "I merely give it as an instance to show that your final and absolute fact is really only conditional on there being no other fact that cancels it."

"Do you think he might have made a third will?"

"It is obviously possible. A man who makes two wills may make three or more, but I may say that I see no present reason for assuming the existence of another will. What I want to impress on you is the necessity of considering all the facts instead of bumping heavily against the most conspicuous one and forgetting all the rest. By the way, here is a little problem for you. What was the object of which these are the parts?"

He pushed across the table a little cardboard box, having first removed the lid. In it were a number of very small pieces of broken glass, some of which had been cemented together by their edges.

"These, I suppose," said I, looking with considerable curiosity at the little collection, "are the pieces of glass that we picked up in poor Blackmore's bedroom?"

"Yes. You see that Polton has been endeavouring to reconstitute the object, whatever it was, but he has not been very successful, for the fragments were too small and irregular and the collection too incomplete. However, here is a specimen, built up of six small pieces, which exhibits the general character of the object fairly well."

He picked out the little irregularly shaped object and handed it to me, and I could not but admire the neatness with which Polton had joined the tiny fragments together.

I took the little "restoration" and, holding it up before my eyes, moved it to and fro as I looked through it at the window.

"It was not a lens," I pronounced eventually.

"No," Thorndyke agreed, "it was not a lens."

"And so cannot have been a spectacle-glass. But the surface was curved – one side convex and the other concave – and the little piece that remains of the original edge seems to have been ground to fit a bezel or frame. I should say that these are portions of a watch-glass."

"That is Polton's opinion," said Thorndyke, "and I think you are both wrong."

"What do you say to the glass of a miniature or locket?"

"That is rather more probable, but it is not my view."

"What do you think it is?" I asked. But Thorndyke was not to be drawn.

"I am submitting the problem for solution by my learned friend," he replied with an exasperating smile, and then added, "I don't say that you and Polton are wrong, only that I don't agree with you. Perhaps you had better make a note of the properties of this object, and consider it at your leisure when you are ruminating on the other data referring to the Blackmore case."

"My ruminations," I said, "always lead me back to the same point."

"But you mustn't let them," he replied. "Shuffle your data about. Invent hypotheses. Never mind if they seem rather wild. Don't put them aside on that account. Take the first hypothesis that you can invent and test it thoroughly with your facts. You will probably have to reject it, but you will be certain to have learned something new. Then try again with a fresh one. You remember what I told you of my methods when I began this branch of practice and had plenty of time on my hands?"

"I am not sure that I do."

"Well, I used to occupy my leisure in constructing imaginary cases, mostly criminal, for the purpose of study and for the acquirement of experience. For instance, I would devise an ingenious fraud and would plan it in detail, taking every precaution that I could think of against failure or detection, considering, and elaborately providing for, every imaginable contingency. For the time being, my entire attention was concentrated on it, making it as perfect and secure and undetectable as I could with the knowledge and ingenuity at my command. I behaved exactly as if I were proposing actually to carry it out, and my life or liberty depended on its success – excepting that I made full notes of every detail of the scheme. Then when my plans were as complete as I could make them, and I could think of no way in which to improve them, I changed sides and considered the case from the standpoint of detection. I analysed the case, I picked out its inherent and unavoidable weaknesses, and, especially, I noted the respects in which a fraudulent proceeding of a particular kind differed from the *bona fide* proceeding that it simulated. The exercise was invaluable to me. I acquired as much experience from those imaginary cases as I should from real ones, and in addition, I learned a method which is the one that I practise to this day."

"Do you mean that you still invent imaginary cases as mental exercises?"

"No, I mean that, when I have a problem of any intricacy, I invent a case which fits the facts and the assumed motives of one of the parties. Then I work at that case until I find whether it leads to elucidation or to some fundamental disagreement. In the latter case I reject it and begin the process over again."

"Doesn't that method sometimes involve a good deal of wasted time and energy?" I asked.

"No, because each time that you fail to establish a given case, you exclude a particular explanation of the facts and narrow down the field of inquiry. By repeating the process, you are bound, in the end, to arrive at an imaginary case which fits all the facts. Then your imaginary case is the real case and the problem is solved. Let me recommend you to give the method a trial."

I promised to do so, though with no very lively expectations as to the result, and with this, the subject was allowed, for the present, to drop.

563

Chapter XII
The Portrait

The state of mind which Thorndyke had advised me to cultivate was one that did not come easily. However much I endeavoured to shuffle the facts of the Blackmore case, there was one which inevitably turned up on the top of the pack. The circumstances surrounding the execution of Jeffrey Blackmore's will intruded into all my cogitations on the subject with hopeless persistency. That scene in the porter's lodge was to me what King Charles's head was to poor Mr. Dick. In the midst of my praiseworthy efforts to construct some intelligible scheme of the case, it would make its appearance and reduce my mind to instant chaos.

For the next few days, Thorndyke was very much occupied with one or two civil cases, which kept him in court during the whole of the sitting, and when he came home, he seemed indisposed to talk on professional topics. Meanwhile, Polton worked steadily at the photographs of the signatures, and, with a view to gaining experience, I assisted him and watched his methods.

In the present case, the signatures were enlarged from their original dimensions – rather less than an inch and a half in length – to a length of four-and-a-half inches, which rendered all the little peculiarities of the handwriting surprisingly distinct and conspicuous. Each signature was eventually mounted on a slip of card bearing a number and the date of the cheque from which it was taken, so that it was possible to place any two signatures together for comparison. I looked over the whole series and very carefully compared those which showed any differences, but without discovering anything more than might have been expected in view of Mr. Britton's statement. There were some trifling variations, but they were all very much alike, and no one could doubt, on looking at them, that they were all written by the same hand.

As this, however, was apparently not in dispute, it furnished no new information. Thorndyke's object – for I felt certain that he had something definite in his mind – must be to test something apart from the genuineness of the signatures. But what could that something be? I dared not ask him, for questions of that kind were anathema, so there was nothing for it but to lie low and see what he would do with the photographs.

The whole series was finished on the fourth morning after my adventure at Sloane Square, and the pack of cards was duly delivered by Polton when he brought in the breakfast tray. Thorndyke took up the pack somewhat with the air of a whist player, and, as he ran through them, I noticed that the number had increased from twenty-three to twenty-four.

"The additional one," Thorndyke explained, "is the signature to the first will, which was in Marchmont's possession. I have added it to the collection as it carries us back to an earlier date. The signature of the second will presumably resembles those of the cheques drawn about the same date. But that is not material, or, if it should become so, we could claim to examine the second will."

He laid the cards out on the table in the order of their dates and slowly ran his eye down the series. I watched him closely and ventured presently to ask, "Do you agree with Mr. Britton as to the general identity of character in the whole set of signatures?"

"Yes," he replied. "I should certainly have put them down as being all the signatures of one person. The variations are very slight. The later signatures are a little stiffer, a little more shaky and indistinct, and the B's and k's are both appreciably different from those in the earlier ones. But there is another fact which emerges when the whole series is seen together, and it is so striking and significant a fact, that I am astonished at its not having been remarked on by Mr. Britton."

"Indeed!" said I, stooping to examine the photographs with fresh interest. "What is that?"

"It is a very simple fact and very obvious, but yet, as I have said, very significant. Look carefully at number one, which is the signature of the first will, dated three years ago, and compare it with number three, dated the eighteenth of September last year."

"They look to me identical," said I, after a careful comparison.

"So they do to me," said Thorndyke. "Neither of them shows the change that occurred later. But if you look at number two, dated the sixteenth of September, you will see that it is in the later style. So is number four, dated the twenty-third of September, but numbers five and six, both at the beginning of October, are in the earlier style, like the signature of the will. Thereafter all the signatures are in the new style, but, if you compare number two, dated the sixteenth of September with number twenty-four, dated the fourteenth of March of this year – the day of Jeffrey's death – you see that they exhibit no difference. Both are in the 'later style,' but the last shows no greater change than the first. Don't you consider these facts very striking and significant?"

I reflected a few moments, trying to make out the deep significance to which Thorndyke was directing my attention – and not succeeding very triumphantly.

"You mean," I said, "that the occasional reversions to the earlier form convey some material suggestion?"

565

"Yes, but more than that. What we learn from an inspection of this series is this: That there was a change in the character of the signature, a very slight change, but quite recognizable. Now that change was not gradual or insidious nor was it progressive. It occurred at a certain definite time. At first there were one or two reversions to the earlier form, but after number six the new style continued to the end, and you notice that it continued without any increase in the change and without any variation. There are no intermediate forms. Some of the signatures are in the 'old style' and some in the 'new', but there are none that are half-and-half. So that, to repeat: We have here two types of signature, very much alike, but distinguishable. They alternate, but do not merge into one another to produce intermediate forms. The change occurs abruptly, but shows no tendency to increase as time goes on, it is not a progressive change. What do you make of that, Jervis?"

"It is very remarkable," I said, poring over the cards to verify Thorndyke's statements. "I don't quite know what to make of it. If the circumstances admitted of the idea of forgery, one would suspect the genuineness of some of the signatures. But they don't – at any rate, in the case of the later will, to say nothing of Mr. Britton's opinion on the signatures."

"Still," said Thorndyke, "there must be some explanation of the change in the character of the signatures, and that explanation cannot be the failing eyesight of the writer, for that is a gradually progressive and continuous condition, whereas the change in the writing is abrupt and intermittent."

I considered Thorndyke's remark for a few moments, and then a light – though not a very brilliant one – seemed to break on me.

"I think I see what you are driving at," said I. "You mean that the change in the writing must be associated with some new condition affecting the writer, and that that condition existed intermittently?"

Thorndyke nodded approvingly, and I continued, "The only intermittent condition that we know of is the effect of opium. So that we might consider the clearer signatures to have been made when Jeffrey was in his normal state, and the less distinct ones after a bout of opium-smoking."

"That is perfectly sound reasoning," said Thorndyke. "What further conclusion does it lead to?"

"It suggests that the opium habit had been only recently acquired, since the change was noticed only about the time he went to live at New Inn, and, since the change in the writing is at first intermittent and then continuous, we may infer that the opium-smoking was at first occasional and later became a a confirmed habit."

566

"Quite a reasonable conclusion and very clearly stated," said Thorndyke. "I don't say that I entirely agree with you, or that you have exhausted the information that these signatures offer. But you have started in the right direction."

"I may be on the right road," I said gloomily, "but I am stuck fast in one place and I see no chance of getting any farther."

"But you have a quantity of data," said Thorndyke. "You have all the facts that I had to start with, from which I constructed the hypothesis that I am now busily engaged in verifying. I have a few more data now, for 'as money makes money' so knowledge begets knowledge, and I put my original capital out to interest. Shall we tabulate the facts that are in our joint possession and see what they suggest?"

I grasped eagerly at the offer, though I had conned over my notes again and again.

Thorndyke produced a slip of paper from a drawer, and, uncapping his fountain-pen, proceeded to write down the leading facts, reading each aloud as soon as it was written.

> *"1. The second will was unnecessary since it contained no new matter, expressed no new intentions and met no new conditions, and the first will was quite clear and efficient.*
> *"2. The evident intention of the testator was to leave the bulk of his property to Stephen Blackmore.*
> *"3. The second will did not, under existing circumstances, give effect to this intention, whereas the first will did.*
> *"4. The signature of the second will differs slightly from that of the first, and also from what had hitherto been the testator's ordinary signature.*

"And now we come to a very curious group of dates, which I will advise you to consider with great attention.

> *"5. Mrs. Wilson made her will at the beginning of September last year, without acquainting Jeffrey Blackmore, who seems to have been unaware of the existence of this will.*
> *"6. His own second will was dated the twelfth of November of last year.*
> *"7. Mrs. Wilson died of cancer on the twelfth of March this present year.*
> *"8. Jeffrey Blackmore was last seen alive on the fourteenth of March.*
> *"9. His body was discovered on the fifteenth of March.*

> *"10. The change in the character of his signature began about September last year and became permanent after the middle of October.*

"You will find that collection of facts repay careful study, Jervis, especially when considered in relation to the further data:

> *"11. That we found in Blackmore's chambers a framed inscription of large size, hung upside down, together with what appeared to be the remains of a watch-glass and a box of stearine candles and some other objects."*

He passed the paper to me and I pored over it intently, focusing my attention on the various items with all the power of my will. But, struggle as I would, no general conclusion could be made to emerge from the mass of apparently disconnected facts.

"Well?" Thorndyke said presently, after watching with grave interest my unavailing efforts, "what do you make of it?"

"Nothing!" I exclaimed desperately, slapping the paper down on the table. "Of course, I can see that there are some queer coincidences. But how do they bear on the case? I understand that you want to upset this will, which we know to have been signed without compulsion or even suggestion in the presence of two respectable men, who have sworn to the identity of the document. That is your object, I believe?"

"Certainly it is."

"Then I am hanged if I see how you are going to do it. Not, I should say, by offering a group of vague coincidences that would muddle any brain but your own."

Thorndyke chuckled softly but pursued the subject no farther.

"Put that paper in your file with your other notes," he said, "and think it over at your leisure. And now I want a little help from you. Have you a good memory for faces?"

"Fairly good, I think. Why?"

"Because I have a photograph of a man whom I think you may have met. Just look at it and tell me if you remember the face."

He drew a cabinet size photograph from an envelope that had come by the morning's post and handed it to me.

"I have certainly seen this face somewhere," said I, taking the portrait over to the window to examine it more thoroughly, "but I can't, at the moment, remember where."

"Try," said Thorndyke. "If you have seen the face before, you should be able to recall the person."

I looked intently at the photograph, and the more I looked, the more familiar did the face appear. Suddenly the identity of the man flashed into my mind and I exclaimed in astonishment, "It can't be that poor creature at Kennington, Mr. Graves?"

"I think it can," replied Thorndyke, "and I think it is. But could you swear to the identity in a court of law?"

"It is my firm conviction that the photograph is that of Mr. Graves. I would swear to that."

"No man ought to swear to more," said Thorndyke. "Identification is always a matter of opinion or belief. The man who will swear unconditionally to identity from memory only is a man whose evidence should be discredited. I think your sworn testimony would be sufficient."

It is needless to say that the production of this photograph filled me with amazement and curiosity as to how Thorndyke had obtained it. But, as he replaced it impassively in its envelope without volunteering any explanation, I felt that I could not question him directly. Nevertheless, I ventured to approach the subject in an indirect manner.

"Did you get any information from those Darmstadt people?" I asked.

"Schnitzler? Yes. I learned, through the medium of an official acquaintance, that Dr. H. Weiss was a stranger to them, that they knew nothing about him excepting that he had ordered from them, and been supplied with, a hundred grammes of pure hydrochlorate of morphine."

"All at once?"

"No. In separate parcels of twenty-five grammes each."

"Is that all you know about Weiss?"

"It is all that I actually know, but it is not all that I suspect – on very substantial grounds. By the way, what did you think of the coachman?"

"I don't know that I thought very much about him. Why?"

"You never suspected that he and Weiss were one and the same person?"

"No. How could they be? They weren't in the least alike. And one was a Scotchman and the other a German. But perhaps you know that they were the same?"

"I only know what you have told me. But considering that you never saw them together, that the coachman was never available for messages or assistance when Weiss was with you, that Weiss always made his appearance some time after you arrived, and disappeared some time before you left, it has seemed to me that they might have been the same person."

"I should say it was impossible. They were so very different in appearance. But supposing that they were the same, would the fact be of any importance?"

"It would mean that we could save ourselves the trouble of looking for the coachman. And it would suggest some inferences, which will occur to you if you think the matter over. But being only a speculative opinion, at present, it would not be safe to infer very much from it."

"You have rather taken me by surprise," I remarked. "It seems that you have been working at this Kennington case, and working pretty actively I imagine, whereas I supposed that your entire attention was taken up by the Blackmore affair."

"It doesn't do," he replied, "to allow one's entire attention to be taken up by any one case. I have half-a-dozen others – minor cases, mostly – to which I am attending at this moment. Did you think I was proposing to keep you under lock and key indefinitely?"

"Well, no. But I thought the Kennington case would have to wait its turn. And I had no idea that you were in possession of enough facts to enable you to get any farther with it."

"But you knew all the very striking facts of the case, and you saw the further evidence that we extracted from the empty house."

"Do you mean those things that we picked out from the rubbish under the grate?"

"Yes. You saw those curious little pieces of reed and the pair of spectacles. They are lying in the top drawer of that cabinet at this moment, and I should recommend you to have another look at them. To me they are most instructive. The pieces of reed offered an extremely valuable suggestion, and the spectacles enabled me to test that suggestion and turn it into actual information."

"Unfortunately," said I, "the pieces of reed convey nothing to me. I don't know what they are or of what they have formed a part."

"I think," he replied, "that if you examine them with due consideration, you will find their use pretty obvious. Have a good look at them and the spectacles too. Think over all that you know of that mysterious group of people who lived in that house, and see if you cannot form some coherent theory of their actions. Think, also, if we have not some information in our possession by which we might be able to identify some of them, and infer the identity of the others. You will have a quiet day, as I shall not be home until the evening, set yourself this task. I assure you that you have the material for identifying – or rather for testing the identity of – at least one of those persons. Go over your material systematically, and let me know in the evening what further investigations you would propose."

"Very well," said I. "It shall be done according to your word. I will addle my brain afresh with the affair of Mr. Weiss and his patient, and let the Blackmore case rip."

"There is no need to do that. You have a whole day before you. An hour's really close consideration of the Kennington case ought to show you what your next move should be, and then you could devote yourself to the consideration of Jeffrey Blackmore's will."

With this final piece of advice, Thorndyke collected the papers for his day's work, and, having deposited them in his brief bag, took his departure, leaving me to my meditations.

Chapter XIII
The Statement of Samuel Wilkins

As soon as I was alone, I commenced my investigations with a rather desperate hope of eliciting some startling and unsuspected facts. I opened the drawer and taking from it the two pieces of reed and the shattered remains of the spectacles, laid them on the table. The repairs that Thorndyke had contemplated in the case of the spectacles, had not been made. Apparently they had not been necessary. The battered wreck that lay before me, just as we had found it, had evidently furnished the necessary information, for, since Thorndyke was in possession of a portrait of Mr. Graves, it was clear that he had succeeded in identifying him so far as to get into communication with some one who had known him intimately.

The circumstance should have been encouraging. But somehow it was not. What was possible to Thorndyke was, theoretically, possible to me – or to anyone else. But the possibility did not realize itself in practice. There was the personal equation. Thorndyke's brain was not an ordinary brain. Facts of which his mind instantly perceived the relation remained to other people unconnected and without meaning. His powers of observation and rapid inference were almost incredible, as I had noticed again and again, and always with undiminished wonder. He seemed to take in everything at a single glance and in an instant to appreciate the meaning of everything that he had seen.

Here was a case in point. I had myself seen all that he had seen, and, indeed, much more, for I had looked on the very people and witnessed their actions, whereas he had never set eyes on any of them. I had examined the little handful of rubbish that he had gathered up so carefully, and would have flung it back under the grate without a qualm. Not a glimmer of light had I perceived in the cloud of mystery, nor even a hint of the direction in which to seek enlightenment. And yet Thorndyke had, in some incomprehensible manner, contrived to piece together facts that I had probably not even observed, and that so completely that he had already, in these few days, narrowed down the field of inquiry to quite a small area.

From these reflections I returned to the objects on the table. The spectacles, as things of which I had some expert knowledge, were not so profound a mystery to me. A pair of spectacles might easily afford good evidence for identification, that I perceived clearly enough. Not a ready-made pair, picked up casually at a shop, but a pair constructed by a skilled optician to remedy a particular defect of vision and to fit a particular face. And such were the spectacles before me. The build of the frames was peculiar, the existence of a cylindrical lens – which I could easily make out from the remaining fragments – showed that one glass had been cut to a prescribed shape and almost certainly ground to a particular formula, and also that the distance between centres must have been carefully secured. Hence these spectacles had an individual character. But it was manifestly impossible to inquire of all the spectacle-makers in Europe – for the glasses were not necessarily made in England. As confirmation the spectacles might be valuable, as a starting-point they were of no use at all.

From the spectacles I turned to the pieces of reed. These were what had given Thorndyke his start. Would they give me a leading hint too? I looked at them and wondered what it was that they had told Thorndyke. The little fragment of the red paper label had a dark-brown or thin black border ornamented with a fret-pattern, and on it I detected a couple of tiny points of gold like the dust from leaf-gilding. But I learned nothing from that. Then the shorter piece of reed was artificially hollowed to fit on the longer piece. Apparently it formed a protective sheath or cap. But what did it protect? Presumably a point or edge of some kind. Could this be a pocket-knife of any sort, such as a small stencil-knife? No, the material was too fragile for a knife-handle. It could not be an etching-needle for the same reason, and it was not a surgical appliance – at least it was not like any surgical instrument that was known to me.

I turned it over and over and cudgelled my brains, and then I had a brilliant idea. Was it a reed pen of which the point had been broken off? I knew that reed pens were still in use by draughtsmen of decorative leanings with an affection for the "fat line." Could any of our friends be draughtsmen? This seemed the most probable solution of the difficulty, and the more I thought about it the more likely it seemed. Draughtsmen usually sign their work intelligibly, and even when they use a device instead of a signature their identity is easily traceable. Could it be that Mr. Graves, for instance, was an illustrator, and that Thorndyke had established his identity by looking through the works of all the well-known thick-line draughtsmen?

This problem occupied me for the rest of the day. My explanation did not seem quite to fit Thorndyke's description of his methods, but I could think of no other. I turned it over during my solitary lunch, I meditated on it with the aid of several pipes in the afternoon, and having refreshed my brain with a cup of tea, I went forth to walk in the Temple gardens – which I was permitted to do without breaking my parole – to think it out afresh.

The result was disappointing. I was basing my reasoning on the assumption that the pieces of reed were parts of a particular appliance, appertaining to a particular craft, whereas they might be the remains of something quite different, appertaining to a totally different craft or to no craft at all. And in no case did they point to any known individual or indicate any but the vaguest kind of search. After pacing the pleasant walks for upwards of two hours, I at length turned back towards our chambers, where I arrived as the lamp-lighter was just finishing his round.

My fruitless speculations had left me somewhat irritable. The lighted windows that I had noticed as I approached had given me the impression that Thorndyke had returned. I had intended to press him for a little further information. When, therefore, I let myself into our chambers and found, instead of my colleague, a total stranger – and only a back view at that – I was disappointed and annoyed.

The stranger was seated by the table, reading a large document that looked like a lease. He made no movement when I entered, but when I crossed the room and wished him "Good evening," he half-rose and bowed silently. It was then that I first saw his face, and a mighty start he gave me. For one moment I actually thought he was Mr. Weiss, so close was the resemblance, but immediately I perceived that he was a much smaller man.

I sat down nearly opposite and stole an occasional furtive glance at him. The resemblance to Weiss was really remarkable. The same flaxen hair, the same ragged beard and a similar red nose, with the patches of *acne rosacea* spreading to the adjacent cheeks. He wore spectacles, too, through which he took a quick glance at me now and again, returning immediately to his document.

After some moments of rather embarrassing silence, I ventured to remark that it was a mild evening, to which he assented with a sort of Scotch "Hmm – hmm," and nodded slowly. Then came another interval of silence, during which I speculated on the possibility of his being a relative of Mr. Weiss and wondered what the deuce he was doing in our chambers.

"Have you an appointment with Dr. Thorndyke?" I asked, at length.

He bowed solemnly, and by way of reply – in the affirmative, as I assumed – emitted another "Hmm – hmm."

I looked at him sharply, a little nettled by his lack of manners, whereupon he opened out the lease so that it screened his face, and as I glanced at the back of the document, I was astonished to observe that it was shaking rapidly.

The fellow was actually laughing! What he found in my simple question to cause him so much amusement I was totally unable to imagine. But there it was. The tremulous movements of the document left me in no possible doubt that he was for some reason convulsed with laughter.

It was extremely mysterious. Also, it was rather embarrassing. I took out my pocket file and began to look over my notes. Then the document was lowered and I was able to get another look at the stranger's face. He was really extraordinarily like Weiss. The shaggy eyebrows, throwing the eye-sockets into shadow, gave him, in conjunction with the spectacles, the same owlish, solemn expression that I had noticed in my Kennington acquaintance, and which, by the way, was singularly out of character with the frivolous behaviour that I had just witnessed.

From time to time as I looked at him, he caught my eye and instantly averted his own, turning rather red. Apparently he was a shy, nervous man, which might account for his giggling, for I have noticed that shy or nervous people have a habit of smiling inopportunely and even giggling when embarrassed by meeting an over-steady eye. And it seemed my own eye had this disconcerting quality, for even as I looked at him, the document suddenly went up again and began to shake violently.

I stood it for a minute or two, but, finding the situation intolerably embarrassing, I rose, and brusquely excusing myself, went up to the laboratory to look for Polton and inquire at what time Thorndyke was expected home. To my surprise, however, on entering, I discovered Thorndyke himself just finishing the mounting of a microscopical specimen.

"Did you know that there is some one below waiting to see you?" I asked.

"Is it anyone you know?" he inquired.

"No," I answered. "It is a red-nosed, sniggering fool in spectacles. He has got a lease or a deed or some other sort of document which he has been using to play a sort of idiotic game of Peep-Bo! I couldn't stand him, so I came up here."

Thorndyke laughed heartily at my description of his client.

"What are you laughing at?" I asked sourly, at which he laughed yet more heartily and added to the aggravation by wiping his eyes.

"Our friend seems to have put you out," he remarked.

"He put me out literally. If I had stayed much longer I should have punched his head."

"In that case," said Thorndyke, "I am glad you didn't stay. But come down and let me introduce you."

"No, thank you. I've had enough of him for the present."

"But I have a very special reason for wishing to introduce you. I think you will get some information from him that will interest you very much, and you needn't quarrel with a man for being of a cheerful disposition."

"Cheerful be hanged!" I exclaimed. "I don't call a man cheerful because he behaves like a gibbering idiot."

To this Thorndyke made no reply but a broad and appreciative smile, and we descended to the lower floor. As we entered the room, the stranger rose, and, glancing in an embarrassed way from one of us to the other, suddenly broke out into an undeniable snigger. I looked at him sternly, and Thorndyke, quite unmoved by his indecorous behaviour, said in a grave voice, "Let me introduce you, Jervis, though I think you have met this gentleman before."

"I think not," I said stiffly.

"Oh yes, you have, sir," interposed the stranger, and, as he spoke, I started, for the voice was uncommonly like the familiar voice of Polton.

I looked at the speaker with sudden suspicion. And now I could see that the flaxen hair was a wig, that the beard had a decidedly artificial look, and that the eyes that beamed through the spectacles were remarkably like the eyes of our factotum. But the blotchy face, the bulbous nose and the shaggy, overhanging eyebrows were alien features that I could not reconcile with the personality of our refined and aristocratic-looking little assistant.

"Is this a practical joke?" I asked.

"No," replied Thorndyke, "it is a demonstration. When we were talking this morning it appeared to me that you did not realize the extent to which it is possible to conceal identity under suitable conditions of light. So I arranged, with Polton's rather reluctant assistance, to give you ocular evidence. The conditions are not favourable – which makes the demonstration more convincing. This is a very well-lighted room and Polton is a very poor actor, in spite of which it has been possible for you to sit opposite him for several minutes and look at him, I have no doubt, very attentively, without discovering his identity. If the room had been lighted only with a candle, and Polton had been equal to the task of supporting his make-up with an appropriate voice and manner, the deception would have been perfect."

"I can see that he has a wig on, quite plainly," said I.

"Yes, but you would not in a dimly lighted room. On the other hand, if Polton were to walk down Fleet Street at mid-day in this condition, the make-up would be conspicuously evident to any moderately observant passer-by. The secret of making up consists in a careful adjustment to the conditions of light and distance in which the make-up is to be seen. That in use on the stage would look ridiculous in an ordinary room, that which would serve in an artificially lighted room would look ridiculous out of doors by daylight."

"Is any effective make-up possible out of doors in ordinary daylight?" I asked.

"Oh, yes," replied Thorndyke. "But it must be on a totally different scale from that of the stage. A wig, and especially a beard or moustache, must be joined up at the edges with hair actually stuck on the skin with transparent cement and carefully trimmed with scissors. The same applies to eyebrows, and alterations in the colour of the skin must be carried out much more subtly. Polton's nose has been built up with a small covering of toupée-paste, the pimples on the cheeks produced with little particles of the same material, and the general tinting has been done with grease-paint with a very light scumble of powder colour to take off some of the shine. This would be possible in outdoor make-up, but it would have to be done with the greatest care and delicacy – in fact, with what the art-critics call 'reticence'. A very little make-up is sufficient and too much is fatal. You would be surprised to see how little paste is required to alter the shape of the nose and the entire character of the face."

At this moment there came a loud knock at the door, a single, solid dab of the knocker which Polton seemed to recognize, for he ejaculated, "Good Lord, sir! That'll be Wilkins, the cabman! I'd forgotten all about him. Whatever's to be done?"

He stared at us in ludicrous horror for a moment or two, and then, snatching off his wig, beard and spectacles, poked them into a cupboard. But his appearance was now too much even for Thorndyke – who hastily got behind him – for he had now resumed his ordinary personality – but with a very material difference.

"Oh, it's nothing to laugh at, sir," he exclaimed indignantly as I crammed my handkerchief into my mouth. "Somebody's got to let him in, or he'll go away."

"Yes, and that won't do," said Thorndyke. "But don't worry, Polton. You can step into the office. I'll open the door."

Polton's presence of mind, however, seemed to have entirely forsaken him, for he only hovered irresolutely in the wake of his principal. As the door opened, a thick and husky voice inquired, "Gent of the name of Polton live here?"

"Yes, quite right," said Thorndyke. "Come in. Your name is Wilkins, I think?"

"That's me, sir," said the voice, and in response to Thorndyke's invitation, a typical "growler" cabman of the old school, complete even to imbricated cape and dangling badge, stalked into the room, and glancing round with a mixture of embarrassment and defiance, suddenly fixed on Polton's nose a look of devouring curiosity.

"Here you are, then," Polton remarked nervously.

"Yus," replied the cabman in a slightly hostile tone. "Here I am. What am I wanted to do? And where's this here Mr. Polton?"

577

"I am Mr. Polton," replied our abashed assistant.

"Well, it's the other Mr. Polton what I want," said the cabman, with his eyes still riveted on the olfactory prominence.

"There isn't any other Mr. Polton," our subordinate replied irritably. "I am the – er – person who spoke to you in the shelter."

"Are you though?" said the manifestly incredulous cabby. "I shouldn't have thought it, but you ought to know. What do you want me to do?"

"We want you," said Thorndyke, "to answer one or two questions. And the first one is: Are you a teetotaller?"

The question being illustrated by the production of a decanter, the cabman's dignity relaxed somewhat.

"I ain't bigoted," said he.

"Then sit down and mix yourself a glass of grog. Soda or plain water?"

"May as well have all the extries," replied the cabman, sitting down and grasping the decanter with the air of a man who means business. "Per'aps you wouldn't mind squirtin' out the soda, sir, bein' more used to it."

While these preliminaries were being arranged, Polton silently slipped out of the room, and when our visitor had fortified himself with a gulp of the uncommonly stiff mixture, the examination began.

"Your name, I think, is Wilkins?" said Thorndyke.

"That's me, sir. Samuel Wilkins is my name."

"And your occupation?"

"Is a very tryin' one and not paid for as it deserves. I drives a cab, sir, a four-wheeled cab is what I drives, and a very poor job it is."

"Do you happen to remember a very foggy day about a month ago?"

"Do I not, sir! A regler sneezer that was! Wednesday, the fourteenth of March. I remember the date because my benefit society came down on me for arrears that morning."

"Will you tell us what happened to you between six and seven in the evening of that day?"

"I will, sir," replied the cabman, emptying his tumbler by way of bracing himself up for the effort. "A little before six I was waiting on the arrival side of the Great Northern Station, King's Cross, when I see a gentleman and a lady coming out. The gentleman he looks up and down and then he sees me and walks up to the cab and opens the door and helps the lady in. Then he says to me: 'Do you know New Inn?' he says. That's what he says to me, what was born and brought up in White Horse Alley, Drury Lane.

"'Get inside,' says I.

578

"'Well,' says he, 'you drive in through the gate in Wych Street,' he says, as if he expected me to go in by Houghton Street and down the steps, 'and then,' he says, 'you drive nearly to the end and you'll see a house with a large brass plate at the corner of the doorway. That's where we want to be set down,' he says, and with that he nips in and pulls up the windows and off we goes.

"It took us a full half-hour to get to New Inn through the fog, for I had to get down and lead the horse part of the way. As I drove in under the archway, I saw it was half-past-six by the clock in the porter's lodge. I drove down nearly to the end of the inn and drew up opposite a house where there was a big brass plate by the doorway. It was Number Thirty-one. Then the gent crawls out and hands me five bob – two 'arf-crowns – and then he helps the lady out, and away they waddles to the doorway and I see them start up the stairs very slow – regler Pilgrim's Progress. And that was the last I see of 'em."

Thorndyke wrote down the cabman's statement verbatim together with his own questions, and then asked, "Can you give us any description of the gentleman?"

"The gent," said Wilkins, "was a very respectable-looking gent, though he did look as if he'd had a drop of something short, and small blame to him on a day like that. But he was all there, and he knew what was the proper fare for a foggy evening, which is more than some of 'em do. He was a elderly gent, about sixty, and he wore spectacles, but he didn't seem to be able to see much through 'em. He was a funny 'un to look at, as round in the back as a turtle and he walked with his head stuck forward like a goose."

"What made you think he had been drinking?"

"Well, he wasn't as steady as he might have been on his pins. But he wasn't drunk, you know. Only a bit wobbly on the plates."

"And the lady, what was she like?"

"I couldn't see much of her because her head was wrapped up in a sort of woollen veil. But I should say she wasn't a chicken. Might have been about the same age as the gent, but I couldn't swear to that. She seemed a trifle rickety on the pins too, in fact they were a rum-looking couple. I watched 'em tottering across the pavement and up the stairs, hanging on to each other, him peering through his blinkers and she trying to see through her veil, and I thought it was a jolly good job they'd got a nice sound cab and a steady driver to bring 'em safe home."

"How was the lady dressed?"

"Can't rightly say, not being a hexpert. Her head was done up in this here veil like a pudden in a cloth and she had a small hat on. She had a dark brown mantle with a fringe of beads round it and a black dress, and I

579

noticed when she got into the cab at the station that one of her stockings looked like the bellows of a concertina. That's all I can tell you."

Thorndyke wrote down the last answer, and, having read the entire statement aloud, handed the pen to our visitor.

"If that is all correct," he said, "I will ask you to sign your name at the bottom."

"Do you want me to swear a affidavy that it's all true?" asked Wilkins.

"No, thank you," replied Thorndyke. "We may have to call you to give evidence in court, and then you'll be sworn, and you'll also be paid for your attendance. For the present I want you to keep your own counsel and say nothing to anybody about having been here. We have to make some other inquiries and we don't want the affair talked about."

"I see, sir," said Wilkins, as he laboriously traced his signature at the foot of the statement. "You don't want the other parties for to ogle your lay. All right, sir, you can depend on me. I'm fly, I am."

"Thank you, Wilkins," said Thorndyke. "And now, what are we to give you for your trouble in coming here?"

"I'll leave the fare to you, sir. You know what the information's worth, but I should think 'arf a thick-un wouldn't hurt you."

Thorndyke laid on the table a couple of sovereigns, at the sight of which the cabman's eyes glistened.

"We have your address, Wilkins," said he. "If we want you as a witness we shall let you know, and if not, there will be another two pounds for you at the end of a fortnight, provided you have not let this little interview leak out."

Wilkins gathered up the spoils gleefully. "You can trust me, sir," said he, "for to keep my mouth shut. I knows which side my bread's buttered. Good night, gentlemen all."

With this comprehensive salute he moved towards the door and let himself out.

"Well, Jervis, what do you think of it?" Thorndyke asked, as the cabman's footsteps faded away in a creaky diminuendo.

"I don't know what to think. This woman is a new factor in the case and I don't know how to place her."

"Not entirely new," said Thorndyke. "You have not forgotten those beads that we found in Jeffrey's bedroom, have you?"

"No, I had not forgotten them, but I did not see that they told us much excepting that some woman had apparently been in his bedroom at some time."

"That, I think, is all that they did tell us. But now they tell us that a particular woman was in his bedroom at a particular time, which is a good deal more significant."

"Yes. It almost looks as if she must have been there when he made away with himself."

"It does, very much."

"By the way, you were right about the colours of those beads, and also about the way they were used."

"As to their use, that was a mere guess, but it has turned out to be correct. It was well that we found the beads, for, small as is the amount of information they give, it is still enough to carry us a stage further."

"How so?"

"I mean that the cabman's evidence tells us only that this woman entered the house. The beads tell us that she was in the bedroom, which, as you say, seems to connect her to some extent with Jeffrey's death. Not necessarily, of course. It is only a suggestion, but a rather strong suggestion under the peculiar circumstances."

"Even so," said I, "this new fact seems to me so far from clearing up the mystery, only to add to it a fresh element of still deeper mystery. The porter's evidence at the inquest could leave no doubt that Jeffrey contemplated suicide, and his preparations pointedly suggest this particular night as the time selected by him for doing away with himself. Is not that so?"

"Certainly. The porter's evidence was very clear on that point."

"Then I don't see where this woman comes in. It is obvious that her presence at the inn, and especially in the bedroom, on this occasion and in these strange, secret circumstances, has a rather sinister look, but yet I do not see in what way she could have been connected with the tragedy. Perhaps, after all, she has nothing to do with it. You remember that Jeffrey went to the lodge about eight o'clock, to pay his rent, and chatted for some time with the porter. That looks as if the lady had already left."

"Yes," said Thorndyke. "But, on the other hand, Jeffrey's remarks to the porter with reference to the cab do not quite agree with the account that we have just heard from Wilkins. Which suggests – as does Wilkins's account generally – some secrecy as to the lady's visit to his chambers."

"Do you know who the woman was?" I asked.

"No, I don't know," he replied. "I have a rather strong suspicion that I can identify her, but I am waiting for some further facts."

"Is your suspicion founded on some new matter that you have discovered, or is it deducible from facts that are known to me?"

"I think," he replied, "that you know practically all that I know, although I have, in one instance, turned a very strong suspicion into a certainty by further inquiries. But I think you ought to be able to form some idea as to who this lady probably was."

"But no woman has been mentioned in the case at all."

"No, but I think you should be able to give this lady a name, notwithstanding."

"Should I? Then I begin to suspect that I am not cut out for medico-legal practice, for I don't see the faintest glimmer of a suggestion."

Thorndyke smiled benevolently. "Don't be discouraged, Jervis," said he. "I expect that when you first began to go round the wards, you doubted whether you were cut out for medical practice. I did. For special work one needs special knowledge and an acquired faculty for making use of it. What does a second year's student make of a small thoracic aneurysm? He knows the anatomy of the chest, he begins to know the normal heart sounds and areas of dullness, but he cannot yet fit his various items of knowledge together. Then comes the experienced physician and perhaps makes a complete diagnosis without any examination at all, merely from hearing the patient speak or cough. He has the same facts as the student, but he has acquired the faculty of instantly connecting an abnormality of function with its correleated anatomical change. It is a matter of experience. And, with your previous training, you will soon acquire the faculty. Try to observe everything. Let nothing escape you. And try constantly to find some connection between facts and events that seem to be unconnected. That is my advice to you, and with that we will put away the Blackmore case for the present and consider our day's work at an end."

582

Chapter XIV
Thorndyke Lays the Mine

The information supplied by Mr. Samuel Wilkins, so far from dispelling the cloud of mystery that hung over the Blackmore case, only enveloped it in deeper obscurity, so far as I was concerned. The new problem that Thorndyke offered for solution was a tougher one than any of the others. He proposed that I should identify and give a name to this mysterious woman. But how could I? No woman, excepting Mrs. Wilson, had been mentioned in connection with the case. This new *dramatis persona* had appeared suddenly from nowhere and straightway vanished without leaving a trace, excepting the two or three beads that we had picked up in Jeffrey's room.

Nor was it in the least clear what part, if any, she had played in the tragedy. The facts still pointed as plainly to suicide as before her appearance. Jeffrey's repeated hints as to his intentions, and the very significant preparations that he had made, were enough to negative any idea of foul play. And yet the woman's presence in the chambers at that time, the secret manner of her arrival and her precautions against recognition, strongly suggested some kind of complicity in the dreadful event that followed.

But what complicity is possible in the case of suicide? The woman might have furnished him with the syringe and the poison, but it would not have been necessary for her to go to his chambers for that purpose. Vague ideas of persuasion and hypnotic suggestion floated through my brain, but the explanations did not fit the case and the hypnotic suggestion of crime is not very convincing to the medical mind. Then I thought of blackmail in connection with some disgraceful secret, but though this was a more hopeful suggestion, it was not very probable, considering Jeffrey's age and character.

And all these speculations failed to throw the faintest light on the main question: "Who was this woman?"

A couple of days passed, during which Thorndyke made no further reference to the case. He was, most of the time, away from home, though how he was engaged I had no idea. What was rather more unusual was that Polton seemed to have deserted the laboratory and taken to outdoor pursuits. I assumed that he had seized the opportunity of leaving me in charge, and I dimly surmised that he was acting as Thorndyke's private inquiry agent, as he seemed to have done in the case of Samuel Wilkins.

On the evening of the second day Thorndyke came home in obviously good spirits, and his first proceedings aroused my expectant curiosity. He went to a cupboard and brought forth a box of Trichinopoly cheroots. Now the Trichinopoly cheroot was Thorndyke's one dissipation, to be enjoyed only on rare and specially festive occasions, which, in practice, meant those occasions on which he had scored some important point or solved some unusually tough problem. Wherefore I watched him with lively interest.

"It's a pity that the 'Trichy' is such a poisonous beast," he remarked, taking up one of the cheroots and sniffing at it delicately. "There is no other cigar like it, to a really abandoned smoker." He laid the cigar back in the box and continued, "I think I shall treat myself to one after dinner to celebrate the occasion."

"What occasion?" I asked.

"The completion of the Blackmore case. I am just going to write to Marchmont advising him to enter a *caveat*."

"Do you mean to say that you have discovered a flaw in the will, after all?"

"A flaw!" he exclaimed. "My dear Jervis, that second will is a forgery."

I stared at him in amazement, for his assertion sounded like nothing more or less than arrant nonsense.

"But the thing is impossible, Thorndyke," I said. "Not only did the witnesses recognize their own signatures and the painter's greasy finger-marks, but they had both read the will and remembered its contents."

"Yes, that is the interesting feature in the case. It is a very pretty problem. I shall give you a last chance to solve it. To-morrow evening we shall have to give a full explanation, so you have another twenty-four hours in which to think it over. And, meanwhile, I am going to take you to my club to dine. I think we shall be pretty safe there from Mrs. Schallibaum."

He sat down and wrote a letter, which was apparently quite a short one, and having addressed and stamped it, prepared to go out.

"Come," said he, "let us away to 'the gay and festive scenes and halls of dazzling light'. We will lay the mine in the Fleet Street pillar box. I should like to be in Marchmont's office when it explodes."

"I expect, for that matter," said I, "that the explosion will be felt pretty distinctly in these chambers."

"I expect so, too," replied Thorndyke, "and that reminds me that I shall be out all day to-morrow, so, if Marchmont calls, you must do all that you can to persuade him to come round after dinner and bring Stephen Blackmore, if possible. I am anxious to have Stephen here, as he will be able to give us some further information and confirm certain matters of fact."

I promised to exercise my utmost powers of persuasion on Mr. Marchmont which I should certainly have done on my own account, being now on the very tiptoe of curiosity to hear Thorndyke's explanation of the unthinkable conclusion at which he had arrived – and the subject dropped completely, nor could I, during the rest of the evening, induce my colleague to reopen it even in the most indirect or allusive manner.

Our explanations in respect of Mr. Marchmont were fully realized, for, on the following morning, within an hour of Thorndyke's departure from our chambers, the knocker was plied with more than usual emphasis, and, on my opening the door, I discovered the solicitor in company with a somewhat older gentleman. Mr. Marchmont appeared somewhat out of humour, while his companion was obviously in a state of extreme irritation.

"How d'you do, Dr. Jervis?" said Marchmont as he entered at my invitation. "Your friend, I suppose, is not in just now?"

"No, and he will not be returning until the evening."

"Hmm, I'm sorry. We wished to see him rather particularly. This is my partner, Mr. Winwood."

The latter gentleman bowed stiffly and Marchmont continued, "We have had a letter from Dr. Thorndyke, and it is, I may say, a rather curious letter, in fact, a very singular letter indeed."

"It is the letter of a madman!" growled Mr. Winwood.

"No, no, Winwood, nothing of the kind. Control yourself, I beg you. But really, the letter is rather incomprehensible. It relates to the will of the late Jeffrey Blackmore – you know the main facts of the case, and we cannot reconcile it with those facts."

"This is the letter," exclaimed Mr. Winwood, dragging the document from his wallet and slapping it down on the table. "If you are acquainted with the case, sir, just read that, and let us hear what you think."

I took up the letter and read aloud:

Jeffrey Blackmore, Decd.

Dear Mr. Marchmont,

I have gone into this case with great care and have now no doubt that the second will is a forgery. Criminal proceedings will, I think, be inevitable, but meanwhile it would be wise to enter a caveat.

If you could look in at my chambers to-morrow evening we could talk the case over, and I should be glad if you could bring Mr. Stephen Blackmore, whose personal knowledge of the events and the parties concerned would be of great assistance in clearing up obscure details.

I am,

Yours sincerely,

John Evelyn Thorndyke
C.F. Marchmont, Esq. "

"Well!" exclaimed Mr. Winwood, glaring ferociously at me, "what do you think of the learned counsel's opinion?"

"I knew that Thorndyke was writing to you to this effect," I replied, "but I must frankly confess that I can make nothing of it. Have you acted on his advice?"

"Certainly not!" shouted the irascible lawyer. "Do you suppose that we wish to make ourselves the laughing-stock of the courts? The thing is impossible – ridiculously impossible!"

"It can't be that, you know," I said, a little stiffly, for I was somewhat nettled by Mr. Winwood's manner, "or Thorndyke would not have written this letter. The conclusion looks as impossible to me as it does to you, but I have complete confidence in Thorndyke. If he says that the will is a forgery, I have no doubt that it is a forgery."

"But how the deuce can it be?" roared Winwood. "You know the circumstances under which the will was executed."

"Yes, but so does Thorndyke. And he is not a man who overlooks important facts. It is useless to argue with me. I am in a complete fog about the case myself. You had better come in this evening and talk it over with him as he suggests."

"It is very inconvenient," grumbled Mr. Winwood. "We shall have to dine in town."

"Yes," said Marchmont, "but it is the only thing to be done. As Dr. Jervis says, we must take it that Thorndyke has something solid to base his opinion on. He doesn't make elementary mistakes. And, of course, if what he says is correct, Mr. Stephen's position is totally changed."

"Bah!" exclaimed Winwood, "he has found a mare's nest, I tell you. Still, I agree that the explanation should be worth hearing."

"You mustn't mind Winwood," said Marchmont, in an apologetic undertone, "he's a peppery old fellow with a rough tongue, but he doesn't mean any harm." Which statement Winwood assented to – or dissented from, for it was impossible to say which – by a prolonged growl.

"We shall expect you then," I said, "about eight to-night, and you will try to bring Mr. Stephen with you?"

"Yes," replied Marchmont, "I think we can promise that he shall come with us. I have sent him a telegram asking him to attend."

With this the two lawyers took their departure, leaving me to meditate upon my colleague's astonishing statement, which I did, considerably to the prejudice of other employment. That Thorndyke would be able to justify the opinion that he had given, I had no doubt whatever, but yet there was no denying that his proposition was what Mr. Dick Swiveller would call "a staggerer."

When Thorndyke returned, I informed him of the visit of our two friends, and acquainted him with the sentiments that they had expressed, whereat he smiled with quiet amusement.

"I thought," he remarked, "that letter would bring Marchmont to our door before long. As to Winwood, I have never met him, but I gather that he is one of those people whom you 'mustn't mind'. In a general way, I object to people who tacitly claim exemption from the ordinary rules of conduct that are held to be binding on their fellows. But, as he promises to give us what the variety artists call 'an extra turn', we will make the best of him and give him a run for his money."

Here Thorndyke smiled mischievously – I understood the meaning of that smile later in the evening – and asked, "What do you think of the affair yourself?"

"I have given it up," I answered. "To my paralysed brain, the Blackmore case is like an endless algebraical problem propounded by an insane mathematician."

Thorndyke laughed at my comparison, which I flatter myself was a rather apt one.

"Come and dine," said he, "and let us crack a bottle, that our hearts may not turn to water under the frown of the disdainful Winwood. I think the old 'Bell' in Holborn will meet our present requirements better than the club. There is something jovial and roystering about an ancient tavern, but we must keep a sharp lookout for Mrs. Schallibaum."

Thereupon we set forth, and, after a week's close imprisonment, I once more looked upon the friendly London streets, the cheerfully lighted shop windows and the multitudes of companionable strangers who moved unceasingly along the pavements.

Chapter XV
Thorndyke Explodes the Mine

We had not been back in our chambers more than a few minutes when the little brass knocker on the inner door rattled out its summons. Thorndyke himself opened the door, and, finding our three expected visitors on the threshold, he admitted them and closed the "oak".

"We have accepted your invitation, you see," said Marchmont, whose manner was now a little flurried and uneasy. "This is my partner, Mr. Winwood – you haven't met before, I think. Well, we thought we should like to hear some further particulars from you, as we could not quite understand your letter."

"My conclusion, I suppose," said Thorndyke, "was a little unexpected?"

"It was more than that, sir," exclaimed Winwood. "It was absolutely irreconcilable either with the facts of the case or with common physical possibilities."

"At the first glance," Thorndyke agreed, "it would probably have that appearance."

"It has that appearance still to me." said Winwood, growing suddenly red and wrathful, "and I may say that I speak as a solicitor who was practising in the law when you were an infant in arms. You tell us, sir, that this will is a forgery, this will, which was executed in broad daylight in the presence of two unimpeachable witnesses who have sworn, not only to their signatures and the contents of the document, but to their very finger-marks on the paper. Are those finger-marks forgeries, too? Have you examined and tested them?"

"I have not," replied Thorndyke. "The fact is they are of no interest to me, as I am not disputing the witnesses' signatures."

At this, Mr. Winwood fairly danced with irritation.

"Marchmont!" he exclaimed fiercely, "you know this good gentleman, I believe. Tell me, is he addicted to practical jokes?"

"Now, my dear Winwood," groaned Marchmont, "I pray you – *I beg you* to control yourself. No doubt – "

"But confound it!" roared Winwood, "you have, yourself, heard him say that the will is a forgery, but that he doesn't dispute the signatures, which," concluded Winwood, banging his fist down on the table, "is damned nonsense."

"May I suggest," interposed Stephen Blackmore, "that we came here to receive Dr. Thorndyke's explanation of his letter. Perhaps it would be better to postpone any comments until we have heard it."

"Undoubtedly, undoubtedly," said Marchmont. "Let me entreat you, Winwood, to listen patiently and refrain from interruption until we have heard our learned friend's exposition of the case."

"Oh, very well," Winwood replied sulkily, "I'll say no more."

He sank into a chair with the manner of a man who shuts himself up and turns the key, and so remained – excepting when the internal pressure approached bursting-point – throughout the subsequent proceedings, silent, stony, and impassive, like a seated statue of Obstinacy.

"I take it," said Marchmont, "that you have some new facts that are not in our possession?"

"Yes," replied Thorndyke, "we have some new facts, and we have made some new use of the old ones. But how shall I lay the case before you? Shall I state my theory of the sequence of events and furnish the verification afterwards? Or shall I retrace the actual course of my investigations and give you the facts in the order in which I obtained them myself, with the inferences from them?"

"I almost think," said Mr. Marchmont, "that it would be better if you would put us in possession of the new facts. Then, if the conclusions that follow from them are not sufficiently obvious, we could hear the argument. What do you say, Winwood?"

Mr. Winwood roused himself for an instant, barked out the one word – "Facts" – and shut himself up again with a snap.

"You would like to have the new facts by themselves?" said Thorndyke.

"If you please. The facts only – in the first place, at any rate."

"Very well," said Thorndyke, and here I caught his eye with a mischievous twinkle in it that I understood perfectly, for I had most of the facts myself and realized how much these two lawyers were likely to extract from them. Winwood was going to "have a run for his money", as Thorndyke had promised.

My colleague, having placed on the table by his side a small cardboard box and the sheets of notes from his file, glanced quickly at Mr. Winwood and began. "The first important new facts came into my possession on the day on which you introduced the case to me. In the evening, after you left, I availed myself of Mr. Stephen's kind invitation to look over his uncle's chambers in New Inn. I wished to do so in order to ascertain, if possible, what had been the habits of the deceased during his residence there. When I arrived with Dr. Jervis, Mr. Stephen was in the chambers, and I learned from him that his uncle was an Oriental scholar

589

of some position and that he had a very thorough acquaintance with the cuneiform writing. Now, while I was talking with Mr. Stephen, I made a very curious discovery. On the wall over the fire-place hung a large framed photograph of an ancient Persian inscription in the cuneiform character, and that photograph was upside down."

"Upside down!" exclaimed Stephen. "But that is really very odd."

"Very odd indeed," agreed Thorndyke, "and very suggestive. The way in which it came to be inverted is pretty obvious and also rather suggestive. The photograph had evidently been in the frame some years but had apparently never been hung up before."

"It had not," said Stephen, "though I don't know how you arrived at the fact. It used to stand on the mantelpiece in his old rooms in Jermyn Street."

"Well," continued Thorndyke, "the frame-maker had pasted his label on the back of the frame, and as this label hung the right way up, it appeared as if the person who fixed the photograph on the wall had adopted it as a guide."

"It is very extraordinary," said Stephen. "I should have thought the person who hung it would have asked Uncle Jeffrey which was the right way up, and I can't imagine how on earth it could have hung all those months without his noticing it. He must have been practically blind."

Here Marchmont, who had been thinking hard, with knitted brows, suddenly brightened up.

"I see your point," said he. "You mean that if Jeffrey was as blind as that, it would have been possible for some person to substitute a false will, which he might sign without noticing the substitution."

"That wouldn't make the will a forgery," growled Winwood. "If Jeffrey signed it, it was Jeffrey's will. You could contest it if you could prove the fraud. But he said, 'This is my will,' and the two witnesses read it and have identified it."

"Did they read it aloud?" asked Stephen.

"No, they did not," replied Thorndyke.

"Can you prove substitution?" asked Marchmont.

"I haven't asserted it," answered Thorndyke, "My position is that the will is a forgery."

"But it is not," said Winwood.

"We won't argue it now," said Thorndyke. "I ask you to note the fact that the inscription was upside down. I also observed on the walls of the chambers some valuable Japanese colour-prints on which were recent damp-spots. I noted that the sitting-room had a gas-stove and that the kitchen contained practically no stores or remains of food and hardly any traces of even the simplest cooking. In the bedroom I found a large box

590

that had contained a considerable stock of hard stearine candles, six to the pound, and that was now nearly empty. I examined the clothing of the deceased. On the soles of the boots I observed dried mud, which was unlike that on my own and Jervis's boots, from the gravelly square of the inn. I noted a crease on each leg of the deceased man's trousers as if they had been turned up halfway to the knee, and in the waistcoat pocket I found the stump of a 'Contango' pencil. On the floor of the bedroom, I found a portion of an oval glass somewhat like that of a watch or locket, but ground at the edge to a double bevel. Dr. Jervis and I also found one or two beads and a bugle, all of dark brown glass."

Here Thorndyke paused, and Marchmont, who had been gazing at him with growing amazement, said nervously, "Er – yes. Very interesting. These observations of yours – er – are – "

"Are all the observations that I made at New Inn."

The two lawyers looked at one another and Stephen Blackmore stared fixedly at a spot on the hearth-rug. Then Mr. Winwood's face contorted itself into a sour, lopsided smile.

"You might have observed a good many other things, sir," said he, "if you had looked. If you had examined the doors, you would have noted that they had hinges and were covered with paint, and, if you had looked up the chimney you might have noted that it was black inside."

"Now, now, Winwood," protested Marchmont in an agony of uneasiness as to what his partner might say next, "I must really beg you – er – to refrain from – what Mr. Winwood means, Dr. Thorndyke, is that – er – we do not quite perceive the relevancy of these – ah – observations of yours."

"Probably not," said Thorndyke, "but you will perceive their relevancy later. For the present, I will ask you to note the facts and bear them in mind, so that you may be able to follow the argument when we come to that.

"The next set of data I acquired on the same evening, when Dr. Jervis gave me a detailed account of a very strange adventure that befell him. I need not burden you with all the details, but I will give you the substance of his story."

He then proceeded to recount the incidents connected with my visits to Mr. Graves, dwelling on the personal peculiarities of the parties concerned and especially of the patient, and not even forgetting the very singular spectacles worn by Mr. Weiss. He also explained briefly the construction of the chart, presenting the latter for the inspection of his hearers. To this recital our three visitors listened in utter bewilderment, as, indeed did I also, for I could not conceive in what way my adventures could possibly be related to the affairs of the late Mr. Blackmore. This was

591

manifestly the view taken by Mr. Marchmont, for, during a pause in which the chart was handed to him, he remarked somewhat stiffly, "I am assuming, Dr. Thorndyke, that the curious story you are telling us has some relevance to the matter in which we are interested."

"You are quite correct in your assumption," replied Thorndyke. "The story is very relevant indeed, as you will presently be convinced."

"Thank you," said Marchmont, sinking back once more into his chair with a sigh of resignation.

"A few days ago," pursued Thorndyke, "Dr. Jervis and I located, with the aid of this chart, the house to which he had been called. We found that the late tenant had left somewhat hurriedly and that the house was to let, and, as no other kind of investigation was possible, we obtained the keys and made an exploration of the premises."

Here he gave a brief account of our visit and the conditions that we observed, and was proceeding to furnish a list of the articles that we had found under the grate, when Mr. Winwood started from his chair.

"Really, sir!" he exclaimed, "this is too much! Have I come here, at great personal inconvenience, to hear you read the inventory of a dust-heap?"

Thorndyke smiled benevolently and caught my eye, once more, with a gleam of amusement.

"Sit down, Mr. Winwood," he said quietly. "You came here to learn the facts of the case, and I am giving them to you. Please don't interrupt needlessly and waste time."

Winwood stared at him ferociously for several seconds, then, somewhat disconcerted by the unruffled calm of his manner, he uttered a snort of defiance, sat down heavily and shut himself up again.

"We will now," Thorndyke continued, with unmoved serenity, "consider these relics in more detail, and we will begin with this pair of spectacles. They belonged to a person who was near-sighted and astigmatic in the left eye and almost certainly blind in the right. Such a description agrees entirely with Dr. Jervis's account of the sick man."

He paused for the moment, and then, as no one made any comment, proceeded. "We next come to these little pieces of reed, which you, Mr. Stephen, will probably recognize as the remains of a Japanese brush, such as is used for writing in Chinese ink or for making small drawings."

Again he paused, as though expecting some remark from his listeners, but no one spoke, and he continued, "Then there is this bottle with the theatrical wig-maker's label on it, which once contained cement such as is used for fixing on false beards, moustaches, or eyebrows."

He paused once more and looked round expectantly at his audience, none of whom, however, volunteered any remark.

"Do none of these objects that I have described and shown you, seem to have any significance for us?" he asked, in a tone of some surprise.

"They convey nothing to me," said Mr. Marchmont, glancing at his partner, who shook his head like a restive horse.

"Nor to you, Mr. Stephen?"

"No," replied Stephen. "Under the existing circumstances they convey no reasonable suggestion to me."

Thorndyke hesitated as if he were half-inclined to say something more, then, with a slight shrug, he turned over his notes and resumed. "The next group of new facts is concerned with the signatures of the recent cheques. We have photographed them and placed them together for the purpose of comparison and analysis."

"I am not prepared to question the signatures." said Winwood. "We have had a highly expert opinion, which would override ours in a court of law even if we differed from it, which I think we do not."

"Yes," said Marchmont, "that is so. I think we must accept the signatures, especially as that of the will has been proved, beyond any question, to be authentic."

"Very well," agreed Thorndyke, "we will pass over the signatures. Then we have some further evidence in regard to the spectacles, which serves to verify our conclusions respecting them."

"Perhaps," said Marchmont, "we might pass over that, too, as we do not seem to have reached any conclusions."

"As you please," said Thorndyke. "It is important, but we can reserve it for verification. The next item will interest you more, I think. It is the signed and witnessed statement of Samuel Wilkins, the driver of the cab in which the deceased came home to the inn on the evening of his death."

My colleague was right. An actual document, signed by a tangible witness, who could be put in the box and sworn, brought both lawyers to a state of attention, and when Thorndyke read out the cabman's evidence, their attention soon quickened into undisguised astonishment.

"But this is a most mysterious affair," exclaimed Marchmont. "Who could this woman have been, and what could she have been doing in Jeffrey's chambers at this time? Can you throw any light on it, Mr. Stephen?"

"No, indeed I can't," replied Stephen. "It is a complete mystery to me. My uncle Jeffrey was a confirmed old bachelor, and, although he did not dislike women, he was far from partial to their society, wrapped up as he was in his favourite studies. To the best of my belief, he had not a single female friend. He was not on intimate terms even with his sister, Mrs. Wilson."

"Very remarkable," mused Marchmont, "most remarkable. But, perhaps, you can tell us, Dr. Thorndyke, who this woman was?"

"I think," replied Thorndyke, "that the next item of evidence will enable you to form an opinion for yourselves. I only obtained it yesterday, and, as it made my case quite complete, I wrote off to you immediately. It is the statement of Joseph Ridley, another cabman, and unfortunately, a rather dull, unobservant fellow, unlike Wilkins. He has not much to tell us, but what little he has is highly instructive. Here is the statement, signed by the deponent and witnessed by me:

"'My name is Joseph Ridley. I am the driver of a four-wheeled cab. On the fourteenth of March, the day of the great fog, I was waiting at Vauxhall Station, where I had just set down a fare. About five o'clock a lady came and told me to drive over to Upper Kennington Lane to take up a passenger. She was a middle-sized woman. I could not tell what her age was, or what she was like, because her head was wrapped up in a sort of knitted, woollen veil to keep out the fog. I did not notice how she was dressed. She got into the cab and I led the horse over to Upper Kennington Lane and a little way up the lane, until the lady tapped at the front window for me to stop.

"'She got out of the cab and told me to wait. Then she went away and disappeared in the fog. Presently a lady and gentleman came from the direction in which she had gone. The lady looked like the same lady, but I won't answer to that. Her head was wrapped up in the same kind of veil or shawl, and I noticed that she had on a dark coloured mantle with bead fringe on it.

"'The gentleman was clean shaved and wore spectacles, and he stooped a good deal. I can't say whether his sight was good or bad. He helped the lady into the cab and told me to drive to the Great Northern Station, King's Cross. Then he got in himself and I drove off. I got to the station about a quarter-to-six and the lady and gentleman got out. The gentleman paid my fare and they both went into the station. I did not notice anything unusual about either of them. Directly after they had gone, I got a fresh fare and drove away.'

"That," Thorndyke concluded, "is Joseph Ridley's statement, and I think it will enable you to give a meaning to the other facts that I have offered for your consideration."

"I am not so sure about that," said Marchmont. "It is all exceedingly mysterious. Your suggestion is, of course, that the woman who came to New Inn in the cab was Mrs. Schallibaum!"

"Not at all," replied Thorndyke. "My suggestion is that the woman was Jeffrey Blackmore."

There was deathly silence for a few moments. We were all absolutely thunderstruck, and sat gaping at Thorndyke in speechless-astonishment. Then – Mr. Winwood fairly bounced out of his chair.

"But – my – good – sir!" he screeched. "Jeffrey Blackmore was with her at the time!"

"Naturally," replied Thorndyke, "my suggestion implies that the person who was with her was *not* Jeffrey Blackmore."

"But he was!" bawled Winwood. "The porter saw him!"

"The porter saw a person whom he believed to be Jeffrey Blackmore. I suggest that the porter's belief was erroneous."

"Well," snapped Winwood, "perhaps you can prove that it was. I don't see how you are going to, but perhaps you can."

He subsided once more into his chair and glared defiantly at Thorndyke.

"You seemed," said Stephen, "to suggest some connection between the sick man, Graves, and my uncle. I noted it at the time, but put it aside as impossible. Was I right. Did you mean to suggest any connection?"

"I suggest something more than a connection. I suggest identity. My position is that the sick man, Graves, was your uncle."

"From Dr. Jervis's description," said Stephen, "this man must have been very like my uncle. Both were blind in the right eye and had very poor vision with the left, and my uncle certainly used brushes of the kind that you have shown us, when writing in the Japanese character, for I have watched him and admired his skill, but – "

"But," said Marchmont, "there is the insuperable objection that, at the very time when this man was lying sick in Kennington Lane, Mr. Jeffrey was living at New Inn."

"What evidence is there of that?" asked Thorndyke.

"Evidence!" Marchmont exclaimed impatiently. "Why, my dear sir – "

He paused suddenly, and, leaning forward, regarded Thorndyke with a new and rather startled expression.

"You mean to suggest – " he began.

"I suggest that Jeffrey Blackmore never lived at New Inn at all."

For the moment, Marchmont seemed absolutely paralysed by astonishment.

"This is an amazing proposition!" he exclaimed, at length. "Yet the thing is certainly not impossible, for, now that you recall the fact, I realize that no one who had known him previously – excepting his brother, John – ever saw him at the inn. The question of identity was never raised."

"Excepting," said Mr. Winwood, "in regard to the body, which was certainly that of Jeffrey Blackmore."

595

"Yes, yes. Of course," said Marchmont. "I had forgotten that for the moment. The body was identified beyond doubt. You don't dispute the identity of the body, do you?"

"Certainly not," replied Thorndyke.

Here Mr. Winwood grasped his hair with both hands and stuck his elbows on his knees, while Marchmont drew forth a large handkerchief and mopped his forehead. Stephen Blackmore looked from one to the other expectantly, and finally said, "If I might make a suggestion, it would be that, as Dr. Thorndyke has shown us the pieces now of the puzzle, he should be so kind as to put them together for our information."

"Yes," agreed Marchmont, "that will be the best plan. Let us have the argument, Doctor, and any additional evidence that you possess."

"The argument," said Thorndyke, "will be a rather long one, as the data are so numerous, and there are some points in verification on which I shall have to dwell in some detail. We will have some coffee to clear our brains, and then I will bespeak your patience for what may seem like a rather *prolix* demonstration."

Chapter XVI
An Exposition and a Tragedy

"You may have wondered," Thorndyke commenced, when he had poured out the coffee and handed round the cups, "what induced me to undertake the minute investigation of so apparently simple and straightforward a case. Perhaps I had better explain that first and let you see what was the real starting-point of the inquiry.

"When you, Mr. Marchmont, and Mr. Stephen, introduced the case to me, I made a very brief *précis* of the facts as you presented them, and of these there were one or two which immediately attracted my attention. In the first place, there was the will. It was a very strange will. It was perfectly unnecessary. It contained no new matter, it expressed no changed intentions, it met no new circumstances, as known to the testator. In short it was not really a new will at all, but merely a repetition of the first one, drafted in different and less suitable language. It differed only in introducing a certain ambiguity from which the original was free. It created the possibility that, in certain circumstances, not known to or anticipated by the testator, John Blackmore might become the principal beneficiary, contrary to the obvious wishes of the testator.

"The next point that impressed me was the manner of Mrs. Wilson's death. She died of cancer. Now people do not die suddenly and unexpectedly of cancer. This terrible disease stands almost alone in that it marks out its victim months in advance. A person who has an incurable cancer is a person whose death may be predicted with certainty and its date fixed within comparatively narrow limits.

"And now observe the remarkable series of coincidences that are brought into light when we consider this peculiarity of the disease. Mrs. Wilson died on the twelfth of March of this present year. Mr. Jeffrey's second will was signed on the twelfth of November of last year, at a time, that is to say, when the existence of cancer must have been known to Mrs. Wilson's doctor, and might have been known to any of her relatives who chose to inquire after her.

"Then you will observe that the remarkable change in Mr. Jeffrey's habits coincides in the most singular way with the same events. The cancer must have been detectable as early as September of last year, about the time, in fact, at which Mrs. Wilson made her will. Mr. Jeffrey went to the inn at the beginning of October. From that time his habits were totally changed, and I can demonstrate to you that a change – not a gradual, but an abrupt change – took place in the character of his signature.

"In short, the whole of this peculiar set of circumstances – the change in Jeffrey's habits, the change in his signature, and the execution of his strange will – came into existence about the time when Mrs. Wilson was first known to be suffering from cancer.

"This struck me as a very suggestive fact.

"Then there is the extraordinarily opportune date of Mr. Jeffrey's death. Mrs. Wilson died on the twelfth of March. Mr. Jeffrey was found dead on the fifteenth of March, having apparently died on the fourteenth, on which day he was seen alive. If he had died only three days sooner, he would have predeceased Mrs. Wilson, and her property would never have devolved on him at all, while, if he had lived only a day or two longer, he would have learned of her death and would certainly have made a new will or codicil in his nephew's favour.

"Circumstances, therefore, conspired in the most singular manner in favour of John Blackmore.

"But there is yet another coincidence. Jeffrey's body was found, by the merest chance, the day after his death. But it might have remained undiscovered for weeks, or even months, and if it had, it would have been impossible to fix the date of his death. Then Mrs. Wilson's next of kin would certainly have contested John Blackmore's claim – and probably with success – on the ground that Jeffrey died before Mrs. Wilson. But all this uncertainty is provided for by the circumstance that Mr. Jeffrey paid his rent personally – and prematurely – to the porter on the fourteenth of March, thus establishing beyond question the fact that he was alive on that date, and yet further, in case the porter's memory should be untrustworthy or his statement doubted, Jeffrey furnished a signed and dated document – the cheque – which could be produced in a court to furnish incontestable proof of survival.

"To sum up this part of the evidence. Here was a will which enabled John Blackmore to inherit the fortune of a man who, almost certainly, had no intention of bequeathing it to him. The wording of that will seemed to be adjusted to the peculiarities of Mrs. Wilson's disease, and the death of the testator occurred under a peculiar set of circumstances which seemed to be exactly adjusted to the wording of the will. Or, to put it in another way: The wording of the will and the time, the manner, and the circumstances of the testator's death, all seemed to be precisely adjusted to the fact that the approximate date of Mrs. Wilson's death was known some months before it occurred.

"Now you must admit that this compound group of coincidences, all conspiring to a single end – the enrichment of John Blackmore – has a very singular appearance. Coincidences are common enough in real life, but we cannot accept too many at a time. My feeling was that there were too many in this case and that I could not accept them without searching inquiry."

Thorndyke paused, and Mr. Marchmont, who had listened with close attention, nodded, as he glanced at his silent partner.

"You have stated the case with remarkable clearness," he said, "and I am free to confess that some of the points that you have raised had escaped my notice."

"My first idea," Thorndyke resumed, "was that John Blackmore, taking advantage of the mental enfeeblement produced by the opium habit, had dictated this will to Jeffrey, It was then that I sought permission to inspect Jeffrey's chambers, to learn what I could about him and to see for myself whether they presented the dirty and disorderly appearance characteristic of the regular opium-smoker's den. But when, during a walk into the City, I thought over the case, it seemed to me that this explanation hardly met the facts. Then I endeavoured to think of some other explanation, and looking over my notes I observed two points that seemed worth considering. One was that neither of the witnesses to the will was really acquainted with Jeffrey Blackmore, both being strangers who had accepted his identity on his own statement. The other was that no one who had previously known him, with the single exception of his brother John, had ever seen Jeffrey at the inn.

"What was the import of these two facts? Probably they had none. But still they suggested the desirability of considering the question: Was the person who signed the will really Jeffrey Blackmore? The contrary supposition – that someone had personated Jeffrey and forged his signature to a false will – seemed wildly improbable, especially in view of the identification of the body, but it involved no actual impossibility, and it offered a complete explanation of the, otherwise inexplicable, coincidences that I have mentioned.

"I did not, however, for a moment, think that this was the true explanation, but I resolved to bear it in mind, to test it when the opportunity arose, and consider it by the light of any fresh facts that I might acquire.

"The new facts came sooner than I had expected. That same evening I went with Dr. Jervis to New Inn and found Mr. Stephen in the chambers. By him I was informed that Jeffrey was a learned Orientalist, with a quite expert knowledge of the cuneiform writing, and even as he was telling me this, I looked over his shoulder and saw a cuneiform inscription hanging on the wall upside down.

"Now, of this there could be only one reasonable explanation. Disregarding the fact that no one would screw the suspension plates on a frame without ascertaining which was the right way up, and assuming it to be hung up inverted, it was impossible that the misplacement could have been overlooked by Jeffrey. He was not blind, though his sight was defective. The frame was thirty inches long and the individual characters nearly an inch in length – about the size of the *D-18* letters of Snellen's test-types, which can be read by a person of ordinary sight at a distance of fifty-five feet. There was, I repeat, only one reasonable explanation, which was that the person who had inhabited those chambers was not Jeffrey Blackmore.

"This conclusion received considerable support from a fact which I observed later, but mention in this place. On examining the soles of the shoes taken from the dead man's feet, I found only the ordinary mud of the streets. There was no trace of the peculiar gravelly mud that adhered to my own boots and Jervis's, and which came from the square of the inn. Yet the porter distinctly stated that the deceased, after paying the rent, walked back towards his chambers across the square, the mud of which should, therefore, have been conspicuous on his shoes.

"Thus, in a moment, a wildly speculative hypothesis had assumed a high degree of probability.

"When Mr. Stephen was gone, Jervis and I looked over the chambers thoroughly, and then another curious fact came to light. On the wall were a number of fine Japanese colour-prints, all of which showed recent damp-spots. Now, apart from the consideration that Jeffrey, who had been at the trouble and expense of collecting these valuable prints, would hardly have allowed them to rot on his walls, there arose the question: How came they to be damp? There was a gas stove in the room, and a gas stove has at least the virtue of preserving a dry atmosphere. It was winter weather, when the stove would naturally be pretty constantly alight. How came the walls to be so damp? The answer seemed to be that the stove had not been constantly alight, but had been lighted only occasionally. This suggestion was borne out by a further examination of the rooms. In the kitchen there were practically no stores and hardly any arrangements even for simple bachelor cooking, the bedroom offered the same suggestion, the soap in the wash-stand was shrivelled and cracked, there was no cast-off linen, and the shirts in the drawers, though clean, had the peculiar yellowish, faded appearance that linen acquires when long out of use. In short, the rooms had the appearance of not having been lived in at all, but only visited at intervals.

"Against this view, however, was the statement of the night porter that he had often seen a light in Jeffrey's sitting-room at one o'clock in the morning, with the apparent implication that it was then turned out. Now a light may be left in an empty room, but its extinction implies the presence of some person to extinguish it, unless some automatic device be adopted for putting it out at a given time. Such a device – the alarm movement of a clock, for instance, with a suitable attachment – is a simple enough matter, but my search of the rooms failed to discover anything of the kind. However, when looking over the drawers in the bedroom, I came upon a large box that had held a considerable quantity of hard stearine candles. There were only a few left, but a flat candlestick with numerous wick-ends in its socket accounted for the remainder.

"These candles seemed to dispose of the difficulty. They were not necessary for ordinary lighting, since gas was laid on in all three rooms. For what purpose, then, were they used, and in such considerable quantities? I subsequently obtained some of the same brand – Price's stearine candles, six to the pound – and experimented with them. Each candle was seven-and-a-quarter inches in length, not counting the cone at the top, and I found that they burned in still air at the rate of a fraction over one inch in an hour. We may say that one of these candles would burn in still air a little over six hours. It would thus be possible for the person who inhabited these rooms to go away at seven o'clock in the evening and leave a light which would burn until past one in the morning and then extinguish itself. This, of course, was only surmise, but it destroyed the significance of the night porter's statement.

"But, if the person who inhabited these chambers was not Jeffrey, who was he?

"The answer to that question seemed plain enough. There was only one person who had a strong motive for perpetrating a fraud of this kind, and there was only one person to whom it was possible. If this person was not Jeffrey, he must have been very like Jeffrey, sufficiently like for the body of the one to be mistaken for the body of the other. For the production of Jeffrey's body was an essential part of the plan and must have been contemplated from the first. But the only person who fulfills the conditions is John Blackmore.

"We have learned from Mr. Stephen that John and Jeffrey, though very different in appearance in later years, were much alike as young men. But when two brothers who are much alike as young men, become unlike in later life, we shall find that the unlikeness is produced by superficial differences and that the essential likeness remains. Thus, in the present case, Jeffrey was clean shaved, had bad eyesight, wore spectacles and stooped as he walked, John wore a beard and moustache, had good eyesight, did not wear spectacles, and had a brisk gait and upright carriage. But supposing John to shave off his beard and moustache, to put on spectacles and to stoop in his walk, these conspicuous but superficial differences would vanish and the original likeness reappear.

601

"There is another consideration. John had been an actor and was an actor of some experience. Now, any person can, with some care and practice, make up a disguise, the great difficulty is to support that disguise by a suitable manner and voice. But to an experienced actor this difficulty does not exist. To him, personation is easy, and, moreover, an actor is precisely the person to whom the idea of disguise and impersonation would occur.

"There is a small item bearing on this point, so small as to be hardly worth calling evidence, but just worth noting. In the pocket of the waistcoat taken from the body of Jeffrey I found the stump of a 'Contango' pencil, a pencil that is sold for the use of stock dealers and brokers. Now John was an outside broker and might very probably have used such a pencil, whereas Jeffrey had no connection with the stock markets and there is no reason why he should have possessed a pencil of this kind. But the fact is merely suggestive – it has no evidential value.

"A more important inference is to be drawn from the collected signatures. I have remarked that the change in the signature occurred abruptly, with one or two alterations of manner, last September, and that there are two distinct forms with no intermediate varieties. This is, in itself, remarkable and suspicious. But a remark made by Mr. Britton furnishes a really valuable piece of evidence on the point we are now considering. He admitted that the character of the signature had undergone a change, but observed that the change did not affect the individual or personal character of the writing. This is very important, for handwriting is, as it were, an extension of the personality of the writer. And just as a man to some extent snares his personality with his near blood-relations in the form of family resemblances, so his handwriting often shows a subtle likeness to that of his near relatives. You must have noticed, as I have, how commonly the handwriting of one brother resembles that of another, and in just this peculiar and subtle way. The inference, then, from Mr. Britton's statement is, that if the signature of the will was forged, it was probably forged by a relative of the deceased. But the only relative in question is his brother John.

"All the facts, therefore, pointed to John Blackmore as the person who occupied these chambers, and I accordingly adopted that view as a working hypothesis."

"But this was all pure speculation," objected Mr. Winwood.

"Not speculation," said Thorndyke. "Hypothesis. It was ordinary inductive reasoning such as we employ in scientific research. I started with the purely tentative hypothesis that the person who signed the will was not Jeffrey Blackmore. I assumed this, and I may say that I did not believe it at the time, but merely adopted it as a proposition that was worth testing.

I accordingly tested it, '*Yes?*' or '*No?*' with each new fact, but as each new fact said '*Yes*' and no fact said definitely '*No*', its probability increased rapidly by a sort of geometrical progression. The probabilities multiplied into one another. It is a perfectly sound method, for one knows that if a hypothesis be true, it will lead one, sooner or later, to a crucial fact by which its truth can be demonstrated.

"To resume our argument. We have now set up the proposition that John Blackmore was the tenant of New Inn and that he was personating Jeffrey. Let us reason from this and see what it leads to.

"If the tenant of New Inn was John, then Jeffrey must be elsewhere, since his concealment at the inn was clearly impossible. But he could not have been far away, for he had to be producible at short notice whenever the death of Mrs. Wilson should make the production of his body necessary. But if he was producible, his person must have been in the possession or control of John. He could not have been at large, for that would have involved the danger of his being seen and recognized. He could not have been in any institution or place where he would be in contact with strangers. Then he must be in some sort of confinement. But it is difficult to keep an adult in confinement in an ordinary house. Such a proceeding would involve great risk of discovery and the use of violence which would leave traces on the body, to be observed and commented on at the inquest. What alternative method could be suggested?

"The most obvious method is that of keeping the prisoner in such a state of debility as would confine him to his bed. But such debility could be produced by only starvation, unsuitable food, or chronic poisoning. Of these alternatives, poisoning is much more exact, more calculable in its effect and more under control. The probabilities, then, were in favour of chronic poisoning.

"Having reached this stage, I recalled a singular case which Jervis had mentioned to me and which seemed to illustrate this method. On our return home, I asked him for further particulars, and he then gave me a very detailed description of the patient and the circumstances. The upshot was rather startling. I had looked on his case as merely illustrative, and wished to study it for the sake of the suggestions that it might offer. But when I had heard his account, I began to suspect that there was something more than mere parallelism of method. It began to look as if his patient, Mr. Graves, might actually be Jeffrey Blackmore.

"The coincidences were remarkable. The general appearance of the patient tallied completely with Mr. Stephen's description of his uncle Jeffrey. The patient had a tremulous iris in his right eye and had clearly suffered from dislocation of the crystalline lens. But from Mr. Stephen's account of his uncle's sudden loss of sight in the right eye after a fall, I

603

judged that Jeffrey had also suffered from dislocation of the lens and therefore had a tremulous iris in the right eye. The patient, Graves, evidently had defective vision in his left eye, as proved by the marks made behind his ears by the hooked side-bars of his spectacles, for it is only on spectacles that are intended for constant use that we find hooked side-bars. But Jeffrey had defective vision in his left eye and wore spectacles constantly. Lastly, the patient Graves was suffering from chronic morphine poisoning, and morphine was found in the body of Jeffrey.

"Once more, it appeared to me that there were too many coincidences.

"The question as to whether Graves and Jeffrey were identical admitted of fairly easy disproof, for if Graves was still alive, he could not be Jeffrey. It was an important question and I resolved to test it without delay. That night, Jervis and I plotted out the chart, and on the following morning we located the house. But it was empty and to let. The birds had flown, and we failed to discover whither they had gone.

"However, we entered the house and explored. I have told you about the massive bolts and fastenings that we found on the bedroom doors and window, showing that the room had been used as a prison. I have told you of the objects that we picked out of the dust-heap under the grate. Of the obvious suggestion offered by the Japanese brush and the bottle of 'spirit gum' or cement, I need not speak now, but I must trouble you with some details concerning the broken spectacles. For here we had come upon the crucial fact to which, as I have said, all sound inductive reasoning brings one sooner or later.

"The spectacles were of a rather peculiar pattern. The frames were of the type invented by Mr. Stopford of Moorfields and known by his name. The right eye-piece was fitted with plain glass, as is usual in the case of a blind, or useless, eye. It was very much shattered, but its character was obvious. The glass of the left eye was much thicker and fortunately less damaged, so that I was able accurately to test its refraction.

"When I reached home, I laid the pieces of the spectacles together, measured the frames very carefully, tested the left eye-glass, and wrote down a full description such as would have been given by the surgeon to the spectacle-maker. Here it is, and I will ask you to note it carefully.

"'*Spectacles for constant use. Steel frame, Stopford's pattern, curl sides, broad bridge with gold lining. Distance between centres, 6.2 centimetres, extreme length of side-bars, 13.3 centimetres.*

"'*Right eye plain glass.*

"'*Left eye -5.75 D. spherical -3.25 D. cylindrical, axis 35°.*

"The spectacles, you see, were of a very distinctive character and seemed to offer a good chance of identification. Stopford's frames are, I believe, made by only one firm of opticians in London, Parry & Cuxton of

Regent Street. I therefore wrote to Mr. Cuxton, who knows me, asking him if he had supplied spectacles to the late Jeffrey Blackmore, Esq. – here is a copy of my letter – and if so, whether he would mind letting me have a full description of them, together with the name of the oculist who prescribed them.

"He replied in this letter, which is pinned to the copy of mine, that, about four years ago, he supplied a pair of glasses to Mr. Jeffrey Blackmore, and described them thus: *'The spectacles were for constant use and had steel frames of Stopford's pattern with curl sides, the length of the side-bars including the curled ends being 13.3 cm. The bridge was broad with a gold lining-plate, shaped as shown by the enclosed tracing from the diagram on the prescription. Distance between centres 6.2 cm.*

"*'Right eye plain glass.*

"*'Left eye -5.75 D.* spherical -3.25 D. cylindrical, axis 35°'.

"*'The spectacles were prescribed by Mr. Hindley of Wimpole Street'.*

"You see that Mr. Cuxton's description is identical with mine. However, for further confirmation, I wrote to Mr. Hindley, asking certain questions, to which he replied thus: "'You are quite right. Mr. Jeffrey Blackmore had a tremulous iris in his right eye (which was practically blind), due to dislocation of the lens. The pupils were rather large, certainly not contracted.'

"Here, then, we have three important facts. One is that the spectacles found by us at Kennington Lane were undoubtedly Jeffrey's, for it is as unlikely that there exists another pair of spectacles exactly identical with those as that there exists another face exactly like Jeffrey's face. The second fact is that the description of Jeffrey tallies completely with that of the sick man, Graves, as given by Dr. Jervis, and the third is that when Jeffrey was seen by Mr. Hindley, there was no sign of his being addicted to the taking of morphine. The first and second facts, you will agree, constitute complete identification."

"Yes," said Marchmont, "I think we must admit the identification as being quite conclusive, though the evidence is of a kind that is more striking to the medical than to the legal mind."

"You will not have that complaint to make against the next item of evidence," said Thorndyke. "It is after the lawyer's own heart, as you shall hear. A few days ago I wrote to Mr. Stephen asking him if he possessed a recent photograph of his uncle Jeffrey. He had one, and he sent it to me by return. This portrait I showed to Dr. Jervis and asked him if he had ever seen the person it represented. After examining it attentively, without any hint whatever from me, he identified it as the portrait of the sick man, Graves."

"Indeed!" exclaimed Marchmont. "This is most important. Are you prepared to swear to the identity, Dr. Jervis?"

"I have not the slightest doubt," I replied, "that the portrait is that of Mr. Graves."

"Excellent!" said Marchmont, rubbing his hands gleefully, "this will be much more convincing to a jury. Pray go on, Dr. Thorndyke."

"That," said Thorndyke, "completes the first part of my investigation. We had now reached a definite, demonstrable fact, and that fact, as you see, disposed at once of the main question – the genuineness of the will. For if the man at Kennington Lane *was* Jeffrey Blackmore, then the man at New Inn *was not*. But it was the latter who had signed the will. Therefore the will was *not* signed by Jeffrey Blackmore – that is to say, it was a forgery. The case was complete for the purposes of the civil proceedings. The rest of my investigations had reference to the criminal prosecution that was inevitable. Shall I proceed, or is your interest confined to the will?"

"Hang the will!" exclaimed Stephen. "I want to hear how you propose to lay hands on the villain who murdered poor old uncle Jeffrey – for I suppose he did murder him?"

"I think there is no doubt of it," replied Thorndyke.

"Then," said Marchmont, "we will hear the rest of the argument, if you please."

"Very well," said Thorndyke. "As the evidence stands, we have proved that Jeffrey Blackmore was a prisoner in the house in Kennington Lane and that some one was personating him at New Inn. That some one, we have seen, was, in all probability, John Blackmore. We now have to consider the man Weiss. Who was he? And can we connect him in any way with New Inn?

"We may note in passing that Weiss and the coachman were apparently one and the same person. They were never seen together. When Weiss was present, the coachman was not available even for so urgent a service as the obtaining of an antidote to the poison. Weiss always appeared some time after Jervis's arrival and disappeared some time before his departure, in each case sufficiently long to allow of a change of disguise. But we need not labour the point, as it is not of primary importance.

"To return to Weiss. He was clearly heavily disguised, as we see by his unwillingness to show himself even by the light of a candle. But there is an item of positive evidence on this point which is important from having other bearings. It is furnished by the spectacles worn by Weiss, of which you have heard Jervis's description. These spectacles had very peculiar optical properties. When you looked through them they had the properties of plain glass, when you looked at them they had the appearance

606

of lenses. But only one kind of glass possesses these properties, namely, that which, like an ordinary watch-glass, has curved, parallel surfaces. But for what purpose could a person wear 'watch-glass' spectacles? Clearly, not to assist his vision. The only alternative is disguise.

"The properties of these spectacles introduce a very curious and interesting feature into the case. To the majority of persons, the wearing of spectacles for the purpose of disguise or personation, seems a perfectly simple and easy proceeding. But, to a person of normal eyesight, it is nothing of the kind. For, if he wears spectacles suited for long sight he cannot see distinctly through them at all, while, if he wears concave, or near sight, glasses, the effort to see through them produces such strain and fatigue that his eyes become disabled altogether. On the stage the difficulty is met by using spectacles of plain window-glass, but in real life this would hardly do, the 'property' spectacles would be detected at once and give rise to suspicion.

"The personator is therefore in this dilemma: If he wears actual spectacles, he cannot see through them, if he wears sham spectacles of plain glass, his disguise will probably be detected. There is only one way out of the difficulty, and that not a very satisfactory one, but Mr. Weiss seems to have adopted it in lieu of a better. It is that of using watch-glass spectacles such as I have described.

"Now, what do we learn from these very peculiar glasses? In the first place they confirm our opinion that Weiss was wearing a disguise. But, for use in a room so very dimly lighted, the ordinary stage spectacles would have answered quite well. The second inference is, then, that these spectacles were prepared to be worn under more trying conditions of light – out of doors, for instance. The third inference is that Weiss was a man with normal eyesight, for otherwise he could have worn real spectacles suited to the state of his vision.

"These are inferences by the way, to which we may return. But these glasses furnish a much more important suggestion. On the floor of the bedroom at New Inn, I found some fragments of glass which had been trodden on. By joining one or two of them together, we have been able to make out the general character of the object of which they formed parts. My assistant – who was formerly a watch-maker – judged that object to be the thin crystal glass of a lady's watch, and this, I think, was Jervis's opinion. But the small part which remains of the original edge furnishes proof in two respects that this was not a watch-glass. In the first place, on taking a careful tracing of this piece of the edge, I found that its curve was part of an ellipse, but watch-glasses, nowadays, are invariably circular. In the second place, watch-glasses are ground on the edge to a single bevel to snap into the bezel or frame, but the edge of this object was ground to a

607

double bevel, like the edge of a spectacle-glass, which fits into a groove in the frame and is held by the side-bar screw. The inevitable inference was that this was a spectacle-glass. But, if so, it was part of a pair of spectacles identical in properties with those worn by Mr. Weiss.

"The importance of this conclusion emerges when we consider the exceptional character of Mr. Weiss's spectacles. They were not merely peculiar or remarkable – they were probably unique. It is exceedingly likely that there is not in the entire world another similar pair of spectacles. Whence the finding of these fragments of glass in the bedroom establishes a considerable probability that Mr. Weiss was, at some time, in the chambers at New Inn.

"And now let us gather up the threads of this part of the argument. We are inquiring into the identity of the man Weiss. Who was he?

"In the first place, we find him committing a secret crime from which John Blackmore alone will benefit. This suggests the *prima-facie* probability that he was John Blackmore.

"Then we find that he was a man of normal eyesight who was wearing spectacles for the purpose of disguise. But the tenant of New Inn, whom we have seen to be, almost certainly, John Blackmore – and whom we will, for the present, assume to have been John Blackmore – was a man with normal eyesight who wore spectacles for disguise.

"John Blackmore did not reside at New Inn, but at some place within easy reach of it. But Weiss resided at a place within easy reach of New Inn.

"John Blackmore must have had possession and control of the person of Jeffrey. But Weiss had possession and control of the person of Jeffrey.

"Weiss wore spectacles of a certain peculiar and probably unique character. But portions of such spectacles were found in the chambers at New Inn.

"The overwhelming probability, therefore, is that Weiss and the tenant of New Inn were one and the same person, and that that person was John Blackmore."

"That," said Mr. Winwood, "is a very plausible argument. But, you observe, sir, that it contains an undistributed middle term."

Thorndyke smiled genially. I think he forgave Winwood everything for that remark.

"You are quite right, sir," he said. "It does. And, for that reason, the demonstration is not absolute. But we must not forget, what logicians seem occasionally to overlook: That the 'undistributed middle', while it interferes with absolute proof, may be quite consistent with a degree of probability that approaches very near to certainty. Both the Bertillon system and the English fingerprint system involve a process of reasoning

608

in which the middle term is undistributed. But the great probabilities are accepted in practice as equivalent to certainties."

Mr. Winwood grunted a grudging assent, and Thorndyke resumed.

"We have now furnished fairly conclusive evidence on three heads: We have proved that the sick man, Graves, was Jeffrey Blackmore, that the tenant of New Inn was John Blackmore, and that the man Weiss was also John Blackmore. We now have to prove that John and Jeffrey were together in the chambers at New Inn on the night of Jeffrey's death.

"We know that two persons, and two persons only, came from Kennington Lane to New Inn. But one of those persons was the tenant of New Inn – that is, John Blackmore. Who was the other? Jeffrey is known by us to have been at Kennington Lane. His body was found on the following morning in the room at New Inn. No third person is known to have come from Kennington Lane, no third person is known to have arrived at New Inn. The inference, by exclusion, is that the second person – the woman – was Jeffrey.

"Again, Jeffrey had to be brought from Kennington to the inn by John. But John was personating Jeffrey and was made up to resemble him very closely. If Jeffrey were undisguised, the two men would be almost exactly alike, which would be very noticeable in any case and suspicious after the death of one of them. Therefore Jeffrey would have to be disguised in some way, and what disguise could be simpler and more effective than the one that I suggest was used?

"Again, it was unavoidable that some one – the cabman – should know that Jeffrey was not alone when he came to the inn that night. If the fact had leaked out and it had become known that a man had accompanied him to his chambers, some suspicion might have arisen, and that suspicion would have pointed to John, who was directly interested in his brother's death. But if it had transpired that Jeffrey was accompanied by a woman, there would have been less suspicion, and that suspicion would not have pointed to John Blackmore.

"Thus all the general probabilities are in favour of the hypothesis that this woman was Jeffrey Blackmore. There is, however, an item of positive evidence that strongly supports this view. When I examined the clothing of the deceased, I found on the trousers a horizontal crease on each leg as if the trousers had been turned up halfway to the knees. This appearance is quite understandable if we suppose that the trousers were worn under a skirt and were turned up so that they should not be accidentally seen. Otherwise it is quite incomprehensible."

"Is it not rather strange," said Marchmont, "that Jeffrey should have allowed himself to be dressed up in this remarkable manner?"

"I think not," replied Thorndyke. "There is no reason to suppose that he knew how he was dressed. You have heard Jervis's description of his condition, that of a mere automaton. You know that without his spectacles he was practically blind, and that he could not have worn them since we found them at the house in Kennington Lane. Probably his head was wrapped up in the veil, and the skirt and mantle put on afterwards, but, in any case, his condition rendered him practically devoid of will power. That is all the evidence I have to prove that the unknown woman was Jeffrey. It is not conclusive but it is convincing enough for our purpose, seeing that the case against John Blackmore does not depend upon it."

"Your case against him is on the charge of murder, I presume?" said Stephen.

"Undoubtedly. And you will notice that the statements made by the supposed Jeffrey to the porter, hinting at suicide, are now important evidence. By the light of what we know, the announcement of intended suicide becomes the announcement of intended murder. It conclusively disproves what it was intended to prove – that Jeffrey died by his own hand."

"Yes, I see that," said Stephen, and then after a pause he asked, "Did you identify Mrs. Schallibaum? You have told us nothing about her."

"I have considered her as being outside the case as far as I am concerned," replied Thorndyke. "She was an accessory. My business was with the principal. But, of course, she will be swept up in the net. The evidence that convicts John Blackmore will convict her. I have not troubled about her identity. If John Blackmore is married, she is probably his wife. Do you happen to know if he is married?"

"Yes, but Mrs. John Blackmore is not much like Mrs. Schallibaum, excepting that she has a cast in the left eye. She is a dark woman with very heavy eyebrows."

"That is to say that she differs from Mrs. Schallibaum in those peculiarities that can be artificially changed and resembles her in the one feature that is unchangeable. Do you know if her Christian name happens to be Pauline?"

"Yes, it is. She was a Miss Pauline Hagenbeck, a member of an American theatrical company. What made you ask?"

"The name which Jervis heard poor Jeffrey struggling to pronounce seemed to me to resemble Pauline more than any other name."

"There is one little point that strikes me," said Marchmont. "Is it not rather remarkable that the porter should have noticed no difference between the body of Jeffrey and the living man whom he knew by sight, and who must, after all, have been distinctly different in appearance?"

610

"I am glad you raised that question," Thorndyke replied, "for that very difficulty presented itself to me at the beginning of the case. But on thinking it over, I decided that it was an imaginary difficulty, assuming, as we do, that there was a good deal of resemblance between the two men. Put yourself in the porter's place and follow his mental processes. He is informed that a dead man is lying on the bed in Mr. Blackmore's rooms. Naturally, he assumes that the dead man is Mr. Blackmore – who, by the way, had hinted at suicide only the night before. With this idea he enters the chambers and sees a man a good deal like Mr. Blackmore and wearing Mr. Blackmore's clothes, lying on Mr. Blackmore's bed. The idea that the body could be that of some other person has never entered his mind. If he notes any difference of appearance he will put that down to the effects of death, for every one knows that a man dead looks somewhat different from the same man alive. I take it as evidence of great acuteness on the part of John Blackmore that he should have calculated so cleverly, not only the mental process of the porter, but the erroneous reasoning which every one would base on the porter's conclusions. For, since the body was actually Jeffrey's, and was identified by the porter as that of his tenant, it has been assumed by every one that no question was possible as to the identity of Jeffrey Blackmore and the tenant of New Inn."

There was a brief silence, and then Marchmont asked, "May we take it that we have now heard all the evidence?"

"Yes," replied Thorndyke. "That is my case."

"Have you given information to the police?" Stephen asked eagerly.

"Yes. As soon as I had obtained the statement of the cabman, Ridley, and felt that I had enough evidence to secure a conviction, I called at Scotland Yard and had an interview with the Assistant Commissioner. The case is in the hands of Superintendent Miller of the Criminal Investigation Department, a most acute and energetic officer. I have been expecting to hear that the warrant has been executed, for Mr. Miller is usually very punctilious in keeping me informed of the progress of the cases to which I introduce him. We shall hear to-morrow, no doubt."

"And, for the present," said Marchmont, "the case seems to have passed out of our hands."

"I shall enter a *caveat*, all the same," said Mr. Winwood.

"That doesn't seem very necessary," Marchmont objected. "The evidence that we have heard is amply sufficient to ensure a conviction and there will be plenty more when the police go into the case. And a conviction on the charges of forgery and murder would, of course, invalidate the second will."

"I shall enter a *caveat*, all the same," repeated Mr. Winwood.

611

As the two partners showed a disposition to become heated over this question, Thorndyke suggested that they might discuss it at leisure by the light of subsequent events. Acting on this hint – for it was now close upon midnight – our visitors prepared to depart, and were, in fact, just making their way towards the door when the bell rang. Thorndyke flung open the door, and, as he recognized his visitor, greeted him with evident satisfaction.

"Ha! Mr. Miller, we were just speaking of you. These gentlemen are Mr. Stephen Blackmore and his solicitors, Mr. Marchmont and Mr. Winwood. You know Dr. Jervis, I think."

The officer bowed to our friends and remarked: "I am just in time, it seems. A few minutes more and I should have missed these gentlemen. I don't know what you'll think of my news."

"You haven't let that villain escape, I hope," Stephen exclaimed.

"Well," said the Superintendent, "he is out of my hands and yours too, and so is the woman. Perhaps I had better tell you what has happened."

"If you would be so kind," said Thorndyke, motioning the officer to a chair.

The superintendent seated himself with the manner of a man who has had a long and strenuous day, and forthwith began his story.

"As soon as we had your information, we procured a warrant for the arrest of both parties, and then I went straight to their flat with Inspector Badger and a sergeant. There we learned from the attendant that they were away from home and were not expected back until to-day about noon. We kept a watch on the premises, and this morning, about the time appointed, a man and a woman, answering to the description, arrived at the flat. We followed them in and saw them enter the lift, and we were going to get into the lift too, when the man pulled the rope, and away they went. There was nothing for us to do but run up the stairs, which we did as fast as we could race, but they got to their landing first, and we were only just in time to see them nip in and shut the door. However, it seemed that we had them safe enough, for there was no dropping out of the windows at that height, so we sent the sergeant to get a locksmith to pick the lock or force the door, while we kept on ringing the bell.

"About three minutes after the sergeant left, I happened to look out of the landing window and saw a hansom pull up opposite the flats. I put my head out of the window, and, hang me if I didn't see our two friends getting into the cab. It seems that there was a small lift inside the flat communicating with the kitchen, and they had slipped down it one at a time.

"Well, of course, we raced down the stairs like acrobats, but by the time we got to the bottom the cab was off with a fine start. We ran out into

Victoria Street, and there we could see it halfway down the street and going like a chariot race. We managed to pick up another hansom and told the cabby to keep the other one in sight, and away we went like the very deuce, along Victoria Street and Broad Sanctuary, across Parliament Square, over Westminster Bridge and along York Road, we kept the other beggar in sight, but we couldn't gain an inch on him. Then we turned into Waterloo Station, and, as we were driving up the slope we met another hansom coming down, and when the cabby kissed his hand and smiled at us, we guessed that he was the sportsman we had been following.

"But there was no time to ask questions. It is an awkward station with a lot of different exits, and it looked a good deal as if our quarry had got away. However, I took a chance. I remembered that the Southampton Express was due to start about this time, and I took a short cut across the lines and made for the platform that it starts from. Just as Badger and I got to the end, about thirty yards from the rear of the train, we saw a man and a woman running in front of us. Then the guard blew his whistle and the train began to move. The man and the woman managed to scramble into one of the rear compartments and Badger and I raced up the platform like mad. A porter tried to head us off, but Badger capsized him and we both sprinted harder than ever, and just hopped on the foot-board of the guard's van as the train began to get up speed. The guard couldn't risk putting us off, so he had to let us into his van, which suited us exactly, as we could watch the train on both sides from the look-out. And we did watch, I can tell you, for our friend in front had seen us. His head was out of the window as we climbed on to the foot-board.

"However, nothing happened until we stopped at Southampton West. There, I need not say, we lost no time in hopping out, for we naturally expected our friends to make a rush for the exit. But they didn't. Badger watched the platform, and I kept a look-out to see that they didn't slip away across the line from the off-side. But still there was no sign of them. Then I walked up the train to the compartment which I had seen them enter. And there they were, apparently fast asleep in the corner by the off-side window, the man leaning back with his mouth open and the woman resting against him with her head on his shoulder. She gave me quite a turn when I went in to look at them, for she had her eyes half-closed and seemed to be looking round at me with a most horrible expression, but I found afterwards that the peculiar appearance of looking round was due to the cast in her eye."

"They were dead, I suppose?" said Thorndyke.

"Yes, sir. Stone dead, and I found these on the floor of the carriage."

He held up two tiny yellow glass tubes, each labelled "*Hypodermic tabloids. Aconitine Nitrate gr. 1/640*".

"Ha!" exclaimed Thorndyke. "This fellow was well up in alkaloidal poisons, it seems, and they appear to have gone about prepared for emergencies. These tubes each contained twenty tabloids, a thirty-second of a grain altogether, so we may assume that about twelve times the medicinal dose was swallowed. Death must have occurred in a few minutes, and a merciful death too."

"A more merciful death than they deserved," exclaimed Stephen, "when one thinks of the misery and suffering that they inflicted on poor old uncle Jeffrey. I would sooner have had them hanged."

"It's better as it is, sir," said Miller. "There is no need, now, to raise any questions in detail at the inquest. The publicity of a trial for murder would have been very unpleasant for you. I wish Dr. Jervis had given the tip to me instead of to that confounded, over-cautious – but there, I mustn't run down my brother officers. And it's easy to be wise after the event.

"Good night, gentlemen. I suppose this accident disposes of your business as far as the will is concerned?"

"I suppose it does," agreed Mr. Winwood. "But I shall enter a *caveat*, all the same."

The End

About the Author

Richard Austin Freeman was born on April 11th, 1862 in the Soho district of London. He was the son of a skilled tailor and the youngest of five children. As he grew, it was expected that he would become a tailor as well, but instead he had an interest in natural history and medicine, and so he obtained employment in a pharmacist's shop. While there, he qualified as an apothecary and could have gone on to manage the shop, but instead he began to study medicine at Middlesex Hospital.

Austin Freeman qualified as a physician in 1887, and in that same year he married. Faced with the twin facts of his new marital responsibilities and his very limited resources as a young doctor, he made the unusual decision to join the Colonial Service, spending the next seven years in Africa as an Assistant Colonial Surgeon. This continued until the early 1890's, when he contracted Blackwater Fever, an illness that eventually forced him to leave the service and return permanently to England.

For several years, he served as a *locum tenens* for various physicians, a bleak time in his life as he moved from job to job, his income low, and his health never quite recovered. However, he supplemented his meager income and exercised his creativity during these years by beginning to write. His early publications included *Travels and Live in Ashanti and Jaman* (1898), recounting some of his African sojourns.

In 1900, Freeman obtained work as an assistant to Dr. John James Pitcairn (1860-1936) at Holloway Prison. Although he wasn't there for very long, the association between the two men was enough to turn Freeman's attention toward writing mysteries. Over the next few years, they co-wrote several under the pseudonym *Clifford Ashdown*, including *The Adventures of Romney Pringle* (1902), *The Further Adventures of Romney Pringle* (1903), *From a Surgeon's Diary* (1904-1905), and *The Queen's Treasure* (written around 1905-1906, and published posthumously in 1975.)

In approximately 1904, Freeman began developing a mystery novella based on a short job that he had held at the Western Ophthalmic Hospital. This effort, "31 New Inn", was published in 1905, and it is the true first Dr. Thorndyke story. In 1907, the first Thorndyke novel, *The Red Thumb Mark*, was published.

From Thorndyke's creation until 1914, Freeman wrote four novels and two volumes of short stories. Then, with the commencement of the First World War, he entered military service. In February 1915, at the age

617

of fifty-two, he joined the Royal Army Medical Corps. Due to his health, which had never entirely recovered from his time in Africa, he spent the duration of the war involved with various aspects of the ambulance corps, having been promoted very early to the rank of Captain. He wrote nothing about Thorndyke during this period, but he did publish one book concerning the adventures of a scoundrel, *The Exploits of Danby Croker* (1916).

Following the war, he resumed his previous life, writing approximately one Thorndyke novel per year, as well as three more volumes of Thorndyke short stories and a number of other unrelated items, until his death on September 28th, 1943 – likely related to Parkinson's Disease, which had plagued him in later years. He is buried in Gravesend.

If you enjoy Dr. Thorndyke, then you'll love
The MX Book of New Sherlock Holmes Stories

"This is the finest volume of Sherlockian fiction I have
ever read, and I have read, literally, thousands."
– Philip K. Jones

"Beyond Impressive . . . This is a splendid venture for a great cause!
– Roger Johnson, Editor, *The Sherlock Holmes Journal,*
The Sherlock Holmes Society of London

Part I: 1881-1889
Part II: 1890-1895
Part III: 1896-1929
Part IV: 2016 Annual
Part V: Christmas Adventures
Part VI: 2017 Annual
Part VII: Eliminate the Impossible
Part VIII – 2018 Annual
Part IX – 2018 Annual (1879-1895)
Part X – 2018 Annual (1896-1916)
Part XI – Some Untold Cases (1880-1891)
Part XII – Some Untold Cases (1894-1902)

In Preparation

Part XIII – 2019 Annual (Spring 2019)
Part XIV – Whatever Remains . . . Must Be the Truth (Fall 2019)

. . . and more to come!

Publishers Weekly says:

- Part VI: *The traditional pastiche is alive and well . . . .*
- Part VII: *Sherlockians eager for faithful-to-the-canon plots and characters will be delighted.*
- Part VIII: *The imagination of the contributors in coming up with variations on the volume's theme is matched by their ingenious resolutions.*
- Part IX: *The 18 stories . . . will satisfy fans of Conan Doyle's originals. Sherlockians will rejoice that more volumes are on the way.*
- Part X: *. . . new Sherlock Holmes adventures of consistently high quality.*
- Part XI: *This is an essential volume for Sherlock Holmes fans.*
- Part XII: *Marcum continues to amaze with the number of high-quality pastiches that he has selected.*

The MX Book of New Sherlock Holmes Stories
Edited by David Marcum
(MX Publishing, 2015-   )

 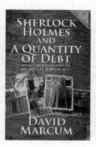 

Sherlock Holmes in Montague Street
by Arthur Morrison
Edited, Holmes-ed, and with Original Material
by David Marcum

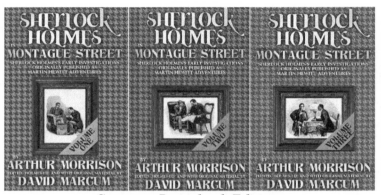

Separate Paperback Editions

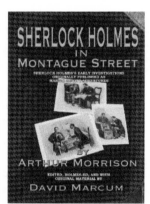

Combined Hardcover Edition

"It's been suggested that Hewitt was the young Mycroft Holmes,
but David Marcum has a more plausible and attractive theory
– that he was Sherlock, early in his career as an investigator
. . . these are remarkably convincing in their new guise."
– Roger Johnson, Editor, *The Sherlock Holmes Journal,*
The Sherlock Holmes Society of London

Thanks to all the Kickstarter backers,
especially
The Mysterious Debra Werth
for their support.

MX Publishing

MX Publishing is the world's largest specialist Sherlock Holmes publisher, with several hundred titles and over a hundred authors creating the latest in Sherlock Holmes fiction and non-fiction.

From traditional short stories and novels to travel guides and quiz books, MX Publishing caters to all Holmes fans.

The collection includes leading titles such as *Benedict Cumberbatch In Transition* and *The Norwood Author*, which won the 2011 *Tony Howlett Award* (Sherlock Holmes Book of the Year).

MX Publishing also has one of the largest communities of Holmes fans on *Facebook*, with regular contributions from dozens of authors.

www.mxpublishing.co.uk (UK) and *www.mxpublishing.com* (USA)

CPSIA information can be obtained
at www.ICGtesting.com
Printed in the USA
BVHW072112060319
541988BV00001B/2/P